The Bride of Texas

The Bride of Texas
Josef Skvorecky

Translated by Kaca Polackova Henley

F
Skvo

 Alfred A. Knopf   New York   1996

3/96   Brodart   27.00

THIS IS A BORZOI BOOK
PUBLISHED BY ALFRED A. KNOPF, INC.

Copyright © 1995 by Kaca Polackova Henley
All rights reserved under International and Pan-American
Copyright Conventions. Published in the United States
by Alfred A. Knopf, Inc., New York. Originally published in
Czech as *Nevesta z Texasu* by Sixty-Eight Publishers Corp.,
Toronto, Canada. Copyright © 1992 by Josef Skvorecky. First
published in English in Canada in 1995 by Alfred A. Knopf Canada,
Toronto. Distributed by Random House Inc., New York.

Library of Congress Cataloging-in-Publication Data
Škvorecký, Josef.
[Nevěsta z Texasu. English]
The bride of Texas / by Josef Škvorecký: translated by
Káča Poláčková-Henley. — 1st U.S. ed.
p.   cm.
ISBN 0-679-44411-4
I. Poláčokvá-Henley, Káča.   II. Title.
PG5038.S527N4713   1996
891.8635—dc20   95-49296
CIP

Manufactured in the United States of America
First U.S. Edition

To my brother-in-law Lumir Salivar, a veteran of the penal uranium mines in Joachimstal, because he loves America, and for all the years of friendship.

★

The following friends have rendered me help, advice and support: Zdenek Hruban from the University of Chicago, Svatava Jakobson from the University of Texas at Austin, Clinton Machann from Texas A & M University, Patrick D. Reagan from Tennessee Technical University, George Kovtun from the Library of Congress, Josef Andrle from the University of North Carolina, the late Vít Hrubín from California, and Emma Barborka from Chicago. And, last but not least, my editor-friends of many years Louise Dennys and Barbara Bristol.

I received much precious information from Vlasta Vráz from Chicago who, unfortunately, did not live to see the day for which she worked all her long life. She died in the late fall of 1989.

Sail On, O Union, strong and great!
Humanity with all its fears,
With all the hopes of future years,
Is hanging breathless on thy fate.
    —*Henry Wadsworth Longfellow*

. . . life, that monster made up of beauty
and brutality . . .
    —*Kate Chopin*

. . . though my digressions are all fair, as
you observe, —and that I fly off from what I am about,
as far and as often too as any writer . . .
yet I constantly take care to order affairs so, that
my main business does not stand still in my
absence.
    —*Laurence Sterne*

Contents

A Historical Foreword and a Note on the Characters

The Bride of Texas *is a romantic fictitious story, but it is set in a world that is as real as I know how to make it.*

I chose General William Tecumseh Sherman to be the central character of this novel based on the American Civil War—indeed, I don't hesitate to call him the hero—for obvious reasons. It was Sherman who commanded the huge army that marched through Georgia to the sea, and then up through the Carolinas to its final engagement, the Battle of Bentonville. And with him marched my Czechs.

Of the many other real-life commanders who appear in this book, I shall name here only those who took part in the Campaign of the Carolinas and the Bentonville battle, which greatly contributed to the final victory of the Union armies.

At the end of the war, Sherman's forces consisted of three armies: the Army of the Tennessee, the Army of Georgia, and the Army of the Ohio.

The Army of the Tennessee's commander was Major-General Oliver Otis Howard, a pious, one-armed officer who took part in many battles of the war, including Gettysburg and the bloody assault on Marye's Heights at Fredericksburg. Howard's army was divided into three corps, one of which, the Fifteenth, under the command of Major-General John Alexander Logan, included Major-General William Babcock Hazen's Second Division.

The Army of Georgia was commanded by Major-General Henry Warner Slocum and consisted of two corps: the Fourteenth, with Major-General Jefferson Columbus Davis commanding, which included the division headed by Brigadier-General William Passmore Carlin and Brigadier-General James Dada Morgan; and the Twentieth, under Major-General Joseph Anthony Mower—Sherman's favourite, whose rash action almost changed the course of the Bentonville battle. In Mower's Third Division fought the Twenty-sixth Wisconsin Volunteers, with numerous Czech soldiers in its ranks.

The Army of the Ohio's commanding General was Major-General John McAllister Schofield. It was composed of two army corps: the Tenth, under

Major-General Alfred Howe Terry, and the Twenty-third, under Major-General Jacob Dolson Cox. Part of this army was the Cavalry Division of Major-General Judson Kilpatrick, a flamboyant and fearless womanizer.

Quite a few other Union officers are mentioned in the novel, but since this note cannot be a Who's Who of the Civil War I refer interested readers to the many non-fiction books on the subject, particularly the magisterial three-volume The Civil War: A Narrative *by Shelby Foote.*

Among the very few fictional Union officers in these pages are Captain Warren Baxter II, Colonel Browntow, Captain Bondy, Lieutenant Williams, Lieutenant Szymanowsky, and Lieutenant Bellman. The latter is important because he later wrote a fictitious book on the Bentonville battle, from which I quote freely.

On the Confederate side, the most prominent historical figure is one of the South's best commanders, General Joseph Eggleston Johnston, who eventually withdrew from Bentonville not for lack of courage but for lack of soldiers. Also frequently mentioned are his three brilliant cavalry generals: Matthew Calbraith Butler, Wade Hampton, and Joseph Wheeler.

A note on the characters

Lorraine Henderson Tracy, the successful author of humorous novels for young women, is not entirely fictional. According to some sources (or perhaps rumours), the real-life General Ambrose Everett Burnside did have a fiancée who ran out on him when the couple were just about to take their vows. Lorraine's literary career is my invention, although some problems of the craft she struggles with (and never really solves) are very real. Naturally, since she herself is not quite real, neither are her husband and her children. Most other characters around her, however, actually lived—from the peacemonger Clement Laird Vallandigham to Burnside's subordinate, General Milo Smith Hascall; to the bloodthirsty Colonel Jennison, who had been with John Brown in "bleeding Kansas" and promised that Chicago streets would "be carpeted with Copperhead corpses"; and, finally, to the luckless Jeremy and Elihu Lecklider, and the murderer Thomas McGehan. On the other hand, the lovely Jasmine, her unworthy fiancé, Hasdrubal, and her mother-in-law, Gospel, never lived, although their problems are not fictional. Made up also is Vallandigham's young colleague in the legal profession, Snopes, though I did not invent his name.

Real too are the Czech soldiers in the Twenty-sixth Wisconsin Volunteers, except for Jan Amos Shake, who anglicized his name from Schweik; he too is a good soldier—at least when he describes actions like the Perryville battle to his companions. Otherwise these men actually lived and fought: Jan Kapsa, Fran-

tisek Stejskal, Vojtech Houska, Frantisek Fiser (Fisher), Adolph B. Chladek, Jan Dvorak, Vaclav Svejkar, Josef Paidr, Frantisek Javorsky, Frantisek Kouba, Ondrej Salek, Frantisek Zinkule, and numerous minor characters like the gunboat gunner Pechlat, who was determined to volunteer for submarine duty as soon as the Union had submarines. Very real also is the commander of the Lincoln Slavonic Rifles, Captain Geza Mihalotzy (in various sources the company is also called the Lincoln Slavonian Rifles or—as in Mihalotzy's letter to Lincoln—the Lincoln Riflemen of Slavonic Origin). Mihalotzy was probably Hungarian, or he may have been Slovak, and sometimes he even claimed Czech nationality— depending, allegedly, on who was paying for his drinks; he ended up as a colonel in the German Twenty-fourth Illinois Infantry. Though his ethnic background is unclear, he was a capable and valiant soldier; he was killed in action at Buzzard Roost, where a small fort commemorated his name.

The sources are similarly unclear as to which men actually went to the field with Mihalotzy, when the original number of pre-war volunteers dwindled after Fort Sumter. Apparently they numbered about ten, and the names most often mentioned are those which appear in the novel: Filip, Neuman, Kouba, Uher, Kukla, Dvoracek, Hudek, Smola, Kafka, and Jurka. (I added Shake and Salek.) They fought valiantly, and some were wounded.

Most Czech civilians who appear in these pages likewise lived. Charles Sealsfield, whose real name was Karel Anton Postl, was an adventurer who travelled in Texas and Lousiana probably as early as 1823, and later became a popular fiction writer under his Americanized name (though he wrote in German). Anthony M. Dignowity took part in the Polish uprising of 1830 and was forced to flee to America, where he became a jack-of-all-trades, his trades including that of medical doctor and writer (in English). At the beginning of the Civil War, Dignowity, an outspoken enemy of slavery, narrowly escaped public hanging in San Antonio, and he spent the rest of the war as an employee of the federal government in Washington D.C. His two sons had been conscripted into the Confederate army, but they both managed to escape, and joined the Union army. Another early Czech pioneer, Josef Lidumil Lesikar, came to Texas in 1851 and was also threatened with hanging, as the New Ulm, Texas, correspondent of an abolitionist Czech paper published in St. Louis. Lesikar survived the war. Ladimir Klacel, an ex-Augustinian monk (he once lived in the same Moravian cloister as Gregor Mendel, the founder of genetics), spent the second half of his life in America, where he edited Czech papers sympathetic to the free-thinkers movement.

The actions of the Kakuska family of Chicago are well documented, including the moving of their cottage; among the twelve strong men who carried it were Matej Barcal, Frantisek Hejduk, Kristuvek, and Jakub Padecky. Even the

Czech-speaking black slave Breta who helps Zinkule cleanse himself of skunk stench is real, although he has no name in my source.

On the other hand, Lida Toupelikova, her brother Cyril, and her lost love Vitek Mika are characters I lifted from a nineteenth-century Czech magazine story, "Reunion on Texas Soil", written by Josef Bunata and published in Chicago in 1898. It is a simple, rather Victorian story which sheds much light on the life of the early Czech settlers in Texas.

Of the two important non-Czech characters, Mme Sophie Sosniowski (sometimes spelled Sosnowski) actually ran a school in Columbia and asked Sherman for protection; Ursula von Hanzlitschek never existed.

Fictional are the de Ribordeauxs and their black slaves Dinah and old Uncle Habakuk. But very little in the latter characters' stories is my fantasy; there were slaves who outwitted their masters, and there were slave girls who learned a lot by listening to their young mistresses' tutors. Finally, I have used the word "Negro" thoughout this historical novel because it was the term used at that time by both African-Americans and whites.

The Bride of Texas

Savannah

IT WAS RAINING on the sycamores. A fog crept along the ground from the Salkehatchie River and out of it came the sound of tin cups clanking against haversacks. The soldiers themselves were invisible except as shadows, with the occasional flash of a bayonet when the sun broke through the clouds. Above the low blanket of fog, a flagstaff floated slowly forward, and on top of it, on a horizontal perch, sat a wet red squirrel scratching its ear with a hind leg. A piglet squealed. Still it rained on the sycamores.

"The fifteenth," said Sergeant Kapsa. "Logan. Good chance the old man will show up after all."

"Who is he, anyhow?" asked Kakuska. "A nephew twice removed?"

Kakuska pointed a bandaged hand at the white tent and said, "Kil's inside there. They can start now."

They both looked at the tent. Beside it, under a canopy the engineers had put up when the rain started, stood the bride. She wore a snow-white dress, and Kapsa deliberately avoided looking at her face. He understood why Vitek had been blinded by the girl's loveliness, the cascade of gold setting off her cornflower eyes, serpent's eyes though they were. It wasn't the colour—Kapsa had never in his life seen a snake with blue eyes. But that day in front of the shop on Savannah's Bay Street with the sign saying MADAM

RUSSELL'S BAKERY, when she had cast a sharp, narrow look at her brother, she had hissed like a snake, "Shut up this minute, Cyril, d'you hear?" Cyril had repeated, "You shameless wench. . . . For her! You say you did it for her sake?" The cornflower-blue concentration of—what? Selfishness? The eyes she had narrowed when she hissed, "Shut up this minute, Cyril!" were not the pools of girlish innocence that had once reflected the clouds over Mount Radhošt. And now the sergeant knew why.

"See? He got himself a new one!" Kakuska's voice drove away the memory, and the sergeant watched the diminutive cavalryman in a general's uniform stride over to the canopy. The incessant South Carolina rain falling on the sycamores around the tent had faded his uniform, but hadn't had time to saturate his black plumed hat.

"He could have been shorter by a head, my friend," he heard Kakuska say. "Last time I saw his old hat, it was flying over me like a crow, and out of the corner of my eye, I saw a sword graze that shiny noggin of his." Kakuska chuckled. "I watched the hat spin away and thought: his head could have been in it, and goodbye Kil. Well, next thing I knew, this fool thing happened," and he raised his bandaged left hand.

With a flourish more typical of a Southerner than a Yankee officer, the tiny general swept off his splendid hat and bowed deeply before the bride. Even from behind, the sergeant could see the carefully brushed whiskers on either side of his face—whiskers that would do even that dandy Burnside proud.

Yesterday, Sherman had run out of his tent calling, "General Logan! Come here!" Logan had turned and, with two of his staff officers, marched past the sergeant, who was standing guard, into Sherman's tent. There they'd been treated to Kilpatrick's story-telling prowess, and so had the sergeant, since Sherman's voice carried right through the canvas walls. Everyone knew Aiken had been a catastrophe, and if some frightened rebel in the last bunch of sixty-year-old conscripts hadn't opened fire prematurely, the tiny general would have been caught in an ambush and Kakuska's vision might have come true, except that Kakuska would have been done for too. Kilpatrick's version, however, was very different. Though short on tactical information, it echoed with the clang of blades, the flowery oaths of General Wheeler's retreating cavalry, and the neighing of their horses—and above all this, the reassuring voice of the diminutive Kil, ordering the retreat. Why both sides were retreating wasn't clear. And not a word about the hat. After the fray, the ambulances brought in one load of dead cavalrymen and two loads of their severely mangled comrades. Kakuska sat beside the driver, carefully resting his left elbow in his right palm, his left hand pointing skyward and wrapped in a dirty rag that turned out to be his puttee.

"Don't know how I'll ever live this one down," Kapsa heard him say.

"What do you mean, live it down?" he asked. "Now, being shot in the hind quarters, that . . ."

"Getting your trigger finger shot off?" wailed Kakuska. "Can you think of anything worse?"

Looking at Kakuska's hand, now wrapped in clean white calico, the sergeant made a face. Ever since Fort Donelson, a strange epidemic of shot-off fingers had plagued the Union army. At Vicksburg they'd heard about it from young Dignowity, who had deserted to the North on principle. Before that he'd been assigned to the sharpshooters in Waul's Texas Legion, after word got out that he'd once won a hunting competition in San Antonio. "The minute I was in uniform," Dignowity had explained as they stood under cover, watching the Vicksburg palisades, "my eyesight got worse. Never did hit one of those fingers. But the Rebs thought it was great. Best target practice in the world. Really!" Dignowity slapped his thigh like a farmhand. "Some Yankee was always poking his finger up over the parapet, like he was trying to tell which way the wind was blowing. Trouble was, there wasn't so much as a breeze. So we'll do them a favour, said the Rebs. One more Yankee with an honourable discharge, and one less finger on the trigger."

"But they shot off your left one," said the sergeant. "So it ain't part of the epidemic."

"Well, I guess that's so," said Kakuska with a rueful look at the bandage. "Do you think I'll have to see this war through?"

"You were awful keen to get into it," said the sergeant. "Surely you're not going to quit now?"

It was still raining on the sycamores, but the sun broke through right over the tent, making it gleam white, and as the wedding party lined up, a rainbow appeared in the sky, arching over the lovely bride with the serpent's eyes. A hand in a cavalryman's glove pointed to the heavenly phenomenon and a murmur of excitement rippled through the company. From the low fog along the road they could still hear the tinkle of tin cups and the muffled, rhythmic thud of marching feet. By now the squirrel's flagstaff was far down the road. The animal itself had scrambled down and vanished into the fog.

Kapsa and Kakuska stood up and walked over to the tent. Behind the canopy a wet band huddled in the rain, the bells of their instruments freshly polished. Towering over the wedding guests ahead of him was the tall figure of Franta Stejskal, who had mended his ragged uniform for the occasion. The holes were patched with scraps of green velvet, apparently the remains of some plantation lady's evening gown, but their unseemly contrast to the faded hue of his coat was lost among the older patches, which reflected all the colours of the heavenly phenomenon overhead except red. Stejskal's comrade, Vojta Houska, exhibited no such respect for the bride, for a hairy white thigh showed through a tear in his trouser leg. The last member of the threesome concluding the short procession had patched the seat of his trousers with two crossed stripes of bright blue silk that bore a remarkable resemblance to the bars on the Confederate flag. The sergeant wondered if this was pure coincidence. Hardly, knowing Jan Amos Shake.

"A Czech day," grumbled Kakuska.

"A Czech bride," said the sergeant, and they joined the threesome. A lieutenant unfurled a fancy parasol and held it over the bride, and the sergeant tried to remember where he had last seen that article of Southern finery. It was pink with little blue flowers on it, with a strip of white lace around the edge. The inside was lined with blue satin set with tiny gold stars that glistened over the bride's coiffure. Then the scene came alive in his mind. A funny war—horrible, but funny all the same. Shake, the clown, loping among stinking corpses of mules, wearing a lady's huge yellow chapeau with bright green plumes and carrying the very same parasol that was now protecting the bride's immaculate dress as she crossed the open space between the canopy and the tent. Behind Shake had been an indignant Negress—a handsome, pale brown hunk of woman holding her skirts above her knees so you could see an occasional flash of white underwear—screaming something in a dialect the sergeant didn't understand, but he didn't need to, it was obvious. Then Shake tripped, the hat fell off and rolled in the dust, and the brown beauty let go of her skirt and dived for the hat while Shake covered his face with his hands, thinking she was about to tackle him. But she just picked up the plumed chapeau and dusted it off. Shake got up and stood there warily while the woman shook her fist at him. finally he understood what she was saying: "Robbing us poor niggers. My Sunday go-to-church hat!"

"Sorry, ma'am, sorry!" Shake muttered, and the woman's gaze fell on the parasol he had dropped in the dust.

"You-all can keep that," she said, and strode off, carrying the hat before her like a holy relic. They watched the proud figure walking away towards the white plantation house, and it occurred to the sergeant that perhaps she had beaten the scavengers to it and helped herself to her mistress's chapeau and the fancy dress she was wearing. But God knew. She was obviously a house nigger, the aristocracy of the slave world.

That was the last time he'd seen the parasol, until it resurfaced above the golden locks of Linda Toupelik.

Kakuska said, "Another Moravian girl finds happiness."

"And another Yankee dunce sticks his head in the yoke," Shake grumbled, then added, "and it's going to be one hell of a yoke, my friend. A Moravian yoke."

The parasol was snapped shut and the bride, on her brother's arm, followed the groom into the tent, accompanied by the diminutive Kil. There was room inside for the groom's fellow officers, but the enlisted men had to stay outside in the rain. The front of the tent was open, though, so they could see old Reverend Mulroney waiting behind the prie-dieu, holding his well-thumbed Bible and smiling an appropriate smile.

It was still raining on the sycamores.

Then the clergyman's gaze fell on the bride, and suddenly his smile didn't seem so appropriate to the sergeant after all. It was as if the chaplain were looking at one of those smutty pictures Corporal Gambetta carried in his haversack and rented to soldiers for a penny when they felt the need to take off into the bushes. The minister looked from bride to groom and, when he spoke, his voice confirmed the sergeant's suspicion.

"Dearly beloved," he intoned, "listen while we read from the Book of Ezekiel the Prophet, chapter sixteen, verse thirteen," and there was a gleam in his eyes as he recited in a singsong voice, *"Thou wast exceeding beautiful, and thou didst prosper into a kingdom. . . ."*

Shake gave a quiet chuckle.

"What is it?" whispered the sergeant, but Shake placed a finger on his lips and listened to the chaplain, who was speaking the words as if he had a mouth full of butter. The sergeant decided he'd better start paying attention too. He recalled the preacher's first sermon for the military, before Kennesaw Mountain—the one that had made him famous, practically a legend. Mulroney had joined the army in a fit of patriotism, forsaking the safety of his parish, where his duties had included caring for the spiritual welfare of the wards of Mrs. Terrence-Willoughby's Academy for Young Ladies, a responsibility that had certainly not prepared him for life in the army. On the eve of the bloody massacre he chose the loss of virginity as the subject for his maiden sermon. With a sheaf of yellowing paper trembling in his fingers, he stumbled over every other word, even though he was reading from his notes. As a matter of fact, since everyone's sphincter muscles were clenched in dread of the upcoming battle, it wasn't such a bad topic. There was none of the usual coughing and throat-clearing, and Lieutenant Matlock even quit picking his teeth with a splinter of wood, as was his custom when listening to the word of God. Even the colonel listened with interest, at least as long as the preacher stuck to virginity, its loss, and the social and physical consequences thereof. But then Mulroney switched to the consequences that lay in the hereafter, and unfortunately he departed from his yellowed notes. Perhaps it had finally dawned on him that when he'd written this sermon so many years ago, he hadn't done so with an audience of soldiers in mind. Now he addressed his warning to men who, in his words, had sunk so low as to rob some poor maiden of her maidenhead or, worse, had actually paid money to commit a mortal sin. The association between virginity and sin was pretty flimsy, but the clergyman made up for it with a colourful description of the torments awaiting the sinner in hell. That was when the colonel began coughing meaningfully, louder and louder, until the reverend noticed and returned to his notes, concluding with a fervent plea to virgins to preserve their treasure till marriage. Then a cannonade sounded from beyond the woods. Sergeant Kapsa thought the colonel had been set coughing by the mention of sin for sale—he was a notorious customer of the camp followers, regardless of their colour—but he was wrong; the colonel's displeasure was moral and praiseworthy. He thanked the chaplain—very curtly—and in his most sonorous voice announced that of course those boys who went straight from the impending battle to the other world would, without exception—deflowered virgins notwithstanding—go straight to heaven. The soldiers' sphincter muscles tightened again, and all thought of the succulent pleasures of peacetime vanished.

The chaplain had improved since Kennesaw Mountain. Not that he'd abandoned his favourite themes, but there were no more notes. Nowadays he spoke of virginity extempore, and sounded to the sergeant like someone reading from one of those blue novels Corporal Gambetta rented out for three cents a day, though the chaplain cleverly shrouded the erotic details in biblical allegory. The sergeant watched the ears of the two men flanking the bride—the groom, Baxter Warren, and the best man, Cyril Toupelik—grow redder and redder. *"How beautiful are thy feet, the joints of thy thighs are like jewels, the work of the hands of a cunning workman"*—even the sergeant could recognize Mulroney's departure from Ezekiel—*"thy two breasts are like two young roes that are twins—"* sighed the preacher, gazing at the bride with lascivious eyes. None of this brought so much as a blush to the bride's cheeks.

It was still raining on the sycamores.

At last the blushing groom kissed his pale bride, and the best man kissed his sister and spoke aloud, but in Czech: "Well, Lidunka, you've humped your way into the upper classes after all!" Now it was the bride's turn to blush, and cold fire flashed in her blue eyes. She turned her back on him and planted a kiss right on the mouth of the diminutive general. Kilpatrick flushed. The sergeant thought it over. That evening, at the campfire, Shake said, "So Kil was one of her . . . ?"

"But he didn't pan out, he couldn't have," declared Kakuska. "He's the biggest wick-dipper in Sherman's army. He'll never get hitched."

"That's what I can't figure," said Stejskal. "Ugly runt like him, practically a hunchback, and women—"

"He ain't a runt where it matters," said Kakuska. "Believe me, I saw it with my own two eyes." The sergeant had heard the story before—how, one November night, little Kil had come galloping up to the house by the train tracks leading another horse bearing two black girls mounted like men. A platoon of the Twenty-sixth Wisconsin was marching past, led by Corporal Gambetta, and the sight of those dark thighs in the moonlight drew an almost unanimous whistle of appreciation from the unit. Laughing, Kilpatrick hopped down from his saddle and helped the two beauties dismount.

Kakuska saluted and said, "A good night to you, general, sir!"

Kilpatrick's smile flashed in the gathering darkness. "And to you, corporal." He turned and ushered the two young women to the other side of the building, where the door was. Soon the upstairs windows were filled with light and Kakuska could hear the tinkling of glass and the sounds of girlish giggles. Later on, silence fell, bedsprings creaked, and conquered women moaned. Then several shots rang out in the distance. Apparently Braxton Bragg's sharpshooters were practising over near Augusta, or maybe Wheeler's cavalry had brushed up against Kil's skirmishers. Kakuska felt horny, and he cursed his general, though it wasn't his fault. In the end he relieved himself and fell asleep.

He was awakened by a terrible racket. From the barricades on the other side of the train tracks he could hear the ringing of horses' hoofs, the clash of metal on metal, shouting, the crack of pistols. He jumped up as someone tossed a burning torch over the fence onto a woodpile near a chicken coop. Terrified chickens flapped and cackled loudly as they shot out the door. Kil's cavalrymen, who had been sleeping in blankets around the dying fire, woke up. The horses strained at their tethers in panic. On the other side of the house someone slashed at the door with a sword, and an upstairs window flew open. In the moonlight a group of riders carrying a banner with two crossed bands of stars galloped around the fence. Kakuska untied his horse but, before he could mount, a figure in a white nightshirt jumped out of the upstairs window, the nightshirt ballooning, and by the light of the burning woodpile and the full moon Kakuska caught a glimpse of his general's natural endowments.

"But he sure knows how to brawl," Kakuska said later. "He was still there come dawn, yelling orders at the troops, in his nightshirt. Finally we fell back to Waynesboro, where the Wisconsins had built light fortifications, and he strutted about half-naked behind the palisades until his orderly found him another pair of trousers. Wheeler took Kil's own trousers as booty, along with those two black tarts, but they got away from him and when we took Augusta, Kil had them in tow again, this time in a carriage."

The flames of the campfire flickered on the faces of these soldiers, all of them from a distant land. Long, tall Stejskal, ten years in the land of the Yankees, more than two in the army, a veteran of General Sigel's Eleventh Corps, a survivor of Chancellorsville. He'd almost met his Maker there, but in the end it only cost him a silver pocketwatch and twelve bucks and he'd ended up in Libby prison. Actually, he didn't end up there, because back then they were still exchanging prisoners. He made the whole march from Georgia and now he was in his general's bodyguard. The sergeant glanced over to Vojta Houska, another South Bohemian. He looked just as Kapsa had always imagined Silly Jack in the fairy-tales—narrow forehead, hair down to his eyebrows, but, like the inveterate fairy-tale hero, he was no coward. He had volunteered for Farragut's insane expedition along the unnavigable rivers and bayous around Vicksburg. Beside Houska sat Paidr, tireless writer of letters home to his mum in Iowa, letters he'd read aloud at the drop of a hat to anyone who'd listen. Item by item, they contained his entire military career: Gettysburg under General Howard, Chattanooga with the Twenty-sixth Wisconsin, Wauhatchie, McLaren's nocturnal assault on General Hooker, the battle for Lookout Mountain. Not an undistinguished military record. And Kakuska, whose love of horses dated back to his native village near Tabor in Bohemia, and later the farm near Manitowoc where he'd enlisted when Lincoln issued his first call for volunteers. Why? In his knapsack he carried a picture of his pretty young wife, who had set out all by herself across the pond to join him, and whom he hadn't seen in almost three years. Why? Once he had tried to get some leave. By then he'd been in the army a year and three months.

"A year and three months?" smiled the benign General Ritchie, famous for having had his life saved by the Bible in his breast pocket. He used to show it around—there was in fact a piece of lead shot, a minnie, buried in it, as though a jeweller had mounted it there. "A year and three months? I haven't seen my wife in two years, corporal. If a general can lay a sacrifice like that on the altar of the Union, so can a corporal."

"Well, general, sir," Kakuska responded circumspectly in his South Bohemian accent, so that the pious general apparently wasn't sure he quite understood, "I don't know you and your missus, but the good God made me and my wife a little bit different." Perhaps the devout general understood the words but not the idea. The sergeant wondered what the pretty farmer's wife in Wisconsin was sacrificing on the altar of the Union, but he quickly suppressed the nasty thought and moved his attention to the next soldier. Jan Amos Schweik—known in the army as Shake—veteran of Lincoln's Slavonic Rifles of Chicago, who, unlike almost everyone else in the company, hadn't deserted, though there was hardly a greater coward in all of Sherman's army. Once he had held up an attack at Vicksburg for twenty minutes by starting to pray very loudly; his colonel, who was more pious than General Ritchie and a Catholic to boot, deferred to that sublime piety, distressed by the rosary Shake was shifting through his fingers. Finally, at the sixth decade, he broke into Shake's pleas to the Almighty with a vigorous "Amen!" and "Forward!", at which point everyone jumped up and charged the palisades except for Shake, who kept right on praying. Finally a canister shot exploded behind him, pushing him in the direction of the assault. By this time, however, the others were all rushing back, led by the colonel, so Shake ended up leading the retreat. Now he was sitting by the campfire, puffing on an oddly incongruous meerschaum pipe—which he carried in his haversack in three segments—and by the light of the fire his smooth, round face looked like a blue-eyed moon.

The bride emerged from the tent on the arm of the groom, who by now had recovered his normal colour, and the band struck up the Wedding March. The rainbow still hung in the sky, its colours reflected in the bells of the trumpets pointing backwards over the musicians' shoulders towards the spectators. A cabriolet arrived, drawn by a white horse and driven by a Negro equerry. The bridegroom helped his bride up onto the seat, then swung up beside her. His youthful face shone with an ingenuous look of bliss.

It was still raining.

On the sycamores.

"God knows where my father is these days," Cenek Dignowity had continued, back in the trench at Vicksburg. "They say he's in Washington, drawing up plans to invade Texas. He got away by the skin of his teeth, so they took it out on me and my brother."

The big guns boomed behind them and the Vicksburg palisades bloomed with fiery grey blossoms.

"Father was a Sam Houston man from start to finish," young Dignowity explained. "He could hardly have been anything else. He grew up in a garrison town back in Bohemia. He watched them torture soldiers. You know what running the gauntlet is?" The sergeant knew all too well. "So when the tsar's Russians were advancing on Warsaw, he got all the way across Prussia, to the famous Fourth Infantry Regiment under Romarin. He watched Polish farmers with nothing but scythes with hooks tied onto them mow down regiment after regiment of the tsar's best cavalry. And the priests were with the revolution. The Fourth Regiment was armed with money the priests collected by selling monstrances to Jews. General Klopocky kept hoping France would lend a hand. No such luck—they had to deal with the enemy on their own. Marvels of courage, they were, but there were just too many Russians, a bottomless supply of cannon-fodder. From the Urals, from Siberia, from the black bowels of that stinking country that thinks it's the salvation of bloody Slavdom and whoever disagrees is their enemy. Father was one of only ten survivors in Romarin's regiment," Dignowity said while Sherman's cannoneers rained canned hell-fire down on the palisades at Vicksburg. "So he lit out for America. Here, we think we do things better than anywhere, and if you can do better, we'll learn from you. Secede from the Union? Considerations for their peculiar institution? Father wasn't having any of that. He'd fought for the Poles, hadn't he? So he talked, he made speeches, he argued with the patients in his dispensary, and then—" Dignowity ran his fingers through his hair—"finally, one afternoon, somebody banged on the back window, damn near broke the glass. It was Judge Collins's slave Sam—the judge was a Sam Houston man too, but not what you'd call brave—and he says, 'They're coming for you, Doc, they want to string you up,' and sure enough, my father looks out on the square and there's this mob gathering, and old man Kearney is waving a coil of rope over his head. Father didn't hang around, he went out the window and onto his horse till all I could see were his coat-tails flapping. That's the last I saw of him. They say he's in Washington now, and I sure hope so. I'm going to try to get there to see him, but—" A petard interrupted him; the heavy artillery had joined in the bombardment. Clumps of dirt and splinters of wood from the palisades came flying through the air onto the roof of their trench.

"Peculiar institution," said Dignowity. "I remember the arguments when it was still okay just to argue. 'So their skin is the same colour as Balthazar's?' yelled my father. 'So what? He worshipped the Baby Jesus too!'"

Another deafening petard. A particularly solid chunk of the fortification rose into the air and they watched as it floated towards them. Everyone ducked. It fell heavily onto the roof and crashed through it. A Balthazar, his eyes wide with fright, landed on the ground in front of them. For a moment he just sat there, stunned by the phenomenal flight, while they stared at him as though he were an apparition. Was this possible?

The Balthazar shook his head. Then, as if he couldn't quite believe it himself, he said, "I's free." He gave his head another shake and exclaimed, "I's free!" He jumped to his feet and they burst out laughing. "I's free!" yelled the Balthazar. Fiery flowers were still blossoming on the Vicksburg palisades.

The cabriolet stopped and the little general strode forward. Two riders were approaching in the rain. The first had the weathered face of a proud beggar, or of an old noncom, the kind who might have led his company into battle under Little Round Top at Gettysburg, into the Wasps' Nest at Shiloh or Bloody Corner at Spotsylvania, slaughterhouses all of them. His name was Sherman.

Captain Warren introduced his bride.

The sergeant had first seen Linda Toupelik standing between two sycamores on Bay Street in Savannah, an emerald against the white background of a sunlit wooden building. The serpent's eyes had grazed his for an instant, then moved across the street crowded with ragged men bearing the insignia of the Twenty-sixth Wisconsin, the fifty-fifth Ohio, and the Thirty-third Indiana, flowing past the white portals of houses set among the green gardens of the city they weren't allowed to torch. Among them he glimpsed Kakuska with a strange load that looked like a big grandfather clock, but he was more interested in the cornflower gaze, and followed it to the white latticework on the building across the street and the red, gold, and ebony heads of the painted women leaning out of the upstairs windows. Then her gaze slid down the façade to a group of officers in brushed blue tunics. In the sergeant's eyes they became a frozen tableau vivant like the tinted engravings in *Harper's Magazine*: Lieutenant Williams, Second Lieutenant Szymanowsky, Captain Bondy, all of them inclined in the same direction, towards the brothel doorway, where the massive madam stood like an evil moon under the sign of her establishment—MADAM RUSSELL'S BAKERY—and beneath it, in smaller letters, *Horizontal Refreshments*, and all three of them were clutching the arms of Captain Baxter Warren II, who was leaning the other way, his legs taut, his heels braced on the curb, and his head turned at an unnatural angle as the cornflower gaze struck him square in the eyes. Later on, going over the moment in his mind, the sergeant realized that he had taken in the entire scene in a single glance, and that memory had shaped it and mingled it with pictures from *Harper's Magazine*. But at the same time his glance shot back to the girl in the emerald-green dress against the white façade, and behind him he heard Cyril Toupelik say, "Well, blow me if it's not our Lida!"

He and Cyril never found out how she managed it, but the second time he saw her, from the bar in the Hotel Savannah, she was dressed in turquoise blue, sitting at a table set with sparkling crystal on spotless linen, opposite the hopelessly smitten captain. A Negro waiter was standing over them, curly silver hair surrounding a fleshy face, pouring champagne from a silver-necked bottle into overflowing flutes. He never did find out how she'd done it, and later just accepted it as a matter of fact that it was Linda Toupelik. Outside the wide windows of the Hotel Savannah, moonlight was pouring down on the sycamores.

By the third time he saw her, he had heard all about her. But in the evening of that first day he knew nothing. Watching Kakuska take apart a huge clock and place one gearwheel beside another on a blue handkerchief spread out on the table, he saw Cyril Toupelik, not here in the room where he lay annihilated by some massa's whisky, but pushing past him to confront the girl. The cornflower gaze faded, the sweetness in her face gave way to surprise, though what kind the sergeant couldn't tell—certainly not pleasant, for the siblings neither embraced nor kissed. The sister just leaned against the pillar holding up the porch roof; Cyril leaned against the pillar opposite her, hands in his pockets, feet crossed. Terse sentences flew back and forth between them. He couldn't understand the words, he only heard the tone—at first questioning, then Linda's voice became defiant, Cyril's irritation increased, and then he caught himself staring at Linda Toupelik and, embarrassed, stepped back into the street and fell in with Sherman's ragtag army, Kakuska's tall clock ahead of him and a squealing pig behind him. He turned around to see Jan Amos Shake striding along with a huge, plundered cigar clamped in his teeth, the elegant hat of a Confederate colonel on his head; on a golden cord from somebody's fancy drapes Shake was leading Clem Vallandigham, the porcine mascot of K Company of the Twenty-sixth Wisconsin, rooting about in the piles of refuse along the street. Kapsa took another quick look at Madam Russell's Bakery, where Williams, Szymanowsky, and Bondy had disappeared—probably inside, since the evil moon in the doorway was gone and in her place stood Captain Baxter Warren II like a blue pillar of salt. Then the sergeant was swept forward in the flow of liquored-up Shermanites, borne along behind Kakuska's clock on the song.

Blank looks in Dixie when Northern troops come!
Sad hearts in Dixie when they hear the victor's drum
Pale cheeks in Dixie when rattle, shell, and bomb
  And down comes the Dixie rag!

Kakuska was taking apart the clockworks he had removed from the shiny case with the etched-glass windows and, one by one, arranging cogs and sprockets side by side on a blue handkerchief, by size, while outside the sun was setting and the sycamores nodded in the wind.

Sergeant Kapsa had never been lucky with women. No, that wasn't it. They never brought him luck. "Oh, you poor, poor man!" said a voice from the dark shadows in the little room at the end of the barracks that housed the infirmary where they had left him to die. "Ach, du mein armer Mann!" He lay on his stomach, unable to turn over. His back felt on fire. And then suddenly he felt cooling water among the flames. He tried to look around but couldn't. The flames flared up again. "Be still!" said the voice in Viennese German, a woman's voice, cooing, consoling, and the water washed his wounds, cooling, soothing, merciful. He felt the touch of a woman's hand. In the gloom a face suddenly surfaced before his eyes, a woman kneeling beside the infirmary bunk, looking at him. It was her. He had seen her that morning on the parade ground, with the other officers' wives and their brats, but he had known her even before that. This encounter over the blood-soaked bed was not the first time their eyes had met. Frau Hauptmann von Hanzlitschek, the captain's wife. When she had first walked past him, accompanied by a maid with a shopping bag, he had been standing guard, forbidden to move even his eyes, but when her grey eyes caught his he had moved them, and had watched her walk away, slender in a long grey dress with a bustle, and before vanishing around a corner she had looked back and smiled. The next time was on the promenade, arm in arm with her husband, with his sabre clanking in its shiny scabbard beneath a huge belly, and his waxed imperial moustache. Hanzlitschek. Another exchange of glances. She dropped her gaze coquettishly, and was that another smile on her lovely lips? A smile in the very shadow of the imperial moustache? And then he saw her one afternoon in the park, with a miniature version of the captain in a little velvet suit and, on a leash, a pug that also looked a little like the captain. A smile, a lowering of the eyes—he mustered his courage but it was impossible, a common soldier in the regiment commanded by her husband, and yet . . . but before he could summon the courage another lady appeared, with another pug on a leash and a little girl in a white lace dress. The pugs began to sniff each other, the miniature Hanzlitschek yanked the bonnet off the little girl's golden curls, a slap, a howl, a yap, a growl; both ladies took vigorous disciplinary action, whereupon Ursula—by then he knew her name—

turned her stern face in his direction and broke into a smile—the situation allowed it—and the smile was clearly meant for him. He reddened, and she turned back to slap the wailing junior Hanzlitschek and stroke the shrieking girl's golden locks. There were a few more encounters, just eyes and smiles. He kept mustering his courage, but still hadn't quite worked up the nerve to speak when the summer of '48 came, and the game that was no longer a game interrupted a full-blown infatuation. They got their orders and marched out of the little town in the Austrian Alps, all the way to Prague, where they joined forces with General Windischgraetz. There he first saw a face sliced in two by a sabre, brains dripping across half-opened lips, two halves of a student cap splattered with pink cranial matter and blood. He was not uninformed. Back home he had read Havlicek's newspaper, his schoolteacher had lectured in the tavern about the Hussites and the noble kings who had ruled the ancient Czech kingdoms long before the Hapsburgs. He knew he was Czech. That was at the root of his crime. No, he hadn't refused to shoot; that would have been impossible. He had simply fired into the air. But Hauptmann von Hanzlitschek was interrogating a grocer they had arrested, lashing his face with a cane. Blood flowed from the wounds, the grocer's teeth were clenched, but he never uttered a sound, though his eyes blazed with a brutal rage. Hatred. Kapsa's own hatred brought some furious words to his lips, and that was all it took. He was sentenced to run the gauntlet three times. Only three times—a mild punishment.

He shuddered. Not from terror, but from the force of the grocer's rage. Back in the alpine town where he was escorted in shackles, it was a murky morning. The grocer with the lacerated face was long behind bars, the student with the severed brain was in his grave, Prague was in abject peace. As he was being escorted back, he saw one of Windischgraetz's cannon-balls fall out of a wall above a bookstore where it had partially lodged, killing a priest who was walking, head bowed, to the Tyn Cathedral. On that murky morning, three hundred of his fellow soldiers stood in two rows facing each other in the courtyard of the barracks, once a Jesuit monastery. Sandstone statues still rimmed the courtyard, a wide-eyed kid perched on each one so as not to miss a thing—who knows why? For the perverse pleasure of it? For the greater hatred of the House of Hapsburg? God knows. Boys like that had been underfoot among the burghers on the barricades in Prague, too, throwing rocks at Windischgraetz's troops. Under the statues stood groups of officers' wives. They were certainly there for the perverse pleasure of it—except for one, whose face was paper-white, her grey eyes almost black in that deathly pallor.

The provost and his henchmen ripped off Kapsa's shirt, stuck a musket-ball in his mouth so he wouldn't bite off his tongue, tied his mouth closed with a rag, and bound his hands in front of him. Then four old-timers hobbled along the rows, distributing willow switches and placing the extras in four piles at either end of the lines, in case somebody's switch broke. Captain Hanzlitschek and two lieutenants marched briskly to the far end of the line. A fine drizzle began to fall. Two corporals stood behind Kapsa with bayonets in case he balked. The drummer started a drum-roll, slowly accelerating to a dance rhythm. Kapsa glanced down the long double row at Hanzlitschek, who seemed quite small. All the men were staring straight in front of them, and some of them were pale too; others were flushed with hatred. Everyone felt hatred. This could happen to any soldier. To many it already had. Some of those were gone. The drum-roll turned into something like a quickstep—an image that had occurred to him only here, in America, where this kind of discipline was unheard of—and then a quick gallop, and then the order came, barked in German, "Lauf!" Run! He started running, and the two corporals ran with him but on the outside of the double line, making sure each of his mates did his duty. The drum-roll crescendoed to a frenzy. It was raining.

With the sun setting, Kakuska lit the candles in the porcelain candlestick. Outside, a soldier approached. He was bellowing a song about John Brown, but the words made no sense because the singer, unfamiliar with English, was merely imitating the sounds as he recalled them. The door was kicked open and there stood the singer, an inebriated, staggering Houska. His eye immediately fell on Kakuska's array of gearwheels spread out on the blue handkerchief.

"Is it busted?"

"The hell it's busted," Kakuska retorted.

"You need another clock? I'll get one!"

"Sit down. Thirsty?"

"You guessed it, chum."

"There's some water over there." Kakuska pointed to a huge earthenware demijohn on the floor beside the table. "Fire-water," he added, noting Houska's scowl. They hadn't stolen the demijohn; it was a gift from an old black man, with his old woman and a little chocolate-coloured girl, who couldn't have been her daughter, in tow.

"Go on, take a drink, gentlemen," the old man had said to the ragtag soldiers. "Good stuff from massa's cellar." As they were taking a swig, Sherman galloped by with General Schofield, followed by Lieutenant Dolfa Chladek, another Czech, the general's adjutant.

"Beulah, look dere, chile!" shrieked the old woman, pointing a gnarled finger at the man with the deeply furrowed face on the fast horse. "Dar's the man that rules the world!"

The sergeant was stirred by a soldier's affection for the general. "Long live General Sherman! Hurrah!" he exclaimed, tossing his cap in the air.

Stejskal, Kabinus, and Paidr followed suit. "Hurrah!" Sherman looked back, grinned, saluted. When he disappeared around the corner, their attention returned to the whisky.

The old Negro was kneeling on the ground beside the demijohn, his arms raised to the heavens, hollering, "Mine eyes have seen the glory! Mine eyes have seen—"

"So what's this clock for?" Houska asked Kakuska.

"Well, Gambetta said clocks have wheels in them with sharp teeth, and they're supposed—"

The sergeant's thoughts drifted away. Women never brought him luck. In the distance beyond the window, a band was playing "When Johnny Comes Marching Home". Home? Never, he thought. Wouldn't ever want to. Yes, the meadows smelled sweet there, and so did the forests, a wild mushroom smell, and the frogs in the pond could sing. But what was the point? And anyway everything was fine here, it really was. Yet Annie—her shiny braids, her neat little apples under that blouse with the rosemary embroidery—"Johnny, I love you so much!" He was lucky with women. He'd picked the prettiest one, and she had a dowry. Even her father liked him, he was a farmer's son. True, he was just the second son, but he was from a farm all the same. Annie, the only daughter, came from a big farm, and her father had taken a shine to him. Then, as luck would have it, the crimps took a shine to him too. Nothing worked. Bribes, entreaties, even intercession from as high up as the vicarage in town.

Annie wept: "I'll wait for you, Johnny! If it takes years!" But the seven years he'd be in the army would be too long.

"You must understand, John, Annie's eighteen," said the farmer guardedly, and a little sadly. "When she's out of your sight, she's out of your mind. And besides, you might not come home from the war at all. Annie could wind up an old maid—"

No, women simply never brought him luck. Within a year Annie was hitched. She was nineteen by then. True, she'd held back. She'd wept, she'd despaired, and a friend of his wrote that she'd even wanted to take arsenic. But where would she get it? In the end, she went to the altar and he stayed in the army. And then along came Ursula.

He ran, caught a glimpse of her—two black coals in a white face—felt the first lash, the second, the third, the pain, blood pouring down, and at the end of the line his back was on fire. He stopped before the belly with the imperial moustache, von Hanzlitschek, took a quick glance back—her face was turned away from the spectacle, her head leaning against the robe of a sandstone saint, the sweet arc of her body in a grey dress, the pain—

"Move!" shrieked Hanzlitschek, and Kapsa turned and started running back. He glimpsed the corporal yanking an ashen soldier out of the line. *Can't have done his duty, a limp willow switch in his hand, may find himself running the same gauntlet in a few days.* But the others did their share, vultures flaying his back. At the start of the sixth lap, darkness came over him. He felt them carry him off, lay him face down on a slab. An order was barked out and he felt the rhythm of marching feet, each beat into his burning back like a red-hot saw. His last thought: *if I croak here, my buddies will still have to finish, because I collapsed before they were done. They'll take my carcass and scourge me, under the watchful eye of the corporal, till they've given the corpse its full eighteen hundred lashes.* Darkness embraced him. The very last thought: *I hate—if there's a heaven*—and then a sad, tender, Viennese voice: "Oh, you poor, poor man!" and cooling water soothing body and soul, grey eyes in the grey dusk, a soft, fragrant mouth on his own cracked lips.

". . . and they make better spurs"—it was Kakuska speaking—"than the government-issue ones." Kakuska searched through his collection of shiny gears and picked out a fine small-toothed one. "This should do it!" he said, and pulled off his boots. In the distance the band was playing "Aura Lea". The sergeant looked out the window at the stars. The stench of the rags binding Kakuska's feet struck his nostrils.

After he first set eyes on Linda Toupelik, Kapsa was carried along in the procession of revellers at the end of Bay Street. He walked slowly past the cheery houses, their gardens full of bright evergreens, the sun shining on the sycamores, and past brother and sister framed in the white portico. Cyril was waving his fists in the air. His lovely sister was standing with her back to him. Kapsa walked on. Unenticingly seductive voices came from the brothel, where Baxter Warren II still stood transfixed in the doorway. Kapsa walked to the end of the street, then turned and pushed his way back against the current of Sherman's marching troops, drawn by the emerald-green dress. He pretended not to notice as he walked by, but just then Lida turned on Cyril and hissed at him like a snake, "Shut up this minute, Cyril, d'you hear?" Cyril's voice broke—was it anger? Sorrow? "You shameless wench, . . ." he heard him breathe. Linda Toupelik spun around, and when the sunlight caught her tossing curls they seemed to burst into flame. The flames vanished inside the door, the door closed, leaving the furious Cyril—or was he just desperate?—alone on the portico.

"Cyril," Kapsa said hesitantly.

Cyril turned and looked at him blankly. Then he shrugged, shook his head as if to regain his senses, stepped down onto the sidewalk. "Come on! Let's get out of here."

"Where to?"

"Still got that demijohn?"

And now Cyril lay like a corpse on a cot in the back, while Kakuska, bootless feet wrapped in his foul puttees, replaced the old rowels in the spurs on his riding-boots with gear-wheels from the grandfather clock.

Outside the window, moonlight fell on the sycamores.

It was raining.

They stood in front of the wedding tent and stared after Sherman, with Logan beside him, trotting back towards the low bank of fog and the sound of clanking mess tins. The banner of the Nineteenth Michigan was slowly floating past above the mist. Mr. and Mrs. Baxter Warren stood beside the cabriolet watching the general ride off. A moment before, the bride had dropped a curtsy, the kind the officers' wives used to make in the Jesuit barracks. Sherman's leathery face crinkled into a fleeting smile, he kissed the bride, the band broke into "Glory! Glory!", the general swung onto his horse and rode off. A drenched and dirty little mutt ran up out of nowhere, sniffed at Shake, and tried to sink its teeth into his calf. Fortunately, his leg was encased in heavy cowhide.

"God alive!" exclaimed Shake. "What a country! Even the dogs have ghosts!"

"What are you talking about?"

"That mutt's a ghost!" Shake stared in astonishment as the small dog ran off, stopping only long enough to cast a baleful look back. There was no doubt he was staring straight at Jan Amos Shake.

"I'll be hornswoggled!" Shake declared. "In this war anything's possible. Even the dogs are coming back from the dead!"

And Kapsa recalled his own brush with death.

Every day the doctor looked in to see if he was still alive and, since he was, ordered them to bring him his rations. When a week had passed and he still hadn't kicked the bucket, the regimental physician himself turned up, examined his back, prescribed compresses, and muttered, "It's amazing, lad, you've risen from the dead!"

But it was she who had healed him, with her living water, and then, when the fire in his back had subsided, with the cooling warmth of her body. He never asked her how it could have happened, where the guards had gone, but he couldn't have asked her anyway, for she spoke no Czech and the only German he knew was the gibberish of military orders. He knew only that her name was Ursula, not why she was Hanzlitschek or why she was the way she was (but that was obvious: he was lucky with women, though they never brought him luck), or where Hanzlitschek was (he was probably in the officers' casino; his monumental belly betrayed a beer drinker). Late in the summer, Kapsa returned to his regiment and spent a month in desolate and futile longing. He felt the terrible loneliness of a soldier confined to the company of men. He would catch an occasional glimpse of her walking across the parade square to town. They always exchanged encouraging glances, but it was the same as before, before she had happened, before she had become a wellspring of healing water. Now glances were no longer enough. At times he'd see her with the captain in a carriage, or with the captain's miniature double in the park, but she was always with other wives and she could do no more than add an occasional smile to her glance. He began to doubt that it had ever happened.

One day when he was off duty they called him to the gate. "You have a visitor," the sentry told him. Who could it be? Someone all the way from Bohemia? "If I were you," said the sentry, "I'd stay put, if I were you. This kind of thing leads to missing lights out. And you know what that leads to."

He told the guard to go to hell and went to the front gate. There he found a pretty girl in a Tyrolean dirndl. He was lucky with pretty women, but they never brought him luck.

"Herr Kapsa?" He nodded. "Tomorrow evening you're to be at Gottestischlein at seven o'clock. Um sieben Uhr.*"*

"What?"

"Gottestischlein. Do you know where that is?"

"Ja, but who—?"

"Wiedersehen!" And the vision in white kneesocks turned and quickly walked away. This time, he thought to himself, a pretty girl has brought me luck.

He was mistaken, but he didn't know it yet. Later on, in America, he would realize he hadn't been mistaken after all. It had just been luck of a different kind.

Kakuska strutted back and forth across the room, jingling his new spurs. He stopped and raised one heel, then the other, admiring the spinning little gearwheels.

"What do you think?"

"The most expensive spurs in Sherman's army." The sergeant grinned, pointing to the pile of precision parts spilling out of the blue kerchief and the beautifully finished clock case with its bevelled glass window. "What are you going to do with this?"

Kakuska glanced at the remains of his spur-making. "That's good for nothing now."

The black small hand was pointing to twelve. Noon or midnight? The big hand was bent at right angles to the clock face, pointing at nothing. "That's for sure," the sergeant said.

Houska was asleep face down on the table. Kakuska tipped the demijohn back and took a swig. "Well, I'm off," he said, and strode towards the door. "Good-night."

"Night," said the sergeant. He walked to the door with Kakuska and stood in the doorway, listening to the jingle of the spurs fading in the darkness. Somewhere far away, a band played "The Girl I Left Behind Me". Moonlight fell on the sycamores. An owl flapped silently across the face of the moon. "Anything's possible in this war!" Shake had said at Kennesaw Mountain. They'd been waiting for orders to attack when an owl flew out of a pine, followed by three crows. The owl turned and gave the first crow a peck. The other two attacked the owl. It defended itself bravely. In the quiet before the storm, wild birds' voices hooted and cawed and feathers flew as the birds battled overhead. "Even the birds are at war!" Shake had exclaimed. Now, as Shake examined the shank of his boot for teethmarks, the band played and Sherman and Logan vanished like ghosts into the low fog. Another flagstaff with a banner and perch floated above the fog. This time there was no squirrel on it, but a bald eagle. The Eighty-second Illinois. Sherman's great army was rolling towards Augusta.

"It must be that cur from the farm in Burnville!" Shake complained.

"Animals don't haunt you if you disturb their graves," the sergeant said.

"It was the other one, then, the one in Cedartown. He looked just like him, two peas in a pod. And his mistress pitched a tomato at me."

"In case you've completely forgotten your catechism," said the sergeant, "dogs don't have souls." He remembered all too well the bummers' foray, when Shake had ended up with a tomato splattered in his face—the girl in the white dress had a good arm and true aim, but pretty soon her pride gave way to weeping, her narrow shoulders shook, and they both stared at her with growing shame as the effects of the whisky wore off. Shake's face looked like a clown's, and the smoking pistol was still in his hand as he stood over the little dog's corpse.

"I'm an Emersonian now," said Shake. "The whole universe is filled with one big soul, and all the little souls, even dog souls, come from the big one!"

"We got orders to shoot every hunting dog," Shake had explained. She stood in tears on the path to the plantation house while Shake held the little pug by its embroidered leash. "It's your own fault, you taught them to go after people and it's too late to break the habit now." Behind Shake's back, Fisher had just wrung the neck of a gabbling goose and Stejskal was coming from the house with a big box of cigars.

"But this isn't a hunting dog," the girl wailed. "It's Tippy, he's a lap-dog."

Shake glanced down at the growling little beast, then at the plantation belle, flushed red with anger and dismay. "Sure," he said, "but how do we know he won't grow up to be a mastiff?" With a deliberately mean look on his face, he put the pistol to the little dog's head, took a step towards its mistress, and tripped. The gun went off. The girl reached into the basket on her arm and then Shake was standing there looking like a circus clown. She turned away proudly, and then broke down in tears. The pug's legs twitched. From around the corner of the big white house came a Negro family laden with bundles. They headed towards the road to join the procession of creaking wagons full of worthless booty, munitions, and provisions. The oxen moved their heads from side to side, the tattered remains of women's hats and silk ribbons dangling from their horns. A soldier limping beside a wagon wore a huge medallion on a glittering chain around his neck. Behind a group of Negroes came a soldier holding a bayonet with a roast suckling pig skewered on it. Sherman's great army was rolling towards Atlanta. Stejskal pried the box open with his bayonet and pulled out a cigar almost as big as a police truncheon.

The sergeant hadn't seen the tragedy at Burnville, but he'd heard about it around the campfire. The woman was no longer young, and the plantation house had burned to the ground but it was still smouldering. She was sitting on a bench in the garden with three paintings leaning against the rosebushes beside her. A bummer was walking off with a fourth that depicted a naked woman on a huge seashell. The three paintings the bummer had left behind were portraits of old men in lace collars. The woman sat motionless, watching them contemptuously. Shake poked the toe of his boot into a rectangle of freshly turned earth, then pulled the ramrod out of his gun, stuck it into the middle of the damp rectangle, and gave the woman an enquiring look. For all he could read from her face, she might have been a sphinx. Shake scowled and poked the ramrod around. It struck something solid.

"Rings on my fingers, bells on my toes, and I shall have music wherever I goes!" fisher sang. The woman didn't budge, so they set to work. In their lust for booty, they failed to notice that the wooden box their spades turned up bore traces of having already been forced open. They removed the lid, also overlooking how easy this was. In the box was a little dog, stiff with rigor mortis. "Poor Dribble," the woman said finally. "I see he is destined never to rest in peace. You gentlemen are the fourth ones today."

Irritated, they slammed the lid shut. Shake felt like kicking a hole in one of the portraits, but he held back and instead drew a pair of charcoal spectacles on one of the old men. The sun, low on the horizon, was turning a fiery red, and thin columns of smoke were rising from the smouldering house. The woman sat as still as a statue. No, a pug would not grow up to become a mastiff. But they did set dogs on them. She sat like a statue by the portraits of her forefathers. Like a statue face to face with violence.

God knows, he said to himself. It was raining on the sycamores. The band was playing. The two-wheeled carriage started down the path, and Linda Toupelik turned and waved. Blue serpent's eyes under the arch of a rainbow.

She was waiting for him. He couldn't see her until he had climbed all the way to the top of the hill called Gottestischlein, God's Little Table, and then there she was, sitting on a bank of moss among the pine trees. Ursula's grey eyes had probably followed him all the way from the outskirts of the alpine valley town in the reddening sun, for it had been early autumn then too. Deeper in the woods was a little habitation, a strange, improbable place, too fancy for a gamekeeper's lodge, too modest for an aristocrat's summer home. It had only two rooms—one with a pot-bellied stove, some dishes, pots, pans, and kettles, and a tall grandfather clock, the other with a modest four-poster bed freshly made up with sheets of fine linen, and a porcelain washbasin in a carved oak commode. It made no sense as a place to live, but he asked no questions. He could see Gottestischlein from his barracks window. Later, on evenings when she couldn't get away, he would lie on his bunk and stare at the wooded hill, and the house would glow in his mind like a holy chapel. On evenings when she couldn't come, he would wonder whether his tearful mates hadn't actually been flogging a corpse on that slab, and whether this wasn't really heaven, for although he neglected church and read godless books, perhaps he had never truly wronged anyone. Like everything wonderful, heaven was measured out in tiny portions, the evenings she could come. The cottage glowed among the pines beneath the dark, looming crags of the Alps, white-capped in the early autumn of that miraculous year, and she was the lovely messenger who brought him luck. But no, it wasn't heaven, for like a cold pistol at the back of his neck he could feel the chill certainty that it couldn't last as heaven must last. He was neither lucky nor dead, but luckily, unluckily, alive, since misfortune is always a matter of time and time is always short.

Perhaps she was a sorceress. He didn't know and wouldn't ask. But it turned out she wasn't. During drill on the parade ground, Captain von Hanzlitschek showed up—moustache, belly, beady, evil eyes—and strode past the company. The provost raised his voice. The orders came faster and their legs flashed back and forth. "Left turn!" "Right turn!" "Present arms!" And Hanzlitschek stopped, but this time he didn't begin bellowing orders, as he usually did on the rare occasions he left his office and came out to the parade ground in the rain. He merely stood there and watched. Kapsa felt, then knew, that he was the one being watched. Nasty eyes, sure of their right, their truth, their property—

—he stared back into those same eyes, reflecting the red sunlight coming through the window. With one hand Hanzlitschek ripped the eiderdown off Ursula, grabbed her by the hair, yanked her off the bed and onto the floor, and Kapsa saw the bullwhip in his other hand, heard the hideous swish and crack, and a bloody welt appeared on Ursula's back. Hanzlitschek drew his arm back again, another wicked swish, a second welt, but Ursula uttered not a sound. Kapsa leapt out of bed, naked as Adam; the third swishing blow never connected, the tip of the bullwhip grazed Ursula's white back but the rest of it snaked around his body as his right hand grabbed Hanzlitschek's wrist, and Hanzlitschek yanked away and turned the whip against him. The next blow caught him on the shoulder and the leather snake cracked across his bare back— his back caught fire, he recoiled, the captain raised his arm and brought the whip down hard on his flaming wounds. He was instantly filled with strength and a bitter, burning hatred. He flung himself on the officer and struck him a cannon-ball blow to the face. Hanzlitschek's body rose from the ground as though he were being blown out of hell, he spread his arms like a crucified Lucifer, and as he fell the back of his skull struck the sharp point of a decorative oak column on one corner of the commode. As he slid to the floor, the blackness of his eyes seemed to drain away into his head; a shaft of red sunlight caught the glassy eyes, a bat fluttered near the ceiling. Ursula rose, her naked loins glistening golden in the reddish light, and they stood over the dead officer like Eve and Cain in paradise gazing at the dead serpent. He felt not a tremor of fear, not a touch of terror. He had no feelings at all about the corpse that lay there, staring at the ceiling—

—so he numbly lifted the corpse onto his back, as she instructed, and carried it deep into the woods, and there he created a story for those who would, at Ursula's behest, go looking for the officer. With the heel of the captain's shoe he gouged a furrow in the moss on a slippery, slanted rock; then he arranged the corpse on the ground with the back of its head against the sharp edge of another rock, a little farther down the slope. He even put the captain's boots on his own feet and made a set of prints to the rock, and then laced them back on the dead man's feet. All this time he never felt a thing, except desperate rage that this fallen angel had driven him out of his paradise.

It was almost morning before they parted, knowing it would be for ever. At dawn he slipped out into the woods, wearing a pair of the officer's baggy civilian *trousers pulled tight around his waist with a belt, and the officer's threadbare coat with the officer's gold pieces in his pocket, and a nest of what looked like crystal eggs. She had gone to fetch all these things in the night.*

Years later, in the barracks of the Thirteenth Army, he began letting his imagination roam. He wrote a letter; no answer came. He waited, then he wrote again. He had never asked her about anything. He had never understood the mysterious little house in the woods, her mysterious visits to the infirmary. She must have been able to work miracles, and she could surely accomplish another one. But no answer came, not even to his third letter.

Why? Had they discovered what had actually happened in the woods on Gottestischlein? Or had she forgotten? Or was she exercising in some prison court-yard, walking in circles in a canvas skirt? Did she have another captain now? Or a colonel, perhaps? Any general could be proud to have her as a wife. Had he, a mere seven-year private, been a trifle to sweeten her life with the paunch? Had he any grounds at all for hope? Had she been a "von" before she became von Hanzl-itschek? Would she ever come to join him? How much more was a sergeant in the Thirteenth U.S. Army than a common soldier in the Royal Imperial Regiment of the Alpine Infantry?

Then the America in him revolted. Havlicek's articles and Charles Sealsfield's books had prepared him for America, but in Europe America had been a mythical Utopia on the far side of a Utopian ocean. It had taken necessity born of murder to make it a reality, a real land where farmers didn't kowtow to officials in the castle, and not just because there were no castles.

He was broken by sorrow because Ursula didn't know that this land on the other side of the ocean could be a Utopia for her too. No, he was being unfair. Something had happened, otherwise she would surely have come. He must have been more than just a spoonful of honey to sweeten a bitter marriage. He sat on the bank of the Susquehanna, and waves of remorse and guilt washed over him for thinking ill of her. Something must have happened. He wrote her another letter, and another. Then he stopped writing.

It was raining on the sycamores. The third time he saw Linda Toupelik, she was in a carriage with the blushing Captain Baxter Warren II at the reins. It was evening, and the house lamps along Bay Street, extinguished when Sherman's great army rolled into Savannah, were lit again. This time there was no looting—or almost none, except for a grandfather clock here and there. Otherwise there were only polite officers, their presence now acknowledged by the local ladies with solemn nods, and soldiers back from the great picnic in Georgia, their good mood maintained by quantities of voluntarily proffered Negro moonshine, a joyful libation to the troops of the Ruler of the World.

The plunking of banjos called from the windows of Madam Russell's beautiful brothel.

"My sister," Cyril Toupelik growled. "My sister, the gentleman's whore. My monstrous little sister." He turned to watch the lovely monster, her cornflower eyes reflecting the bright brass buttons on Captain Warren's tunic. Suddenly—and it all happened so fast that again it seemed to the sergeant like a *tableau vivant*—a man in a green coat hobbled quickly down the three steps from the white house. The sergeant noticed the knob-end of a wooden leg sticking out of one of his trouser cuffs, but otherwise he was a tall, statuesque, downright handsome man with long hair cascading onto his broad shoulders. He stumped past them, and the sergeant saw Cyril step up to the cripple just as he pulled a pistol from his unbuttoned coat. Cyril's fist shot up, and the gun went off as it flew through the air. The sound of shattering glass came from across the street, and one of the lanterns outside Madam Russell's went out. The sergeant glanced at Lida Toupelik and saw her flinch; her eyes seemed to double in size. Then he looked at the captain, who had turned his head with mild interest towards the gunshot. By then Cyril was holding the cripple by the shoulders, so the captain turned back, still glowing with infatuation like a pious convert.

Lida pulled herself together and tossed her golden curls confidently as Cyril said in English to the small crowd that had formed, "He's had a few too many and he felt like firing a couple of shots in the air, that's all."

The crowd looked doubtful, but they'd had a bit too much to drink as well. They started to disperse while the one-legged man stood there, pale as death. Cyril picked up the pistol, stuck it in his belt, took the man by the shoulders, and turned him towards the steps leading to the white building.

From inside the brothel came a spirited version of *When Johnny comes marching home again. . . .*

It was raining on the sycamores.

The cabriolet disappeared around some bushes. Linda Warren's white veil fluttered in the breeze. The mist over the road was thinning out now, and the men of Mower's division were marching under the plane trees, their filthy boots tracing regular arcs in the remaining wisps of rapidly dispersing fog as they sang:

The Union forever, hurrah, boys, hurrah!
Down with the Traitor, Up with the Star,
As we rally round the flag, boys, rally once again,
Shouting the battle cry of freedom.

Behind them came a squad of Kil's cavalry, their banner riddled with bullet holes; then a battery of field artillery rattled by, the butt of a huge smoked ham sticking out of a caisson, the black cannon barrels glistening in the rain. Behind them came three scrawny young drummers followed by a solid file of bearded soldiers singing "The Battle Cry of Freedom". Out of step, tin cups clanking against knapsacks, a frying-pan stuck handle down in the barrel of a rifle, came men from the mountains, men from the plains. Kapsa recalled an ancient, gloomy battalion, gloomy but polished, polished and gloomy, marching smartly in step down an alpine valley, with corseted Imperial officers on horseback. The Eighty-second Illinois began singing too, a terrible disharmony of wonderful voices, and he knew there had probably never been such an army, ever, since the days of Caesar. . . .

We will welcome to our numbers
The loyal, true, and brave,
Shouting the battle cry of freedom. . . .

They moved—men, guns, horses—out of step, rolling on like the mighty Mississippi, Sherman's great army rolling north to Atlanta.

"Look at him there!" he heard Shake say.

Reverend Mulroney was having trouble with his filly. Behind him the engineers were striking the wedding tent; the filly was prancing skittishly and the chaplain was struggling to control her. Shake chuckled and ran over to settle the filly, and the chaplain scrambled up into the saddle.

The rain kept pouring down on the sycamores.

"What struck you so funny?" the sergeant asked Shake later that evening, around the campfire. "The bride was beautiful, wasn't she?"

"Oh, that!" Shake chortled again. "You can't have done much church-going, right, sarge?" He turned to rummage in his haversack. "Fact is, what he read the Holy Church won't allow to be read on any Sunday after Pentecost, or any other time, for that matter." He took out a well-thumbed Bible, and flipped through the pages. "Listen," he said. "Here it is: the Book of Ezekiel the Prophet, chapter sixteen, verses thirteen to sixteen. He took a little piece of verse thirteen because he knows damn well you heathens never opened a Bible in your lives."

The flames flickered across Shake's moon-face, dancing in his blue eyes like cherubs in swaddling clothes.

"'*Thou wast exceeding beautiful,*'" he intoned in the mock singsong of a preacher, then noted in a conversational tone, "Mulroney read that, all right. But the part that comes right after that he kept to himself. '*But thou didst trust in thine own beauty, and playedst the harlot because of thy renown, and pouredst out thy fornications on every one that passed by; his it was.'"*

"Stop, you're corrupting us!" Stejskal chimed in.

"No, wait! Here's the main thing he left out." Back to the mocking singsong: *"And of thy garments thou didst take, and deckedst thy high places with divers colours, and playedst the harlot thereupon; the like things shall not come, neither shall it be so.'"*

He looked around at his comrades. They were silent. Shake stuck the meerschaum in his mouth and sent a little cloud of blue smoke towards the stars.

Stejskal said, "What I can't figure is how come you know the Bible by heart, you pagan."

"Me? A pagan?" Shake replied. "Were you knocked in the head by a cannonball, or what?"

Outside, the moonlight fell on the sycamores.

The Writer's First Intermezzo

NO GENERAL took part in as many battles as Ambrose; had regulations not required him to be at the command post, he would have spent every minute in the thick of it, with his troops. In Cincinnati, he once told me that he never felt right about it. "Soldiers are dying, and I'm watching this from a distance through a glass. I feel like a dodger. I'll never get used to it, Lorraine, though it's logical, of course. But I reckon it's just as logical to bolt as soon as the Reaper takes the field. No one wants to die."

"It's not logical," I said, "it's only psychological. It is logical, though, to protect your generals, because it costs a great deal of money to teach them their trade."

Ambrose sighed. "That all depends."

"On what?" I asked, annoyed because I knew what he meant. He had never wanted to be commander-in-chief but, naturally, he obeyed Lincoln. An order from him was like one of the Ten Commandments. Lincoln was fond of Ambrose. He also thought he was smarter than Ambrose. And he was—except for one thing. Ambrose knew himself better than anyone else did, including Lincoln.

Dear Ambrose. He was simply the most honourable, the most truthful, the most loyal, and the bravest soldier in the Union army.

He also cut quite a figure.

I count myself among the many who have wronged him in his lifetime, although in my case there was an extenuating circumstance: I was young at the time, and correspondingly foolish. Perhaps more so than average.

A time would come when Ambrose would take embarrassment in his stride. But back then—

2

It was ghastly. Rather than strength of nerves, it must have been some kind of physical spasm that kept me on my feet after I turned and fled up the aisle from the altar, with those appalled faces gaping at me on either side. Nothing like this had ever happened in Liberty for as long as anyone could remember, and most of the congregation, perhaps all of it, had never even thought it possible. That spasm held me together as I ran outside into the searing sunshine and climbed into the carriage, where I even managed to wait for my maids of honour, Maggie and Sarah, who came rushing out of the church behind me. Only after they plopped down on the seats across from me did I instruct Sam to drive us home. And it was not until I got back to my own room that it all sank in, and I became so hysterical that I thought I could simply run back and put everything right again. But for the first time in my life, my legs wouldn't obey me. And besides, there was that letter from the publisher in Boston on my writing desk.

"Good Lord! Maggie, Sarah! I have to explain to him!"

"How?" asked Maggie curtly, and stared at me without an ounce of sympathy.

A good question.

"I'll go get him," said Sarah, sweet soul that she was.

"Save yourself the trouble," said Maggie, but Sarah was already out the door. Maggie turned to me. "You really are a prize idiot, you know!"

There was no point in arguing. She was right.

So I burst into tears.

"Stop bawling," said Maggie, "it's not your style."

She was right again. But nothing like this had *ever* happened in Liberty. It was an extraordinary circumstance.

I bawled. Mama came into my room, sat down on the bed beside me, and stroked my hair.

"You've really done it now, girl," she said. "Papa went to the cellar and then upstairs. He's locked himself in his study."

That meant Papa had taken a gallon of whisky from the cellar. If we were lucky, he'd drink himself speechless. If not, he'd have all too much to say. This was his easy solution to everything, from a toothache to family problems to metaphysical questions, if and when any occurred to him. When my little brother ran away from home and we got a letter from Santiago, where he'd dropped anchor with the whalers, Papa made the trip to the cellar and back up to his study and that settled the matter, as far as he was concerned.

"Go ahead, get those tears out," said Mama. There was no reproach in her voice. Perhaps she was feeling sorry for herself. She could have done what I'd just done, twenty years ago, except in those days Papa hadn't yet taken to retreating into his private alcoholic haze. Or if he had, Mama didn't know about it.

She stroked my hair a little longer and then left.

"If I did something that cuckoo, my folks would tear me apart," Maggie said. "Be thankful for the parents you've got, you dimwit."

By then I wasn't sobbing so hard. I knew I deserved this. Then Sarah rushed in, all out of breath, and said that Ambrose was gone by the time she got to the church. The moment he'd come to his senses, they said, he was out of there like a shot. So good old Sarah rushed over to the Burnsides', but Bob wouldn't even let her in. The lieutenant had just stopped by for his valise, and then left for the station.

I looked at the clock on the dressing table. It was almost three. The train to Connersville would leave at a quarter past. Ambrose would have to wait an hour in Connersville for his connection.

I could catch him there.

I had no idea what I would say.

3

The truth is, it wasn't fair. I wasn't ready to marry Ambrose. But that's how life is: not exactly fair.

Ambrose had gone off to West Point before he turned eighteen. He was a thin lad, a tailor, and his shop, which wasn't even on Main Street, wasn't what you'd call elegant. Business was only fair, and his hairline was already receding. Not that any of this bothered me at the time. I was twelve and considered a tomboy. Girls didn't interest me, boys did, because they would take me fishing and let me play soldiers and Indians. But when one of those Huck Finns suggested I play an abducted beauty that the American cavalry would rescue from the clutches of the Shoshones, I got mad and said I was no beauty and just let anyone try to abduct me. I said they should ask Becky Thatcher. She was the beautiful one, and she read her older sister Jocelyn's romance novels. So they did, and of course Becky said yes and dressed up in her Sunday best for it. I was Chief Flat Feet of the Shoshones, and I abducted Becky in order to slay her. I was well brought up, I knew the only reason beauties were abducted was to be slain.

Or, if the abductors were Indians, to be tortured to death at the stake.

What actually happened to abducted beauties was something I didn't learn until my mother noticed that it was time to tell me the facts of life. Still, I remained a tomboy until I was almost seventeen and started reading articles by Margaret Fuller. Instead of flirting with young men, which I was now inclining towards, I decided to fight for the rights of women. I also decided never to marry, so that nothing would distract me from the struggle. This decision wasn't just because of Margaret Fuller; Mama's position in the family had something to do with it too. Papa was—well, inaccessible to reason. His cellar was too well stocked for any rational conversation.

I may have been a case of arrested development, rather than the great intellect that poor Margaret Fuller was. Be that as it may, my life till then had not prepared me for the figure I saw one sunny morning in front of Mr. Jenkins's saloon on Main Street.

His head was the first thing I noticed—I had never seen anything like it. It was beautifully framed by a dense chestnut moustache that seemed to spread from below his nose, then swoop down across both cheeks and up past his ears, and meet over his forehead. No one in Liberty had ever seen a moustache like it. Nor, for that matter, had they ever seen such chestnut-brown eyes under eyebrows so dense. The eyebrows emphasized his high forehead. It never entered my head that this signalled the beginning of baldness.

The young man, or rather his exquisite head, bowled me over completely.

Only then did I note how well the uniform of a United States Army lieutenant suited him, and how thrilling the low-hung pistol looked in its holster at his waist.

And only then did I—no, I didn't actually notice Mr. Jenkins standing beside the young man, I only heard him call, "Lorraine! Come here!"

I recall hearing someone behind me sigh deeply, and I suppose I responded. In any case, I found myself standing in front of the young man. Those chestnut-brown eyes were looking down at me and Mr. Jenkins was saying, "Now, do you know this young lady, lieutenant?"

"I can't say as I've had the pleasure," said the young man, shaking his head. "I'd surely never have forgotten such a lovely young lady." He sounded smitten already.

"The butterfly emerges from its chrysalis," said Mr. Jenkins. "This is the Hendersons' Lorraine."

"Ah," went the handsome lieutenant. Someone behind me sighed again. The lieutenant bowed from the waist and kissed my hand.

And that was all it took.

There and then—for a time—I lost interest in women's rights.

4

That was all it took. I was caught in the eye of a hurricane; he spun me like a top, and I couldn't find my feet. That very same evening there was a ball at the Campbells'. He came for me in a hired carriage and I, who was essentially against men, who avoided balls and therefore had never learned to dance properly, I floated across the dance floor with him all evening like a feathery cloud. The next day brought an excursion on horseback to Green Springs, where he declared his love for me in a romantic valley, a love that was fresh but all the more profound. The following day . . . well, to make a long story short, we went through the whole gamut of romantic courtship in a single week—including love letters, though we spent only a few hours each night apart.

He had only two weeks' leave.

A champagne picnic—it was summertime—and under the August moon he recited a carefully memorized poem. I didn't like the poem, but I loved his moustache. An awful lot. An outing on horseback to Gloucester Valley, croquet in the garden of the Methodist manse, and Sunday afternoon he came over to ask for my hand and we were engaged. The wedding was set for the following week, after which we were to go straight to join his garrison at the Jefferson Barracks in Missouri. More champagne, my father tearful, his appetite for whisky stronger than usual after champagne, my mother dry-eyed. But that didn't strike me as odd.

Then on Monday the letter from the publisher in Boston arrived.

The thing is, I had written a novel. Secretly. Inspired by literature—

Margaret—and by life—Papa, his cellar, and the increasing frequency of decreasingly adequate jugs. When I was writing the novel, I began, for the first time in my life, to dream. Not about romantic or even just ordinary lovers, the way Sarah and almost everyone else, perhaps even Maggie, did. As young as I was, I was overcome by the spell of pen and ink, the ecstasy of giving birth on paper. The advantage is that you can create your children any way you please. You can make them clever but naughty, beautiful, foolish, generous, ugly or plain, and no matter what they become, you love them all. I dreamed, as my characters appeared and grew under my fingertips, that this magic would make me an independent woman, freed from the necessity of choosing between some drunken but well-heeled bridegroom and a quiet but defeating life of poverty as an old maid.

By then Papa was up to his ears in debt and was beginning to see white mice. I dreamed that my novels would make me rich, that I would do nothing but fight the good fight with my pen, and have Mama come to live with me. That was my fantasy.

For a week, Lieutenant Burnside—quite unlike the former young tailor, now the perfect embodiment of an Achilles, a comely warrior and lover— changed all that.

But on Monday the letter from the publisher arrived. Thirty dollars in advance, ten per cent on every copy sold.

A peculiar change came over me. It may well have been a chemical change.

5

Though at seventeen and a bit I could be a gentle beauty when the need arose, there was still a little of the tomboy in me. I ripped the bridal veil over my head, pulled on my everyday calico dress, and saddled my little filly, Andromeda. Mama appeared in the doorway.

"Don't tell me you've changed your mind again, Lorraine?" she asked me.

"No—but I did such an awful thing to him!"

Mama didn't say a word. From Papa's upstairs window came the sound of singing. Lately, he'd taken to singing to his white mice and watching them dance.

"I must talk to him!" I shouted, like a truly hysterical female. I jumped into the saddle as Mama retorted drily, "What about? The weather?"

Then Andromeda was trotting along the path beside the tracks. In the distance ahead of me I could see smoke pouring out of the locomotive's smokestack. There was still time. I'd make it.

As I rode along in that uncomfortable side-saddle, my mind continued to work, for of course the mind can't be stopped, and it recapitulated on its own that awful week before the wedding that didn't happen. Poor Ambrose was a victim of the chemical change in me, and all that remained of the spell he'd cast was that aura of—what? Masculinity? Ingenuousness? Ambrose embodied all the best masculine virtues, but he was such an innocent.

And I had written a novel, and Mr. Little in Boston was going to publish it.

The first week of our acquaintance, I had paid no attention to what Ambrose was saying. All I could hear was that velvet voice. The poems he'd swotted up so eagerly from some handbook for young men in love didn't impress me much, but that voice!

The second week I began listening to what he was saying.

He was babbling inanities, probably from the same handbook. They were mostly about the glories of nature and the individual components of it deemed to possess a particular beauty, such as roses, butterflies, stars, and the full moon. He would intersperse these with his memorized poems and, because I happened to be reading Poe at the time, my mind involuntarily set Ambrose's verses against "Ulalume" and "Israfel". Ambrose lost in the comparison. Slowly at first, and then with increasing intensity, panic began to set in, and by Wednesday it had become abject terror. Good heavens! Was I to listen to this drivel for the next half-century, some of it in rhyme? I realized that his sumptuous side-whiskers had intoxicated me, and as I sobered up my rational powers returned. I knew that sooner rather than later Ambrose would stop reciting bad poetry and talking about the mellifluous song of the nightingale—but then what in heaven's name would he talk about?

Of course, I was young and foolish myself and should have known that love turns most men, temporarily, into gibbering idiots. Most women too, as I'd discovered for myself. It turned out later that, although Ambrose was an innocent, he was no fool. He went on to design a breech-loading rifle that was better than any other manufactured at the time. When the war began, they armed several divisions with it. So take that rifle: he designed and built it, but he didn't know how to sell it. After six years of struggling to stay on its feet, his munitions factory in Bristol, Rhode Island, closed down and he found himself in such dire straits that he had to sell his sword and the epaulettes from his dress uniform for thirty dollars so that he and his young wife, Mary, wouldn't starve. Then he took a job with the railroad.

He had a wonderful weapon but he couldn't sell it. Why? For all practical purposes, the sole customer for this type of product is, of course, the army. The army commission that tested all the various weapons systems ranked Ambrose's patent as the best. So Ambrose went to Washington with the naive idea that he need only sign a contract with the Secretary of War, John Buchanan Floyd, and the Rhode Island factory could start production in earnest. Floyd's assistant, however, indicated to him—in fact, he was unabashedly candid about it—that the quality of a weapon is one thing, and its sale something else entirely. The sale can only be made by someone who has certain army contacts. This someone would be available for twenty per cent of the profit Burnside stood to make from the contract.

Ambrose was horrified. "But—that's bribery!" he said with rising indignation.

"I wouldn't go that far," said the man with the contacts. "Let's just call it a commission?"

"And if I refuse?"

"The army has several other models to choose from."

"But my system is the best! That's what the commission decided. No one tried to influence them, nor would it ever have occurred to me to try!" Ambrose's blood was boiling now. "This weapon will enhance the army's firepower. The army's effectiveness—indeed the lives of its soldiers—will depend on it!"

The assistant looked at Ambrose as though he were a figure in a fairytale. "Exactly, sir," he said. "Aren't the lives of those soldiers worth twenty per cent of the profit?"

"But that—but that—Bribery is not consistent with military honour!"

"Hmm," said the secretary pensively. "Am I to understand that your private sense of honour is more important than soldiers' lives?"

Ambrose took a deep breath but couldn't come up with a coherent response. Instead he walked out and slammed the door behind him, which ultimately led to the sale of his sword and epaulettes for thirty dollars. But even as he was going through the door, he was aware—he wasn't *that* innocent—that his military honour might cost him dearly. And yet. . . .

It was still bothering him in Cincinnati, when the old wounds had long since healed and I, past thirty, was no longer a tender beauty, or even much of a campaigner for women's rights any more, although I smuggled many a radical idea into my tales of bright young women and handsome young men, ideas the wise men of this world would hardly have approved of had they happened onto them. I had learned to camouflage such ideas carefully, and I had abandoned entirely my struggle in the cause of temperance, which had been the secondary theme of my first novel. The critics had approved, but it was far less lucrative than Eros.

"Dear Ambrose," I told my former fiancé, "the bribe would have been a specific amount in hard dollars. How could you possibly calculate how many more soldiers died because they used an inferior system, say one of Smith and Wesson's, instead of one as undoubtedly superior as yours?"

"They ended up using my rifles anyway," said Ambrose. "When I went bankrupt, the patent was one of the assets I had to turn over to my creditors. In time I paid the rest off in cash."

"And what did they do with the patent?" I asked.

"Well," said the general, stroking his magnificent side-whiskers, "well, Mrs. Tracy—"

"Lorraine."

"Lorraine." He said it almost as melodiously as he had years before in Liberty, and a delicious shiver went up my back. "When the war broke out, the army had a serious shortage of weapons. Smith and Wesson signed a contract for two thousand units a month—"

"Without a bribe?"

"I don't know for sure, but I'd say yes, without a bribe. After Lincoln's appeal there were suddenly seventy-five thousand volunteers who had to train with sticks instead of rifles. The army was buying up everything it could lay hands on. I suspect that was the end of bribes for a while."

"So two thousand of your rifles a month—"

"At the beginning. The demand was far greater; the manufacturers started producing more and pretty soon they were delivering five thousand a month. At Bull Run about a third of the infantry regiments had my breech-loaders."

"So you indirectly saved a lot of lives, and your honour too."

"Well," said the general, again fingering the fringe around his face, "the casualties at Bull Run were still too high. I managed an orderly retreat." There was a slight trace of pride in his voice . . . poor Ambrose. Bull Run was one of his very few military successes, and at that it was only partial. He kept his regiment from panicking while others—they were all volunteers—fled in disarray. Unlike most commanders, he emerged from the defeat with his professional reputation more or less intact. "But otherwise," I heard him say, "some units got mixed up—there was great confusion—"

"You saved your honour, and on top of it the soldiers got your splendid rifle. Did you get anything out of it yourself? I mean in dollars and cents?"

He shook his head. He was perplexed, I thought. "I told you, the patent

wasn't mine any more," he said. "I'd given it to my creditors as partial payment of my debts."

So there you have Ambrose. He knew how to make a better gun. But he
could never quite fathom matters of honour and bribery, and the life and
death of soldiers.

So how could he have fathomed the problems awaiting him in
Cincinnati?

6

But back then, on the way to the Connersville railway station in the
uncomfortable saddle, I gave no thought to this side of Ambrose's personality. What was going through my mind was how the horror of the
second week of our courtship had given way to the horror of what I had
done to him.

The nightmare of that second week had urged me to break off this engagement while there was still time, but I couldn't bring myself to do it.
Once, I interrupted one of those abominable poetry recitations in the middle of a would-be sonnet. "May I recite a poem for you, lieutenant?" I said
and, without waiting for a reply, I began. I hadn't consciously memorized it,
either, I'd simply fallen under Poe's spell:

> *It was many and many a year ago*
> *In a kingdom by the sea*
> *That a maid there lived whom you may know*
> *By the name of Annabel Lee. . . .*

When I finished, he just stared at me in silence with his beautiful, guileless eyes.

That was Wednesday. After that he stopped reciting poems to me, and
he pruned back his odes to the glory of nature, too. So now it was I who
babbled, about everything except what I wanted to say, what I should have
said. I'd look at those devoted and suddenly desperate eyes of his—and I just
couldn't bring myself to do it. Once, when I was ten, some boys were jumping off a cliff that must have been twenty feet high, showing off and daring
me to do the same, and teasing me for being just a girl, and they made me so
mad that I climbed the cliff, but once I got to the top I looked down and I
was terrified. The boys were like the seven dwarfs at the bottom of a chasm,

egging me on. I took a deep breath and shut my eyes, but I was afraid to jump. I tried again, but the same thing happened. I could hear their voices mocking me, but I still couldn't do it. Then, when the voices became a single, huge, taunting roar, I opened my eyes and saw the whole gang walking away, chanting, "Girls are fraidy-cats! Girls are fraidy-cats!" So I shut my eyes again, and this time I—or someone—shoved the fear away and I was flying, my skirt filled with air, falling for what seemed like ages; then I opened my eyes and hit the ground with a crash. Something in my leg went crunch, and when I tried to get up I fell back like a ninepin. The boys had to carry me home on an improvised stretcher made of branches. My right foot was a swollen lump. Luckily I had only sprained an ankle and bruised my tailbone.

That was the kind of fear that stopped my tongue every time I tried to tell Ambrose that it was all a mistake, that I couldn't marry him because I was actually fond of him and if we did marry—

But there was no chorus of little boys mocking me, and I couldn't push away the fear.

Saturday came and they dressed me in white lace. I got out of the carriage half conscious. Sarah and Maggie held up my train as I stumbled down the aisle. I stood before Reverend Morris. . . . I could hear him asking me if I took this man . . . and I finally mustered the strength to leap into the chasm. I said, clearly and unequivocally, "No!"

And now, as I rode side-saddle down to Connersville, the memory gave me shivers of mortification.

7

I could see him from a distance. He was sitting on a crate by the tracks, near a couple of farmers smoking their pipes on a pile of logs, and a little farther away a Negro family with about eight children warmed themselves in the evening sun. I reined in Andromeda, slid out of the saddle, hitched her to the railing, and walked over to him.

What on earth would I say?

He was staring at the ground, but some sixth sense must have told him I was coming—the vile person who had shamed him in front of all Liberty. He looked up and jumped to his feet, visibly embarrassed. I stopped two steps away from him.

"Ambrose—" My voice came out in a squeak.

"Yes, Miss Henderson. . . ." There was a despondent note of defeat in his voice. Unfortunately it wouldn't be his last defeat, though the later ones weren't caused by an arrow from Greek mythology.

"Lorraine," I corrected him.

He said nothing, but looked at his feet.

"You know, Ambrose, I—" Then it burst out of me. "My novel is going to be published," I said, encapsulating the whole tangle of reasons in a single sentence.

"Novel?"

"That's right. I wrote a novel and Little and Brown in Boston are going to publish it. They—they even sent me an advance—thirty dollars."

"My congratulations," said Ambrose.

I must have seemed demented. "I'm not fishing for compliments. I'm telling you to—to explain—"

"There's nothing to explain, Miss Lorraine," he said helpfully. "I was— tried and found wanting."

"You were not found wanting!" I exclaimed, so loudly that one of the farmers looked around at us. "You deserve someone better than—"

"No, no," he interrupted me again, "I deserve exactly what I got. How could I have been so vain? I know my limits—"

"You aren't the least bit vain, Ambrose! And what I did—well, it was awful. Dreadful!"

The train whistle sounded from a distance. I didn't have much time. I was supposed to be a writer, but I couldn't find the right words. What could I possibly say in the few moments before the train arrived?

"I was a vain fool. You're bright and I—Those verses I recited . . . and you responded with 'Annabel Lee'—"

The pain struck me like lightning. He had recognized it! I thought he'd hardly read anything except those verses from his handbook, yet he recognized real poetry when he heard it. Oh, God! It must have been worse for him than I realized. This handsome, honourable, sensitive mountain of a man—how did he ever end up a soldier, anyway?

Should he have remained a tailor?

"You know, Miss Lorraine, I'm not very smart," he said sadly. "But unlike a lot of other fools, I'm smart enough to know that I don't have a whole lot up here," and he tapped his forehead.

"That's not true!" I exclaimed, but I was interrupted by the shriek of the locomotive braking. He bent down and picked up his valise. "You're intelligent and sensitive," I insisted. "Any girl would be proud to—but I—" How do you explain the inexplicable, when it's as clear as a slap in the face?

"They're going to publish your novel," he said sadly.

"That's not the point," I said. The stationmaster was calling all aboard. "It's just that I don't really want to get married! I want to be independent! I want to write novels and work for—"

Ambrose had mounted the steps to his car when he said something unexpected. "You'd be wasted on me. I'd be no good for you. I'm not up to it."

The train started to pull out.

"That's not the reason, Ambrose, believe me!" I called after him.

He waved.

"Forgive me, Ambrose! Ambro-o-o-ose!" I was screaming like a hysterical female. I could hear Andromeda neigh uneasily from the railing.

The train and Ambrose vanished, and that was the last I saw of him until thirteen years later, in Cincinnati, when he was named commander of the Department of the Ohio. By then he had his only real military success of the war, the capture of Roanoke Island, under his belt. And he'd been through Fredericksburg, probably the worst military catastrophe ever endured by a Union general. I had been married to Professor Tracy for years, had two children, Jimmy and Loretta, and under the pseudonym Laura Lee I was the country's most popular author of novels for young girls. I wove into these novels my mildly subversive messages about young men who were invariably described as "handsome". That was all that remained of my dream of being a great champion of women's emancipation. I was now a lady, the wife of a college president and professor of philosophy at the Academy in Cincinnati.

8

My curiosity about the impact of time on his beautiful side-whiskers moved me to send him my calling card when he arrived in Cincinnati. I was somewhat nervous about it, but I believe that time is a sieve that allows the bad things to pass through and retains only the good ones. I also knew that he had married not long after the disaster in Liberty, that he was a model husband, and that his marriage was a happy one and as solid as the rock of ages. In the meantime, side-whiskers had become all the rage, both in the army and outside it. People had taken to calling them "sideburns", a word they'd coined by twisting Ambrose's surname, thus ensuring him a place in history long after everyone but the historians had forgotten that he'd botched the job at Fredericksburg, or at least earned the reputation of having done so.

Actually, when you stretch the chain of cause and effect to the limits, the catastrophe at Fredericksburg was Lincoln's fault.

"As long as he was merely offering me the supreme command," Ambrose admitted in a weak moment, while he was trying to sort out the conundrum of Vallandigham, the traitor in his eyes, and *The Chicago Daily Times*—which he finally resolved like Antigone, correctly, so my husband says. "As long as he was merely asking me to take it, I kept saying I wasn't worthy of the honour. But Lorraine, the president had little choice—and then there was Roanoke and the retreat at Bull Run. I was only in command of a division there, that's something I'm up to—but the president didn't consider that. He probably said to himself, 'If he can do that well with a division, he won't be likely to do much worse with an army.' In any case, he ordered me to take the command. I'm a soldier, Lorraine."

After that he lost ten pounds. I knew something about how that had happened, but I didn't tell him; the immediate cause of his weight loss was an inappropriate topic of conversation in mixed company. But among the officers with whom my philosopher husband liked to smoke his pipe, it was an open secret that Ambrose had caught dysentery in the Mexican war, and that its unpleasant consequences continued to torment him. They never returned in the heat of battle; mortal danger wasn't something that inspired fear in Ambrose. They came back when he was attempting to follow orders that brought him up against his own limitations.

In my company, of course, he spoke only of an undefined ailment that had temporarily struck him down in the Mexican War; had it not been for his orderly, Robert Holloway, who had also been with him in New Mexico on the campaign against the Apaches, he said, heaven knew he might well have succumbed to the—ah—affliction.

Robert Holloway was a Negro, a circumstance that—albeit indirectly—may have played a role in the dramatic events of the spring of 1863 in Indiana, Ohio, and Illinois.

Ambrose arrived and, as they say in novels (even in mine, I admit), my heart skipped a beat. Time and suffering had done him no damage. On the contrary, they had only enhanced his masculine charms. True, his forehead now went all the way back to the nape of his neck, but his magnificent chestnut beard was the same as ever and his eyes held a wealth of experience garnered between that hysterical conversation at the Connersville train station and this afternoon in my parlour in Cincinnati. He had indeed lost weight, a fact that was underlined by the cut of his dark blue uniform, and the gold belt with a pistol slung low on one side and his sword, with a big gold tassel, on the other. He held a Union general's hat in his hand and his smile seemed to indicate that he was actually pleased, after all those years, to see the cause of the first major disgrace in his life. Time is indeed a sieve; the horrors of that courtship were a thing of the past. He turned his radiant gaze to little Jimmy, who bowed politely, and then to Loretta, who took after me and, despite the frills and bows that made her look like a sugarplum, was turning into a shameless tomboy. Still, she managed a relatively passable curtsy, and Ambrose then turned to me. "You didn't want to marry, Lorraine, but you couldn't escape it. With all the consequences."

9

To my own surprise, I lost my head again at the sight of him and I felt—though briefly—as I had years ago in front of Mr. Jenkins's saloon on Main Street. When he sat down in the armchair and crossed his legs in those shiny boots, he was surrounded by that aura of charm so mysteriously irresistible to ladies—and I was now a lady. I exercised self-control, of course. After all, romantic love was the coin I dealt in, and that is a far better protection against losing one's head entirely than motherhood is. In fact, motherhood, as our daily press constantly confirms, is no protection at all. We began reminiscing—in other words, gossiping—about mutual friends and, as we drifted together down the stream of time, I overcame my momentary weakness and landed back on my feet. "And did you hear that Sarah Withers married and moved to England?" I asked.

"Sarah? Wasn't she your bridesmaid in . . . ?"

I flushed and said quickly, "Sarah, quiet but deep, and now she's a countess."

I told him her story. It sounded as though it might have come from one of my novels, and Ambrose wondered aloud at the paradoxes of marriage-brokering in Liberty, which did not surprise me in the least, and led me to ask, "Do you have any news of Maggie Rogers? I somehow lost track of—"

"She married some officer in St. Louis," Ambrose said, almost curtly, and my cheeks flushed again. You idiot, I said to myself, and quickly changed the subject to my children. Ambrose sat in the plush armchair, the very picture of a general, but the hypnotic charm was gradually wearing off and a different kind of flame was kindled inside me. It was only later, when he had left to attend to his conflicting responsibilities—those he devoted himself to enthusiastically because he felt at home in them, like organizing units for the coming battle at Vicksburg, and those that tormented him because they were connected with his position as military commander of the civilian department of Iowa, Ohio, and Illinois—that I was able to define the feeling. There was nothing original about it: it was friendship, which is supposed to be impossible between a man and a woman. How did ours come to exist, then? I don't know. And when he was still sitting there in my parlour, toying with the golden tassel on his sword, I said, "And of course there was the Morton boy, Oliver, who's now Governor of Indiana."

He laughed. "Did you know I was once given a hat by the Honourable Governor? Of course, it happened before he was governor. Back in Liberty."

"I had no idea," I said. "How did that happen?"

"Because he got a waistcoat from me," said Ambrose.

"You bought each other Christmas gifts?"

"Not bought," said Ambrose. "Made. He was apprenticed to a hatter, I to a tailor. And we were friends. And now—"

I tried to imagine Ollie Morton, whom I could no longer picture in anything but tails, in that little wooden town among the fields, and I said, "Now that friendship may stand you in good stead, with him the civilian head and you the military one."

Ambrose's sunny mood clouded over. "Yes, we're still friends. But that's exactly why—" He was about to continue, then apparently decided it was something he couldn't discuss. "Lorraine, do you know General Carrington?"

"General Carrington? I know a Colonel Carrington—"

"Wright promoted him yesterday. My predecessor."

I laughed. "Well, Carrington can't botch things, not even as a general." Then I bit my lip. Talking with Ambrose about generals who can't botch things—but Ambrose said, "Well, Halleck thinks—" and he stopped himself again.

10

Halleck, Lincoln's general-in-chief, played a black role in Ambrose's tragedy. As soon as Ambrose had recovered from the shock of being named Commander of the Army of the Potomac, he declared war on his own sense of inadequacy by mapping out the details of an offensive against Fredericksburg. His plan assumed a rapid march along the northern bank of the Rappahannock to put his army opposite the town before Lee could figure out what Ambrose was up to and order Longstreet—who was then located thirty miles west of the town—to move his troops up to reinforce Fredericksburg. Pontoons would be waiting on the northern bank; Ambrose's engineers would build a bridge; the army would cross the river and take the town by storm, since it was defended by no more than a few Confederate companies and a single battery of light artillery. This would open the way to taking Richmond and striking at the heart of the Confederacy.

I had opportunity enough to hear all kinds of strategic plans like this in our parlour, since they fascinated my husband, Humphrey, and the officers he invited over for brandy and cigars. To me these plans always seemed rudimentary and transparent. There was never anything surprising or innovative about them, probably because the so-called art of war is more like a polka than a symphony, though it does sometimes thunder like Beethoven. Flanking manoeuvres from the left, strikes from the right, feints down the centre to trick the enemy into shifting his forces, and then a main offensive to outflank him on the right and strike at his rear—it was all a kind of abracadabra. I could never understand where the brilliance of the individual tactic lay, so Ambrose's plan, as he described it to me afterwards in my parlour, seemed as clever as if Napoleon himself had come up with it.

At the outset, everything went according to plan. General Sumner's Grand Division, the vanguard of Ambrose's army, covered the forty miles from their camp in Warrenton to the little town of Falmouth across the river from Fredericksburg in two and a half days. No general had ever moved so many troops so far in such a short time. Large bodies of troops were expected to cover no more than six miles a day, so Sumner should have taken a week. But—

Either Halleck, or Old Brain, as the generals had nicknamed him, was too important to listen carefully to the likes of Ambrose, or his big brain was too preoccupied with other problems, which the war supplied in ample amounts. Afterwards he told Ambrose that he had understood that Ambrose had agreed to a change of plan: Ambrose's army would ford the Rappahannock some twenty miles above Fredericksburg, march the rest of the way along the southern bank, and then simply attack. "He must have been listening with half an ear," Ambrose told me bitterly later on, "because the refrain of the song I sang was 'pontoons'. I never changed that refrain. 'Pontoons' was the last word I said to him before I launched the campaign. Maybe—" and then he stopped, for there were limits to complaining about superior officers, and he was reluctant to say aloud what I was saying to myself—that maybe Halleck, with his big brain full of other concerns, simply forgot about the pontoons and made up the story about a change in plans. The truth was never determined, nor could it have been, for there were no witnesses to the conversation.

And so, when the great army arrived opposite Fredericksburg on November 17, exactly according to plan, the pontoons were conspicuously absent. It was the same the following day and the day after that. They didn't arrive until a week later, on November 24, because Halleck hadn't realized his mistake until November 20. General Woodbury, who was charged with delivering the pontoons, did what he could but, by the time his wagons finally arrived in

Falmouth, the astute Lee had long since figured things out. The moment the engineers began assembling the bridges, they were mown down by Longstreet's artillery.

And that was as far as Ambrose's art as a commander took him. His estimate of an army's marching capacity had been unorthodox but correct. His assumption that Lee, used to the snail's pace of Ambrose's predecessor, McClellan, wouldn't grasp what was happening in time, and that Longstreet would be at least two days' march from Fredericksburg when they were ready to move on the town—all that had been correct. But the pontoons hadn't arrived.

What Ambrose should have done, I don't know. Or rather, I do. He should have been given an order. He was better than almost anyone else at carrying out orders. But generals in the field were not given specific orders.

Napoleon might have come up with something brilliant, and Hooker, Ambrose's successor, would have improvised something and managed to look valiant in the attempt. Less than four months later, Hooker botched everything he could at Chancellorsville, at a cost of four thousand more casualties than there were at Fredericksburg. Two months after that, he was removed and the inconspicuous Meade swung into the commander-in-chief's saddle, truly a last resort. Such are the paradoxes of war: it was this last resort who finally defeated Lee. A bloody, glorious, and fatal defeat. Gettysburg.

His inability to carry out the plan paralysed Ambrose. It was as if his brain had seized up. Yet he had to come up with an adaptation of the plan, and he did come up with a new idea of sorts. He decided to build three more pontoon bridges about three miles downstream, east of the town, where Stonewall Jackson's units had taken up position on a rise overlooking the river. The new plan depended on two simultaneous strikes: one against Jackson, led by General Franklin across the additional bridges, which would divert attention from the other, the main strike along the long hillside opposite the fortifications at Marye's Heights.

The problem was that it was General Longstreet's army that was now waiting for them, instead of a few frightened companies. They'd had two weeks to dig in and fortify their positions, for it had taken that long to build the new bridges under constant fire from Lee's artillery.

On paper it still looked possible, though only barely so. When he told the story later in my parlour, beads of perspiration broke out on Ambrose, as if he were still standing on the river bank opposite Fredericksburg, looking through field-glasses in horror at the hillside below Marye's Heights. Franklin's strength was almost double that of Jackson, Ambrose explained.

He could have taken the heights south of Fredericksburg, and then attacked Longstreet's flank while Ambrose concentrated on a frontal assault at Marye's Heights. But there was a dense fog that morning; Franklin waited under its cover until half past eight and then, of all his massive army, dispatched only Meade's division against Jackson. Ambrose pulled a blue handkerchief out of his sleeve and wiped his forehead.

"Why in the name of heaven did he do that?"

Ambrose tucked the handkerchief back in his sleeve. "It was my fault, Lorraine. Just imagine, I, who was the first to use the field telegraph in my army, decided that the situation was too grave to entrust my orders to an unreliable mechanical device, so I sent General Hardick with a message to Franklin." Ambrose shook his head as though he couldn't believe his own stupidity. "It never occurred to me to send the order by telegraph at the same time. I bypassed the machine entirely, and of course Hardick couldn't find Franklin and didn't get to him until around half past eight, and by that time he'd forgotten the exact wording of the order and got everything mixed up—"

Ambrose fell silent. I looked sharply at him. He seemed to be flushed.

"—or perhaps I didn't make the order clear enough," he said. "That's probably it. It was probably my fault too." He turned his brown-eyed gaze to me. "In all honesty, Lorraine, I didn't know what to do. On one side there was Lincoln, who needed a victory badly. On the other, there were my own commanding officers." The blue handkerchief came out again. "I called a council. I'd have welcomed any reasonable advice, but they didn't know what to do either."

Instead, they gave voice to his greatest unspoken fears, because the responsibility wasn't on their shoulders. "An attack on Marye's Heights will bring about the worst carnage of this war," said Colonel Hawkins. "The entire Army of the Potomac hasn't enough troops to force through a single man," said Colonel Peters, casting a meaningful glance at the long hillside bristling with Longstreet's palisades.

"Gentlemen," said Ambrose desperately, "I'm looking for advice, not—" He fumbled for words.

Lieutenant-Colonel Taylor broke the silence. "It's going to be murder, not warfare."

"Gentlemen, counsel, not—"

I honestly don't know what Ambrose would have done if an old hand, the fifty-year-old General French, hadn't lost patience and spoken up. In the language and images of cheap, heroic adventure tales, he expressed full confidence in the soldiers of the Union army and predicted that they would wipe out Lee's army in a couple of days. Then he called for three cheers for Ambrose. The younger officers had all been taught at West Point by the great opponent of frontal attacks, Dennis Hart Lahane; the good-looking General French was challenging their sober judgement with some old-fashioned Napoleonic spirit. In the face of Ambrose's visible gloom, his desperate but still loyal staff officers mumbled agreement.

Ah yes, the art of war. A miracle almost took place: by sheer coincidence, Meade attacked at a spot where there was a gaping hole between the rebel units and managed to penetrate to Jackson's rear. But Franklin sent no reinforcements through the gap, and the rebel counter-attack forced Meade's troops back down the hill to the river. At half past two in the afternoon, Ambrose, half crazed, ordered a new attack. He used the telegraph this time, but there were such discrepancies between his first and second sets of orders that the flustered Franklin, having lost what little confidence he had left in Ambrose's ability to command, simply ignored him.

Meantime, a dance of death was going on below Marye's Heights. The northern flank, following the plan, waited until the battle to the south seemed to be in full swing—seemed, because the entire battlefield was wrapped in fog. The telegraph was working but the situation wasn't clear even in Franklin's headquarters, and at eleven o'clock General Sumner issued the order for a frontal attack. All afternoon unit after unit was thrown into the fray. Some got to within a hundred feet of the breastworks of the rebel position, but they were relentlessly and ruthlessly mown down. As evening fell, thirteen thousand dead and wounded lay on the hillside while the living pushed forward in that *danse macabre*—or, if you prefer, marched valiantly to their own execution. They must have known that they were no longer on a battlefield, that they were advancing into the path of a huge, mechanical, thundering scythe—but they advanced all the same. It was incomprehensible. At least, I can't comprehend it.

Ambrose? After the war, they wrote that this battle had been a clear demonstration of his stubbornness. I'm not so sure. I think that his brain, never quick at the best of times, was inhibited even more by his intense desire not to disappoint the president. It was a fear that came not from rebel guns but from his soul. A loyal soul, but unendowed with the attributes of a successful general.

The night after the battle was a dark night indeed for that soul. Ambrose wandered from commander to commander, a stiff smile between his splendid sideburns. Towards dawn, he assembled his staff and announced that the attack on Marye's Heights would continue. With one difference. He would lead it himself, not from his command post, but at the head of his troops.

II

The fact is, Ambrose was born too late. He should have come into this world when kings still rode off to battle on armoured horses at the heads of slow processions of mounted warriors in coats of mail. In those days a general could be a simple soul. He only had to be brave. And he could never have found himself in the situation Ambrose got into in Chicago, soon after Fredericksburg, when he capped a military débâcle with a political one.

On that morning of December 14, they finally dissuaded him from leading a new attack on Marye's Heights. He executed the final manoeuvre of the Battle of Fredericksburg—a complex retreat—and he did it magnificently. It was straight out of the textbook; Ambrose had always done his homework. Late that morning, when the fog lifted and General Longstreet looked down from his position on top of the heights, there wasn't a living federal soldier in sight. In my parlour in Cincinnati, perspiring as though he were living it all over again, he told me why he hadn't joined his fallen troops back in Fredericksburg.

"Later, some people claimed I'd wanted to commit suicide," he said. "Perhaps I had, but it wasn't a conscious thought. I kept seeing those soldiers, Lorraine, those dead soldiers, and I had sent them out there to die. I still see them now, at night, often at night. Back then, I felt that the only place left for me was among them, among the dead. But then—"

He fell silent and stared into the distance. His eyes were probably seeing that hillside again.

"But what?"

"Then I—simply—" He paused, and his eyes returned to the room. He smiled sadly at me. "At least I conquered my own arrogance."

"You were never arrogant, Ambrose," I said.

"Maybe I was, maybe I wasn't," he said bitterly. He placed his finger on his temple. "Thirteen thousand men had to die before the light went on inside this foolish skull. It was a terrible price, Lorraine, a terrible price to pay just so a man could come to his senses. But then I realized that this gesture— dying at the head of my troops—would have cost—what? Another thousand? Another five thousand? So I called off the attack."

"Oh, Ambrose, dear Ambrose," I said, because there was nothing else I could say.

"I could always have used my pistol," said Ambrose. "But that would have been too easy an escape—from the troops and from the responsibility. It would, in fact, have been a cowardly act, Lorraine. And I'm not a coward. I may be a fool, but—"

"Ambrose!"

"—I'd rather be a fool than a coward and a traitor. So I took it all upon myself. I was in command. I was responsible for everything."

After that disaster and its complicated aftermath, the president sent Ambrose to the Midwest to organize an army to pull a thorn out of Grant's paw, for Grant was stranded at Vicksburg. In addition, he was given the job of maintaining order in the civilian sector of Ohio, for it was bubbling with discontent with the war and dissatisfaction with Lincoln, and there were dozens of newspapermen clamouring for peace at any price.

He came like a bull in a china shop, and that afternoon in my parlour he started to say, "Halleck thinks—" and then stopped himself.

12

"What does Halleck think?" I asked, when Ambrose had remained quiet for too long.

"What I meant to say," he said awkwardly, apparently realizing the indiscretion of divulging to a woman what one general thought of another general. I didn't press him. I was sure I could piece together what Halleck thought from Ambrose's clumsy questions. "What I meant to ask was—do you know Congressman, or rather ex-Congressman, Vallandigham?"

"Comely Clem?" I did indeed. He was a charmer, and among women the most popular Ohio congressman. Women may not have the vote but, once charmed, they can certainly influence their husbands.

"Comely Clem?"

"That's what they sometimes call him here. He's a handsome man."

"He's critical of the government," Ambrose said. "Sometimes, in a way, that amounts to aiding and abetting the rebels."

"That's natural. He's angry at the government," I said. "He lost the October election because the Republicans ran General Schenck against him. Clem was a general in the militia before the war, besides holding many other functions. After Fort Sumter, he pretty much lost interest in military matters and threw himself into politics."

"You say he was in the volunteer militia? A general?" Ambrose mused with interest.

"You can be sure they brought it up," I said. "But he still didn't have a chance against Schenck. Schenck was a hero. In the second battle of Bull Run, a piece of iron from an exploding canister nearly sliced his hand off at the wrist; he dropped his sword, but he got his aide to improvise a bandage, picked up his sword with his left hand, and charged the rebels at the head of his troops. Clem's babbling in Congress didn't amount to much beside that."

"That explains a lot," remarked Ambrose, stroking his sideburns with satisfaction. "Did you hear about the speech he made last week in Hamilton?"

I shook my head. "I'm not particularly interested in Vallandigham," I said, "though I probably should be. He wouldn't make a bad—" "character in a novel" was what I'd started to say, but I suddenly remembered that Ambrose didn't know about this other part of me, or at least he hadn't asked about it yet. Either my pen-name had protected my secret, or he had forgotten what I'd said at the Connersville station. It also struck me that Ambrose would make a far better character for a novel than Vallandigham. Fortunately, he was so preoccupied with framing his questions discreetly that he never noticed my sudden silence.

"In that speech he denounced General Carrington's order prohibiting civilians from carrying weapons."

"Ah," I said, "so Clem invoked the Constitution."

"How did you know?"

"I inferred as much," I said. "Thanks to Miss Wright, the Constitution is one of the few things I remember from school: *'the right of the people,'*" I recited solemnly, "*'to keep and bear arms shall not be infringed.'*"

Ambrose gave me a look that may have been one of admiration. I had the feeling he was measuring the circumference of my head with his eyes, which of course would deceive him, for I was wearing a fashionable hairpiece.

"Precisely," he said. "Of course, Carrington had a damn—a darned good reason for issuing that order. Besides, he'd talked it over with Ollie Morton. He got a report from Sergeant Perkins, who was in charge of an eight-man detail that was supposed to arrest deserters in Franklin. When word got out that Perkins and his men were there, a mob of at least two hundred horsemen gathered in the town square, all of them armed, and not only did they stop Perkins from carrying out his orders, they even cheered, 'Long live Jefferson Davis!' That traitor and leader of traitors, Lorraine!"

"Are you sure it happened?" I said. "Don't forget, Carrington's notorious for his vivid imagination—especially after he's had a few too many."

"Ollie confirmed it. And it wasn't an isolated instance. The day before, another armed mob stopped them arresting some deserters in Putnam County."

"But that's—"

"Treason!" he said, looking straight at me. It suddenly dawned on me that my friend was rushing headlong into a new catastrophe.

"It could hardly be called anything else," I said.

"In the face of treason, all available means must be used. That was why General Carrington issued the order," he said stiffly.

And I could see where the rub was. "But there's the Constitution," I said.

"Well—yes, there is," admitted Ambrose. "Of course—"

"Didn't General Carrington declare martial law?" I interrupted.

"Well—no, he didn't."

"That was a mistake."

"Maybe so," said Ambrose. "No! It *was* a mistake. But treason *was* committed, and treason is treason!"

"But the Constitution is the Constitution."

Ambrose's brow furrowed. He crossed his legs—his shiny boots and the gold tassel of his sword glinted in the afternoon sunlight, the scabbard rang against the Chinese vase beside the armchair. I imagined him running along the hill at Marye's Heights in those polished boots, his sword drawn, the boots spattered with blood.

He recited, "'*On the orders of the United States and the people of the United States, George Washington, Commander.*' Now, whom do we obey: Carrington or Washington?"

"I beg your pardon?"

"That was the question Vallandigham posed at the town meeting in Hamilton." He was looking straight into my eyes.

There was a long pause, then I said, "What do you think, Ambrose?"

"What do *you* think, Lorraine?" He looked at my sizeable coiffure.

"I don't know." Outside the window, a cool spring rain had begun to fall. Raindrops trickled down the windowpane, picking up the occasional ray of sunlight. "But I do wonder," I said slowly. "Suppose George Washington had found himself in a situation like that of the sergeant who was sent out to arrest deserters, and a mob of armed men had started cheering General Cornwallis—"

"Precisely, Lorraine," said Ambrose gratefully.

Not precisely. Analogies like that can be dangerous.

But they needn't be.

Not if they're applied by someone like Ambrose.

It wasn't precise, but there was something to it.

"What else do you know about Vallandigham, Lorraine?"

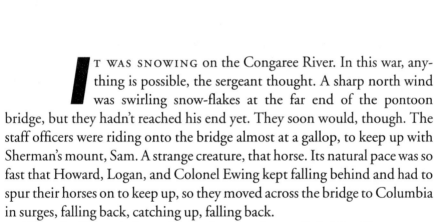

Columbia

IT WAS SNOWING on the Congaree River. In this war, anything is possible, the sergeant thought. A sharp north wind was swirling snow-flakes at the far end of the pontoon bridge, but they hadn't reached his end yet. They soon would, though. The staff officers were riding onto the bridge almost at a gallop, to keep up with Sherman's mount, Sam. A strange creature, that horse. Its natural pace was so fast that Howard, Logan, and Colonel Ewing kept falling behind and had to spur their horses on to keep up, so they moved across the bridge to Columbia in surges, falling back, catching up, falling back.

Then the fifteenth Army Group thundered onto the bridge. The sergeant looked back and he saw the first four men, four bearded soldiers in Sherman's great army, which had broken stride so as not to rock the bridge—but being out of step was hardly unusual for them—and ahead of them, striding beside his horse, was Captain Baxter Warren II, under the banner of the Ninety-second Iowa, carried by Sergeant Waleski. Sergeant Waleski had no ears. He'd lost one in the Battle of Warsaw, in Poland, and the other at Fort Donelson. Kapsa looked back again. The fifteenth Army Group wound across the countryside like a snake with quills, grey bayonets aimed at grey clouds overhead. An unfinished fortress dominated the landscape. Yesterday, they had watched from its tower as Negroes from Columbia helped themselves to sacks of corn and hams piled neatly by the railroad depot. Just below the fortress, Captain DeGress had unlimbered a battery of twenty-pound Parrot guns and was lobbing shot into the town as clusters of Butler's Cavalry appeared and reappeared in the streets. Sherman had put down his field-glasses and ordered the captain to stop firing, and to put the fear of God into the black looters instead; those hams and that corn were the property of his army. South Carolina, drenched, grey, the unfinished fortress standing there like an old Roman ruin under clouds that ran from grey all the way to black. But there were no signs of a snowstorm anywhere. A strange war. The sergeant turned, spurred his horse, and saw a swirl of snow envelop the general. Everything was topsy-turvy. The white flakes were not falling from the sky but rising from the ground like feathers, as the north wind swirled them into tiny cyclones. Then they fell onto the Congaree River.

Soon the sergeant was caught in the snowflakes too. For a moment they made it hard for him to see the generals cantering away, Sherman's sweaty hat in the lead and, farther off, the unfinished Confederate government building in the centre of town. A snowflake got up his nose and he sneezed.

King Cotton. Someone had torn the king's ermine robe into shreds and tatters. A foul smell hit him, and he saw smoke rising from the town. A flash of flame burst through the wall of smoke. Burning cotton fell on the Congaree River.

By night-time, the air was alive with sparks swirling and falling towards the dark waters.

★

Zinkule believed in ghosts—and in premonitions, prophetic dreams, telepathy, and miracles. He had come to this state after an act of heroism at Kennesaw Mountain, important enough to have been mentioned in the colonel's report. "Although lying on the ground, semi-immobilized by a canister exploding nearby," the colonel had written, "Corporal Zinkule brought down a Rebel flag-bearer with his bayonet and took possession of the banner." Shake maintained that the report was essentially true, except that Zinkule had been stunned not by an exploding canister but rather by a Minnie that ricocheted off a rock, hit him on the head, and knocked him down. Yes, Zinkule had been on the ground, and yes, the Rebel sergeant had ended up on his bayonet, but the Rebel had actually skewered himself. It had happened like this: Shake, lying unhurt beside Zinkule and merely scared out of his wits, had decided to flee the field of glory, but as he was getting to his knees the standard-bearer, thinking him dead, stepped over him and tripped over his rising behind. He fell and impaled himself on Zinkule's bayonet. *The Rebel flag fluttered down on top of Zinkule and, when he recovered enough to stand up, he got tangled up in it, lost his bearings, and set out towards where he thought the enemy was. Shake tagged along because he saw that in fact they were heading back towards the reserves. Shortly thereafter, the rest of the unit arrived running. Nobody noticed anything amiss, and Zinkule got the glory for capturing the flag. Shake maintained that he himself should have got the credit, since he had set the action in motion, or his behind had. But he couldn't be bothered making the effort to get his name in the report.*

Zinkule, meanwhile, took the incident as a sign and started believing in his dreams, in which he was always dying a hero's death, and he recounted them at great length around the campfire. Finally Salek got so fed up that he told him, "If you don't watch out, you'll wind up like the village idiot in Brnives. Remember him?" Zinkule shook his head. "Surely, you old fool, you remember the petrified devils in the chapel under Saint Prokop's church in Sazava?" Zinkule shook his head again, so Salek went ahead with the story: "Once Saint Prokop was serving mass there, and these two devils come in and start tempting him, so Saint Prokop makes the sign of the cross over them and they turn into stone. They're still there today. They look more like bears, but in fact they're devils. One time—"

When they ushered the lady in to see Sherman, the sergeant suddenly felt that maybe Zinkule was on to something. Was this a sign? A vision? He knew he'd seen her before, but he couldn't remember where. He cast his mind back through the confusion of his life. When had he met her? A long time ago, that was for sure, but where? Then she spoke to the general.

"I am surprised and indignant, general," she said, "that your army should behave so towards a conquered people who have surrendered their city and do not resist. I have always told people we had nothing to fear except the accidents of war—but I do not consider the deliberate burning of a city an accident." Her tone was haughty, her accent heavy. What sort of accent was it? He couldn't put his finger on that, either.

The general looked at the lady. He was exhausted and had to force himself to remain calm. Dawn was coming and the sky was red, but it wasn't just the sunrise, it was the fires that the fire brigades hadn't managed to put out yet. The general's face was like a desert gullied with dry river-beds. Outside, they could hear the crackle of burning beams.

"I have told my friends," the lady went on, "private property and women would be protected when you came. But no, instead of this—"

He knew the general was sensitive to criticism, but deep in his heart he also knew the general was right. It was a different war now. Even the Southern officers, who used to consider digging trenches cowardly and undignified, now dug in when canned hell started exploding overhead.

There had never been anything as horrifying as Pickett's charge at Gettysburg, when the neat ranks of Georgians were mown into huge bloody heaps by canisters at short range and volley after volley from repeating rifles, when musket balls and shrapnel ripped into corpses and the wounded alike. The general was determined to end that horror once and for all, and he had a single recipe. The sergeant agreed with him.

"Instead of this, you have waged warfare," the lady continued contemptuously, "that is a disgrace to our history."

"What do you mean by that, madam?" the general growled finally, with barely suppressed anger.

"I mean exactly what I have said."

The general was silent. He was always civil with women, and it wasn't just because he had spent long years in the South. The general really liked women—not the way Kilpatrick did, but the way most of his soldiers did. Gentle female beauty was a light beyond the black smoke of the barking Parrot guns.

The general looked at the cigar smouldering in the ashtray, and killed it. The air in the room was already hazy, and the smoke hung over the table like mist over the pond in far-away Roznice. The general had probably never set foot outside America, the sergeant thought, or seen a country where churches were made of stone, not wood, where black cathedrals stretched to touch the sky in mountain valleys. But in fact he had, as a young man. Around the campfire once, while chewing on hardtack and smoked meat, Sherman had told a tale about eating in a fancy restaurant called Faroux, at the foot of a mountain called Sugar Loaf, in Rio de Janeiro. They had been rookie officers, fresh out of West Point and sailing round Cape Horn to join their garrisons in the backwoods of California. Until this point, their idea of the height of elegance had been the Willard Hotel in Washington, with its brass spittoons. Now their dreams of a new world, hovering above the fruit on the table, were interrupted by the arrival of the bill, worked out in a foreign currency and presented to them on a small silver tray by a dark-skinned waiter. The general's eyes had twinkled in the light of the campfire at Kennesaw Mountain. He was describing the panic that came over the young officers as they looked at the size of the bill and dug deep into their pockets. All they could come up with were a few gold coins, adding up to less than a couple of sawbucks. The general laughed, took a bite of meat, and puffed on his cigar. The dark-skinned waiter had come back with a mountain of copper and gold coins on the silver tray. "There was almost seven thousand rei in change!" In the firelight the general's face looked haggard and gaunt, like the face of a hungry beggar. "A dollar was worth about a thousand rei in those days," he laughed, gazing off into the distance. It was the only time he'd ever been away from his beloved America. Their guide had taken them to the nearby Rua da Ouvadar to see a local speciality: artificial flowers made of brightly coloured parrot plumes. "But it was the sight of those lovely girls making the flowers," mused the general, "those beautiful Brazilian girls, so clever with their hands, that ebony hair"—a sharp glance from General Howard, who had just joined the campfire, reminded him that he was a married man. General Howard was the kind of fellow who would skip the parts of the Bible that a good Christian could only read as allegory; he would not have understood that his commanding officer was reminiscing about an aesthetic, not a carnal, experience. He would not have understood that in the twilight of memory, mulatto girls weaving flowers out of parrot plumes glowed like a bright beacon beyond the ugly confusion of battle. Like the beacon—no longer carnal—named Ursula.

"I thought you commanded an army of disciplined soldiers," the lady continued, while the sergeant searched his mind further. "But what I have seen with my own two eyes, general. . . . My late husband was also an officer. Whenever possible, his soldiers were expected to mind their manners, but also their appearance. His officers knew how to keep discipline. I know that soldiers everywhere like to have a drink, but what I saw yesterday and today in Columbia. . . . Those are not soldiers. They are riff-raff." She said the word with disgust. "Inebriated, ragtag soldiery, general. . . . I even saw an officer who was no longer in control of himself."

The sergeant, still searching his mind, recalled one of many images from a night that had etched itself into his memory: the huge General Giles A. Smith on his motionless black horse, lit by flaming buildings on both sides of the street, raising to his lips a bottle glinting gold with whisky. He emptied it, tossed the bottle into the fire, and shouted, "Down with the Confederacy!" Then he glanced at an old Negro who was holding another bottle up for him. The old man's eyes were wide with admiration. "Well, what do you say, Sambo? What do you think of the night?"

"I thinks the day of redemption and jubilation has come, massa," the old black man said respectfully.

"You speak of a disgrace to American history, madam." The general's voice was cold. "But it appears you have not considered that this city which 'surrendered without a fight' was only recently spoiling for a fight. Not so long ago this very state of South Carolina drowned out all the sensible and loyal voices in the South, madam." He put the cigar back in his mouth but did not light it. The lady was immobile, reminding the sergeant of those proud plantation women they had seen on the march through Georgia, then to the sea and Savannah, then through South Carolina. They all had a similar look about them. The general said, "It was your own cavalry in retreat that set fire to the cotton. But the stocks of whisky, cussed big stocks of whisky for a God-fearing city like this, madam, were left untouched. Now, if I were a suspicious man—" He fell silent.

The general's train of thought led the sergeant to recall another scene. "What do you expect?" the general had practically shouted at Mayor Goodwin. "What can I expect? What can anyone expect?" That was before dawn, when the mayor had come running to the house where Sherman had spent a sleepless night and begged him to do something about the fires, the looting, and the pillaging. "What do you want? You set fire to the cotton, but you leave enough whisky to last ten years!" "I begged them, general, and so did General Beauregard. We pleaded to be allowed to destroy it, pour it out, set fire to it instead of the cotton. Because I knew what it could—"

The sergeant could read the general's thoughts. "Let me tell you, madam, I had the opportunity to talk to many of your soldiers, those taken prisoner. Many, perhaps most of them, were sick to death of the war. Had it been up to them alone, perhaps—but it was you, the ladies of the South, who kept egging them on to fight a war in which they were already whipped. And still you drive them to persist"—he put the extinguished cigar back into the ashtray—"to the bitter end. Perhaps you do so because you yourself have never experienced what that phrase conceals."

Howard stood engulfed in the smoke which filled the room, his knuckles white as he tightened his grip on his Bible.

The general went on. "Now you have that opportunity. Perhaps—I'm hoping—you ladies of the South, now that you've sampled a little of that bitter end, will use your celebrated persuasiveness to help shorten the course of this war. As I am trying to do with my"—the general made a face—"ragtag soldiery."

Now it was the lady's turn to be silent. She stiffened her proud back like someone whose pride had just been stung. The sergeant's memories leapt back through the years—

"*—our village idiot went there on a pilgrimage, and to the fair," said Salek. "Well, he wasn't Francek, the real village idiot, but this farmer Matej fellow was a close second. He walks into the chapel and the first thing he sees is that all the statues of the saints have candles burning in front of them. So Matej buys a couple of candles from the monks, but then he sees the two stone devils and he gets feeling sorry for them. 'The saints get all the attention here, and you're stone for eternity and you get nothing' is what he's thinking. So he sticks a candle in each of their paws and kneels in front of them and says a prayer. That night, he dreams that* *these two critters come alive and get into his room and entice him out into the garden, where they tell him, 'Matej,' they say, 'you're the only one who's ever lit a candle to us in a thousand years or so, and we're going to make you rich. On this very spot is buried treasure. When you wake up tomorrow, come out here and dig.' 'But Your Eminences,' says Matej, 'how will I find this spot again? My head is full of holes.' 'You'll find it, Matej,' says one of the devils. 'Pull down your pants and take a shit. In the morning you'll find your treasure underneath it.' There's a cloud of smoke and sulphur, and the devils are gone. So the old fool pulls his trousers down and takes a squat. Suddenly, by the living Jesus, he feels a burning pain in his bunghole, like he's sat in a hornet's nest. His first thought is he should never have taken up with the devil, and now the fires of hell are burning him, but then he wakes up and what does he see? He sees himself sitting astride his wife, but not for the reason you think. He's actually taking a crap on her, and she's howling and holding a burning candle under his balls. Now, how about that, Zinkule?"*

Zinkule shrugged his shoulders.

"Did that stop Matej from believing in his dream? Not on your life. Next day, instead of going to work in the fields, he starts digging in his garden, and he keeps at it for two months, until his garden is one enormous hole—never found a thing, of course—and he finally stops believing in his dream. But by then it's past harvest time and he doesn't have his crops in, so that winter they all damn near starve to death."

Everyone howled with laughter, but Zinkule looked as if he knew more than he was telling.

"You misjudge me, general," the lady said. "I was never in favour of this war. And I have suffered for that. I am not a lady of the South, as you say. I came to America as an adult, and I ended up in the South not by choice. My husband"—she swallowed, and the sergeant racked his brains but still found nothing—"my husband was not an American officer."

She fell silent again. A gold crucifix rose and fell on her heaving bosom. The general was silent too. Finally she asked, "So will you not provide me with a guard detail to protect my school, general?"

"You won't need one," snapped the general, then added, "Unless something unforeseen happens, I'm leaving tomorrow, and all my soldiers must be ready to march out."

"They must be, but they are not," said the lady. "Unless, that is, you need them prowling around private homes, looting and stealing, and destroying what can't be taken, and committing acts that I as a lady am reluctant to mention. I have two daughters who are barely twenty years old. And tomorrow is a long time away. But I won't keep you any longer, general."

She turned, and the crucifix glistened. The general's face darkened and he opened his mouth as if to call her back, then caught the sergeant's eye and wordlessly conveyed an order. The sergeant opened the door for the lady and walked out behind her.

The sergeant thought of the previous night, remembered yelling, "Stop it, men!" and pulling out his pistol. Five or six faces turned towards him with derisive laughter. He knew rank wouldn't be enough on this drunken, barbarian night. He didn't recognize the men, and looked in vain for any identifying insignia on their tattered uniforms. They started yelling back at him, "Bugger off, sarge!" Then they saw the pistol. "Dismissed! Want me to make it plainer?" He swept the pistol in a broad arc so that, one by one, they stared down its barrel. The man who had been pumping away at the black woman like a steam piston froze, then his naked buttocks lifted slowly. "Dismissed!" shouted the sergeant again. "Easy, sarge! We're going," growled a plump one, buckling his belt. "What's the problem? She was willing. More than willing. We emancipated her, didn't we?" *Move!* he bellowed. The fellow with the bare buttocks climbed off the woman and pulled on his trousers. "We're going, we're going." Drunken faces, weaving bodies, staggered out of the yard. The black woman lay on the bench, stunned, her legs apart, her skirt up over her belly. The sergeant walked over to her and pulled her skirt down over her knees. A pretty young face, African features mixed with heaven knows what. Her eyes were pinched shut, her lips sucked in, her mouth thin with restrained agony. "Can you get up?" he asked her gently. Her eyes opened, large, white with dark irises, but he couldn't see what was in them. It was too dark. The voice sounded meek. "Yes, sir." "You live here?" "Yes, sir." She rose and stood there. What was she waiting for—an order? She couldn't stop shaking. He thought of the old black man he'd met earlier that night, who'd called this a day of redemption and jubilation. The girl was quivering like an aspen. Day of redemption. An alabaster angel had cast aside its golden wig and lifted its white robe to reveal a cloven hoof. No, it wasn't that simple. After all, he knew them. Today they advanced against the enemy, fearless in the face of exploding canisters; tomorrow they were beneath the earth, blown to pieces, dead. But how did this creature see them now? What could she be thinking? That her "massa", the plantation owner, was right about them? He stuck his pistol back in its holster and touched the black girl's smooth cheek. "Run home and hide. In a day or so we'll be moving out." "Yes, 'sa." She turned and ran towards the scorched house and disappeared in the shadows.

The sergeant shut the door behind him, then walked quickly to catch up with the lady. "Ma'am," he said, "I'll find a guard detail for you."

She looked at him. His mind spun back through time. "Against your general's orders?"

"He didn't give me any orders. And he won't mind."

They walked outside into the yard. He looked around. Several soldiers were sitting on crates, puffing on looted cigars that still had gold bands around them.

"You say you run a school?"

"Yes. The Barnham Academy for Young Ladies."

He glanced at the crucifix. "Catholic?"

"That's right."

"Wait here, please."

He strode over to the soldiers. "Hi, sarge," said a soldier with red hair, pleasantly. His cap bore the insignia of the Seventeenth New York. The sergeant knew they were mostly Irish.

"You fellows Catholic?"

"Sure are. You too?"

"See that lady?" the sergeant said. "She's a Catholic. She's got two young daughters and she's worried about them."

The redhead looked at the gold crucifix glowing in the light of the dawn and the burning buildings. He rose to his feet. "Pat!"

A second soldier got up. The sergeant took them both over to the lady. "These men are Catholics, ma'am."

Her unhappy face brightened. "Are you Polish?"

"No ma'am, we're Irish," the redhead said politely.

The sergeant's mind suddenly found what it was looking for.

★

It was snowing on the Congaree River. The Doric pillars of the Columbia statehouse were no longer holding up anything but the black sky. The gabled façade had received a direct hit from Captain DeGress's cannoneers, who were as accurate with their Parrot guns as Logan's sharpshooters were with their rifles. Sherman wanted to destroy the heart of Columbia, and on his order Captain DeGress had tried to smash it with an iron cannonball. The ball now lay on the street amid the ruins. A black tomcat was perched on it, staring with devilish eyes at the sergeant, the lady, and the two Irishmen. A blizzard swirled through the dark sky. A swarm of sparks shot out of the burning buildings, setting the flakes on fire.

The lady stopped. "Mr. Komarowski!"

On the sidewalk in front of an ornate building sat a row of bottles and pails filled with amber liquid that flickered in the light of the flames. A man in a black overcoat had raised a bottle to his lips, but at the sound of the woman's voice the hand with the bottle dropped to his side. Two bearded, musket-bearing men in blue rags were holding him up on either side. He babbled something, then slouched precariously. A soldier at the end of the row of bottles took a swig and fell on his back. One of the bearded soldiers poked the man in the black overcoat in the ribs with his rifle barrel. With some effort the man raised the bottle to his lips again. Whisky dribbled onto his white shirt-front adorned with a red and white stick-pin.

"Mr. Komarowski!"

"You know him, ma'am?" asked the sergeant.

"Mr. Komarowski is General Wade Hampton's major-domo," said the lady. "This is General Hampton's headquarters," she added, indicating the house, which had white pillars topped with ornate capitals. "Mr. Komarowski has always been a teetotaller. I've known him since—" She stopped, her eyes welled with a bitter light.

"He's drinking to forget the débâcle," growled one of the Irishmen.

"What's going on here?" the sergeant asked sharply.

One of the bearded soldiers looked at him closely. "He put poison in the whisky," he replied. "He uncorked them bottles, lined them all up here on the sidewalk, and he was putting poison in them." He glanced at the soldier lying on his back at the end of the row. "If that man dies, we'll—"

The sergeant walked over to the supine figure. A snore emerged from his whiskers.

"He's soused, not poisoned," he said. The two Irishmen laughed.

The man leaning on his musket barrel waved his hand. "Maybe he is, maybe he ain't," he said. "He should've waited till this bastard tasted them all. If he don't croak, we'll know for sure."

The burning snow arched across the black sky like a wide rainbow of ruby and gold. "If he's a teetotaller and you make him drink all this"—the sergeant pointed to the long row of bottles—"he'll croak, poisoned or not."

The major-domo suddenly seemed to come to his senses. "It was my intention to pour them out. That's why—I uncorked—" He turned pale and bent over. A gush of yellow-green liquid poured from his mouth, and the lady closed her eyes.

"Let him go," ordered the sergeant, "and dump those bottles out."

The bearded soldiers balked. "Aw, come on, sarge!"

Without a word, he kicked over the nearest pail, spilling the whisky onto the sidewalk. His two soldiers did the same. But as he turned his attention back to the lady, he noticed each of them corking a bottle and sticking it into his knapsack. He said nothing.

"Let's go, ma'am."

The lady looked at the major-domo. He weaved towards the house, where he collapsed on the marble steps. The sergeant felt she had wanted to say something to him, but she lifted her head, glanced at her escort, and said, "General Sherman's great army."

"They're not my slaves, Your Honour. They're my soldiers," General Sherman had said to the trembling mayor of Columbia. "I cannot order them out of the city. They have fought bravely, and an old tradition says that the first units to enter the city have the right to police it." The sergeant knew that "policing" meant clearing the streets of snipers and other obstinate champions of the cause who preferred death to surrender. But with all the whisky available, law and order had rapidly degenerated into brutal and drunken debaucheries in the streets and alleyways. As the sergeant and the lady walked eastward, they saw more and more bottles lined up along the sidewalks. The city, or at least its black population, had become an army of waiters offering the soldiers wine from plantation cellars and whisky imported from the hills of Scotland, and they sang and danced as they did so. The sergeant knew the songs were religious, but they sounded more like square-dance calling. Beneath its aurora of burning snow, Columbia was pulsing with music like a gigantic tavern. The sergeant and the lady walked on—

—and before Cyril, done in by plundered whisky, fell asleep in the house in Savannah where Kakuska was making spurs out of clock gears, he talked about his little sister, Lida the dragoness, and how her blue reptilian eyes had captivated Étienne de Ribordeaux the moment she walked into the parlour. She had looked around the room, at the paintings in gilded frames—portraits of gentlemen in which the painters had lavished at least as much attention on the lace shirt-fronts as on the fleshy faces set against landscapes more beautiful and ordered than any in this part of the world. Then she looked back into the eyes of the man with the wooden leg and the lace shirt. She gazed at the many heavy candelabra, and then back at Étienne, her blue eyes brilliant with the splendour of the candlelight. It was as if she had always belonged here, surrounded by velvet and the fragrance of verbena, although she was tightly laced into a Moravian folk costume that caused her bosom to swell temptingly beneath the floral embroidery on her white blouse. The one-legged man didn't know that those breasts had known the lips of an infant, and even had he known . . .

"Tell him," said Cyril's father, and Cyril translated for him as he said that he didn't care for the "peculiar institution", that it was the only thing here he didn't

care for, because as a young man he had experienced another "peculiar institution" and knew what it meant to work for masters, not in exchange for wages but because he was a serf and had no choice. Étienne hid his wooden leg behind his good one, and the older de Ribordeaux twirled his cigar in his fingers, waiting for Cyril to finish translating his father's ponderous speech into an English that by now was almost fluent. The dinner was over and it was time for brandy. Cyril finished by saying that the best work is done by a worker who is free.

Mr. de Ribordeaux was finally able to take the floor, and his words were like poetry. Cyril translated them into Czech for his father while his sister's eyes played with the candles and the dark gaze of the man with the wooden leg and the lace shirt. Mr. de Ribordeaux was no slave-driver, and he didn't make his slaves work their fingers to the bone. They glowed with well-being. Of course, they were all still young, having been purchased on the way to Texas, to the new plantation. The old ones had stayed behind in Louisiana. No, Mr. de Ribordeaux was no slave-driver. He was a thoughtful man who read books and could quote from the classics. "Of course, the serfdom of Europe is something entirely different from our system of servitude," he said, avoiding the word "slavery"— that was how Cyril had first translated his father's references to the "peculiar institution", until he realized the word wasn't pleasing to Mr. de Ribordeaux's ears. "It's not a matter of master and slave, but of master and servant. Serfdom is an unfortunate amalgam of freedom and servitude," explained Mr. de Ribordeaux, and Cyril noticed that Mr. Carson, who had brought them here, winced but remained silent. "Each condition carries an obligation with it. Neither carries any inherent rights. A serf is at the mercy of crop failure on his own fields, and has to beg from his master in time of need. The first harvest is for his master, and only then can he harvest his own. There is nothing like that here," said Mr. de Ribordeaux. "I bear the risk of crop failure myself. The servants are like my children, and I am obliged to care for them. For that matter, mentally, they . . ." Mr. de Ribordeaux drew a deep lungful of cigar smoke. "When their children fall ill—you've seen for yourself, after all, Mr. Tuplick." Before dinner he had taken them around the plantation, and in the nursery they had seen two little black girls and two little white girls covered with the same rash, all in the care of a fat black woman and a young white lady, the daughter of a friend of Mr. de Ribordeaux who was visiting from Louisiana. The small quartet was howling because Dr. Wilmonton, who had been called in from Austin, was just examining them with tickly fingers.

"Yes," said the elder Toupelik. "All well and good. But the best thing of all is freedom."

"Freedom and property," said Mr. de Ribordeaux solemnly. "What is freedom without property? Of course, you haven't been to the North, but—"

Lida was now studying the lace crinolines of the Meissen figurines on the mantelpiece. Étienne's good leg had fallen asleep, and he crossed the wooden limb over the good one but then hid it again, though it was beautifully carved. He squirmed in his armchair.

"I have," continued Mr. de Ribordeaux. "I don't base my conviction on the legacy of tradition alone. We live in the age of empiricism. I have visited factories in the North. Freedom without property, Mr. Tuplick, when there are no jobs to be had, is something I don't think you'd like to see. Free workers? My servants couldn't survive under those circumstances. They're used to security, Mr. Tuplick, from the cradle to the grave." Mr. de Ribordeaux's cigar had gone out, and he reached for a candle to relight it. "Where is Dinah?" He pulled a purple cord and a mellow-sounding gong rang. As he drew on his cigar, the tip turned red, casting a ruddy glow on his face. It was the face not of a slave-driver but of a thoughtful conquistador.

"We had a neighbour in Louisiana—in fact," he chuckled, "he was an anomaly of sorts, a rare bird—he owned a sugar plantation and he was"—another chuckle—"a contradiction in terms, sir, a Southern abolitionist."

"Freedom and property," echoed Mr. Carson, who had been silent until now. "In the North, some Negroes have acquired property with hard work, and—"

"One in a thousand, at best, Mr. Carson," said Mr. de Ribordeaux. "Now, this friend of mine, Mr. Collet—"

—past another house, also with decorative pillars. On the sidewalk in front of it, in a gilt armchair, Captain Henry of the Twenty-sixth Wisconsin sat teaching a group of house slaves to sing "John Brown's Body". He was an abolitionist and he was plastered, keeping time with a bottle and splashing its contents onto the pavement, where it evaporated rapidly. The sergeant thought of Windischgraetz's captains—brandy-drinkers as well, but only in the officers' mess, never in the streets of a conquered city, where Sergeant Kapsa and the others could see them. Sherman's great army. The captain sang a battle hymn of freedom while a chorus of voices transformed it into a barely comprehensible dialect. There was even a fiddler, and his squawkings made the melody sound like a jig.

John Brown's body lies a-mouldering in the grave—

The sergeant and the lady stopped. Among the singers the sergeant saw Jan Amos Shake.

John Brown's body lies a-mouldering in the grave—

Standing stiffly at attention, Shake was holding a tall pendulum clock close to his side like a rifle, and singing tenor in his beautiful seminary-trained voice.

But his soul goes marching on!

"Private Shake!" Captain Henry tried to sit up in the armchair, but slumped to one side. One of the servants rushed over and propped him up. In the same sharp voice he used to read orders, he hollered, "Private Shake! You're promoted to corporal. No, as you were! To sergeant!"

That evening, over a disassembled clock—Kakuska had broken one of his new spurs in a skirmish with Hood's men and he'd asked Shake to keep his eyes open for another clock—Shake was sewing a set of sergeant's stripes on his sleeve. He spent most of the evening learning to bark orders—not very successfully, for his voice was better suited to liturgy than to military drills—and didn't finish with the clock until morning.

"*—conducted something of an experiment,*" *Mr. de Ribordeaux went on, "though of course it was his second plantation, the smaller one he had just inherited. He had only about twenty servants there, and he gave them all their freedom and hired white farm labourers. And do you know what those labourers did, first chance they got?"*

Cyril translated. His father shook his head. Lida flipped her golden braid around so that it lay on her bosom, retied the red ribbon to make a prettier bow, then suddenly raised her eyes to look directly into the eyes of the one-legged man. He was caught in the lasso.

"*They waited till the harvest and then went on strike. Double our wages, they said, or harvest the crop yourself. Fortunately, the 'liberated'*"—*Mr. de Ribordeaux's tone put quotation marks around the word*—"*servants had spent their days of freedom hanging around the plantation, stealing chickens, and several had gone to the big plantation, where their relatives lived, and when the strike was two weeks old Mr. Collet called off the experiment. He fired the white labourers, gave the servants a chance to return, and all of them did, except for two that Mr. Collet had apprenticed to a carpenter; they'd gone to New Orleans. The crop was saved at the last moment.*"

The elder Toupelik shook his head stubbornly, and Mr. de Ribordeaux continued: "Servitude is simply the most stable form of labour, and the high degree of care required by cotton or sugar-cane cannot be achieved with any less stable form."

Cyril's little sister tossed the braid with its fresh bow back over her shoulder, and the man with the wooden leg emerged for a moment from his trance and recited, as if quoting from a textbook: "Our system is consistent with the interests of both capital and labour." He was no slave-driver either, but part of the younger, better-educated generation. He had studied in France, where he had had the accident that cost him his leg and prevented him from finishing his studies. "Our system of servitude," he said, but his textbook explication began to falter as the blue eyes opposite stared more intently into his, "our . . . system of . . . servitude has resolved the problem that statesmen have wrestled with since the beginning of organized society, that philanthropists have . . . tormented themselves with for centuries. . . ." His voice wavered, dissolving in blueness.

"Mr. de Ribordeaux," Cyril interrupted, "I've noticed that the plots of ground where your servants grow their own melons and greens—now, I could be wrong, but they seem far better kept than your larger fields. I also hear complaints about how, on some plantations, your servants' tools keep breaking, how they trample the crops, abuse the livestock—"

Mr. de Ribordeaux didn't wait for Cyril to finish. "Some do, Mr. Tuplick. As I've said, they're like little children. They even suffer childhood illnesses unknown to white men. Dysaesthesia aethiopica—"

Next morning, Captain Henry was walking briskly past Sergeant Shake's tent. Shake was sitting outside, still taking apart the clock. Captain Henry suddenly stopped and did an about-face.

"Shake!" he demanded. "What is this supposed to mean?"

"I'm taking apart the clock, captain, so I—"

"I mean this! What is *this* supposed to mean?" He pointed at the new stripes on the sleeve of Shake's tunic.

Something inside the clock clanged as Shake jumped to his feet. "You promoted me yesterday, sir. To sergeant, sir."

"You?" The way he said it suggested that the captain had regained his senses if not his memory. "I must have been drunk."

Shake made no effort to persuade him otherwise. "It was yesterday, when you were teaching the niggers how to sing 'John Brown's Body'. Sergeant Kapsa was there. . . ."

A blank in the captain's mind began to fill with a street scene in Columbia. His face darkened. He's sunk, thought Kapsa. Suddenly the captain looked at what Shake was doing and his dilemma was resolved. He scowled. "Are you familiar with General Sherman's orders before the attack on Columbia?"

Shake's usually quick wit failed him.

"He said he would punish anyone caught stealing from civilians, except for material needed by the army!" He pointed to the disembowelled timepiece. "Sergeant Shake," the captain intoned, "for disobeying an order"— though strictly speaking it hadn't been an order at all, merely something Kapsa had overheard Sherman mention to General Howard—"I hereby demote you to private!"

He turned on his heel, setting aflutter the gorgeous peacock feather in his hat—which he had probably taken, against regulations, from a lady's fan. Shake glumly watched him go. Then he ripped off the clumsily applied stripes and sighed, "Ah well, the Lord giveth, the Lord taketh away."

"Shouldn't it be booze giveth?" asked the sergeant. "But then what taketh way? A hangover, maybe."

Shake's face broke into a grin. He had survived his demotion with a minimum of shame.

"*—is something overseers sometimes mistakenly attribute to the Negro sense of mischief," continued Mr. de Ribordeaux. "These things may appear deliberate. In fact, however, they're symptoms of an illness caused by the infantility of the Negro mind and his nervous insensitivity."*

Cyril interpreted as best he could, and his father responded, "Well, I don't know." But he was impressed by the plantation owner's erudition.

"Or take drapetomania," said Mr. de Ribordeaux. "The symptoms are repeated attempts to escape. It was always rare on my plantation, and with proper medical care it is curable."

"Well, I don't know," Mr. Toupelik repeated.

"As a matter of fact, I have had only one case," said Mr. de Ribordeaux. "Jean. I had apprenticed him to a locksmith. My late wife taught him to read and write, so he could avail himself of the literature on his trade. How else would you explain it, Mr. Tuplick? Unfortunately, I failed to get him back. But he did write to me from Canada." Mr. de Ribordeaux ground out his cigar in a shell-shaped alabaster ashtray with a naked Venus perched on the rim. His son was gazing, mesmerized, at the golden braid. "He worked in a factory up there," said Mr. de Ribordeaux. "He had lost his hand in an accident. I mustn't hold it against him, he said. He was grateful for everything, but he'd had to leave. I sent him the money to come back, but he never did. I learned that they made him a sexton in a Methodist church in a place called St. Catharines." Cyril translated. Mr. Carson held his tongue.

"Well now, I—" said Mr. Toupelik.

The door opened and a maid walked in. She was wheeling a cart holding a round bottle of brandy, snifters, and a burning alcohol lamp. "At last!" declared Mr. de Ribordeaux.

"Sorry, monsieur," said the maid. "They had to get a new bottle from the cellar." She poured some brandy into a snifter and warmed the liquid over the flame. Cyril saw but scarcely noticed the bottle, the snifters, the flame licking the curved side of the glass, the warm brown liquid; what he noticed was the hand that held the glass, a hand the colour of a tea-rose. Mr. de Ribordeaux was saying something about the brandy—cognac, he called it—and Cyril heard the words but didn't listen, for what he saw was an arm in black silk, a lace bodice, a long

neck with a velvet ribbon, and above it a face the colour of a tea-rose and bur-
nished copper. He forgot that they had come to talk about cooking oil, for all the
beauty of the white world and the black was combined in that face.

The general did not explain the tradition that gave his army the right to
police the city. "As a matter of fact," he said to the trembling mayor, "I am
known for turning a blind eye to sins of intemperance and fornication when
they're committed by soldiers who risk their lives every day. But don't you
find it extraordinary that your God-fearing metropolis has supplies
of whisky that would last all the taverns of Dublin half a century?"

Sherman's soldiers had nailed an irregular row of silver salvers to a fence
surrounding a deserted warehouse. Behind it was a tall building spouting a
column of flames that looked like the hand of Satan reaching for heaven.
Fifty yards from the fence stood a ragged line of threadbare soldiers, half of
them shoeless, one with a dead goose tied to the back of his belt by its neck.
They were shooting at the plates, and they looked like a firing squad except
that each of them had a bottle at his feet. The sergeant watched the rifle barrels wobble, perhaps to the rhythm of the dancing flames reflected in the
polished silver targets. A short distance away stood another threadbare soldier, holding aloft a sword that had once belonged to a general, with a general's spyglass sticking out of his pocket. He barked an order and there was a
ragged chatter of musket fire, but only two of the plates were struck. It must
have been the whisky.

"So this is Sherman's great army," said the lady, shaking her head.

"Ma'am, are you by any chance German?" asked Kapsa. "Or Austrian?"

★

Burning snow was falling on the Congaree. It fell too on a black and white
procession that emerged from around the corner of a building devastated by
cannon fire and headed towards the house the lady had stopped in front of.
It was one of the many manor-houses that, in the sergeant's mind, blended
into a white avenue of luxury stretching from the Georgia line to Savannah,
then through South Carolina to this burning corpse of a city. This house appeared to be undamaged except for the symbolic statue on the gable, which
an exploding shell had reduced to a scorched wire skeleton of uncertain
significance, one arm raised to the black sky, the other still gloved in plaster.
They stopped. A group of officers galloped up to the house, among them
General Logan. The sergeant recognized him by his drooping moustache,
like two Turkish scimitars pointed downwards, parallel to the sharp grooves
of his frown. Two sentries—who were sober, and looked as if they belonged

in a different army—saluted, and the general and his escort walked in through the doorway between two etched-glass lanterns with brass fittings.

The lady looked at the intact building and the sergeant now remembered where he'd seen her. "No, I'm Polish," she replied. "My name is Sosniowski."

Ursula in the park with the miniature Hanzlitschek and the little girl whose bonnet had fallen off. Two ladies and their wailing offspring. He saw her again with Ursula in the municipal park, and one evening, after the miracle at Gottestischlein, he asked, "Who is that lady in the park?" He spoke a halting German which had begun to differ from the harsh, parade-ground vernacular of her husband, for he was spending his free time studying a German grammar for beginners. The lady herself was of no particular interest to him; he was merely avid to know anything that had to do with Ursula.

"Which lady in the park?" she asked.

"The one with the little girl and the pug dog," he said.

Ursula laughed and it sounded like sleigh-bells. "Oh, you dear man! You're even making progress with the German language!"

"For you," he replied solemnly. More sleigh-bells, and the hand that had recently spread healing water on his burning back now stroked his hair.

"She is Frau Doktor Sosniowski," said Ursula in the deepening twilight, which cast the only shadow on his paradise, that brief interval in which Hanzlitschek drank beer in the officers' mess. By now, since the sun was almost setting behind the Alps, he was probably tucking into his first nightcap. Ursula rose and, as she put on her clothes, she explained that the woman was the wife of a Polish doctor from Austrian Galicia. They had moved into the garrison town about twelve years before, and she was Ursula's good friend. "It was she who gave me the salve for your back. Her husband knew what it was for. He's a good man. They have endured a great deal."

She never told him what it was they had endured, and he didn't really care. The red fringe of sunset was shrinking behind the mountain peaks; Hanzlitschek would be finishing his second nightcap, and wouldn't down the third one till he got home. The sergeant watched Ursula through the window as she ran down the hill and disappeared into the outskirts of Helldorf. Soon after that, Hanzlitschek appeared in paradise with a bullwhip.

The black and white procession came to a halt in front of the manor-house. It was a cluster of little girls in soiled white dresses, surrounded, like the border on a funeral notice, by nuns in black habits. Their heads were bowed meekly, their gowns speckled with holes made by burning snowflakes. The procession was headed by a statuesque Mother Superior with a face that was anything but meek, just like the lady he'd finally remembered was—or had been—Frau Doktor Sosniowski.

"Is this the residence of General John S. Preston?" the Mother Superior asked a second lieutenant who was leaning against a pillar.

"No, Reverend Mother," replied the officer. "This is the headquarters of General John Alexander Logan, Commander of the Fifteenth Corps of General William Tecumseh Sherman's army."

"You are mistaken, lieutenant." The tall nun pulled a piece of paper out of her sleeve. "I have here a letter from your General William"—she made a slight pause—"Tecumseh Sherman, in which he assigns me General Preston's house as compensation for my convent school, which your soldiers set ablaze after General William Tecumseh Sherman promised me that both our convent and our school for young Catholic ladies would remain unharmed."

The lieutenant, nonplussed, took the paper.

"My name is Sister Baptista Lynch," the nun continued as he tried to decipher the general's scrawl. "Years ago, in Ohio, I taught Miss Minnie Sherman, daughter of your General Sherman—"

The second lieutenant yanked himself erect and ran into the house. They could hear him calling, "General! Just a moment!"

Sister Baptista looked around and saw the lady. "Ah, Madam Sosniowski! I do hope your academy has been spared such barbarism!"

The sergeant listened and remembered.

General Sherman finished reading the letter, and said, "It's true, she did teach Minnie, and now she suddenly remembers. In '61, though, she conveniently forgot, just like her brother, Patrick Lynch, the Bishop of Charleston." He turned to Colonel Ewing. "He's a friend of my wife's." He stared out the window at the burning city. "He also bears part of the blame—and no small part—for this devastation."

"Tecumseh Sherman," said Mother Baptista contemptuously. "He and his bandits—they're like the Roman soldiers who ridiculed Our Lord Jesus Christ," and she made the sign of the cross. "Would you believe it, madam? They blew their cigar smoke in the sisters' faces—and the little girls' faces too—and they laughed at us. They said, 'We're just as holy as you are, Reverend Sister! And, now what do you think of God? Ain't Sherman greater?'" The Mother Superior made the sign of the cross again. "Tecumseh Sherman. The pagan name suits him all too well."

The sergeant had never seen his general pray. Except maybe once—

"That was only on account of old Abe," insisted the newly pious Zinkule. "Sherman is in league with the Devil."

"How would you like a punch in the nose?" Houska offered.

"Leave him alone," said Stejskal. "He may be right."

"I am," declared Zinkule. "Remember Kennesaw!"

"And what's there to remember from Kennesaw?" Houska asked suspiciously.

"Things happened. Mysterious things."

They were sitting in the parlour of yet another white manor-house some-where near Savannah—the sergeant had lost count already. A large, scowling Negress towered over them, sulking because they had kept her from relieving the daughter of the house of some bed linens she was about to carry up to the master bedroom, where Vendelin Kabinus was about to deflower his new bride. Her wedding dress had belonged to the daughter of the house, whose husband-to-be was off fighting with Hood's army to the south, and it was quite dirty but still manifestly white. The bride's freshly scrubbed skin, on the other hand, was as black as tar.

"Woman! You're free now!" Stejskal snatched the comforter the black woman was still holding and put it on the rest of the linen in the daughter's arms. "You're not a slave any more, you have to drop those slave habits."

"I's part of the family," the black woman protested.

"You are? Let her take it anyway. She's younger than you are."

The Negress pouted, and Houska said, "Isn't this a waste of fine sheets, mess-ing them up on a wedding night?"

"It's none of your business," said Stejskal. "Do you have any idea what this means to Vendelin? He had to travel halfway around the world and fight his way from Wilber to Southern Georgia before he managed to talk anyone into it."

The plantation-owner's wife walked through the parlour. She was taking a blanket, as they had ordered her, to the rear of the house, where the Negro mem-bers of the family were sleeping. During the entire march from Georgia, Vendelin Kabinus had scarcely spoken; according to some, he had delivered one brief and not entirely coherent speech. That was when he fled inside his tent to escape the young vivandière that Kapsa and Svejkar had bribed. That was also when he explained the reason for his continuing chastity, which had always mystified them. How could he ever get a woman to marry him, he said, not to mention seduce her, when he had no idea what to talk to her about? He didn't know what he would talk to his bride about either, but that didn't trouble him because he spoke no English. Shake, whose Yankee tongue was nearly as smooth as his Czech one, had arranged the marriage. One of the few times Kabinus had spoken during the march through Georgia had been when he saw a young black girl in a green turban eyeing Sherman's troops. "What a piece!" he'd said, and that was all Shake needed to hear. He delegated himself to propose to her on Kabinus's behalf. Stejskal put her age at seventeen, Shake at twelve, and when

Reverend Mulroney asked her just before the ceremony, she said, "I ain't exactly sure. My ma says I's sixteen." Shaking his head, Mulroney recorded her age in the marriage registry as sixty.

They thought of the incredible things that had happened at the foot of Kennesaw Mountain, and the sergeant knew that Zinkule was right to imply that the general's display of piety in the Methodist church in Memphis was not religiously motivated. The general was simply a patriot like himself.

★

He had attended the Methodist holy of holies because of a sermon of Bishop Lynch's, published in the Charleston newspaper, about the states' inalienable right to freedom. The sergeant had read it and thought that he would be inclined to live among the subjugated Czechs if Austria were free, not as it was now, but as America was. He couldn't understand how two freedoms could be so different. And what kind of freedom was Bishop Lynch talking about? He glanced at the Negress in the corner of the dining room, taking out her rage on a silver tray so that, when they left the following day, her master would count that tray among the damages caused by the Unionists, along with the voluptuous nude statue that the virtuous Zinkule had covered with whitewash.

The sermon had unexpectedly driven the general to visit the nearest church. With an escort of four men from his personal bodyguard (two Czechs, two Irishmen), he sat in the front pew, and when the preacher, unnerved by his presence, concluded his circumspect sermon with a prayer for unspecified "soldiers on the field of battle" but without the usual prayer for the victory of an unspecified side, the general rose and, in a voice he usually only employed to be heard above artillery fire, launched into the prayer prescribed by the Union Army Command for the battlefield: "Almighty God, I beg you, grant strength, health, and long life to the President of these United States of America, Abraham Lincoln!" The soldiers thundered "Amen!" in two accents, and the preacher braced himself to be arrested.

★

They mused about the curious things that had happened to them at the foot of Kennesaw Mountain. Late on the afternoon of June 22, the veterans of Carter Stevenson's Confederate division had moved up along both sides of the Powder Springs Road to engage with Alpheus Williams's division. It was an old-fashioned attack, elbow to elbow, perhaps because they were veterans, but in Zinkule's eyes there was no accounting for it. Williams's division, supported on the right by Milo Hascall and on the left by John Geary, had the advantage of numbers. General Hood, who had ordered the attack, must have lost his mind. Otherwise his order could only be explained as inspired by a malicious God who was siding with the Union on Kennesaw Mountain. The Union artillery let Stevenson's men advance to within five hundred yards of their position before they cut loose with all forty cannon and hammered them, first with conventional ammunition and then, because that didn't stop them, with explosive canisters. Those forty cannon fired a record ninety salvoes a minute, yet the grey-clad ranks, with gaps like a mouthful of rotten teeth, got to within fifty yards of Williams's fortifications before the butchery was ended in a hail of minnies. Only then did the Rebels retreat to a muddy hollow, regroup, and attack again. The next fusillade they faced was worse, Paidr swore later, than the one at Chickamauga or on Missionary Ridge at Gettysburg. They retreated again, with more gaps in their ranks, and then attacked a third time. It couldn't have been mere insanity on Hood's part, Zinkule maintained. The barking of the cannon became the roar of a wild beast, and the madmen got to within thirty yards of the fortifications, where they were cut to ribbons. The survivors fell back a third time to the gully, where it was already dark. Soon darkness descended on Williams's palisades as well. But before it did, the rocks on the hillside glowed red with blood. In the dark, Rebel litter-bearers carried the moaning and the silent wounded back into the gully. Paidr climbed over the palisade and gave some water to a groaning Rebel lying a short distance from the barricade; when he had taken a sip of the lukewarm water in Paidr's canteen, he gave up the ghost. Paidr set out down the hill and didn't return until he ran into the Rebel litter-bearers. On the way back, his foot caught in the strap of an abandoned knapsack, and when he'd untangled it he took the knapsack back with him. Next morning, when the first rays of sunlight emerged, Paidr opened the knapsack and turned pale at what he found inside. There was a scrap of newspaper with a sketch of a man resembling Lincoln, and surely meant to be Lincoln, judging by the name printed under the picture in angular German script. But that wasn't what horrified Paidr. After all, there were Germans on both sides, and in the North there was an entire German division under the command of the Prussian General Franz Sigel—or so Stejskal, who had served under him briefly, claimed. No, what horrified him was the poem under the crude image of Lincoln. It too was printed in German script, but the words were Czech.

Paidr read it out loud:

Like the ancient fabled Phoenix, Freedom
Is born again in smoke and flashing flame,

And no man calls another man his brother,
Unless his hand with human blood is stained.

Thus has it ever been: Bohemia's hero,
John Hus, was burned to death for his ideal,
And here John Brown, for principle and honour,
Did bravely 'neath the looming gallows kneel.

And yet, when both these heroes bowed their heads
To bravely meet their cold and brutal fate,
Did bigotry and reason clash around them,
Brother shed brother's blood for love and hate.

Yet reason shall prevail as always,
Though blood-drenched soil and graves abound,
As friend and foe lie side by side, beneath the ground;

And broken shackles are the signs
Our dauntless efforts must obey.
Our quest for justice follows where they point the way.

"Boys," said Paidr, his voice catching, "there's Czechs on the other side too. Maybe we did this one in yesterday—"

"Why did he join up?" growled Stejskal.

"Join up?" said the sergeant. "Why do you think he carried this around in his knapsack?"

And he repeated the line to himself:

Like the ancient fabled Phoenix, Freedom—

He tried to understand the different freedoms: Bishop Lynch's freedom and the freedom of the black bride. That night the conundrum kept him awake, and in the morning he decided that there should be two different words for it.

★

Houska thought it over. At the top of the hill, bright cherries were glistening temptingly. Cherries in July? In Georgia? Houska's boyhood cravings were awakened. They were sitting in trenches at the bottom of the hill, and above them hung this bounteous tree with its mysterious red fruit, a perfect target. Hood's artillery were watching from the opposite hillsides. Houska's mouth was watering.

Later, Shake claimed Houska should have been court-martialled for trying to poison himself with inedible fruit—how could they possibly have been cherries, when the birds were ignoring them? But Houska started crawling up the hill towards the Tree of Paradise.

A bit farther on, at the foot of Kennesaw Mountain, Svejkar became the victim of an uncanny incident. One of Hood's sharpshooters had fired on Lieutenant Bondy in his observation post among the rocks, after he carelessly let his field-glasses catch the sun. The poorly aimed musket-ball glanced off the granite cliff face just above a ledge where Svejkar was tanning his stomach; it ricocheted upwards at an absurdly sharp angle, then fell back and landed directly on Svejkar's solar plexus, fortunately striking the book lying on his chest while he dozed. That, together with the projectile's decreased velocity, cushioned the impact, like General Ritchie's famous Bible—except that Svejkar had borrowed his book from Gambetta and it wasn't suitable for public display. He had to pay Gambetta a whole dollar for the damage, and on top of it all, the incident gave him a savage case of the runs.

★

Strange things had indeed happened at the foot of Kennesaw Mountain. Fisher, for instance, had managed to avoid the battle at the village of Dallas, though not deliberately, for he was frozen by supernatural terror. At the moment the order to attack arrived, Fisher was aiming his musket at a Rebel in a flagrantly piratical hat, when he realized that the man was aiming his musket directly back at fisher. Before Fisher could pull the trigger, he saw a flash in his sights and the butt of his musket kicked him in the shoulder. Squinting down the barrel, he saw that a bulge had appeared in it. He dodged behind a boulder and discovered that the pirate's shot had gone straight into the muzzle of his own musket; since it was of a larger calibre, it had plugged the barrel like a cork, making the weapon almost useless. Fisher mounted his bayonet and listened in disgust to the racket his unit was making as they advanced to a low stone wall a hundred yards ahead. He poked his musket out from behind the boulder, then peered carefully over the edge. The pirate must have been waiting for him to emerge, for he saw another flash and the musket flew out of his hands. By now Fisher was terrified—the pirate had hit the very tip of the bayonet, and a minnie was impaled on the point of his bayonet like a sugar plum. He retreated behind the boulder again and gave up all thought of heroism. Indeed, he experienced a sudden conversion to Zinkule's faith. He now believed that there was indeed some kind of black magic going on out there beyond the boulder. When the rest of the

*men set out from the low wall they had just taken, he remained behind his cover,
stunned by metaphysical terror.*

*Despite his absence from the battle, the attack made him famous throughout
the regiment. The amazing musket travelled from hand to hand, until Colonel
Connington confiscated it for his collection of war memorabilia, which included
a tiny bottle containing his own little finger, bitten off by a Washington society
lady who had come out to observe the first battle of Bull Run and, when her carriage had suffered a direct hit, had bolted in terror towards the Rebel lines;
Colonel Connington had grabbed her and tried to prevent her from screaming
with his hand.*

"The Devil is on Sherman's side," Zinkule insisted solemnly.

"How would you like a punch in the nose?" Houska asked again.

"He is!" the mystic repeated.

*"So you think Lucifer is helping our sacred cause?" chimed in the normally
taciturn Javorsky. He took everything seriously. "Whose side is God on, then?"*

*"Both," said Shake. "God, as you know, is a Jew, and wants to be on good
terms with everybody."*

"Are you asking for a punch in the nose too?" asked Houska.

*"What leads you to draw such erroneous conclusions about my desires?"
countered Shake.*

"Seriously, friends," said Zinkule, "the signs are obvious."

"You mean hell is on our side?" Javorsky asked ominously.

*"No, Jindra," said Zinkule, rolling his eyes to the ceiling as if he were in the
midst of a vision. "God Almighty sides with our cause as such. It's just that Sherman has the Devil on his side, because he's sold his soul just like Faust did. The
signs are obvious."*

*Upstairs in the master bedroom, the bedsprings began creaking as though an
elephant were rolling around on them.*

"Vendelin is vandalizing the bed," said Shake.

*"Put two and two together," Zinkule went on. "What happened the day be-
fore the canister buried Honza Dvorak? And what happened the day after?"*

*They recalled the resurrection of the boy from Milwaukee. He was sniping at
Rebels from a spot below a rocky overhang when a Rebel cannoneer made short
shrift of the overhang with a supernaturally well aimed shot. It lodged in a crack
below the overhang and exploded, burying Dvorak in a rock slide. When they
tried to free him, Rebel fire forced them to take cover. Fisher tapped out a message
with a pebble on rocks, and called out, but no sound came from the stony sarcophagus and he assumed the sharpshooter had been crushed to death. Then
some Rebel skirmishers showed up outside their palisades and they had to deal*

*with them. The Rebels forced them to retreat to their second line of defence, and
they opened fire from there, driving the Rebel swarm back behind their own palisades. The sarcophagus, with Dvorak inside, ended up in no man's land. As
night fell they exchanged a few more volleys, then it was dark, and next morning
they pushed the Rebels back once more. Scarcely had they caught their breath
when they heard the rattle of stones, and Dvorak emerged from his tomb with
nothing worse than a monumental bump on his head.*

"What happened the day before?" asked Paidr.

*"The nigger, remember?" Zinkule was still gazing at the ceiling. "All the
omens are there for the reading."*

*Now the sergeant remembered. A shirtless Negro in tattered trousers, with his
hat deferentially clasped to his bare chest, had stood in a meadow about ten feet
from Sherman. The general took a step towards him, and then several things happened at once: he slipped on a slimy mushroom and sat down with a thump, there
was the sound of a pine tree snapping in two, the general looked up to see the
Negro standing there headless. Behind him a black cannonball was rolling away
in the grass, and along with it a bloodied black head.*

*"Read the signs!" Zinkule urged. "The Devil is protecting Sherman. That
poison mushroom was the Devil's work."*

*"How do you know it was poison?" asked Stejskal. "How do you know what
kind of mushrooms grow in Georgia?"*

*The mystic ignored him. "Read the signs, friends," he said. "And the very
next day—"*

*The next day, the general had been inspecting his forward lines. Not half a
mile away stood Pine Mountain, and on its summit he could see a group of
officers in grey. They were unrecognizable at that distance, but their noncha-
lance irritated Sherman.*

*"Look at them!" he fumed. "Do they think we can't shoot straight, Captain
Dilgher?" he barked. "Unlimber your cannon. I want to see them drop!"*

*"Yes, sir!" replied the captain, formerly one of Sigel's officers back in Baden.
His white shirt-sleeves were rolled up to his elbows, perhaps to indicate that operating a cannon was hard work as well as risky. He gave the order to fire in a private code he had laboriously taught the thick-headed farm boys from Ohio, and
to Zinkule, the mystic, it sounded like diabolical abracadabra. Two slow claps,
three rapid ones, and two more slow ones, the boys set the gun for proper eleva-
tion, the cannon roared—*

*—and on top of Pine Mountain the fighting bishop, General Polk, was felled
by a cannonball that went right through him.*

*When they read about it in one of the Rebel newspapers, Zinkule adapted the
facts to suit his theory better. "The cannoneer says, 'Abracadabra,' and more than*

a mile away General Polk drops dead—the shot goes through him from his right hip to his left—and he's a bishop!" he said, his eyes wide, his index finger in the air. "One day a cannonball rips the head off a liberated slave, the next day it drills a hole through a bishop. When we pray, we say, 'The Lord Jesus descended from heaven to earth to lead the people from the left side to the right.' The cannonball goes into his right side and exits from the left. It's back to front, like the crucifix is upside-down at a witches' sabbath, and like—"

The bride's moans rose above the sound of creaking bedsprings.

"He's really giving it to her!" said Paidr.

Just then, Kabinus whinnied like a horse.

"She's the one giving it to him!" said Stejskal.

"Read the signs," the mystic declared.

★

Houska had just climbed up the hill to the tree with the alluring red berries and begun picking the fruit when he heard a loud crack. The red crown of the tree toppled over onto him as he was stuffing a handful into his mouth. Down inside the palisades, they could see a cannonball rolling down the hill towards them, and at that moment a swarm of iron bees buzzed over the hilltop. Houska dropped to the ground and rolled down the hill like a barrel of beer, and was greeted by a volley of laughter. Although he had had only a handful of the fruit, he, like Svejkar, fell victim to the Georgia quickstep.

"Strange are the ways of the Lord," said Shake.

Strange things indeed happened at the foot of Kennesaw Mountain.

★

The massa's whisky put them to sleep. They stretched out on the parlour floor and, when they woke up in the morning, each of them had one of the massa's pillows under his head. The Negress might be in a sulk, but she had taken pity on these soldiers who spoke a strange language.

The staircase creaked. Vendelin Kabinus, who seemed only half present, was coming down the stairs. The remains of a ham lay on the table, and when Kabinus was done with it only the bone was left for his bride to gnaw on. That day, they began the strenuous march to Savannah. Four hours later, when Colonel Connington ordered a rest and they all collapsed in the grass beside the road, Kabinus kept on marching. For a minute Lieutenant Bondy stared in amazement at the marching groom (the bride in the turban, furnished with a letter to the Wilber sheriff that Shake had translated into English for Kabinus, was hard at it again back in the master bedroom) and then he yelled, "Kabinus!" When the private didn't respond, the lieutenant ran after him, took him by the shoulder, and turned him around. Kabinus was still marching, this time in the opposite direction. As he was about to pass them, Shake stuck out his foot and tripped him. Kabinus fell flat on his face, looked up, blinked, and said, "Boys, I'm so tired I could cry!"

It was the longest sentence he uttered during the whole march through Georgia.

★

From the depths of the elegant house came the sound of profanity. The Reverend Mother Baptista's face stiffened. General Logan appeared between the brass lanterns, his moustache bristling like Hauptmann von Hanzlitschek's. He was clutching Sherman's letter and uttering words that the sergeant wouldn't have dared use in the presence of ladies.

Then Logan saw the Reverend Mother Baptista, and the gentleman in him prevailed.

"Forgive me, madam," he said. "Or Reverend Mother. This house belongs to the traitor Preston, and was to be burned down. Were it not for this letter"—he shook the paper under the scowling nun's nose—"the job would have been done today. So kindly forgive me my use of certain expressions." He looked around. The wind had picked up and the burning flakes of cotton were swirling through the air like swarms of lightning bugs. "It would have made a splendid torch!" He pointed at the devil's fist smouldering on the horizon. "But if General Sherman wishes otherwise—so be it!" He pushed the paper into the Reverend Mother's hand and jumped into the saddle. The group of officers followed; the foot soldiers formed a ragged line and, enveloped in smoke and soot, marched off behind the riders. A group of Negroes emerged from the intact Methodist church across the street, singing:

I am bound for the Promised Land
Bound for the Promised Land.
Oh, who will come and go with me,
I am bound for the Promised Land. . . .

On horseback, the general seemed larger than life. The soldiers didn't look back, marching eastwards through the smoke and the burning snowflakes.

Somewhere deep inside himself, the sergeant heard a different song, in a different language which was—perhaps still—his own.

Freedom, freedom, for dear sweet freedom,
Noble throngs faced martyrdom,
Noble throngs, dying to be free.
Freedom, dear mother, stand by me.

In his mind he saw a skull split in two by a cavalryman's sabre, the grey bubble of the student's brain. Hauptmann von Hanzlitschek; the bloodied grocer, his lips a barely perceptible line; the gauntlet formed by his fellow soldiers armed with willow switches. He gave his head a shake, then saw General Kilpatrick hunched over on horseback beside the pontoon bridge as his cavalry galloped across it. The general was looking down at a crater in the road, the mangled corpses of the sergeant's fellow soldiers scattered on either side, farmers' brains splattered across the South Carolina mud. The general yelled, "When I annihilate that hellish cesspool of secession, Johnny Reb, there won't be much of you left to wipe out!" He saw the towering General Slocum staring at the astonished face of a dead soldier from Ohio, the bottom half of whose body was missing. "This is no way to make war!" Then the sergeant saw his own general writing an order, his gaunt face crumpled into a scowl. "Nothing but war matériel and public—" and a courier rushed in with news that Rebel mines buried in the road by the pontoon bridge over the Savannah River had exploded as a platoon of the Eighth Ohio was approaching the bridge, tearing seven soldiers to pieces. Sherman tossed the uncompleted order on the floor. Behind him, General Howard made the sign of the cross: "This is no way to make war!" Sherman dipped his pen and began a new sheet, and Howard opened his Bible. He read softly, "'*Behold, the day of the Lord cometh, cruel both with wrath and fierce anger, to lay the land desolate: and he shall destroy the sinners thereof out of it.*'" Sherman stopped writing and engaged in a struggle with the Lord, while General Howard prayed softly. Then Sherman reached under the table, picked up the discarded order, dipped his pen in the ink, and went on writing—"buildings in Columbia should be burned." The sergeant knew that the fire that had destroyed a third of the city was the will of the Lord, not that of General Sherman. In Charleston, in the home of a brother of a friend of the general's, a white-collared Episcopalian clergyman had stood in the corner of the room. Sherman was saying his farewells when the clergyman said, "General, could you please order your men not to destroy our seminary library? It contains many rare volumes of American history and the history of the classical world, and European history—" The general spun around. A week earlier, Father Toomer Porter had still been preaching, and the sergeant wondered what his sermon had been about. The rough face scowled. "Have no fear," he said. "But since you have so many history books," he continued bitterly, "you should have seen to it that your students read them better. They might have learned enough history to keep them from starting a war."

Logan's soldiers marched through the fire, smoke, and dusk. Voices came from the Methodist church behind them:

> *Oh freedom, oh freedom, oh freedom over me*
> *And before I'd be a slave*
> *I'll be buried in my grave*
> *And go home to my Lord and be free.*

"Madame Sosniowski," asked the sergeant, "have you ever lived in Helldorf, in the Tyrolean Alps?"

Burning snow was falling on the Congaree River.

★

Cyril had shown up that night and, over the night sounds of Savannah coming through the window, the Negro bands, the cries of delight from the gay ladies of Madam Russell's Bakery and the Dutch Maids Riding School, had told the story of his little sister while Kakuska snored away in the corner over the disassembled cuckoo clock. Cyril reminisced about that time long ago, before they had left for America. Kapsa knew the countryside Cyril was talking about. He was from a different region, but the miles and the years had shrunk the tiny land into a single bittersweet picture of fragrant manure piles and dark forests, of tiny mountainous fields beneath a brutal August sun, torture chambers where old, overworked men of thirty had one foot in the grave. A brief youth, a brief old age. He knew the life. He had never felt homesick for the mushroom-filled forests, the undulating foothills, young women redolent of fresh wild thyme—not even in the garrisons of Louisiana, Dakota, or California, or in the rocky valleys of Arizona. He longed neither for the old country nor for Annie, torn from his grasp by the army, by a realistic father, by obedience; he couldn't even remember what she looked like. Ursula was the only one he ever missed. For years he had nightmares about what had become of her, her years in prison or possibly her last few moments on the gallows. But eventually Ursula too became no more than a picture in a locket at the bottom of his knapsack, beneath a pile of images from his new life. Gradually even the locket faded into half-memory, and besides, there were the cyprians in establishments like Madam Russell's, and skilful professionals from Mexico, and once he'd even been consoled by a Czech woman in Chicago, the wife of a buddy, but it wasn't consolation he was after, just relief. The land itself was his consolation. Unlike the country he came from, this land was endless. He had marched through it, ridden over it on horseback, by railroad, from garrison to garrison. A kaleidoscopic land. The army—once a trap in which his brief, almost happy youth had ended—became a mother to him, the Thirteenth Regiment of the United States Army—

—so that when Cyril told the story about Zalesni Lhota, a picture came to his mind, a bitter greyness shrouded the dawn, and he felt not a hint of homesickness. He only felt again, for the thousandth time, a sense of home. The rasping scream of the cicadas joined in the exotic music of the bands in the beautiful city of Savannah, under the fabulous sky with its plethora of stars. This was home now. Before this he'd never really had a home, just the kind of bad dream Cyril was talking about—a crofter's cottage, a piece of land three roods square, an ill-used father, and a headstrong sister.

★

Lida had been different then, very different. Blue eyes that were more like turquoise dandelions, with an innocence that had captivated Vitek Mika of the Mika estate. The Toupeliks owned only the tiny field and a cottage. A little world of its own. "It couldn't have happened," Cyril was saying. "Besides, you had to have an official form for everything. The groom had to be exempted from military service or discharged, and by that time he'd be a pretty old bridegroom. And he had to have an official document saying he had the means to support his bride. Of course, everything was possible with bribery and barter. I could never have married there; the most I could hope for was a roll in the hay with the hired girls. Remember all the ones that got pregnant? My uncle Thomas and his regiment were in Kutna Hora for three years, and during that time there were so many illegitimate kids born, they started calling it 'Bastard Hill'. Seven hundred, my uncle said. Of course, that wasn't a problem with Vitek. But Lida didn't have a dowry. How could she, with our place only three roods square? Things were going from bad to worse for us. We'd had crop failures three years in a row, then our cow died. Little Josef and I had to pull the plough for Father, and Josef wasn't even fourteen. And then—" Old man Mika became suspicious of his only child, his only son and heir. And Cyril began to suspect his sister. The Toupeliks all slept in the same room, for the cottage had only one. Mother and Father on the bed, Cyril and little Josef on a ledge above the tiled stove. Lida slept on a bench in the corner. At night she began going to the outhouse, and she'd al-

ways tie a skirt around her nightshirt. It was perfectly clear to him what was
going on. But the mother and father were heavy sleepers, and suspected nothing.

Lida wouldn't come in from the outhouse until after midnight; then she'd slip
out of her skirt and very quietly climb back onto her bench. Little Josef slept the
deep sleep of an overworked child. When they stopped ploughing at noon and
took out their dry bread and onion, he'd barely finish eating before he lay back
on the grass between mouthfuls and was dead to the world. Only Cyril knew
what she was up to. His young body could take the extra work it had to do now
that the cow was dead. He also drew strength from his passion for Marie, the
hired girl on the Mika farm, except that Marie had a soldier who was supposed
to come home in two years, and she was one of those stubborn maids who frit-
tered away their Sundays off by praying in church, and spent all her free time on
winter evenings reciting litanies, and attended the May masses in the spring: a
bull-headed faith, but what else was there? She was so different from Lida, who
went to church on Sunday only out of duty, and had no time for litanies. One
night, as soon as Lida closed the cabin door softly behind her, he got up and
watched her run past the outhouse towards the woods.

That night, picking his way through the low spruce trees and occasionally
catching a glimpse of Lida's bare feet flashing in the moonlight on the path, he
suddenly saw the shadow of old man Mika behind a tree on the other side of the
path. He stopped. Lida disappeared among the taller spruce trees and the old
man came out onto the path and followed her silently. Then Cyril lost sight of
him too, and he ran down the forest path because he was certain of the reason for
Lida's nocturnal outings. He'd been certain before, he merely hadn't known who
the fellow was.

Then he saw old Mika creeping into the underbrush on the edge of the tiny
meadow. He left the path on the opposite side and crept through the brush as
stealthily as the old man.

There they were. They stood so close that they looked like a single entity, protected by the night and the woods, protected, they thought, by their parents' heavy
sleep after hard labour, one soul but not yet one body in the middle of the tiny
meadow, observed only by owls. Under the harvest moon they melted into each
other, lulled by the soft woodwinds of the nocturnal birds.

Slowly, with the tenderness that precedes a frenzy, they lay down on a patch of
moss. He glimpsed Lida's thighs as Vitek lifted her skirt—and a brief, incestuous
pang tingled in his crotch—but old Mika burst out of the bushes and, with his
strong farmer's grip, tore his only son and heir from the undowried thighs. He
heard a resounding slap.

"Father!" That was Vitek's voice.

"Silence!" The bark of a drill sergeant. Mika twisted Vitek's arm up behind *his back and drove him wordlessly down the path towards the village and their farm.*

Lida pulled down her skirt and sat up. Cyril jumped out of the bushes and ran over to her. Her teeth were chattering and she was trembling violently but she wasn't crying. Was it fright that made her shake? Terror? He knelt beside her, put his arm around her. She showed no surprise at his presence, and it was a while before she could even weep. "Oh God, Cyril, you won't tell on me, will you? Say you won't tell. . . ." He assured her he wouldn't, and kept reassuring her all the way down the path and across the fields to the cottage. "Promise me, Cyril—as silent as the grave!" The incestuous desire had been no more than a momentary lunacy and a brief vision of white thighs in the moonlight. She was his sister, after all.

It wasn't until years later, in Texas, that he figured out that it hadn't been fright or terror that had made her quake. That night, she had been touched by a terrible Austrian form of death. The death of the pursuit of happiness.

He didn't tell on her. How could he? But next day, though it was haying time, the farmer appeared in the Toupeliks' field and called out to Cyril's father. The father put down his scythe and walked over to the hedgerow. Cyril stopped work as well. Little Josef, in the middle of binding a sheaf, dropped to the stubble-covered ground and fell asleep. Lida turned white as death, and glanced at Cyril. Was it fright or hatred? Then she bent over a sheaf, picked up a piece of straw, and bound the sheaf. Her entire body was trembling, as it had the night before. The rich farmer was talking urgently to the poor farmer by the edge of the field. Of course, Cyril knew what he was saying. Then the father returned, his face a deep, dark red, but he said nothing. He picked up the scythe and set to work again. He didn't say a word until that evening.

Cyril's father was good-natured, but there was a tradition in such matters. He ordered everyone but Lida to leave the cottage. Outside they could hear her whimpering, and the whistle of Father's strap. Mother crossed herself, and little Josef asked, "What has Lida done?" And Cyril replied, because that too was part of the tradition, "Quiet! You're too young to understand." So now little Josef knew too, for he was a country boy, and already twelve. Father called them back inside. They sat down to supper and ate their potatoes in silence, without sour milk, because the cow had died. Lida lay on the bench, facing the wall, her entire body heaving and shuddering.

The memory of running the gauntlet flashed through the sergeant's mind, and the red gash on Ursula's white back. It was a tradition. The faded side of the locket. He gave his head a shake, and looked over at the diligent Kakuska, his clockwork gearwheels gleaming brassily in the candlelight. The hullabaloo outside, in Savannah. "Shut up this minute, d'you hear,

Cyril!" Blue eyes, no longer innocent—serpent's eyes now, cruel, and the Negro voices outside the window, . . . *and before I'd be a slave I'll be buried in my grave*. . . . Plunking banjos, cicadas, moonlight pouring down on the sycamores.

Something had happened. At mass on Sunday, his sister usually stifled yawns or flirted with the boys across the nave, and paid attention only when the singing began. This Sunday she remained on her knees for the whole mass except when the liturgy required her to stand. This went on Sunday after Sunday. On the opposite side of the church, in the corner, there was another kneeler, another rosary passing through the unaccustomed fingers of Vitek Mika. Then came spring.

Can piety be evil?

"I'd never been on a pilgrimage, there wasn't time for it," said Cyril. "It never entered my mind that Lida would try to put one over on God just to get her own way."

"What else could she do?" asked the sergeant. "And what did they plan to do, anyway?"

"To run off to America. What they forgot was that money can buy anything. And it looked like real one hundred per cent repentance. Mother watched her like a hawk at mass but Lida never even glanced at Vitek. In autumn, Mother heaved a sigh of relief because Lida's screwing about hadn't had any consequences."

In the spring, Lida began making her case.

"Lida, you've never ever been the slightest bit interested in pilgrimages, and now you want to go all the way to Amberice?"

"I have to beg forgiveness from the Virgin Mary," she said, without as much as a blush. Her eyes weren't yet reptilian, but they were no longer innocent either.

"Father wouldn't hear of it. So my terrible little sister—"

"Terrible?" said the sergeant. "Isn't she just pitiful?"

Cyril gave a nasty laugh. "Wait till you hear. So she managed to bewitch the padre. He was young, and of course he was crazy about her, but he was a good priest and didn't let on. She bewitched him, all right. He came to see us to plead her case. Said he'd keep an eye on her himself, since he was going to lead the procession to Amberice that year. Keep an eye on her! The very first night—it was three days' walk to Amberice, the fourth day was for prayers, and then three days back, that meant six nights spent sleeping in barns, the women in one, the men in another, and of course Father Bunata couldn't stay with the women. Keep an eye on her! Mother Fidelia of the Franciscans was chaperoning the women, but she had trouble with her feet and by evening all she could think of were her bunions."

"Wasn't it risky? Couldn't they have waited till they were out of the country?"

"*They were young. And besides, how could they know that Father Bunata wasn't the only one keeping an eye on them? An old army veteran named Svestka went along on the pilgrimage, for money. Old man Mika's money.*"

"*Odd that old man Mika let them go in the first place,*" *said the sergeant.*

"*Could you ever stop someone in Austria from going on a pilgrimage? Lida, maybe. She wasn't of age yet. But Vitek was twenty-two. He didn't ask his father, he just signed up. They were going after the crops were in, so what could old Mika do? Besides, when Father Bunata was at the Mikases' for Sunday dinner he had nothing but good to say about Vitek, how he'd changed so much for the better, what a devout lad he was now, how he helped carry the banner in the Corpus Christi procession. Bunata certainly knew what had happened between Vitek and Lida. There was no chaplain in Lhota, so he was the only one to hear confessions—*"

"*What makes you so sure they confessed to him?*" *the sergeant interrupted him.*

Cyril frowned and thought it over. "*Well,*" *he replied,* "*I was an altar boy as a child. I'd never have thought of not confessing. But you see what she's like? She may well have lied. And you don't even know why I'm telling you all this. Isn't it awful? Adding the sin of sacrilege to fornication.*"

"*But was it fornication?*" *asked the sergeant.*

Cyril waved a hand dismissively. "*Well, anyway,*" *he said,* "*old Mika was left with no choice but to hire a spy. But the spy wasn't that good, and they almost got away with it.*"

Amberice was only three kilometres from the district capital, where the train to Vienna stopped. That would be the escape route. But they couldn't wait. Three nights in a row they snuck out of the barns. Mother Fidelia was asleep, a victim of her bunions, and old Svestka was asleep too, drowned in the gin he'd bought with Mika's money. In the woods that lined the road to Amberice, Vitek and Lida at last became more than just one soul. Services were held from early in the morning of the fourth day, in the Church of the Holy Mother on the Hill, who, among her other titles, was the Patroness of Fortunate Conception. It was as though God, deceived as he was, was having his little joke. Lida sat conspicuously in the first row, clearly visible to Father Bunata. The priest warmed to her unearthly piety, sensing that God was bestowing a special mercy upon her. He sang the litany in his lovely, resonant tenor: "*Hope of sinners . . . Sweet Virgin of virgins . . . Virgin of the Immaculate Conception. . . .*"

"*Intercede for us!*" *responded the women, and from the first row came Lida's lovely soprano, though by* "*us*" *she only meant her and Vitek. If she was a believer at all, that is. But she probably was. The ways of the Lord are strange.*

Meanwhile, all but unnoticed, Vitek slipped out of the church and ran to-

wards the railroad station in the district capital. Unfortunately the old soldier had exhausted his supply of gin, so he was sober and alert. He slipped out behind Vitek and followed him under the cover of the hedgerows that lined the road.

God—or the Devil, depending on how you look at it—intervened once more, and almost saved the enamoured sinners. When Svestka discovered why Vitek had gone to town, he waited until the young man had left the little railroad station and started back to the church. Svestka himself was no longer in any hurry. He was no genius, but he could put two and two together, so he took a walk through the town. He had at least until dark.

There were several taverns on the town square. As luck would have it, under the sign reading "The Horn of Plenty" stood retired Oberleutnant von Meduna, examining the menu posted in the window. Svestka's high spirits—his discovery at the railroad station had sparked his sense of adventure and improved the prospect of an additional reward for a job well done—rose to dizzying heights as he remembered old campaigns, for military memory is always beneficently selective. He completely forgot how once, during the advance against Garibaldi, this very same Oberleutnant had had him put in irons. The only thing he could recall was the Oberleutnant's Lombard mistress, the wife of his superior officer, whom he, as the Oberleutnant's orderly, had successfully blackmailed. So he ran over to him, stood at attention, and clicked his heels. "Herr Oberleutnant, reporting for duty, sir!" The same kind of selective memory was operating in the Oberleutnant. His rank upon retiring had been so low because, having failed to find himself a suitably wealthy bride, he had led a life of restless desperation that exceeded even the norms of promiscuity permissible to officers. He selectively forgot that he had caught his former orderly, who was now standing at attention before him, red-handed stealing cigars (the orderly was not a smoker, and had been selling the cigars to Feldwebels at half price), sneaking drinks of cognac and topping up the bottle with water, and in dozens of similar transgressions. All he could recall was how discreet the orderly had been in procuring women for him, and so he said, "At ease!" and took the old soldier into the tavern for goulash.

They had more than just goulash, of course, but Svestka had plenty of time till sunset. He learned, in fact, that he had till dawn, because the first and only train to Vienna wasn't due to arrive at the little railway station until half past four in the morning. He learned this from his Oberleutnant, who was planning to take the same train back to the imperial capital. Over brandy and gin, recollections unfolded of cannonades without casualties, painless injuries, and the glorious fallen, while in the church of the fortunate conception Father Bunata grew more ardent as Vitek secretly showed Lida their two tickets to paradise.

They all had time till dawn.

★

Madam Sosniowski stopped and looked at the sergeant. "Helldorf! How did you know?"

"I serv—I lived there for some time too. In '48. Your husband was a doctor, I believe."

"Did you know him?"

"Not personally. I used to see you in the park. You had two little girls."

Madam Sosniowski smiled. They were walking past the last building on the outskirts of Atlanta. The street curved around towards an isolated white building surrounded by trees.

"Those little girls have become young ladies," she sighed. "What were you doing in Helldorf?"

"I was stationed at the garrison there. Until the spring of '49."

She looked at him curiously. "And then you came to America?"

"Yes."

"You deserted." It wasn't a question.

"I came in search of freedom."

She was silent. A unit of Kil's cavalry galloped past, pulling a small cannon behind them.

"My husband did the same," said Madam Sosniowski. "He wasn't deserting, of course. He wasn't even in the army. At least not in Austria. But he didn't want to stay there any longer, not after the revolution in '48. When Bach came to power in Vienna, with his secret police and all—after what my husband had gone through—he decided it was time to leave."

"But why are you here? Why did he come to the South?"

She looked at his regimental insignia. "Are you surprised that I've become a dyed-in-the-wool Southerner?"

He shrugged.

"I haven't," she said. "It simply troubles me—it sickens me, in fact—that your army doesn't behave as one would wish if one were concerned about—" She fell silent again, almost as if she couldn't bring herself to say the word "freedom". "Did you hear those Negroes singing?"

"I did, but war is war," he said, parroting his general. "We're not here to be loved."

"Is a war like this one still war?"

He felt a sudden desire to stand up for his drunken companions, because he'd walked all the way across Georgia with them, and they'd been together at Chickamauga and Spotsylvania. He repeated his general's words: "War must be waged effectively, or not at all." He felt something like anger rising in him. "It can't be waged to suit Southern ladies."

Madam Sosniowski looked up at the sky, black with the smoke that swirled out of Columbia. Another of Kil's squadrons galloped past them towards the city.

"I am not a Southern lady," she replied softly, "and my husband was once a soldier too. An army doctor. But—you may be right. Once you see Sherman's army, you lose your taste for war. Only, you know, there are some things you simply can't accept. This is how the Cossacks behaved in Poland. My husband often spoke of it in Siberia. Of the brutality, but also of why different people wage different kinds of war."

"In Siberia?" he asked, astonished.

Still the flakes of burning cotton drifted down on the Congaree River.

★

The old veteran twitched in his sleep and woke up with a start. He could see the spring stars overhead, and each one had a twin. He didn't know what had woken him up, and didn't know where he was, but he was lying in a hedgerow between two fields, shivering with cold. Then he remembered. He jumped up and ran towards the church, its four steeples towering against the double stars like a black reproach. That night, instead of sleeping in barns, the pilgrims had bedded down in the convent refectory.

He ran, his heart skipping beats. He arrived at the convent gate and rushed inside, then into the dining hall. One of the straw mattresses was empty. He surveyed the room in alarm. In the moonlight, the clock on the wall showed five to four. He panicked. He ran to the mat closest to the door, where Father Bunata lay moaning softly. He shook him.

"Reverend Father! Wake up!"

The priest opened his eyes wide. He too had forgotten where he was.

"They're trying to run away to Vienna together!"

"What? Who?"

The priest sat up on his straw mat, still not quite awake.

"The Toupelik girl and young Mika!"

"What?" The priest was returning from a paradise of inappropriate dreams to the waking world, a world that was suddenly falling apart. "Little Lida Toupelik?"

"Yes, yes! Hurry! We may be too late already!"

They ran together towards the dark town. The priest's boots were untied and his cassock was unbuttoned; the old soldier was as sober as he could remember ever being, though he was short of breath and kept falling behind the clergyman—for the priest was young and strong, and driven by an undeclared love. Looking like a big black rooster, he raced ahead with his skirts flying, so that by the time Svestka reached the town square, gasping for breath, the priest's cassock was just flapping out of sight around the corner at the far end. The old soldier's strength gave out and he stumbled and fell, and then, by sheer force of will, he scrambled back to his feet, with his heart in his throat, and dragged himself to the little railroad station. He staggered through the waiting room, but he didn't fail to notice the sign on the wall. "DELAY:" and beside it, in chalk lettering on a black background, "30 minutes". It was exactly four-thirty. He heaved a sigh of relief and opened the door onto the platform.

Father Bunata was sitting on the ground, blood streaming from his nose. Lida Toupelik was standing behind Vitek, whose fists were clenched, but it was Oberleutnant von Meduna who was wiping his right hand with a handkerchief. A gendarme in a plumed hat was pounding down the platform towards them. As Svestka ran out onto the platform, Lida said something to the Oberleutnant. Von Meduna bowed and replied, "Frauendienst ist Gottesdienst—*to serve a lady is to serve God."*

"Das ist Gotteslästerung! *That's sacrilege!" wailed the downed priest, holding his hand to his nose. The gendarme ran up, helped the priest to his feet, and asked, in German, what was the matter.*

The priest rummaged under his cassock for a handkerchief, forgetting that in his haste he had neglected to put on his trousers. The Oberleutnant gallantly offered a handkerchief of his own.

"What's going on here?" the gendarme repeated, in Czech this time.

"He's going to take her away!" exclaimed the old soldier.

"What business is it of yours, Svestka?" the Oberleutnant snapped.

"But she's not even seventeen!" the old veteran said feebly.

"Since when are you so moral, you old fool?"

"It's not that I—but I was supposed to keep an eye on him."

"You were supposed to what?"

"Keep an eye on him," replied Svestka miserably. "They almost got away. It's your fault, sir, for pouring all that liquor into me."

"Me? You poured it into yourself!" roared the Oberleutnant. "You were so drunk they had to throw you out of the tavern!"

The old soldier couldn't remember. But beyond the black hole in his mind, he did remember being paid to keep an eye on Vitek Mika—and what he was paid to do, he did. Not for the credit that came from a job well done, but because, in his experience as an orderly, a job well done meant a bonus.

"I've got to make sure he gets home!" he whimpered. "His father ordered me to!"

Now Vitek spoke for the first time. "My dad can't tell me what to do. I'm of age!"

"But she's not!" old Svestka whined, pointing at Lida. In the murky light of the approaching dawn, her blue eyes were as cold and inscrutable as a basilisk's.

"Go to hell, Svestka!" said Vitek. "She's my wife, or she will be before the day is out."

Now the gendarme entered the discussion. "The Fräulein is under age," he declaimed officiously. "In the absence of parental consent this constitutes abduction."

"No one," declared the Oberleutnant righteously, "has the moral right to stand in the way of young love."

"The parents do," said Svestka, determined to fight for his bonus to the very end.

In the distance they could hear the clanging of an approaching locomotive. The priest gently pushed the gendarme away, took the handkerchief from his nose, and said heavily, "Parents have the moral responsibility to prevent a sin from being committed. Sins may be forgiven"—blood began dripping from his nose again and he caught it in the handkerchief—"but they mustn't be condoned or concealed, or actively aided and abetted. Lida, dear—" He turned to her, and it sounded like a plea for forgiveness.

"Leave me alone!" snapped Lida.

The priest turned pale and shrank, as though he'd been struck a mortal blow.

"Polizei!" cried the old soldier desperately. "Do your duty!"

The train sounded close at hand, and the gendarme finally made up his mind. He stepped over to Lida and took her by the arm. "Fräulein, how old would you be?"

"Six!" hissed the girl.

"Let her go!" the Oberleutnant said, ominously but not persuasively. "Do you know who I am?"

"I do, sir," said the gendarme, "but the law is the law. The Reverend Father here will be my witness." He gave Lida Toupelik's arm a tug, and she grabbed Vitek and hung on. Vitek threw a punch at the gendarme, but the gendarme was well trained and ducked the blow.

"In the name of the law," he said, raising his rifle, "you are under arrest!" And he slammed Vitek across the head with the stock.

Vitek went down.

Lida pushed the priest away, and he attempted no more than to make the sign of the cross in her direction. She just stuck her tongue out at him.

She returned to Lhota alone. Well, not quite alone, for she had a shadow. The old soldier hobbled along behind her the whole way, and slept at the door of the stable where she spent the night. By midnight the following day they were in Lhota. The old soldier got his bonus. Old Mika went to the town jail to pick up his son in the buggy. Lida stopped going to mass. Within a month, she knew that the Patroness of Fortunate Conception had done her work well.

★

Dr. Sosniowski had treated the Polish wounded. Finally there were more wounded than able-bodied, and he was captured by the Cossacks with a rifle in his hands. They exiled him to Siberia for ten years. Because he was an educated man, the tsar (who didn't believe in equality between the classes) allowed his young wife to accompany him into exile. They rattled across the vastness of Russia in a carriage, in the company of indifferent, desperate, and desperately rough Russian soldiers. It took them three months to get to a remote village in the far northern reaches of the taiga, where smelly muzhiks caught scrawny fish in a half-frozen river and the couple had to report each week to the tsar's local agent, who reeked of vodka. There were four other exiles in the village: a writer, two lawyers, and a mad priest. They were all Russians. The writer owned a handful of books: Voltaire, Rousseau, a Russian translation of Tom Paine, and the Declaration of Independence. Dr. Sosniowski was often in poor health. His wife looked after him as best she could, and brought him remedies from an old vodka-soaked herbalist, but they always made him feel worse; in the end she tended him only with love. It wasn't even physical love any more, because in exile it was mainly the soul that clung to life.

"We often talked about the brutality of the Cossacks," she said as they approached the white school. "And also about America."

"We're fighting this war to rid America of everything that's like Russia," said the sergeant.

"But must you fight it so brutally?"

"The more brutal it is, the shorter it will be," he replied, quoting his general again. "And Sherman's not a murderer. He does everything he can so as few of his men are killed as possible. He's convinced that the life of one soldier is worth more than—" He looked around. On the bank of the Congaree River, a luxurious summer place stood burning as the fiery snow floated down on it. "—than this. Sherman isn't a killer. He destroys things, maybe, but he doesn't kill. Not like the Russians. Just remember."

She sighed. "Perhaps you are right."

The sergeant's anger quickly subsided. "He gets no pleasure out of destroying things, either," he added. "He does what he has to, to end the war fast. Sometimes people suffer. But he finds no pleasure in their troubles. Never!"

That was not entirely true.

★

In the long run—in the very long run—the conception was indeed a fortunate one. Otherwise old Toupelik would never have got moving, if only because there wasn't the money. It was haying time again, and this time it was he who appeared at the edge of Mika's field. And it was old Mika who laid aside his scythe, knowing that only something urgent would make the man leave his work at midday and trudge the three kilometres through the July heat from his three roods square to the farmer's ample fields. In any case, Mika knew what had brought him. Now, in the middle of haying, it couldn't be anything else.

"Father'd been thinking about America for a long time. Everyone who was poor thought about it," said Cyril. "But two things got in their way. One was money. Boat tickets for five adults cost a fortune. The other thing was that people didn't know much about America; the Austrian authorities saw to that. They hardly ever let the papers write anything about America, and when they did it was usually an article translated from a German newspaper about the horror emigrants could expect to face, how many died on the voyage, and how those who survived were scalped by Indians. But some things got through to the general public." Cyril laughed. "I know you've been here since '50, but you did say you used to read Havlicek's newspaper—"

"I did," said the sergeant. "That's what got me thinking about going to America in the first place. Except I was in the army."

"Lesikar and Klacel," said Cyril. "Those two are the ones to blame, or give the credit to, depending on your point of view. Klacel was a monk and a jack-of-all-trades. He wrote poems, and later on, they say, he and his abbot played God. They used to experiment with peas in the monastery garden; then Abbot Mendel wrote it up in German. Lesikar was my father's third cousin. He was a tailor and farmed a small piece of land, but he got mixed up in politics, so, after the revolution of '48 fell through, the gendarmes never gave him any peace. Lesikar had piles of books, and that's mainly what they were after. He was hand in glove with some woman writer called Bozena Nemcova, a real beauty, and Lesikar told me later on, when we were in Texas, that she had a fun-loving little snatch. But she was involved in politics too, and so was her husband. Anyway, Lesikar put one over on the gendarmes. He put the banned books in a box in the root cel-

lar, then he borrowed some harmless books from an old woman in the neigh-
bourhood who was a Protestant like him, and stuck them in his shelves. The gen-
darmes went straight for his books, but what could they do to him for stuff like
The Courage of Brunclik, The Farmer's Almanac, The Loves of Countess
Tubing, *or* Jirik's Vision? *They confiscated a dream book,* Your Dreams Explained, *but he got it back later—with illegible German scrawls in the margins,*
and one dream blacked out with India ink. Even they couldn't arrest him for a
single dream in a seven-hundred-page book. Anyway, Lesikar dissolved the cen-
sor's ink with Hoffman drops, and guess what the page said? "If you dream of see-
ing a jackass on the throne, misery will engulf the land."

Outside, banjos were kachinking. "I'd have arrested him," the sergeant said.
"After all, that dream came true, didn't it?"

"They didn't arrest him, but they kept harassing him," Cyril continued. "So,
just for the fun of it, he kept adding to his collection. The Glory of the House of
Hapsburg, Amusing Incidents in the Life of the Monarch. *And for all he was*
a Protestant, The Meaning of the five Stars in the Crown of our Patron
Saint, St. John of Nepomuk. *The gendarmes weren't interested in any of them.*
So after a while they left him alone, and he gave the old woman back her dream
book, and to be on the safe side he kept Amusing Incidents, *and he even dug up*
a copy of its sequel, Sad Moments in the Life of the Monarch. *Once he stopped*
by our place before he left for Texas, in '50, and he translated passages from one of
his subversive books for us, Das Kajutenbuch *by Charles Sealsfield. Lesikar said*
Sealsfield was a Czech whose real name was Karel Postl, but he started calling
himself Charles Sealsfield after he came to America. He was one of the first; he
came here sometime in the '20s. Lesikar translated bits of what he wrote about
Texas. And that was what put the bug in Father's ear about coming to America."
Cyril fell silent for a while, and they listened to the Negroes singing.

> There are rocks and hills
> And brooks and vales
> Where milk and honey flows,
> I am bound for the Promised Land
> I am bound for the Promised Land. . . .

"That's it," nodded Cyril. "Printing articles about America in the newspa-
pers was forbidden, but Lesikar got a crafty idea. Back then, Klacel was editor of
The Moravian News. *It used to come to our village. Mika would read it and*
then pass it on to his neighbours, including my father. Lesikar got his hands on a
letter from Reverend Bergman, a Lutheran pastor from Skruzna who'd emi-
grated to Texas in '50, got the job of pastor for the German Lutherans in Cat

Springs in Austin County, and started writing letters back home about what life was like in Texas. The letters passed from hand to hand but only a few people ever got to read them, so Lesikar and Klacel decided to publish one in The Moravian News *in a section called 'From our Readers'. Lesikar figured that a letter wasn't news, but to help them get away with it they published an anti-emigration article in the same issue to pacify the censor. It worked. True, they never let them print any more of his letters, but one was enough. It put the Texas bug in a lot of people's ears. The paper got into every village and pretty soon the letter had done its work. In spite of the horror stories, people began emigrating in droves. Lesikar went too. Fine, but to emigrate you had to have a little money, at least, and Father didn't have a bean. Our cow was dead, we couldn't afford another one, the crop had failed three years in a row, and boat tickets for five adults were out of the question," said Cyril.*

> . . . rocks and hills
> And brooks and vales
> Where milk and honey flows. . . .

    "*But they say every cloud has a silver lining,*" *Cyril said,* "*and it sure was true for us.*"

    For me too, thought the sergeant. If the Hauptmann hadn't gone snooping and—well, slipped on the moss—or if his suspicions of cuckoldry had been dampened by alcohol and the sergeant had been able to spend months in the paradise called Gottestischlein, and then if von Hanzlitschek's regiment had been transferred somewhere else, he'd have been out of sight. He would never have thought of deserting, and being out of her sight would have put him out of her mind. . . .

    Then, Cyril explained, two things happened to decide matters. First, Lida was pregnant, and something had to be done about it. Cyril could see that his father was making up his mind about something. The crimps were snooping around the district, and Cyril's own future was inevitable: he was about to turn twenty, so it would be a soldier's white tunic for him. But he had no idea what his father had in mind. Old man Toupelik wasn't one to confide in his family.

    Then the second thing happened. It turned out his distant cousin in faraway Texas hadn't forgotten him. The day before Toupelik abandoned the mid-afternoon haying and walked almost three kilometres to the edge of Mika's field, a letter had arrived from Lesikar. Toupelik read it aloud to his family over their dry potatoes:

    "*Cat Spring is neither a town nor a village, as we understand them. The countryside is wild and beautiful with numerous trees, hills, and enchanting valleys, and there is a winding road all the way to Galveston, though no railroad as yet. It was not easy here at first, dear cousin, but beginnings are always difficult. We lived in a simple log cabin that we built without using a single nail. It had only holes for windows, and the doors were made of scraps of wood or pieces of cloth, regular lumber being scarce. None of this was to my dear wife's liking, but she never once complained, and I sought and found solace in our freedom. I never once felt homesick, for in my case there was nothing I could do to be of any aid to my former homeland, nor could it have helped me one iota. I relish the liberty and freedom here. I am not one of those people who, I dare say, are immature, who cling to their mothers' apron-strings. I have never complained and our circumstances have constantly improved. The only thing we missed were our Czech books. But there have to be some sacrifices, and otherwise I was doing well. Wheat thrives here, and so do rye and corn, but the most highly valued crop is cotton. In two years I was able to buy seventy acres of land."*

Cyril's father stopped reading. The size of Lesikar's holdings had stunned him. He stared at the bowl of potatoes, a look of astonishment on his face. It was more than Mika had, and at home the Lesikars had had no more than four roods square, though he had made a bit of money on the side with his tailoring. Toupelik went on reading:

"As soon as possible my two sons and I started building, and now we live in a decent farmhouse with four rooms to it. We have a stable and a team of oxen and riding horses, and a cotton gin. I was able to buy more land and now I have 109 acres."

That was the moment old Toupelik made up his mind. He folded the letter carefully, placed it in a chest along with some other documents, and, though it was already dark, went outside to his field.

★

The truth was that his general sometimes did find pleasure in other people's troubles. Once, before Vicksburg, trouble caught up with three reporters who were stirring things up in his army. Sherman believed in two things, both sensible in his profession: accuracy and secrecy. Journalists are not famous for either. But whereas a half-fabricated news story could at worst destroy a man's reputation as a commander, or perhaps, on the other hand, confuse the enemy, the premature disclosure of facts could bring despair to the very mothers, wives, and children the journalists loved to appeal to. The general came by his convictions honestly. For example, he hadn't known that he was launching the attack on Chickasaw Bluffs alone, which would have been madness, because neither Grant's nor Banks's courier had arrived.

Perhaps the two generals had forgotten to send them in the confusion, or maybe they had been killed on the way. Forrest and Van Dorn's cavalry had cut Grant's supply routes and his telegraph link, so Grant was unable to join Sherman's attack from the east. Nor did Sherman know that Banks, softened by the gentler New Orleans climate, had fallen ill in the harsh Mississippi weather, so that his attack from the south, which was to have taken place at the same time as Sherman's, had to be postponed. The reporters knew nothing of these things either, nor had they made any effort to find out. All they knew was that the offensive that was intended to catch Pemberton's division in a three-way vice and thus open the way to Vicksburg had dwindled to Sherman's lone attack on Chickasaw Bayou. Pemberton was able to shift his division quickly from the front to face the immobilized Grant. Sherman, convinced that Grant was attacking with him from the east and Banks from the south, attacked as planned and suffered the consequences. He lost 1,899 soldiers, and he was superseded—though only temporarily—by McClernand, intent on taking Vicksburg as a wedding present for his bride, who was with him on the battlefront.

The solo attack on Chickasaw Bayou seemed like insanity, but Sherman wasn't insane. Yet the war correspondents tried to make him look as though he were, because, in their ignorance of the facts, they had no other explanation. Moreover, they included some persistent backroom gossip about the state of Sherman's mind, because a mad (and, if possible, drunken) general sold more papers than a man who had all his wits about him. They therefore portrayed him as a butcher who brought tears to the eyes of the mothers and widows and children who were, of course, nearest to the journalists' hearts.

Sherman had a low opinion of correspondents, and banned them from his army camps. He described them in words they themselves couldn't print. And he found considerable pleasure, and let it be known that he did, when he heard that three "damned scribblers" (one of his milder expressions) named Richardson, Browne, and Colburn had attempted to slip down the Mississippi past the Vicksburg batteries on a boat that night—an act of insanity, though they weren't insane, just ignorant—to escape Sherman's clutches (with good reason) and seek refuge in the camp of General McClernand, who enjoyed seeing his name in print. Their boat, of course, did not elude Pemberton's gunners, who were experienced in shooting at floating targets and turned it into a sieve. Sherman was delighted: "Good! Now it's news from hell that we'll have before breakfast!" He only regretted that he had already banished Thomas W. Knox from his camp. Sherman had had Knox, a reporter for the *New York Herald*, arrested and court-martialled as a spy, but the man had been released by the court. In his eagerness for a scoop, Knox would certainly have ended up in hell with the drowned trio.

In fact, however, the trio were not in hell, for they hadn't drowned. They had merely dropped, one by one, into the Mississippi and, confused by the barrage, had swum to the wrong shore. There the Rebels seized them and locked them up in Andersonville Prison for almost two years, without benefit of a trial.

The capture of the trio was an innocent divertimento that may have relieved Sherman's boredom during the forty-seven-day siege of Vicksburg. A few days before, however, other reporters had caused some mischief that might well have brought extraordinary anguish and grief to mothers, fiancées, and orphans—and blame to Sherman—had the Confederate Captain Grimfield controlled his urge to practise the gentleman's art of sarcasm.

The general had discovered the Achilles' heel in the Vicksburg fortification, and had decided to take advantage of it. To do this, he needed to move three batteries of artillery into position unseen. He came up with a devious scheme—devious, that is, considering the Southern code of honour. But, thought the sergeant, what was left of that code by the spring of '63?

The general called a truce and sent negotiators into Vicksburg, and then went himself and deliberately got involved in lengthy and repetitive talks about an exchange of prisoners. While negotiations were going on, a cease-fire was in force. At Rebel headquarters the general became very argumentative about the terms of the exchange. He demanded time to think them over, continually took offence and then was conciliated; he made excessive demands, and protested against excessive demands made of him. The Rebels welcomed these protracted negotiations. It gave them a chance to rest and round up provisions, for supplies were dwindling inside Vicksburg. And all the time he was putting on this show of diplomacy, Sherman was silently, cannon by cannon, repositioning his artillery.

But he forgot—and this may be an unforgivable lapse, given his familiarity with the ways of journalists—that a few correspondents remained in his camp, all of them hungry for a scoop. One afternoon, after two hours of talk, Sherman once more demanded a recess until the following day and prepared to return to his camp. That night he planned to move the last cannon into position. As he was leaving, the Confederate Captain Grimfield approached him in an unusually clean uniform. (The negotiations had given his black orderly, Billy, a chance to attend to the captain's appearance.) Smiling like a gentleman, Grimfield suggested that the general not use his recently repositioned guns the next day, since he was scheduled to be best man at his commanding officer's wedding and it would be rather unpleasant if the wedding was disrupted by artillery fire.

The general looked like a beggar caught stealing apples red-handed. He regained his composure, however, and said coldly, "I congratulate you on your spies, captain."

"And I, sir, congratulate you on your correspondents," declared Captain Grimfield.

The general rushed back to his headquarters and ordered up all the newspapers, which he hadn't had time to read that morning because he'd been conferring with Captain DeGress about putting the last cannon in place. *The Memphis Bulletin* contained a strategic analysis by its reporter (one of the rats who, a few days later, failed to drown in the Mississippi) which concluded from the secret gun emplacements that an attack on the Achilles' heel of the Vicksburg fortifications was imminent.

The general exploded. He ordered the arrest of the correspondent, who got wind of his wrath and went into hiding until he could board the boat that, regrettably, did not take him to hell. The general started to call loudly for censorship or, better still, for all war correspondents to be barred from the theatre of operations, or, best of all, for a ban on all war reporting until victory had been declared. And he called for violators to be shot. (The sergeant wondered if that was possible here in America; three times through the gauntlet would have been a more suitable punishment, since the correspondents' writings were always dangerous, often demonstrably damaging, and usually wrong.)

Everything civilians needed to know about the war, the general felt, they could learn from the letters that soldiers wrote home, for, unlike men in the armies of Europe, most were literate. They enjoyed writing letters and, because they were risking their lives in battles, they were notably more accurate than journalists.

Thus the general did not call for censorship of soldiers' letters to their loved ones at home.

★

"What do you intend to do about it, neighbour?" asked old man Toupelik. Mika stood scowling and silent. Sweat ran down his forehead, but it may have been just because of the hot noonday sun.

Despite the vast difference in wealth between the two men, Toupelik and Mika were friends. Both of them fiddled at village dances, Toupelik for the extra income, Mika because he had music in his blood. When times were bad, he had even been known to help Toupelik out. Though Toupelik's daughter had done him this mischief—as Mika saw it—he would certainly not have her father roast in hell for it. So Toupelik waited for Mika to speak.

"Do you want to marry her off?" Mika growled after a while.

His reaction was just what Toupelik had expected. "You mean to your Vitek?" Mika didn't reply, and finally Toupelik said, "Or are you saying you'd give the mother of your grandson a dowry, maybe even help find her a husband?"

He knew Mika had thought of that. In those years finding a husband among the poor who lived in cottages on small holdings for a girl with a small dowry would have been child's play, and even if the bride was pregnant, that obstacle could be easily resolved by throwing in a few ducats. And Mika had plenty of ducats to throw.

"How much?" Mika growled.

"Fifty gold pieces," said Toupelik.

Mika's eyebrows rose. "That's hardly enough for a husband."

"She doesn't need a husband," said Toupelik. "What I want for her and the rest of us is boat tickets to America."

Mika put out his hand to shake on the deal.

"That's not all," said Toupelik.

"What else?"

"There's Cyril," said Toupelik, "and the crimps are on the prowl. Last week they were conscripting in Petakov."

Mika furrowed his brow. "That won't be easy."

"No, but it can be done," said Toupelik.

It could be done and it was, though what it cost to bribe the doctor, added to the price of the boat tickets, would have made a handsome dowry. The doctor discovered that Cyril had a weak heart, rheumatism in his left leg, extreme myopia, and chronic enuresis. And so the fictitious cripple wound up in Texas instead of in uniform, where he was suddenly and miraculously cured. Before spring planting began, his sister gave birth to a daughter, and christened her Deborah to remind her as little as possible of the old homeland. Lida began calling herself Linda, and not long after that she began signing herself Linda Towpelick.

"Linda Towpelick," Cyril mimicked bitterly. "We came to America young enough to pick up English. If I'd come years later I'd probably be talking like my old man, right, Corporal Kaykashka?"

"Dat's right," said Kakuska, switching from Czech to English without looking up from his spurs.

Outside, moonlight poured down on the sycamores.

... rocks and hills
And brooks and vales
Where milk and honey flows. ...

★

Flaming snow was falling on the Congaree River. Madam Sosniowski was reminiscing about Siberia. Her husband had become desperately ill and even the most basic treatment had been unavailable. After six years the tsar, who still didn't believe in equality between the classes, took pity and let him go home. Dr. Sosniowski, however, didn't want to live in Galicia any more; it was too close to his vanquished Poland. He got a letter from a fellow student who had built up a practice in Helldorf but then married a wealthy Bavarian woman. Dr. Sosniowski bought him out and paid the debt over time.

In Helldorf his thoughts were increasingly on America. He got himself the English originals of the Declaration of Independence and the American Constitution, and together they studied English, read de Tocqueville—in the original because, of course, they both knew French. They had a child—a little girl—and then another. When he'd paid for the practice, he sold it and they emigrated to America. That was in 1850.

"But why did you come here, to the South?"

"We had a friend here, the only person we knew in America. He'd fought in '30, and after the defeat he was lucky enough to get out. You saw him in front of General Hampton's house."

The sergeant wasn't ashamed. He was never ashamed of his general's army. Glancing back, he caught one of the Irish soldiers drinking from a bottle. Grinning at the sergeant, the soldier quickly hid the bottle and gestured with his hand. The sergeant turned back to Madam Sosniowski.

"What does your husband think of this war?"

Madam Sosniowski looked at the burning city, sighed, and said, "My husband died less than a year after we arrived. Siberia had destroyed his health. For him, America came too late."

★

The general knew that depriving his soldiers of the right to write home would have been like arming them with popguns instead of rifles. Letter-writing went on everywhere—at campfires, in tents by candlelight, even outside in the pale light of the full moon. Houska, sitting beside the sergeant, had several pages of a letter laid out on his knapsack, and the sergeant knew what his comrade's problem was. The elder Houskas couldn't read or write but they were famous throughout Wilber County as scandal-mongers and gossips who left the reading up to their children. Not only were Houska's nine brothers and sisters literate, but the family gift of the gab had transformed their literacy into a passion for letter-writing. Each of them, from forty-year-old Lojza down to eight-year-old Ferda, sent Houska at least one letter a month, and although they all lived in the same village near Wilber, Houska never thought of simply writing one letter to the whole family. To make matters more complicated, the youngest could only read English, and Houska had to employ the linguistic services of Shake, who was a powerhouse in that language. Houska only knew enough English to understand orders and the names of the foodstuffs the sutlers sold around the camp. He wrote often to a fiancée too, but behind Houska's back Shake expressed some doubts about her ability to read and write; instead of answering his letters, she sent him jelly doughnuts that always went stale before they arrived. Shake was wrong—the fiancée eventually did write Houska a letter—but it was a letter of farewell.

★

During the assault on Kennesaw Mountain, Houska fell stunned into the bushes. When he came to, the Rebels had counter-attacked, leaving him lying in a no-man's land which for the moment happened to belong to the Confederacy. So he stayed in the bushes and watched events unfold from behind a tree. A Rebel soldier stopped a few steps from his hiding-place. On the ground in front of him lay a bulging military knapsack with a Rebel flag sewn on the pocket. The man may well have been a gallant soldier in the cavalier tradition, but he looked like the King of the Beggars. His feet were bare; his trousers, once long, now barely reached below his knees, with a few tatters of the original legs reaching his ankles. He was shirtless under a tunic patched with butternut cloth. He wore a partially scorched straw hat, and to Houska he looked like one of the scarecrows he remembered from the fields around his native village near Tabor. Then a canister exploded nearby. A fragment whistled through the undergrowth, ripped open the knapsack, and embedded itself in Houska's tree. The knapsack yielded up its contents like guts spilling out of a slaughtered animal. The Rebel swore angrily and, with canisters now exploding all along the edge of the woods, started examining what turned out to be a sartorial treasure trove. Houska knew he wasn't dreaming—in this war, after all, everything was possible—but later on, when he told the story, he said he felt like an intruder at a nancy-boys' bazaar. The ragged soldier pulled something white out of the pile of things on the ground and unfolded it, and Houska saw a fine set of Confederate officer's linen under-

wear, complete with a blue embroidered monogram. The Rebel set it down carefully on the grass, checking it thoroughly for bloodstains. Next he held up a shirt
with a ruffled lace front. One by one, more quickly now, he unfolded the garments—there was even a moustache band and a mesh nightcap and a spotty,
hand-coloured daguerreotype of a pale beauty who looked as if she had the
measles. Finally the Rebel pulled out a bottle with a label on it. Act Two of the
performance began. The crack of rifle fire was still coming from the trenches
where Houska's buddies were bathed in sweat, while behind them, like Roman
tubas, the Parrot guns roared defiantly. The ragged Rebel seemed deaf to all this.
He quickly stripped to the skin and pulled on the white underwear (he wore
none of his own), and before long Houska was staring at a man in a lace shirt,
and trousers with crimson cording and razor-sharp creases made by some Negro
orderly. Next came the headgear, a brimless top hat with a broad red band and a
red, white, and blue plume. Finally, the man put on a double-breasted frock-
coat with two rows of gold buttons down the front and thick gold epaulettes, and
he was just buckling on a belt woven with gold threads in it when all hell broke
loose overhead and the first ranks of dishevelled Rebels started running past in retreat. The attack had been repelled. The Rebel sat down on the ground and
struggled to get his feet into the fine leather boots with shiny knee protectors.
More Rebels rushed past. Many were limping and bleeding, and one carried on
his back a comrade with an arm missing, probably shot off by a
cannon-ball. Blood was spurting from the stump, leaving a glistening red trail
on the grass. The once-beggarly Rebel, now properly shod, jumped to his feet just
as the fleeing ranks began to thin. He took one more look at the picture of the girl
with the spotty red cheeks, tucked it inside his shirt, stuffed the bottle in the
ample coat pocket, and grabbed his musket. Houska decided to act. Aiming his
rifle directly at the gilt belt, he stepped out of the bushes and in a heavy Czech accent said, "Hands up!"

A few days later the Rebel was traded for Sergeant Karpeles. They let him
keep the uniform and the picture of the red-cheeked beauty, but Houska
confiscated the whisky. It went the rounds at the campfire, and the only one to
suffer any ill effects was Kakuska.

★

According to Stejskal, Kakuska was like a wild stallion who won't carry on with
mares outside his own herd. He had remained faithful to his wife, despite the services offered in city bakeries and by the women in their camp like Easy Lizzie, or
the aptly nicknamed Bubbly Babsy. Kakuska suffered passively at first, then mustered the courage to ask General Ritchie for furlough. That didn't work, and af-

terwards he suffered twice as much. But unless onanism is considered infidelity, he remained a good Catholic spouse. They drank the captured whisky and, because there were five of them and only one bottle, no one got really soused. There was just enough to make the familiar conviction that all was well with the world rise from their stomachs to their heads. Kakuska drank his share and for a while he was silent like the rest of them, enjoying that pleasant world where distant cannon-fire can sound almost playful. But all at once he jumped up, looked around with a wild expression on his face, then tore off among the trees. The next day they found out that he'd ended up in the infirmary. As long as he was under medical care they couldn't explain his sudden flight, and more or less accepted Zinkule's explanation that Kakuska had been temporarily possessed by a demon distilled into the Tennessee whisky. Two days later he got out, however, and the mystery of his disappearance was cleared up.

When he vanished among the trees, Kakuska had not been headed for the latrines, as the many who had been stricken by the Kansas quickstep assumed. Instead, he ran straight to the creek and jumped in. But it was shallow—and it was summer in Georgia, and the water wasn't cold enough. So Kakuska climbed out and chinned himself frantically on an overhanging branch until it broke under his weight, dropping him to the ground, where he began doing grunting push-ups. He called so much attention to himself that, by the time he set out on a marathon sprint through the encampment, he had a mob of followers curious to know what he'd been drinking. At the other end of the camp he ran into Bubbly Babsy, who was just emerging from Colonel Curtiss's tent, and flung himself on her. Bystanders jumped him and subdued him after a lengthy struggle, then dragged him off to the infirmary. There Kakuska found himself in a straitjacket. But Dr. Blake, observing his most evident symptom, brought Kakuska's torment back to its normal state with a medication of his own devising.

So they deliberated on the dangers of whisky and arrived at an essentially racist theory which Houska was the first to voice, although he hadn't thought it up. It was based on a lesson that the lad from Wilber County had learned from Doc Paddock, an Irishman whose clinic, where he also lived, was on the second storey of the first building ever built in Wilber, right over the Homestead Saloon. Doc Paddock's choice of location was deliberate: the saloon was his main source of clientele.

One of the casualties was Houska, when a conversation over a glass of whisky between him and a Norwegian farmer, Olaf Heglund, ended prematurely in a ripped ear. (Heglund was now serving with the Fifteenth Wisconsin, and when the two men had resumed the conversation after Chancellorsville the outcome had been reversed.) The bill for the surgery on Houska's ear came to an exorbitant ten dollars, an amount he didn't have on him—he had rarely seen that much cash in one place—so he offered instead two paintings he happened to be carrying with him in a laundered potato sack. Actually, the paintings were the reason he had walked the twelve and a half miles from Bee Grove to Wilber that day; they were to be a gift for his father's sixtieth birthday, and Houska's brother Vincek had commissioned a jack-of-all-trades called Josef Prokes (whose affinity for rye whisky was the main reason he was master of none) to paint his father's portrait on the basis of a youthful daguerreotype. In addition to doing portraits, Prokes also painted stage sets for an amateur theatrical group called Wilber Thalia, and on Saturday nights he played the accordion at the Homestead Saloon and took his pay in rye. He also built houses, made furniture and shoes, and distilled slivovitz, some of which he consumed himself; the rest he sold in Chicago. When Vincek found out how much Prokes charged—two dollars for a portrait measuring three feet by five—he had the artist do his portrait as well, and when they were done he sent his younger brother to pick them up.

Doc Paddock liked the pictures. The portrait of the father depicted a stocky, round-faced fellow in a flowered vest sitting at a table, holding, in his left hand, a glass of beer with a perfect head of foam. The father radiated good cheer and good health, and on the wall in the background hung a miniature portrait of his son Vincek. The second painting showed a considerably younger man seated at the same table, with a gaunt, sallow face marred by a sketchy goatee. On the wall behind him hung a miniature copy of the portrait of his dad. There was a glass in Vincek's hand as well, containing a yellowish but foamless liquid. To ensure full comprehension, a bottle stood on the table with a label that said, "Visky".

Doc Paddock looked approvingly at the pictures, and then he looked at Houska. "Tell me, Vojta, are you a beer drinker or a whisky drinker?"

"A whisky drinker," admitted his patient.

"Take my advice: stop while there's still time," the physician said, pointing to the stitched-up ear. "You're young and you can still escape its clutches. Drink beer instead!" He looked again at the portrait of the healthy father, then at the portrait of his haggard son, and finally at the still rosy-cheeked son before him. "Just remember, you're not Irish!" he declared. "As long as a Czech sticks with beer, he'll be as sound as an oak. But the moment he starts drinking whisky, he's paying for a plot in the cemetery."

Houska was startled by this advice and resolved to follow it—and he did, too, at least until he found himself in uniform.

"If I were to start drinking beer," Doc Paddock continued, "I'd soon look like this"—he pointed to Vincek—"and not like this!" He pointed to Houska's dad. Doc Paddock was a pinkish, plumpish man with a head of thick ginger hair. "Because I'm Irish," he went on, "I only drink whisky. If I were to take all the

whisky I've drunk so far in my life and pour it into a cask, it would kill off all the Czechs in Bee Grove—and that's the entire village, because the only one who isn't Czech is black Freddy—like sick chickens. And so would Freddy—the only thing that's good for Negroes is mint julep."

Houska never found out what a mint julep was until he reached Georgia, and then, because he drank himself sick on it, his faith in Doc Paddock's theory was confirmed.

That day in Wilber, Doc Paddock offered to take the pair of two-dollar paintings as full payment of his ten-dollar fee. Houska wasn't authorized to agree to this, but when he arrived home that evening he communicated the offer to Vincek, who thought for a while and concluded that the doctor was making six dollars on the deal. The next morning, Houska's father was presented with a problem in mathematics, instead of his portrait. They worked on solving it all day during the birthday celebrations, and the next morning, bright and chipper, the father rose with the chickens (he'd been celebrating with beer) and set out for Wilber. In the evening he returned jingling six silver dollars. He'd refused to let the doctor bamboozle him, so all in all, Houska explained, the paintings had wound up costing Doc Paddock six dollars apiece. The doctor hung them in his office and used them to educate his patients and visitors.

"How do you see six bucks apiece?" asked Paidr.

"Well, the six I owed him and the six he gave Dad," said Houska.

"And what about the paintings? You have to add four bucks, so that makes it four bucks apiece."

"Subtract four bucks," said Shake.

"Bunk, you add them," maintained Paidr. For a while they sat and thought about it, then Fisher said, "You got taken. Your dad doesn't know how to haggle. He should have realized that the doc didn't so much like the pictures as he needed them for his livelihood. Your dad should have squeezed at least ten bucks out of him, on top of what you owed him."

"Six dollars?" asked Stejskal.

"Ten. Plus twenty bucks in cash."

"And the paintings," Houska asked tentatively, "add them or subtract them?"

They worked for a while on the mathematical puzzle, but resolved nothing. So they returned to the racial theory.

"The fattest man in Wilber is a guy called Baloun," Houska said, elaborating on the theory. "He's the blacksmith. He's seventy, but nobody can shoe a horse like he can. When he was young he used to play in a Russian military band, and one time when he was playing in Rome the mere sight of the Pope blessing people from a balcony brought on a huge thirst; he's been guzzling beer ever since. Ten litres a day and more."

"What did he drink before that?" asked Shake.

"Different things," said Houska. "Pine gin, mostly."

Shake gave Zinkule a telling look. "If he'd stuck with pine gin, he wouldn't be shoeing horses any more. He'd be dead and gone."

The Pope's miraculous influence seemed to confirm Doc Paddock's theory, but then Svejkar poked a hole in it. "Pine gin isn't whisky," he said.

"What's it made of?" asked Salek.

It turned out that they had all left their homeland too young to know this basic fact, so they speculated. Was it made from pine bark? Pine cones? They finally concluded that it was distilled from rye, with some kind of evergreen essence—pine needles, perhaps—added.

The theory held.

They assigned beverages to nationalities. For General Sigel's Austrian divisions they chose schnapps; no one knew what it was made from, but all the troops, including the general, drank it and flourished. Fisher added the persuasive evidence that General Blenker, who was as German as Sigel, had brought on his own premature death by his frequently issued "Ordinanz Numero eins!", following which champagne was always served in his tent, while his troops, quite properly, drank schnapps. They had difficulty agreeing on whether champagne or brandy was more appropriate for the French, but unanimously agreed that red wine suited the Italians. And there was no doubt about the Irish: they all recalled the incident on the march to Kennesaw Mountain. An overturned sutler's cart lay beside the road. A cannon-ball had killed the horse and the sutler had gone for help. Among the crates of dried fruit and sacks of coffee and tea was a small cask of whisky. Private O'Malley jumped onto the cart, but before he could unstop the cask the bloody-minded teetotaller Captain Parry ordered two sergeants to seize it and spill the whisky out onto the road, where the dry earth quickly drank it up.

When they resumed their march, Private O'Malley turned to Sergeant Mac-Manus and said, "If I'm killed tomorrow in battle, Billy, bring me back and bury me here," pointing to the rapidly disappearing pool of aromatic liquid. It was a wish Sergeant MacManus was unable to fulfil, for both men were killed in the fray at Cherry Grove.

So the Irish were a clear case, as were the Scots and the English. They decided that bourbon was harmful to Canadians. They never resolved the mystery of the fellow from Tristan da Cunha, who by some fluke of war joined the Twenty-sixth Wisconsin and drank a whitish liquid that he carried around in a leather bottle. The erudite Shake identified the man's native island as a whaler's port somewhere between Tierra del Fuego and the Cape of Good Hope, and they decided that the most appropriate drink for a man from Tristan da Cunha would be fermented fish oil, which Shake said was exactly what the fellow had in his leather bottle.

But despite their collective wisdom, they were unable to explain satisfactorily the dramatic effect that Southern whisky had had on Kakuska.

★

Their beginnings in Texas were difficult. Little Josef fell ill as soon as they arrived in Galveston, and that cost money. Property prices had risen in the five years since Lesikar's arrival, and what they had left from the proceeds of their property in Moravia was only enough to buy them about thirty acres. Like Lesikar, they started out in a log cabin, but Cyril and his father studied the neighbouring farmhouses and soon built themselves a house that was better than the one they'd had at home. Cyril even made a cradle for little Deborah, and in the evening, under the amber Texas moon, he would listen to Lida singing lullabies. The work on the new farm was back-breaking, and he often fell asleep even before the baby. While dozing off he would think for a while about his sister's voice. Was it love he heard in it, or some other emotion, less benevolent but more profound? Then he thought about his old homeland. Like Lesikar, he had no particular feelings for it. Perhaps he felt exhausted by having to work like a slave in the land of the free. He already knew the lullabies, and preferred the Negro songs that floated across the cotton-field on Mr. Carson's plantation down the road. They stirred him deeply, though he couldn't understand a word of them as yet. The singing was different, as different as Texas was from the Lhota foothills, as the bright Texas stars were from the sad, smudgy little points of light over their cottage in Moravia.

He'd left nothing behind, not even a girl. The balmy nights of those first months, Lida's homesickness—or whatever it was—and the harmony of the incomprehensible voices beyond the waves of cotton, all that merged into a single overwhelming feeling that he had managed to escape from a cage into a vast wilderness, that while life so far was harder than in that tiny village redolent of manure and wild sage, somewhere out there, in the flow of time, the future was waiting. He had never felt that way back home.

Aside from that, calamity followed calamity. The ox broke a leg and had to be put down. They were late getting the cotton in, but that was from lack of experience. Disaster and woe—but with the future awaiting them somewhere out there.

One day, while working in the field, Cyril saw a gig jouncing merrily down the road from the Carsons' place, probably headed for Austin. In the driver's seat was a girl in a red dress. As he straightened up to get a better look, the bones in his spine cracked like an old man's. Just then something spooked the horses. They reared, and the gig went off the road and tipped over. Cyril saw the girl fly through the air like a red bird and land in the cotton-field.

By the time he'd caught the horses and calmed them down—something he was good at, for he'd often helped out at the count's estate in Dvorec, back home—she was standing on the road, ruefully examining her raw and bleeding hands. She was cursing, though he still couldn't hear what she was saying. She was no delicate flower, that girl.

She wasn't much of a beauty, either. She looked, in fact, a little like her horses. But she was slender and had a shapely bosom. She walked over to him and said, "How can I thank you?"

That much he understood. She might vaguely resemble her horses, but they were handsome, spirited horses, still breathing heavily from their recent fright. When she patted their noses, they licked her bloodied hand.

"Good," she said, and repeated, "How can I thank you?" Then she said something he didn't understand.

"Is okay," he said, using up about a tenth of his English vocabulary in a single phrase.

"You're German?" That he understood too.

"No, Moravian."

"Oh," said the girl, with another annoyed glance at her injured palms.

"Come," he said, "wash hands."

So Rosemary Carson found herself in the log cabin, and while Cyril was fetching water from the pump in a wooden bucket (they had been lucky to find water right away) she examined Deborah's cradle. Lida had decorated it by burning designs into it with a red-hot nail—they had brought a box with them to Texas, because Lesikar had warned them that nails were hard to get there— little black hearts surrounded by garlands of tiny black blossoms. He poured the water slowly over the girl's injured hands. Rosemary nodded towards the cradle.

"Very nice design!" she said, and something else he couldn't understand. She pointed at the sleeping baby and said, "Your baby?"

"No, sister baby."

Her face softened.

Much later, mainly thanks to Rosemary, he was even able to talk Southern politics, which were gradually slipping, unwanted, into the Toupeliks' world. But by then he knew all the beauty of the black and white worlds, and where the horses were. In the meantime, an improbable love story—they were in America, the Carsons didn't even seem to mind the disgraceful memento of Linda's sin—and the flow of time would give way to the future. But back at the cabin—

He bandaged Rosemary's hands with a piece of linen torn from one of the baby's little shirts, not thinking how angry his sister would be when she got back from working in the field; the linen, brought with them from Lhota, was a real rarity here. As he held the horses, waiting for her to climb into the gig, she pointed at the reins with her bandaged hands.

So he got into the gig with her and drove her back to the Carson plantation. He couldn't catch a word of the rapid exchange between Rosemary and her mother—Mr. Carson was out in the fields—but Cyril could guess what they were talking about.

He waited in the vestibule of the white house. It was big, but not as extravagant as Mr. de Ribordeaux's mansion with the white pillars along its façade, on the road to Fayette. Still, it was a spacious home, fragrant with the smell of the smokehouse. On the vestibule wall hung paintings of men in red coats and white trousers, riding through unfamiliar scenery with packs of dogs. Mrs. Carson poured him a glass of something that tasted like apple cider, and left the room. Rosemary smiled at him. He said, "I must go work. In field."

The girl kept on smiling. Her teeth were small and white. "Just wait a minute," she said. "Wait, please!" Her mother came back with something large wrapped in a piece of linen.

"No, no!" he protested.

"Yes, yes," said Rosemary, mimicking him, and then, noticing that he was blushing, she added, "You must take this. You—saved—my—life!"

As he hurried home towards the distant field with the big bundle under his arm, he realized how exaggerated Rosemary's words had been. After all, she had merely scraped her palms. But he didn't mind, and could even forgive her mild mockery of his accent.

The bundle contained a whole smoked ham. For the first time in a long time, they had a proper dinner. Back home, they wouldn't have had a meal like that even on a feast day.

"She's fallen in love with you," said Lida, when he recounted the story over supper, and told her how Rosemary had enticed him into the gig to drive her home. As charmed as he was—less by the girl than by the adventure that had briefly brightened the monotonous slavery of his days—he was still worried about what Lida would say when she discovered what he had used to bandage Rosemary's hands. But Lida didn't discover her loss until three days later, and by that time the adventure had produced a healthy return.

"You don't say," replied Lida, licking her fingers, when he protested. "You think she gave you a present like that for no reason?"

"I saved her"—he almost repeated her exaggeration, but caught himself in time—"her team. The horses bolted and pretty near got away."

"You don't say! And bolting horses run for ever, do they?"

The next evening, as they were having supper, they heard a horse whinny outside the cottage. A knock came at the door. Cyril's father opened it and a man in a cowboy hat stood silhouetted against the Texas sky. "My name is John Carson," he said in English.

"Toupelik," said Cyril's father, and then, in Czech, welcomed him with a country saying: "Come on in so you don't steal our sleep."

"May I come in?" asked Carson. By now Cyril was beside his father.

"Yes, please come in."

He had come to offer Cyril a job. Carson's overseer had fallen ill and wanted to return to New Orleans, where his sister, widow of a rich tobacco merchant, lived. Carson needed a replacement. Later, Cyril discovered that Carson's blacks didn't need much overseeing.

Even though his farm-hands were his property, Carson wasn't much of a slave-driver. He was a gentleman plantation-owner; originally a farmer in England, neither rich nor poor, he had inherited a huge Louisiana plantation from his childless brother. He didn't like Louisiana. When Texas opened up to slave-owners, he sold the plantation, bought one in Fayette County, and brought his slaves with him.

"They didn't like Louisiana either," he grinned, and by this time conversation came more easily to Cyril, because he'd picked up English quickly, the way small children pick up a new language. Rosemary teased him for talking like the Negroes (there were too many of them on the plantation and they talked a lot), though her own King's English, acquired back in Miss Meacham's boarding school in Devonshire, was coloured with a Texas twang and Negro syntax, especially when she tried to get a word in edgewise with her father's garrulous slaves.

"Not many Negroes like Louisiana, and they have good cause not to," said Mr. Carson. Cyril still didn't understand why. After all, Carson's Louisiana Negroes seemed to like it in Texas, at least in that tiny piece of Texas owned by Mr. Carson. The reasons gradually became clear as the Toupeliks became acquainted with the politics of the South, and as Cyril came to understand that Mr. Carson was not a slave-driver.

Carson put two young Negroes at the elder Toupelik's disposal to replace Cyril's labour, and in exchange for half of Cyril's new wages. They didn't seem like slaves, either, and they had nice names: Washington White and Jefferson Black. They were so talkative that even the elder Toupelik picked up some English from them—their English, of course. They had clever hands and they helped him fix his cotton gin, a rickety old machine that had already had five owners and was a cotton gin in name only. They laughingly encouraged Mrs. Toupelik to teach them Czech, and they picked it up as quickly as Cyril had picked up English, which seemed to confirm the theory that Mr. Carson put forward with true British irony—that if they were children, as most Southerners claimed, they were the wiliest of children.

There was one way in which Mr. Carson was a typical slave-owner: he thought more about politics than about his plantation. The plantation ran as well as it did mainly because he was the kind of slave-owner he was, and the slaves were the kind of slaves they were. Behind their cabins—not the standard, cramped, dirt-floor cabins, but spacious wooden structures—were verdant vegetable plots and clucking chickens.

Cyril was fascinated by how a large plantation worked, even though it wasn't his own. He was always poking around and asking questions.

Under a shelter in the corner of the Carson farmyard stood a cotton gin. Beside it was a deep pit filled with layer upon layer of cotton seeds, the remains of several bountiful harvests.

"What do you do with them?" Cyril asked the Negro operating the machine one day.

"Nuthin'," replied the man, whose name was Franklin Adams. "They ain't no use at all."

Cyril picked up a handful of seeds from the top layer and rubbed them between his palms. "No use at all?"

Franklin shook his head, "We tried usin' them for fertilizer, but cotton plants come in too tall and the bolls don't make much cotton. No need to fertilize here anyways. It's fresh soil. Massa told us to feed them to the stock, but they won't eat them much, and the milk tasted bad. Too much fat," said Franklin. "So here they sets."

In the old country, nothing went to waste. He mulled it over. He started playing with a corn crusher. In the old country he had learned how to fix anything, so now, by tightening some screws and readjusting the plates, he got the crusher to remove the shells from the cotton seed. He roasted the kernels in something he rigged up from an old metal stovepipe, then pressed them by hand.

A few days later, he turned up in the Carson kitchen, where Hester the cook was preparing dinner under Rosemary Carson's scrutiny. Chicken was frying on the stove.

"Try this," he said, handing them a small bottle.

"What is it?"

He explained that it was oil from the cotton seeds. Rosemary wrinkled her nose and pretended to gag.

"Just try it," he said. "No one will know."

He was sure of that. He had tried the new oil out on Washington and Jefferson the day before.

Rosemary stopped making faces and began to wonder when Cyril would approach her father.

Franklin stood by the corn crusher and watched in amazement as the cow gobbled up the cottonseed mash.

"Look at that, Massa Cyril," he said. "Look how she love it!"

And so they started making cottonseed oil on the Carson plantation. It turned out to be the first production site of its kind in the South. Soon Cyril had improved the cleaning process and found a way to eliminate the mild but unpleasant taste. He and Mr. Carson formed a partnership. His reputation reached the ears of Monsieur de Ribordeaux, at whose house Cyril first set eyes on all the beauties of the white world and the black. That was when everything else faded in importance.

He put the question delicately to Washington, because he knew he could hardly ask the Carsons.

"Dinah?" Washington winked at Jefferson and they both laughed. "She was a birthday present," said Jefferson, "for young Massa Dribordo."

Cyril didn't think their laughter sounded very genuine. And he didn't like what he'd found out.

★

Sergeant Kapsa couldn't bring himself to ask the question. Was it for fear of opening the old wound? Time and this huge land had healed it for him long ago; all that remained was the scar. He could feel it but it no longer hurt. It was merely a memento of the paradise in the mysterious little house on the hill at Gottestischlein, not a reminder of the hardship of his escape, Hanzlitschek's clothes flapping loosely about him, with none of the officer's documents, no official papers to provide him with security. That had been a land where sundry uniforms with eyes and ears—or so Kapsa saw it, evading the authorities on alpine footpaths and forest trails and later, in Germany, fleeing in coaches and even leaping from moving trains—existed only to annoy travellers who were doing nothing suspicious (which in itself aroused suspicion) by demanding stamped papers of the sort the fugitive did not have. All he had was money, the hundred and eighty gulden in gold and silver coins that Ursula had taken from the Hauptmann's cash-box. But the money could only help him on his way, not protect him from uniformed spies. He managed to cross two borders and reach Holland—by then he was wearing new clothes he'd bought for three of Hanzlitschek's gulden from a discreet Jew in a small town in southern Germany, where he'd finally mustered the courage to emerge from the woods. He spent several anxious hours at a tiny railway station, realizing that the eyes beneath the derbies could be more dangerous than eyes in uniform. In a dubious effort to disguise himself, he returned to the merchant and bought himself a derby like the ones the police agents wore. But now, in Amsterdam, his anxiety almost completely vanished.

He still had well over half the gulden, and under his shirt, against his bare skin, was the velvet pouch she had pressed into his hand during their last kiss, their final farewell: "*Jetzt lauf!* Run now! And don't forget me, *mein liebster Mann!*"

He hadn't looked inside the pouch until he was well into the woods. Under the alpine moon, the diamond necklace had glittered like a nest of crystal eggs.

He heard the distant report of a Parrot gun and braced himself to ask the question. He didn't want to hear of death from the Polish woman's lips. In the nightmares that had haunted him all the way from the haystacks and stables he'd hidden in, on the Atlantic crossing and even in the garrisons of the Thirteenth Regiment, he had hellish visions of Ursula facing the gallows. What if the maid had talked? What if there had been gossip? What if the colonel investigating the tragic accident in the forest had failed to believe the evidence of the bloody rock and the bootmarks in the moss? Kapsa had sweated in mortal terror as he tried to sleep in the garrisons of the United States Army. In a hot summer, he imagined Ursula standing in prison garb under the malevolent imperial eagle, before an awful judge. His own safety only made his fear worse. Once, in a fit of madness, he decided to desert the army once again, cross the ocean and two borders to Helldorf, and then, like some Robin Hood or Janosik, carry Ursula off through her prison window, down a rope, and back across two frontiers and the Atlantic. But it had been no more than a momentary fantasy.

That had been long ago. Now, here in the burning city of Columbia, his fears were revived.

They had almost reached the white building when a terrified young woman in a blue-grey dress came running out of the door, screaming, "Mama, Mama! Something terrible has happened!"

★

Shake came up with a hypothesis that had nothing to do with the relationship between race and alcohol, but rather with the linguistic abilities of Kakuska's young wife. It was based on something Kakuska, chastened and humiliated but now released from the infirmary, had let slip.

"Medicine? What for?" Stejskal wondered. *Kakuska was one of the healthiest men in Kil's cavalry; he'd never had a cold, or even diarrhoea, a common complaint during the march through Georgia. There was a surplus of hogs on the farms and, despite the rigours of war, these animals were well fed. While others cut the fat from their pork, Kakuska tended to trim the lean bits off his, and stuff his cast-iron innards with bacon and pork rinds. It never seemed to bother him. Even as they talked now they were roasting big chunks of fatty smoked sausage over the fire.*

"What kind of medicine was it?" Stejskal pressed.

"From my Bozenka," mumbled the oddly subdued Kakuska.

"What was it for?"

"I don't know," he replied, turning red.

Shake noticed. "Don't you know lying is a mortal sin?"

"I'm not lying," declared Kakuska.

"Does anybody believe him?" *Shake turned to the others. They shook their heads.*

"Kakuska! The truth now! You put something in your booze. What was it?"

"A powder."

"What kind of powder?"

"I told you, something Bozenka sent me."

"We heard you. But why—"

"I—" *Kakuska tried to interrupt Shake, but he wouldn't let go.*

"—and what was it supposed to cure you of? The itch in your pants?"

Kakuska was now the colour of fresh blood. Shake, thanks to his dirty mind, had hit the nail on the head.

They were finally able to drag it out of him. They knew that Kakuska had gotten married three years before, mainly because, after he'd enlisted, Bozenka had informed him that she was pregnant. He couldn't de-enlist, so he made a respectable woman out of the deflowered virgin and then, straight from the altar, galloped off to join Kilpatrick. All this time he stayed away from the pleasure parlours and girls with nicknames, and instead became a regular user of Corporal Gambetta's library. But that made him feel guilty too, so he decided to write to his wife and their son, Matej, two and a half years old.

"You idiot, why didn't you go to Dr. Fishbach?" Fisher asked. "He has just the thing for it."

"Fishbach's only a doctor," said Kakuska. "He's not bound to keep the secrets of confession, like a priest. He'd shoot off his mouth someplace, and I'd feel like drowning myself for shame."

"Weren't you ashamed to write to your old lady about it?" asked Paidr.

"Yes, I was," admitted Kakuska. "But a husband and wife aren't supposed to have any secrets."

"Did you ever think she'd feel ashamed to ask the doctor for your stupid powder?" Fisher snapped. "I'd rather go jerk myself off." Fisher was a bachelor.

Shake, who was usually talkative, just listened.

"Bozenka has a smooth tongue in her head," said Kakuska, "not like me. I figured she'd know how to ask the doctor without blushing."

Now Shake spoke. "In English?"

Kakuska stopped. "Well, yes, in English. The doctor back home is German, Schlaflieber, but Bozenka can't speak German."

"So she'd have spoken English with him?"

"Sure."

"Who speaks English the best," asked Shake, "the doctor, your little lady, or you?"

Kakuska admitted that he might. He'd picked up some in the army, though not very much. Like every soldier, he had had several brushes with death, and one of those had been caused by his poor English. He had gone to the woods for firewood. A sentry (a Scot) had challenged him and Kakuska, not understanding, had replied in Czech, "Kiss my butt." The sentry had fired at him. Fortunately his aim was rotten.

The sausages roasting on the sticks smelled wonderful. "Dr. Schlaflieber doesn't actually need English that much," Kakuska explained. "There aren't hardly any Yankees in the county, just Czechs and Moravians, a few Swedes in the south, Germans in Ulm, and one Pole in Halden. Most of them don't speak English anyway, except maybe the Swedes. But the doctor can always find a way to make himself understood."

"What exactly did you write to your wife?" said Shake. "How did you phrase it?"

"Well, ah"—Kakuska turned pink—"I said I needed something so I wouldn't always have this—this—need—you know. When Bozenka and I can't—"

"Screw?" Stejskal prompted.

"That's not what I wrote!"

"When I cannot make love to my wife?" Shake offered, and Kakuska nodded.

"That's right." Embarrassed, he pulled his sausage out of the fire and took a bite, squirting some pinkish juice into Paidr's eye. Paidr swore.

"So I hope it's clear to you now what happened," Shake said to Kakuska.

"Well," Kakuska replied, "something must have gone wrong."

"You bet it did," said Shake, and then he explained his hypothesis: of Bozenka's awkward English explanation Dr. Schlaflieber had understood only the words "husband" and "cannot make love to me", and had assumed that Kakuska, apparently home on furlough and traumatized by the war, had potency problems. He had therefore mixed up a dose of Spanish fly big enough for a horse, and—

"How much did he tell her you were supposed to take?" asked Shake.

"An inch," said Kakuska confidently.

"An inch?"

"Yes, an inch," repeated Kakuska firmly. "There was about an inch in the vial she sent. So I figured it was one dose, and I dropped it all in my whisky."

"Jesus Christ!" exclaimed Stejskal. "What a jackass! Supposing Dr. Schlaflieber had understood your old lady and given her what you wanted. You'd have been limp till the day you died!"

Kakuska froze.

"The good Lord was watching over you," said Shake. "Or if you're in the free-thinkers' camp these days, you're luckier than you are smart. But—did the doctor really tell Bozenka you were to take an inch?"

"That's what she said," replied Kakuska. "But there's a good chance she didn't understand him."

"A very good chance," said Shake. "Couldn't he have said 'a pinch'?" Kakuska slowly turned his sausage over the coals. "So you swallowed an inch of Spanish fly instead of a pinch, and mixed it with whisky. Just be glad you didn't attack Jeff Davis, with that little porky butt of his."

He was referring not to the Rebel president, but to a young swine they had found on the farm where they'd liberated the sausages. That afternoon they'd christened the pig with bourbon also liberated from the farm, whereupon Jeff Davis had fallen asleep—grunting, so Shake maintained, to the tune of "Yankee Doodle".

★

A white horse stood in the upstairs parlour, and behind it on the carpet lay a pile of horse buns. Slumped on a divan, beneath a large portrait of an officer in a foreign uniform, was a corpse in a tattered Union uniform. A sabre sheathed in a decorative scabbard lay on the floor beside the divan. The sergeant had never seen anything like it in Sherman's army, or since Helldorf, for that matter. A blonde young woman with curly hair, in a blue-grey dress, stood trembling over the corpse. Her teeth were chattering. An open satchel with silver spoons spilling out of it lay on the floor in front of the horse, along with a big doll in a folk costume and a bronze American eagle. One of its wings had blood on it. The sergeant felt as though he'd landed in the middle of a bizarre dream.

"What happened?" asked Madam Sosniowski, running to embrace the girl. "Are you all right? And what is Ferdy doing indoors?" She pointed to the horse, which tossed its head and whinnied.

The young woman who had greeted them with screams outside said, "The Yankees took Linda and Dapple. So we brought Ferdy up here—" She looked over at the man on the divan. Madam Sosniowski turned to look at the pale corpse.

"And him—?"

The girl cleared her throat. "We didn't try to stop him from stealing the silver, or the Polish doll. But—" She stopped, trembling.

"Did he—did he try to force you to do something you didn't want to, miss?" asked the sergeant. He realized that she hadn't really taken account of his presence, or that of the two Irishmen, who were looking around the parlour. The white horse gave another whinny and the Irishman who'd been caught drinking on the street walked over and stroked the horse's nose.

"No, he didn't," she replied. She turned to Madam Sosniowski. "But he took Papa's sabre off the wall. I begged him to leave it, but he pulled it out and waved it at me, so I tried to get it back from him." The Irishman took something messy from his pocket and offered it to the horse.

Madam Sosniowski turned to her other daughter.

"I didn't mean to kill him!" wailed the young woman, covering her mouth with both her hands. The sergeant walked over to the divan and unbuttoned the corpse's tunic. There was no shirt underneath it. The sergeant placed an ear to the bare chest. He turned to the other Irishman, who was staring raptly at the girl with the blonde curls.

"Give me that whisky!" he snapped.

"What whisky?"

"The whisky in your pocket," said the sergeant impatiently. "Give it! Give it here!"

"Oh, that whisky," said the soldier, pulling the flask from his tunic. The sergeant reached for it, uncorked it, and placed it to the corpse's lips. Madam Sosniowski put her arms around her daughter.

★

*"Ever since I found out from Doc Paddock that Czechs shouldn't drink whisky,"
said Houska, "nobody at our house drank it. Not even Vincek, and I tell you it
wasn't easy for him."*

"Did he switch to water?" asked Shake. "Or vodka?"

"Just as Doc Paddock advised," said Houska, "he switched to beer. And he lasted almost two months. Then one fine day—"

One fine day Father Houska had to go to Wilber for the christening of the sixth son of Ezekiel Kohak, who owned the Wilber general store. In keeping with Doc Paddock's advice, he got half drunk on beer at the christening, and as he set out for Bee Grove at four in the afternoon, he found himself craving more of the kind of conversation he had so recently enjoyed in Ezekiel Kohak's garden. He then allowed himself to be drawn into the Homestead Saloon. He was carrying home a gift, a bottle of Scotch whisky in a brown paper bag—from Kohak's wife, who was from Scotland and could therefore imbibe it unharmed—and he put it on the windowsill beside his table. Then with a foursome of his Wilber cronies he sat drinking beer and gossiping until dusk. With another superhuman effort, he overcame his irrepressible urge to go on talking and set out for home, forgetting the bottle on the windowsill. He arrived home at dawn and had three bottles of beer for breakfast. Meanwhile the foursome at the Homestead Saloon sat around until midnight, when the saloonkeeper tossed them out. By this time they were three sheets to the wind, having exhausted the saloon's supply of beer and gin, and then having found the bottle of whisky in the brown bag on the windowsill. As they staggered off into the night, neighbour Vejrobek's conscience got the better of him, and he went back and refilled the whisky bottle with some cooking oil he had with him that happened to be roughly the same colour. He corked it up, put it back in the paper bag, and managed to replace it on the windowsill before the sleepy saloonkeeper noticed him and threw him out the door again.

Three months later old man Houska remembered his gift, but had no plans to go to Wilber, and because he knew the saloonkeeper to be an upstanding citizen he decided to wait and pick up the bottle next time he had reason to be in town. This happened a week later when he went in for a new batch of beer. He drove the cart in for that, but once more forgot about his trophy because the session with the foursome of Wilber neighbours repeated itself with an even less sober outcome.

For the next two months he had no cause to make another trip to Wilber, and then, when he did, he had to send Vojta, because he got a severe case of lumbago. He was reluctant to subject a minor like Vojta to the temptation of the forgotten bottle, because until Doc Paddock had made his diagnosis, the lad had been well on his way to becoming a drunkard. Finally, after another two months, the opportunity arose. Old Auntie Vejlupka's daughter was getting married, the one from Spider Web near Wilber, and Dad Houska remembered the bottle and, to keep it in sight, placed it in the centre of the table where another gathering of the *foursome was taking place. Towards morning, he finally succeeded in getting it home.*

At home, Doc Paddock's warning did its work: like a hungry cat Vincek stalked the kitchen cabinet where the whisky stood on the top shelf, without touching the forbidden beverage. But the bottle possessed a strange power that drew Vincek closer and closer on his rounds. The circle tightened, until one evening Cousin Martin appeared unexpectedly, along with his very old father, on the way to Wilber from the distant town of Cuba in Dakota, and they needed a place to stay the night. That called for a celebration—they hadn't seen one another for more than three months—but, true to Doc Paddock's advice, they started with beer. Then Martin's father, who had never in his life needed a doctor, expressed the desire for something a little sharper. The circle tightened down into a point without dimensions and the bottle, twice forgotten and once denied, found its way to the kitchen table. Vincek poured a generous measure for his ancient uncle, Martin, Vojta, and his dad, and then for his two younger brothers, and what was left (quite a bit) he poured himself. The old uncle held up the glass and smacked his lips. "Quality whisky," he remarked knowingly, "leaves a film on the glass. Here's to you!" Vincek felt bad, but he couldn't insult his relative. They all emptied their glasses in one gulp and they all got sick.

"From that day forward," said Houska, "I don't think Vincek has touched a drop of whisky, Dad is sworn to stay dry, and so was I, before I enlisted. Here it doesn't make much sense to look after your health, since you're always risking your neck anyway."

All that was left of the campfire was a few glowing coals. Kakuska, with his castiron stomach, was roasting the last two sausages over them.

★

It was raining in Amsterdam. The Hotel Savoy faced onto a small square, its paving-stones set alight by the brilliance of the large café in the nearby Grand Hotel. Kapsa still had well over half of Hanzlitschek's gulden left. In an upstairs room, a candle in a pewter candlestick on the commode shed its light on a framed alpine landscape with the sun setting behind a snow-capped peak.

The rain poured down. Beyond the wall of rain—unseen, but Kapsa could feel its presence—was the sea. In the opposite direction, to the south and east, night had descended over Germany and Austria. He knew he would never go back. Ursula was there, but she had never been even a possibility. In her he had had a brief glimpse of a beautiful life, a green oasis, an island in the grey ocean of his existence.

He was terrified for her but there was nothing he could do. And he still had more than half of Hanzlitschek's gulden left.

In the rainy Amsterdam night, his choice was clear. Tomorrow a travel agent, a ticket, a boat, America.

He went downstairs to the dining room. The hotel had an imposing name, but it was small, no more than a refuge for the modest traveller whose means did not extend to the porter's services at the Grand Hotel.

He sat down at the bar and, because his money couldn't buy what he really wanted, he ordered a whole bottle of brandy, to help him forget the grey ocean, until only the green island with Ursula remained.

Then he heard the sound of someone speaking his mother tongue.

It scared him.

He couldn't make out the words. It wasn't the language of his paradise—no, that was German, so hated, so loved ("Ach, du lieber Mann! Mein Liebster! You know, don't you! Or are you that dumb? Do I have to tell you? You barely under-stand German, mein Liebster!") That was the gentle tongue of Ursula von Hanzlitschek. Home was no paradise, but in the language of his homeland he was at home. Seven men sat at a corner table, the oldest not quite thirty, as far as he could tell through the dense cloud of cigar smoke that enveloped them. They were puffing on huge cheroots with gold bands around them, which contrasted with their threadbare clothes. There was one exception. His cheroot set off an aris-tocratic face with an aquiline nose. He wore a new suit of Irish tweed, and it was his voice that led the conversation. In front of him on the table sat a box of cigars and two bottles of brandy.

The words were clearer now: ". . . nsky has a brickyard in New York. He needs fellows who don't have two left hands. . . ."

Kapsa took his bottle from the table and his derby from the back of his chair, and walked over.

"Fellow countrymen?" he asked.

The sound of their mother tongue startled them, and seven pairs of suspicious eyes peered at him from behind a smokescreen. They saw the tell-tale derby and were frightened.

Then one of them said, "Kapsa, is that you?" An echo from the not too distant past. Not a city face, but one he had last seen under the two brass apples on an Austrian cap.

"Salek?"

"That's me! What the devil are you doing here?"

And what the devil are you doing, Kapsa thought. Last time he'd seen Salek had been in Prague, when Windischgraetz was blasting the barricades with his cannon. Kapsa's unit had been marching past the battery towards their attack position and, in the heightened awareness that the tension of battle brings, he had taken in the image of a huge man from his neighbouring village, a blackened muzzle-loader in his hand, urgently ramming a ball down the barrel. That was Salek. He glanced around the table. Kapsa could imagine little brass apples twinkling over each of the country faces, except for the man in the tweed suit.

"Probably the same as you, Ondra."

He sat down and listened to their simple stories. They had all deserted together from Mohuc, an Austro-German garrison, where they were members of Klevenheuller's Thirty-fifth Pilsen regiment, which had joined to it nine artillery companies from the first Prague Regiment. All of them, that is, but the sharp-nosed man in tweed, who said he was from General Hartmann's artillery but wasn't a gunner, something he needn't have added because Kapsa could see that he didn't have a gunner's hands. What were they—a priest's hands? He held his cheroot in a silver cigar-holder with an ivory snake curled around it. Was he a chaplain? Why would an Austrian chaplain desert from an army in which chaplains were second only to God and the emperor? Perhaps this chaplain had another von Hanzlitschek at the beginning of his story, and another—but no, there was only one Ursula.

There were short, simple tales about endless soldiering, about misery that became unbearable following the débâcle at the Prague barricades in '48. There were reports of misery at home. Havlicek was forbidden to publish his newspaper. A slight man from Nymburk told them the jails had swallowed up hundreds of patriots now that this swine Bach was at the helm in Austria. They were on their way to America. They even had work waiting there for them.

Kapsa placed his bottle on the table beside the two others, and he saw the man with the aquiline nose—who could have been some retired lieutenant—eye the bottle and then Kapsa's face.

"That's true," he said. "Four years before we took off, before '48, Touzimsky left the Mohuc garrison all by himself. Well, he wasn't alone—he took the regimental strong-box with him. Now he owns a brickworks in Brooklyn."

The men around the table chuckled.

"Help yourselves," said Kapsa, pointing to his bottle.

"And you, have a cigar," said the retired lieutenant emeritus—or was it chaplain?—and he pushed the box in his direction, then took a puff on his own cigar in its silver holder with the ivory snake.

"He sounds like a crafty devil," remarked Kapsa.

"Touzimsky? I know what you mean," said the lieutenant-chaplain. "But he's a patriot all the same."

Kapsa lit a cigar. "Is that so?" The cigar reminded him of von Hanzlitschek, and he set it aside on the ashtray. "You say he left before '48?"

"Why not? America was there long before '48. He didn't need a kick in the butt from General Windischgraetz, the way we did."

"All he needed was a chance at the regimental cash-box."

The lieutenant looked at the bottle again, as though there was some significance to it, Kapsa felt. "Right, that was all he needed."

They were silent, then one of the six said, "He only hires Czechs to work for him in the brickworks. We're all sure of a job."

"And he's looking for Czech investors," said the lieutenant. "He's expanding." He took a sip of his drink and looked at Kapsa's bottle again.

Later, the two of them were left alone. The lieutenant was staying at the same hotel as Kapsa, while the others were lodged in a doss-house down by the harbour. "Where did you take off from?" the lieutenant asked.

"If you don't mind, I'll keep that to myself."

Another glance at the bottle. "I won't press you. You must have had good reason."

"We all did."

"It's all in how you look at it," the lieutenant said, pulling a gold watch out of his tweed vest. "Those fellows"—he gave a toss of his head towards the door—"it was misery for them. Life is tough in the Austrian army these days, and will be for a long time yet. Hard outside the army, too. And even if it weren't, when they finally finish their service and go home, their sweethearts will have married the clever ones, the ones who could afford to bribe the crimps and avoid conscription. And what do these men have to look forward to? Drudgery, my friend. Drudgery and the hope that, if they work extra hard, they'll live until they die. Do you think any of them comes from an estate?"

"I'm a smallholder too," said Kapsa. "That's why I was in uniform."

"Why aren't you still in uniform?" The eyes—were they a priest's eyes?—looked right through him. "Because you didn't want to go back to the farm? Because you got the urge to go to America?"

Kapsa said nothing. A suspicion was taking root in his mind. What if he, or all of them, had fallen into a trap? What if the tweed coat was just like the derby, a disguise? He shivered. But this was Holland, after all—

"I'll tell you how it is with you, my friend," said the retired lieutenant, sticking a fresh cheroot in the silver cigar-holder with the ivory snake creeping around it. "You can't go back to the farm now!"

★

When the mail arrived, the sergeant was standing guard by the general's tent, staring out at the Vicksburg palisades. The city towered over the broad river like *a fiery triangle. They couldn't seem to conquer it. Lieutenant Williams walked out of the tent.*

"Sergeant," he said, "are you Bohemian?"

"Yes, I'm Czech, sir."

"The general wants to see you."

Inside the tent, his general was sitting at a camp table, puffing on a cigar. He raised his eyes to the sergeant, eyes that were clear and bright even through the smoke that hung in the air. He repeated Lieutenant Williams's question. The sergeant repeated his reply.

"There are quite a few of you Czechs in the Twenty-sixth Wisconsin, aren't there?" *asked the general. The question caught the sergeant off guard. The general was looking at a letter that appeared to be from a parish registry office, but he couldn't tell which one—the letter was upside-down. The general studied the letter.* "Do you know a vivandière who calls herself—Busty Betsy?"

"I think. . . ." *The sergeant tried to recall if any of the camp women went by that name, maybe even a Czech, but he couldn't.* "I think I don't, sir."

"But of course you do know there are women like that in camp."

"Of course," *the sergeant admitted,* "Easy Lizzie, Bubbly Babsy, Hot Bottom Lynn. . . ."

"I'm not looking for a list," *the general interrupted.* "I just need to know if there's such a person as Busty Betsy."

"I can't help you with that one, sir. But I will check."

The general exhaled and went back to the letter. They could hear the tinkle of tin cups as a platoon marched by. "Soldiers will always surprise you," *the general said.* "Let me read you something." *He laid aside the letter from the parish. Beneath it lay another letter, on pink paper, with a picture of Cupid holding a bow and arrow—part of a folder that Corporal Gambetta sold to soldiers who wanted to write love letters. Cupid's arrow, made of yellow metal, could be removed from his bow and stuck into the heart embossed on the other half of the folder. The recipient was supposed to write an answer on this half, tear it off, and return it to the archer. The general read:* "'Each evening, dear brother, I whisper to my sweetheart—a kind and lovely nurse who ministers to the ill and the afflicted in the regimental dispensary: Behold thou art fair'"—*the general looked briefly at the sergeant*—"'Busty Betsy, ah, how fair—'" *As the general read on, the intriguing nickname popped up again and again, while the sergeant wondered furiously who it could be.* "'Thy two breasts are like two young roes that are twins, Busty Betsy, which feed among the lilies'—well," *said the general, putting the letter down,* "I don't have to continue, do I? I assume you recognize the passage. You're a Christian, are you not?"

The sergeant shook his head, wondering what the consequences of admitting the truth would be. "I used to be a Catholic. Now I call myself a free-thinker. I'm a theist, sir."

"Have you been to college?"

"No, but I've read a lot. And I know the passage."

"Even if you're not a Christian, will you agree with me that there's a fine bit of blasphemy here, when you consider that this is a Christian army, in name at least? And when you consider what it is we're fighting for? It's one thing to get mixed up with a Busty Betsy, and even to blow off a little about it to your comrades, but it's quite another thing to write such improprieties in a letter to your brother"—he perused the covering letter from the parish office, and the sergeant could feel an impending calamity—"especially," the general went on, having found what he was looking for, "when the brother is only eight years old."

He put the letter down and looked the sergeant in the eye. "I can't just ignore this," he said ominously. "The child couldn't make head or tail of the letter, so he showed it to an older sister. She translated it for the parents and they took it to their priest and asked him to give the writer a good talking-to. The priest, in turn, has asked me to do it for him. Shall I read you what he wrote?"

"You don't have to," replied the sergeant hoarsely.

"Do you know a private in the Twenty-sixth Wisconsin by the name of"—the general peered at the priest's letter, and then spelled out, "V-o-j-t-e-c-h How-ska? He's a fellow countryman of yours in K Company."

"It wasn't him!" blurted the sergeant. He stopped himself, but under the general's glare his principles dissolved and he gave voice to his suspicions.

In fifteen minutes, Shake, the pale practical joker, stood in front of the general, swearing up and down that he hadn't known how young Vojta's brother was. The general didn't believe him and, although he was normally quite succinct, this time he delivered a lengthy lecture on the corrupting of innocents. An hour later, Shake was marching around the camp wearing a barrel around his waist with a sign that said, "I AM A LIAR."

He had admitted to the general that he had invented Busty Betsy.

The general didn't bother to summon Houska, and the sergeant was relieved. Perhaps Vojta would remain happily ignorant of what had happened. But then—letters! The garrulous parents would send letters. Sharing it with the priest wouldn't be enough. True, they didn't know how to write, but what are sons for?

As long as his sweetheart didn't write! But surely the parents wouldn't have told her.

A few days later, he ran into Houska sitting in front of his tent with a letter in his hand, scowling and shaking his head.

"What's the news from home, Vojta?"

"I can't figure it out," said the private from Wisconsin. "Ma's preaching to me like a priest. She says I should stay away from easy women and wash in cold water. And not put pepper or spices on my meat—" Houska raised his sad eyes from the page. "As if we had spices in the army!"

"Does your ma mention any easy woman in particular?"

"No," said Houska. "I'd give a lot to know what's eating her. After all, I'm engaged."

You're in dreamland again, the sergeant thought, but out loud he said, "You know mothers, they worry."

So much for the home front. Now the sweetheart.

A week later more mail arrived. Houska was again sitting in front of the tent with a letter, this time looking like a farmer whose barn had just burned down.

"Something wrong, Vojta?"

"Read it," said Houska gloomily.

It contained a single sentence, written in the copperplate calligraphy of someone who had gone to a one-room school but no further: "Vojta I had no idea you are such a swine goodbye for ever I am marrying fredy houzvicka from cedar rapits your not for never more Rosie."

"I can't understand—" Houska sat there like an undertaker. "Sarge, did I get drunk and do something I don't remember? But how could anyone not remember something like that?" He thought a moment, then added angrily, "And what bastard would have written her about it if I did?"

For the next two months—except for two weeks when they were skirmishing with the Rebels and the mail wasn't getting through—Houska ignored his family and concentrated on winning Rosie back.

When the sergeant read Rosie's letter, he went looking for Shake, who had served only half his barrel penalty. Shake sat down and meekly wrote a long letter. But right after that the Rebels struck, the mail was blocked, they fought, they bled, and it was two months before letters started arriving again.

Houska sat in front of his tent, crushed. "So much for my bride," he told the sergeant, showing him the letter.

It said: "dear Vojta forgive me I was wrong but its two late now I got married last week to fredy from rapits with a baby coming for chrismas dont send me any more leters as I am a married woman now your forever Rosie."

That was the end of September. The sergeant wondered if the lad from Bee Grove ever realized the implications of what Rosie had written him. If he did, he never let on.

★

"I couldn't help myself, sarge, I got so mad," said the tattered soldier. He had regained consciousness and was sitting up on the divan, while Madam Sosniowski wound a strip of white linen around his head. He was barefoot except for a dirty rag wrapped around the big toe of his right foot. "When I see paintings of those stuck-up Rebel mugs, I go crazy! I've sliced up at least fifty of them since Kennesaw Mountain. You would too, sarge. They killed my kid brother at Kennesaw."

As hardened as he had become, the sergeant felt some sympathy for the man. He saw the bandaged toe on the bare foot. Harshly he said, "This time you were wrong. This is no Rebel officer."

"Come on, sarge, I know their faces and their feathers. And that sabre—"

"This man fought in another war," said the sergeant. Madam Sosniowski had finished binding his head, and pinned the bandage down. The soldier carefully turned his head to look at the portrait.

"The Mexican War?"

"No," said the sergeant.

The soldier examined the portrait. "They never wore uniforms like that in the Revolution."

"That is my late husband," said Madam Sosniowski, her Polish accent heavy. The soldier scowled. "He fought in Poland." He didn't seem to understand. "In Europe," she said, "against the Russian tsar."

Perhaps that word, anathema to America, meant something to the soldier. He rose heavily from the divan and growled, "I'm sorry, ma'am." He looked around, noticed the spilled spoons, bent down and started to put them back into the case. "If only your daughter had said something—" He got up, handed Madam Sosniowski the case, and turned uncertainly back to the sergeant. "Sarge—"

"Go sleep it off," said the sergeant. "Tomorrow we're on our way to North Carolina."

"Thanks, sarge!" The soldier turned and stumbled towards the door.

"Private," said Madam Sosniowski softly. The soldier stopped and turned back to her with obvious effort. Madam Sosniowski picked up the doll and, without a word, handed it to Sherman's shabby soldier.

"But ma'am, I couldn't—"

"Take it," she said, "as a souvenir."

Once again the sergeant had the impression—with the horse, the bloodied eagle, the horse dung on the green carpet—that this was somebody's crazy dream.

In this war anything was possible.

The tattered soldier might not understand these images. The sergeant did.

★

"Quit staring at me like a heifer at a new gate, and light yourself a cheroot!" The lieutenant—if that was what he was—handed him a cigar with a gold band. Kapsa let him light it for him, although the man with the sharp nose reminded him more than ever of the man he had killed in the house on Gottestischlein. "You're in it up to here, just like me, isn't that so?"

"I don't know what you're in," Kapsa said, looking at his tweed jacket rather than into his eyes. "All I know is where you're not from. You're not a small-holder," he said. "I know that."

The lieutenant chuckled. "You guessed correctly. I grew up on an estate."

He was a lieutenant then, for certain.

"A butler's son," he added, and, noticing renewed suspicion in Kapsa's eyes, he continued, "Look here, you're telling me you're an ordinary soldier, and yet you've rented a room at the Hotel Savoy and bought a bottle for two gulden. Either you're lying and you're no ordinary soldier, or you're not lying and—well, the alternative that suggests itself—"

The same alternative had just suggested itself to Kapsa.

"What about you? You're also an ordinary soldier?"

"A general's orderly. An ordinary soldier with a leg up."

Kapsa felt relief wash over him. He took a deep pull on the cigar and his head began to swim a little. He pointed to the half-empty cigar box. "You stole this from the general?"

The lieutenant-orderly grinned. "The same way you stole this bottle from the bartender."

The tweed suit was just a tweed suit again. Kapsa realized that the other man's assessment of his situation was far more logical than the truth about what had happened on Gottestischlein, which Kapsa might have revealed in a moment of madness.

"But you did steal something, didn't you?"

"The general's strong-box. And you?"

"Me? Just a captain's."

"Let's drink to that!" The orderly refilled their snifters with Kapsa's cognac and the glasses rang like a bell.

"How much have you got?" the lieutenant asked him.

Kapsa didn't tell him till they were halfway across the Atlantic.

★

Standing before the white façade flickering yellow in the flames of burning Columbia, the sergeant finally mustered his courage. A squadron of Kil's cavalry was trotting down the road, with Kakuska at the rear in his new riding boots and shiny spurs that clearly were not government issue. They were headed off to the north, where the sky on the horizon was already black, with billows of burning snow glowing like a dying comet against the dark.

"Madam," said the sergeant, and paused as his throat tightened in apprehension. "Madam, did you, when you lived in Helldorf, did you know a"— a final pause before he came out with it, in German—"Frau Hauptmann von Hanzlitschek?"

"Ursula?" asked Madam Sosniowski, and the sergeant's heart galloped like a horse.

Burning snow was fluttering down on the Congaree River.

The Writer's Second Intermezzo

V A L L A N D I G H A M   B E L I E V E S—or claims to believe—that our dispute with the South will be resolved not by war, but by peaceful negotiations," said my husband, Humphrey, over pork chops, which they had naturally complimented me on before getting into the serious part of the conversation. The dinner in honour of Ambrose Burnside had actually been prepared by Jasmine, our housekeeper and general factotum. She had been in charge of the kitchen ever since she had come to work for us, allowing me to limit my culinary activity to making tea, which I know how to do. I had hired Jasmine as a maid, but back at Mr. Carmichael's mansion in South Carolina, where she came from, she had picked up a great deal from Gospel, who was a champion cook. Mr. Carmichael's late wife had made a discriminating gourmand out of her husband, and when she died young, a victim of her own culinary skills, Mr. Carmichael was willing to pay the exorbitant sum of five thousand dollars for the famous Gospel from Georgia, though she had only one leg. He came to regret spending such an outrageous amount; as soon as he brought her to his plantation, Gospel's culinary skills evaporated—or rather, they appeared to be based uncertainly on magic of some sort, which was apparently affected by her moving to South Carolina.

I knew Ambrose had a soft spot for Negroes. It may even have been hereditary. His father had set out along what they called "the Quaker Road" from his native South Carolina to Indiana, where he had given the slaves he inherited from his parents their freedom. Ambrose continued the tradition in his friendship with his orderly, Robert Holloway, who Ambrose exaggeratedly maintained had saved him from the ravages of dysentery in Mexico. The friendship did not turn Ambrose into a militant abolitionist, but he found slave-owners offensive and he simply couldn't abide nigger-haters like Vallandigham. So, as he was praising the pork chops to the skies, I decided not to take credit, but to introduce him to Jasmine after dinner. I assumed the girl would be in seventh heaven in the company of a Union general, since she not only had a natural interest, which she shared with her race, in the victory of the North; she had a strong personal interest as well.

"But Vallandigham is wrong," my husband was saying. "Even if Jeff Davis agreed to peace talks with Lincoln, which I find hard to imagine, he would enter them with some ulterior motive, not an honest desire to come to a settlement. His real intention would be to give his troops a rest, or to export cotton to England undisturbed by hostilities and so forth. He's crossed his Rubicon."

"I agree," said Ambrose.

"There were no fundamental philosophical reasons for the South's decision to secede," Humphrey continued. "There is no theory here, either, based on the biblical notion of hewers of wood and drawers of water, or on any paleological or psychological speculations about the inequality of human races. Slavers know that's all rubbish, even better than we do. We consider Negroes mostly as concepts. They know them as people of flesh and blood, and they know only too well that they're human. There's no philosophy here, general. Slavery is simply very profitable!"

The concept called Jasmine entered with a tray, and I was reminded of her five-thousand-dollar mentor, whose miraculous abilities had suddenly vanished when she was transplanted. I imagined Gospel serving chicken burnt to a crisp, sauces with too much salt, overcooked rice.

"What's the matter with you, Gospel?" Mr. Carmichael had asked, annoyed.

"It be black magic, massa!"

Mr. Carmichael did not believe in magic, white or black. He saw Negroes as uneducated and therefore primitive people, and believed he had only to invent a fairy-tale that would undo the spell in order to enjoy again the delicacies for which he had acquired Gospel. So with a perfectly straight face he asked Gospel where the black magic was coming from.

"My son Hasdrubal, massa."

"Oh, is he a sorcerer?" asked Mr. Carmichael.

"He learn it from Nausika, a bad nigger-woman on Massa Roberts' plantation. She can put the evil eye on anybody. She even bewitched massa."

"Is that a fact?" Mr. Carmichael still maintained a solemn face. "And just how did she bewitch him?"

"She fixed it so he can't have no babies," Gospel replied with equal solemnity.

Mr. Carmichael hesitated, wondering if his cook was as dense as she seemed, or as impertinent as he was beginning to think. He knew Nausika and her five high-yellow children well. All of them had their mother's huge eyes and Mr. Roberts's aquiline nose. They were the only children on the plantation with noses like that, since Mr. Roberts had never had any children by his wife.

"So now your son has put the evil eye on you, Gospel. How?"

"I surely don't need to explain it to you, massa."

No, indeed she didn't. Mr. Carmichael wondered if his cook believed in magic any more than he did. And an unpleasant suspicion began to take hold. "I meant to say, what kind of curse was it?"

"Well, if I get sold and he don't get sold with me, I can't never cook another thing, not even a decent mess of grits," she explained, her face a stony mask of gravity.

Furious, Mr. Carmichael rejected then and there the existence of a causal nexus between lack of education and lack of intelligence. "I'll show you, Gospel!" he said to himself, but then realized he was helpless in the face of the one-legged virtuoso.

Roberts was a gambler, and had sold Carmichael the cook because he had urgently needed eight thousand dollars. The cook had begged her new owner to buy her son as well. Hasdrubal was young, good-looking: footman material. But Roberts wanted three thousand for him. Carmichael didn't need a footman, and spending that much money for a field hand went against the grain. So a tearful Gospel went alone to South Carolina, where she fell victim to Hasdrubal's remote version of black magic.

"Why didn't you tell me about the spell back in Georgia?" Mr. Carmichael asked angrily.

"I didn't think Hasdrubal could do it. He never put the evil eye on nobody before this."

In other words, thought Carmichael, the ploy hadn't occurred to her until later.

Carmichael knew he was trapped. Gospel was also an excellent seamstress, but Hasdrubal's magic would undoubtedly paralyse her needle as well, and he had no intention of going around in ill-fitting trousers. Soon the story about the evil eye would spread and nobody would take Gospel off his hands at any price. She stood there looking at him, her expression inscrutable, but he knew what she was thinking.

"And besides, massa," she said, "I didn't think you'd believe me. You don't even believe in the evil eye. Leastwise, you didn't used to," she added—solemnly, but with what struck him as triumphant irony.

There was nothing to do but buy himself a footman. Fortunately, Roberts's luck at cards had changed and in a good mood he let Hasdrubal go for a mere twelve hundred.

"Vallandigham doesn't understand that it's the captains of industry who are in control of the war right now," my husband was saying. "Slavery and capitalism are mutually exclusive in America. Lincoln may not realize all the implications of his famous dictum about how we cannot endure permanently half slave and half free. The captains of industry would take this noble though somewhat abstract thought and give it substance. In the slave half, you have Negro labourers in the fields—and in factories now, too—who won't go on strike and who are paid in kind; and in the other half, quarrelsome, greedy whites using what amounts to blackmail to drive wages as high as possible. For all his backwoods shrewdness, Lincoln is an idealist, although in his own way so is Vallandigham."

"Ha!" I interrupted my husband.

"What do you mean by that, Lorraine?" my husband asked sternly.

"A story is what I mean," I said. "From real life."

2

I was a witness of sorts, because the murder victim, Jeremy Lecklider, used to deliver farm produce to our kitchen. He was a shrivelled little man of fifty but, like many with a farm too small to support a hired hand and too large to run without back-breaking drudgery, he looked at least seventy. He lived with his widowed father, who for twenty years had been crippled with gout. At the time of the murder the father was almost eighty-one, and the only tasks his crippled fingers and stiff knees were up to were feeding the chickens, cooking the porridge, and cleaning the shotgun that Jeremy used to hunt grouse with in the fall. Anything heavier or more delicate was left to Jeremy.

They both appeared to be good, quiet people, and bore the futility of their existence—because there was no one to inherit the farm—with Christian humility. Or so it seemed to a woman who wrote romantic stories. And yet, in Jeremy's story, tragedy smouldered under his apparent resignation.

But no one knew that, especially an authoress who never looked to real life except for useful details about handsome lads and clever lasses and was uninterested in the lives of the elderly. It was only after old man Lecklider's trial that I thought to try my hand at realism, and then I discovered that it's easier to write fiction on the basis of imagined experience. So I consigned my unfinished tales drawn from real life to my desk drawer, apparently for ever.

The one person to have any idea of the impending tragedy on Elihu and Jeremy Lecklider's farm was a travelling salesman who peddled patent medicines for humans and livestock from farm to farm. The evening he arrived on his mule at the Lecklider farm, he spent almost an hour outside an open window listening to an argument between the father and the son. Finally he decided it wasn't the right time for a sales call; he could still make it to the neighbouring farm before dark. The next day he returned to the Leckliders' and found the farmhouse in total silence. He knocked on the door. He knew that young Lecklider would be working in the field, but that the old man would be home, since he had great difficulty moving about, even with the crutches his son had made for him. No one answered. The salesman opened the door and went inside. Young Lecklider was at home after all. He was lying on his back on the floor, and where his head was supposed to be was a bloody pool with fragments of skull and clumps of grey hair in it. Old Lecklider was sitting over the corpse in an armchair, with a shotgun in his lap, staring at nothing.

3

The Indiana state prosecutor asked Clement Vallandigham to take the case, and he accepted. He wasn't one to turn down a chance for a public display of his skills. "That was what made me laugh, Humphrey," I said, turning to my husband. "Vallandigham may be an exceptional lawyer, but would you call him an idealist? He can get a man to the gallows as easily as he can tear him from the hangman's clutches. It all depends on what suits his purpose at the time."

"I heard about the case," said Ambrose. "Vallandigham won it."

"That's right," said Humphrey. "Doesn't it seem to you, Lorraine, that his almost obsessive devotion to duty is the sign of a certain—"

"Vallandigham wants to be the hero of the day, no matter what," I said. "He's prepared to walk on dead bodies if need be, sometimes literally. He got old Lecklider hanged."

"Because Elihu actually murdered Jeremy."

"Do you really think that's the right word for it?"

In an old article in the *Cincinnati Daily Gazette* I had seen Vallandigham's name connected with John Brown. The article was published shortly after the incident at Harpers Ferry, before Brown was hanged. They'd captured him, and he lay wounded in jail awaiting the gallows. By that time Vallandigham was a congressman, and although he was hurrying to an election meeting in Dayton he got off the train at Harpers Ferry and went straight to the jailhouse.

"He wanted to see Brown with his own eyes," said Humphrey. "He was interested in him. Vallandigham is one of the most determined opponents of emancipation."

"If he'd merely wanted to set eyes on him, we might call it curiosity—though in dubious taste, considering that Brown was staring death in the eye. But he tried to extract information from him to use in the campaign."

"Brown was no politician," said Ambrose.

"But some of his people came from Ohio. Brown himself had once spent some time in Ashtabula County, which was the election district where Joshua Giddings was running, a man Vallandigham couldn't abide."

"Did he think Giddings had a hand in Brown's uprising?" asked Ambrose. He was trying to get his bearings in the hornets' nest that was the pro-peace Midwest.

I responded, "He hoped to be able to cast a shadow of suspicion on Giddings. He knew that the idea of a Republican congressman who cared about his career conspiring with a religious fanatic was utter fantasy, but Vallandigham was a master of transforming suspicion into the illusion of fact. He hoped to get Brown to admit to having met Giddings in Ashtabula County. Brown was no fool, though, and wouldn't admit to anything. And that's my argument, Humphrey," I turned to my husband. "Vallandigham doesn't care a fig for the Union or emancipation, and certainly not for truth. The only thing he cares about is the career and future of Clement Vallandigham. If that is idealism, then I agree, Comely Clem is the most idealistic politician in this land."

"It's a bit too apparent that you don't care for him, Lorraine," said my objective husband. He was right—call it female intuition, but I simply didn't like him. "Aren't you being a little unfair to him?"

Jasmine entered the dining room. She smiled pleasantly at Ambrose and placed a carafe with brandy on the table, while Ambrose ran his fingers through the dense whiskers framing his face. It was the face of a bandit from a schoolboy's adventure novel.

4

The story of Jasmine is in my drawer too. She had been assigned by Mr. Carmichael to help Gospel. Not long before, Hasdrubal had arrived on the plantation and removed the spell from Gospel. He hexed her again, briefly, when Mr. Carmichael, who already had a footman, tried to put him to work in the fields. He removed the hex as soon as he received permission to dress in silk stockings and assist the former footman—now elevated to head footman—by standing in the dining room and looking decorative.

He was decorative indeed, and it turned out that, although he was redundant as a footman, he was not totally without his uses. Mr. Carmichael had no intention of remarrying. He liked to say that one yoke per lifetime was enough, by which he meant the marriage that had produced his only daughter, who was now married to a Yankee factory owner in Cleveland. But he enjoyed chatting with the opposite sex, and he discovered that Hasdrubal tended to draw colour-blind ladies to the plantation for visits, despite Mr. Carmichael's legendary unwillingness to marry.

Black or white, it was Jasmine who enjoyed looking at Hasdrubal most of all. Just when their romance was in flower, Mr. Carmichael's daughter, Beate Morris, arrived with her husband and two little boys to celebrate her twenty-eighth birthday.

The discussion around the dinner table on the eve of the birthday celebration would have been civilized had it remained between the two men, who were gentlemen in the British mould, unwilling to raise their voices though they might be ready to burst with rage. Mr. Carmichael defended the "peculiar institution" and Mr. Morris attacked it, not out of some inner conviction but for purely practical reasons. But then Beate got involved. Physically and emotionally the living image of her temperamental mother—who during a happily brief marriage had nearly driven Mr. Carmichael insane—Beate had fallen under the sway of passionate abolitionists in Cleveland, and was not prepared to hold her tongue. So the dinner discussion became heated, and erupted in a minor family upheaval when Beate Morris said something that her principled father did not deserve to hear:

"I'm leaving tomorrow and I'll not come back until all the disgusting slave-owners like you, Papa, are hanged!"

"Beate!" said her husband, shocked.

"And you're not coming back either!" she snapped at him over her shoulder. She stormed out, slamming the door. Mr. Carmichael, looking as pale as death, sat stunned while Mr. Morris tried to control his temper. Then the slave-owner, damned by his own daughter, pointed to the liquor cabinet. Hasdrubal and the head footman understood without a word, and until long past midnight continued topping up the two gentlemen's glasses with bourbon, while they went on with their discussion. Mr. Carmichael defended himself from unspoken accusations of cruelty by saying that he was kind to his slaves and wondered what would become of them if he were to give them their freedom and turn them out into a world that was cruel to Negroes. Mr. Morris assured him that there was nothing personal in his position, but that he was simply opposed, on principle, to slavery. Mr. Carmichael declared that he too was opposed on principle to slavery, and suddenly the two men weren't sure any longer what they were arguing about, or even if they were arguing at all. Mr. Morris, used to drinking scotch, was the first to succumb to the bourbon, and Mr. Carmichael followed suit a few minutes later. The two footmen had to carry them to their bedrooms.

Next morning, Jasmine traded jobs with the chambermaid, Lucretia, and brought Beate her breakfast in bed. The manufacturer's wife was propped up on her pillows, still annoyed by last night's arguments.

"Ma'am, . . ." Jasmine said shyly.

"What is it, child?"

"Ma'am, you be celebrating your twenty-fifth birthday today, is that right?" said Jasmine, intentionally making her younger.

"Twenty-eighth," said the young matron, beaming, "and I don't know that I'll be celebrating. . . ."

"You mean after last night?"

"Well, well, now," Beate said, sitting up straight, "and what do you know about last night?"

"Well, that young footman, Hasdrubal, he's my sweetheart."

"Congratulations, child," the woman said, like an old hand.

"But I doesn't want to marry him till I's free. And neither do he." Jasmine burst into deliberately heart-rending tears.

Beate put her arms around the girl and the tears dripped down into the woman's décolletage.

"I hoped, . . ." sobbed Jasmine, "but I dasn't ask you. . . ."

"Please ask me, child!"

"It's awfully impertinent—"

"I like impertinence," she said. "The awfuller the better."

"I got to thinking, since you're such a friend of us niggers—" Jasmine paused.

"Why, of course I am, child."

"That—if you could ask for me and Hasdrubal for your birthday. Hasdrubal is extra here. Massa don't really need him. . . ."

"My God!" exclaimed the young matron.

"We'd work for you till we could buy our freedom, ma'am," Jasmine added quickly.

"What an idea!" exclaimed Beate. "But after yesterday—"

"Oh, I know," Jasmine said, with a touch of calculated despair in her voice.

Like all fanatics, Beate was prepared to lose face if she could get her way. The role of the liberator of young lovers moved her abolitionist heart. She bathed quickly and, perfumed and penitent, went to Mr. Carmichael's bedroom, where he was attempting to cure the effects of the previous night's bourbon with a diluted solution of the hair of the dog. With him in this condition, it was not difficult for Beate to make amends. He allowed her to kiss his cheek and she began: "Papa, I'm sure you got me a birthday gift."

"I did," said Mr. Carmichael. "I forgive you, but you still deserve to be punished."

"You're so right, Papa. You can punish me by keeping my present till next year—"

"Well—" said Mr. Carmichael.

"— and this year, you can give me something else instead, something that won't cost you anywhere near as much as the jewellery."

"How did you know I was planning to give you jewellery?"

"Because that's what you've always given me."

Mr. Carmichael frowned. "Aren't you being just a little too clever, Beate? You remind me of your mother."

"You've always said I'm just like her."

Mr. Carmichael nodded gravely. "Hmm. And what is it you want, Beate?"

"In October we're moving to a new house. Incidentally, you must come to the house-warming," said Beate. She knew very well that her father did not care for Yankee cooking and probably wouldn't take her up on it. "It's twice as big and we'll need a lot more servants than in the old place. For sentimental reasons, I'd like a pair of real southern Negroes."

"Hmm," said Mr. Carmichael, "yesterday I'd have said you were a damned abolitionist!"

"Of course, I'd give them their freedom. Once Tony and Billy grow up."

"And you want me to give them to you today, as a birthday present, is that it?"

"You will, won't you, Papa?"

"Hmm," said Mr. Carmichael again. "Who will choose them? Me or you?"

"I thought I would. I know exactly what I need."

"Who would you choose, then?"

"Well," said Beate, pretending to think, "I thought the cook's helper, Jasmine, and the second footman, Hasdrubal, would make a nice pair. And besides, what do you need two footmen for?"

"I don't," replied Mr. Carmichael. "Jasmine, well, all right. But Hasdrubal cost me fifteen hundred."

"Papa! You mean you'd only give me a present if it cost you nothing?"

"I've fed and clothed Jasmine for seventeen years. She'd bring at least as much as Hasdrubal today, she can cook—"

"But, Papa—"

"Of course"—Mr. Carmichael smiled craftily—"if your husband agrees, I'll sell him Hasdrubal. For three thousand," he added quickly.

"You said you only paid fifteen hundred for him!"

"Yes, but I paid five thousand for his mother. I have to recoup something." And with that, he refused to discuss the matter any further.

But Mr. Morris objected. It was a matter not of money but of principle, he insisted; he was opposed to buying and selling people. A principle was a principle.

"But we'd set him free as soon as we got to Cleveland."

"First I'd have to buy him, though."

Beate looked searchingly into her husband's eyes until he had to look away. "Morris," she said, "what if he were to let you have him for a hundred dollars?"

"Well—" said her husband.

"A principle is a principle," said Beate.

But Mr. Carmichael had not forgotten Hasdrubal's magical powers, and the sale never materialized. The next day, Mr. and Mrs. Morris left for the North with Jasmine and a plan. Once at home, Beate would use her contacts in the abolitionist movement to help Hasdrubal escape to Cleveland on the Underground Railroad. Then Hasdrubal and Jasmine would save up to buy Gospel's freedom, which, in the light of Hasdrubal's magic, wasn't likely to be too expensive.

But a week after returning to Cleveland, Mr. Morris, Beate, and both their sons were drowned in a storm on Lake Huron. I hired Jasmine.

Shortly after that, the war broke out.

So Jasmine's yearning for a Union victory was based on more than just the natural interest of her race.

5

I may have been the only other person to have caught a glimpse, before the murder, into what lay beneath the apparently peaceful life of the aged father and the ageing son. But my testimony would hardly have changed the fate of the poor old man. That was in Vallandigham's capable hands.

Once, when Jeremy showed up with eggs and chickens to sell, I noticed he was wearing a black rosette on the lapel of his coarse farmer's jacket. He placed the packet of eggs on the table and his creased face seemed more sombre than usual.

"Has someone died, Jeremy?"

He shook his head and looked away. "It's ten years today since my Mary was killed. And young Jeremy."

It was a simple story. Their cart hit a hole in the road, the axle broke, the cart overturned and rolled over and over down the embankment to the river. The horse went over too, but the harness broke and it survived without so much as a broken bone. The farmer's wife broke her back, and the ten-year-old boy was knocked unconscious and drowned in the river.

How can one respond to a story like that? I mumbled something about the inscrutable will of God, and the mild-mannered Jeremy suddenly became a heretic, spewing metaphysical hatred.

"The will of God, you say?" he replied. "I say He's a rogue. A dastardly murderer." It took my breath away.

"Inscrutable, you say?" Jeremy continued. "What did He give us reason for, if not to understand His ways?"

"Jeremy—Jeremy! I understand that—"

"He's worse than a murderer!" yelled the farmer, not to be interrupted. "He's omnipotent! What did my Mary do to Him? What did little Jeremy ever do to Him?" His eyes were burning.

I decided to say nothing more until he calmed down. Then, as quickly as he had lost control, he became quiet. The rage in his eyes subsided, giving way to sorrow.

"Forgive me, Mrs. Tracy," he said in his usual meek voice, "but it's been ten years today."

It gave me something to think about. In the face of the farmer's tragedy my romantic love stories seemed like wisps of lace and filigree. His terrible hatred had clearly been triggered by an equally powerful love. Why had he never remarried? He had been only forty when his wife was killed. In the simple formula that novels are written by, country folk take these things philosophically—a farmer needs a wife, a farm needs a homemaker. In life, however, there are always exceptions.

At the time I still knew nothing about old Elihu Lecklider, and I didn't until the trial.

The salesman's testimony was confused. Father and son had been arguing as if a million dollars were at stake, but the salesman hadn't really understood the point of the disagreement. Yet from his testimony its metaphysical essence became clear: Jeremy had not accepted the death of his wife and son with appropriate Christian humility. Radically exceeding the limits of his inherited faith, he had called God a murderer to his aged father's face, as he had done in the amazing conversation with me in the kitchen. It never entered his mind that God might have had nothing to do with his tragedy because—

Because there was no God. That was what the half-crippled eighty-year-old Elihu Lecklider had insisted in a steely voice. There simply was no God in the universe. It wasn't God that killed Mary and Jeremy, but a broken axle. If it's anyone's fault, Jeremy, it's yours. You should have kept the cart in better repair. But you're not the murderer either. Nobody is the murderer. The universe is blind, cruel, indifferent. There is no hope anywhere. There is only death, and whether it happens now or a hundred years from now makes no difference, for it will always happen. That's the way the universe is.

All this came out at the trial. It seemed to me that the notion of a God that didn't exist was less blasphemous than the notion of a God who was in fact the Devil. Theologically speaking, which was less acceptable? God the illusion, or God the murderer?

Vallandigham took the tortured philosophies of these two old men who had somehow lost their grip on the meaning of life, and made of them a dichotomy that lent itself to great oratory. The victim was a Christian who had blasphemed out of understandable pain. The murderer was an atheist, anathema in a Christian society; a pagan, someone lacking in values, unworthy of the benefit of mitigating circumstances.

The old man was obviously in agony. He denied nothing, confessed to everything. He obviously wanted to die. I just don't know if he wanted to die on the gallows. Perhaps Vallandigham was doing him a favour, though it was hard to tell. Shattered by his own deed, old Lecklider would not have lived much longer anyway. They brought him to the gallows on a stretcher.

"Vallandigham walks over dead bodies," I said. "Literally."

6

From our dining room you could step out onto a small balcony with three wicker chairs and a round table. It was only the last week in April, but the evening was mild, more like May. We sat down and the gentlemen lit their cigars.

"He'd like to walk over the dead body of the United States," said Ambrose. "I'm no philosopher, Professor Tracy, and no politician either. But peace now would be tantamount to a Union defeat."

Jasmine came out onto the porch with a fresh bottle of cognac. She was listening to the conversation intently. The glasses on the tray rattled lightly.

"The only way peace would be possible now would be if one side capitulated," said Ambrose. "Our side, or their side. And we—"

"And we won't, of course," my husband interrupted. "Because it would be more than just a defeat for the Union, it would be a defeat for the nineteenth century."

Jasmine set a glass down on the table before him.

"We have far more factories," my husband continued, "and we can place far more soldiers in the field. And in the final analysis—though, unfortunately, to many ears in the North this may seem the weakest argument of all—we are fighting for the liberation, not the enslavement, of the human race. The only advantage the Confederacy holds over us is that so far their generals"—he halted, feeling awkward about saying this in Ambrose's presence, then he went on—"have enjoyed better fortune in war than ours."

The glasses sparkled in the light of the candles. It was a balmy night; the stars overhead were reflected in Ambrose's polished boots. Humphrey raised his glass to the moon. Nothing seemed to me lovelier than a glass of cognac shimmering with little blue and amber flames. It was so peaceful.

"Here in the Middle West," Humphrey continued, "many people have been affected by the collapse of river commerce. The Union gunboat patrols the river to prevent it from serving the rebels and their northern suppliers, but to many it represents violence, usurpation, freedom denied, misery, and bankruptcy. It's difficult to explain why they should face ruin here for the victory of the Union, when Yankee manufacturers in the East are lining their pockets. Now Lincoln has tossed the Emancipation Proclamation into the pot. Workers fear a rapid drop in wages if the Middle West is flooded with Negroes who have no idea what wages are, and who are prepared to work for a mere caricature of a decent day's pay."

"There's a war on!" said Ambrose, frowning, swirling the sparkling liquid around in his glass. "The troops are sacrificing far more. When the war is over, everything will return to normal, including river traffic on the Mississippi."

"Yes," my husband said, "but if too many freed slaves move north, it's going to cause problems. The main problem, for now at least, is that those who want peace with the South are only fanning the flames of these fears. You've read those newspaper articles, haven't you, general?"

Ambrose nodded gravely.

"At the Democratic Convention where Vallandigham tried unsuccessfully to win the nomination," said my husband, "an old anti-Lincoln slogan turned up: 'The Constitution as it is, the Union as it was.' Vallandigham's supporters added, 'And the Niggers where they are!' There can be no misconstruing that." Humphrey gave a dry chuckle and took a sip from his glass. "There are paradoxes everywhere. Here, workers are afraid of competition from the Negro. Many entrepreneurs in the East fear it too, for some factories in the South are beginning to use slave labour and that could bring down international prices. That's why they're for emancipation in the East, and against it in the Middle West." He paused and sighed. "No one really cares what happens to the Negroes, neither the factory owners in the East nor the peace-makers in the Middle West. Hatred for the Negro race is actually artificial. Or rather, it's secondary."

I rose and walked over to the newspaper stand by the balcony door, and took out a copy of the Indianapolis *Daily Sentinel.* I had marked some articles in red pencil. My two men watched me in silence as I read aloud: "'Congress has the negro-phobia. It is nigger in the Senate, and nigger in the House. It is nigger in the forenoon and nigger in the afternoon. It is nigger in motions and nigger in speeches. It was nigger the first day and it has been nigger every day. Nigger is in every man's eye, and nigger in every man's mouth. It's nigger in the lobby and nigger in the hall. . . . The nigger vapor is a moral pestilence that blunts the sense of duty to the Constitution and destroys the instinct of obedience to the law.'" I put down the newspaper. "Thus saith Vallandigham. Does that sound like secondary hatred to you? Or even artificial? Vallandigham voted against emancipation in Congress. That might be explained by your hypothesis, Humphrey, but he also voted against recognizing the Negro Republic of Haiti—"

"That was Lincoln's proposal," my husband interrupted. "And the abolitionists were pushing for it."

"But, my darling," I asked, "what does that tell you?"

My husband paused to think, then smiled. "You're probably right. His distaste may well have deeper roots. Because"—he paused again—"if you look at his voting record, he was in favour of eliminating the inhumane treatment of sailors, for granting Jews full rights of American citizenship, and as a matter of fact he even voted to allow the Mormons in Utah to practise polygamy. You might even say"—he made a wry face—"that Vallandigham is a champion of the underprivileged as long as their skin isn't black. Although, in a sense, he ought to be grateful to the Negroes."

"Why?" asked Ambrose.

"He ran for Congress three times unsuccessfully," said my husband. "He was defeated a fourth time too, by Lewis Campbell. But Vallandigham found out that, all over Ohio, many of those who voted for Campbell were Negroes, even though the local regulations prohibited it. He challenged the results and after a recount he came off about two votes ahead of Campbell. He hadn't won the confidence of the voters, but the law was on his side."

I thought for a moment. "Humphrey," I said, "you're the philosophy professor. What's the name of that Greek play where the sister wants to bury her murdered brother and—"

"What play?" said Ambrose.

7

When we were saying our farewells that evening under the lantern at the doorway, and Ambrose stood there in his glittering uniform, he seemed to have made up his mind about something. He swung onto his horse and galloped off into the shimmering darkness. Such a lovely uniform. Soldiers deserve it. Their lot in war is terrible.

Humphrey went to bed and was soon sound asleep, while I sat in the parlour, thoughts chasing around in my brain like naughty children.

Was I being unfair to Vallandigham? One thing you couldn't deny: he had opposed this war for a long time, and what had it brought him? He had once tried to explain his position in an army camp in Washington, and a sergeant had slapped his face and he had almost been lynched. A grocer in Dayton where he'd shopped for years refused to serve him, saying he wouldn't take money from traitors. When Clem tried to talk the matter over with him, the grocer pulled a pistol on him; Vallandigham stepped back, tripped on the doorstep, fell to his hands and knees, and crawled along the sidewalk into the next shop. Unfortunately it was a fashionable milliner's, and the sight of the congressman entering the establishment on all fours was far too delightful for the ladies to keep to themselves.

To that point, of course, the war had been one calamity after another: Bull Run, Antietam, Chickamauga, Fredericksburg, with no more than fleeting glimpses of victory. Many in the North were growing weary of the war, and the Copperheads—the fanatics and the Democrats advocating peace with the South—were gaining in strength. Unless the North started winning, the Democratic candidate stood to beat Lincoln in next year's presidential election. Was this what Vallandigham was betting on? Whatever it was, so far things were going his way.

One time at Eunice Jarrett's, where Vallandigham was invited as the guest of honour, he explained his theory of the war to us. Negro slavery isn't the issue at all, he said. It's over things like import tariffs, which the North insists on and the South rejects, because the North opposes importing cheap industrial goods from Europe, while the South welcomes it. It's over the transcontinental railroad, which the North wants to run from Chicago to San Francisco while the South wants to go across Texas to New Mexico. To enforce their will, the Northern capitalists need to whip up a war fever—but who would go to war for an import tariff or a railroad route? That's where abolitionism suits their purpose. Slavery can't be considered with a cool head, and abolitionism adds the element of righteous indignation that clouds the mind. But with the North less than successful in the war so far, hot heads have begun to cool. The soldiers have come into contact with Negroes and had their eyes opened. They see the horrors of the bloody casualties. . . .

"Does this mean you are not opposed to slavery, Mr. Vallandigham?" asked Eunice, and her voice trembled. She had recently been host to Harriet Beecher Stowe, and was considering inviting the other Harriet, Harriet Tubman, to her salon.

"Of course I am," replied Clem, "but I have also always been opposed to unleashing this terrible war for the sake of abolitionist fantasies."

"And yet—" said Eunice, but Vallandigham wasn't finished.

"Any dispute can be resolved through discussion," he declared with deep conviction. "Even slavery."

"But—" Eunice tried again, but Vallandigham talked on and on, while the ladies in Eunice's parlour stared at him as if they'd been bitten by a snake.

I thought of the snake with the lovely coppery head, called by the same name as the copper coin worn in the lapels of those who strove for peace with the South. Unlike the bombastic rattler, which gives a noisy warning before it strikes, this attractive reptile gives no warning at all.

The Bavarian pendulum clock struck midnight. I sighed. I had resolved nothing; I just wanted to be fair.

And Ambrose had come to a decision of some sort. He was going to do something foolish.

Jasmine tiptoed into the room. I wondered what she was doing up so late. I had sent her to bed hours before.

She hesitated, her hands folded at her waist.

"Is something the matter, Jasmine?"

"I can't sleep," she said, "I keep—"

"What is it, child?"

The fear in her eyes was obvious. "Miz Tracy—do you think—"

"Think what?"

"Think they'll make peace with the Rebels?"

"Oh dear, whatever gave you that silly idea?" I said, putting an arm around her. "Of course they won't make peace. We would have to surrender for that to happen, and you saw General Burnside tonight, didn't you? Men like that don't surrender, Jasmine."

8

I would go to the library at my husband's college and read the newspapers. They had a good selection of Democratic and Republican papers, from Illinois, Indiana, and Ohio, and the major dailies from New York and Boston—entertaining reading if you weren't too concerned whether the outcome of the war would suit Jasmine and her lazy footman.

The newspapers siding with the anti-war Democrats called for peace, which they would qualify as "honourable" and "mutually acceptable" and "sensible" and so on. But they also ran articles that demanded peace "at any price". I imagined Ambrose diligently trying to work out what that price would be, furrowing his brow as he read lines directed at Lincoln's government: "fight your own battles. The Democratic press of this country refuses to support the interests of the abolitionist traitors any longer. This paper

will do everything in its power to stop the wave of desolation that threatens
to sweep the land!" In his Washington office Halleck may have thought
these were just words—strong words, but no more than words. But people
here were mesmerized by them.

I was visiting my sick aunt in Dayton when Vallandigham arrived, fresh
from Congress.

"You say they gave him ovations?" Ambrose asked bitterly. We had run
into each other while I was out for a stroll along the river.

"It was a hero's triumphal return to his home town," I said. "No one has
ever been welcomed in Ohio like that before. They fired a cannon in front
of the hotel in his honour. I counted the number of salutes for a while, then
gave up. They couldn't stop."

"I hear the Copperheads had an allegorical float," he said with evident
distaste.

"They did indeed."

"There was apparently a white man in chains and a Negro standing over
him with a bullwhip."

"It was nothing very original. It was supposed to illustrate Vallandigham's slogan about the war being waged to free the slave and enslave
the white man. But it had very little impact," I said. "There was a banner
over the wagon that said EMANCIPATION IN THE SOUTH—STAR-
VATION IN THE NORTH. The Negro was real, but he was so terrified
that the white man in chains had to kick him to make him raise the whip
and crack it feebly, and it obviously never connected, and many people
must have thought, as did I, that plantation overseers would hardly be that
ineffectual."

"How could he have allowed himself to be used like that?" Ambrose said,
shaking his head.

"An editor of the *Dayton Journal* who was at my aunt's house said they
held the Negro's wife hostage at *The Empire* until the parade was over. I
heard that he'd already had some trouble with the Copperheads on a farm
near Dayton—"

We stopped by an iron railing where there was a nice view of Cincinnati.
The April wind played with the tassel on Ambrose's sword. I had heard the
story of the allegorical Negro's troubles from Jasmine. He had run away
from a Georgia plantation with his wife, with the help of the abolitionists
and their Underground Railroad, along the same route Jasmine's footman
would have taken if things had gone according to plan. The abolitionists arranged for the man to work for a farmer named Palme, an abolitionist him-

self and an exception in Ohio. Word of the black farmhand spread through the district like wildfire, and a few days after he got his first pay, a mob gathered in Palme's field—some were white workers, most were just white brawlers—and Palme's assurance that he was paying the black man the same wages he paid his white hands just added fuel to the fire. The workers who had come to protest low wages for the former slave, which could bring down their own wages, thought equal pay was an insult to the white race. It was an interesting clash of two unacceptable opposites, but it didn't lead to deeper thinking. On the contrary, the labourers drove the Negro off the farm, and the brawlers tried to pick a fight with the farmer, but he brought out a shotgun. The Negro and his wife went on to make their living in Dayton, doing odd jobs provided to them by militant local Republicans. Now and then the couple also hewed wood for militant Democrats, which was supposed to remind the population of Joshua, chapter nine. Finally they made the Negro play another symbolic part, for the greater glory of Clem Vallandigham, and they even paid him to do it. Of course, they paid him less than the piece of white trash they hired to symbolize the enslavement of the white race.

"They had someone on the float representing Lincoln," said Ambrose. "I heard it was downright insulting."

"It made even less impact than the Negro with the whip. Lincoln stood behind him, appearing to approve of how the former slave was whipping the white tramp. But the one playing Lincoln was the shortest of the three on the float. Maybe they don't have enough tall men in Dayton. They put an extra high top hat on his head, but it collapsed and, all told, it was—"

"I heard they also slandered the president," Ambrose interrupted. "Speaker after speaker. They called him 'usurper', 'tyrant', 'demagogue', 'fool'—"

"The one I liked best was 'the ugliest head of state in the world'. That may well be the truth."

Ambrose spun round to face me. "Lorraine," he said intensely, and then he quoted an article he had memorized. His voice was bitter: "'The miserable imbecile that now disgraces the President's chair . . . raw-boned, shamble-gaited, bow-legged, knock-kneed . . . one who has no intellect and less moral nature. . . .'" His pink face turned red with rage. "That's what some of them are saying about Lincoln! The man who bears all this superhuman responsibility on his shoulders! The commander of our brave army, bleeding and dying on the battlefronts!"

He spoke in the clichés of a general, but what is a cliché? Perhaps it's a truth so truthful it has become self-evident. Of course, to those who never knew blood-soaked hillsides like the one at Marye's Heights, such truths may mean nothing.

"At the very least, it was in poor taste," I said.

9

Once when he was having tea at our house Ambrose showed me a pair of shiny cuff-links. One of them depicted the head of the goddess Liberty on an old copper coin, the other a little snake (it looked more like a worm) with a triangular head, which everyone knows conceals poisonous fangs. I thought of the evening at Eunice Jarrett's. The symbol had inspired some enterprising soul, because Ambrose handed me an advertisement for the strange cuff-links clipped from the Indianapolis *Daily Sentinel*: "Let every white man accept 'the insult' and wear the grand old emblem of Liberty—the Copperhead!"

"Since when is a poisonous snake a symbol of liberty?" I asked. "Our American bald eagle eats those creatures for dinner."

There were rings of fatigue under Ambrose's eyes, but he laughed aloud. "You should have been a journalist, Lorraine! That would never have occurred to me. Too bad you aren't a man!"

"Really?"

"Well, you know what I mean," he said, his face turning a pleasing red.

"I probably do, even though I'm just a woman," I said. "And you're welcome to use that line. Maybe you can inscribe it in some lady's autograph book, or include it in one of your orders—"

He nodded. I knew the military situation was on his mind. He had just returned from Kentucky two days ago; he'd gone on the urgent request of General Rosecrans, who was currently in Murfreesboro, Tennessee. He had needed Ambrose's units in position along the Cumberland River, down in the south of Kentucky. I learned this from the papers. I only prayed that the Northern papers were delayed in getting to the South.

"I just issued an order," said Ambrose morosely. "Order Number Thirty-eight. It's a pity I didn't come to see you first."

I had already heard about that order. It had been provoked by a firebrand speech delivered in Hamilton by Vallandigham, who had run for governor and was therefore trying to get himself arrested. As a martyr, he could scarcely fail to win the nomination. My husband commented on Burnside's order with the word "Ouch!" and then read the order aloud: "'All persons found within our lines who commit acts for the benefit of the enemies of our country will be tried as spies or traitors and, if convicted, will suffer death.'"

"Somewhat bloodthirsty," I said, "but of course treason is—"

My husband went right on reading: "'. . . Likewise, anyone declaring sympathy for the enemy will be subject to arrest and trial, with conviction carrying the death penalty or expulsion beyond federal lines "into the lines of their friends".'"

10

The evening of May 4, as I was walking past the central telegraph office in Cincinnati, I saw Ambrose's chestnut mare tied to the railing outside, its shiny coat as brown as the general's whiskers. I walked up to the door; WESTERN UNION was stencilled on its glass pane. Inside, Ambrose and his aide were leaning over the telegrapher's desk. I thought I might be able to have a few words with him, but just then they finished what they were doing and hurried towards the door. Ambrose rushed past without noticing me. They jumped on their horses and galloped off.

Something was up.

Three hours later, I was strolling up and down the platform at the railway station, waiting for Humphrey to arrive from Indianapolis on the eleven-fifteen. Just before eleven, a large unit of soldiers marched onto the platform, led by a captain I had met at a party—Hutton was his name. A short while later, Ambrose and his aide came out of the stationmaster's office and talked to Hutton, apparently giving him some urgent instructions. I was standing in the shadows so again Ambrose didn't notice me.

A locomotive with two passenger cars pulled in and Hutton and his men got on board. As the train started moving, Hutton appeared on the rear platform and Ambrose and his aide returned his salute.

When the train had gone, I walked out of the shadows and called his name. "I hope your birdie doesn't fly away!" I sang out, waving a hand with my fingers crossed. I have to admit, though, I wasn't much in a singing mood.

Ambrose and his aide looked at me in horrified astonishment. Then the train from Indianapolis pulled into the station and I had to watch for Humphrey. But out of the corner of my eye, I could see the two men still staring at me, though not for the usual reasons.

I knew that I had witnessed a historical moment.

That night Hutton arrested Vallandigham.

II

"Do you think Ambrose will have Clem shot?" I asked my husband the next day. Vallandigham was safely under lock and key in a well-guarded room in Bennet House, the most famous hotel in the Middle West. Ambrose, always the gentleman, had had him moved there from the cell at the Kemper barracks, where Hutton had put him. He was being held in comfort, but under arrest all the same.

"With cholerics like your Ambrose," said my husband, "one never knows."

"Will you have him shot?" I asked Ambrose the next evening, when I arranged an accidental meeting with him on the street.

He replied with unaccustomed venom, "You don't shoot rats like Vallandigham. You hang them. And a court of law will decide, not I. But he won't get the death penalty. We'll lock him up in a fortress till the war is over." There was regret in his voice now.

"What a shame," I remarked.

"I agree," said Ambrose.

"It would have been a more elegant solution to send him to his friends on the other side. Clem ought to have the mark of Cain put on him."

"For you it would be the mark of Cain. But not for the Copperheads. Did you see how they rejoiced over Hooker's defeat at Chancellorsville? They actually celebrated it, Lorraine!"

Less than two months later, General Meade would defeat Lee's army at Gettysburg and Grant would put an end to the siege of Vicksburg. The Copperheads would be silenced—once and for all, as it turned out. But back then we couldn't foresee that.

"It was awful," I said, "but there's a good side to it. Vallandigham's arrest didn't get nearly as many inflammatory headlines as it would have if Lee had waited another week at Chancellorsville."

12

That evening my husband was supposed to speak at the Republican Club in Dayton, but it was cancelled because everyone hurried to watch the fire. In the Dayton *Empire*, the editor, Logan, exhausted the entire inventory of English curses (to the best of my knowledge, of course) to condemn the "infernal insult" of Vallandigham's arrest. He cursed "the cowardly abolitionist scoundrels" and called on the supporters of peace to defend the civil rights that were jeopardized by the general's action, even at "the cost of blood and massacre". Storey, of the Chicago *Times*, added, "at any cost."

That moved the controversy into the streets, and the "potential treason"—as Ambrose called something he sensed was so, but could not logically define—turned into something that looked like rebellion. Of course, the law books would probably call it civil disobedience rather than treason, just as Thoreau had long before the war, though his purposes had been entirely different. But—

I glanced at Jasmine, who stood by the window, ready to pour the drinks, and I said to my husband, "Ambrose once spoke rather incoherently about unwritten laws."

"Such laws are usually dangerous," said my husband.

"More dangerous than written ones?"

He didn't reply.

Logan's invective inflamed the Dayton mob, and the Copperheads poured fuel on that metaphoric fire by distributing free whisky in the many taverns along Main Street. On one side of the street was the *Empire* building, the headquarters of the Democrats, and across the street the *Journal,* where the "Republican nigger-lovers" gathered. Several very drunk defenders of the peace took paper and tar and made turpentine balls, and the metaphorical flames became real. By then it was almost night, and the flaming balls started flying across the street in the darkness, bouncing harmlessly off the walls of the *Journal* building and rolling down the street like fallen comets. But finally one flew through a broken window and vanished inside. In a supernaturally short time, the window looked like a view into the first circle of hell, and shortly afterwards the roof was in flames.

"Diabolical!" I said.

"And it was not without bloodshed, either," said Ambrose. "Some rascal tried to cut the firemen's hose and Sergeant Liverside shot him."

"Dead?" I asked.

"No," replied Ambrose. "He was shot in the buttocks."

13

I smiled at Jasmine, but she merely lowered her eyes and poured my husband some brandy. Then she withdrew to the window again to watch the May stars—a mournful silhouette, broken by the news from Chancellorsville. In less than two months she would be able to stand straight again. And two years later: "Write to him before you do anything else, Jasmine."

"He don't read, Miz Tracy."

"Then wait. I'm sure he's already on his way. He does know where you are, doesn't he?"

"No, 'cause I didn't come to work for you till after Fort Sumter. By then I couldn't get word to him."

"Wait, I'll ask Ambrose," I said impetuously. "He'll arrange it."

"General Burnside got more important things to do," Jasmine said. "No, Miz Tracy. You pay me well, and I saved up for the train fare. I'll go looking myself."

Back then, she'd been pouring a drink for Ambrose, staring at him as though he were Saint Nicholas, and the brandy overflowed onto his beautiful trousers. "'Therefore I stomp on General Burnside's orders, I spit on them!'" Ambrose was quoting Vallandigham as his spies had reported. "Evidently he wanted to insult me personally," he said. "He apparently doesn't know me. I know I have a short fuse. But I am certainly not in the habit of mixing personal matters in with our cause." He brushed aside Jasmine's embarrassed apologies with a smile. He wiped the drink from his trousers with a napkin and said, in a voice befitting a general, "We're waging a civil war here, and we have a crisis on our hands that requires a force that can act more quickly than civilian power can. No one has ever won a war by hesitating to use that kind of force when necessary."

14

My heart went out to my general, but my brain, always skeptical and only briefly clouded by emotions, woke me up in the night. Ambrose—with the unwritten and hence abusable law on his side—was marching straight into another one of his predicaments, this time in conflict with the written law. I couldn't get back to sleep. Was it really possible that men's matters, like war and the rules of war, were too much for the female brain? I balked at the thought, bolstered by my long-standing friendship with Margaret Fuller, an utterly unsullied friendship because we had never met. It's probably just as well. The kind of stories I write would make a travesty of such a friendship. Though I hadn't intended this to be the case, they are sugary stories, with a drop of arsenic in the sugar—just a drop. Now and then a critic notices that my heroines are always "clever" and the heroes always "handsome", and that the plots unfold accordingly. But none of them draws any radical conclusions from that. They mention my charming irony and other such qualities. Thanks to some inexplicable talent bestowed on me by the Creator, or by Providence, my little novels are always entertaining, and as a result no one ever takes them seriously, or bothers to analyse them.

Humphrey was sleeping contentedly beside me, but I was wide awake with anxiety, so I got up and went to the dining room, where the carafe holding the lovely liquid stood on the sideboard. I poured some into a snifter and stood where Jasmine had, by the window, staring up at the Cincinnati sky. The starry sky above me—the splendid starry sky over Cincinnati, in my native land. Where had I heard that before? From the lips of the brandy-loving scholar I am married to, quoting some sage from over the sea. I was an American. What is the essence of that condition, if not that the world and life are measured by the world and by life and not by Order Number One, the Constitution, when appealed to by Clement Vallandigham? Even though the order is hallowed by the authority of the glorious and the dead—glorious perhaps because they are dead. Is that dangerous? Everything is dangerous. There is something in the heart of an American that says: danger cannot be avoided. All those dead soldiers. Danger is not to be sought out, but once it is there you cannot dodge it.

So I stood sipping the lovely liquid and philosophizing, and I thought of Ambrose giving orders and getting into trouble again. He keeps giving them because he is afraid—perhaps wrongly—that this land of ours will wind up in trouble.

Someone upstairs lit a lamp, for a soft glow of light suddenly fell on the spring leaves of the elm tree outside. Jasmine probably couldn't sleep either.

The starry sky above me.

I went back to bed.

The
Burning
Forests

THE TURPENTINE FORESTS were ablaze. The sound was
like the roar of a waterfall.

The forests lay across North Carolina, in a thick green
carpet. The trunks of the pines oozed resin that the bummers, that brazen
spearhead of Sherman's army, had set ablaze. The flaming countryside had a
wild beauty about it. The sergeant remembered the huge landscape painting
over the dining-room fireplace in the château where he had once helped
move a new pianoforte. It had looked as though the painter had observed the
scene from a flying balloon. But they hadn't had balloons in those days; it
wasn't until this war—in which everything was possible—that they had
begun to use them. Lieutenant Williams watched the burning forests
through his field-glasses. All the way to the horizon, billows of black smoke
were bursting out of the dense green canopy. Large black mushrooms of
sooty smoke rose above the forest cover, turned grey, and quickly dispersed in
the overcast sky.

The sergeant could see the endless blue line of Sherman's great army
snaking through the trees, sometimes obscured by the smoke. It too reminded him of the painting in the château, yet it was so different. In the
painting, the sun shining through broken banks of cloud had made patches
of light and dark on the ground, and in these patches soldiers in white had

battled soldiers in red. They had covered the land from foreground to horizon, while above it, hidden in the azure sky, God was perhaps looking down, amused. Here there was nothing but smoke, clouds of it near the ground, columns of it reaching miles into the air and touching the leaden clouds like the buttresses of a burning cathedral. The turpentine forests were ablaze.

The standard of the Twenty-sixth Wisconsin emerged from the smoke. Through a rift in the smoke the sergeant spied a group of four men marching in long strides and swaying as if to the music of a dance band. Axles on munitions carts creaked, yoked oxen groaned in discomfort. The caravan of wagons wound back to the horizon, and beyond it smouldered what was left of Columbia. North Carolina was ablaze. Lieutenant Williams trained his field-glasses on the edge of the forests. Owls were flying in and out of the smoke, their nocturnal eyes huge as if they were horrified at this vision of Armageddon. And pervading it all was the rhythm of that strange percussion, the clanking of tin cups and canteens. Sherman's great army was rolling northwards.

"War is beautiful," said Lieutenant Williams softly, perhaps to himself.

The sergeant overheard him and wondered if he was right. The painting in the château had shown war in its beautiful aspect. So did the view from the hilltop that was his general's vantage-point. The sergeant remembered a long, lazy afternoon at the edge of a spruce grove above Dvorec, the countryside stretching towards the July horizon. Between two spruce trees a spider had woven a work of art that glistened in the sun like silver. He was just a boy and he lay there waiting as the spider rested in the heart of its magnificent web. At last a fly, green and shiny as brass, landed on the web, and the web enfolded it while it buzzed loudly and in vain. The spider darted over and solicitously wrapped the fly in a funeral shroud. The beautiful world around them was alive with the drone of bees and bugs and beetles and dragonflies, with birdsong and the rustle of leaves. Vain calls for help. The battle-cry of spiders. If this was beautiful, why not war?

The endless blue line of ragged men marched with a rocking gait. The blue in their tattered uniforms had almost faded to grey, but from up here on the hillside the grey still looked blue; the clanking of the canteens was everywhere. A bayonet flashed silver through the black smoke. A squirrel dropped a pine-cone, which hit Jefferson Davis on the buttock; the young hog snorted as it trotted along beside the blue line. The sergeant heard a song over the fire's persistent roar:

In the beauty of the lilies, Christ was born across the sea
With a glory in His bosom that transfigures you and me;

As He died to make men holy, let us die to make men free
While our God is marching on. . . .

It is a beautiful war, the sergeant thought. The song came from wagons with groaning axles at the foot of the hill where he stood. These were ambulances carrying soldiers with minor wounds who had refused to stay behind in plantation houses transformed into field hospitals because they wanted to move with their general. They bumped and rattled along in the creaking ambulances, dangling their bandaged legs over the sides, heads wrapped in turbans of bandages and bobbing up and down in rhythm with the wheels. A beautiful war. The soldiers on one of the carts saw the general through the smoke and yelled, "Long live Sherman!" The general's horse neighed, tossed its head, and a smile flashed through Sherman's rust-coloured beard. He saluted. A thicket of bandaged hands answered his salute, and—

—the cart rattled along a narrow street in the Old Town, close to where an embedded cannonball had fallen from the building façade and killed the young priest. They moved forward, stumbling, the little apple insignias on their caps, dragging the muskets they would have to clean and polish that evening, when the battle was over. Hauptmann von Hanzlitschek was at the head of the column. They passed a cart carrying students bloodied from the barricades, maimed or dismembered by Windischgraetz's artillery. One of them was already dead, his mouth agape, his head lolling backwards over the rungs. Behind him, the grocer was wiping blood from a nasty wound in his skull—the same fellow he would later see being interrogated by von Hanzlitschek. They passed another cart loaded with horrors, two legs dangling over the sides, one shot off at the ankle, the stump wrapped in a shirt, the blood oozing through. With rising tears, he noticed the folk embroidery on the shirt as blood from the stump dripped onto the oval paving-stones—signalling the end of—

—and another wagon appeared, full of wounded who saw the general and cheered. They had heard cheers like this when the war began, but not often afterwards. Not after Shiloh, or Antietam, or Chancellorsville. Not until now, at the very end of a beautiful war. The wounded who refused to be left behind rode towards Bentonville, singing.

Mine eyes have seen the glory of the coming of the Lord;
He is trampling out the vintage where the grapes of wrath are stored;
He hath loosed the fatal lightning of His terrible swift sword;
His truth is marching on. . . .

Sherman's great army rolled towards Bentonville. The bummer spearhead set fire to the forest, billows of smoke rose from the blazing resin, pushed through tangled branches and burst into the air above—great black mushrooming clouds, wide-eyed owls, the jangle of canteens and cups, and in the smoke the band of the Twenty-sixth Wisconsin playing "The Battle Hymn of the Republic". Sherman's great army was rolling towards Bentonville.

★

Dinah ran her index finger—its underside pink, its top the colour of a golden tea-rose—down Cyril's cheek.

"Well, will you buy me, white boy?" she said. "I don't come cheap, though. Eight, nine hundred." She placed the pink side of her finger on his lips. "Maybe a thousand."

He kissed her. "If you're nice to me, . . ." he said. "Meantime, I'm saving up for you."

"You that poor?" she asked. "You don't even have a thousand bucks?"

"Well, I will have if the oil business gets going—"

"Maybe they'll let me go cheaper, now that. . . ." She stopped. Moonlight poured in the open stable window. They were leaning against fragrant bales of hay, and the moon reflected off the satin dress hanging from a hanger that Dinah had tied to a beam with a piece of string. His own clothes lay in a heap underneath the dress.

"Now that what?"

A firefly lit on Dinah's breast. They both watched the tiny insect trace the curve of her bosom with a faint point of blinking light, then drop to her belly and move lower.

"Scat!" Dinah flicked the firefly off her belly. It spread its wings and flew off, a cool, winking spark in the darkness.

"Now that what?" he repeated.

"Now that your sister has charmed Étienne. Maybe they'll let you have me cheaper."

This was news to him. After all, he himself had been charmed.

"I thought," he began nervously, "she was coming here to paint those—" It hadn't occurred to him that the young aristocrat could have fallen in love with a girl who was disgraced. Cyril only knew he'd expressed an interest in the designs she had burned into the shutters of their cabin with a red-hot nail, just as she'd done the hearts on Deborah's cradle. Because he was charmed himself, Cyril had thought nothing of it when colourful Moravian designs of hearts and flowers and doves and four-leaf clover suddenly began winding up the white columns

of the Ribordeaux mansion. Linda's imagination left something to be desired. In Moravia they would have laughed at her, but this was another country. Once she tried drawing a buffalo head among the hearts and doves and flowers, and it looked a lot like the Devil. Still, it was another country and it didn't matter.

"She comes here to set a trap for him with her abracadabra, so he'll never get away," said Dinah. "And she'll get rid of me once she knows. Oh, she'll mind, all right. She ain't no real Southern lady." She shrugged her tea-rose shoulder. "Even some real Southern ladies mind. Matter of fact, most of them do."

"I mind too."

"That's because you ain't no true Southern white massa."

"Why, I'm white as cheese!"

She laughed aloud. It was a simile from another world. "Cheese ain't white," she said. "I'm closer to cheese than you."

"You're the colour of a rose."

Dinah opened her hand and looked at her palm, then gave him a questioning glance.

"I mean a tea-rose," he said, kissing her breast. "And I'm jealous. I'm going to kill that one-legged son of a bitch."

"You better save up and buy me instead."

"All loved up by a cripple," he said bitterly.

"He's quitting," she said, "now that he's all wild over your sister."

"What do you mean, quitting?"

"Quitting loving me."

"What do you mean by that?"

"He really did love me, white boy, I wasn't just some nigger-girl he took to bed. The stories I could tell!"

"I don't want to hear them!" he snapped.

"Oh, you dear white boy of mine," she sighed. "Why not just look at it like I'm cheating on him with you. That should make you feel better right away. Or are men jealous of the husbands of the wives they're cheating with, back where you come from?"

"I don't know," said Cyril. "I never did it!"

"She's pretty foxy, your Dinah!" laughed the sergeant.

"Was," said Cyril bitterly. "And not foxy. She was wise. It really did help me. Oh, God!" He raised his head to look at the moon, which was just like a Texas moon. They were sitting on a hillside while the Ninth Iowa marched below them like a torchlight parade, their fire-brands soaked in turpentine resin. They were headed for Fayetteville.

• • •

"Well, you're doing it now," said Dinah. "I belong to him, and you've got me. You've got me and you never even paid for me."

"I have got you!" He grinned blissfully.

"Because I love you, and I only belong to him. Do you love me?"

"I do, Dinah."

"See what a fool nigger-woman I am? I believe you."

"You're not a fool nigger-woman. And I do love you."

"Come to Mammy!" She reached out for him, and he did.

Afterwards, she said, "Maybe you'll get me cheaper. High-yellow girls are cheaper."

"That's not true."

"Is too."

"Why?"

"And the cheapest of all are practically white. Like Pompey."

Pompey was a white shadow in the home of Monsieur de Ribordeaux. He polished silver and served meals wearing white gloves. He looked like a footman in the prince's château in Dvorec.

"But why?" he pressed.

"Because it's easier for them to run away. In town, nobody can tell they're niggers," she said, and Cyril suddenly grasped the logic of the market-place, if not of the ideology. "Unless they happen to know them," Dinah added.

And it rained. It poured and yet the forests went on burning. They were still in South Carolina. The engineers laid down a corduroy road, row upon row of logs in mud that could have stopped the caravan of wagons, that seven-mile snake with its tail still in Columbia. What he had seen just north of Columbia drowned out Cyril's reminiscences. Beneath them rolled the flaming river of the Eightieth Ohio with their turpentine torches, and it had been pouring rain, then as now. He had galloped along with Sherman's officers, who were cursing in their beards as they surged forward, then reined in their horses to keep pace with the general on his mount. Suddenly the general had halted, so abruptly that the sergeant had almost gone flying out of his saddle. The general had looked ahead through his field-glasses and cursed loudly. They had started off again across the soggy meadow to the plantation house in the middle of the garden. Then he had seen what the general had seen.

★

They were swinging from the massive lower branches of a mighty tree—
seven dead men in rags, puffy tongues lolling between heavy black lips. The
tallest had one leg chopped off at the knee. Blood mixed with rain trickled
thin and pink from the stump. It couldn't have happened long ago, or perhaps the rain had kept the blood from coagulating. No, the wound was
much too big. The huge dead man had a board hanging around his neck
and written on it in charcoal, only partly smeared by the rain, were the
words "HERE'S YOUR EMANCIPATION!" The white plantation house
looked haunted, its front door wide open in the rain. They approached cautiously, the sergeant with his Enfield at the ready, the lieutenant with his revolver drawn. In the spacious foyer there were portraits of gentlemen and
oddly unattractive beauties. On the floor lay a number of brutally beaten
Negroes, some dead, some unconscious. Under a painting of the Good
Samaritan performing his deed of mercy, a young Negro woman in a silk
chambermaid's dress sat on a chaise longue. Her face was large and sallow;
her widely set eyes had an oriental cast, a little like his Annie with her pretty
Tatar features, the sergeant thought. But the Negro girl's cheek had been cut
open with a whip, and blood stained her white apron. Her eyes were
terrified, still staring at things no longer there. She trembled and her teeth
were chattering. Lieutenant Williams went up to her; she saw his revolver
and started to scream. The lieutenant quickly holstered his gun and took
her by the shoulders.

"What happened here?" he asked.

She kept on screaming. An old man with frizzy white hair, wearing livery, sat up on the chaise longue. "It was Chisholm's cavalry, massa," he said.
"General Cheatham's division. I see young Massa Burdick. His daddy, old
man Burdick, he got a plantation five miles down the road."

"But what happened here?" Lieutenant Williams repeated, because he
knew something strange must have happened. Rebels did not destroy their
own property.

★

*"Maybe you'll buy me and not give me my freedom anyways," said Dinah,
pulling on her white corset. She turned her back to him and awkwardly he
started to lace her up.*

"You're right, I won't," he said. "I'll marry you instead."

"That'll be the day," she said.

"We'll move up north."

"You don't say."

He pulled the laces tight, and a lovely little gully formed between her breasts. "Ouch!" said Dinah. "You'll end up treating me like Auntie Bramwell's children treated her."

"Do I know them?"

"How could you?" she said, carefully removing her dress from the beam. "That was back in Louisiana. She had five—three boys and two girls. And she could embroider real nice, too. Miz Bramwell taught her that before she died."

She disappeared inside the dress and emerged at the neck. The moon split in two and settled in her eyes.

"And what about her children? What did they do?"

"Nothing," said Dinah. "But when Miz Bramwell died, old Massa Bramwell remarried with Miz Bourbon. They married for love, white boy. I only wish you loved me as much as old man Bramwell loved Miz Bourbon."

"I love you more!"

"You don't say!" Pearly teeth flashed a smile in the moonlight. "Well, they didn't have no children," said Dinah, "and old Massa Bramwell kind of lost interest in the estate. Actually he wasn't that old either. Before Miz Bramwell died they just had their tenth anniversary, and him only ten years older than her. Massa was forty. Well," said Dinah, "I have to go now, white boy. Will you buy me? Cross your heart?"

"Cross my heart! If they'll sell you. If not, I'll steal you!" said Cyril.

"I'll be for sale. You can bet your life."

"You'd better be!"

"You can bet on it," said Dinah. "Your sister will make sure of that."

The torchlight procession at the foot of the hill moved towards Fayetteville. Beyond it the turpentine forests were ablaze. Because it was night, they could see the flames inside the bursting grey mushroom clouds. The fires roared like a storm in the dense forests, and the low clouds lit from beneath looked like an inverted Niagara Falls, with pink and orange whirlwinds descending on a topsy-turvy world. If the sergeant had still believed in such things, it would have seemed like hell. But as hells go it was a splendid one, and anyway the sergeant no longer believed in the god of the priests. He believed in the general. Sherman had no particular love for the Negro, but with the fire in the turpentine forests he was reforging the broken Union, while the Union violently purged itself of the illogical logic that so perplexed Cyril, who was bewitched by a bewilderingly free spirit in a body worth eight hundred, maybe a thousand dollars. The fire and brimstone of this splendid hell were burning that logic out of an ugly world.

The sergeant remembered carrying a dispatch for General Slocum. Towards evening, just outside Winnsboro—a large village about forty miles north of Columbia—he had caught up with Sergeant Metcalfe's skirmishers, among them Stejskal with his long legs and a bright yellow silk patch on his back, Paidr, Shake, and Houska. They entered Winnsboro together, and found they'd been preceded by bummers, the drifters of Sherman's great army, who were already wandering the main street and throwing things at each other that looked like uncooked dumplings. Sacks of flour were scattered in the road. They had been sliced open and the flour was spilling out of them. On the corner in front of the Episcopalian church, a tattered man with a porcelain chamber-pot on his head was mixing dough in a wash-tub. The bummers, apparently deranged, were grabbing fistfuls of the dough, and flour was flying through the air. All around them houses burned like flaming Christmas trees, and from somewhere—not the church—came the sound of a pump organ.

"Looks to me like old Slocum liberated the local madmen instead of the local slaves," said Shake.

One bummer, covered from head to toe in flour, rolled up a big barrel of molasses. Right behind him was another with a vinegar barrel. The street ran downhill to the south. Soon a strange mixture was flowing downhill in a trough, and the bummers were floating hardtack biscuits down the stream like toy sailboats.

The organ was still playing. They arrived at the corner just as flames burst through the church roof. Three men came rushing around the corner carrying turpentine torches, and a chorus of military voices sang in unison with the organ:

> *Hurrah! Hurrah! we bring the Jubilee!*
> *Hurrah! Hurrah! the flag that makes you free!*
> *So we sang in chorus from Atlanta to the sea,*
> *While we were marching through Georgia.*

They finally saw the organ around the corner. It was out in the street, a short distance from the church, and on either side of it were carefully stacked pyramids of smoked hams doused in turpentine. A bummer put his torch to the one on the left and it burst into flames; then he ran over to the other side and set fire to the second pyramid. A small bummer sat at the organ with his back to them, playing. The chorus of soldiers, who looked like weather-beaten devils, sang facing the organ, the two in the middle supporting something that looked like a coffin standing on end. When they came closer, they found it was indeed a coffin, still damp from the graveyard behind the church. The bummers had dug it up and pried open the lid and had found a fresh corpse dressed in the brand-new uniform he'd been buried in. It was a Rebel captain, his face twisted in a grimace of death, his teeth bared at the sizzling hams. One eye had been incompletely closed and he looked as if he were winking mischievously. The smell of roasting ham filled the air, along with the roar of the fire inside the church. The organist kept hitting wrong notes, and the pedals creaked behind the diabolical chorus.

"Local madmen," said Shake. "Dangerous lunatics, I'd say."

"Didn't I tell you?" Zinkule chimed in. "He's sold his soul to the Devil!"

This time Houska didn't object. He was staring, flabbergasted, at the grimacing captain in the coffin. He rubbed his eyes with his fists.

"A smoked Apocalypse," Shake remarked.

"I told you so," said Zinkule darkly.

Yet the Devil is a mere servant of God, thought the sergeant. A helping hand when there's dirty work to be done.

"Stop!" he yelled, but the crazy singers went on singing, in soldiers' discordant harmony:

How the darkeys shouted
When they heard the joyful sound!
How the turkeys gobbled
Which the commissary found!
How the sweet potatoes even
Started from the ground,
While we were marching through Georgia.

"Stop it!" the sergeant yelled again. That brought Sergeant Metcalfe to his senses. He barked an order, the men shouldered arms. With a final wheeze the organ fell silent.

"What's the matter?" asked the organist.

"Break it up!" ordered Metcalfe.

Half an hour later, the main street was cleared of bummers. By then, of course, it was too late. As Zinkule and Paidr lowered the coffin back into its grave—after tying the lid back on with a piece of rope—the smell of burnt ham hung over the cemetery. Zinkule made the sign of the cross over the coffin and shovelled the dirt back over it with a village drudger's steadfastness. Though it was a long way down the road, the sergeant, when he looked back over his shoulder, could see the fires of Winnsboro dying down. He felt no regrets. Everything was possible in this war. Everything was at stake.

"*Just like Auntie Bramwell's ungrateful children,*" *Dinah said, as they walked out of the barn into the moonlight.*

"*But what did they do that was so awful?*"

"*They did the awfullest thing in the world. They didn't set her free.*"

"*And they could have?*"

"*That's just it,*" *said Dinah.* "*See, they used to hire Auntie out to do sewing for young plantation ladies even back when Miz Bramwell was still alive. And more after she died. Old Massa Bramwell let Auntie keep half of what she earned, sometimes even more when she asked real nice. So she saved her money. First she bought her oldest son, Bob, and freed him. He was a carpenter, and he took off north right away.*" *Suddenly Dinah jumped behind a bush and gestured for him to join her.*

The man with the wooden leg was limping out of the white manor-house. Cyril's sister was holding his arm. They strolled to the carriage shed. A groom stood waiting with a horse and buggy, which shone in the moonlight.

"*See? What did I tell you? Old Massa Ribordeaux is in Austin today,*" *whispered Dinah.* "*While I was cheating on the young massa with you, white boy, he was busy with your Linda.*"

Cyril was confused but he was beginning to understand, and it terrified him. His sister jumped up into the buggy and held out her arms to the man with the wooden leg, and helped him onto the seat beside her.

"*I don't want you to call me white boy,*" *whispered Cyril.*

"*Why not? You are my white boy.*"

"*What if I started calling you black girl?*"

"*You couldn't. I'm pale yellow.*"

"*I'm not white either. I'm darker than you are, after all this time in the Texas sun.*" *It was all Dinah could do not to burst out laughing.*

"*So Auntie Bramwell saved up to buy all of them their freedom?*"

"*Sure she did,*" *said Dinah.* "*After Bob took off, Tom followed him north, then Beulah, who knew how to embroider like Auntie did, then Clothie—she sang real pretty—and finally Jim. He didn't do nothing. But he was only fifteen. In fact,*" *she said,* "*he wasn't the least bit to blame. As soon as he got up north, they locked him up for getting into the chicken coop at the Methodist manse. They say he got ten years. So it wasn't his fault.*"

"*What do you mean, it wasn't his fault? He was a thief.*"

"*No, he wasn't,*" *Dinah shook her head.* "*He took from white folks, and that ain't stealing.*"

The buggy started down the road, the man with the wooden leg at the reins. Lida's lovely head glimmered like silver. She had made up her mind about some-

thing, but what was it? Was it this? It couldn't be love. After all, love had stayed behind in Moravia. Suddenly everything fell into place.

"But the rest of them—they could have done something," Dinah continued. "Tom and Bob, they started up a carpentry shop in Boston. Beulah got work with a fancy dressmaker in Philadelphia and Clothie married a minister in Buffalo. They say he sang better than he preached. They even say he used to get hired along with some other freed slaves to sing at white folks' weddings. What I mean is," sighed Dinah, "they done fine. And they forgot all about Auntie." The tiny moons in her eyes narrowed to silver slits. "Think of that, white boy!"

"Don't call me white boy!"

"Okay, brown boy. They started out saying they'd save up and buy her out together. But Bob and Tom, just as soon as they got a whiff of freedom, they went crazy over women—slave women, of course, two fancy little maids back in Massa Carruthers' house in Louisiana. Carruthers set their prices real high, so Auntie had to wait while the boys saved up for Phillippa and Brigitte. Next they had to save up for a nice house for Bob, and another one for Tom. Clothie started having babies and Beulah had left two back on Massa Bramwell's plantation, so they had to save up for them, too. Meantime things were going bad on the plantation because old Massa Bramwell didn't care about nothing but Miz Bourbon any more, and she didn't give two hoots for the property. The niggers in the cotton-fields lollygagged around, watching the clouds roll by, because when the meanest overseer, Mr. McDrummond, saw how everything was falling apart, he quit. The other two overseers was old and married like Massa Bramwell, and they started loafing around with the niggers. The crop was ruined, Massa Bramwell got deep in debt and come to his senses, left Miz Bourbon in the parlour and went out in the cotton-field where the overseers were down playing poker with the niggers."

A whip snapped in the moonlight; the carriage, a gold and silver blossom in the night, vanished around a bend in the road and rattled off towards where the Toupeliks' farmhouse stood, five miles away.

This tea-rose, thought Cyril, would be too refined a creature for his father, and his mother would probably call her "Miss" because Dinah looked like the countess from the château at Lhota, only prettier.

"What are you thinking about, white boy? You're not listening to me."

"I'm thinking about how we'll go north," he said. "I probably couldn't marry you here."

"Sure, go north," sighed Dinah. "Question is, can I believe you, or will you turn out like Auntie Bramwell's rotten children?" She scowled. "Except for Jim. He was behind bars, so he couldn't save up for nothing."

"May God strike me down if I'm like Auntie Bramwell's rotten children!"

"He will, too! Like He did to Bob and Tom—sneaky, ungrateful niggers."

"Did they lose their carpentry business?"

"They lost Phillippa and Brigitte. Soon as Bob and Tom bought them their freedom, the two girls ran off to Chicago. I hear they got work in some fancy house there, as whores or nannies, I ain't sure which."

"You're making this up, I bet," he said. "What happened to Beulah and Clothie?"

"Nothing, of course. In the South, the Good Lord is a gentleman. But Jim got his reward."

"Jim the thief?"

"I told you Jim never in his life stole nothing!" This time she seemed genuinely annoyed. "But he got his freedom too, like Phillippa and Brigitte. The jailer's ugly daughter fell in love with him and unlocked his cell door one night."

"Where do you get these stories?"

"I read the books that Missy de Ribordeaux left here when she married and left for Louisiana," said Dinah. "But Jim got away and ran all the way to Canada. He went way up north, where I hear there's niggers who milk whales. So he got work as a whale-herder."

"Now, I'm positive you got that from a book!"

"No, it just came into my head."

"Where did you learn to read?"

"When Missy de Ribordeaux was little, she didn't want to play with nobody but me. And she had a tutor, Mam'selle Seulac. Missy was a mite slow, so you had to repeat everything ten times over. All I had to do was listen."

"But this mam'selle must have been French, with a name like that?"

"Sure. The novels are in French too. I don't read English so well. Everything is spelled funny in English."

Cyril couldn't believe what he was hearing. "Let me touch you," he said.

"Why?"

He reached out and touched her. She was real—he hadn't dreamed her up. But nobody else knew about her. Just him.

★

"That's Brutus," said the old black man in livery. "When they put that sign around his neck, he kick young Massa Burdick, and the young massa haul out his sword and slice off his leg." He pointed a black finger at the stump, which was still dripping pink drops, like a water-clock measuring time on the cross. "Then they hang him."

"Was it all his own idea?" asked Lieutenant Williams.

"He always a bad nigger," said the old man. "He got this trick, colonel." The lieutenant did not correct him. "He throw his arm out of joint and put it in a sling and get off work. Bad nigger. He talk about Nat Turner sometime, too."

"What happened to your master? And his family?" asked Lieutenant Williams.

"Nothing, colonel. Brutus don't want to kill 'em. He say he don't need to, now that Massa Lincum give us freedom. He just tell the white massas the plantation belong to us now, and he drive 'em off it."

Lieutenant Williams glanced at Sherman. The general frowned and said nothing.

"I tell him it ain't ours," said the old man. "The only thing we is, is free, because Massa Lincum's soldiers come in and do the job. That's what they tell us, Gen'ral Kilpatrick's cavalry. Trouble is, they ride right off again. Cato join Brutus." He pointed to the corpse hanging next to the man with one leg, and then recited all the names like a litany: Caligula, Marcus, Aurelius, Cicero, Catiline, and the last one, with ebony skin and a horrifying postmortem erection, Hannibal. Their master had had a classical education.

"I do what I can," said the old man. "We only got freedom, and freedom ain't property. But Brutus, he don't want to hear this. We work till we bleed, he say. That's true—some do. But not him. He got this trick, and other tricks too. Never go to the fields much. He sweep and pick up, fix the gins, help out in the kitchen—"

A wave of hot wind blew in from the burning forests. The corpses began to turn slowly.

"Cut them down!" snapped the general. The little band of Negroes started taking the wretched corpses down one by one.

"So they drive them away," said the old man. "Brutus, he don't let them take the carriage, or the horses neither. They has to walk. They walk straight to the Burdick plantation. I knowed it," the old man sobbed. "I tell Brutus, but he don't listen. They each take a room in the big house, and Brutus take Claudia right into his—poor girl, he drive her crazy, I think." The old man turned to look at the girl. She was sitting on the steps now, moaning softly through clenched teeth. "Next morning, they back up with Chisholm's cavalry. Young Massa Burdick, he with them." The old man began to cry.

The Negroes carried off the dead bodies. General Sherman said, "Leave a guard here. Send a unit to the Burdick plantation."

The blistering wind from the turpentine forests chased clouds of black smoke in their direction. The general's horse reared and pivoted, and he galloped off towards the long blue line of his great army.

They forded a creek in which the water was almost boiling. The horses galloped across, scalding their hoofs. Gigantic cathedrals of fire roared against the sky. *"Mene, mene, tekel . . ."*

★

His beautiful Dinah said, "He never even yelled at them. He just told them, 'You're wallowing like hogs in the mud while the cotton's rotting, and you're going to get off your backsides and work till I'm out of debt or I'll sell you off to a rice plantation and move to New Orleans.' And that was that. He walked away, they all got scared. Big Wellington yelled, 'Get crackin'!' and he clapped his hands, his palms are five foot square—"

"Come on, yellow girl, you're making that up!"

"Inches, then. The only ones who never got crackin' were those two overseers. Nobody needed them. The niggers worked so hard you could see the steam rise off them. You know, brown boy, niggers on rice plantations die like flies. By the time Massa Bramwell passed on three years later, he wasn't even forty-five and he had the richest plantation in Louisiana."

"Fear is the best overseer," said Cyril.

"Maybe," said Dinah. "He also told them he'd give them their freedom in his will, because he had no children, but if they didn't work hard he'd change his will and sell them to the rice plantation, because he didn't mean to spend his old age begging."

"So what made them work? Fear, or the hope of freedom?" asked Cyril.

"Fear they wouldn't get their freedom," said Dinah. "And you know, white boy—or brown boy, or whatever you are—in the end, Auntie didn't have no use for her ungrateful children. When old Massa Bramwell died, she got her freedom like all the rest, and she used what was left of her savings and bought herself a train ticket to Canada. But she went all the way north to where the niggers milk whales, because that's where her good son was working, as a whale-herder. Auntie Bramwell spent the rest of her life nursemaiding whale puppies."

"Whales don't have puppies, yellow girl," said Cyril. "And if you say they do, I'll have to touch you again."

"They do," said Dinah.

★

Kapsa was trying to work up the resolve to take the final step. Had it not been for the eagle over the door, he would have long ago turned away and walked down

Broadway, where the casino was, to the Lower East Side, where he would have lost his way, died, vanished. But you can only vanish from the world, not from yourself. So he would have hanged himself there.

This eagle was different, but how or why he didn't yet know. Odd that his memory of that other eagle was already so vague after such a short time. The sign on the door to the little stone building said U.S. RECRUITING OFFICE, but he couldn't bring himself to walk through the door. If it hadn't been for the eagle and how different it was, he would have turned around, walked away, hanged himself. What else was there? The brickworks in Brooklyn? Why? For what?

"Yes, Touzimsky's still hiring, and he's only hiring Czechs. He has more orders than the brickworks can fill. They say he's expanding."

"But twenty-five cents a day? For a fourteen-hour day?"

"Well, I know it's not a lot. But the work is steady. Longshoremen make two or three times as much, but they never know if they'll have work the next day. Half the time, they don't."

"If he's doing so well, why doesn't he pay you better?"

"That's exactly why he's doing so well. He can sell his bricks cheaper than the competition, so he doesn't have to lay people off. And a place to sleep comes with the job, too."

He looked around the bunkhouse. There were eight men there at the moment. Some had already gone to bed. Along the front wall was a long military pallet for ten, but twelve slept on it. A colour print of George Washington hung askew over the pallet. Kapsa sat at the table with one of the twelve workers, a fellow called Zrubek. He could see through the open doorway to the brickworks. The stacks were belching smoke into the approaching night, and black shadows danced like devils around the bright squares of fire as kiln doors were opened and closed. There were several clay tumblers, a stoneware pitcher, and a candlestick on the table.

"Night shift pays forty cents," said Zrubek. He was covered with dust and looked as if he were made of brick, and so did the others. Brick dust is hard to wash off—if the men ever washed.

"Where's Salek?" asked Kapsa.

"He didn't like it here. He left the day before yesterday. Said he was heading for Chicago."

"You like it? Can you save any money?"

Zrubek shrugged, reached for the pitcher, and poured himself a tumbler of beer. The pitcher was nearly empty.

"We could if we didn't have to drink so much. It's hellish hot in the works now in summer but the work is steady. I can last for"—he hesitated—"a year or so, save up—"

"And then?"

Zrubek took a drink. "Then we'll see. Maybe get something better when I pick up a little more English. Cigar-making isn't bad, they say, but you need some money to start out with. Here, you know you got steady work and steady pay."

"Where are you going to pick up English in this place?"

Zrubek shrugged again. "I haven't even been here a year—"

"And how much do you know?"

"'Tzenk you'," said someone sitting on the bunk. "And 'beer pleeze'."

Devils danced around the open kiln doors. Why, he asked himself.

"Well, I wish you luck," Kapsa said, and rose. His mind was made up. In the course of the night and the long morning and afternoon previous, he had changed his mind several times, but by evening, standing outside the gates of that tolerable hell, he finally made up his mind.

"Goodbye."

Zrubek walked out of the bunkhouse with him. Kapsa could smell the ocean and feel the hot breath of the brickyard on his face. Zrubek glanced at the sky. The brickyard smoke blurred the stars.

"If you want to live, you've got to get born, and you mustn't die," said Zrubek.

Why? Exhausted in body and soul, he couldn't think it through. He could only wonder: why?

"Well, goodbye, neighbour."

He set out back to Manhattan.

On the ship, he and the butler's son, Eduard Frkac (he registered himself in the passenger list as Ed Fircut), had shared a cabin with two other tycoons, one a German, the other an Englishman by the name of James Smithie. It was a foolish extravagance but, like the hotel in Amsterdam and the bottle of cognac, he thought it was worth it. The hicks going to work in Touzimsky's brickyard travelled steerage. Even after paying for his cabin, he still had more than half of von Hanzlitschek's money left, and he carried the case with the diamonds under his shirt. He had no intention of giving that up, not now that Ursula was dead, as he knew she must be. With the passage of time, he realized how clumsy his attempt to cover up his crime had been. How could the man have been killed by striking his head on a moss-covered rock in the forest? What would von Hanzlitschek have been doing there anyway, so far from his usual haunts at the officers' casino or the promenade? And the maid must have been too terrified to remain silent. Ursula must be dead, even though she might still be technically alive in a jail cell somewhere.

At that time Eddie Fircut had some irrational, magical power over him. "In the hold? Think again, man! You can afford better, and it's an investment that will pay off a hundred times over. A cabin passenger is in an entirely different class from some stinking refugee in steerage. Besides"—by then they knew who would be sharing the cabin with them—"in these three or four weeks you'll pick up some English from the Englishman, and that makes it an even better investment."

He was right about that. Smithie was a garrulous, pompous man who never looked them in the eye. He felt superior to them, of course, yet he also felt flattered in his role as teacher. He was the son of a wholesale wine and whisky merchant and he'd brought several kegs of the latter along. The captain allowed him to keep it in the pantry in exchange for the privilege of free access. Smithie had a long journey ahead of him, for he was going to California to prospect for gold. He talked too much and was conceited, but he wasn't stingy.

The crossing was stormy and took six weeks instead of the usual four. Kapsa had English lessons every day and was quick to learn. By the time he reached New York, he was reasonably fluent. In the evenings he drank scotch to drive out the vision of the gallows that haunted him, waking or sleeping, and listened to Fircut and Smithie tell stories.

Fircut, who never actually drank, told tales of erotic conquests, and helped to take Kapsa's mind off the gallows. But one stormy night Smithie told a story that began as an English romance, about Evelyn, a woman he had loved and lost because he hadn't been her social equal. In an act of pure vengeance, he had helped her and her lover to the gallows. Fortified by Smithie's whisky, Kapsa didn't know whether to believe him or not. But the story horrified him, and revived all his old fears. He tossed back more whisky, hoping to punch a hole in his memory and let his fear for Ursula escape.

His only recollection of the rest of that night was a storm at sea, the cold wind of the North Atlantic, whitecaps reflecting flashes of lightning on their slick coal-black slopes, hands grabbing him in the air above the water. He was flying, but he never landed, merely tumbled into darkness.

When he awoke Fircut was standing over him, smoking a cigar in a holder. The next thing he knew, Kapsa was sitting at a table, eating something he couldn't identify, and Fircut was saying, "What's the problem, my friend? You have one foot in America, and Austrian imperial justice can't touch you there." He smirked and added, "Not unless somebody turns you in to the Austrian consul."

Kapsa broke out in a cold sweat. Could he have babbled something in his sleep? Did Fircut know about Ursula? Would he blackmail him? How could he know?

Fircut reassured him somewhat. "Even if they did, you could disappear," he said. "In America, nobody ever asks to see your papers. Change your name." He paused. "But you ought to hide this a bit better. If it weren't for me, it would be inside some shark's stomach by now, along with you."

He pulled the pouch from his pocket. Kapsa reached out to grab it, but Fircut handed it to him without a struggle. When he opened it, the nest of diamonds lay intact in the blue velvet. His terror began to fade.

"So you did your commander in, did you? Robbed him and rubbed him out? He caught you in the act, right? Scared of the gallows, are you? More than of the galleys?"

Kapsa gave a sigh of relief. Fircut was only guessing, and he wasn't about to put him straight.

He stared at the eagle over the entrance to the little stone building. It was holding a bundle of arrows in one claw, an olive branch in the other. It was so different from the eagle on von Hanzlitschek's cap, and on the banners that had fluttered over the conquered barricade that cannoneer Salek, as black as a demon, had destroyed with well-placed shots from Windischgraetz's heavy artillery. But Kapsa still couldn't make up his mind.

★

Rain, snow, hailstones. For three days the engineers worked on a pontoon bridge over the Pee Dee River between North and South Carolina, and Kakuska got another glimpse of little Kil in his night-shirt. This time it didn't fly up, but by now Kakuska knew what he knew; he just grinned to himself when the jealous Lieutenant Jamison wondered out loud what the Columbia beauty Kil had just bundled into a confiscated carriage saw in that dwarf with a monkey's forehead. Between wild forays into the countryside in pursuit of General Wade Hampton's scattered troops, Kil fed the beauty delicious meals cooked by his French chef. When she was satiated, he would close the tattered curtains on the carriage. Kakuska couldn't see inside, but he knew better than the rest what the homely general was using to charm his high-class whore.

They crossed the Pee Dee River and stirred things up. Hampton divided his Confederate cavalry into small units that rode through the countryside in the cold downpour, attacking, skirmishing, withdrawing, attacking again—something they'd become virtuosos at during the four years of warfare. Kil's veteran cavalry swarmed towards Fayetteville but they were harassed and impeded by a rash of attacks, and forced to counter-attack. At one point they had taken a prisoner, an unhorsed cavalryman who now trotted along tied behind the carriage with Kil's whore inside, a black driver in the driver's seat and, beside him, the French chef, smoking a Russian cigarette that some kindred spirit had taken from the prisoner, along with his riding boots, also imported from Russia—a gift from the tsar's army to the worthy Confederate cause. Now the prisoner was stumbling along in Irish boots of untanned leather, cursing Kil, the whore, and the chef.

Before they put him to work helping to push the carriage out of the mud, they learned from him that the main body of Wade Hampton's corps was behind them. Kil knew he now had a chance to surround Hampton, cut off his approach to Fayetteville, force him to battle, and then destroy him. He broke up his cavalry into three brigades and fanned them out across the countryside, with orders to secure all access roads to Fayetteville and, as soon as they made contact with Hampton's massive corps, to snap the fan shut like a trap. But Hampton either anticipated Kil's plan and changed direction, or got lost in the fog that set in after the rain and hail that evening when Kil's carriage and staff arrived in Solomon's Grove. The same fog veiled their camp, like blue-grey cotton wool soaked in twilight.

Kil had chosen Solomon's Grove because he only needed to post sentries at the west end of the village, since approaches to the east, south, and north were protected by swamps. But the swamps generated fog. The captive cavalryman took advantage of it, gnawed through the rope tying him to the carriage, and vanished into the mist, leaving behind the pair of bloody Irish boots. But then, the sergeant thought, half the Confederate army was used to fighting barefoot.

Kil established his headquarters and his bedroom (but mostly his bedroom) in a small stone cottage in the heart of the village, and the cavalrymen settled down in a circle around the house. They were expecting a peaceful though somewhat chilly and damp night, and for the first time in several days they undressed down to their underwear (if they had any). They wrapped themselves in horse blankets and were soon fast asleep.

Kakuska crawled into the empty carriage.

Night began to fall, a peaceful night with the swamps exhaling fog that rose to drown the Carolina stars, and the moon along with them.

The dawn came, scarcely worthy of the name. The light was dull and veiled in fog and the first illumination came from small fires started, with much coughing and farting, by men hungry for breakfast. Kakuska was still asleep. A small detail of sentries coming off duty emerged from the mist and quickly found places to sit around the barely flickering fires. Someone under the carriage sneezed and Kakuska awoke, still dreaming of Wisconsin and Bozenka's warm embrace. But when he looked out of the carriage, he saw Kil's bugler wetting his lips and raising his battered horn, and blowing not "Reveille" but "Attack". Kakuska jumped up but immediately fell back into the velvet cushions as the bugle call was answered by a terrible din. It was as though the gates of hell had opened: the Rebel war yell. He groped for his rifle.

Horses tore through the fog from the south and west. Swords flashed, pistols cracked, and the air was filled with bloodcurdling shouts. Out of the house, where moments ago, Kakuska knew (with some envy), his commander had been tupping his whore, flew a familiar figure clad in a night-shirt. The figure raced towards the tethered horses, which were whinnying and straining at their ropes, as riders raced through the camp. Three Rebel horsemen stopped the figure, shouted something at it, and then galloped off. The night-shirt swung onto a horse and rode north towards the swamps.

It was only after the fray that Kakuska learned of the foolish mistake Wheeler's horsemen had made after wading through an apparently impassable swamp. They must have taken the man in the night-shirt for a villager; the fog probably obscured Kil's face with its characteristic nose. "Where's General Kilpatrick spending the night?" one of the three riders had yelled at the general. "That way!" Kil had shouted, "less than half a mile from here!" Then he had leapt on his horse and ridden off to hide in the swamp.

From his vantage-point in the carriage, Kakuska could see Wheeler's horsemen plunging this way and that way through the fog. By the light of the fires, men dressed only in drawers crawled out of their blankets, some of them holding their hands over their heads. The main cluster of riders galloped through the camp, then turned and galloped back. Behind them ran the Rebel prisoners they had freed. Meanwhile, a few of the men in drawers had come to their senses and picked up their weapons, and bullets whistled through the foggy dawn. Another night-shirt emerged from the stone house. This one was silk, and in it Kil's woman ran through the rain of bullets to the carriage. Perhaps she thought she could drive to safety, but when she saw that the horses were unhitched she turned and started back, halting when a group of Rebels galloped past, firing as they rode. A Rebel officer leapt off his horse and dragged the girl to safety in a ditch, then ran back to his horse, but as he was riding off he suddenly threw up his hands, toppled off his mount, and lay on the ground. Another clutch of riders, rifles blazing, came galloping in from the opposite direction. Kakuska raised his repeater to his shoulder and knocked two of the riders off their horses with three shots in rapid succession. He noticed a blonde head peeking cautiously out of the ditch. Curiosity, he thought to himself, but then he had to turn his attention to more Rebel horsemen riding in from the south. For the next while, he and his rifle were fully occupied and he forgot about the girl.

The fog grew thicker with gunsmoke. Wheeler's cavalry was still charging through the encampment like demons. Despite the fog, however, Kakuska and many of his comrades, who were now fully awake, could see that there weren't as many riders as the noise had suggested. They also saw that the Rebels were armed with single-shot carbines that were hard to reload on a moving horse. Kakuska, concealed in the carriage, fired away as if he were in a shooting gallery. The sun, now higher in the sky, burned off the last wisps of fog. Suddenly, from the west, another bugle sounded the attack.

Around the campfire at Bentonville, Kapsa picked up the story from there, because he had been riding behind the bugler and little Kil, now in his coat with the night-shirt still showing beneath it. They arrived after it was all over, when the repeaters had already done their work. The sergeant saw men dressed in their underwear advancing south towards the swamps. A few had put on their clothes by now, while others were just pulling on their trousers. As the sergeant stepped over a corpse, he glimpsed a general's stars in the firelight. Moving aside to make way for a small herd of stampeding horses—one of them still dragging a dead rider with his foot caught in a stirrup—they continued south, then took cover because bullets were swarming out of the swamp. A line of grey uniforms advanced towards them but the repeaters toppled them like playing-cards, and when they fell the swamp swallowed them up. The sergeant heard someone shout, "This ain't fair!" He saw the man stand up, drop his carbine, and dive into the swamp; an instant before it swallowed him, the back of his head blossomed red and disappeared. The repeating rifles kept firing away, and before long a bloody mass of Wheeler's riders lay piled up on the edge of the swamp. There were no more Rebel yells, only moaning.

Kakuska jumped out of the carriage. He saw the girl climb out of the ditch and run towards the stone house, her nightgown clinging to her body. The gunfire fell silent, and he could even hear some indecent remarks directed at the fleeing little whore; the survivors had regained their composure. Then, in an ankle-length coat with his night-shirt showing at the hem like a fancy petticoat, Kil strode in from the swamp.

They counted a hundred and thirty dead Rebels, sixty of them in the bloody cluster at the edge of the swamp. There was no telling how many the marsh had swallowed up. Retreating to the west, the horsemen of Humes's brigade drove a hundred and three of Kil's riders ahead of them into captivity. General Humes himself lay in front of the stone house with a bullet in his head. They found two other dead Confederate generals, Hannon and

Hagan, and when they counted the fallen officers they realized that the Rebel brigade must have withdrawn without its commanders.

"The Battle of Kil's Night-shirt"—which was how the infantry late-comers christened the encounter, and how it entered history—was not a strategic success for the North. It opened the way of retreat to Fayetteville for General Wade Hampton and the fan did not snap shut as planned. Hampton repositioned his forces, waited for Sherman's army in Fayetteville, and finally withdrew to Bentonville.

The rain, snow, and hail were soon overtaken by the fire in the turpentine forests.

★

The torchlight parade at the foot of the hill as Sherman's army advanced on Bentonville; the fragrance of turpentine resin; the forest on the horizon in glorious flames.

"It wasn't easy for me," said Cyril. "There was nothing like it at home. What did we know!" He sighed. "Life was regimented. Getting a girl from one of the big farms was out of the question. Look how Lida ended up. But here?"

The clanking of tin cups tied to knapsacks. From the north-east, where the torchlight parade became a thin golden line, came the sound of singing:

"Sherman's dashing Yankee boys will never reach the coast!"
So the handsome rebels said, and 'twas a handsome boast.
Had they not forgot, alas, to reckon with the host
While we were marching through Georgia. . . .

"It's different here," came Cyril's voice out of the dusk and the tang of turpentine. "I mean, nothing is fixed. There are no rules. Things are exactly the opposite for Lida and me. What she ran into at home, I didn't run into till I got here. But there are no rules about that either. Not really."

"Maybe," said the sergeant, remembering how their old homeland had been a land of iron certainties. Here there were no guide-posts. But most of those old certainties—all of them, maybe—hadn't been worth a damn. Here there was no framework, nothing. Everything was an unknown. Yet almost everything—maybe everything—had some value. It was a game of chance.

"So you weren't really in love with Rosemary?"

"Now I know I wasn't," said Cyril. "And that's the strange part. Now I'm fonder of her than I ever was then. But"—Cyril leaned his head on his hands—"the Devil only knows!"

The buggy rattled down the road towards Austin. The cotton-field sun was blazing, the air was silent. Rosemary was at the reins. The horses had coloured ribbons tied to their harnesses, the way they used to do it at Mika's around fair-time. His little sister had embroidered the ribbons a month before, as a birthday present for Rosemary; the Austin district was starting to look more and more like Moravia. Rosemary liked the beribboned fillies. They spoke to her of a land where a harness was inevitable, so to lighten its load they decorated it. In Texas everything was plain, and only the horses were harnessed. And the Negroes, of course. In the fragrant stillness of the bougainvilleas, Rosemary had placed a warm hand on his, and he had turned to her, gazed at her equine beauty, then kissed her.

Now, silence and the rattle of the buggy.

"What are you thinking about?" asked Rosemary.

"About Negroes," he lied. He was thinking about how nothing at home had prepared him for this. For the affections of a farm girl. A girl from a big estate. But he wasn't a boy from a small holding any more. Besides, it wasn't love. Love was when—Rosemary was cheerful, voluptuous, certainly no delicate flower. A pretty little filly in a beautiful red dress. An only daughter. He was a partner in an oil manufacturing company, and then suddenly all the beauties of the black and white world had overwhelmed him.

"Negroes?" asked Rosemary. She was as pretty as a filly and no delicate flower, but—

"Last night your father and I were talking about them, Rosemary."

They had been standing behind the oil-pressing shed on the hilltop, with a view of the rolling Texas countryside, fields of cotton, a sea of conifers, clusters of cactus, the white shirts of Mr. Carson's Negroes, and the music of their song:

When Israel was in Egypt land
—the bass voice of Goliath, and then the chorus:

Let my people go . . .

"Beautiful, isn't it?" Cyril heard Mr. Carson say, and he felt the music pulling him in. These were songs he had always liked, but now that something had happened to him that had never happened before, the music made him feel like crying. A tear ran down his cheek and he wiped it away with his finger.

"Instrumentum vocale," he heard Mr. Carson say. "I studied Roman Law at Cambridge. The Romans called tools, ploughs, wagons, instrumentum mutum—*mute tools. Horses, cattle, sheep, and mules were* instrumentum semivocale. Servi—*or slaves—were* instrumentum vocale." *Mr. Carson stopped and listened to the singing again, the bronze voice:*

Oppressed so hard they could not stand
and the chorus:
Let my people go!
"But," *Mr. Carson said,* "if something is vocale, *can it still be an* instru-mentum?"

Go down Moses, way down in Egypt land,
Tell old Pharaoh,
Let my people go!

"Is that why you're so good to them?" asked Cyril.

"I'm not good to them at all," said Mr. Carson. "Come with me."

They walked down the path to the cotton-fields. Soon they were strolling beside a line of cotton-pickers. Were the black faces he saw happy? They didn't look miserable. At the end of the line, a tall young man was working beside a big girl with a nice little protruding behind like his own Dinah's.

He shook his head. "You're good to them!" He had been present when the tall youth had pleaded with Mr. Carson and Carson had complied at once. The bride had cost him six hundred dollars, and he had already had more Negroes than he needed.

"No, I'm not. If I were, I'd set them free. Someday I will, but not now." He took Cyril by the arm. "There's going to be a war, son."

"Do you think so?"

"What else?" said Mr. Carson. "I got to know those people in Louisiana. They're stubborn as mules. If they don't get their own way, they'll split the Union. And then there's going to be a war. And these people"—he waved his hand to indicate his Negroes at work in the fields—"in the meantime will be better off, or at least have some security, if they stay with me."

"But if there is a war, what if they"—he realized that he referred to most of his new compatriots, the Southern whites, as "they", just as Mr. Carson, who was British, did—"what if they defeat the Yankees?"

Mr. Carson smiled. "That will hardly happen, son. All they have is cotton. The Yankees have factories, and you can manufacture weapons in factories. But even that's not as important," he said, "as the fact that the secessionists wring the Bible like a piece of laundry to get a drop of truth they can stomach out of it. And what they get isn't even truth, it's self-delusion. The real truth lies with the North, and when all is said and done, that's more important than factories when it comes to winning. What I mean to say"—Mr. Carson picked the blossom of a cotton plant and stuck it in his buttonhole—"is that, without the factories, truth would be rather academic. The important thing is that the self-delusion of the South doesn't have any factories behind it."

"And you think the Yankees care enough about these people"—pointing at the fields of cotton—*"to go to war?"*

"They won't go to war over the Negroes," Mr. Carson said. *"But people don't have to know the truth to be on the side of truth."*

"Now I know what Mr. Carson meant by that," said Cyril, pointing to the long line of Sherman's great army moving on Bentonville. "He was a wise man. He could see things others couldn't. I still feel ashamed today when I think about it."

"Can a fellow help what he does?" asked the sergeant, and Ursula's face flashed in his memory as if illuminated by the torchlight of Sherman's great army. By now he knew she was still alive.

"Maybe you have to consider other people. Particularly when they mean as much as Dinah meant—" He stopped, and in the half-light the sergeant noticed a trickle of moisture in the stubble of Cyril's beard. "I wonder what became of her? They say she went to Jamaica. I don't even know where that is."

"You'll find out, don't worry. The war's almost over."

Sherman's great army was advancing north-west. In the distance, not far away, lay Washington.

"That's one of the stupidest passages in the Bible," said Cyril. "About love not seeking its own. It does seek its own," he said. "It isn't patient. It does behave itself in unseemly ways, and maybe it even thinketh evil."

She was no longer a faded picture in a locket tucked away in Kapsa's knapsack. After all those years she had risen from the dead, and the thought of her still hurt.

Burning snow was falling around them and Madam Sosniowski said, "Ursula? Of course I knew her. When her husband died, she married Baron Hofburg-Ebbe. A diplomat. I think, though I'm not certain, that he's a consul somewhere in the North."

"The North?" he breathed. *"What do you mean, the North?"*

"In the Union," said Madam Sosniowski. *"In New York. Or was it Chicago? I'm not certain. Somewhere."*

Burning snow was falling on Columbia.

"Heaven knows how the Bible means it," said Cyril. "But the Bible is right in one thing; what am I without love? Nothing. But I do think evil. If she weren't my sister, I could throttle Lida. She'll be punished, though. God will punish her."

"He already has," said the sergeant. "She didn't get Vitek."

Cyril looked up. "Vitek?" He thought for a moment. "Unless, in His wisdom—but you don't believe in God, do you?"

"In the priests' god? No."

"What could He have punished her for back then? She hadn't done anything yet. Not till she got here."

The Negroes were singing as they worked. A cheerful song of despair.

"It is not entirely out of the question," said Mr. Carson, "that I am simply rationalizing an evil practice, just as my colleagues do—if they even think about it. Deep in my heart, son, I may indeed have become a slave-driver."

"No, you haven't," said Cyril.

"I am afraid I have," said Mr. Carson. "Sometimes I catch myself thinking about them as if they were my children. Children! That's what they call them!"

"That's different and you know it is. The slave-drivers think of them as children who will never grow up, and you know that they eventually will."

Mr. Carson squeezed his arm. "I don't like all of them," he laughed. "Take Amanda. She's been pregnant now for—how long?—twelve months. She hasn't worked in the fields since last harvest." He laughed some more. "She must take me for a fool."

"She takes you for what you are," said Cyril.

"And she's actually mistaken," said Mr. Carson. "Deep in my heart, if I weren't a slave-driver I'd have set them free as soon as old Whigham"—he paused to listen as a bronze-toned voice sang:

Ezekiel saw a wheel a'rollin'
Way up in the middle of the air,
A wheel within a wheel a'rollin'. . . .

They walked in silence towards the Carson house. It was silent and inviting against the azure sky of north Texas.

"As soon as old Whigham what?" Cyril asked.

Mr. Carson stopped. "Where do you think all this comes from?" With a sweep of his arm he indicated the house, the barns, the fields of cotton.

"You inherited it," said Cyril.

"But originally where did it come from?"

"Your—" Cyril hesitated.

"Great-uncle."

"Your great-uncle came to America and made his fortune like a lot of others," said Cyril. "My dad is a rich man too, compared to what he was in Lhota; he's a property owner. That's the kind of place America is. And your great-uncle's son had no children so he left his plantation in Louisiana to you—"

Mr. Carson interrupted him. "That's it. Old Whigham was my great-uncle's American partner. He made his fortune too, but he didn't invest it in land and slaves, he put it into tobacco. My great-uncle bought a plantation. But you know how those two characters originally made their fortunes?"

Cyril shook his head but he could guess. He hoped they might have been pirates, or might have robbed a bank in London and escaped across the sea. Anything but what he already knew they'd done—

"They owned a ship that carried cargo from Africa to New Orleans. Almost two-thirds of the cargo got spoiled on each trip, so they had to throw it overboard. But the one-third that was left was enough to make their fortune. Two fortunes. Their cargo, son, was instrumentum vocale."

"So you're not thinking about me?" the girl in the red dress asked softly.

"I am," he said, and in fact he was, for he was thinking about how to end their relationship, though he didn't put it that way to himself. He finished telling her about his conversation with her father, but he knew she wasn't interested. Not that she was insensitive, but love seeketh its own. He couldn't think of anything else to talk about. The buggy rattled on. In Austin they bought candles, salt, sugar, vinegar, thread—everything on Mrs. Carson's list. They didn't speak. Rosemary gave the order to the shopkeeper for three pounds of salt, and he felt shame, the worm of bad conscience. But he knew what he had to do. There was nothing else to be done—

As they walked back to the buggy, they passed a shop that sold flowers.

"Wait a minute, Rosemary."

He returned with a nondescript bouquet.

The buggy rattled off towards the darkening sky. They were still silent. The horses tossed their heads, the gaily coloured ribbons fluttered sadly in the cooling evening breeze. He stared at her tanned arm, the hand holding the reins, the shapely bosom under the bright red fabric, the pretty face, the breeze tossing the fringe of hair on her forehead. When they pulled up at the house, he leapt down and reached out his hand to help her. She didn't need it but she took it, jumped down, and the lace on her petticoat flashed white. Then she reached up to the seat for the flowers. She had tears in her eyes. He wished he could turn to stone. She handed him the bouquet.

"Cyril," she said, "I don't know who she is, but give these to her."

And she walked away towards the white house, straight as a candle in her bright red dress.

"Love," said Cyril. "Is there any escape from it? Does anyone ever find true love?"

Ursula.

Who ever found true love?

"But from what you said, Étienne—"

"He too. He too lost everything," said Cyril.

They could hear the sound of a band coming from the foot of the hill. Saxhorns, trumpets, bass horns. The disparity of a world where everything existed simultaneously. Blazing turpentine forests. Annie, who obediently didn't wait. Ursula. The general—his beloved general and his great army. It was transformed into truth, with truth's repeating rifles. Dinah. Lincoln in Washington, which they were getting nearer to every day. All of it, it all belonged together.

A rose in a crown of thorns, and, on the thorns, impaled little beetles foolishly waving their legs in the air.

Shake said, "I signed up even before there was an army."

"There was always an army," said the sergeant.

"I don't mean you. You're a professional soldier. I mean the ones who signed up after Lincoln's appeal, like Franta Stejskal. The only reason Joska Paidr's here is because, when they called him up, he didn't have the money for a substitute."

"You're wrong!" Paidr objected. "I could have found the money. I was doing my duty."

"Then why didn't you sign up after Lincoln's appeal?" asked Houska.

"No one had a duty to join then," said Shake, "so Paidr wouldn't have been doing his duty. I signed up back in the fall of '60, with Lincoln's famous Slavonic Rifles in Chicago."

"I know them," said Kakuska. "They weren't all that famous."

"But they could have been. In any case," said Shake, "they were one of the first militias."

"There wasn't a war in the fall of '60," said Kakuska. "It was easy to sign up then. Any spineless fool can play soldier in peacetime."

"And what do you think I'm doing here?" asked Shake. "Playing soldier?"

"Weren't your famous Lincoln's Slavonic Rifles founded by some valet?" asked Kakuska. "Some Hungarian?"

"He was a Slovak," said Shake. "That's like a Czech, and vice versa. Mihalotzy. He was about as Hungarian as Tonda Pokorny of the Eighth New York or Honza Fiala of the Seventh. Or as much as you're an Austrian, Kakuska. His real name was Mihalik, probably. They made him a Hungarian when he joined the army."

"They'd have made him into a Mitchell, not a Mihalotzy," said Kakuska.

"I mean the Hungarian army. Geza Mihalotzy. He was mixed up in the trouble in '49. That's why he had to hightail it to America."

"And take a job as a valet? Here?"

"What did you do when you came here, stupid?" asked Paidr.

"Same thing I did at home," said Kakuska. "Worked like a dog."

Kapsa knew that Kakuska had been brought to the States when he was twelve. His dad had worked like a dog back home and had worked just as hard here. In Kapsa's mind, his buddy Kakuska was part of a cluster of memories—not all of them pleasant—of the time when he'd travelled to Chicago from his garrison in Ohio, after getting a letter signed "Andrew Cup".

The first thing he looked at was the signature, because he never got letters. A postscript explained the name: "alias Ondrej Salek, I changed my name to what it means in English, since all my customers are American anyway, so now I'm Andrew Cup; at least it doesn't bring Austria to mind, and everything I suffered there."

In his mind's eye, Kapsa recalled a black-smudged beanpole holding a ramrod in the smoke of Windischgraetz's cannon as they pounded the barricades to smithereens. And then he remembered that Sunday afternoon in New York City, on Broadway, when Mrs. McCormick, Fircut's landlady, said, "That spalpeen! Where is he?"

"I don't know," Kapsa said. "We were supposed to meet last night at the Bohemian Casino and he never showed up. I thought I'd find him here."

"Did he rob you blind too?" the old Irishwoman snapped. The question made his heart sink. He had almost convinced himself that Fircut was honest, and hadn't shown up because he was ill.

"Daylight robbery it was. He walked away with the silver crucifix my dear late husband brought over from Kilkenny and treasured till the day he died. Never sold it even when we was deep in debt. May the Good Lord punish him! Would you take a look at this?" She led him into the parlour and pointed at a chest with metal reinforcements. A hole had been freshly chopped in its side. "This is what he was doing yesterday afternoon while I was at mass. He knew I was away at church every Saturday afternoon. Two hundred dollars in cash and the crucifix he took. What's he stolen from you?"

"Nothing," he lied, and felt all his hope vanish. He knew that he and Tuma had waited in vain at the casino. "He just borrowed a few dollars," he added, so the Irishwoman wouldn't feel so bad. He stumbled out into the street, not caring where he went or how, and on the corner of Third Avenue and Twentieth Street he ran into Salek.

"Good to see you, Honza!" Salek said. "They say there's a Czech tavern

around here some place, the Bohemian Casino. Ever heard of it?"

"Why would you want to go there?" He was rather abrupt with Salek. Suddenly everyone in the world seemed suspicious.

"I'm sick of all this American grub, and they say they cook our kind of food there. If I don't get some good plain Czech food soon, I'll starve to death!"

He went back to the beginning of the letter: "Frkac told me you might have joined up. So I thought to write you that if you ever find your way to Chicago, you're always welcome. I have a grocery store at the corner of Clinton and Randolph and, besides, me and a fellow named Franta Rehacek have opened a bakery. I got married, too, but take it from me, never marry a widow. I'll tell you all about it if you ever happen to find yourself in Chicago, there's lots to tell but I'm not much for letters."

So Fircut was in Chicago; it was half a day by train from Carlington barracks. He put in for some furlough. The letter had been following him around for six months—it was simply addressed to him "Care of the U. S. Army"—but the army mail was reliable; slow but reliable. The army was small then, too, with barely eighteen thousand men. Supposing Fircut had done his dirty work in Chicago and then disappeared again? But this was a clue he couldn't ignore. He realized he had no proof that Fircut had done anything wrong. Maybe he'd just give him a good thrashing; he was back in shape now. Maybe. But more likely just look him in his sneaky butler's face, catch his shifty butler's eye, and say, "Frkac, you're a real spalpeen!" He had to go to Chicago.

"Yes," he had said in New York City to Ondrej Salek—later Andrew Cup—"down this street a bit and you'll see it on the corner. They have a Czech lion on the sign, but the sign is in English. 'Bohemian Casino'."

"And do they have Czech food?"

"They sure do."

"Then let's go," said Ondra.

He shook his head. "I've just come from there," he lied. They stood and talked a little while longer.

"Are you working?"

"Not just now," Kapsa said.

"Well, if worst comes to worst, they're still hiring at the brickworks. But I wouldn't unless it does come to the worst," said Salek. "Touzimsky's a slave-driver. Maybe I'll go to the harbour, sign on with the longshoremen. But I'm not staying at the brickyard much longer. So—only if worst comes to worst, Honza." Off he went, in search of real Czech home cooking. Kapsa started walking, but he didn't know where he was going. It was Sunday afternoon in Manhattan and he was all alone. It took him a while to pull himself together. A week? Two? He'd *lost track. He was looking for Fircut, although he didn't really care any more. He stopped in at the Casino every day, but Tuma just shook his head. Soon he realized that it was foolish to expect Fircut to show up. The hole in Mother Mc-Cormick's wooden chest spoke for itself. Still, he kept wandering the streets from tavern to tavern, from one side of town to the other, and once he passed a one-storey stone building with an American eagle over the door. At first he put the idea out of his mind, for he still thought of the army as a black Austrian hell. Then one morning he woke up in a flophouse in the Bowery with only a few cents in his pocket. It was a maddeningly sunny morning, the city was humming. He realized that it must be his destiny. He got up and walked slowly through the busy streets to the building with the eagle. It was different from the Austrian eagle, although it too had talons and a sharp hooked beak. It felt like destiny. Home? He had no home. He had lost it far away a few years back, in the narrow streets of Helldorf, in the gauntlet and the bloody bench and Ursula, who was certainly dead, and must have died an awful death. And in the storms of the North Atlantic. He hesitated one more time. Should he try the brickyard? Was this the worst it could get? He returned to the shelter of the eagle's wings, and a week later he was in uniform.*

The grocery store on the corner of Clinton and Randolph had large windows made of smaller panes of glass in shiny red frames. Outside the store there were sacks of potatoes, onions, beans, and flour under a wooden awning supported by red poles. A long sign that said in yellow letters: "ANDREW CUP—Vegetables, Fruits, Groceries" was affixed to the awning. Inside, the counters were stacked with produce from Iowa vegetable gardens, along with bunches of bananas and pyramids of oranges. A tall man wearing a black suit with a canary-yellow vest and a massive, glittering loop of chain that ended in his watch pocket walked through the strings of coloured beads that curtained the doorway. Salek, now known as Cup, was wider and bulkier than he had been, with a moustache that extended across his face and vanished into thick black hair hidden under a yellow hat. Holding his arm was a woman dressed in lace. As the two of them emerged into the sunlight, she opened a parasol. It cast a shadow on her face, and from that shadow peered a pair of curious eyes. That was when Salek saw him.

"Honza! Wonderful to see you!"

He saluted. "Sergeant Kapsa, at your service." The woman held out a small hand in a mesh glove, and he saw a familiar invitation in her grey eyes. He could guess what Cup's "lots to be told" would be about.

They bounced along the streets of the big city, the woman inside the carriage, Kapsa up beside Salek in the driver's seat, where he listened to the grocer's success story interspersed with commentary on the sights. For the moment, he put all thought of Fircut aside. They were approaching the outskirts of the city; the buildings thinned out and the street, which was still under construction, suddenly ended in a dirt road with houses scattered along it. On their right was a lake so enormous it could have been the sea, with blue water stretching to the horizon. Salek finished his success story and began talking about the Kakuskas, who were holding the christening of baby Anna, old Bartolomej Kakuska's newborn daughter. They turned into a driveway leading to a small white frame house surrounded by beds of red and white carnations. Over the door was a sign that said THERESA KAKUSKA, MIDWIFE. They pulled up in front of the house.

"They're doing well now," said Cup-Salek. "But that's mainly her doing. Old man Kakuska's a hard worker but he's got no ambition. Been working in Calwell's frame factory for ten years now, and he finally made foreman. But she brings in most of the money. She's the first Czech midwife in Chicago. She has plenty of American customers too, and she managed to stake their oldest son, Jakub, to some property in Wisconsin. This is his second year farming. He'll be here for the christening."

The house was long and narrow and had obviously been built in stages—the embodiment of American progress. The front section was actually nothing more than a wooden shack. Behind that was a section built of bricks with a veranda facing west.

In the shack section stood the housewife, midwife, and mother of the baby, who now lay sound asleep wrapped in a white binding quilt edged with pale blue lacing. Around her stood other members of the family: the grizzled and bony father, Bartolomej; the attractive daughter Molly in a calico dress, beside a rather slick-looking young man who turned out to be her fiancé, Franta Kouba; the younger son, Vavrinec (now known as Larry), who had just finished his apprenticeship as a gunsmith; and the novice farmer, Jakub, who had indeed come all the way from Manitowoc, Wisconsin, for his baby sister's christening. The occasion was special because, as Tereza declared with a solemn gesture towards the infant, "This is our first little American!" There had been an earlier American-born baby, Matej, but he had survived only two days.

Jakub showed Kapsa and Salek through the house. "Dad and I hammered this front section together first, every evening for a week, but it was on Sixth Street then. It had no floor, it just sat on the ground like a doghouse or a shed. But it was home, a roof over our heads. We were happy, but happiness—well, it never lasts long."

"We arrived in Chicago completely beggared," Kakuska said. "All I had left was a silver half-dollar and a two-dollar bill I hid in my clothes. We'd been three

months on the ocean, hungry and thirsty most of the time, but the thirst, my friend, was the worst. And then, wouldn't you know it, just as we docked in New York, some people on the boat broke out in a rash and a bunch of them died— and the boat was put in quarantine. For ten days. Some poor wretches breathed their last looking out at America, at Manhattan. We survived, praise God. But the shipping company had to pay our room and board for the extra days. We had no money left, except for what I'd hidden in my clothes, and I wasn't going to part with that for anything. We had train tickets paid all the way to Chicago, and we needed the money for those first days there. They accepted our feather beds as security, but we were real greenhorns and of course we never saw the feather beds again, and all we got in exchange for them was one salt fish a day and a slice of bread each."

At first they slept in a dormitory that a philanthropist had built for Czech immigrants—a single large room, a stove for cooking in the centre, broad bunks along the walls for eating, sitting, and sleeping. They shared it with six other immigrant families, but at least they had a roof over their heads.

"We'll be grateful to that kind man till the day we die," said Tereza. "Next day Father went to the docks and got a job unloading the ships. It was hard work. I didn't have the connections to practise midwifery yet, and besides, I was carrying Matej at the time. Father didn't make much, but we saved enough for lumber and Father and Jakub put up this shack. They built it on the prairie, not far from the dormitory. But we were happy. We were in America, and we knew this was only the beginning."

One afternoon, someone came pounding on the door. Tereza, eight months along, opened the door, and there were two men dressed in knickerbockers and tweed caps.

"We'd like to talk to Bartholomew Kakuska," said one of them in an official-sounding voice. Tereza was frightened by the tone and put her hand on her stomach.

"Not home. Is working," she said.

"What—time—will—he—come—home?" said one of the men. He looked disdainfully around the single room until he saw a printed picture of George Washington carefully nailed to the wall under a crucifix they had brought from home with a painted metal Christ on it. The contemptuous expression faded. Molly, who was fifteen, walked in from the vegetable garden, where she had been hoeing.

"Molly, tell them Father won't be home till dark. I hope he's not in trouble of any kind," Tereza said, in Czech.

"My father comes home after sunset," said Molly.

The men asked if they could wait and Molly invited them in. By the time Kakuska and Jakub returned from the dock after sunset, the women knew all about the two men.

One of them, an engineer called Schroeder, was a Bavarian, a forty-eighter, who after the defeat of that revolution left for America along with Fritz Sigel, who had commanded the rebel force and whose neck was on the line. Schroeder was now a surveyor for the City of Chicago. The other man was Schroeder's assistant, a Yankee called Trevellyan. They had come to tell Bartolomej Kakuska that his dwelling was standing right in the middle of what was to become Sixth Street, along which the future metropolis of Chicago would expand westwards, and that he had three days to remove it from the road allowance.

Nothing lasts for ever. Schroeder talked Kakuska out of his first idea—to ask the authorities to run the street elsewhere (Kakuska valued his home so highly, or else his notion of American democracy was so preposterous, that his idea didn't seem outlandish to him)—and then Tereza talked him out of his second—to ask that they widen the street and leave his house as an island in a river of traffic. She couldn't imagine stagecoaches and carriages, carts and buggies flowing past her door, drowning them in constant racket. Bartolomej Kakuska decided with a heavy heart to take the building apart and reassemble it farther out on the prairie. Now that they had tasted the joy of owning their own roof and four walls in a free country, they could not face returning to the shelter and starting again from scratch. Tereza wondered if they should buy a tent to tide them over, but Bartolomej was strongly against it. "What good would a tent do once we've built the house again? It's a complete waste of money!" He began making calculations with the stub of his carpenter's pencil. The structure had to be taken apart carefully, so as not to damage the valuable boards; nails had to be pulled out and straightened so they could be hammered back in; and it all had to be dismantled like a puzzle so it could be reassembled. It went against everything the poor pragmatist knew to waste anything but his own efforts. He decided that he and Jakub couldn't manage to dismantle it carefully in three evenings, because they had to earn their living by day. So they set out to Slavik's Tavern on Van Buren Street to ask their fellow countrymen for help.

They found five of them in the tavern: Barcal, Hejduk, Kristuvek, and Padecky, and a fifth that the Kakuskas didn't know—a black-haired, sprightly young man with a round, canny face, and a pair of guileless eyes. At first Kakuska thought he might be Father Zdeborsky from the parish in Prachen, who had been rusticated for a pious swindle he had run back in Bohemia. Father Zdeborsky—a handyman with a commercial bent—had created a crucifix with a Christ figure that wept tears of blood whenever a coin of sufficient size was dropped into a coin box that carried the words IESUS EST HOMINUM SAL-

VATOR. *The deacon intervened when pious old widows began to go hungry, spending their mite to see the Lord weep. Father Zdeborsky was threatened with excommunication for blasphemy, but the Bishop of Budejovice settled for exile. However, this gnome with the clever, guileless eyes of a con man was not Zdeborsky. He was introduced as Shake, and as Kakuska came in he was telling his skeptical countrymen of his plans to set up a readers' society that would subscribe to a magazine called* Czech *that a veteran of the '48 rebellion had just started up in Paris. But the rest had other things on their minds, so they were deaf to Shake's contention that without a literature there was no nation. Kakuska's problem, on the other hand, was close to their hearts, and though it was nearly midnight they set out to the site of the endangered house. Reluctant to stay behind in the tavern alone, Shake went along.*

The night was dark and they had to look over the structure by torchlight. They examined the nails that Kakuska had hammered in (much too securely) and began to discuss the problems of taking the building apart without damaging the materials.

Meanwhile Shake walked around the little house and went inside. Moments later a rather loud slapping sound came from the cabin, but nobody paid much attention to it.

Shake emerged from the cabin and rejoined the men. He listened to them talk about the number of nails they would have to cut around and pry out, and how they would have to take the roof off in one piece because Kakuska had nailed the shingles on too meticulously. Then Molly came outside in her nightshirt, with an oversized wool shawl tossed over it. She looked around, stepped over to her mother, and whispered something in her ear. The torch in Tereza's hand wavered. Shake looked on warily. Barcal was explaining that the inner beams would have to be turned around so the nail-holes wouldn't match, otherwise they wouldn't be tight enough. Tereza stepped over to Shake and was just about to speak when Shake said, "Why do it the easy way when you can do it the hard way?" Tereza hesitated.

"What do you mean?" asked Barcal.

"How much can it weigh?" speculated Shake.

"How much can what weigh?"

"The whole building."

"Mind your own business," said Padecky irritably.

"Well," said Shake, "if you think harder is better than easier—"

"What kind of nonsense is that?" Padecky snapped.

"It's a favourite Czech saying," said Shake. "I collected them back home."

"So stick it in your ear and let's help the Kakuskas," barked Padecky.

"The cabin has no cellar, . . ." Shake observed.

"It doesn't have a steeple with a clock on the roof, either," Padecky said drily.

". . . because it has no floor," said Shake.

"Didn't have enough boards for a floor," said Bartolomej Kakuska.

"It's just sitting there on the ground like a doghouse," said Shake.

"Oh yeah! I'll show you a doghouse!" yelled Padecky.

"Can we get hold of two long beams somewhere?" asked Shake.

"Oh, you mean—" Barcal responded, frowning thoughtfully.

Tereza finally had an opening. *"Mr. Schweik, you're never to set foot in our house again!"*

"My fellow countrymen," said Shake, *"man is by nature a vessel of weakness. The shame is mine."*

"How much can it weigh? A couple of hundred pounds? Four, maybe?" Barcal wondered.

"I can tell you how much your brain weighs," snarled Padecky, enjoying his annoyance.

"Even if it weighed six, . . ." said Barcal, turning to Shake.

"Don't change the subject," declared Tereza. *"You're a wicked man, Mr. Schweik, and you're no longer welcome in our house!"*

"How many men do you think it'll take?" asked Barcal.

The next day, before sunrise—before the men left to unload ships and push wheelbarrows—both the Kakuska women, along with Mrs. Hejduk and Mrs. Barcal (Shake was a bachelor and Padecky's young wife had left him and returned to Bohemia two years after their marriage), called on seven other Czech households. That evening Schroeder went to visit the Kakuskas' domicile, drawn by compassion for the hard lot of the industrious immigrant, but also by his memory of the immigrant's daughter. Twelve Czechs, armed with hammers and mallets, were hammering big carpenter's nails into two large beams that were longer than the Kakuskas' cabin. Then they nailed the beams along two opposite walls of the structure. Then they lined up, six to a side, and on the command of Geza Mihalotzy—a former Feldwebel who had deserted from Paloczy's regiment in Budapest after the débâcle in '49—they all bent over and, like twelve weight-lifters, heaved the Kakuskas' little house onto their shoulders, and on the order *"Marschieren, marsch!"* they started off, left foot first. Backlit by the setting sun and its reflection in Lake Michigan, the caterpillar with twenty-four legs moved slowly westward across the prairie, away from the unfortunate Sixth Street allowance. The admiring Schroeder strode along behind the women and the wives of the men who bore the dwelling on their shoulders (Shake, granted partial clemency as the man who had come up with the idea, was one of them) and young Larry Kakuska, who wasn't yet big enough to be part of the caterpillar.

That night, half a mile farther out in the prairie, the little house was settled

down like a bird in a nest, half buried in sagebrush, and in its one room they celebrated a job well done with two bottles of schnapps contributed by Schroeder,
who was gratified by their Bohemian ingenuity. The chastened Shake, still in
disfavour, sat in the sagebrush beside the little house, which was rocking with
laughter, and soothed his pride with a third bottle of schnapps from the generous
Schroeder, which he had all to himself.

"What had he done?" Kapsa asked Jakub Kakuska years later, at the christening.

"I can't tell you here in front of everybody," said Jakub. "Maybe some other
time."

He never did. Much later, after the great battle of Bentonville, Kapsa heard
the story from Jan Amos Shake himself, freshly decorated with a medal.

★

The Bohemian Casino on Twelfth Street in Manhattan was not, as its name
suggested, a gambling den. It was just a tavern, and the only game the patrons
indulged in was Marias, a card game they played for matchsticks, since no one
had money for more than supper and ten or at most fifteen beers. Above the bar
was a portrait of Frantisek Palacky, the father of the Czech nation, with the
Czech heraldic lion on its right and the Moravian eagle on its left. Underneath
it were two small star-spangled banners, crossed. At the end of the bar lay a
stack of Havlicek's liberal newspapers, Narodni noviny, for which the
pubkeeper, Tuma, was a secret correspondent. Some of the tables were occupied
by beer-drinkers reading newspapers, others by beer-drinkers playing cards.
Kapsa and Fircut sat drinking whisky at a table in the corner. Tuma would
occasionally toss them a glance from his place behind the bar.

"If you think I'm trying to rob you—which is what you apparently think,"
Fircut was saying, "then go pawn them or sell them yourself. What else would
you do with them?"

"Nothing," Kapsa replied. "For now." He was annoyed.

"So what are you going to do? Break your back at the brickyard like the rest of
those clowns?"

Kapsa had got so used to Smithie's whisky on the boat that he'd developed a
taste for it, and had only a handful of Hanzlitschek's gulden left, and now that
he'd entrusted them to Fircut to invest, he had only twelve dollars left in his
pocket. The whisky helped him drive away the visions of the gallows, but it also
addled his brain.

"So what are you doing—just hanging onto them for luck?" Fircut persisted.
"There's no luck without money, you know." It was a favourite Czech proverb.

"That's exactly what I'm doing. And besides, what's luck?" Through a golden fog of scotch, Kapsa saw Fircut thinking hard.

"You know what I think? I think that commander of yours had a wife."

"I don't know what you're talking about."

"Of course. He did, didn't he? A looker!"

"He did not!" Kapsa almost shouted.

"A commander without a wife?" said Fircut. "He must have been a widower."

"Yes, he was."

"I'll bet he was!" said Fircut.

Kapsa took a sip of whisky but it didn't help him come up with a reply.

"I think you were schtupping his wife."

"He was a widower, I said!" he almost shouted again.

"I don't think he was. But I'll bet she's a widow now," said Fircut. "And I think it was your doing."

Kapsa tried to tell him to shut up but he tripped over his tongue.

"So that's how it was!" said Fircut. "Of course, that—"

Tuma came over and sat down.

"So, neighbours, have you made a deal?" he asked.

"Almost," said Fircut. "First I have to stop off at the Austrian consulate. There's something I have to take care of."

"Wonderful," said Tuma. "The building next door is going cheap. We'll cut a door between the two buildings, we'll make a dance hall out of the storage space, maybe even a theatre, book in those minstrel shows. They're all the rage now. Ever seen one?"

"Of course," said Fircut. "I just have to take care of one small matter with the Austrian consul."

"I'd stay out of there if I were you," said Tuma. "The consul won't lift a finger for you, especially not since '48. He thinks anyone who ran off to America can't have much love for Austria."

They hadn't admitted to Tuma that they were deserters. Fircut had passed himself off as a nouveau-riche merchant who had outgrown Austria. He had cast Kapsa as the heir to a fortune left to him by a wealthy aunt. He embellished his story with frequent references to the captain's cabin, implying that their only contact with life in steerage on their way across the Atlantic was the stench they could smell on their walks on deck.

"You're right," said Fircut. "But there's one matter I must take care of. It concerns a certain lady and her late husband. My friend Kapsa here knew them both well." He placed his hand on Kapsa's shoulder. "I'm still owed a fair sum of money. But my friend Kapsa here has been a big help. The Austrian consul can

hardly refuse me now, especially since the Austrians stand to make some tax on the money, but even so . . ."

"Well"—Tuma glanced at Fircut suspiciously—"I don't know about things like that. All I did was confiscate the regimental treasury. But like I say, the building next door is for sale cheap. It's a good location and it's a gold mine. I need backers and I'd prefer my own countrymen."

He got up and went back to the bar.

"Well," said Fircut, "what do you think? Should I write a love letter to the consul?" He grinned. "Of course, you're beyond the imperial jurisdiction. But what about her? What's her name? Not that it wouldn't be easy to find out."

"I'll throttle you!" Kapsa growled.

"That would make it a double murder," Fircut smirked. "You won't tell me? No matter. As I say, it won't be hard to find out."

Kapsa finished his drink and poured another, emptying the bottle.

He gave up.

After that, all he could remember was sitting on a bench on the edge of a park. He remembered triple gold balls over the entrance to a shop. That was Friday afternoon. He remembered Fircut coming up to the bench, and hearing the sound of the chimes as the shop door opened and closed.

"Here's the ticket," Fircut said. "Look, I'm putting it in your wallet." He flashed a piece of paper.

Then a ride—in a hack?—and being carried—did Fircut carry him?—and then darkness. He woke up in a doss-house.

The next evening he and Tuma waited in the tavern for Fircut to show up. He never did.

Kapsa still had the ticket. He hadn't looked at it yet, but he had it.

Twelve dollars was all he had left now—ten, actually. He'd bought dinner and a bottle of whisky at the Bohemian Casino.

Then he found out about the hole in Mother McCormick's chest.

He still had the ticket.

By Monday he had only six dollars left. The rest had gone for whisky and food after his encounter with Salek. At eight o'clock he was standing beneath the gold balls on Sixth Street. A gilt sign in the window said PAWNSHOP— COHEN AND SON, and behind it, in the sleepy morning sun, he could see a dusty violin along with some alarm clocks, mandolins, and a faded frock-coat on a chipped mannequin sporting a real monocle set in a wooden eye socket. Moments later, Cohen arrived and opened his shop. Kapsa hurried inside with him, almost knocking him over from behind. He handed the pawnbroker the ticket.

"Two dollars at forty percent a month," said Cohen. "That's eighty cents. You

pawned it Friday evening, Saturday, Sunday—I have to count Monday too—
that's a tenth of a month—eight cents, counting Friday. That'll be ten cents. Two
dollars and ten cents altogether."

And he placed a silver cigar-holder with an ivory snake coiled around it on
the counter.

Kapsa handed him the money and stuck the cigar-holder in his pocket.

★

Rain and more rain. It was a warm rain, as in South Carolina, but wet
enough to put out the fires in the turpentine forests. Now they were just
smouldering. The nature of the terrain had changed. The endless wagon-
train of Sherman's great army now wound its way among pine groves, along
carpets of logs laid down by the engineers where the road became marshland, across freshly repaired bridges spanning flooded rivers, through meadows just starting to turn green, northward towards Goldsboro. The sergeant
was galloping ahead with a dispatch for General Davis from Sherman, who
was riding on his huge horse, Sam, beside General Slocum, in the ranks of
Howard's Twelfth Corps. Davis's Fourteenth Corps, with General Morgan's
division leading it, was up ahead, snaking its way deeper and deeper into
North Carolina. By morning, the sergeant arrived at the house where General Davis was conferring with Major Belknap. The major's foragers had
met a man going to Springfield on a mule. He'd been more than willing to
talk, because he owned a small farm south of Raleigh, and hoped the war
would end before Sherman's bummers got to it. The man had confirmed
that a large force led by General Joe Johnston was gathering at Bentonville,
with every indication that they were preparing for a battle.

But Sherman no longer believed that General Johnston or his subordinate commanders had large forces at their disposal. Hundreds of miles and
three months had gone by since Kennesaw Mountain, since the bitter battles over Atlanta. His own army was now moving into North Carolina in
three long columns—Slocum's battalion in the north, Howard's to the
south, and Schofield's closer to the coast. They were marching at some distance from each other, like three independent armies rather than a single
one, and in all that time they had had only minor skirmishes with Hampton's and Wheeler's cavalries. Spies and prisoners brought them tales of
an epidemic of desertion infecting the Confederate infantry, with only
Wade Hampton's skirmishers remaining immune, the cream of the cavalry
patrolling the margins of the Rebel army. Most of its infantry was dying
of attrition.

Sherman had always tried to avoid major battles; he left those to Grant out in the wilderness, where regiments numbering tens of thousands rolled over one another, bleeding each other dry on carefully constructed palisades and earthworks, and filling their trenches with fresh blood from units that were marched to the battlefronts past corpses there had been no time to bury properly. Spring downpours washed them out of their shallow graves, leaving half-decayed skulls to grin at the earnest newcomers as if to say: soon you'll look like us.

Sherman no longer believed in the power of huge, ponderous armies engaging in monstrous battles that had no decisive outcome. The sergeant would listen to him when he joined them around the campfire and philosophized about war, while Lieutenant Williams surreptitiously took notes in a leather-bound book. "Let's give Pyrrhus credit where credit is due," said the general. "He was a soldier, and a brave commander. But what kind of general pays for every five feet his troops advance—and five feet is the height of a very small soldier—with a dead man or a cripple? War is an art, a terrible art. It ought not to exist at all but, since it does, it ought to be practised as an art. It is not an exercise in mass execution, the winner being he who has more men to sacrifice and more executioners who are, in turn, also condemned to die. To my mind Pyrrhus was an executioner of that calibre," said the general, placing a cigar in his mouth and enshrouding his creased face with smoke. "Caesar was the real artist," he said from behind the smoke. "His soldiers were superlative marchers first, and only then soldiers."

And yet, mused the sergeant, looking over the newspaper that had caught up with them north of Savannah, the general had the reputation of being a gambler, an adventurer, even a madman. Counter to the rules of war, he had plunged into the backwoods of Georgia, cut himself off from his supply routes and lines of communications, and driven his soldiers on long daily marches to the south. As they went they plundered the countryside and impoverished the farmers, so as not to have to wait for the arrival of unwieldy supplies. They did not have to rely on vague, uninformed orders from strategists working in safety far from enemy territory. They did not allow the Rebels time to manoeuvre or concentrate their strength and force the hand of battle, which could transform an art into a bloodbath on some fixed field of glory and of death. Kil's skirmishers and armed bummers spearheaded Sherman's army and rode in small battle groups threading through the countryside. And so the great but agile army drove quickly and deeply into Georgia, then on to South Carolina, and then northward. The general avoided major battles, not because he feared them, but because he was an artist practising an art that, although it shouldn't exist, did exist, and demanded artists, not bloodied tyros, to be properly applied.

Sometimes the sergeant was ambushed by memories of long-ago times in the one-room schoolhouse of his childhood, where their patriotic teacher, Erazim Kozel, used to tell them stories of another great military leader, Jan Zizka of Trocnov. Under the Georgia stars, the sergeant imagined Zizka's fifteenth-century battle-carts filled with stones, careering down the hillside and crashing into the ironclad phalanxes of crusaders, smashing swaths of death through their ranks. What if his general had that kind of battle-cart? What if Georgia and the Carolinas were full of smooth, steep hillsides? What if the general had light wagons, perhaps powered by steam instead of oxen—wagons that could ply the roads of the Carolinas like gunboats plying the Mississippi, and carry soldiers armed to the teeth with repeating rifles. The sergeant shook off the idea, but the vision of an army with armed wagons arrayed in small battle groups like Kil's cavalry, penetrating like lightning in all directions throughout the burning Carolinas, made him shake his head again. He knew that Sherman's headlong drive into the unknown was a lesser risk to life and limb than the slow, prudent, well-supplied steamroller that called itself the Army of the Potomac.

Even less did the general believe in a grand pitched battle now, in the twilight of the war. He simply waved his hand and sent the sergeant with instructions to General Davis to keep a sharp eye out.

The sergeant caught up to General Davis at dinner-time in a charming farmhouse about twenty miles outside Bentonville, where he was in the company of General Carlin and an alarmed farmer who hadn't the slightest desire to see his land become a field of glory.

"It weren't," said the farmer, "I mean, it weren't just the cavalry. There was infantry too, three regiments at least, gentlemen. I seen them yesterday, moving towards Bentonville."

"All Morgan came across was cavalry," said General Carlin.

"It was them set fire to my barn at Pete's Bend this morning," said the farmer. "They were covering the infantry. I seen them yesterday. They come back to give the infantry time to gather at Bentonville. I'm telling you, gentlemen, there's a battle brewing. If it happens here—and I'm damned sure it will—it'll cost me a lot more than an old barn."

On his way back to General Sherman, the sergeant rode with General Davis and his aide. Sherman heard his account of the conversation with the farmer, and Major Belknap brought up his own experience with the man on the way to Raleigh.

But just as Sherman didn't believe in big pitched battles now, in the twilight of the war, he was convinced that the other side didn't believe in them either.

"No, Jeff," he told Davis. "Johnston won't risk a battle, with the Neuse rising at his back and only one bridge across it, if I can believe my scouts. There's no infantry standing in our path, Jeff. All they have is a few squadrons of cavalry. Sweep them aside and you're fine. We'll meet tomorrow at Cox's Bridge."

★

"'If I were to tell you!'" The sergeant impatiently knocked the ash off his cigar into a tin ashtray fashioned to resemble a heart pierced by an arrow. "You keep saying, 'If I were to tell you. . . .' All right, tell me!"

So Salek told him. The tavern was in a large building on the corner of Randolph and Desplaines. The owner stood behind the bar in a cloud of smoke with just his head showing, a scimitar moustache, his hand on the tap guiding the draught beer into quart-sized mugs. A band was playing a loud polka on the podium, also surrounded by a cloud of smoke: a flugelhorn, a clarinet, a tuba, violin, drum, and an accordion. On a plank floor in front of the band, couples were swirling energetically to the music. A Czech Sunday in Chicago. Act One of Salek's Chicago story hadn't been Czech, but his present wife, Vlasta, was— Vlasta who never left the dance floor, and whose grey eyes kept firing shafts at the sergeant as he tapped his ashes into the tin-heart ashtray. Act One had been Deirdre.

"If only she hadn't died on me!" said Salek sorrowfully over his two-pint glass of beer, his fifth this afternoon, each one spiked with a shot of gin. Deirdre—who had opened the door at five o'clock one morning, sleepy-eyed but dressed in a grey skirt and faded blouse, while he stood on the step holding the two loaves of warm bread he was supposed to deliver every other day to that large, hungry house on Dearborn Street. On the street was his cart, pulled by an old mule. The morning was as murky as the Vltava River after a rainfall. She had a freckled nose and green eyes.

"Good morning," he said in a heavy accent, and she took the loaves from him, yawned, and turned to close the green door while he, enchanted by her reddish braids, went on staring long after the door, with its heavy polished brass knocker, had shut behind her.

The sergeant felt Vlasta's eyes upon him, as she kicked up her black-stockinged legs in the smoky mist and the band played the polka.

"If only she hadn't died on me!" Two days later, when Salek was delivering

the loaves of bread again, he noticed that her thumb was bandaged. He took out a fragrant braided poppyseed roll he'd made especially for her the night before. She shook her head and said something he didn't understand. He knew only a few words of English, but her speech had an Irish lilt.

He shook his head too, pointed to her, and said, "Is for you!"

She was startled but then she smiled and took the roll from him. "Thank you!" She hesitated. He was standing there like a lump, unable to think of anything to say in English. She gave him another smile, then turned away and closed the door: two reddish braids tied with green shoelaces, the green door, the brass knocker.

Two days later: "Was good?" This time she smiled as soon as she opened the door. Another beautiful roll didn't catch her off guard.

"Oh yes, it was very good!"

He pointed to his chest and said, as he'd planned to, "Ondra."

"I'm Deirdre," she replied and waited.

"I bring you again, yes?" he said.

"You're very kind," she said.

No chess master, he hadn't thought of his next move, but when she turned away he saw that she'd replaced the laces in her braids with shiny green ribbons. Two days later, he brought her a big poppyseed kolach.

She died less than a year after they were married. It had been a late-evening wedding, with one tallow candle in an out-of-the-way Irish church, the only other glow coming from the priest's red nose. Salek couldn't afford a better wedding by daylight. The bride wept with disappointment. Deirdre went on living with her master on Dearborn Street and he lived with the baker, Rehacek, in a furnished room. They saved their money and saw each other once a week. Their dream was a bakery of their own, where she would sell bread and pastries.

"All I have left now is Annie," sobbed Salek, pouring another shot of gin into the two-pint glass of beer. "If it weren't for how kind Vlasta is to Annie . . ."

The sergeant didn't press him to continue. Instead, he said, "Don't you and Vlasta have any children of your own?"

"Thank heavens, no," said Salek. "I'm sure about Aninka. I know she's mine. If Vlasta and I had—I mean, if Vlasta had a child—I couldn't be sure." The sergeant saw a black-stockinged leg flashing through the smoke. The grey eyes, darker than the smoke, caught his for an instant.

"I'll divorce her, I will!" Salek said bitterly. "But what about Annie?"

The memory of Salek's sad voice was driven out by Shake's high-pitched tenor, and the sergeant's mind returned to the present, to the campfire a few miles from Bentonville.

"Nobody ever said so out loud," Shake was saying, "but deep down we were all surprised that Salek stayed with us. Especially Mihalotzy. By that time Salek was pretty well off, better than Honza Talafous, and nobody thought Honza's sudden concern for his family's welfare was odd. We all knew he had a prosperous shop on Randolph Street. Or Kabrna, whose cigars were selling so well that he'd hired twenty people. Nobody even thought it was strange when Kabrna tried to get the Austrian consul to get him out of military service. But he wasn't the only one in Chicago to give the Czechs a bad name."

"What about you?" asked Paidr.

"Me? I was the wonder of the town," said Shake.

"You mean," Kakuska said, "the whole town wondered about you."

"But I knew they'd wonder and I wanted them to wonder," said Shake. "I like being the centre of attention. Besides, everyone knew I'd bought some armour, so I had no reason to be afraid."

"They say you wore it backwards at Perryville," said Kakuska sarcastically.

"I didn't know how to put it on properly," said Shake. "It was supposed to fasten in the back with a buckle, but I couldn't reach around to do it up."

"Why didn't you get help?" asked Fisher.

"I didn't want to be laughed at," said Shake. "So I put it on backwards and buckled it in front, and then I couldn't get it turned around properly. But it saved my life all the same."

"Is that so? When?"

"During the attack on Perryville. I got a direct hit but the armour held fast."

"If you try to tell me someone on our side accidentally shot you in the back," said Houska, "you're going to get a direct hit in the nose from my fist."

"I'd just turned around to urge my fellow soldiers on," said Shake calmly. "I got shot right in the back—a solid shot, my friends. I lay there, stunned."

"But in one piece," said Kakuska.

"Take a sniff!" warned Houska, sticking a clenched fist under Shake's nose.

"Why don't you still wear it, if it saved your life?" asked Paidr.

"I don't have it any more," said Shake. "You remember the winter we had in '63? It got rusted."

"I said, take a sniff!" Houska challenged him again.

"I want to hear more about Salek," the sergeant said, averting the impending conflict.

"He was practically a wealthy man," said Shake. "You don't think that grocery store of his was something he earned by the sweat of his brow, do you?"

The sergeant cast his mind back to Chicago, back to that afternoon before the dance, when Cup-Salek was bragging about business and took him on a tour of the bakery.

"You need to be a little bit lucky and a little bit shrewd," he said. One morning five wagons loaded high with sacks of flour had stopped in front of his bakery, when it was still tiny.

"What's this?" he asked the driver.

"You ordered flour?"

"Yes."

"Well, here it is," said the driver, handing him a purchase order. It said, "2000 sacks of flour". The last two zeros had been squeezed in before the word "sacks".

"The wheat crop that year was excellent," Salek-Cup explained to Kapsa. "Flour was going cheap. But I had an almanac from back home that had long-term weather predictions in it." So he said nothing and had them carry the flour into the bakery. When they ran out of space, he rented the empty shop next door. Then he went to the wholesaler's, but entered by the back door so that the agent who had taken his order didn't have a chance to sneak away. The agent was a little guy with a tic, and Salek towered over him menacingly.

"He knew I always paid cash," said Salek, "and never took anything on credit, so he thought I was feeble-minded. I held the purchase order under his nose and said, 'Look, you made a mistake.' He turned pale. I said, 'I wanted twenty thousand sacks, not two thousand.' 'You—you don't need that much,' stammered the agent. 'You're right,' I said, 'I may have overdone it a little. So I'm only going to pay you for the two thousand. But I want the discount for twenty thousand. After all, it was your mistake.' The discount he gave me was so big that each sack of flour only cost me a few pennies. And the almanac was right. Next year the harvest was terrible, and the price of flour went way up." Salek moved from the little shop on Goat Street to the one on the corner of Clinton and Randolph.

"What was wrong with that?" asked Fisher. "If anyone was dishonest, it was the agent."

"But it wasn't honest work," said Shake. "It was cunning."

"Is it dishonest to be cunning?" asked Paidr. "If it were, you'd have been in jail long ago."

"You're quite right," said Shake. "I've gone to pot mentally since I joined the army. Sometimes working with your mind can be honest, yes—and you can make more that way than working with your hands."

"Making shady deals isn't working with your mind," said Paidr.

"What is, then?"

"Teaching, maybe," said Paidr. "Or preaching. Priests work with their minds."

"What makes you think priests are honest?"

"Watch what you say!" the devout Houska broke in, brandishing his large farmer's fist an inch from Shake's nose.

The sergeant intervened again. "So why didn't Salek quit Lincoln's Rifles when the shooting started? You say he was richer than Kabrna or that butcher."

"That's what surprised everyone," said Shake. "It's like the Copperheads used to say: rich men wage wars, poor men fight them."

"Not always," Zinkule chimed in. "Especially the ones who inherit their money. Look at General Millgate—he put up a whole regiment out of his own pocket, never took pay, and to top it all, he lost a leg at Shiloh. The real weasels are the ones who never made a cent till the war started. But worst of all are the substitutes. They get paid to take someone's place, get whatever bonus they can for it, then desert and sign up all over again. Some of them have done it ten times over, I've heard."

"You're right," said Shake. "The rich-by-inheritance have military honour in their blood. But the ones who've earned their money by mental work or by being smart appreciate it more, and they try to stay alive to enjoy it."

"You think poor men don't want to stay alive?" grumbled Houska.

"Wealthy men have more to lose," said Shake. "All the poor man has is his life, and that's not something you can bargain with. That's why poor men are so eager to join the army. Their lives are worth something for a change."

"Poor men are stupid," declared Zinkule.

"Are you saying I'm stupid?" Houska turned to him angrily.

"You're an exception," Shake said hurriedly. "Like Salek was. But why?" He looked at his stupid companions, and the sergeant was compelled to wonder just what America would be like without their kind of stupidity. "Did you know that Salek was the very first American Czech to divorce his wife?" asked Shake.

"I didn't know you could do that," said Houska.

"Not in the church you can't. He got a civil divorce. It just goes to show you that, for all he's a Christian, Salek had grounds for divorce that were stronger than his fear of burning in hell."

"He sure did," said Kakuska. "She screwed every Czech in Chicago."

"She wasn't that patriotic," said Shake. "She put out for Polacks too, and even for married men without a single drop of Slavic blood."

The sergeant said nothing. He knew more about it than Kakuska.

And he knew why the general was so quick to dismiss the likelihood that Slocum's battalion would encounter Johnston's infantry at Bentonville, instead of just a few squadrons of Wheeler's cavalry. Less than a year after the general had chosen him to join his staff, the sergeant had come to understand the two faces of war. In his first fifteen years of soldiering—first under Windischgraetz and his beadle, von Hanzlitschek, and then in tiny outposts of the small regular army of the United States—he had been exposed to only one of them: the face seen by the foot-soldier and the noncom. He brought one thing from the Royal Imperial Austrian Army that served him well in America: drill. All he had to do was replace von Hanzlitschek's brutal and punitive style with straightforward discipline—though the bellow remained. He soon became a drill sergeant. When the war started, he mastered the art of transforming rural romantics and urban adventurers into soldiers, men who no longer saw military orders as an imposition on their personal liberty as Americans, and who came (kicking and screaming) to the conclusion that courage would lead to victory far more quickly if it was shaped by some good old-fashioned Austrian-style authority.

The face of war that the foot-soldier and the noncom saw was the face of confusion, marches here and there for no apparent purpose, building fortifications, tearing them down, skirmishing, confusion in which death was imminent and victory remote, and it all seemed like pricking an elephant with a hat-pin. The sergeant knew this face of war all too well, but in this new American war not everything he had learned from von Hanzlitschek still applied. Rifles had a greater range and accuracy than they had had at the barricades in Prague, and they could be reloaded faster. In Europe the slow advance against a kneeling enemy (though here the enemy didn't kneel but lay flat on his belly, in a rifle pit or behind a palisade) became, at the range of a hundred yards, an awkward charge with ranks closed tight together, crouching elbow to elbow. Here—

In the American war, new weapons were constantly appearing on the battlefields. Once, at the Yazoo River, they brought something to Sherman's tent that seemed at first like an expensive joke. The muzzle of an ordinary breech-loader was mounted on a two-wheeled gun-carriage. Attached to the weapon at the breech was a tin funnel topped with a rectangular box. It looked like an oversized coffee-grinder, with a crank handle on one side and a rudder-like device protruding from the hind end. The artillery officer who had come to demonstrate the weapon took it down into a narrow valley that formed a natural shooting-range, and had a row of empty biscuit barrels placed on the opposite slope; then he stood behind the device. He grasped the rudder while an artillery sergeant took hold of the crank. The general's staff formed a semicircle around them and the general positioned himself beside the man with the crank. He nodded for them to begin.

"Fire!" the officer shouted. His assistant began turning the crank and, inured though they were to the noise of war, all of them jumped when the machine began exploding like a whole squad of riflemen, emitting a steady stream of flashes, belching smoke like a chimney, as the artillery officer slowly moved the rudder from one side to the other and the barrels on the opposite slope toppled one by one. The officer barked another order, and his assistant stopped turning the crank.

The officer turned to the general. "General, sir?"

"Hmmm," said the general. "If every battery had two of these. . . ." He paused while the sergeant tried to estimate how many men it would take the place of. "Let me try it," said the general.

The officer stepped away from the rudder, but the general reached for the crank and began to turn it. The officer took the rudder again. Again the machine let off its thrilling staccato racket, while smoke poured out of the muzzle and the reset barrels toppled over again. Then something happened: a part flew off the barrel, the general gasped and let go of the crank, the noise stopped suddenly, and there was General Sherman hopping around the contraption on one leg, filling the air with curses.

For three days after the demonstration the general walked with a bad limp. The contraption did not become part of the armament of Sherman's great army.

By this time, as a member of his staff, the sergeant was also getting to know the face of war most familiar to the general. By night, civilians would arrive on horseback and slip inside the general's tent; when the wind blew the tent flaps open, the sergeant sometimes saw the general's reddish head by the light of a candle, as Sherman watched intently while a civilian's finger traced a path across a map. Next day the army would make a large detour. There would be a lot of grumbling about how unnecessary it was but the sergeant knew it made sense, even though it often didn't in the long run. He was gradually learning the art that the general was studying—by a process of trial and error that often had the ambulances filled and dripping with blood. There was confusion, but now and then the confusion would settle into patterns that could be understood, briefly, before reverting to chaos again. Maps were less than precise; reports from the scouts and spies who came by night were often full of inconsistencies. Cleverness distorted the art, faulty observation distorted intelligence. On one occasion the enemy fortifications seemed to bristle with cannon, but when the frustrated general captured the position in a dangerous attack the cannon turned out to be wooden—yet when Lieutenant Bain delivered an angry kick to one of the harmless muzzles, hornets swarmed out of the hollow interior and stung him so badly that he died a hero's death. After the battle, they found a prostrate Rebel bass-horn player on the battlefield. He told them how General Beauregard compelled his one band to make exhausting marches up and down the long meandering battlefront, stopping every quarter of a mile to play a different tune, fortissimo, to make General Butler, who was listening closely from the Union palisades, think there were many different regimental bands and hence many different regiments facing his depleted ranks. That night the Union general withdrew his division from the battlefront, defeated by a single weary band.

Kapsa, having retreated to the infirmary with a violent two-week bout of the Kansas quickstep, heard a story from General Rosecrans's cook, who was recovering from a bayonet wound he'd received at Chickamauga. Rosecrans was another apprentice in this nascent art, and he'd stood restless and impatient listening to a sharp-eared old woman outside a rough-hewn log cabin on a hilltop near Chickamauga. A cannon boomed from the woods in the valley, and the woman said, "That there, that would be from some place near Reed's Bridge." General Rosecrans nervously examined his poorly drawn map but couldn't find Reed's Bridge. Another cannon sounded from the woods and the old woman said, "Now that there, that could be from Kelly's farm." But the farm wasn't on the map; instead, the general found Reed's Bridge where the farm should have been. A third cannon roared. The old woman fingered the warts on her chin and shook her head. "Now that there, I can't rightly say. Could be Connolly's Grove—but then again, maybe not." General Rosecrans found Connolly's Grove on the map but it was a long way from where the sound of the third cannon had echoed from. Then he remembered that the old woman had admitted having a son with Hook's division; although she'd sworn her loyalty to the Union cause, she might well be—indeed, everything suggested that she was—deliberately misleading him. So he gave up on her information but not on her method—he simply began listening for himself. The individual cannon blended into a basso profundo, interrupted now and then by the crackle of rifle fire. The old woman scowled at him through the window of the log cabin as he paced back and forth shouting, "That's Brownlow attacking!" And a while later, "No, Brownlow is just starting his attack now!" And then, "That's Negley! Running a little late!" In the end, the method proved a complete failure. Ordinary courage and butchery prevented the worst, but the

Battle of Chickamauga was won, without much glory, by Braxton Bragg.

And yet the apprentices were gradually becoming journeymen, if not masters, of the art, which was why the sergeant understood his general's certainty when he reassured General Davis: "There's no infantry standing in our path, Jeff. All they have is a few squadrons of cavalry. Sweep them aside and you're fine. We'll meet tomorrow at Cox's Bridge."

★

Several days earlier, in a house near Cheraw that he had chosen for his quarters that night, Sherman had found evidence that General Hardee had recently stayed there. The evidence included a New York *Tribune* only a few days old, and the paper made him as angry as he'd been at Vicksburg. "God damn that scoundrel Greeley!" he cursed as he read the editorial. "Journalistic scum!"

Hardee had in fact slept in the little house the night before, and had undoubtedly read the paper as well. By sending Slocum's battalion towards Raleigh, Sherman had hoped to trick Hardee and Johnston into thinking that he intended to force a battle for the capital of North Carolina. They would then have diverted their weary regiments towards Raleigh, and cleared his way to Goldsboro and the port and Morehead City, where he planned to meet up with a flotilla carrying supplies from Savannah, put his men in new uniforms, and, thus refreshed, strike the decisive blow of the war and smash the Confederacy to a pulp. But the publisher of the Tribune had tried his hand at strategic analysis with unfortunate accuracy: "The next time we hear from Sherman will be from Goldsboro," Greeley wrote. "We have determined that the supply-vessels from Savannah are to rendezvous with Sherman's forces in Morehead City."

The general was all the more furious the next day, when he found indications that Hardee had read and understood the editorial all too well. Six miles south of the village of Averasboro—at a spot where the two rivers on either side of Slocum's advance, the Cape Fear River and the Black River, were less than four miles apart—Hardee had posted General Taliaferro's infantry division right in the way of General Kilpatrick's reconnaissance units, and had forced a battle the general would gladly have avoided.

Damn Greeley!

During the battle, Sherman behaved in a way Kapsa had never seen before. While Kakuska sweated to help put up the barricades Kil had ordered to halt the advance of Taliaferro's infantry, and while Shake in the Twentieth Corps sweated with fear because he desperately wanted to live to see the war's end, which was now indisputably imminent, and while the pandemonium of battle—the first the Twentieth Corps had seen since the battle of Atlanta almost nine months before—continued long into the night and started again early the next morning, Sherman and his staff sat well beyond the range of the guns. The general wore a grim expression and seemed to be in a trance. The sergeant knew why. Thanks to one man's journalistic ambitions, his work of art was being destroyed in the bottleneck between Cape Fear and the Black, and his soldiers were paying for Greeley's scoop with their blood.

Indeed, the main reason Hardee engaged Sherman at Averasboro was to find out if Greeley was right in speculating that Sherman's apparent march towards Raleigh was just a feint. When Hardee ordered a retreat, and when the spies and prisoners began to trickle into the woods where Sherman sat frustrated amid his bewildered staff, the stories they told revealed a surprising fact: Slocum's successful resistance had convinced Hardee that Greeley had been wrong. Evidently, Hardee had concluded from the encounter that Sherman was not heading for Goldsboro after all, but intended to fight a decisive battle at Raleigh.

They were all still learning the art of war.

At noon on March 17—St. Patrick's Day—the general ordered Slocum's battalion to move north-east, towards Bentonville and Cox's Bridge, while Hardee and Johnston's troops—so the general thought—were marching north-west to protect Raleigh. The work of art was salvaged, and the regiments and companies and gun batteries and the column of supply wagons of Sherman's great army rolled on towards Bentonville in the drenching spring rain.

The rain stopped, the moon appeared and lit the blossoming apple trees, while in the distance in Bentonville a few tiny lights glimmered in the dark, and Shake was telling the others about how his Readers' Circle scheme had failed.

He used to lend his five books out, but at that time Latin script was all the rage in Bohemia, and when he finally succeeded, with the help of Molly Kakuska, in assembling a Readers' Circle, Padecky came to him and said, "Look, man, I can't read this, it's impossible!"

"What do you mean?" Shake was offended. "Such a beautiful story, so moving! Weren't you moved by Viktorka's fate? What are you, insensitive?"

"Bugger insensitive. I can't read it!" said Padecky, putting his spectacles on his nose.

"Maybe you need to clean your specs," advised Shake, and Padecky lost his temper.

"Here, dammit, Molly, take a look at this," he said, shoving the book into the

hands of Molly Kakuska, who hadn't gotten a book since there weren't enough to go around, even though she was the heart and soul of the Readers' Circle. She opened the book eagerly, but stared at the pages like the proverbial calf at a new barnyard gate, related Shake at Bentonville.

"Mr. Schweik," she said, "it's not in Czech! It must be German."

"What do you mean, German?" Shake grabbed the book out of Molly's hand.

"Just a minute," Sergeant Kapsa interrupted Shake's story. "I thought you weren't allowed to cross the Kakuskas' threshold."

"I wasn't," said Shake. "But I didn't have to. With a single hold, I scared the wits out of her, but I also charmed her, so she used to come to me for advice."

"What 'hold'?" asked Houska suspiciously. "You wrestle? You?"

The army coarsens a man, and war even more so.

This was when the sergeant finally learned why Mother Kakuska had banned Shake from her house.

The moon had been shining into the Kakuskas' modest castle while, outside, the Czechs were trying to figure out a way to pry out the nails. Shake already knew what should be done; he just needed to look inside to see if the structure had a floor and any foundations that would complicate his ingenious solution. He walked around the cabin to the door, and entered. In a shaft of moonlight he saw a firm young breast, like alabaster, but when he touched it—how could one resist touching it?—it was warm and resilient. Molly gave a sigh, opened her eyes, and was terrified to see Shake looking at her like an obscene Jesuit. He wasn't the least bit obscene, just young and horny. She smacked his hand, covered her breast with her nightie, then gave Shake a resounding slap across the face. He ran out of the little house while Molly went to Tereza to complain.

Shake didn't appeal to Molly, but it was the first time in her life a man had touched her like that, and something in her was aroused. So when she happened to meet the culprit on the corner of Van Buren and Canal streets, instead of sticking her nose in the air she said, "Good afternoon, Mr. Schweik." Shake caught fire, and they began to meet. She never let him get anywhere, of course, since by this time Schroeder, the engineer, was expressing serious interest in her too. She merely started to help Shake with the Readers' Circle, because, when he wanted to, Shake could be extremely persuasive—although in Molly's case it did him no good. "German, what do you mean, German?" he asked woefully.

"'Cause I can't read it!"

That was how Shake discovered that his compatriots were literate only in Gothic type. In the meantime, Latin type had come into fashion in Bohemia, from where his sister, patriot that she was, had sent his book.

★

The sergeant looked northward, past the burning turpentine refineries. Somewhere out there General Howard's army was spending the night, but there was no sign of his campfires. The distance between Howard's and Slocum's armies must have increased during the day. The two corps were moving north-east like two immense pincers closing in on Goldsboro. Slocum marched along the only road. Ahead of him was the Fourteenth Corps of General Davis, who, despite Sherman's reassurances, couldn't shake from his mind the farmer's stubborn insistence that Johnston was concentrating his infantry at Bentonville. Davis kept slowing down, his units advancing awkwardly along the narrow road towards the eastern horizon among the pine groves. Every so often a squadron of Wheeler's riders would appear just within range, fire at the soldiers in Davis's van, and withdraw to the pines. Davis and Morgan, who was commanding the forward line, couldn't agree on what this meant. Were they simply random forays by a desperate cavalry, something to be swept out of the way, or were they trying to distract attention from the massing of Confederate infantry units under cover of the woods and scrub oak covering the countryside?

While Morgan and Davis pondered Wheeler's raids, the Twentieth Corps at the rear of Slocum's army and the Twenty-sixth Wisconsin under General Coggswell laboured on the muddy road. They filled impassable holes with logs, and reinforced bridges that were collapsing under the weight of munitions and supply wagons. At the campfire that evening a cursing Shake rubbed tallow on his bleeding calluses. The conversation turned to the armour which he claimed had saved his life at Perryville. It had stopped the projectile but had buckled under the impact, unfortunately leaving an indelible reddish badge of courage between the hero's shoulderblades. Shake pulled up his shirt and the mark was visible in the firelight, almost like the traces of a crown of thorns.

"I also nearly lost my hearing, friends," Shake said. "Have you any idea of the noise a minnie ball makes when it hits armour?"

"You said it was a solid shot that hit you," said Paidr.

"A slip of the tongue," replied Shake. "I meant a minnie ball."

"What you meant was that you think we're stupid," said Houska.

"Cenek Pechlat really went deaf," Javorsky chimed in. "In an ironclad gunboat. They were bombarded by a shore battery at Fort Donelson. No one got hurt but they all went deaf. Pechlat says the din was indescribable. You have to imagine yourself being shut up inside a tin drum while some sadist is learning how to play it. He was as deaf as a post after that."

"Did he get a discharge?" asked Fisher.

"He didn't want one," said Javorsky. "He said that now he couldn't hear the hellish racket, he felt right at home in the ironclad boat. Later on he served with Farragut's flotilla—it was Farragut who wanted to dig a canal at Vicksburg so they could get past the city. Last time I saw Pechlat, he said some Rebel engineer in Charleston had invented a boat that could go under water, and he said that when our side came up with something like that he was going to sign up for it, not to miss all the fun."

"Did he volunteer?"

"Yep," said Javorsky, "but before he could join up the underwater boat sank and they lost it. They're supposed to be working on a new one, and as far as I know Pechlat is still waiting for his chance."

They put more wood on the fire, and the conversation turned back to Shake's armour and the famous Battle of Perryville.

"The smart ones," said Shake, "went back to being Austrian subjects, and us dumb Americans, like the twelve Apostles, went into battle." He continued, counting on his fingers: "Ferda Filip, later to become Mihalotzy's lieutenant, Joska Neuman, Franta Kouba, Lojza Uher, Franta Kukla, Pepik Dvoracek, Prokop Hudek, Franta Smola, Eda Kafka, Salek-Cup, Josef Jurka, and me. 'Lincoln's Slavonic Rifles'. But we weren't Slavonic any more. There were five times as many Germans in the company as Czechs, a few Hungarians, one Wend, and the commander, Captain Geza Mihalotzy. When he was three sheets to the wind on whisky at Slavik's Tavern he claimed to be Czech, when he was hung over he said he was Slovak, and sober he'd claim to be a Hungarian-speaking American formerly of the Thirty-seventh Infantry Regiment garrisoned in Nagyvarad. So we had to drop the word 'Slavonic' from our name. They stuck the company with the Twenty-fourth Illinois, promoted Mihalotzy to lieutenant-colonel, and in September of '62 we marched off for our trial by fire as part of Major-General Charles C. Gilbert's division in the celebrated army of General Buell, who was famous at Perryville for falling off his horse the day before the battle, which might explain the hullabaloo that followed."

Shake took a swig from the wooden canteen on which he had carved the Czech word for water, WODA, and choked on it as the stink of tallow on his calluses was overpowered by the smell of whisky.

"We were driven by patriotism," he said, "and by thirst."

"Were you drinking that much back then?" asked Fisher. "I thought it was the horrors of war that turned you to booze."

"I meant thirst in the original sense of the word," said Shake. "That year there hadn't been a drop of rain in Kentucky. The wells were empty, the riverbeds had dried to a trickle that smelled like dung-water and tasted like it too. What's worse, all we had to eat was herring, so we were starving as well. A seven-day march through bone-dry countryside and even Major-General Gilbert's tongue was hanging out, never mind us ordinary soldiers. Finally the scouts brought us some really good news: near the village of Perryville there was a creek that was still running, called Doctor's Creek. General Buell—who was riding in a wagon in the rear because, as I said, he'd fallen off his horse and suffered an injury of a delicate nature so he was unable to continue on horseback—decided to throw his entire army at Perryville. The scouts also said that Doctor's Creek was defended by General Polk."

"The same one who got shot through with a cannonball later, at Kennesaw Mountain?" asked Stejskal.

"The very same," said Shake. "But even so, Buell's army advanced on Perryville without complaint. Gilbert's division led the charge with the Twenty-fourth Illinois in the van, and spearheading the whole thing, rifles at the ready, were none other than Lincoln's famous, formerly Slavonic, Rifles. And in the very front ranks, bayonets fixed, Geza Mihalotzy leading them, were us twelve Czech volunteers."

"You did all this for water?" asked Houska.

"Czechs are capable of even that!" declared Shake.

The sergeant took a cigar-holder out of his pocket and stuck a stubby cigar into it. The silver was tarnished, the ivory was yellowed, but the snake still twined around the shaft—

—and he tapped his ashes into the heart-shaped ashtray. Through the smoke and the music, which had drifted off key in the late hour, he caught another signal from the grey eyes. He looked at Salek, who was weeping into his gin-laced beer for his dead Deirdre.

"Listen," Kapsa said. "You've been in Chicago for quite a while now. You said in the letter you'd run across a fellow called Frkac."

Salek looked up at him with blank, bloodshot eyes.

"Tall, probably well dressed. Probably pretty well off by now, too," said the sergeant.

Salek was trying to concentrate on what he was saying.

"He goes by the name of Fircut."

"That swine!" exclaimed Salek. "I could tell you stories!"

"So," urged the sergeant, catching another blinding signal from the grey eyes, "tell me!"

He had seven dry months of duty behind him, and his cuckolded friend's tipsy grievances cast Vlasta in the best possible light for Kapsa's needs.

"We ran to the top of the rise overlooking Perryville," Shake went on. "We went over, and on the other side there was a steep drop down to the bottom, where there were lovely clean pools of water on either side of Doctor's Creek, which otherwise was bone-dry. Water! And it looked drinkable! But the water was surrounded by armed Rebels, and as soon as they saw us they started scooping up water into their canteen cups, mocking us."

A distant cannon boomed from the north-east.

"What was that?" the sergeant wondered.

"It's just the devil farting," declared Shake. "Well, gentlemen, we didn't hesitate. We couldn't have anyway, our thirst made us reckless. We didn't wait for orders, but tore down the hillside." Shake took a puff from his meerschaum, then nodded to Paidr for a light. "That hillside was so steep you couldn't keep your balance. Eda Kafka tripped, and as he tried to get his balance he went flying over our heads right into one of the puddles and just lay there drinking from it. As it turned out, he was the only one who got a drink that night. The Rebs took him prisoner but just for an hour. We set him free on our second charge."

"How could they stop you on a steep hillside like that?" asked Houska.

"They outnumbered us and they were in a better position. We had to re-treat," sighed Shake.

"But dammit!" asked Houska irritably. "How did you stop yourselves from literally falling into their hands?"

"The boys sat down on their butts and managed to skid to a stop, then did an about-face and scrambled back up the hill and over the top on all fours," Shake replied coolly. "I was ashamed of them, though. That's why I turned my back to the Rebs for an instant, to inspire our boys to greater feats of courage."

"On a steep hill like that?" Houska said ominously. "How come you didn't fall on your ass?"

But Shake replied calmly, "The minnie kept me from falling. The im-pact knocked the wind out of me and drove me back up the hill like a bil-liard ball. At the top I rolled over to the other side of the rise and just lay there gasping for breath. I was so winded I couldn't join the second charge."

"And you were gasping for breath the whole time," said Fisher.

"I was indeed," Shake assured him. "I wasn't able to fight again until next afternoon, and then I almost took General Polk prisoner."

"I'll bet you did!" said Javorsky.

Salek's account of Fircut's activity in Chicago was delivered under the influence of too many gin-spiked beers, and all the sergeant could tell was that there had been some money at stake, perhaps as much as five hundred dollars. The exact nature of the con game wasn't clear, however, and it was Vlasta who ended up throwing some light on that. They left Slavik's Tavern with Salek as dawn was beginning to tinge the ragged skyline with gold. When they reached the building with the red shutters, which were closed on Sundays, they banged on the door, and the maid who opened it exclaimed, "Oh, not again, Massa Cup!" (she had arrived by the Underground Railroad and still hadn't lost her planta-tion habits of speech). They put Cup to bed in the master bedroom and left him in the care of the maid, whose black eyes gave the sergeant a quick glance and got the picture.

In the guest room, after making love, Vlasta shared his cigar with him. "Not that I doubt you, sergeant. Not at all. I believe you. But in this case Fircut was as pure as a lily. It was an honest investment in an honest deal—"

"Fircut? Honest?"

"Everybody has his own way to drum up capital. Some do it like Cup, and depend partly on hard work and partly on luck. Others like Fircut aren't cut out for work, they just trust to luck. Did you say he was a valet? Did you ever see a valet who worked hard? They come by their capital in other ways. I don't know what he stole from you, or even where you got it in the first place, but after all, darling, you were just a private then. . . ." She turned her grey eyes on him, and they seemed to be laughing at him.

"Never mind," he said. "Just tell me what happened."

. . . Salek, drowning another shot in another beer, had said, "I'm a sucker for stuff like that. Maybe it was a cannonball out of my cannon. I have a bad con-science about it anyway. But what else could you do under Windischgraetz?"

"Don't tell me Fircut was on the barricades in '48. He wasn't even in Prague then. He was serving port to General Uhlmann in Mainz," the sergeant had replied. . . .

". . . whenever Ondra has too much to drink, he's back loading that stinking cannon of his," said Vlasta. "Naturally he and Fircut got drinking, and before he knew it he'd loaded his cannon; Fircut placed himself up on the barricade like a sitting duck, and the shot broke his leg."

"But Fircut hasn't even got a limp," he said.

"Maybe he got some first-class surgery in the imperial prison hospital," said Vlasta. "Or else you fell for Fircut's tall tale like Ondra did. Anyway, Ondra gave him a cheque for five hundred dollars."

Vlasta stretched a bare arm towards Kapsa and held out her hand. A jagged bolt of lightning shot across the Chicago sky. He placed the little cigar between her fingers. He said, "Why do you do this to Ondra?"

She inhaled, stuck the tip of her pink tongue between her lips, and blew smoke rings into the air. "Why did you do it to Ondra?"

Seven months without a woman. But he said, "I'm probably a rat."

"What does that make me?"

He turned to her. She lay on the bed, resting on fluffy pillows. She had small firm breasts and nipples, and he cupped one of them in his large hand. "They're so tiny," *he said.*

"That's because I'm not a cow."

"What are you?"

"Just a woman," *she said.* "With no children. My late husband didn't give me one. Cup didn't. None of the others did. You won't either. All I have is Ondra's Annie. But I want—" *She tapped the cigar ashes into the ashtray on the chair beside the bed.* "Come here," *she said.*

The sergeant, caught between her soft legs, wondered how he would get through another seven months—

"... I can't say no to somebody like that," *Salek had said.* "I have a bad conscience. And besides, everything seemed proper. He showed me an endorsement, a bona fide endorsement from the Doctors' College that said his ointment would restore hair in a month, six weeks at the latest. Six weeks, my arse! The results came in the next day!" *Cup's voice rose and his fist slammed down on the tabletop, making the heart-shaped ashtray jump and scatter its contents.* "By six in the morning, the first bald-headed man was banging on the door with a bagful of what was left of his hair. By nine there was a whole mob in front of Fircut & Co., heads as bald as billiard balls, every one. One of them was pushing a cart with a bucket of melted tar and another was carrying a feather bed and a knife and four bald men were dragging a rail. Fircut snuck out the back way. If he ever shows up here again, I'm going to—"

Later on—by then Kapsa was a drill sergeant in the newly formed Thirteenth U.S. Army Regiment under Sherman—Fircut did show up again. Nothing had happened to him. It turned out that the depilatory effect of the tonic acted like a fertilizer: in the long run, it actually did promote the growth of hair.

Salek, determined either to get his five hundred dollars back or to punch Fircut in the nose, wound up doing neither. In fact he invested more money—this time in the new firm of Fircut, Sanders, & Co., which arranged for the reburial of fallen heroes in special coffins offered in a range of prices. But Cup never saw a single dividend. By then he was a Union soldier.

Shortly after that night with the lightning, he divorced Vlasta.

"Okay," Shake admitted, "I wasn't the one who almost took General Polk prisoner, but I was there when he just skinned out of being taken prisoner by Colonel Shryock, who was sent to us when Colonel O'Sell was taken by General Polk when he reported under his command, as ordered, with his entire brigade."

"You've got it all haywire," said Javorsky.

"All I'm doing is faithfully describing the renowned battle of Perryville.

If anything was haywire, that was," said Shake. "For instance, how would you explain the fact that next day, when the main battle broke out, Lincoln's Rifles, which were part of the Twenty-fourth Illinois in General Gilbert's corps, fought with the Eighty-seventh Indiana in General McCook's corps?"

"How do you explain it?" asked Fisher.

"I can't."

"I can," said Houska. "You simply scrammed, banner and all, and ran into the Indiana troops, who stopped you from scramming any farther."

"You didn't hear me right," said Shake. "The twelve of us were the only heroic ones of the original eighty-two men in Lincoln's Slavonic Rifles, and—"

"Including you, right?" said Javorsky. "You and your armour."

"I admit I was driven to heroism by cowardice," said Shake. "But the mix-up at Perryville was partly the fault of our three commanders, partly the weather conditions, and mainly the powder!"

"Your powder was damp?" said Houska. "I thought you were saying how dry it was."

"I mean the powder, the yellow dust that covered us," said Shake, "because the weather was so dry."

The second day, when Cheatham and Buckner and their veterans came tearing out of the woods with their Rebel yells and woke up the desperately thirsty rookies in General McCook's two divisions, they raised clouds of dusty earth from the ground that turned both the blue and the grey uniforms an indistinguishable greyish yellow. The units got mixed up as individual soldiers moved in and out of the dust clouds, and shortly General Terrill was the first casualty, and no one knew if he died a hero's death or was accidentally shot when some scared rookie fired at a dusty shadow. But Sheridan, who at that time was an artillery commander, not a cavalryman, recognized that the forward ranks of the Confederate troops, mixed in with the Union rookies, were driving McCook's two divisions off the battlefield and towards defeat, so he aimed his cannon at the rear lines of the Rebel army and executed a textbook artillery assault from the flank, where they least expected it. He added to the confusion but he also prevented a rout.

"In a coach far away from the slaughter, General Buell had no idea what was happening," Shake continued, "because, in addition to the powdery dust, there were something like bubbles forming on the battlefield that didn't let any sound through."

"Bubbles? Of what?" Zinkule wondered.

"Hot air," said Houska.

"I don't know," said Shake. "One minute you're deafened by Rebel yells, then you take a step and they look like a chorus of fish. Buell and his coach were right in the middle of one of those bubbles, waiting for the fighting to start, but it had already been going on for an hour and he couldn't hear it. He was confused when his messengers described the start of the operation to him."

Fourteen hundred from both armies died in the battle, and later on almost six thousand more died in field hospitals and infirmaries—legless, armless, gangrene-ridden, thirsty, racked with pain. Around the campfire, the horrors turned into comedy. It was the reverse of the chromotypes printed in ladies' magazines at the beginning of the war, reducing the horrors of the slaughter to one or two symbolic soldiers splayed out picturesquely on emerald-green grass.

Shake said, "In the course of the battle, the Lincoln's Rifles took up a position in the ruins of a farmhouse, and we waited for the right moment to deliver a decisive blow against the enemy. The farmer and his family were trembling with fear in the cellar, but they had a supply of well water, and because they were loyal to the Union they sent their daughter up to bring us water and she ended up staying and watching the battle. So we finally slaked our thirst as we waited for the right moment to attack. Then we gradually got really thirsty."

"You said you already slaked it," said Houska.

"He means figuratively speaking," said Javorsky.

"Exactly," said Shake. "The farmer was prepared for that too. He sent his son up with a jug; the kid put it beside the trap door and went back down into the cellar. So we worked on getting rid of that kind of thirst, and towards evening—"

"What about the girl? I'll bet you tried to seduce her into drinking with you too," said Houska with a frown.

"Not into drinking with us," said Shake, "and anyway, we got nowhere. It was the fighting she was interested in. Just when we thought the moment to attack had come, a fresh brigade headed by Colonel O'Sell emerged from a cloud of dust. We cheered and Colonel O'Sell walked over to Geza Mihalotzy and asked him if he was in contact with the enemy. Mihalotzy didn't want to admit that so far the only contact we had had was with the civilians in the basement—and they were friendly—so he told O'Sell that we hadn't been able to identify the enemy clearly in the raging battle. At that moment one of those sound bubbles rolled over to us, a cloud of dust was blown away, and on a little rise ahead of us was a tall officer in a dark uniform, scouring the valley with a pair of field-glasses, though he couldn't have seen much. 'Isn't that General Terrill?' Colonel O'Sell asked. In his embarrassment, Geza Mihalotzy ran his finger inside his collar and raised his chin. Colonel O'Sell took this for a nod and hurried over to the officer in the dark uniform. Just then the bubble burst and we could hear O'Sell as clear as a bell. 'General, sir, I'm here on your orders with an infantry brigade.' The general looked him up and down, which was unusual, given the battle situation, then asked him which brigade he meant. 'The second brigade of the First Division of General Gilbert's corps,' replied Colonel O'Sell. 'I await specific orders regarding our position in the field.' The general looked him over again, apparently taken aback, and then said, 'There must be a mistake. You, colonel, are my prisoner.' And then we saw O'Sell sheepishly unbuckling his sword and handing it to the general. It was General Polk. With all that dust on his uniform, it looked blue."

"Why didn't you go to O'Sell's rescue?" asked Fisher.

"We intended to start firing but we might have hit O'Sell. So we had to stand by helpless as Polk escorted him to the nearest bubble."

"Why didn't you launch this attack you keep talking about?" Houska asked.

"It didn't seem like the right moment," said Shake. "When the right moment finally came, General Polk was gone with his prisoner, Colonel O'Sell."

More cannon boomed in the distance. Shake inverted the canteen with the word WODA carved on it, ran his finger around the inside of the neck, and licked off the last few drops. He sighed. "The situation got more and more complicated," he said. "It was getting on towards dusk, on the north hillside of the valley a greenish sun crept along the jagged horizon, the moon rose in the south and it—"

"—had polka dots," Stejskal prompted him.

"Damn near," said Shake. "It was kind of a turquoise colour, with strange orange blotches on it. Bubbles were rolling about the battlefield and it turned out that they didn't just block out sound, they could hold it as well. When a bubble burst, it sometimes let loose an order shouted half an hour earlier at the other end of the battlefield, which just made things more confusing. One of the bubbles released some choice bits of profanity uttered by General Braxton Bragg, and then we could hear General Polk interrupting him: 'General Bragg, expressions like that will not be tolerated on my battlefield!'"

"Admit it," said Houska, "your thirst was so quenched that you slept right through the battle and dreamed up the bubbles."

"It's extraordinary that some of you don't believe me," said Shake. "In this war anything is possible."

They sat around the campfire palavering in Czech while farther away, at a respectful distance, was a circle of Negroes they had gathered on their march. They looked like impoverished scarecrows. Tattered shirts were draped over dark sweaty torsos, muscular legs were barely covered by what had originally been trousers. But they were grinning into the fire, for they were free. Then two Negroes got up and moved closer to the fire. They had obviously been listening to the conversation. Their clothes seemed in better repair than the rest and one of them had an embroidered design near the collar of his shirt, stained though it was with the mud and dirt of North Carolina. To the sergeant it looked like a little Moravian dove design. Was it the booze? No, he was quite sober.

"A blessed good evening to you," said the first Negro, in Czech. The sergeant spun around to face the man, whose plump lips framed a shiny white smile. He closed his eyes and opened them again: the little Moravian doves were still there on the grubby shirt.

"Are you Czech?" Kapsa asked, in the same language.

"Oh no, I'm Moravian," the man replied, in a Moravian dialect. "So's Breta here," he added, pointing to his companion.

"Massa was Moravian," he explained, "and so was his missus."

"What's your name?"

"MacHane," said the Negro. "He taught us to read and write, too."

The sergeant was moved by this living evidence of a compatriot's destiny in the depths of the Carolinas, amid the smouldering turpentine forests. He invited the two men over to the fire. Stejskal gave them some roast meat and they downed it hungrily. The story or legend, or whatever it was, emerged gradually. It must have been the truth; after all, both men spoke Czech. Their mother had died young; Massa MacHane had bought them as kids. He only had five slaves, all male, and they worked on his steam-powered sawmill on the Charleston River. He bought the two little boys for his kind missus, for the couple had no children of their own.

"What was her name?"

"Ruzena. She died five years ago, a year before the war started."

"And where is your massa?"

"He had to join up. He's a colonel with Massa General Braxton Bragg."

The name was still confusing him. "You know how to write?"

They both nodded. He handed them a pencil and a notebook. "Write down your massa's name, his whole name."

The Negro wrote, in a large schoolboy's hand, *Jindrich Machane.* Then he said aloud, "Ma-khah-nee-yeh. But everybody called him MacHane. So we did too. Sunday he'd read the Bible to us. Massa was a Moravian Brother."

An odd story to come across here, in deepest North Carolina. Massa MacHane had been born here. Maybe his father came from the old country, the Negroes weren't sure. Now he was the enemy in Braxton Bragg's corps out there somewhere. Colonel Henry MacHane. Kapsa glanced at the Negroes gnawing away at the generous hunks of plundered meat roasted over a campfire. Freedom. The respectful circle of black men hung back in the black darkness, singing pianissimo:

> *Oh Freedom, oh freedom, oh freedom over me*
> *And before I'd be a slave, I'll be buried in my grave. . . .*

Ursula's face emerged from the darkness. Freedom. No von Hanzlitscheks.

> *There are rocks and hills*
> *And brooks and vales*
> *Where milk and honey flow. . . .*

Sucking on a cold meerschaum pipe, Shake was finishing his wild dream: "Clouds of dust that started out yellowish brown turned blue when the spotted moon rose over the battlefield, and suddenly out of one of those clouds came a swarm of attacking soldiers in pale green uniforms. It was an optical illusion, of course, but we recognized them from their hats. Not even the zouaves from New York wore anything like that, and they'd wear practically anything. No, these were Rebels. So Colonel Shryock, who had replaced Colonel O'Sell when he got taken prisoner, gave the order to fire, and all of us Lincoln's Rifles obeyed to the last man."

"How big was that jug?" asked Javorsky, but Shake went on unperturbed.

"The Rebs took cover behind a low stone wall dividing two fields and returned our fire. Then all at once an officer in a dark general's uniform emerged from a dust cloud on our right and looked around, and when he saw Colonel Shryock hiding behind a wayside cross—"

"Aren't you getting this mixed up with the Hussite Wars?" asked Stejskal. "A wayside cross in Perryville?"

"The farmer was from Moravia," Shake retorted calmly. "The general walked over to Colonel Shryock behind the wayside cross—it was a pillar depicting the agony of Christ on the cross—and yelled, 'What's going on here, colonel? Can't you see you're firing on your own men?' Colonel Shryock was startled, uncertain, and glanced over at the low stone wall and the unmistakable hats showing behind it. 'I do not think, general, that we are mistaken here,' he reported in an official tone. 'I have no doubt whatsoever that these soldiers are indeed the enemy!'"

"Sounds like a book," said Houska.

"That's because Shake tells stories straight out of story-books," said Javorsky.

Shake just shrugged. "'Enemy soldiers!' the general shouted, annoyed. 'What nonsense! Colonel, hold your fire, at once! And what is your name?' Beside me Pepik Dvoracek jumped up and tried to alert Colonel Shryock to something, but he and the English language didn't get along too well, because he never had much use for it tapping beer at Slavik's Tavern. 'Sir, Sir,' Pepik shouted, 'He . . . he. . . .' 'What do you want to tell him, Pepik?' I asked, but he was so eager to speak that he couldn't get it out. 'Sir! He . . . sir!' As Pepik was stammering away, I heard Colonel Shryock say, 'Colonel Shryock, Eighty-seventh Indiana Regiment. And might I ask who you are, general?' 'Sir! Sir!' Pepik Dvoracek kept saying. The general looked at the Lincoln's Rifles and scowled. He rode over to Colonel Shryock, shook his fist in the colonel's face, and declared, 'You don't know me, but you will!' He turned his horse, did a slow gallop along our battle position, calling, 'Hold your fire! Hold your fire!' We obeyed and, oddly enough, so did the fellows in the hats behind the wall. 'Sir! Sir!' Pepik kept trying, but still couldn't get out what he wanted to say. The general slowly vanished in a dust cloud, with a neigh and the sound of galloping hoofs. And Pepik Dvoracek gave up and shouted in Czech at Colonel Shryock, 'Colonel, sir! That was General Polk. I know him because once, before the war, he dropped in for a drink at Slavik's.'"

"And a bubble burst and translated it into English, right?" said Fisher.

"Wrong," said Shake. "I translated it into English. Shryock ordered us to resume firing, but meanwhile a bubble of dust had drifted over and hidden the wall, and by the time it burst the hats were gone. Bragg had ordered a tactical retreat."

The sergeant glanced down the row of campfires that lay across the dark landscape like a fiery arrow pointing at Bentonville. The war was ending. Somewhere beyond the tip of that flaming arrow, General Johnston was devising some desperate defensive action, Wheeler's wild riders were galloping about, and a nervous Leonidas Polk was counting heads in his battalion, mired in the blood-drenched Carolina mud.

★

Benjamin ran down the hill to the plantation house: "They're coming! They're coming!" So they lined up outside, at the foot of the front steps. As the youngest, Dinah stood at the end of the line, in a new black silk dress and a new starched white apron. She was curious about young massa. She had last seen him four years before, when she was twelve and wasn't even allowed to stand in the line of the house niggers to wave goodbye, so she had waited with a bunch of the other children by the road for young massa, proud on his horse, in a grey top hat and grey boots with red cuffs. Riding behind him was Gideon, happy to have been chosen to go to Paris.

Now Gideon sat dejected on the jump-seat and young massa was inside the coach, sunk back in the pillows, looking grim. Before the coach came to a stop, Gideon jumped down and put down the step. He wore soft leather riding boots and was dressed in red livery. The coach stopped. Old Moses, who had been riding beside the driver, took up a position by the step; young massa reached out, put his left arm around Moses' shoulders, hopped onto the step, and lowered himself to the ground. His left leg was gone. With Gideon and Moses supporting him on either side, he moved slowly towards the house, with old massa behind him, a pained expression on his face.

They didn't know if they should cheer his arrival, so they were silent and grave. Old Abe bowed. "Welcome home, massa!" But young massa barely nodded. He hobbled past the line, up the steps, and through the front door. The left leg of his white riding pants was pinned up in the back.

Dinah felt sorry for him. She pictured it in her mind. The horse had broken its leg jumping a wall and had gone down so fast massa hadn't had time to pull his foot out of the stirrup. The bones in his leg were so badly smashed not even the famous Paris surgeon could save it. That was the story. But Gideon couldn't hold his tongue, and the day after they came back everyone knew the truth. It had happened in a duel, and the duel had been over a woman, of course. Dinah imagined someone fighting over her. She had read about such things in the French novels that belonged to Mademoiselle Hortense de Ribordeaux, who had just gotten married and gone off to live in Louisiana.

"It was Count Lissex," said Gideon.

"Lissieux," she corrected him.

Gideon exclaimed, "Listen, girl, was it you in Paris or me?" He looked at her as though he had never properly seen her before. "Tell me your name, anyway."

"Dinah. I never been to Paris, but you say it Lissieux. He's famous. He fought

three duels." *She counted them off on her fingers:* "*Baron Fleury, Prince Jean-Paul de la Roche, and the Spaniard Don Carlos.*"

"*What is this nonsense?*" *he interrupted her.* "*Massa, he only fight one duel. I never heard of no Jean-Paul!*"

"*I read about it!*"

"*Whereabouts you read it? The newspaper? We don't get no Paris newspapers here.*"

"*No, it was in a novel that Miss Hortense had—*"

"*A novel!*" *Gideon exclaimed.* "*My, ain't we smart!*"

Young massa lay on the big four-poster canopy bed smoking slender Parisian cigars, staring out the open window at the dismal trees with their beards of moss. He did not come down to dinner. Gideon took it to his room on a wheeled cart, while old massa sat alone at the huge dining table, between the candlesticks, permanently grim. When she came upstairs with the coffee, she saw that Gideon had just been whispering something in young massa's ear, and massa watched her so intently as she walked over to the table that she felt self-conscious and almost tripped over the carpet.

"*You speak French?*" *he barked at her abruptly.*

The man's tone scared her. She should have kept it to herself. What if—"*No sir, massa.*"

"*She lying,*" *said Gideon.* "*She corrected my French.*"

"*Don't lie,* ma petite,*" said Massa, still gazing at her.*

"*I'm not lying, sir,*" *she said, pouring the coffee with a trembling hand.*

"*Fais tomber une goutte de cognac dans mon café,*" *said massa. She walked over to the liquor cabinet and opened it.*

"*You are lying,* ma petite,*" he said.* "*Where did you learn French?*"

She finally told him, but it was like pulling teeth.

"'*You see, Cyril, I was scared to tell him. There's a kind of law about it. Negroes can't learn how to read and write and speak French. Our massa doesn't respect the law much, but I thought to myself, he may not like it.*'" *Cyril said later, quoting her. In his mind the sergeant rearranged the story into scenes and dialogues, evocations of nights and events.*

That evening after dinner, Beulah, the cook, who was in charge of the girls like her in the big house—the kitchenmaids, parlourmaids, chambermaids—told her, "*You gonna take care of young massa. You bring him his food, his drink, and*"—*she made a face*—"*you empty his thunder-jug.*"

"*Me?*"

"*Who else? You the youngest.*"

"*On top of that,*" *said Benjamin,* "*you've got the prettiest tits.*"

"*But it's mainly because she knows French," said Gideon. "Young massa won't feel like he back in Texas so much.*"

"*He didn't lose his leg in Texas.*"

"*He lost his heart in Paris. Dinah gonna read him love stories.*"

"*Read?*" smirked Sarah. "*That I want to see.*"

Benjamin licked his lips. "*Me too!*"

She emptied his chamber-pot, but massa read his books to himself. He didn't read a lot. Mostly he sat in his armchair staring out the window. And he drank a lot. She brought him cognac and carried out the empty bottles. Once a week Dr. Webber came from Austin to examine his stump. The wound was still slightly infected and she changed his dressing twice a day, bathed the stump in a cleansing solution, and rubbed ointment on it. She felt sorry for young massa but she never said anything, because he never spoke to her. He would just look at her, watch her nursing his wound, follow her with his eyes as she walked across the room. She was aware of his attention. She knew that he watched her carrying out the dirty bandages, that he watched her from the window as she walked among the trees with a basket of apricots from the orchard. She watched him, too. She would stand by the dining-room window as he hobbled across the lawn swinging on his crutches like a pendulum, a slender French cigar clenched between his teeth. Then he stopped using the chamber-pot. She thought nothing of it until the day he began talking to her. She had come in with his cognac and caught him staring at a picture. He quickly stuck it in the drawer of his nightstand and let her pour him some cognac. As she was gathering up the coffee service she saw him looking at her more intently than usual. The next morning she came to change the bedsheets when he was downstairs, and she opened the drawer. The picture was there, in an ebony frame, face down. She turned it over and was startled. Her first impression was that the picture was of her. Instead of a black dress and starched apron, however, the woman wore a gown like the ones the ladies used to wear when the Ribordeaux held a ball. The complexion of the skin in the décolletage was a bit lighter than hers, but not much. She stared at the picture and lost track of time.

"That's not you," she heard a voice from the door saying. She looked up, unperturbed.

"Forgive me, Massa Étienne. The drawer was open—"

"Don't lie," he said, and swung into the bedroom on his crutches.

She put the picture back in the nightstand, but before she could shut the drawer he said, "Give it here!" He sat down in the armchair, rested the crutches against the armrests, and stared at the portrait. "Come over here!" She came nearer. "Closer," he said. "I want to take a good look."

She leaned over the chair, and he held the picture close to her face.

"*This could be you if you weren't black,*" *he said.* "*As a matter of fact, you're not even that black. Maybe she wasn't completely white. I couldn't have brought her to Texas.*"

Much later, he told her that the woman's name was Doña Jorge de Castiello and that her colour came not from the sun of Southern Spain—because since she was five she'd lived in Paris, where her father was a diplomat—but from the Moorish blood in her veins. She could hardly become a Texas bride. Besides, she had lost interest when he lost his leg, even though it was on account of her.

"*Who is she?*" *Dinah asked.*

"*A countess.*"

"*Can a Negro woman be a countess in Europe?*"

He didn't reply. She knew that the idea of a Negro countess violated the hypotheses that existed as absolute truths over glasses of bourbon and cigar smoke. "*Come up after supper,*" *he said.*

She knew what that meant.

Reading aloud from French romances.

That evening, a moon hung over the blossoming cotton-fields like an etching illustrating the French novels Mademoiselle de Ribordeaux had used to read, tearfully mouthing each syllable. Dinah had read over her shoulder and then, later, borrowed them without permission and reread them by the light falling on the front lawn from the big windows of the master bedroom, where old massa was reading something, though not French romances.

She knew there was nothing she could do. That was just the way it was. Black countesses only existed in Europe. But being sixteen and full of those French romances, she decided that, while she did it, she would be a French countess.

He was lying on the bed, already naked, and he said, "*Take off your clothes.*"

The moon over the cotton-fields shone on the muscular body of the young man with one leg. His stump was healing well now. The day before, a cabinet-maker from Galveston who also manufactured artificial limbs had measured it.

She pulled her dress over her head, removed her corset and her underwear. Aroused, he said, "*Come here. Sit down on me.*"

He grasped her by the hips, lifted her up, and lowered her down slowly. She was a virgin and she hissed with pain. Massa started to writhe, his palms on her breasts.

The white moon was shining, a night bird called out, and the cotton rustled in the breeze. The novels never described this moment, but if they did it surely wouldn't be like this. That night she didn't become a black countess. He kept his eyes closed the whole time. But then, perhaps I am, she said to herself. It hurt a lot, as she had known it probably would. Later on, she would enjoy it. Before she left his room that night, she changed the bedclothes. Of course, the washer-woman, Mother Terrill, had to tell everyone.

"*He really give it to you,*" *Benjamin sniggered.*

"*I give it to him. His stump started bleeding.*"

She would never again say anything so cynical. But then, he had merely as-serted his right of ownership, and besides, it was only painful for her, and noth-ing more. Later on, they always did it the same way. They could have reversed positions, but he would have been too aware of his stump. He would embrace her, hold her close, and even kiss her. She enjoyed it, but he was the one who began falling in love.

Of course, she never thought it could be anything else, as it might have been with the real black countess in Europe, the one he saw behind his closed eyelids. Soon, though, he stopped closing his eyes. When he married—the stump would be no obstacle; the plantation was the second-largest in the state and he was the only son—three things could happen. He could put her away in a little house in Austin, or maybe farther away, in Galveston, and under one pretext or another come to see her once or twice a month, and his wife would be either stupid enough to believe him or smart enough not to pry. The second possibility was that she would not exist for the wife; she would be no more than a piece of prop-erty kept in one of the shacks on the plantation to soothe his nerves, the way he kept French cigars in a humidor. The third and worst possibility: Étienne would fall in love with his wife, and Dinah would be demoted back to the status of a chambermaid who did nothing but make beds and serve cognac and empty the chamber-pot again. When time passed, and along with it the charms that re-minded him of his Moorish countess, she would end up with the others in a shack on the plantation, perhaps the mother of a few of his bastards, perhaps along with the children of a Negro husband.

She couldn't—fortunately—imagine any other possibility.

And he was the one who started it. Actually, it was started by a letter sent to old massa from Louisiana. The story—the horror, the bloody and costly tri-umph—spread through the plantation from a single source: Gideon, who, after old massa had read the letter, took it to young massa in the summer-house, where he sat over a big book smoking and copying things out. That was how they first heard the story of the costly triumph. She heard it all again late that night in Éti-enne's room. That night he wasn't naked on the bed, but was sitting in the arm-chair, smoking. He told her how the Negroes on the plantation of M. de Ribordeaux's cousin in Louisiana had rebelled. Not all of them had, just eight. They took massa and his two overseers hostage, and massa, with a knife at his throat, gave them their freedom, all eight of them. He gave it to them in writing, in black and white. They weren't foolish enough to think that would be enough.

It was more like insurance in case someone stopped them on the road before the word got out. Word wasn't supposed to get out until morning, when the house niggers, who weren't in on it, would start wondering why massa hadn't come down to breakfast yet; the field niggers would assume the overseers had had too much to drink and were sleeping in. The men had stolen horses and intended to ride all night and all day through the woods until they reached the Underground Railroad. An itinerant abolitionist preacher had told them where to go. They picked an evening when the young massa had taken his sister and the planta-tion-owner's wife to visit relatives in New Orleans. They tied up massa and the two overseers, gagged them, buried them in the hay, took several pistols from massa's room, and set out. Their downfall was their need to stay together. They hid the pistols under their shirts, but eight well-dressed Negroes—like M. de Ri-bordeaux, the cousin didn't treat his slaves badly—riding handsome plantation horses were rather conspicuous in the Louisiana countryside. Early the next morning, while massa and his two overseers were still bound and gagged in the hay, three white men on horseback stopped the eight of them. The manumission papers aroused even more suspicion. How could all eight of them have been granted freedom on the same day? The horses were obviously well bred, more likely to be found at the races than under nigger butts.

"Hmm"—*one of the riders spat on the ground*—*"everybody knows Ribor-deaux's crazy and spoils his niggers. But I can't believe he'd have gone this far."*

The three riders agreed and the oldest, with a military-style moustache, turned to the runaways. "Okay, you'll ride back with us and we'll ask Mr. de Ri-bordeaux how much he had to drink last night." And he waved in their faces the papers that had represented their hopes.

The plan had failed and their only recourse was the pistols. Jim and Luke pulled theirs out and shot the rider with the moustache; the other riders were quick on the draw and shot Jim and Luke. Two others reached for their weapons, but one fell off his horse with a bullet in his head, and the other spun around and managed to gallop away. The remaining four surrendered.

The one who had escaped was picked up that evening by a posse of planta-tion-owners. He resisted but they shot the pistol out of his hand and clapped him behind bars along with the four who had surrendered, though in a separate cell. His fate was certain. One of the other four would share the gallows with him— the one who had started it.

"What's that?" she asked. She couldn't let on that she had already heard the heroic story in the kitchen, so she simply asked him to define a word he had used to explain it all away. And she added—unable to keep the disbelief out of her voice—"Is that a sickness?"

"That's right," he replied uncertainly. "There's a book about it, written by a

physician, Dr. Samuel W. Cartwright. It's a sickness of the mind. Drapetomania. After all, they had no reason to run away."

She said nothing. She looked out the window at the lovely row of trees, and the cotton-fields beyond it rising slowly to the horizon, rimmed with beautiful woods. Beyond lay an even more beautiful world, at the end of the Underground Railroad.

"Or did they?"

"I don't know, massa."

"Uncle Jean-Jacques is no fool. His overseers had instructions not to beat his slaves. Six of the eight could read and write. Three of them had learned a trade," said young massa. His voice betrayed growing uncertainty.

She said nothing.

"Were they lacking anything?"

She shrugged.

"Are you?" By the time he got to this point, he had lost all hope of trusting his own beliefs. Because he would always know that the only way she could be a black countess was when he closed his eyes. She could never have what the black countess in Europe had—beautiful clothes, jewels, a carriage. The privilege to sometimes say no.

"No," she said softly.

"So you see," he said, but he knew she saw nothing. *"Damn!"* he swore, and stood up. He had his artificial leg by then. It was made of fine wood, and elegantly carved and polished, but it was artificial all the same. He turned to the window and lit a cigar.

She asked, *"Should I take off my clothes?"*

Silence.

"Massa?" she whispered.

He turned. *"Do you want to?"*

"If you do, massa—"

"Do you?"

Oh, what do I want? To have what the black countess has, even if she were suddenly very poor. But in her clever mind she knew that Étienne was going through something his books didn't explain, something they never dealt with, something that never came up over bourbon and cigars, something the worst gossip wouldn't mention. Fool nigger-girl, she said to herself, but she couldn't help it; she felt sorry for him. His dark, defeated silhouette against the window and the Texas sky. Despite everything, she pitied him. Silly nigger-girl.

She nodded.

Then she pulled her dress over her head, unlaced her corset; he tore his clothes off and unfastened his wooden leg; she climbed on the bed and sat back on her *heels, waiting for him to lie down on his back. But he knelt beside her on his knee and, supported by his stump, he gently laid her down on her back and gently spread her legs. She embraced him.*

That night he was the slave.

It wasn't love she felt, just pity.

"You were a silly nigger-girl," Cyril said later.

"You'd have been too," Dinah said. "How was I to know your little sister was going to show up in Texas?"

That night Étienne told her everything—how he had collapsed with a bullet in his shin, but Lissieux had fallen too, beyond help; how he had to leave Paris, and his leg was given hasty treatment by the physician he'd brought along for just such an eventuality. He waited for his mistress in Rennes. She never showed up. He expected a letter from her, at least. They amputated the leg, then at last news arrived that she'd left for Cordoba, where she would be getting married. So it had just been a flirtation. She had only been pulling his leg. He hadn't known then of a fiancé, who was now a bridegroom. Only then did he understand Lissieux's remark, the remark he had taken as a mortal insult, not recognizing the truth in it. Now Lissieux was dead and the woman was in Cordoba. Gideon found out when the next ship was due to leave and they sailed for Galveston.

Dinah didn't love him, but she was rather fond of him, and besides, she found that he was the best at it. She tried it with young Ezekiel, mainly to see if massa was as good as she thought he was. He was. Now Ezekiel spent his nights howling outside her window but she refused to give in again, and when he tried to obtain by force what he felt entitled to (she was hanging out laundry behind the big house and Ezekiel had feigned a toothache and left the fields to find her) she kicked him in the groin, and he fell to the ground and whimpered in such pain that she was afraid she'd damaged him for good. She was relieved, a month later, when he got a silly field-nigger pregnant. Massa Étienne might be a virtuoso, but in this sphere it was she who was free and he who was the slave. In fact, as she would soon discover, he was a born slave. He started talking about a little house he had seen for sale in Austin, about the garden with a stable where he could put his horse.

That was after old massa's friend came to visit from Louisiana and brought along his daughter. About the same time, old massa would often, at dinner, raise the subject of a grandson and heir, whose appearance on the scene would not be unwelcome. The friend's daughter, whose name was Scarlett, was pretty enough—quite lovely, in fact, except for her freckles. But in the evening, when they were assessing the situation in the kitchen, Beulah said white men liked freckles.

And Benjamin said, "Pretty soon no more screwing for you, Dinah. Least-wise not twice a day and four times a night like now."

"You sure don't think much of us, Benjy. We ain't a hundred years old like you," she snapped at him.

That was when Étienne started talking about a little house in Austin. Well, she said to herself, it could be worse.

Then Mr. Carson came to call, and brought with him a foreign beauty with stunning blue eyes and a long braid she liked to play with. And her brother. Suddenly there were two slaves, and they weren't both hers.

The Writer's Third Intermezzo

I WAS SITTING in the parlour working on my correspondence when Jasmine brought in a grey calling card.

"This lady wants to talk to you, Miz Tracy. She says she's sorry to arrive unannounced, but she says you were friends years ago, in Liberty."

The calling card read:

> Mrs. L.A. Brumble
> 217 Main Street
> Sanderstown, Rhode Island.

On the reverse, my visitor had added a handwritten note: "Maggie Rogers—remember me, you lucky girl?"

How could I forget Maggie's exasperated outburst? "You dimwit!" she'd said, on an occasion when I had indeed displayed singular dimness of wit. No, you don't forget moments like that.

"Don't bother showing her in, I'll go myself, Jasmine." In the front hall stood a broomstick of a woman dressed in dark green velvet. She had a fat black handbag in one hand, a fat black book in the other. Her dark eyes stared at me out of unfathomed depths. She had rings under them the likes of which I had never seen. Maggie had never been a beauty, but a picture like this—

"Maggie, . . ." I breathed.

"Yes, it's me, all right," said my old friend.

I got my second shock when she sat down at the coffee table and put her book on it. It had a spine of pink leather (or something that looked like pink leather) and the title was in gilt lettering. . . . Good God!

"Don't tell me you read this kind of thing?"

Maggie smiled. She still had pretty white teeth, though they had looked prettier in Liberty. Back then, she had some colour to her complexion; now she was ashen. "Are you surprised?"

"It's just that you never were much for romance novels."

"That's because I thought I was above all that. As sometimes happens, though, life has disabused me of that illusion."

Then she noticed another book on the table that I hadn't thought to conceal. Its spine was also of pink pseudo-leather but the book was slightly thicker. Maggie squinted at the title. The golden letters on the spine said *Getting Even* by Laura A. Lee. She looked at me and said, "I'm more surprised at you."

I felt myself beginning to blush. "Well, you know—" I began defensively, but Maggie interrupted: "I'd have expected to find Thackeray, or Poe. But not this."

My shame was ridiculous. Although I spoke of my books as little romances, I was proud of them, and besides, I enjoyed writing them—I was on the verge of lying when Maggie started talking again. "I haven't read this one yet. What's it like?"

The identity of Laura A. Lee had apparently remained a mystery to my old friend. Thank heavens I had responded to my publisher's wish to satisfy numerous readers' requests for a picture of me by giving him a daguerreotype of my late aunt, Rosemary Wayne, who had been killed at nineteen in a fall from a horse. She had been a platinum blonde who insisted on having her picture taken with a pince-nez to hide the fact that she was cross-eyed, which was the only flaw in my poor aunt's beauty. That was why I had chosen her picture.

"It's not bad," I said. "The heroine is a little more intelligent than usual, I think."

"But not the hero, I hope."

Her critical perspicacity warmed my heart. I said, "It wouldn't be Laura Lee then, would it?"

"She must be an insufferable woman," said Maggie. "I imagine her as fat as well as cross-eyed."

"I saw her picture in *Ladies' Companion*," I said. "She's fairly pretty, and she doesn't really look fat."

"But she is cross-eyed."

Was she toying with me? Did she know that Laura Lee was me, and intend to confront me with it? "I never noticed," I said.

"Why do you think she wears a pince-nez? I've seen that picture too. True, you can't see anything below the neckline, but—"

She looked at me with her deep, dark eyes and I couldn't tell what she knew.

"—but that beautifully alliterative name doesn't fit somebody fat," she said. "It would go better with someone like you."

I felt the blood rush to my face again.

"But you're a redhead," she added. Maggie ran her fingers over the gilt letters on the spine of the book. "God knows if it's her real name."

"What makes you say that?"

"She's probably from high society and isn't anxious to be known for silliness like this. Even though it's not sheer silliness. You probably don't think so either, otherwise you'd be reading Thackeray instead."

I felt a wave of authorial pride. "It isn't Thackeray, but it does have—"

"Guts," said my friend. When we were girls, she was always the vulgar one. "Even though she is—at least I hope she is—a woman."

I still wasn't sure if she knew, but then Maggie sighed, "I used to turn up my nose at this kind of reading, until it saved my—well, not my life, exactly, but my sanity."

"Really!"

"I lost a baby, did you know?"

"Maggie!"

"It was a miscarriage."

2

In my privileged position as a friend of the commanding general, I didn't have to rely on an unreliable press. I heard the report of Vallandigham's arrest straight from Captain Hutton. I found out about things that weren't public knowledge, like the crinoline Mrs. Vallandigham had left hanging in the hall that Hutton got tangled up in when he came to arrest her husband, and how his soldiers were stumbling around in the dark because Comely Clem had

hidden in the bedroom and no one had thought to bring a lantern. Ambrose
was busy writing his speech for court that afternoon, but two other men with
moustaches sat in my parlour, adding their own distinctive commentaries to
Captain Hutton's dry report. The young, rosy-cheeked Lieutenant Pettiford
was there too. In fact, my Loretta appeared to find him fascinating, which I
took as a sign that her congenital tomboyishness was beginning to wane.
One of the moustaches, a black one contrasting with the silver hair above it,
belonged to the handsome General Hascall, who had clearly noticed Jasmine
as soon as he came into the room. The second moustache graced the face of a
legend, Colonel Jennison of Kentucky, who had volunteered to help Hascall
catch deserters in Ohio. Before the war he used to ride with one of John
Brown's bands of desperadoes, but they never caught him. He was said to
suffer from chronic itchiness of the trigger finger.

"I hear," he said, when Captain Hutton finished his report, "that Burnside is preparing to try that wretch before a military commission?"

Lieutenant Pettiford laughed. He laughed whenever anyone made a
joke, or whenever he thought they had.

"The trial starts tomorrow," said Hascall. "The general convened the tribunal yesterday. They're good men, one and all." He raised an empty snifter
and Jasmine poured him some cognac. "Thanks, dearie!" General Hascall
said, twirling the end of his moustache around his index finger. Jasmine
flashed him a flirtatious smile, which surprised me because that morning, as
I looked out the window, I'd seen her resolutely reject the advances of Judge
Parker's black coachman from next door. I hadn't heard what the coachman
said, but the rejection was clear, and it was hand-delivered.

"A waste of time," declared Colonel Jennison. "You should have hanged
him on the spot. Or"—he turned to Captain Hutton—"at the Kemper barracks at the latest."

Hascall laughed. "That would have been a solution—not a legal one,
perhaps, but under the circumstances an ideal one." Lieutenant Pettiford
guffawed and slapped his shiny boot. General Hascall wound the other tip
of his moustache around his finger, and gave Jasmine a sidelong glance. She
smiled again, then turned and went to get the coffee, wiggling her behind as
she walked, though she usually moved like a nun.

3

"Oh, Maggie! I'm so sorry to hear this!"
"You have two children, don't you?"

I nodded. Maggie looked around and the portraits of Jimmy and Loretta on the cabinet caught her eye.

"What do you call them?"

I told her.

"Mine would have been Lorraine. Or Ambrose, depending."

I was touched. Maggie nodded towards Humphrey's portrait. "Is that your husband?"

"Humphrey." I rang for Jasmine. "Can I offer you some coffee?"

"It doesn't help," said Maggie. She looked around the parlour again. On the table by the window stood a decanter of cognac. She started to say something, but Jasmine came in and I instructed her to bring coffee and some pastry.

Maggie picked my book up off the table and said, "It's a good thing Laura Lee is so prolific."

"There's no shortage of prolific women writers in America."

"I've tried a few, but I keep going back to Laura Lee."

"Surely you don't mean the woman can bear a second reading?" I asked, trying to sound condescending.

"She's even better the second time around. I've even read some of them three times."

I was elated, but also suspicious. Jasmine walked in with the coffee. "Thanks, Jasmine."

"You're welcome, Miz Tracy."

"Like Thackeray," said Maggie.

"How do you mean?"

"He's better the second time around."

"Maggie, you're exaggerating." I got up and walked over to the table by the window. She had lost a baby. A woman in that situation might well read some sort of opium like Laura Lee. I came back with the decanter and poured some of that other opium into her coffee.

"Why spoil good fire-water?" said Maggie. "Put a drop in a glass for me, will you?" When I did, she said, "I said a 'drop' just to be polite." I corrected my error and, after a brief hesitation, I poured a drop for myself as well. Maggie wrapped her thin fingers around the snifter and looked again at the portrait of Humphrey between my two cherubs.

"He's nearly as handsome as the one you jilted," she said. "On the other hand, he hasn't got as much on his conscience, either."

"Ambrose—" I started, huffily, but Maggie just waved a hand.

"I know. A fellow can't help it if he's a bit wet. And your husband is all right. Maybe if he grew some side-whiskers—"

"And what about your husband?" Then I thought, what if she's a widow? A war widow? But would she be wearing a green dress?

"Do you want to see what he looks like?"

"Of course I do!"

She opened her bag, pulled out a framed photograph, and handed it to me. It was not a conventional portrait, but more like those photographs by Matthew Brady that had so appalled New York society when they were shown in public. It showed a meadow, and a hillside sloping up to a low stone wall. On the meadow lay a pile of dead soldiers. Above them on the empty hillside, by the stone wall, lay an isolated corpse in the uniform of a Union officer.

"He's the one by the wall," said Maggie. "The name of the place is Marye's Heights."

4

I went over the bare facts again. A unit of the United States Army, on orders from their military commander and without the authorization of a civilian court, enters the private quarters of a lawfully elected member of Congress, and arrests him without a warrant for exercising his constitutional rights in a manner which was not to the liking of the military commander. All this flouting the first Amendment, issued almost three-quarters of a century ago by another general, more important and certainly more renowned. And here am I, an intelligent American woman, a writer, in fact, though only of books for adolescents, but still a woman whose life is in the written word—

I returned to the reality of the parlour.

"Moved him? Where to?" Colonel Jennison asked, in dismay.

"To Burnett House," replied General Hascall.

"That scoundrel? To the best hotel in the Middle West?"

"Vallandigham's a prominent prisoner," said Hascall, "and General Burnside—"

"Burnside is soft!" yelled Colonel Jennison. "If he could, he'd have the noose lined with velvet!"

Lieutenant Pettiford roared with laughter. I glanced at the seasoned officers around me and felt very ill at ease.

5

An hour later the decanter on the table was empty, and I saw my surroundings through the prism of memories of Liberty, that town of frame houses. Jasmine appeared with a fresh pot of coffee and then, seeing we didn't need two full pots of coffee, took it back to the kitchen and returned with a full decanter of cognac.

"Head over heels, Lorraine," my old friend was saying. "It happened to me exactly when it happened to you. I was a few steps behind you, and what Ambrose had become in the few years he'd been gone swept me off my feet as well. But Mr. Jenkins introduced him to you. Nobody paid any attention to me. Not Mr. Jenkins, not you, and certainly not that beautifully transformed ex-tailor."

I wanted to say something appropriate, but nothing came to mind.

"Back then I could live with it," said Maggie. "But then you left him standing at the altar and the world began to seem awfully unfair. That was why I called you a dimwit."

"It fit perfectly well," I said.

"What really happened?"

I almost told her about the letter from the Boston publisher, but stopped myself in time. I took another sip of cognac. "You know how it is," I said.

"No, I don't know how it is. But I suppose it was the doggerel rhymes that opened your eyes, the stuff he memorized and then spewed out for you in the grove."

"My God, how did you know that?"

"I was so mad about him that I used to follow you and hide in the bushes. You were always so literary. I wasn't, but even I saw what was going on when you started quoting Poe at him."

I smiled at the memory, although it hadn't been funny at all. *"'It was many and many a year ago, in a kingdom by the sea—'"*

I stopped short and didn't continue. But Maggie just said, "I was right, wasn't I? It was something like that, wasn't it?"

"Something like that."

"As soon as you left Liberty—" Maggie stopped. "It was the disgrace of jilting him you were running away from, wasn't it?"

"Something like that."

"Well, I made a bee-line for St. Louis. I got my cousin Clara to invite me, she was always telling me about going dancing Saturday nights with the handsome young officers from Jefferson, which you must know was where Lieutenant Burnside had gone to lick his wounds."

6

I wasn't feeling well at all. Lieutenant Pettiford's laughter was even worse than Colonel Jennison's loud offers of Kentucky hangmen. At the top of his voice he explained to General Hascall that in Kentucky they'd hanged all the traitors like Vallandigham, and now that they were at loose ends they'd love to keep in practice. I could see that even Hascall was wearying of this blood-thirsty guerrillero, and I was grateful when he suddenly rose to his feet and said he had an urgent commitment elsewhere. Jasmine saw the visitors to the front door, where General Hascall allowed Jennison to precede him and then tried to do the same with Pettiford. The young lieutenant politely re-fused, and Hascall unceremoniously shoved him out into the street. I watched through the half-open door of the parlour as the general took my chambermaid by the hand and said something to her. She bowed her head; the general raised her hand and touched it to his moustache-adorned lips. I felt very disapproving. The best that could be said was that at least the gen-eral didn't hold Negroes in contempt, as so many people did, even in the North. Then again, the seduction of black women was never taboo, even in the code of the South.

When Jasmine returned to the parlour, I told her irritably to do some-thing about the smudges the colonel's dirty boots had left on the carpet.

7

"In St. Louis, fortune smiled on me," said Maggie. "Except that fortune has a deceptive smile. It turned out that Clara knew Burnside, and she was a matchmaker by nature. That Saturday, she took me to the public ball given by the Democrats of St. Louis, because she knew Ambrose would be there. And he was. He came with three other lieutenants and, although Clara tried her best, he danced one short dance with me, just for propriety's sake, and then turned his charm on the matchmaker."

"And to think I was consumed with guilt," I said. I was genuinely upset to hear this, for I had drunk more than a little cognac and was having vivid memories of the sad episode at the railway station with Ambrose.

"He was doing what he could to recover from your irresponsible emotional impetuosity, Lorraine," said Maggie, putting me in my place.

"From what you say, he succeeded," I remarked.

"In a manner of speaking," said Maggie. "Meanwhile, I was dancing in the arms of another lieutenant. The only nice thing about him was his name—half his name, at least—Leonidas Brumble. Then four country bumpkins from the South trying to pass for Southern gentlemen came into the ballroom, clearly under the influence. They noticed Clara right away, and one of them, the ringleader, spoke to Ambrose: 'Lieutenant, your lady appeals to me. I believe I'll have a dance with her!' and he reached for Clara. Ambrose caught his wrist and said, 'I beg your pardon, sir!' and reached for Clara. My partner, Brumble, saw what was happening, stopped spinning me around, and pushed his way through the dancers to Ambrose. I followed, and so did the other officers, with their ladies in tow. 'I beg your pardon, sir!' the Southerner said mockingly, and for a while they stared at each other, until finally the Southerner said loudly, 'Didn't you hear what I said, lieutenant?' All the dancing stopped, and the tension in the room became thick as a fog."

"Did they come to blows?"

"Nothing as vulgar as that," said Maggie. "Ambrose asked us ladies to follow him, and he made a way for us through the crowd. The Southerner called out after us, 'The United States Army is scared?' Ambrose ushered us gallantly to the staircase, then turned to confront the Southerner. 'Our ladies don't dance, sir, with the likes of you,' he said in an icy voice. His Yankee accent provoked some bruiser among the bystanders to ask ominously, 'Our gentlemen aren't good enough for your ladies, Yankee?' In his best West Point manner, Ambrose looked him up and down, and his sideburns bristled. 'Gentlemen like you? Certainly not, sir!' Then he turned and followed us up the stairs to the balcony. I spent the rest of the evening watching Clara wind him around her little finger, instead of matchmaking as she was supposed to."

"She didn't succeed, did she?"

Maggie looked at me maliciously. "She just cured him. And I—"

"You what?"

"I left with Brumble."

"Where did you go?"

"I can't tell you because I don't know. I know one thing for certain."

"What's that?"

"I lost my virginity that night."

"My goodness!"
"And something else."
"What?"
"What do you think?"

8

Ambrose wasted no time with Vallandigham. The trial, in early May 1863, lasted all of three days, and as soon as the verdict was reached, Vallandigham's lawyer turned to Judge Humphrey Leavitt of the Federal Court of the Southern District of Ohio seeking a writ of *habeas corpus*. If the judge had granted the writ, the case would have been moved to a civil court where the general had no influence. The sword over Vallandigham's head hung by the thread of Judge Leavitt's decision. Leavitt was faced with a dilemma that no one envied, because after many debates in the press, at political meetings, in taverns, and in private salons, it boiled down to an apparently unanswerable theoretical judicial question: does General Order Number One—as Vallandigham referred to the Constitution of the United States—have the authority of natural law or not?

It later turned out that Ambrose's choice for the tribunal of "good men one and all", as Hascall had put it, was not the happiest. Fortunately, this didn't become obvious until after the fact. By then Clem was residing at the beautiful Clifton House Hotel on the Canadian side of Niagara Falls. Shortly thereafter, he was evicted, because emissaries from Chicago were arriving to visit him under the influence of whisky and the hotel's clientele, mostly wealthy widows, complained. He had to move to the somewhat less savoury Table Rock Hotel, where he finally found out the details about his tribunal.

The first of Hascall's "good men", Captain Mayer, had had a noteworthy military career. Before offering his services to the Union army, he had served in several European battalions and helped in the suppression of a number of rebellions. But he had neglected to become naturalized in America, so his right to sit in judgement over a citizen of the United States was unquestionably questionable. Another member of the tribunal, Colonel Harred, was born in America but just before the war had served a prison sentence for "running a house of prostitution", and hence might have been better addressed as "Madam" than as "Your Honour". But the star of Ambrose's gallery was the military prosecutor, James M. Cutts. Several months after the Vallandigham trial, a bellboy at Burnett House caught him standing on a chair and peering through the transom into a neighbouring suite, where the daughter of Senator Hawkins of Indiana was getting ready for bed.

So Ambrose's choices were less than fortunate, but none of this came out until after Judge Leavitt issued his verdict. He puzzled over the legal conundrum for five days, and finally came to a conclusion that was about as American as General Order Number One. Years later, my grandson (or was it my great-grandson?), a philosophy student at Columbia University, declared that Leavitt's decision was in the spirit of a theory known as pragmatism, which, in the words of my grandson or great-grandson, consists in "modern man's turning away from abstraction, from purely verbal solutions, from pretended absolute knowledge and terms, towards concrete facts". That was somewhat erudite for me, so I told the boy that Leavitt had simply been acting in the spirit of common sense. The honourable judge had written: "If the doctrine is to obtain that every one charged with and guilty of acts of mischievous disloyalty not within the scope of the criminal laws of the land, in custody under military authority, is to be set free by courts or judges on habeas corpus, and that there is no power by which he could be temporarily placed where he cannot perpetrate mischief, it requires no argument to prove that the most alarming conflicts must follow and the action of the Government be most seriously impaired. I dare not in my judicial position assume the fearful responsibility implied in the sanction of such a doctrine. . . ." In other words, he decided not to decide.

9

Maggie got up and started to pace the parlour floor; the second decanter was now far from full. She stopped in front of the marble bust of a Roman girl with one blue eye and stared at it for a long time in silence. Then she walked to the window and gazed out at the May night. Jasmine appeared, assessed the situation, and vanished again. Maggie returned to the armchair.

"The lout that Ambrose confronted turned out to be a journalist," she said. "The next day he wrote an article for the St. Louis *Dispatch* about the ball, 'the dignified course of which was disturbed only by the unseemly behaviour of some snob with grotesque side-whiskers in the uniform of the United States Army who thought that the society of St. Louis was not sufficiently refined for his lady friends to mix with.'"

"I presume Ambrose challenged him to a duel," I said.

"In a manner of speaking," said Maggie. "He showed up at the editorial offices of the *Dispatch* with a bullwhip, and he was charged with assault and battery."

I was surprised. "I had no idea Ambrose was ever behind bars."

"He never was, of course. A man with Ambrose's good looks had too many female admirers in St. Louis for some boor to do him any damage. The judge decided that he had acted in just if somewhat prolonged indignation over the insult to his ladies, and the lout was put to such shame that he had to leave town. I understand he was next seen as an auctioneer at the slave-auctions in New Orleans."

In the candle-light her complexion no longer looked quite as ashen.

"I could probably write novels too," she sighed. "But who would read such tragic stories?"

"You wouldn't write tragic stories. I'm glad that—that in spite of everything you've been through—you're still the same as ever."

"Right. I laugh so as not to cry. It's been less than six months since Fredericksburg, and I'm not in mourning for Leonidas." All the laughter had vanished from her eyes again. "But at the outset, Leonidas didn't behave like a gentleman," she said.

"What do you mean?"

"Ambrose was the one who behaved like a gentleman."

"I don't understand."

"Dear Lorraine, how could you?"

10

The thrashing Ambrose gave the lout from St. Louis was comical. The second thrashing—in fact it was just a slap in the face—was less comical, but that was mainly because the baby died. Our lives, I think, are coloured by our demise. It is our end that sets the tone, not our beginning. The baby survived its deferred death by only a couple of months. Had it died when it should have, Maggie would have been spared twelve years of misery which ended only at Marye's Heights.

Good intentions sometimes—often, in fact—have evil consequences, while evil intentions may lead to fortunate ends. Maggie had left St. Louis. She was living in Cincinnati with her rich though unmarried aunt, Hermione Collins, who had found Jasmine for me after that unfortunate disaster in the lake. I was alone in our large house—my husband was lecturing in Chicago—and I lay in bed, listening to the sad songs coming from Jasmine's little room—"*Sometimes I'm up, sometimes I'm down, Oh, yes Lord! Sometimes I'm almost on the ground, Oh, yes Lord!*"—and I knew that that scoundrel Leonidas had been right, but that Maggie had been saved from a terrible sin and had been punished terribly for it. She was saved not by a guardian angel but by a vision of hell: the pedagogies of our inscrutable Creator, Whose ways are indeed strange.

Leonidas had taken her to a house by the river that resembled a skull: a whitewashed façade, two darkened windows on the second floor, an open door on the ground floor, with a reddish glow behind it that came from a blazing fireplace. Maggie's knees gave out and Leonidas had to push her inside. A bare white cot stood in front of the fire in a spacious room. The cot was clean—the doctor's clientele came from the best families in St. Louis—but it was bare as a catafalque, and behind it stood an old crone dressed in black. The doctor wore a vest, a white shirt with the sleeves rolled up, and a red cravat, and on a table before him lay an open case with his instruments laid out on black velvet. Maggie began to weep. Leonidas held her up, the doctor and the crone exchanged looks, the old woman stepped over to Maggie and cooed to her in the voice of a nursemaid, "There, there, little darling, there, there." She reached out to stroke her cheek, but Maggie pushed her away, screaming. The doctor watched for a while, with the cold eyes of a practised demon, then put his instruments away and snapped the case shut. Maggie kept on screaming.

"Well, lieutenant," said the doctor, "your lady is apparently unwilling." He started to roll down his sleeves and Leonidas replied angrily, "Wait, I'll see to it—"

"Not here, lieutenant," said the doctor, putting on his jacket and pointing to the door.

"I paid in advance!" Leonidas exclaimed.

"And falsely informed me that the lady had agreed."

"Oh, but she will!"

"In that case, when you get her permission you may call on me and we shall arrange another appointment. Of course"—he looked at Maggie—"you don't have much time. You should have had it done much sooner, as it is."

Leonidas allowed Maggie to drag him towards the door. He turned back to say, "And my money?"

"Consider it payment for my lost time. Good evening, lieutenant."

Maggie looked at me. "Had it done much sooner?" she said. "I didn't want to do it at all. To snuff out the flame of a tiny life. . . . Would you have agreed?"

I shivered. "Did you love him, a little at least?"

"I hated him. He never turned up after the ball in St. Louis, and that was fine with me. But when I discovered I was pregnant I wrote him a letter. He came and the only thing he could talk about was that doctor. I started hating him then."

My poor friend had fallen into an eternal female trap, and after fleeing the devil's kitchen she had married Brumble. That was how things were done in Liberty.

"I fell into a gentleman's trap," said Maggie with a crooked smile.

"Again I don't understand you, Maggie—"

"How could you?" she repeated. "I'd been determined to remain alone, unmarried, with the baby. I probably would have moved here to Cincinnati. Aunt Hermione would have taken me in. She was the spitting image of Miss Marlowe, if you've read *Hubris and Humility.*"

My God, how could that early farce of mine remind Maggie of—"I've read it," I said, "but I truly don't understand—"

"Even if life were the kind of comedy Laura Lee, thank the Lord, makes it out to be," Maggie interrupted me, "Aunt Hermione was too down to earth to harbour ideas that silly. My aunt is not from a farm but from Cincinnati. Somebody else got the marriage idea. And it was my fault."

She stroked the pink spine of my latest thick opus. "But what I suffered in that skull-like house—it was like something straight out of your favourite poet—" said my friend, who was probably better read than she admitted. "That may have been an extenuating circumstance. I'd like to have seen you in that situation, Lorraine."

"I'd have fainted," I said, to make Maggie feel better. But she knew me too well.

"You? Chief of the Shoshones? I didn't faint either. I just fell to pieces, and once I was in pieces I confessed everything to Clara. She was certainly the right one to confess to!"

II

When I finished reading Leavitt's verdict, something drew me to Humphrey's library, and I was just about to reach for the shelf where he kept his favourite philosophers when my two youngsters burst into the room screaming. Jimmy was holding his hand over his nose and blood was streaming between his fingers and down onto his brand-new clothes. Still the tomboy despite Lieutenant Pettiford's influence, Loretta defended herself with a classic phrase: "Mama, he started it!"

So I didn't reach for the book among Humphrey's philosophers until years later, when I heard how Comely Clem had met his end. The end sets the tone.

Ambrose had wanted to put Vallandigham away in Fort Warren, a bleak prison in Boston Harbour, but Lincoln, fearing that prison would make him a martyr, amended the sentence and ordered the King of the Copperheads exiled to the Confederacy. Such justice, however appropriate, was too complex for Ambrose's political sensibilities, and he balked. The tribunal, made up of "fine officers" (before they were exposed), had considered deportation and decided against it. If he was obliged to change the decision now, his prestige would suffer—prestige he would need in the coming weeks, when a number of similar trials were expected for which the Vallandigham affair was a precedent. Lincoln held his ground, and Ambrose, as usual, obeyed his president's wishes. On May 22 the prisoner boarded the gunship *Exchange* in the Cincinnati River, and was conveyed to St. Louis, where he was transported by a special train to Murfreesboro and turned over to General Rosecrans. From there he was driven to the nearest front line. Following complications with grudging Southern officers, who found Vallandigham a somewhat distasteful ally, Rosecrans's Major Wiles fobbed him off on Colonel Webb, who hadn't had time to get proper instructions from his commanding officer, General Braxton Bragg. Comely Clem had become a hot potato, and when he left for Canada they were probably glad to see him go.

12

It was *Dayton's Weekly* that pronounced the last word on the Vallandigham trial, when it wrote that through his oratory Vallandigham had been quickly digging his own political grave, and that Burnside had resurrected him. But as the future showed, Ambrose was not such a miracle-maker. The resurrected Clem was far from the old barn-burner of the wild days of May 1863, when the little snake raised its coppery head and Vallandigham gambled on martyrdom. He lost. In the October elections of that year, he ran *in absentia* from Canada. His stay in the South had been brief; he was on to Lincoln's game, and had no intention of compromising his peace-loving followers in the North by fighting for the cause while safe under the wings of Confeder-

ate President Jeff Davis, who in turn wasn't stupid enough to try to keep
him there. But despite the martyr's halo and the juicy anti-Negro slogans
that marked his campaign, he was defeated. So he returned to Illinois—
Georgie Morton "lost his way" en route from Indianapolis to Columbus so
he wouldn't have to arrest him—but he failed again at the Democratic Convention in 1864.

When the war was over, Vallandigham decided to bet on what my
learned husband called *panta rhei*. Though he used to appeal to the past as
though it were holy, a source of divine inspiration, he now said, "The past
must be forgotten. What has been, has been. We need to stop taking it into
account." But there was a less philosophical term for Vallandigham's transformation, and it was applied not only by the Republicans but also—perhaps because they didn't know Greek—by members of his own party:
turncoat. There was no need to explain that Clem himself stood to gain the
most from his "new tasks". His idealism should obviously be taken with a
grain of salt, for the martyr of the Constitution was—and had probably always been—an opportunist.

In that, perhaps his critics were being unfair. Be that as it may, things
went downhill for him from then on. At the first post-war Democratic
Convention, in 1866, he was accused by his long-time colleagues Jewett
and Campbell of having "flirted with high treason", thus confirming,
after the fact, Judge Leavitt's common sense and Ambrose's instincts.
Then he tried to win the Democratic nomination, first for Congress
and later for governor, but he lost both bids and returned to the practice
of law.

And there he won everything.

In 1871 he defended a violent murderer, Thomas McGehan, and saved
him from the gallows. But for himself—

I read a detailed account of his death in the *Dayton Journal* in the college
library in Cincinnati. They quoted Vallandigham's last words before he lost
consciousness: "Oh, Murder! O what a blunder!"

There were only a few students in the library at the time. I got up,
walked over to the shelves, and pulled out the book I had wanted to get long
ago. I took it over to a window that overlooked the college garden. It was
dark already, and the July stars were high in the sky—the same stars the general had once looked up at from my balcony.

Everyone gazes at them, because they shine so brightly. Only a few of us
try to look deeper, to look inside ourselves as well, because, as a rule, the
darkness there is profound. And in that darkness lies something more important than the stars.

13

"There wasn't a lot of time, and Leonidas was having nightmares about what I would do to embarrass him," said Maggie. "He came twice to implore me to change my mind, and the third time I told him I wanted nothing, only to be left alone. You could tell how relieved he was. 'Don't worry, Maggie, I'll take care of the child.' 'How?' I said. 'Will you marry me?' He was startled. 'But you said—' 'Don't worry, I won't force you to the altar with a shotgun.' He looked at me as though he had something to say but couldn't, then at last he blurted out, 'I inherited a little something from my Uncle Bart. If you're going to need money—' 'Of course I'm going to need money,' I said. In the end, he reluctantly gave me three hundred. I was so sick of the whole thing that I took it. That was my worst mistake." Maggie sighed. "Because in the meantime, Clara was matchmaking again."

It was like this: Lieutenant Burnside was Brumble's immediate superior, and Clara had him in the palm of her hand. She stepped into a play that was on its way to becoming the drama of a courageous and independent young woman, and introduced some traditional gentlemanly elements into it—so successfully that the whole play became a melodrama, complete with a so-called happy ending. What followed the happy ending was a tragedy, but melodramas never go that far.

A young woman from St. Louis arrived unannounced at the Jefferson barracks. The black footman jumped down from her carriage and exchanged a few quiet words with the officer on duty, who stepped over to the vehicle, opened the door, and escorted the lady to Lieutenant Burnside's office. The lady spent some time with him behind closed doors, then Lieutenant Burnside escorted her back to her carriage. Lieutenant Burnside's face was red. He locked himself in his office, and word spread through the garrison that the womanizer Burnside had gotten a society lady from St. Louis in trouble. The next morning, Second Lieutenant Brumble returned from a two-day furlough to find that Lieutenant Burnside urgently requested his presence. The office door was closed again, for a long time; then came a sound that an inquisitive sergeant identified as a slap. Voices were raised. The gossip was modified. Next day, two officers in dress uniform were shown into the parlour of Clara's parents, and Lieutenant Brumble asked Maggie for her hand in marriage. She fainted dead away.

"Really?" I wondered. "Did you actually faint?"

"Don't be silly, Lorraine. I had to gain time to think it over. In the end, I finally did say the momentous 'Yes'."

Maggie's gaze fell on Humphrey's humidor. She opened it and took out a slender Virginia cigar. I held a candle for her to light it.

"I simply fell into the gentlemen's trap. Had I insisted on doing what I wanted to—and perhaps that's what I should have done—a lot of people would have been hurt. Mother, Father, in the end even Clara too. She was convinced that she'd done me a tremendous favour. And I wish you could have seen Ambrose. He was an outraged guardian angel, side-whiskers bristling. After all he'd done, I couldn't bring myself to embarrass him. That's probably why I said yes." Maggie exhaled a cloud of smoke and looked me straight in the eye. "What you did to him was bad enough, but it still fit into his picture of the world. He had no room in his brain to understand what I wanted to do. And to be entirely honest," said my friend, "the prospect of matrimony still seemed to me more acceptable than the alternative. Because at the time I still had no idea what matrimony could entail."

"So it was in fact a lady's trap," I said.

"If you insist," said Maggie. "But the trap was set by gentlemen. Was it ever a disgrace to be an illegitimate father?"

14

The dilemma of those stormy days in May 1864, like so many other things, was described best by Lincoln. After the war, we all read his words from his widely quoted letter to Corning: "Must I shoot a simple-minded soldier who deserts while I must not touch a hair on the head of a wily agitator who induces him to desert? This is nonetheless injurious when effected by getting a father or brother or friend into a public meeting and there working upon his feelings till he is persuaded to write the soldier boy that he is fighting in a bad cause, for the wicked Administration of a contemptible Government, too weak to arrest and punish him if he shall desert. I think that in such a case to silence the agitator and save the boy is not only constitutional but withal a great mercy."

Of course, lawyers and historians after them argued that there was no evidence that the peace orators had any direct influence on the morale of the army. I don't know what kind of evidence they meant, but a simple-minded person like Ambrose had no doubts about the adverse effect that the anti-war campaign had on the war effort.

Even less did his subordinate, General Hascall: "As well I might establish a number of smallpox hospitals in the heart of this city, and then punish the people for becoming infected with that loathsome disease, as to allow newspapers and public speakers to belch forth their disloyal and treasonable doctrines, and blame the people for becoming contaminated therewith." Hascall was a tough and forthright fellow. Within a week of Ambrose's blood-thirsty order, which my husband commented on with the word "Ouch", Hascall arrested D.E.Volkenburgh, editor of the *Weekly Democrat*, who had made fun of the edict but soon changed his tune. He gave other papers in his district a choice: stop criticizing the war, or stop publishing. The big dailies in the bigger cities entered the game, particularly Storey's Chicago *Times*. Hascall jumped into printed debates with editors, which he had no experience at, and Vallandigham decided to go for broke.

Direct evidence was still lacking; in fact, there were increasing indications that the rank-and-file soldiers were not reacting as the generals had feared, and the peace-mongers began increasingly to feel the wrath of both individuals and whole units.

The Democratic Party called a convention in Indianapolis for May 20, and Storey couldn't resist editorializing that the Democrats would defend their constitutional rights "peaceably if possible, and forcibly if necessary." It's entirely possible that Storey had let himself get carried away with rhetoric, but that can't be proved. In any case, someone reported to Hascall that the convention was just a cloak to disguise the real purpose of the assembly: seizing the Indianapolis armoury and arming Copperheads with stolen rifles. Ambrose warned Hascall against any use of force, but Hascall's Pythian response was that he was "taking all precautions necessary for the preservation of the peace." Accordingly, on May 20 the centre of the city was swarming with people wearing the familiar Copperhead insignia, but also with troops. Infantry with mounted bayonets occupied the city square; the arsenal was surrounded by artillery reinforced by infantry, and cavalry units cantered back and forth across the city. In addition, individual soldiers stationed in the crowd saw to it that nothing from the rostrum could be interpreted as a call to treason—and the interpretation was up to them. Constantly interrupted and out-shouted by armed, uniformed men in the audience, the speakers were never able to unleash their anti-war rhetoric, and one of them, wearing a big, shiny badge on his lapel, was driven off the stage by a soldier with a bayonet.

It was hard to tell what led to what. At four o'clock Senator Thomas A. Hendricks stood on the main rostrum but then ducked out without saying anything. A unit of scowling infantrymen was approaching the rostrum with bayonets poised, and the senator's flight was the spark that ignited general confusion. A squadron on horseback rode into the crowd and scattered it and, soon afterwards, gunshots echoed from the railroad station. Civilian passengers on a train expressed their anger by shooting out the windows and firing in the air. Hascall ordered the train stopped, and people along the tracks watched in amazement as the men on the train tossed their pistols into Pogue's Run Creek. In his report to Burnside, Hascall described this rain of pistols most vividly of all the events of that day, and he conferred upon it the high-flown title "The Battle of Pogue's Run Creek".

The event could be construed as an attempted coup against the government, or as an encroachment on the people's freedom, and it was seen both ways. But at the time Ambrose had other concerns that he considered more important. He had received orders to establish the Twenty-third Army Corps, take command of it, and join General Rosecrans in western Tennessee as a prelude to driving the Rebels from the eastern part of the state. On June 3 the preparations were complicated by additional orders instructing Ambrose himself to go to Hickman's Bridge, Kentucky, and organize the transfer of units to Vicksburg, where Grant and Sherman were preparing for a decisive battle. Burdened with such complex problems, all within his proper field, Ambrose could hardly be expected to pay much attention to the nuances of constitutional law.

15

Storey of the *Times*, however, paid all the more attention. I met the man personally only once in my life. He was a tall, grey-haired, withdrawn gentleman with a passion to create a great newspaper. He was dominated by two related emotions: a hatred for Lincoln and an aversion to Negroes. When Humphrey and I were in Chicago attending a dinner at Dean Stowell's with Storey, a Methodist clergyman from Virginia (who apparently had no idea who Storey was) came out with a petition to Lincoln, asking him to do away with slavery as a sign of repentance for a great national sin. Before he could start circulating it for signatures, Storey turned to him and, pinning the cleric to his chair with an icy stare, said, "The great national sin for which Providence is punishing the American people is the election of Lincoln to the presidency. The punishment for this sin, sir, is entirely proper."

As my husband remarked, Storey's articles expressed his hostility towards the Rebels purely in terms of a formal libation to the Federation. For his hatred of Lincoln and his "niggers and nigger-lovers", on the other hand, Storey employed expressions suffused with genuine feeling. It is no surprise, then, that Ambrose—who revered, perhaps even loved, the president—paid particular attention to Storey's attacks, the more so since Ambrose's old friend from Liberty, Ollie Morton, now governor of Indiana, was also complaining about Storey. In this Morton was in full agreement with his colleague Richard Yates, who had wired Washington some time earlier that something needed to be done about the *Times* or "the citizens of Chicago would take matters into their own hands". Ambrose was far from alone in seeing Storey as a covert (not so covert, actually) Rebel supporter. But in the end, of course, all of them, Ollie Morton included, left him to stew in his own juice.

The *Times* kept attacking him personally, but Ambrose could tolerate personal attacks. What he could not stomach was a report from "X", the newspaper's Washington correspondent. "X" described Lincoln as a haggard, careworn ruin of a man, consumed by justified remorse, his conscience burdened with sins as heinous as the emancipation of the slaves. Lincoln was nothing more than a servant dancing to the tune of his cabinet; "such are the men who control the destinies of this once-free Republic."

Neither the author nor Ambrose noticed any discrepancy between the cited sin and the conclusion of the article. Ambrose missed it because the journalist's portrait of the president had enraged him. With one foot on the train that was to take him to the Twenty-third Corps in Kentucky, Ambrose issued three orders in rapid succession, suspending the publication of the *Times* and formulating his perhaps simplistic but unwavering conviction that "freedom of discussion and criticism which is proper in the politician and journalist in time of peace becomes rank treason when it tends to weaken the confidence of the soldier in his officers and his government. Citizens are in a sense soldiers, and citizens as well as soldiers have sacrifices to make, and these sacrifices extend to freedom of speech and the press."

After that Ambrose left for Kentucky, where he was to launch his offensive against eastern Tennessee. Except that in the meantime they had changed their minds in Washington, and at Hickman's Bridge a telegram was waiting for him instructing him to move his troops to the Vicksburg theatre of operations.

It would not be the last time in those unsettled days of early June that Washington changed its mind, and the consequences would fall on Ambrose's head.

16

Before she left that evening, Maggie described her marriage. It confirmed my belief that, were she to pick up a pen, she would eclipse Laura Lee. Like every reputedly happily married woman, I have heard my share of reports from friends afflicted with unhappy unions. Although they were all true stories, they were usually, in formal terms, sheer symbolism. The heroine was a pure lily, while her partner was an evil spirit who could teach the Devil a thing or two. Maggie's story was spare and free of symbols, embellished only with touches of irony.

The story started not so much with the wedding as with the miscarriage, the death of the baby who had escaped death only a few months earlier, and it ended with the death of Colonel Brumble a step away from the little stone wall on Marye's Heights. Between the two deaths were years of silence, duties fulfilled only in hopes of another child, which never came. Each found the other's presence unbearable, torture; a trap. And above it all stood an absurd guardian angel with gigantic side-whiskers.

"There's a similar story in *Twilight in Baltimore*," said Maggie. "The marriage between Elvira and Henry. But of course he married her because his parents wanted him to, not because she ran away from the abortionist. Although who's to say? You probably can't write about that in novels anyway."

"No, not in the ones Laura Lee writes. And besides, that's just a sub-plot. The main plot in *Twilight in Baltimore* is the same as in all—in all her other books. It's a simple formula: a trip to the altar after overcoming amusing setbacks."

Maggie got up, the cigar between her lips, and walked around the parlour. She stopped again in front of the blue-eyed Roman girl and blew a cloud of bluish smoke at the bust.

"Why doesn't Laura Lee ever make the trip to the altar the sub-plot, amusing setbacks and all?" she asked.

"Because it's easier to write. At least I think it would be," I added hastily. "Telling about life as it really is—"

"Have you ever tried it?"

I shook my head and replied in what I hoped was a tone of offhand surprise, "You know I don't write."

My voice gave me away. Maggie turned from the Roman bust to face me: "No fibbing, Laura!"

17

In Detroit I heard about a reporter whom Storey sent to cover the murder of a Democratic clerk at City Hall. The newsman filed a report based on nothing but confirmed facts, which were not enough to prove the guilt of the suspect, a bartender and well-known Lincoln supporter. Storey added some details of his own devising which clearly pointed the finger at the bartender. The story was published, the reporter got angry, and he and Storey had it out. Finally Storey fired the man, with a gem of a parting statement, worthy of Mr. Bartlett's attention: "You're forgetting, Mr. Bendix," said Storey to the departing journalist, "that you are not working for the sheriff, and you aren't paid by the city. You're a reporter for the *Times*, and you're paid by me."

In the end the sheriff's men found evidence against the real murderer, and the bartender was released, but the whole affair dragged on for several months and the fabricated news story was forgotten. For Storey the fabrication was worth a few dollars in extra copies sold, thanks to the sensation. Nothing was more valuable to him than that.

In Chicago, Storey didn't have to fabricate anything. After Ambrose's edict, the *Times* failed to appear for two days, but Lincoln revoked the order and the newsboys made the city echo with shouts of "Freedom triumphs!"—and Storey made a few more dollars. Later, Secretary of the Navy Gideon Welles would say that Ambrose's edict was just the kind of regulation that "gives bad men the right to question the actions of good men." Perhaps. Storey, of course, could not have cared less.

I thought about it all in the parlour, and stared at the summer stars outside the tall window. Then I considered the things that are more important than the stars.

Bentonville

ONE MORNING, after days and weeks of rain, the sun finally appeared over the horizon. The landscape looked freshly scrubbed and Carlin's division were shuffling slowly into some semblance of order, readying themselves to march out as the advanced guard for Jeff Davis's Fourteenth Corps at the head of Slocum's Georgia army. It was a fine day, without a trace of fog. Beyond the horizon the turpentine forests were still smouldering, and there was a thin grey haze hanging over the trees. But the sinister black columns of smoke that had towered over them like the buttresses of a gutted cathedral were gone. The march to Cox's Bridge, where Davis was to meet Sherman the next morning, was about ten miles. Even if Carlin had to dispose of some cavalry squadrons that were in the way, they would still make it that day. That would put them barely twenty miles from Goldsboro, where Schofield would shortly be arriving with a fresh army.

"I expect the danger is past," Sherman said that morning. He was convinced that Hardee, Bragg, and Johnston were falling back on Raleigh. They must have concluded—and had that conclusion confirmed by prisoners taken at Ayersboro—that Greeley's article had been a ruse; must have decided to stand and fight a major battle, perhaps the final battle of the war, just outside the state capital.

"It's Sunday." Sherman smiled. "A good time to visit Howard." At the beginning of the war, General Howard had argued that the fighting should stop on the Lord's Day so that soldiers could spend the day in worship. Sundays in Howard's army still began with services when possible, but usually the fighting went on as on workdays.

On his way back from the creek, the sergeant had a tingling sensation in the back of his neck, as though someone were pointing a gun at him. He rode past an apricot orchard in bloom and watched the Twenty-second Wisconsin lining up company by company at the foot of a hill that was glowing with spring green, preparing to scout in advance of Carlin's division. Ragged and caked in mud, the boys from Wisconsin looked more than ever like an army of able-bodied beggars.

An orderly was brushing a new uniform in front of General Carlin's tent, and through the tent flaps the sergeant caught a glimpse of the general buttoning up his fresh white shirt and looking gloomy.

"What's this?" Kapsa asked the orderly. "We're not going on parade."

"That's how the old man always dresses before a battle." The soldier grinned. "If he bites the dust, they'll be able to tell him by the crease in his pants."

"There won't be a battle," the sergeant said loyally. "A few skirmishes with Wheeler, maybe, nothing worse."

"I wouldn't count on that," said the orderly. "The old man has a nose for blood, and he's smelling it right now. Look yonder!" He pointed west. Supply wagons were already moving off towards the rear. "He wants to make sure the Rebs don't get their paws on our ham if the battle goes wrong."

"There won't be a battle," the sergeant muttered again, and walked quickly towards his general's tent, where Sam stood saddled and ready. As Sherman came out of the tent, he put on his hat. A piece of its brim was missing and, where it had once sported a plume, now only the quill was left. The sergeant couldn't remember the original plume—it had always been just a quill sticking out of the band—but he remembered the brim being intact.

The general swung into the saddle and turned his weather-beaten face to the east. At seven in the morning the sun, still low on the horizon, was already warm. They started off.

They had ridden barely three miles—Howard's army was dangerously far from Slocum's, in places as much as twenty miles—through the spring countryside, past pine groves and deserted plantation houses, past swamps where birds sang their first mating songs, past blossoming apple orchards and flowering apricot trees. A cool breeze was blowing but it seemed almost warm after the chill of the rainy days. Waterfowl circled overhead. Up ahead the sergeant could see the general's back and Sam's glistening flanks, the staff officers riding in their usual pendulum motion, falling behind the general's swift horse and then catching up again. The sergeant dozed for a moment in the saddle and dreamed of Chicago after the war. Ursula, who had turned into a faded picture in his memory, had suddenly come alive with the words of Madam Sosniowski. He hadn't found out a lot from her in Columbia— only that Ursula was alive and in America—but it was enough to dispel his worst nightmares into a puff of smoke.

"In New York. Or was it Chicago? I'm not certain. Somewhere."

Somewhere? Anywhere! As long as she's alive!

His heart took off at a joyful gallop. Boldly he asked her, "Was her husband killed? Hauptmann von Hanzlitschek?"

She hesitated. "Did you know her?" she asked. "I mean—did you know her well?"

"A little," he said.

"Hmmm." She stared at Kakuska, who was riding off with his new spurs flashing.

"Every soldier knew her a little. By sight, I mean. After all, she was an attractive woman and she was married to the most obnoxious captain in the Sixth Regiment," he explained.

She looked him square in the eye. "The most hated captain. Or were you fond of him?"

He couldn't help hearing the sarcasm in her voice. He felt a twinge of worry, but only for a moment. They were standing in front of her white house, now yellow in the fires of Columbia—thousands of miles from Helldorf, seventeen years from the moment von Hanzlitschek's bullwhip had branded the emblem of his jealousy into Ursula's back, in the rage of a man deprived of his property.

"I wasn't," he said. "And Ursula"—he hurried to correct himself—"Frau von Hanzlitschek—"

"Ursula," she said, smiling.

Years of living with his fears made him cautious even now. "Ursula—I knew her—quite well. We'd speak sometimes. She—well—I was in the infirmary once and she—she used to bring me ointments—"

Madam Sosniowski looked deep into his soul again. "So you were the one. My late husband mixed those ointments for her. He never asked her who they were for. The first time she came for them, he told me they couldn't be for the Hauptmann because they weren't for piles." She smiled at him. "I had known her since she married the Hauptmann. She'd never been happy. She didn't marry

*for love. It was"—she made a face—"arranged. And then suddenly she was radi-
ant with happiness. But when von Hanzlitschek was killed"—she caught his eye
again—"she almost fell apart. I'd never seen her so miserable."*

He said nothing.

*"Nothing is so bad that it doesn't bring some good with it," said Madam Sos-
niowski. "There were certain suspicions, but everyone could see how badly Ursula was taking it. True, that might have reinforced the suspicions. But Ursula
had a convincing alibi. The maid—do you remember her? She was very pretty.
Heidemarie."*

He nodded.

"She testified that Ursula had been at home all day, writing letters."

Another squad of Kil's cavalry was approaching from Columbia. From the
east came the boom of cannon-fire, and the sergeant was suddenly alert.
They were about a mile from Cox's Bridge and General Howard's camp, but
still twenty miles from Goldsboro, where they were to meet Schofield the
following day. Bentonville, source of the ominous rumble of artillery, was
ten miles to the east. The air was fragrant with cherry blossoms, the spring
breeze rippled through the grass, and the sun, now low in the west, still
filled the air with bright spring light. But the countryside was echoing with
the eerie, mechanical roar of cannon.

They sat still on their horses, their field-glasses trained on Bentonville.
No one said a word. They were waiting for the general to speak.

Yesterday he had said, "Only a few squadrons of cavalry." Could a small
battery of light cavalry artillery be making that much noise? Kapsa looked at
the general. His aides, Audrey and Dobson, exchanged glances over their
field-glasses. Their thoughts were not hard to read.

The burden of decision lay, as always, on the general's shoulders. Not
long ago, he had asked his staff a rhetorical question: "What is strategy?"
They had been complaining about how unreliable their maps of North Carolina were. "Strategy is common sense applied to the art of war."

The sergeant recalled that General Howard's eyebrows had risen sharply,
a disciplined display of disagreement. The general went on, sounding more
like a farmer than a soldier: "You have to do something. You can't go around
asking corporals and sergeants what to do. You have to make it up out of
your own mind, and then give the order. If things don't work out, you can
attribute the disaster to anything you please; the blame will still fall on you,
no matter what."

"And if things do work out, what then?" asked Captain Williams.

The general laughed. "No matter what they attribute the success to, the laurels will land on your head. And quite rightly so. It was your decision, after all." The general looked around at his regiment resting among the trees. "A halo doesn't give you much protection, though," he said. "You issue another order, everything seems to fall apart deliberately, and in a few days the reporters wash your head in a cesspool and the laurels float away, never to be seen again. That's what glory's like." He glanced at a young second lieutenant in a stained uniform who was trying to cultivate a moustache. "Fame—" said the general thoughtfully. "You get killed on the field of battle and your name is spelled wrong in the newspapers. That's fame."

"Not all heroes get killed," said Captain Williams.

"No," conceded the general. "But in the end they all die. After that, they can't give evidence about how they saw things, and the journalists have a field-day." He laughed. "They'll make me out to be a holy terror whose only excuse was being crazy, and they'll explain away my modest successes by attributing them to the luck of the Devil. They'll turn Grant into a drunkard, and how will they explain a drunkard doing anything right unless they call it the luck of the Devil? You, Oliver"—he turned to Howard—"you're the only one who'll come out of it smelling like a rose. They wouldn't dare connect the Devil with your good fortune."

General Howard scowled, apparently displeased by the trivializing tone of Sherman's monologue, and reached for his Bible, which, as usual, was right there in his coat pocket. Sherman added quickly, "And still, no matter what we are, I have to issue an order, Grant has to issue an order." The general's gaze drifted from Howard, whose expression was returning to normal, to his troops, who were taking up their positions. He added, "Without orders it wouldn't work. Even the president has to give orders. Without them America would be lost, and would earn the contempt of all mankind."

Captain Williams raised his field-glasses, and the sergeant looked in that direction. A solitary rider was galloping towards them out of a grove of apricot trees. "It's Burton, of Slocum's staff," said the captain.

Later, when Captain Burton was returning west, growing smaller as he rode, they moved east as the apricot orchard darkened in the twilight. The columns of smoke before them came from Howard's camp. The courier's welcome dispatch now lay folded in the sergeant's knapsack. "The Twenty-second Wisconsin came into contact with units of Rebel cavalry and taught them a lesson," Slocum had written. So Sherman had been right: there were only a few squadrons of horsemen to harass them. But was that unceasing din coming from a few squadrons of horsemen? Still, the general was reassured by the dispatch and rode swiftly towards Howard's campfires, his staff keeping up as best they could. The sound of cannon faded in the distance and soon the sergeant was surrounded by the twilight songs of spring, the crickets and the bird-calls. For the first time in many days, the twilight was sprinkled with stars.

"There were bound to be suspicions at first," said Madam Sosniowski. "Everyone knew that von Hanzlitschek had a mistress in Neuhausen. She admitted it after he died. They used to meet up on Gottestischlein—you remember it?"

He nodded.

"There's a little house up there, a love-nest," she said. "Von Hanzlitschek furnished it for his own purposes, and they met there on Tuesdays and Fridays. He did everything according to a schedule."

"But he died on a Wednesday—" He stopped short, too late.

She smiled at him. "Yes, I believe you're right! Ursula had her alibi from Heidemarie, and then von Hanzlitschek's mistress—who, by the way, was governess to the young Countess Schoenheim, the family with the castle in Neuhausen—you surely recall?"

"Yes, but what about her—the mistress?"

"She had an attack of hysteria in front of the General Commission of Inquiry. It turned out she was expecting von Hanzlitschek's child," explained Madam Sosniowski. "And in her fit of hysteria other things came out as well."

"What sort of things?" It was hard for him to imagine it now, so far away and so long ago.

"I can't tell you and I don't want to. My husband only hinted at what they were. Simply, it came out that Herr Hauptmann von Hanzlitschek had demanded services of his mistress that gentlemen generally don't presume to ask of their wives. Or they may presume, but Ursula would hardly have complied. She did not love him."

Ursula and he had never talked about von Hanzlitschek and he knew nothing about him. But Ursula had come to him of her own free will. That was why it had been such a miracle. Far greater than anything he had ever expected to experience in this world. The sergeant shook his head.

Burning cotton was falling all around them.

"Naturally, such revelations did not make a good impression on General Graetz, who didn't care for von Hanzlitschek in the first place, and who did? So Ursula had all his sympathy. The mistress had an alibi too, and when they looked at the evidence—the slippery moss, the sharp stone—everything looked convincing. The only thing they couldn't explain was what he was doing up there that evening. After all, he was as regular as clockwork, Tuesdays and Fridays."

He gazed right into Madam Sosniowski's dark eyes, and saw showers of burning snow.

"It was the Devil who brought him there," he said. "To give him his due."

Sherman stood in front of the tent with Howard. They were both facing east and listening intently. Darkness had fallen some time ago, the stars were out, but the cannon were still rumbling. This was more than just a skirmish. The two generals conferred in low, inaudible voices far into the night. Artillery sounded sporadically. Slocum had written his reassuring dispatch that morning; now it was night. The decision lay with Sherman. But no more couriers came. The only message lay in the continuing cannonade. An owl hooted. The general threw up his hands, turned, and went into his tent. Howard followed. The sergeant watched their moving shadows on the sides of the tent. Then the lamp was put out. He stretched out on the ground beside the dying campfire, stared up at the stars, and remembered the burning snow.

"I agree," said Madam Sosniowski. "The verdict was 'death by misadventure'. Ursula"—she looked him straight in the eye, and by now she knew everything—"I had never seen her so unhappy."

"I loved her," he said. "I still love her."

"Well, that explains everything, then," said Madam Sosniowski.

He was awakened by the pounding of horses' hoofs, and jumped up. The stars were still out and two riders were approaching from the east. One of them was Captain Farmer, commander of Howard's guard. The second rode a horse that was foaming at the mouth. A courier.

They went into the tent, and a carbide lamp was lit. The sergeant could hear excited voices.

"I wrote her, but she never answered," said the sergeant.

"She left for Vienna right after the verdict," said Madam Sosniowski. "She married again in less than a year. Naturally, there was talk in Helldorf. But Baron von Hofburg-Ebbe is a diplomat, and a month after the wedding she went with him to Stockholm, I think."

He wanted to ask how she could have done such a thing, but then he realized it was a foolish question. What else could she have done? Accepted his wild invitation to America? Besides, his letter had probably gone astray—which was just as well. He shook his head.

"Some wishes come true only in books, sergeant," said Madam Sosniowski. "And some people only belong together in books too—you know?"

That annoyed him. Why just in books?

But perhaps she was right. It was all so long ago. More like a dream. Not much of a reality any more.

The general came tearing out of the tent, looking like a demon in long red underwear, barefoot, charging into the dying embers of the campfire, yelling, "Where's Williams? Report to me! The whole staff! Wake them all up!"

General Howard emerged from the tent stuffing his empty sleeve into his empty coat pocket. In the starlight an officer dashed towards the general's tent, buckling on his sword as he ran.

★

Under Shake's impatient guidance the Readers' Circle, all of them schooled to read Czech in German Gothic script, was gradually learning the Latin alphabet. The only one to have mastered it with any ease was Molly Kakuska, and while the others were still making laborious progress syllable by syllable, she sat in a corner weeping over a popular Czech novel. Padecky wanted to quit. He was furious to find himself illiterate again, after he'd put so much effort as an adult into the Schwabach Gothic script back home. He cursed the Austrian emperor for introducing the Latin alphabet in the first place. In a democracy like America, he insisted, the government would never dare.

"It certainly wouldn't," Shake agreed. "They've used the Latin alphabet since the day they started. So, as a good American, you ought to be glad of the chance to learn it."

"Don't bring that into it!" Padecky said. "Me read English? I can't hardly ask for the time of day in English and I'm supposed to learn to read it?"

"You learn to read Czech first," explained Barcal, who was turning out to be quite the toady.

"I'll tell you what kind of Czech you are, Franta!" barked Padecky. "The emperor makes a decree and you break your neck trying to obey!"

"Incidentally," Shake remarked, "it was the emperor who decreed that Czechs had to use the Gothic script. After the Battle of White Mountain."

"Don't spread mystification just because you're educated," Padecky snapped. "And as for this, I qui—" But before he could say "quit", Kyspersky burst into the pub with the news that a bunch of soldiers was drilling on the green below Monroe Street. "They're wearing bright red floppy trousers!"

"Zouaves," someone said.

Their trousers were indeed bright red and floppy. Each soldier was also wearing a red fez and high white spats. A zouave colonel in gold epaulettes stood in the middle of the green, barking orders in a shrill voice. The white spats executed an "about-turn" and a "left turn" and a "right turn" and the trousers rippled elegantly as they marched back and forth like a big red centipede. A row of carriages was parked on one side of the green, with little fans in fluttering hands at the windows.

"Are they Mohammedans?" asked Kristuvek.

"That's all we need," grumbled Padecky, the free-thinker. "As if America didn't have enough religious maniacs already."

"Don't mock the faith, you pagan!" declared Kafka, a converted Catholic. "But you're right about that—Mohammedanism shouldn't be allowed here. America is and must remain Christian."

This put Padecky in a rage. "If you want to tell people what to believe in and what not to believe in, why don't you march back to old Austria? Everybody else here is enjoying the freedom!"

"Calm down, neighbours," said Shake. "These people don't pray to Allah. They just came up with these uniforms so they'd look good in the war."

"What war? Are you trying to tell us there's a war on?" snapped Padecky.

"There will be soon enough," said Shake.

"The hell there will!" Padecky roared. "The South wouldn't dare break away from the Union."

"Neighbours, take a look at that!" Slavik interrupted, pointing across the green to a sight much more interesting than politics. Several ladies had stepped out of their carriages and, with rapt curiosity, were taking a closer look at the marching men in their red trousers. One of them, a lady in burgundy velvet, was peering at them through a lorgnon. Their colonel barked an unintelligible order, the soldiers' white tunics expanded as chests swelled, and the white spats began flying up and down while the red trousers flapped splendidly. The lady dropped her lorgnon and let it dangle from its golden chain, and began clapping. The others joined her. The colonel gave another order, and the zouaves halted in formation. He dismissed them, then led them over to the ladies. More passengers stepped daintily out of the carriages. The listeners across the green could hear animated conversation interspersed with female laughter.

"They wouldn't dare!" Padecky's irate voice drowned out the congenial sounds. "There ain't going to be a war!"

Nobody felt like arguing with him, for they were all staring enviously at the vivid display of spats and trousers and ladies' dresses. Slavik stroked his moustache as though he were contemplating a complicated military manoeuvre.

"Neighbours," he said, "I've got an idea."

• • •

At the founding meeting it turned out that no one had any experience as a soldier—except for Filip Ferdinand, and he'd been discharged from the Austrian army after six months for flat feet. Then Vasek Lusk came forward and volunteered to lead them.

"You?" Kristuvek asked in amazement. "Vasek, you weren't even seven when your dad brought you to Chicago."

"But we sailed to America to join my uncle," said Lusk.

"So what, kid?" challenged Padecky.

"Uncle Amos was Moravian Brethren," said Lusk. "A staunch one. And it's in our blood."

"What is?" said Slavik.

"Soldiering. My great-great-great-grandaddy was killed on White Mountain," said Lusk. "We were clandestine Moravian Brethren till after the Toleration Patent. But Uncle Amos left for America before that, and Cousin Dianthe married that fellow Brown. So it's in our blood."

"What Brown, you runt?" yelled Padecky.

"The one they hanged!"

"Oh, that Brown!" said Padecky. "But wait a minute. He can't be your blood kin. You ain't got anything in your blood."

"But Uncle Amos was all for it."

"And she was too?" asked Kristuvek. "That cousin of yours?"

"She went nuts," said Lusk. "When she died, Brown married again."

"Look," said Padecky, "the only soldier was your great-great-great-grandfather, and you're just a common busboy at the Swan Hotel."

"I'm a waiter already," protested Lusk.

"Busboy or waiter," declared Padecky, "you're still no soldier."

"But it's in our blood," Lusk insisted. "Uncle Amos came to America on the same ship as Jakub Benjamin, a Jew from Prague who joined Brown in Kansas and fought beside him in a battle against Kentucky slave-owners!"

"A Jew?" Kafka piped up. "Jews don't fight battles."

"In America they do. Everything is possible in America," said Lusk. "They say there were three of them with Brown. Somebody called Weiner—he was older and fat; and then Gustav Bondy—he was supposed to be from Prague too. He was the wildest of them all. He even fought Kossuth in the revolution in '48."

"Do you by any chance happen to be a Jew?" Kafka asked darkly.

"Why?"

"Because you keep going on about having things in your blood!"

But before Lusk could deny it, Padecky asked, "Did your Uncle Amos do any soldiering with them three Jews under Brown?"

"Well, no," admitted Lusk, "he just knew them. Well, at least he knew Benjamin. They were on the same ship."

"So what exactly have you got in your blood?" Padecky was getting mad again. "Was your Uncle Amos a soldier with Brown or wasn't he?"

"No, but my aunt baked bread for him."

Molly Kakuska walked into the pub with Schroeder.

"Why?" asked Slavik.

"Because he loved it," said Lusk. "It was rye bread with caraway seeds, like they make in South Bohemia. Brown couldn't get enough of it."

"Oh, so this is where you all are!" said Molly Kakuska. "I've been waiting for you an hour in the hall—"

"That's how Auntie snared him," Lusk went on. "It was on account of that bread he married my cousin Dianthe. She wasn't much to look at."

"You're all supposed to be in the Readers' Circle," said Molly.

"Let us alone, girl," said Padecky. "We're dealing with more important matters." He turned to Lusk. "Look here, if it's bread-baking you've got in your blood, you can be chief cook and bottle-washer if you want. But commanding us just because your uncle was buddy-buddy with some Jew from Prague who says he fought under Brown in Kentucky—I'd have to see it to believe it! What we need is somebody who knows what the hell they're doing, not some busboy whose great-great-great-great-grandfather croaked on White Mountain!"

"We missed our chance," said Shake later. "We could have had a commander with a direct line to the famous John Brown. Instead we picked a Slovak, a Hungarified one at that, who worked as a valet to Dr. Walenta, who was a Germanized Czech who made his reputation in Chicago as a skinflint on the insurance company's side, fixing the entitlements of the crippled workers in that big train wreck in '58."

"That's what I said, you had a valet for a commander," said Houska.

"Geza was about as much a valet as you are a—" Shake couldn't think of an adequate comparison.

"Me, I'm never any different," said Houska. "Call me an ordinary farmer."

"That's it. That's exactly what Geza said: he was never any different," said Shake. "He was a soldier, first and last. Even in Chicago, when he dressed up in tails and held the door open for Dr. Walenta's classy patients." And he went on to quote Molly Kakuska's reply.

"More important matters? Is bending your elbow more important?" she said, pointing to the empty beer steins that were banned at the Readers' Circle.

"We're drinking for courage, girl," declared Padecky, who was undergoing an opportunistic change of opinion. "There's going to be a war."

"*Jesus in Heaven!*" *exclaimed Molly.*

"*Was sagt er?*" *Schroeder wanted to know what he was saying.*

"*There's going to be a war!*" *Shake translated into German for him.*

"*Well, I should hope so,*" *replied Schroeder in German.*

"*Jesus in Heaven!*" *repeated Molly.*

They told Schroeder what their meeting was about, and the Prussian imme-diately offered to command them. Kafka said it wouldn't be possible.

"Warum nicht?"

"*Because we're going to call ourselves the Slavonic Rifle Company.*"

"*We're going to have red trousers,*" *Kyspersky interjected.*

That was when Schroeder told them about Mihalotzy, Dr. Walenta's valet. He wasn't certain whether the man was a Slovak or a Hungarian, just as he didn't know if Dr. Walenta was a Czech or a German. But they were both Aus-trians, he was sure of that.

"*Are you hanging about with that Hun?*" *Shake asked Molly after the meeting.*

"*I don't hang about with anybody, Mr. Schweik,*" *declared Molly.* "*He just keeps coming around, and besides, Franta went to Cedar Rapids for potatoes.*"

"*Does Schroeder come around when Franta is home?*"

"*Well, he can't then,*" *said Molly, blushing.*

Schroeder walked over to them and Shake backed off with a touch of regret in his heart.

"Poor Franta," said Stejskal.

"Did she marry Schroeder?" asked Paidr. A cannon boomed from the di-rection of Bentonville. The sergeant couldn't shake his ominous thoughts.

"No, she didn't. She married Franta Kouba. But he was taken prisoner at Chancellorsville and died in Andersonville," said Stejskal. "I was there with him. I got exchanged, but by that time Franta was dead. I had the sad duty of telling Molly."

"What happened to Schroeder?" asked Paidr.

"He's fighting with Sigel, as far as I know," said Stejskal. "At least that's what he said. Except that Sigel hasn't been in action for a long time, not since he got knocked on his backside by those cadets from the Virginia Academy."

"And Schroeder?" asked Paidr.

"What makes you so interested?" asked Javorsky. "You got eyes for the young widow Kouba?"

"She must be worth the sinning," Paidr said, "from the way Shake talks about her!"

"Yes, well, there'll be no sinning with her, brother," Shake sighed. "Not for me, anyway."

"Maybe there will be, now she's a widow," said Houska. "Widows are easier."

"What do you know about it, farm-boy?" Javorsky said.

"Nothing," said Houska. "That's what they say."

The sergeant looked at Salek and saw Salek looking at him. But Salek had never found out about the moonlit night the sergeant had spent with his wife. Salek had been dead drunk that night and the sergeant had left early the next morning. Salek had finally caught Vlasta *in flagrante* with the priest of the Polish Church of the Immaculate Conception, and the only reason he didn't cause a scandal in the Church was that Vlasta agreed to divorce him. Salek took his place in Chicago history as the first Czech to divorce his wife. Cup entrusted little Annie to the Kakuskas to raise, and joined Lincoln's Slavonic Rifles on their way to the battlefield at Perryville. Vlasta became a waitress in the fancy Swan Hotel and continued to sin against the fifth and ninth commandments.

Salek dropped his gaze. A horse neighed. A shooting star streaked across the North Carolina sky.

"No, friends, it will never happen," said Shake. "But how could a man hold himself back in the presence of such beauty?"

He went on to describe the second slap in the face Molly had given him—when he tried to steal a kiss from her that night in the dance hall on the corner of Van Buren and Canal, because she looked so beautiful in the costume the ladies had made for the Ladies' Circle Ball to raise money for the Slavonic Rifles' red trousers; Molly's dress was pink with a blue-trimmed white apron and a blue ribbon around the waist.

"Why didn't the women just make the trousers for you and be done with it?" asked Javorsky.

"You can't deny a woman the pleasure of dressing up," said Shake.

"Was it you going to war or was it the women?"

"Nobody much figured on a war," explained Shake. "By that time the Slavonic Rifles had fifty members, and we thought that once we had the red trousers we could draw another fifty to the Union cause and then we'd have enough for a whole company. Mihalotzy even had a Hungarian colonel take a letter to Lincoln asking the president's permission to use his name."

"So Mihalotzy was actually a Slovak?" said Salek.

"I don't know and I don't think he really did either. More than anything he was a soldier, eager to get fighting, and it's like they say—as ye sow, so shall ye reap. . . ."

"Was he killed?"

"At Buzzard Roost Gap, in the spring of '64," said Shake. "He was in command of Hecker's Twenty-fourth Illinois. I wasn't with them any more. He was a real hit at the Ladies' Circle dance, though. He charmed them with the way he spoke Slavic. That whole night it was ladies' choice."

★

As soon as Dinah stepped into the parlour with the brandy on a tray, she noticed the mesmerizing effect Lida's braids had on Étienne. She also noticed the girl's brother looking at her, but she was used to glances from white boys. As the buggy was leaving, she waited in the shadows on the veranda. Étienne stood there waving, and he was still standing there long after the buggy was just a cloud of dust dissipating in the moonlight. Finally he turned and walked past her into the house. He stopped in the doorway and turned back to her. "Not tonight," he said softly. "I'm not—" He hesitated. "Not tonight."

There probably won't be a little house in Austin, she thought. The Louisiana fiancée will have a different kind of competition now. She sighed.

Early the next morning Étienne left the house, but he came back before noon and locked himself in his room. That evening Gideon rode off into the setting sun with a letter fixed with a big red seal.

"No more jassing about for you," Benjamin teased. They were in the kitchen. "Young massa's in heat for somebody else."

"At least I'll get some rest," she snapped.

That night she stayed in the cabin with her family. But the next day—the evening following the afternoon that young Towpelick brought Étienne a letter without a seal on it—Étienne told her, "Come tonight."

Was he in heat? Was Miss Blue-eyes the cause?

Early in the morning after that fateful afternoon, Étienne appeared at the Toupeliks' farm with a bouquet. Standing in the doorway, Cyril could see the patch of purple flowers approaching on horseback along the path between the cotton-fields.

"We have a visitor. I wonder who he is?" he teased Lida, who was on her way back from putting a bucket of fresh milk in the pantry.

"My husband," his little sister replied as she passed him. "Look after him while I change!" And she was gone.

"Who did you say?" he called after her, but she didn't reply.

Étienne reined up his horse in front of the house, wished him a good morning, and said, "Is Miss Linda at home?"

"My sister will be right out," said Cyril. He wondered about asking casually

after the girl who combined all the beauties of both worlds, but he couldn't think of a way. Lida emerged from the house as pretty as a picture in her Sunday best. Étienne climbed down from his horse. He was amazingly nimble for a man with a wooden leg. Cyril now understood what his sister had said.

"I need to ride out to the Ribordeaux place this afternoon," Cyril said in an offhand tone next morning, after the Negro had delivered them the letter with the red seal. "Do you have a message I should pass on to somebody?" And he grinned.

Lida looked him square in the eye. "No, I don't have a message. But you could take him a letter."

"Do you want me to check it for mistakes?"

"No, mistakes don't matter. The more the better."

He could see how she was playing Étienne. She was far more calculating than she had been back home. She was an exotic blossom for de Ribordeaux. She knew the impact of braids and bows and charming blunders in English. She had stuck the flowers in a pitcher of water and put them on a windowsill decorated with pictures of doves and four-leaf clovers. That was all she could draw, but it was enough.

She ran off and returned with a letter. It didn't have a seal, of course, and the stationery came from her father's supply, brought from the old country. Once every three months, he would write a letter home saying how well they were doing in America.

"Give him this."

He made a face at her again and said, "Your husband?" He glanced pointedly at little Deborah, who was playing on the doorstep with the kittens.

"Just you wait and see!" she hissed. He saw the same fire in her eyes that he had seen when the old veteran had brought her home from Amberice. "That won't matter at all," she said. "And you stay out of it!"

"I hope you're right," he said. "But I wonder."

The fire faded from her eyes. "It's worse for you, Cyril." She smiled, without a hint of rancour. "And how come you need to ride to the Ribordeaux place today?"

He felt embarrassed. "I don't know what you're talking about," he said.

"Of course you do. I'm not blind. And I wish you well, big brother. But this is Texas—" She laughed and ran back inside.

He was furious with her, but gradually he calmed down. What if she was right?

The door to the plantation house behind the bougainvillea was opened by Benjamin, though Cyril didn't know his name yet. "No, massa's gone to New Orleans this morning. Oh, you mean Massa Étienne? Massa Étienne's in the summer-house out back." Benjamin took the letter.

"I'll wait for a reply."

She slipped quietly into the front hall, holding a duster made of rooster feathers as if it were a sceptre. An African princess. She gave him a broad white smile.

"Good morning, miss," he said.

She looked around, but they were alone. She looked into his eyes. Perhaps he came from a country with black countesses. "You calling me 'miss'?"

"Well," he said, "you're too young for me to call ma'am."

She laughed, and jiggled the feather duster under her nose. She sneezed.

"Could I—" he said, "could we meet sometime, miss?"

"I don't know."

"Don't you want to?"

She shook her head. "It's not that. It depends on—"

"On what?"

A clock chimed the hour, as pleasant as the sound of music in the night. A door opened and the sun cast a limping shadow on the white stone hall floor. The man with the wooden leg was walking through the doorway, reaching out to shake his hand. The princess with the rooster-feather sceptre vanished into the labyrinth of the big house.

"It was so kind of you to go to the trouble," the man was saying. "I do appreciate it. But I can't ask you to—"

Instead of finishing his sentence he ushered Cyril into a room he knew already—the naked goddess on the seashell hanging over the fireplace and, on the walls, portraits of ancestors in lace and velvet and pearls and shiny buckles and gleaming belts, pearl earrings worn by women as pink as dolls, and paintings of fleshy-faced men and women whom the artist had rendered with much less care than their finery. Étienne invited Cyril to sit in a Louis XIV armchair, though Cyril didn't know this, and opened a carved humidor to offer him a cigar Cyril knew was from Cuba. It was long and fat, with a straw down the centre so the smoke was always fresh, unfiltered by the tobacco which would otherwise have spoiled the taste as the cigar burned down. Mr. Carson smoked the same cigars and offered them to guests as well, though from a more modest humidor.

"I've heard that Mr. Carson has put two servants at your father's disposal. The manufacture of oil from cotton seeds genuinely interests us," Étienne said, broaching a subject he wasn't the least bit interested in. He asked how soon Mr. Towpelick might be able to set up a similar plant on the de Ribordeaux plantation. The smoke from the two cigars mingled with the fragrance of verbena, which reminded Cyril of the perfume Dinah had been wearing.

"A month or two, as I said."

"I'm also interested in your ideas about our system of servitude. True, our opinions differ—" He paused to inhale some smoke and think a bit. "Well, at

least we differ in part," Étienne continued. "Yes, I'd truly enjoy discussing it with you, and other things as well. But next time, have your sister use one of the servants at her disposal. Or have her tell Benjamin to wait for her reply, or have him come for it. That would save you the trouble."

Another pause. Wisps of pure, unfiltered smoke rose to caress the fleshy cheek on one of the portraits, then drifted across a gloomy canvas where names and dates, written in gold and framed in decorative little boxes, represented the de Ribordeaux family tree.

"Our mansion was in the Department of the Seine," Étienne told her. "After St. Bartholomew's Day my great-grandfather had to leave. He ended up in Louisiana."

"Miss Hortense had a novel about that," said Dinah.

By then, the man with the wooden leg knew that his golden-brown girl could read French. He saw her differently now than he had the first or second time she had come to him. He was no longer giving her orders. She was the one who asked, "Do you want me to, massa?"

One day he said, "I don't want you to call me massa!"

"What should I call you?"

"Étienne."

"Massa Étienne?" she said.

"No! Just Étienne!"

So, from then on, he was Étienne.

"Our line," he said, "goes back uninterrupted to the fifteenth century, and there it fades into the dawn of history."

"Mine fades into the dawn of history too," she replied, relishing the phrase, "starting with my mother. I don't know who my father is."

He was standing in front of the dark canvas with the family tree, the evening sunlight on his handsome, proud, and—she sometimes thought—haughty face. She knew already that he was having strange thoughts about her. After his cousin's slaves were caught trying to escape she knew she was no longer just a body to warm his bed, no longer even a "servant". His philosophy was crumbling, but he still couldn't speak the new words aloud.

"It was either Hannibal McGuire or Patrick McGuire," she said, looking at him mischievously. Her power over him was leaking into the cracks in his philosophy. "And, massa—"

"Étienne!"

"Massa Étienne, can you guess which one it was?"

.   .   .

"*Your lovely sister, Mademoiselle Linda,*" *said Étienne awkwardly, "is an extraordinary girl.*" *By then he knew she was from Moravia, in the Austrian Empire. Back in the parlour with the portraits, Cyril had told him the story of the family's move to America, changing only a few details. He had failed to mention the baby, but Étienne's black messenger had sharp eyes.*

"*Or should I call her Madame Linda?*"

So he knew about the baby.

"*Well, to be precise, you probably should,*" *said Cyril. "But her husband was killed in a riding accident two months after the wedding. Deborah was born after he died.*"

"*Deborah,*" *mused Étienne. "That's not a Moravian name?*"

"*She was born in Texas,*" *said Cyril. "When Linda's husband was killed, we were all getting ready to come to America anyway.*"

"And he believed you?" asked Kapsa.

Cyril gave a bitter laugh. "Lida had him figured out. But nobody had Lida figured out."

★

"Because it was ladies' choice, Mihalotzy went from hand to hand. Every one of them wanted to touch him. There was plenty to touch, too. He was nearly two metres tall. And when he had gone around once, they started him round again, so that Bill Trevellyan—guest of honour at the party along with Schroeder—decided that Czech women were a band of Amazons. The prettier they are, the more terrifying they are, and he started trying to talk Schroeder out of Molly Kakuska. Because even though she came from a highly moral family, she got her hands on Mihalotzy too.

"Well," Shake went on, nodding to Paidr for a light for his long pipe, "the dance party was a huge success, and they raised plenty of money for the trousers. Enough, in fact, to inspire thievery. A certain Skotas-Kulhawey offered to keep the proceeds for Marticka Lusk, since the women's dresses had no pockets and Marticka hadn't brought a purse with her. Skotas-Kulhawey kept the money, all right. He ran off with it that very night, presumably to Russia."

"Where?" asked Stejskal, horrified.

"That's right—Russia," said Shake. "It's a long story. Some immigrants were having trouble with English. Most of them were farm people and Chicago seemed like a strange place. They started seeing Russia as a Slavic paradise, and a few benighted souls even wrote to the tsar and asked if he'd let them move there. Of course, he didn't take the trouble to tell them to piss off. Pretty soon there were two camps. The smarter ones began wondering if this idea of a Slavic paradise wasn't a little far-fetched, since the Poles, who are Slavs too and had lived in that Slavic paradise, had been treated like savages by the Russians—and don't forget there were a lot of Poles in Chicago. A man called Tom Plavec, who was a Czech but from some Russian province, escaped to America and said the Russians would make muzhiks out of the Czech Americans if they came, and then they would be serfs again, although not in Austria but in the Slavic paradise. 'Although Siberia,' he added, 'is a wonderful land with lots of forests, even if it's too cold.'

"Most of those who'd been thinking of going to Russia were discouraged by what he said, and Vasek Lusk pointed out that it wasn't so much that they were homesick for their Slavic homeland, it was more that they missed village life. So Lusk and Tonda thought everyone who was unhappy in Chicago should get together, hire wagons and oxen, travel west to Nevada or California, and set up a pure Czech community. They had a name all ready for it: New Bohemia."

"Not a bad idea," remarked Houska.

"Are you kidding? A community of pure Czechs?" said Salek. "They'd be at each other's throats before they even got there. The first thing they'd do is break into two separate communities."

"Or three," said Stejskal.

"As a matter of fact, they did fight," said Shake. "Even before they got the first team of oxen, they fought about whether to build a church to Saint Wenceslas in New Bohemia, which is what the Catholics wanted, or a Shrine to Reason, as the free-thinkers demanded. It got into the newspapers. Kohout, leader of the Catholics, publicly accused Stradal, the free-thinker, in the pages of *Slavia*, of having had a picture of His Imperial Highness Franz Josef on the wall of his cabin in the old country. Stradal replied that indeed he had, but that was before he was living in freedom. In America he had realized the error of his ways, renounced his former admiration of the emperor, and hung a portrait of George Washington in his home instead. Later on that got a bit sticky too, but I'm getting ahead of myself. Kohout wrote in *Slavia* that, as he was a Catholic, the only picture he ever had on his wall was the Virgin Mary. Stradal couldn't resist getting back at him with a few digs at the virginity of the Mother of the Lord. The Kohout–Stradal controversy made *Slavia*'s circulation shoot up, and the paper is still going in Chicago to this day. When the war broke out, Kohout suddenly discovered that his eyesight was bad, and Stradal decided that his admiration for the emperor hadn't been entirely a mistake. He went to the consulate—but that was later. In short"

—Shake puffed some more on his pipe—"thanks to the legendary Czech unanimity and harmony, neither Utopia—Russian or Californian—came to pass, and instead the Czechs gradually put down roots in Chicago. The only one who kept pushing for an exodus to Siberia was Skotas-Kulhawey. And when eventually they all decided to stay in America, he went alone. With the proceeds from the dance.

"And that was a real blow to Lincoln's Slavonic Rifles," said Shake. "When Geza Mihalotzy told us we'd have to pay for our own uniforms, and when a tailor told us a uniform with red trousers would cost three-fifty and one with plain trousers no more than two seventy-five because they could use cheaper fabric from the government stockpiles, the company almost fell apart. Only a few were willing to give up the red trousers and make do with ordinary ones. The rest lost interest. It was only Mihalotzy's strength of personality that saved the Slavonic Rifles from dying before they were even born."

★

North of the only road to Bentonville (he read about it in Colonel Bellman's book one winter long after the war, because winters on the farm were for reading; actually it was Terezka who read it to him. He pretended his eyesight was failing because he loved the sound of her eleven-year-old voice reading fluently, her American accent unblemished by even a trace of Czech, though she spoke Czech too), where the marshy gloom was unaffected by the spring sunshine, stood the remains of the Cole plantation. The pillars of the big house, once pure white, were now grey, with holes in them that showed them to be hollow—nothing, in fact, but the trappings of nobility. The plantation was surrounded on all sides, as if by a crown of thorns, by a tangle of the scrub oak that lined the narrow road for some distance towards Bentonville. A few leaves left over from last fall rustled drily in the tangled branches. The screen formed by the trees was almost opaque. Lieutenant Bellman, commander of the Twenty-second Wisconsin's reconnaissance unit, noted a few dead, dried-out bugs impaled on the twigs of a bush by the road, left there by some satiated butcher-bird. Or perhaps the butcher-bird had died and its victims had been left hanging on hooks, unconsumed. The sergeant listened to his daughter's lovely voice reading words she did not always fully understand. "There were men enough; all dead, apparently, except one, who lay near where I had halted my platoon to await the slower movement of the line—a Federal sergeant, variously hurt, who had been a fine giant in his time. He lay face upward, taking in his breath in convulsive, rattling snorts, and blowing it out in sputters of froth which crawled creamily down

The Bride of Texas

his cheeks, piling itself alongside his neck and ears. A bullet had clipped a groove in his skull, above the temple; from this the brain protruded in bosses, dropping off in flakes and strings. I had not previously known one could get on, even in this unsatisfactory fashion, with so little brain."

Lieutenant Bellman had grown used to this kind of thing—gutted plantation houses, ruins—and it no longer struck him as ominous. On the other hand the butcher-bird's deserted larder was an evil omen, a sign of the battle that General Carlin was so convinced would happen. Carlin now rode right behind the last men of the Twenty-second Wisconsin, in the freshly washed shirt and pressed uniform intended for his coffin.

With his reconnaissance unit right behind him, the lieutenant stepped into the alley between the bushes. They walked along in silence, listening to the skeletal rattle of the dry leaves. Then the lieutenant saw the trench. He jumped backwards into the bushes, but the scrub oak was impenetrable. The men behind him dropped, but before they hit the ground the first shots cracked from the Confederate trench. The lieutenant silently gave the signal to withdraw. The soldier behind him didn't move, then moaned softly, trying to help himself up. But his strength was fading fast and he dropped back. The lieutenant grasped him by the armpits and elbowed his way out of the roadway with the wounded man, while other men opened covering fire. Once outside the alley of scrub oak, they zigzagged towards a low wall bordering a newly ploughed field where the rest of the unit had taken cover. The Rebels stopped firing. The lieutenant lifted the wounded man onto his back and stumbled towards the wall and over it. He turned him over to the litter-bearers in time to see two generals jump off their horses at the forest's edge and run towards the front line. One of them lost his hat; he bent to grab it and in the early sunlight his hair glistened wetly. It was Major-General Slocum, Commander of the Army of Georgia. The other general was someone the lieutenant knew personally: the sharply pressed uniform, a Schlachtanzug—*as drill sergeant Hoenicke used to call it, may he rest in peace. His battle outfit.*

The lieutenant saluted. The generals reached the wall and dropped to their knees. Slocum pulled out his field-glasses.

"There's a trench about fifty yards from where the trees start," Bellman reported. "When we got close, the Rebels opened fire. We have one wounded."

"Thank you, lieutenant," said General Slocum, surveying the area with his field-glasses: the thick hedge, the devastated plantation house, the scrub oaks stretching from the house to the road and farther south, and on the low hills a pine grove here and there, low walls marking the edges of fields. Nothing was moving anywhere.

"What do you think, general?" Slocum asked Carlin.

"I'd be careful if I were you," said Carlin. "The terrain is full of thickets and groves and swamps. It could be hiding a considerable part of Johnston's army."

Slocum continued surveying the landscape for a while. Then he said, "There won't be more than one or two of Wheeler's squadrons. But let's see. Send skirmishers north and south of the road. Let's make contact with the enemy—that is, if he doesn't just silently fade into the underbrush by himself." He laughed. "Johnston's division is at Raleigh. Surely there can't be more than one or two cavalry squadrons here."

The two generals strode calmly back to the woods where their horses stood. They mounted their horses; General Slocum wrote something down and passed it to a rider, who left the group waiting for the generals by the woods and galloped off across a meadow and along the bushes to the south. That would have been the courier who caught up with Sherman's staff later that afternoon with the optimistic dispatch, the sergeant thought as he listened to Terezka reading.

The men of the first Brigade of Davis's corps marched across the meadows to the south and north of the road. They spread out and advanced to the hedges and walls around the plantation fields. The lieutenant followed them with his eyes. Suddenly there was a flash to the north of the hedge, then another, then a third. The men of the first Brigade broke into a run. The thunder of cannon rolled over them, and smoke came spurting out of the long, black, uneven line of bushes. The first casualties dropped to the grass. There was another flash to the south, then farther north, then farther south. Was this one or two squadrons? It was the first time since the taking of Atlanta that the lieutenant had heard the majestic roar of artillery in the full strength of several batteries.

The blue ranks wavered. Some men continued running forward, others turned and fled, crouching and staying close to the walls. The first canisters exploded over the meadow. Now everyone turned and retreated. The brightness of the sun faded as the smoke rose to veil it. Thunder from the west—Carlin's batteries opening fire. They overshot. The men of the first Brigade quickly ducked behind the walls and into the brush of the nearby grove. Several soldiers were writhing in the grass, others lay there motionless.

The courier galloped south with his optimistic dispatch. The roar of the cannon got there before he did. But when he found Sherman, the general chose to believe the dispatch. It strengthened his conviction that he had been right: ". . . a few squadrons of cavalry. Sweep them aside and you're fine. We'll meet tomorrow at Cox's Bridge."

★

Dinah only looked at the letters after they started talking about it in the kitchen and Benjamin asked her, "Well, can he still get it up for you, girl?"

"Just make sure your own tool's working!" she retorted.

"I just wondered what white meat does for him—"

She wasn't sure about that either. His eyelids had started to flicker shut. "Are you getting married, Étienne?" she had asked him.

He opened his eyes and stared at her. "Why do you ask?"

"I thought you and Miss Scarlett got engaged?"

"What do you want to know that for?" he said, raising his voice.

"Don't get upset," she said.

He got up and limped, naked, over to the window on his beautifully carved wooden leg. After a while he said, "I've bought that little house in Austin." He was staring out the window at the cotton-fields in full bloom.

But what did that mean?

"Thank you," she said.

He didn't look at her. She got out of bed and picked up her clothes from the armchair.

"Don't leave yet!" he said. Was it a command? He kept looking out at the moonlit countryside.

She put her clothes back on the armchair and got into the bed.

Finally he joined her there, a shadowy, hobbling silhouette. But it wasn't completely dark, and she could see that he was ready again.

She opened herself to the wild bliss. She always did, but stopped herself from crying out. This time she couldn't help it. "Ahhh!" she cried. "Ohhh, ohhh!"

"Stick a gag in your mouth next time, gal!" Benjamin said in the kitchen the next morning. "I needs my sleep."

Afterwards, Étienne kissed her on both cheeks and rolled over on his back. For a while she lay beside him, then she got out of bed. This time he didn't stop her from leaving. She dressed quickly, crept out of the house, and walked towards the summer-house. White meat? The thought made her cringe. What magic powers lay in that white porcelain skin, those blue eyes?

She walked through the orchard thinking about the white boy who talked funny and called her miss. He spent all his time back there by the stables, putting some kind of machinery together, and whenever she walked by—which was more than she needed to—something strange happened: she had the feeling that his eyes were not undressing her. She knew what the undressing looks were like. Now and then Étienne had visitors from neighbouring plantations, young dandies from Galveston, and she heard them joking about her to Étienne, and he would laugh and not say a thing. This young white boy, covered with black axle-grease, was something different. When he stared at her over the oily metal plates his two helpers were struggling with, it made her feel like a black countess, or a countess in the novels in Mademoiselle de Ribordeaux's bookshelf, at whom the cavaliers always "gazed with veneration". That was it. The white boy looked at her "with veneration". He had already asked her twice to meet him in the evening after she was done working. She hadn't been able to because Étienne had wanted her. But yesterday Étienne had told her he was going to Galveston for three days. If the white boy should ask her again. . . . She walked past the blossoming cactus plants and realized how unhappy she'd be if he didn't.

In the morning, when she was cleaning Étienne's room—he had ridden out early in the carriage—she thought of those letters. After what had happened the previous night, she wanted to be clear about things, so she searched through the drawers in his writing-desk. There they were: ivory-coloured sheets of paper with the name of some town and a picture of church towers and bridges across a river printed across the top. They were written in a large calligraphic hand, four letters in total, the English funnier than the brother's. "Dear Mister de Ribordeaux," said the first one. "Thank you for the letter. I cant meet you day time but tomorrow Tuesday at seven o'clock I coming to were Hardy Creek turn south at weeping willow tree. sincerely, Linda Towpelick." So the boy's name was Towpelick. The rest of the letters were shorter, but all the more eloquent. They started "Dear Étienne," followed by a time and a place, and ended "Your Linda." The last one had been delivered the previous afternoon by Jefferson, one of the men Carson had lent to the Towpelicks. It read: "Seven o'clock Cobson's Grove."

★

"I swear I never snooped around in Lida's things," Cyril declared one of those turpentine evenings. "But she left the letter lying on the chest. She knew it was nothing but gibberish to Mother and Father, and anyway she didn't have to keep secrets any more, like back home."

The letter contained a poem but Cyril didn't understand much of it yet. "Lida? Whatever English she knew she had learned from Washington and Jefferson. They followed her around like puppies. One time in Austin she bought herself a textbook for newcomers, but she learned a lot more from those two lovesick servants. I read that poem over and over until I knew it by heart. Finally I figured out what it was all about. Of course, Lida knew the first time she read it—if she ever read it, for all she had to do was look at the letter. It was obviously a poem. What else can a poem from a young man mean?"

"Do you still remember it?" asked the sergeant.

So Cyril recited it. At the other end of camp, a band was playing taps.

What is love? 'Tis not hereafter;
Present mirth hath present laughter;
What's to come is still unsure:
In delay there lies no plenty;
Then come kiss me, Sweet-and-twenty,
Youth's a stuff will not endure.

★

"Yesterday they were smooching down by the weeping willow," Benjamin said in the kitchen. "I got an awful sneeze and it scared them off."

"Just be glad he didn't break your back with his wooden leg!" Uncle Nero grinned.

"He never seen me. I scuttered down the ravine and on out of there," said Benjamin, "so I missed watching him screw her."

"Massa he never do it like some white trash," said Uncle Nero. "Down by the creek."

"You don't think so? Just ask this little girl here." He turned to Dinah. "Go on, tell Uncle Nero!"

Before she could say something sassy, Uncle Nero said sternly, "I don't abide no dirty stories."

"Anyway," said Benjamin, "now they got scared off the willow tree, they'll find somewhere else."

Cobson's Grove was a miniature French park, one of de Ribordeaux's flights of sentiment, like his big library full of French novels that, for the most part, only Dinah had read. There was an arboretum with a gazebo, where Hortense de Ribordeaux had spent hot afternoons perspiring over her reading lessons. There were places to hide all around the gazebo. That evening, from one of those places, Dinah heard Étienne reading English poetry, and through the leaves she saw him try to steal an ordinary kiss from Miss Blue-eyes between sonnets. But Miss Blue-eyes wouldn't let him. She told him to read her another poem instead.

Dinah was amazed. Was this the way white folks did it? Just the way they did in novels? She recalled his crude command to her that first night and practically laughed out loud. Étienne was so comical now. After all kinds of flirtatious toing and froing she finally let him kiss her, but the moment Étienne put away the sonnets and reached for her bodice she stood up and said she had to go home. The moon had barely risen. Étienne got up too, and limped obediently beside her to the buggy. Miss Blue-eyes climbed in and snapped the reins, but by then Dinah was running along the hedge in the little park, then between the cabins and back to the big house.

That night she tried to control herself, but she cried out again. She owed her pleasure to little Miss Blue-eyes. And this time she even caught herself closing her eyes and imagining it was the white boy under her. She was feeling something strange, and she had no idea that it was happiness. That afternoon the white boy had asked her a third time. This time she had said yes, and had invited him to the arboretum. Étienne was going to Galveston the following day.

★

The sergeant watched his daughter through half-closed eyes as she struggled with the dry sentences of the colonel's memoirs by the light of the kerosene lamp. "The advanced guard of General William Passmore Carlin's division encountered the North Carolina division of General Robert F. Hoke. The latter, having taken advantage of the cover provided by the dense scrub oak which bordered both the road to Bentonville and the fields surrounding the Cole plantation, had taken a position as the axis of a vice that was meant to pulverize Carlin's division. The right arm of the vice was the army of General A.P. Stewart, positioned in the bushes and groves to the north of the road, while the left one was to be the corps commanded by General William Joseph Hardee, which, according to Confederate General J.E. Johnston's plan, would locate along the south side of the road. General Johnston, however, had formulated the plan on the basis of maps of dubious precision, since more precise ones were not available, and thus, to his dismay, General Hardee discovered that the distance he and his men were to cover on their march towards Bentonville was twice that indicated by the maps. When General Carlin's advanced guard came in contact with Hoke's units, only the northern arm of the vice—A.P. Stewart's Tennessee army—was in the position called for in Johnston's general plan. Once the assault of Carlin's advanced guard was thwarted, neither Hoke nor Stewart proceeded with a counter-attack but instead waited in anticipation of the arrival of Hardee's units. Thus Johnston's carefully formulated plan collapsed even before it could be implemented."

The girl put down the book. "Daddy, can I have a drink of cider?"

"Apple juice," the sergeant corrected her and closed his eyes. He could see Carlin's soldiers, whipped by the hot breath of battle, retreating behind bushes and stone walls. Not an orderly retreat, but it had been weeks since they had danced to the roaring music of cannon and sought shelter from the rain of canisters all around them. They re-formed their ranks behind the bushes and the walls, and

attacked again. The countryside, flooded with morning sunshine, was blanketed with running men, and gunfire began crackling in the bushes opposite them. Small clusters of grey-clad soldiers broke out of that cover to counter-attack. The blue of the Union uniforms had faded to a dull grey-blue on the early spring march through the Carolinas, so to General Carlin, watching through his field-glasses, the battling soldiers became a jumbled, indistinguishable mass, punctu-ated by the gleam of a bayonet or the flash and puff of a gunshot.

"Apple juice," the girl corrected herself.

"Go ahead," said the sergeant. "You read very nicely."

The child's smile was lovely. If the war had turned out differently—if—

The sergeant would live to a ripe old age. He would die content in his ninety-seventh year. By then the Austrian Empire was history, and all of them—Ursula, Shake, Paidr, Javorsky, Salek-Cup, Houska—all of them were dead, alive only in the memories of an old soldier. An American-style republic was born back home in the old country, but the sergeant's home had long been America. Or so it seemed to him when another child, a great-granddaughter, read an American newspaper to him, because by then his eyes truly were failing him. Padecky, Stejskal, Fisher, Zinkule—all gone, vanished with a vanished age, forgotten, alive only in the flickering and dying memory of an old sergeant. But if the war had turned out differently—would there have been that new American republic in old Europe?

It wasn't a battle yet, only a prolonged skirmish, but the cannon were firing hungrily. Braxton Bragg, with his inclination to confusion, was in command of Hoke's division, and he sent General Johnston a request for re-inforcements just before the blue ranks wavered, stopped, and turned tail. The path of their retreat was littered with the corpses of men bitterly struck down in the final days, the early spring days, of the terrible war which, had it turned out differently—

The morning courier galloped across the greening meadows, avoiding marshland, taking cover behind scrub-oak hedges, carrying Slocum's dis-patch to Sherman.

Three Rebel soldiers, followed by some men in faded blue uniforms, jumped the stone wall and surrendered. General Slocum looked them over suspiciously. "People who can bury a mine in the ground, and then in safety enjoy the prospect of an infantryman treading on that mine and seeing it blow him to pieces—people who can fight with that kind of base perfidy—" The general waved dismissively. "Are these soldiers? NO! Where would we be if, instead of real soldiers, we had only these spineless cowards who commit cold-blooded murder from a distance!"

Sunbeams shone through bursting buds on the trees. Slocum and his staff sat on tree stumps in a clearing while on the other side, guarded by soldiers with bayonets, stood the three musketeers with their improbable tale. Slocum frowned as he regarded them. "According to them, Howard is supposed to turn around and concentrate all his forces on Bentonville—where, granted, there may be more than a few squadrons of Wheeler's cavalry—and Hoke's division, or part of it, is there too. But in my opinion that's all. They're trying to tell me that as soon as Howard clears the field, Johnston is going to pull some kind of devilry like an outflanking manoeuvre?"

"I don't know," said General Carlin.

"They're spies," said Slocum. "Their task is to mislead us. Why would Johnston have his whole army waiting for us, when all he has behind him is a river with a single bridge?"

The deserters maintained that Johnston's aim was to destroy Jeff Davis's Fourteenth Corps. By itself, their version was not improbable. It only became suspect when Slocum considered it alongside different assessments of the situation, assessments that became certainties in the mind of a confident commander-in-chief. The deserters claimed to be Union soldiers taken prisoner at Resaca. In order to stay out of Andersonville Prison, they'd convinced the interrogating Rebel officers that they were Copperheads, followers of Vallandigham who had never wanted the war with the Confederacy in the first place, and that, now that Vallandigham had been silenced, they wanted to fight on the Confederate side for the old rights guaranteed by the Constitution. So the Rebels had taken them into their army, and since then they'd been waiting for a chance to desert. It had finally come, at Bentonville.

"They're spies," Slocum insisted. "I'll have them shot."

"I don't know," said General Davis.

From not far off came the crash of cannon. A shell fell close to the edge of the woods and exploded. They heard the shrapnel tearing the leaves off the trees. Someone cried out.

"I don't know," said Davis. "Why would he just send Hoke?"

They glanced at the prisoners, who were standing almost at attention, their faces paper-white in the light of the rising sun.

Refreshed, the girl returned, sat down on the stool, kicked her bare feet a couple of times, placed the book on her lap, and searched with her finger for the place where she had stopped reading.

If the war had turned out differently, the old country wouldn't be the American republic it had turned out to be—a dream that had never crossed his mind on that slow sail across the Atlantic, with the wily Fircut, to where a war awaited him and then a long life. Would the expeditionary forces of some Northern States of America have fought in the war that happened much later in Europe? If they had, would the Confederate States of America have sent proud descendants of the victors of '65 to bolster the other side, the Austro-Hungarian monarchy? Even in the new century, officers battling on the side of the imperial armies would have been accompanied by black servants. If his general had lost.

But Sherman could never have lost. Nor could Shake, Kakuska, Paidr, Houska, Javorsky—

The little girl resumed her reading:

"Whereupon General Slocum issued the order for the remainder of the Fourteenth Corps to advance and dig in, and simultaneously, the order for the Twentieth Corps to leave the rear and reinforce the advance units that were in a frenzy of palisade-building."

★

Slocum, Davis, and Carlin stared at the deserters.

"Stand them up against the wall," said Slocum. "Of course—"

Major Tracy of Slocum's staff emerged from the bushes on the opposite side of the clearing. He approached the three men with the paper-white faces. The cannon were still firing. Major Tracy spoke with them for a while and then walked over with one of the spies, or whatever they were.

"I know this man," Tracy said to Slocum. "We grew up together, general. He's telling the truth."

Slocum examined the prisoner. Sunburned skin showed through the days-old growth of whiskers, and his nose was red and peeling.

"Johnston's there with his entire army?"

"Yes, sir. General Hoke's division is right in front of you. North of it is General Stewart's Army of Tennessee. General Hardee is supposed to make up the left flank but he hasn't arrived yet. General Bragg's main force is in Bentonville and General Johnston—"

"OK," Slocum interrupted. "Lieutenant Foraker!" He looked around. A clean-shaven young man jumped up off a stump. "You'll ride to General Sherman!"

Ten minutes later, the courier galloped off to Howard's camp with a second, pessimistic dispatch. General Slocum was urgently requesting reinforcements.

★

The white boy wasn't really that white, at least not in the more visible places. The Texas sun had baked him to a reddish-brown colour, as it did all the white trash. Once in a while she would catch a glimpse of them stripped to the waist and washing themselves at the pump or in the creek: reddish-brown faces and necks, torsos white and freckled, mostly the arms too—just the hands were reddish brown, as if they were wearing brick-coloured gloves. Some were furry like bears, and all of them had some hair on their chests. The only truly white ones were young ladies like Hortense de Ribordeaux, because they never went anywhere without a parasol, and even so, when she was undressed, her face was darker than her milk-white breasts, so that she had to use talcum powder to make it the colour of alabaster. Dinah examined herself in Étienne's mirror, where she was changing before meeting the white boy. She was the colour of tea with milk. The sun merely made her slightly darker, and she didn't have the silly white shirt the poor farmers had, or the brick gloves on her hands. She was the colour of tea with milk all over. A nigger. She doused herself with the French perfume issued to the house niggers after the father of Étienne's fiancée visited the Ribordeaux household, wrinkled his nose, and said, "You can smell a nigger at a hundred paces! We make our house niggers use perfume, even the men. I can't abide the stink of niggers!" So she covered herself with perfume, though who knew—maybe the white boy liked the spicy smell of sweat. He certainly didn't look like a plantation fusspot.

She also got herself a book from massa's library: Poems for Every Occasion. *She wasn't at home with poetry. All she had ever read were French romance novels. But she liked the look of the book, with lots of gilt curlicues on the binding. Having learned from novels that punctuality did not become a lady, she resisted her inclination to be on time, and stepped into the arboretum like a countess, a whole five minutes late, smelling of sandalwood at a hundred paces.*

The young man was sitting there, waiting for her. He had even brought flowers. He had a small nose and a broad face. In fact, he looked a lot like his sister. He even had the same eyes. But, unlike his sister, he had the brick-coloured skin of white trash. And his blue eyes "looked at her with veneration."

"Bonsoir," she said.

He jumped up and gave her the flowers. He hadn't picked them in some meadow. This kind didn't grow in meadows.

"Oh! They are beautiful!" she said, like a countess, and he actually cleared his throat: "I'm—I'm glad you came."

"Me too," she said, with unaristocratic enthusiasm. He said nothing. Birds were singing all kinds of songs in the surrounding treetops. After a pause, she asked, "Do you like poetry?"

"Poetry?" he replied, taken aback.

"Yes, you know, poems." She handed him the gilt-lettered volume. "There are

beautiful poems in this book," she said. "They're for reading on every occasion."

"Oh," he said. He turned the book over in his hands and examined the back cover.

"Read me one," she urged. She was a black countess and he would be Étienne reading sonnets to Miss Blue-eyes. But he wasn't.

"I don't think I know how," he said dubiously.

"Give it a try!"

He opened the book at random and made a heroic effort to read the first poem his eye lit on:

Look 'round thee now on Samarcand!—
Is she not queen of Earth? Her pride
Above all cities?—

He gave her a miserable look: "I don't read much English, miss. I just speak it some."

Miss!

"No, you read beautifully," said the countess. "Are you from the North?"

"No, from Moravia."

"Where's that?"

"That's in Europe. Across the sea."

"Ah," she said. "So you're from France?" There was France, she knew, and there was Africa. Both of them were over the sea. Each of them somewhere else probably.

"No, not France. Austria."

"Ah!" Where was that? Somewhere far away. Austria. They must have black countesses there. "Do they have niggers there?"

He shook his head. "No. I never saw one till I came here."

"Ah!" A world with no black folks. Where could that possibly be?

Later on he told her where. And he also told her about the little cottage where they had all slept in one room. Lida on the bench.

"Lida?"

"My sister. She calls herself Linda here."

"Ah!"

And how they had toiled and drudged and never got ahead. And farmer Mika, and how they had sailed to America. And seen their first Negroes.

"And you saw me, white boy!"

"Yes, I saw you. But you aren't a nigger."

"Yes I am," she said. "But you love me anyway, don't you?"

"Yes, I do! I love you very much, my sweet-smelling tea-rose!"

"That's sandalwood," she said.

But back in the arboretum he hadn't said a word. He was no Étienne.

And she was no Miss Blue-eyes.

She took the gilt-covered book from his hands and patted his cheek.

"Dinah...."

Nor was she a countess. She put her arms around his neck, pressed her black lips to his, and they kissed and then they made love on the green lawn by the arboretum. She hoped the foul-minded Benjamin wasn't spying on them from some place, but nobody sneezed. Only the song of birds hung in the air, and the fragrance of perfume issued to niggers to quench the stench of sweat.

At home, his little sister sniffed the air meaningfully: "Big brother! You've been to a house of shame!"

★

Lieutenant Bellman couldn't get the dead bugs impaled on the branches out of his mind. On the orders of General Slocum, the men wrestled boulders and the trunks of hurriedly felled pine trees into place. Like frozen waves on a green sea, palisades and stone earthworks quickly sprang up in the hilly countryside checker-boarded with black hedges and interspersed with pine groves and steaming marshes, to hinder the progress of the wild Southern troops under Johnston, Taliaferro, Bragg, Hardee, and Wheeler. Slocum was finally convinced of their presence. On his orders General Morgan's division had made a quick, strenuous march forward from the rear of the long column that, only an hour earlier, had been winding through the countryside like a lazy snake. Now they were digging in at the front. The sun stood high in the sky among white clouds that cast their moving shadows on the ground, now and then extinguishing the delicate glitter of dew in the grass. In the melancholy Carolina landscape, men in tattered uniforms toiled as if their lives depended on it, erecting formless structures—traps for other men, Lieutenant Bellman thought—while deep in their souls they were eaten alive by the question: Why? Why so late, when the end is already—

Within arm's reach? Only the sparse columns of black smoke rising from the turpentine forests on the distant horizon reminded them of the butcheries of the rapidly receding past, when such questions would never have arisen. The graves of the many who could no longer ask those questions were far, far away. Lieutenant Bellman watched the men sweating in the fresh landscape of pine groves, green meadows, awakening fields, but he couldn't shake the memory of that graveyard of bugs tortured to death by the butcher-bird. Within arm's reach.

★

Lida sniffed the air in the room.

"Wait outside until I call you," she said. Obediently he limped out.

She slowly took off her clothes. What was going through her head?

"I told him you were widowed," said Cyril.

"Thanks, big brother, but you didn't have to. Pegleg"—she always referred to him as Pegleg, never Étienne—"doesn't mind. How could he? He's crazy about me."

"So he knows you never had a husband?"

"I told him everything. Well, almost everything. I made Vitek a count, to make it easier for him to swallow. The count gave me a little bastard and then the count's father paid our family's way to America."

"Did you love him?" asked the jealous Étienne.

"I don't know," lied Lida. "He was handsome. I liked that. And he was a count."

"You still love him, don't you?"

Lida glanced out the window at the moonlight on the cotton, as Étienne had done the night before. And she lied through her teeth. "No, it's you I love, darling. But I wonder—"

"Wonder what?"

"What's that smell?"

"Smell?" His intonation gave him away.

"Smell," she said. She rolled over onto her side and rubbed her breasts against his chest. "You've had another woman here!"

He had to admit the truth. "But here, in the South, that's nothing important."

"Do you love her?"

"It's you I'm in love with!"

"But you like her," she said. "And where I come from, that's something important."

"I love you, Linda. It was love at first sight, and I love you as I've loved no one else in my life, ever!"

"So it won't be hard to choose."

"Certainly not." But he didn't sound so certain.

The turpentine forests were on fire.

"He was fond of her," said Cyril. "How could anyone not be fond of Dinah? There isn't another woman like her in the whole world. But he was just crazy over Lida."

"So this other woman will go," said Lida.

"What do you mean?"

"You will sell her," she said. "That can't be a problem, can it?" She sniffed the bedclothes. "Sell her somewhere far away, otherwise it will be a problem."

Whatever could have been going through her head?

"Heaven knows," said Cyril. "I don't understand her. Or actually I do."

Enormous turpentine fireballs.

"What about Rosemary?" Lida asked. "Did you throw her over for that nigger girl? Are you crazy, Cyril? You'll never get her."

"I will. I'll buy her and then give her her freedom."

"You will? And then what? Will you both move to the North?"

"That's right," he said. "I don't want to live in this kind of country, anyway. The real America is up north."

"And what about the farm?"

"I'll leave it for Josef. I can always find a way to make a living."

His little sister grew thoughtful. She stared out at the field where their father was walking contentedly among the rows of corn.

She said, "Well, Father won't hold you back, that's for sure. He won't be able to. But think it over. Starting all over again, with a Negro wife—it's not going to be easy, not even in the North."

"Will he sell her to me?"

"He'll have to. But Cyril—" She paused.

"What?"

"You really will move to the North? You wouldn't stay here with her, would you?" She was almost imploring him.

"How could I possibly stay?"

"No one objects to black concubines for white masters around here. And you're a master already."

"I love her."

She gave him an odd look. "Sometimes masters can love their concubines, can't they?"

She didn't know that Étienne would soon prove her right. A few days later, Dinah was sweeping out the little house in Austin, and Gideon, bearing a letter for Miss Towpelick from Étienne, was also carrying a secret note from Dinah to Cyril. It said, "Baywater Street by the river. A dry chrysanthemum on the door. Yours—and ONLY yours, Dinah."

"Sold her? You sold her?" Lida asked, horrified.

"To show you I'm a man of my word, my sweetheart," Étienne lied. "You said either, or. There's no more 'or'. Are you pleased?"

"Étienne!" she exclaimed, almost unhappily. "Where is she?"

"I sold her to a slave-trader. It's better that way; I'll never know where she ends up."

"Étienne!"

★

The sergeant's eyes were stinging.

Was it old age?

No. Because within arm's reach, at the very last minute—a ragged figure rose over the tent, capless but with a dirty bandage around his head, the red badge of ardour soaking through it. The figure broke into a halting run towards him and he reined in his horse. Then he recognized him.

"Sarge!" exclaimed Vojta Houska, his blue, naive, caring eyes full of pain. He also had a dirty bandage around his left leg, visible because his trouser leg had been shot off. "Kakuska's on his last legs."

Kakuska lay in the plantation-house foyer, along with a number of others. He was gasping for breath. A big Negress, probably a member of the household, was wiping his forehead with a wet rag, which was all she could do now except say a prayer—and she was apparently doing that too, for her lips were moving silently while Kakuska's breath rattled in his throat as he breathed heavily in and out. There was a white bandage around his neck, with the red badge of ardour soaking through it.

"I only caught a glimpse of him, sarge," Houska whispered. "Wheeler had just attacked us and we had our hands full and suddenly our cavalry rode up from the right and one of them seemed to float out of the saddle, his arms spread. I heard a nasty crackling sound over all the racket and he was flying through the air like he was crucified, his carbine in his right hand and his left spread out so I noticed he was missing an index finger. Kakuska, neighbour, poor Kakuska!"

Within arm's reach.

The minnie had struck Kakuska in the chest, right below the collar-bone, and had lodged in his spine. The surgeon had extracted it, because that was what they did in those days—the ball must come out—but could do no more. And Kakuska was choking; his throat was rattling and he couldn't talk.

The sergeant bent closer to him: "Jake, man—"

The eyes recognized him. Then the hand missing the index finger reached slowly for the tattered jacket that lay on the floor beside the cot. It felt for something but couldn't find it. Kakuska's eyes implored the sergeant, his lips moved but the sound that emerged wasn't human speech but a gurgle, the kind that heralds our transformation into nothingness, or into angelic beings. Kapsa looked up at the big Negress. It was hard to tell her age. He had seen hundreds like her in plundered plantation houses. Kakuska's hand was still groping. The sergeant leaned over, picked up Kakuska's jacket; Kakuska closed his eyes and opened them again, as if he were nodding. The sergeant unbuttoned the breast pocket and pulled out something that looked like a little book, with wooden covers hinged and tied together with a worn, once golden piece of string. In the middle of the top cover, which Kakuska had cleverly carved with his pocket-knife to look like a miniature altar, were the words BOZENA KAKUSKA in beautiful letters, first lovingly chiselled and then burned, perhaps with a red-hot nail at a campfire, so the words gleamed black against the yellowish wood.

Kakuska lifted his hand and moved his fingers; the sergeant understood that he wanted him to untie the string. Between the covers was a picture of a girl's face, and the sergeant knew who had painted it. She had rosy cheeks, cobalt-blue eyes, red lips, a copy of a folk embroidery around the neckline of her blouse. To her right, on the wall behind her, hung a crucifix. To her left was a tiny portrait of a bearded man in a miniature frame. Kakuska's hand moved again. Behind the picture the sergeant found an envelope, the kind the sutlers sold, with a picture of doves and two hearts pierced with a single arrow. On the envelope, in Kakuska's farmer's hand, it said in English: "Wen I fal delyver to Bozena Kakuska, Kakuska farm neer Manitowoc Wisconsin."

The sergeant put the envelope back and retied the covers and, while Kakuska followed him with his eyes, unbuttoned his own jacket pocket, put the wooden booklet inside, and rebuttoned it. Kakuska closed his eyes. The sergeant thought he smiled. Then the sign heralding the transformation: the brief lull; then, from the throat of the dying horseman, the awful, deep rattle, the abrupt silence. The sergeant took Kakuska's hand by the wrist. It was already lifeless. He searched for a pulse but found none. He looked up into the broad, black face leaning over Kakuska. His eyes met her brown ones.

"*Crucifixus est etiam pro nobis,*" said the black woman.

The sergeant glanced at her in astonishment, for he didn't understand a word—though it reminded him of something he couldn't identify.

"Amen," she added.

The sergeant glanced at the girl still struggling with the colonel's vocabulary. He died for me too, not just for the big black woman. He died for the nothing he had back home, and the farm he had here, so he died for this country even as it was threatened with falling apart. He died for the world. Kakuska.

Once, after the war, his father-in-law had asked, "Tell me, were there a lot of you Czechs in the army?"

"Not a lot," he said. "Maybe a few hundred. A lot more of them found ways to avoid army service." He recalled Chicago, and how Ursula had said in her sweet German, "I thought of you when they turned up in my husband's office, looking for ways out of it. Sunshine patriots!"

"But the ones that didn't seek ways out fought as Union soldiers," he said almost proudly, although he had never been a sentimental sort. And it was true.

After the war, he went from Chicago to Manitowoc with the carved wooden keepsake, and from there he continued to the farm, about three miles outside town.

You died for that too, friend Kakuska.

The sergeant bowed his head. Beside his cot stood a pair of riding boots. On them sparkled the dead man's spurs.

★

"We're off to the North!" said Vincenc. "Dad isn't that young any more, but we're going! Come along with us!"

"I will," said Cyril. He looked at old man Lesikar. What Lesikar had seen on his way to Austin had been the last straw, the last stain on the sweet face of America. It was a slave auction, with able-bodied mulatto women for sale. On command they would stand up and strut back and forth, displaying their breasts, then turning so the buyer could see the curve of their buttocks. Behind a screen stood some elderly slaves having their grey hair blackened to drive up their price. It offended everything that old Lesikar had come here for, and he raged inside. And Cyril had a piece of paper in his pocket, with an address on Baywater Street written on it, a reference to a dry chrysanthemum, and in his ears Lida's uncertain voice: "You wouldn't stay here with her, would you?" So the last stain on the sweet face of America affected him too, Cyril Toupelik, and his tea-rose, who didn't even have a surname of her own, just the trademark "de Ribordeaux".

In the little house on Baywater Street, they wished for war.

But first: "He's going to sell me, I know it. This here, Baywater Street, this won't last long. Your sister will figure it out, but he won't sell me to you. He'll be jealous of you. He'll sell me the way Massa Leclerc sold Auntie Penelope."

She knew nothing. Europe wasn't even a word for her, much less an idea. Just France. She was full of stories no one had ever written. Not yet. Maybe sometime, years later, but by then they'd be half fiction.

"Auntie Penelope," she said, "was in the same predicament as me, except she didn't have you. But she did have two children with Massa Leclerc, a boy and a

girl. And when Massa Leclerc got married, nobody had to tell his new wife who Auntie Penelope was. She drove her out of the house into the fields. The children too. She ordered the overseer to keep them strictly in line."

"Lida wouldn't do that," he said. "Lida goes after what she wants, but she's not mean. She knows what meanness is because she's felt it herself."

"But she's going to want to get rid of me, and he won't sell me to you. He'll sell me exactly the way Massa Leclerc sold Auntie Penelope, though no one was jealous of her. He sold her and her two children to his cousin, who was a Methodist minister in Georgia. Actually, he gave them away. Reverend Leclerc just paid for the journey. And he was good to them. And me"—she wiped away a tear—"I'm going to end up the same way. If I'm really lucky. Just you wait and see."

"No you won't," he said. "There's a war coming. The Yankees will win it. You'll be just as free as me or Lida or Étienne. Nobody will ever be able to sell you again."

"War," she whimpered. *"You'll have to join up. And maybe they'll kill you."*

He took her in his arms. She was trembling, weeping, her shoulders quivering. He had never seen her like this. She had always been cheery, sassy, imperturbable.

"The hell I knew her," he said as the turpentine woods blazed on. "She laughed so she wouldn't have to cry."

"They won't kill me," he said. "I'll run away. We'll run away together. The Yankees will win. They have more men and cannon, and besides, they're in the right. Nobody will ever be able to sell you again, my sweet rose. It's war. Too bad it didn't start a long time ago!"

They invoked war, while outside the window the river rolled lazily past, warm and southern, and the breeze caressed the moss dangling from the mournful trees. They invoked war and dreamed of running off together.

That night, when he got home, his sister was waiting up for him. She sniffed his coat. "Aha!" she said. "Where is she?"

"Who?"

"Who do you think? You smell like a perfume shop."

So he told her about Baywater Street. She would have found out anyway.

His sister's lips grew thin and hard, her eyes filled with tears. Different tears.

"The swine! He thinks I'll be like his colourless Southern belles and turn a blind eye!"

"Why not?" he said. "You don't love him, do you?"

"But you love your yellow girl, don't you? I'm doing this for you, big brother. Or are you willing to share her with Pegleg?"

He was staggered that she should even suggest it. But she had no intention of sharing Pegleg either. He pulled himself together.

"You're not doing it for me, Lida. Your sisterly love doesn't go that far."

She gave him a look that was somewhere between pity and contempt. "What do you know about love?" she said. "But you're right. It's only partly for you. It's not that I'm jealous, for heaven's sake! But he mustn't think I'd let him get away with anything if only he'd marry me. I'd be pretty stupid if I did that, and I got smart a long time ago. You, Cyril," and she took him by the shoulders and the moon flashed red in her eyes, "in this world it's the strong ones that win out. And love? Well, go for love—but if you can't get love, then go for anything you can get."

★

Bugs skewered on thorns—he couldn't get them out of his mind. He lay on his belly behind the palisade of hurriedly felled trees. In front of him was a green meadow, then a twisted ripple in the terrain that ended in black scrub-oak brush and silence. General Carlin stood not far from Lieutenant Bellman, in his neatly pressed *Schlachtanzug*, surrounded by his staff officers. The rays of sunlight coming through the pine branches transformed him into a bright blue target, and sparkled for a moment off the field-glasses he had trained on the line of black bushes. That was where the silence before the storm lay hidden. It was half past two in the afternoon. Carlin put his field-glasses back in their case and Lieutenant Bellman heard him say to his aide, "There's one thing I don't understand: why didn't they take advantage of the element of surprise? Nobody expected them here, and they gave themselves away by shooting at the advanced guard, and now they're waiting. For what?"

★

"Hardee's men proceeded with effort, hindered by marshes that did not appear on the maps, which, as stated earlier, were far from reliable in other aspects as well," *read the girl.* "They only arrived at the assault site in the late afternoon, to take their places on the right wing and provide power for the vise that General Johnston intended to use to pulverize Carlin's division. Moreover, they were delayed by the fact that the only road leading from Bentonville to the battlefield was blocked by the rear guard of General Hoke, whose corps formed the axis of the vise. The left arm consisted of units under the command of General Bragg. The latter, his senses muddled by the fierce battle that ensued when Carlin's reconnaissance units encountered the enemy, was convinced that the axis of the vise—Hoke's corps—

would be annihilated by the counter-attack from Carlin's regrouped units, so he called desperately for reinforcements. Then General Johnston—who would later admit it was an error in judgement—ordered Hardee, who had only just arrived, to send McLaws's regiment to reinforce Hoke. That left the right flank with only the division of Tali—Talifor—" *faltered the girl.*

The sergeant prompted her: "Taliaferro."

"Taliaferro," she repeated in her earnest schoolgirl voice. The sergeant recalled his general bent over the map and Slocum's dispatch, which had just been delivered by Lieutenant Foraker, and which the general had read aloud to his staff: "I consider it crucial that the right flank be repositioned forthwith to join us under cover of darkness. Also send all munitions and all available empty ambulances." The sergeant had noticed how the general nervously ran his fingers through his reddish beard while reading about empty ambulances, and he knew what factor would determine the general's decision. In the final analysis, it was always the same determining factor.

"I have reliable reports," continued Slocum, "that I am facing the concentrated units of Hardee, Stewart, Lee, McLaws, Hill, and Hoke." The general ran his fingers through his beard again.

"McLaws, guided by the same inexact and perplexing map," *read his daughter,* "wandered for a long time among the marshes and swamps unrecorded on the map, before he finally took his place for the attack. So it happened that it was not until a quarter past three in the afternoon that all of Johnston's units were in place and the planned assault could begin. Concealed behind hastily erected palisades, they faced the units of Carlin's division, reinforced by General J.D. Morgan's Second Division. Also approaching the battlefield was Slocum's corps, with the divisions of Williams and John W. Geary as well as that of W.T. Ward, released for the purpose from its role of accompanying and guarding the munitions and supply train. That was the situation on the battlefield at fifteen minutes past three o'clock, when the Confederate troops launched their attack."

★

First, metal showered down on the palisades in the pine groves, and on the stone barricades zigzagging across the open fields. Next, the defenders heard the delayed din of cannon. Then came the Rebel yell, a long ah-aah-aaaah!—the awful battlefield chant of this four-year-old war and perhaps its last cry. And finally they appeared, led by officers on horseback. They were dressed in rags, terribly handsome under their tattered company banners, marching quickly forward, rank upon ordered rank, with the long strides of veterans who had been through everything, Shiloh, Antietam, Perryville, Chickamauga, Chancellorsville, Gettysburg, *morituri* from the Devil's colosseum.

They were handsome and tragic, strange "artists for art's sake" of death. They were fighting only for honour now, their ranks depleted by growing desertions, men abandoning even honour and going home to defend their small farms, every man for himself. Leading them on a black horse, crutches clipped to his saddle, the one-legged General Bate galloped across the field towards Lieutenant Bellman, brandishing a ludicrous bare sword. Behind him the banners of rapidly advancing divisions, regiments, companies, flapped in the dazzling spring afternoon sunlight, as the troops marched with the confidence of veterans of obscure places that were now entries in the Devil's dictionary of history—Little Round Top, Resaca, Lookout Mountain. Under those tattered banners their divisions had the strength of regiments, their regiments the strength of companies, their companies the strength of a mere handful of undermanned squads. And yet above them the terrible Rebel yell still sounded, and before them boomed the metallic explosions of canisters. Before he knew it, the lieutenant was running close behind the fleeing veterans of those same battlefields, leaping with them over the palisades, while behind them veterans were climbing over the palisades they were abandoning. General Bate kept twisting in the saddle, urging on his ragged, sunburned soldiers with his sword and a loud holler, all needlessly, for they knew all was lost, the Confederacy and the human property that most of them had never owned anyway. All was lost but honour. And they fought for that, professionally—that is, courageously. They fought for honour.

But his general didn't see this scene. From Slocum's dispatch he knew that a single division under Carlin was facing the onslaught of battalions under Hardee and Hoke and Lee and Stewart and Cheatham and Hill. He would not see, later that day, the ragged division banners fluttering over the heads of what were scarcely a regiment, or the regimental banners flying over squads. "Hardee," General Howard said. "I taught his son Willie in Sunday School at West Point." The general ignored him and started barking orders. "Hazen! He's closest to the left flank. His division will immediately join Carlin! Woods, Smith, Corse, they're at Cox's Bridge." The Rebels had set fire to the bridge, but while it was burning Logan's engineers erected a pontoon bridge across the Neuse. The sergeant understood the general's intention: "They'll cross the Neuse and hit Johnston from behind. Blair and the entire Seventeenth Corps will move to Bentonville tonight!"

There wasn't much night left. The marathon march of divisions and battalions continued through the day, while the huge battle raged at Bentonville.

★

"Why do you always use that perfume, little rose?"

"Does it bother you?"

"Of course not. I love the smell. But I always end up smelling like it too."

"That bother you?"

"Not me. But you told me Étienne gets jealous."

"He can't tell. He's so used to my perfume he never even notices it any more."

It made him feel sad and angry. *"Yes, he's used to it—I'll never get used to it."*

"Wait till I'm yours," she said. *"I mean, I'm yours and only yours already. It's just that I don't belong to you yet."*

The light hoof-beats of a carriage-horse came in from the road. Dinah ducked down behind the machine he was assembling. She had stopped off at the lean-to on her way to take some medicine to sick Uncle Habakuk, the old patriarch of the plantation, who was at least sixty-five and who used up enormous quantities of rheumatism ointment that M. de Ribordeaux got sent from Galveston for him.

"He smears it on his bread," said Dinah.

"His bread?"

"That's right. Uncle Habakuk has peculiar tastes, all on account of an overseer named Mister Williams, who had it in for him back when Uncle Habakuk was still on Massa Butler's plantation in Louisiana. Mister Williams, he was a mean overseer. He beat the niggers and did all kinds of things to them. He accused Uncle Habakuk of being lazy and, fact is, Uncle Habakuk was lazy, and still is. He'd rather practise fiddling in his cabin than pick cotton, and Saturdays he'd play the fiddle at dances."

"And Williams let him? Maybe he wasn't that mean."

"He had to let him. Uncle Habakuk was so good at faking that he even had Dr. Benson fooled for two whole months, before the doctor caught him making a tongue paste and sent him back to work."

Cyril was puzzled. Did she mean that Uncle Habakuk had a recipe for a spread made out of beef tongue? There were still gaps in his knowledge of English, or perhaps Dinah's pronunciation had something to do with it. When she wanted to she could talk as well as the white gentry, and when she was alone with him that was how she spoke.

"No, it wasn't a beef spread," she said. *"It was something he used to mix from*

mustard, dandelions, and God knows what else. He'd smear it on his tongue and the back of his throat and pretend he couldn't talk and had the shivers. He knew how to fake shivers so bad it looked like he was chilled through to the bone. Dr. Benson tried to scrape the yellow-brown coating off his tongue but it held so strong he had trouble getting it off himself later on, when he was back in the cotton-fields. The only thing that would take it off was whisky. Not even julep would do the trick. So Uncle Habakuk's throat was coated for weeks at a time, because whisky was hard to come by. On the other hand, it stuck so well that he could be sick for days at a time.

"Dr. Benson tried out all his cures on Uncle Habakuk. First he bled him, then he purged him, then he had him fast for a couple of days, bled him again, and when the film in his throat wouldn't go away he sent Uncle Habakuk back to the cotton-fields."

She had told him this story the second time they met in the arboretum; she hadn't brought him a book to read. There were fireflies everywhere, midsummer Texas fireflies. Dinah's eyes were full of mischief and he accused her of making the story up. Her eyes grew grave.

"Why would I make things up?" She glanced across the hedge to the white lights of the big house, and the yellow lights of the cabins beyond it. "I don't need to make anything up."

He realized she was right. With the life she led, why would she need to make things up?

She laughed out loud. "It's Mister Williams who's responsible for Uncle Habakuk's strange tastes. Once he caught him taking a snooze among the tobacco plants. 'You lazy bastard! So this is what you do! And I keep wondering how come there's still so many caterpillars on my tobacco plants. You just wait,' he hollered. 'I'll teach you.' Then he ordered the niggers not to stomp any of the caterpillars they were picking off the tobacco plants, but to put them in a tin pot he gave little Sarah to carry. When the pot was full and it was time for lunch, he pulled out a spoon and ordered Uncle Habakuk to eat the caterpillars. Well, everybody expected him to throw up, but Uncle Habakuk sat down on the ground, set the pot in his lap, dug his spoon into that squirming mess of caterpillars—ugh—I get sick just thinking about it. I'd surely have thrown up if I'd been there. But I only heard about it from Uncle Habakuk."

"And he didn't make this up?"

"Where else do you think he got those strange tastes, like spreading rheumatism ointment on his bread? Anyway, Uncle Habakuk says his stomach did feel pretty awful. But then he shut his eyes, grabbed a caterpillar off the spoon with his fingers, and took a bite. 'It taste a little like blackberries, girl,' he told me.

Uncle Habakuk actually took a liking to them and dug right in. When Mister Williams saw that, he threw up himself."

Cyril burst out laughing.

"And so did five women who were expecting."

"Now you just thought that up!"

"All right, I did," she admitted, "but that was all I made up. That feast didn't make Uncle Habakuk very popular with Mister Williams. In fact, it turned into a feud between the two of them that dragged on and on. But Uncle Habakuk came out on top in the end. You see, he could read, except nobody knew. And he also drew pictures, really beautifully."

★

Lida sniffed. Like a cat. She was wearing a new dress Cyril had given her money for, with a bold décolletage and a hanky tucked into it. Her mother had shaken her head over the dress, and her little brother Josef had whistled when she was looking at herself in a mirror that was too small. She had taken that as a compliment and said, "Thanks."

Now she sniffed. "You had that woman here again."

"No I didn't!"

She looked around the room, stepped over to the wide bed with its silk coverlet. She sniffed again.

"You swear?"

"I swear it!"

"You had no woman here yesterday?"

"I swear I didn't."

Impatiently, he went up to her and put his hands on her breasts. She pulled away and walked over to the window. "I believe you, but. . . ."

Outside Benjamin was walking by. He tossed her a lewd, knowing glance and then quickly looked away, as though he hadn't seen her.

"But what?" asked Étienne uneasily.

"It's not discreet enough here," she said. "I found a sort of an—Absteig—"

"A what?" She sometimes resorted to words he didn't understand.

"A place to meet so your niggers can't spy on us."

"Where?" he asked. He seemed baffled.

"It's in Austin," she replied sweetly. "By the river. In Baywater Street."

He turned beet-red.

"My dear," she said, her voice still sweet. "You will not cheat on me, because you cannot. And you will sell the woman who uses this perfume. Really sell her this time."

He dropped to one knee—something he had learned to do even with his wooden leg—embraced her thighs, and buried his face in the front of her tight skirt. "I'll sell her, Linda my sweet, I swear—"

"But you will sell her where I tell you to sell her," she interrupted. She looked out the window. The cotton-fields sloped away to the setting sun. "I think I know who will buy her."

"I'll sell her to anyone you say, Linda!"

"And you will sell her cheap. As punishment!"

★

As he fled, Lieutenant Bellman could see General Carlin running ahead of him, his *Schlachtanzug* gleaming like a blue target, unstained by battle. The entire division was running away, driven by explosions overhead that sheared the branches off the pine trees. Minnie balls made the air buzz with their discordant funeral music. Just ahead of the lieutenant, a soldier fell to the ground, half his head tumbling bloodied to the grass. The lieutenant jumped over it and ran on. Another soldier beside him fell, grabbed his leg, and howled as blood poured from his wound. They could feel the Rebel yell driving them. General Carlin and a group of his staff scrambled into the black brush. Lieutenant Bellman joined them. All across the green meadow, men in tattered uniforms were rushing forward, their ragged banners flying victoriously in the sunshine. General Carlin pulled out a pistol and fired once, and then again, at the thin but furiously advancing line led by General Bate, his crutches bouncing up and down against his saddle. A group of Union riders tore past, pulling their field-guns behind them. A blue target, General Carlin stood towering over the black bush.

"Get down, general!" one of the mounted artillerymen yelled. "My battery's the last one. Ain't nothing but Rebel troops behind me!"

A rifle cracked nearby and a captain in Carlin's staff grabbed himself by the arm; droplets of his blood spattered the general's *Schlachtanzug* and quickly soaked into the fabric. Carlin broke into a run again, with his staff behind him, including the captain whose arm was spurting blood. Bellman came last, his mind on those impaled bugs. Now, when the end is already—he ran.

He must have run a whole mile, turning now and then to fire. The grey lines kept advancing, their banners shredded by gunfire and fluttering like butterflies high over their heads. General Bate brandished his sword. Lieutenant Bellman reached the palisade at the edge of the woods and clambered over it.

General Carlin was already standing there, talking with two excited men in blood-soaked shirts.

★

His girl told him that Uncle Habakuk had learned how to draw as a boy on the plantation of Massa Ripley, a real strange bird in North Carolina: a patriarchal abolitionist plantation-owner. Ripley was killed suddenly when his carriage overturned, and he didn't leave a will—just a young son, James, at the University of Virginia in Charlottesville, who had managed to rack up a gambling debt of two thousand nine hundred dollars and get expelled, thanks to the company he kept—a poet with the elegant name of Edgar Allan Poe. Fortunately for the young rascal—unfortunately for Habakuk, who was only fourteen and nobody's uncle yet—James inherited the whole plantation, and offered Uncle Habakuk to his creditor as payment for the gambling debt, along with two handsome maids whom the creditor sold at a profit, keeping Uncle Habakuk as his personal servant. The creditor, young Master William Smithson, was, unlike young Master James, a fairly good student. Uncle Habakuk slept on a cot at the foot of the bed in his room when William and his cronies played cards and argued philosophy, so Uncle Habakuk got an education by listening and by reading Master Smithson's books while he was away at classes. Massa Ripley had taught him to read. Master Smithson liked to draw too. He used to copy birds and plants from a book by a man called Audubon. When William had gone to classes, Uncle Habakuk would borrow a sheet or two from the large amounts of drawing-paper that Smithson kept around. He didn't draw birds and flowers, though; he sketched the faces of the debating card-players from memory. One day Master Smithson caught him at it. Fortunately he was in a good humour that day—the night before there hadn't been much discussing, and he had made fifty dollars—so he didn't punish Uncle Habakuk. Instead he started showing him off. He got him to draw portraits of his friends and enemies, and soon the university was flooded with Uncle Habakuk's work. In time, Master Smithson started taking him along to the big houses on nearby plantations, and to the homes of Charlottesville merchants, where Uncle Habakuk drew portraits that enhanced the beauty of the young ladies. He had an almost supernatural ability to draw the homeliest, plainest girl so that she looked like herself but also like a princess.

But the lot of a servant is seldom happy. Master Smithson got himself in the bad books of the stern and uncharitable Zebulon McIntyre, professor of classical languages and history, and persuaded Uncle Habakuk to draw the Latin scholar as Nero, in the nude and engaged in an act of love that may have been common enough in antiquity but was officially deemed not to exist on the campus of the

University of Virginia. Professor McIntyre suited the role of Emperor Nero very well; he was a fleshy epicure who seemed to be modelled out of goose-fat, and was renowned on campus for his capacity for lobster tails and his love of roast pork. There was a pigsty behind his two-storey house, one of the several residences connected by the student dormitory, and the hogs would snort their comments on his students' halting translations of Homer and Horace.

The portrait of Nero in action circulated until it reached McIntyre. It found him suffering a mild case of food poisoning from tainted lobster.

McIntyre was no abolitionist. Although Uncle Habakuk had acted on the instructions of his owner, and although McIntyre originally demanded young Smithson's expulsion from the university, the affair was finally resolved by Smithson discreetly shifting his winnings at cards into McIntyre's pocket. Like it or not—since otherwise he would have had to forgo a classical education—he also had to sell Uncle Habakuk to an infamous slave-trader named Forest, who in turn unloaded him to Frederick Zeno Butler, a Louisiana tobacco farmer. Butler, who was dead set against slaves being able to read and write, wasn't told of Uncle Habakuk's talents. But Forest wasn't risking anything. Butler's distaste for literate slaves was his best guarantee that Uncle Habakuk would keep his education to himself.

★

The wounded men in the ambulance cart slowly rattling its way along the road to Bentonville had been playing cards since morning. There were only five of them. Four sat in front with kerchiefs tied across their noses and mouths. The kerchiefs were badly stained, but none of the stains was blood. The fifth man, Zinkule, sat at the opposite end of the cart. He was stark naked, stubbornly scrubbing himself with a piece of rag he kept dipping in a basin of strange-smelling water. His injury was different.

The night before, he had been sprayed by a skunk.

The bald-headed Sergeant Zucknadel wasn't seriously wounded either. He larded his conversation, full of conversational obscenities, with a stream of heartfelt invective against the Czech nation. He had broken his leg when it got wedged between the logs that K Company had laid across the muddy road. In barely comprehensible English he damned the slipshod handiwork, and when he found out that a Czech squad was responsible for the carelessly laid corduroy he started to curse them as *das boemische Gesindel*—Bohemian scum—and heaped abuse on every famous Czech he'd ever heard of—John of Nepomuk, Jan Hus, Saint Wenceslas, and Princess Libuse. In the scuffle that followed, the outraged Prussian was overpowered by the Czechs and was saved from their rage only by his injury. Houska, patriot that he was, put it succinctly, even if his logic left something to be desired: "If he didn't have a broken leg, I'd bust the other one too!"

The German's anger was not an expression of a blood-thirsty will to fight, frustrated by a broken bone. It turned out that the noncom was worried that the war would end soon and now, thanks to Czech carelessness, he wouldn't be able to march in the victory parade before the president, with troops he'd intended to train in the genuine Prussian *Paradeschritt.*

By then Paidr couldn't stand it any more, and bellowed at the injured man, "You're a Forty-eighter, aren't you?"

"Klar bin ich ein Achtundvierziger!" Zucknadel said at the top of his voice. *"Und was soll sein?"* Or, roughly, "Damn right! So what?"

To enlighten the ignorant Prussian, Shake presented what verged on a scholarly lecture on the ideals of 1848. The Prussian mind, however, remained obstinately unenlightened. It perceived no difference between the beauty of democratic ideals and the equally radiant beauty of high-stepping army boots. The row started up again. It got so loud that they never heard the clatter of cannon-fire coming from Bentonville shortly after dawn, and it came to a head when Sergeant Zucknadel furiously opened his stuffed rucksack and pulled out a spotless sergeant's coat with shiny buttons and silver braiding. The Prussian had carried this dress uniform with him all the way from Perryville, through the main battlefields of the war, inspired by the vision of a closing *Parademarsch* reviewed by the president of a newly united Union. This masterpiece of the tailor's art succeeded in silencing the ragtag crew of Company K, and that was when the sound of cannon-fire got through to them. They listened, bewildered. It grew to the continuous roar they had last heard at Atlanta. Even Zucknadel quit swearing.

Finally Shake ventured, "Pack up the uniform, sarge. The parade's been indefinitely postponed."

Zucknadel grumbled but took the tunic, folded it with care and love, and gently put it back in his rucksack. The rest of them listened. The cannonade showed no signs of letting up.

Stejskal turned to Shake. "That armour, rusty or not, you shouldn't have got rid of it."

"I think it was a stupid thing to do too," said Shake. As they listened, they could hear new cannon joining the fray.

A Negro rushed up to the cart, out of breath, carrying a steaming basin. "Here, pop," he said to Zinkule in colloquial Czech, "I've got some fresh brew for you."

Zinkule dumped out the old basin and took the fresh one from the

Negro. They could smell a blend of skunk spray and that other oddly piercing aroma.

"It's not helping much, Breta," Zinkule told him.

The Negro flared his nose and sniffed. "You don't smell nearly so bad no more, pop. I'll find you a new set of blues some place. Two, three more days and you'll be able to get dressed again."

Resigned, Zinkule slipped the rag back into the basin. The smell of the potion hit them again. Hard to tell if it smelled good or stank.

"I don't know, Franta," said Paidr. "Maybe you just need to wait, get unstunk by yourself. This is sort of like going from the frying-pan into the fire."

The rumble of cannon ahead of them grew louder. An officer on horseback was galloping towards them, down the long, slow column of creaking wagons.

★

"Mister Williams the overseer tormented Uncle Habakuk something awful," Dinah continued. A fat caterpillar was crawling across her skirt. She wrinkled her nose, picked it up gingerly, and tossed it away. *"See, that's just the kind of ugly creature Uncle Habakuk had to eat whenever Mister Williams caught him doing anything bad at all. Especially loafing. But instead of curing him of his laziness, it did the exact opposite. Caterpillars, centipedes, moths, earthworms, maggots, and mashed blowflies—"* she counted them off on her fingers. *"He ate them all."*

Cyril said, *"Until he really got sick."*

"Oh no. Uncle Habakuk got used to it, it was Mister Williams who didn't. Whenever Uncle Habakuk stuffed himself with those creepy little things—he liked daddy longlegs the best; when he chewed them their legs would stick out of his mouth, twitching—Mister Williams threw up, which always made him furious."

Perhaps it was all true. Perhaps it was a little more than the truth. So he said, *"And five pregnant women threw up every time Mister Williams did."*

"Oh no," she said, *"they all got used to it too. Because when Uncle Habakuk took a liking to eating insects, he decided to make a business out of it. He started selling roasted grasshoppers at Saturday-night dances; they tasted something like almonds. And when customers acquired a taste for those, he began to get fancy. Pickled centipedes, earthworms stuffed with ants' eggs, fat caterpillars like those that feed on onions. His greatest success were rain-worms stuffed with some kind*

of tiny fly that migrates up from Mexico. Whenever he had those, the dancers got so happy that some of them forgot their manners and didn't even get drunk. They'd just disappear outside into the bushes, as often as five times in a single evening. So on top of being known as a famous fiddler, he got a name for being an expert insect chef."

"Why didn't Butler put him to work as a cook?"

"Massa Butler had no idea, of course," said Dinah. "He was just glad his niggers were having fun Saturday night. He thought that it made them more pious and enthusiastic when they sang hymns in church on Sunday, and that by Monday they'd go back to work in his tobacco-fields fresh and happy. Except in the end," she said, "everything fell apart. Mister Williams realized he wasn't getting anywhere, all he'd done was create a bug-eating nigger, so he changed his tactics. He forbid Uncle Habakuk to play the fiddle on Saturday nights, made him quit selling fried insects, and forced him to eat supper with the overseers. It worked. The food he had to eat at the overseers' table made him sick. The tongue paste didn't impress Mister Williams any more, so Uncle learned from a nigger on a neighbouring plantation how to dislocate his wrist. But that made it hard for him to play the fiddle, so he decided he'd be better off working. The weak stomach he got from the overseers' food and not being able to play at Saturday dances were too much for him, so he came up with a plan."

He based it on Williams's outstanding weakness: women. Williams left most of his not inconsiderable wages in cat-houses, but even that wasn't enough for him. He had several favourites among the female field hands, and he rewarded them by allowing them to sleep in the shade of the tobacco leaves for several hours each day while the rest had to hoe away in the hot sun. The slaves grumbled about this in their cabins at night, but none of them ever thought of going to Butler to complain; they were too scared of Williams. Justice had to wait until the classically educated, musically and artistically gifted, and vengeful insect chef finally resolved to spread the word. Shrewdly, he put a word in the ear of one of the house niggers about why work wasn't getting done in the tobacco-fields. As he expected, the whispers went straight to the ear of Mrs. Butler. She passed the story on to her husband, who could tolerate a lot from his niggers, but not shirking work.

Butler decided to investigate. He crept up behind the hedge by the field where Mister Williams was overseeing the hands. There he saw one beauty dreaming under the hedge. He left her alone and crept on, and found another one, and more—seven of them sound asleep.

When he got to the seventh sleeper, he stood up and revealed his presence to Williams. He summoned him to the big house for a talk, and there, in the ab-

sence of field Negroes, raked him over the coals and cut two dollars off his wages. But the house niggers were at the keyhole, and the news was whispered back down from the big house to the field hands' cabins.

"*Didn't Uncle Habakuk feel bad that he cost those women their good times?*" *asked Cyril.*

"*No, because now they started getting presents from Mister Williams—calico for dresses, rings for their ears, and things. And on Saturday nights they'd try to see who could catch the handsomest nigger at the dance, and sometimes they even got into fights over it.*"

"*But they did have to work in the fields.*"

"*Everything has its price,*" *shrugged Dinah.* "*But that's when Uncle Habakuk launched the next part of his plan.*"

Part Two of the plan was founded on Uncle Habakuk's culinary knowledge. He was expected not only to eat with the overseers but to serve them as well, so he took some of the tiny dried flies that he'd used to stuff the rain-worms, and put them in with the pepper in the pepper shaker. After a while on that diet, Williams added some older and less attractive hands to his harem. Not only were the fields full of sleeping women, but they were the scene of other activities that kept work from getting done. News of the despised overseer's extraordinary capacities took the usual route back to the ear of Mrs. Butler—who was quite a beauty herself.

"*Fred, what kind of a fellow is that overseer, that Williams person?*"

Butler immediately became jealous, and this was part of Uncle Habakuk's plan. "*Why do you want to know?*" *he asked warily.*

"*Well, I've heard the niggers say all sorts of things about him.*"

"*What sorts of things?*"

"*All sorts,*" *said Mrs. Butler, and in a delicate phraseology acquired from novels she acquainted her husband with his overseer's gargantuan appetites.*

There was another talk in Butler's study, noisier this time, and the news reached the cabins quickly. Butler had nothing against fornication with the young women who were his property, "*But not in the fields, not in full view of the niggers, and not during working hours!!!*" *He hollered at Williams so loudly that the maid listening at the keyhole felt her ears ringing.*

Meanwhile Butler began to nurse a grim suspicion about his lovely wife. The next day he went to the field. Uncle Habakuk noticed him hiding behind a clump of trees, and rubbed his hands in glee.

Butler came to the conclusion that Williams was probably not suited for work on a plantation where the lady of the house was the beautiful Florence.

And that was when Uncle Habakuk struck.

From Beulah, the lady's maid (he was sleeping with her, and used to bring her grasshoppers braised in cognac that Beulah had stolen), he found out that the chronically jealous Butler regularly and covertly checked the secret desk compartment where his wife kept her correspondence. (After she read a short story by the writer with the elegant name, she hid her private correspondence in her husband's desk, in a drawer he never opened—where he kept the Bible.) And so one afternoon when Miz Florence was off visiting her friend Lillian (who had a handsome brother) on the next plantation, the plantation house shook with an outburst of Butler's rage. Soon Othello the footman was running to the fields with more alacrity than usual, and soon afterwards Williams was seen hurrying to the big house.

Without a word, Butler showed Williams a love letter addressed to "My dearest Florence", full of suggestive insinuations (the latter had originally contained a long quotation from Ovid's Ars amatoria, but Uncle Habakuk had realized in time that the overseer didn't have the same classical education he had, and had rewritten it), along with a beautifully sketched portrait of Florence Butler nude from the waist up. Uncle Habakuk's imagination, fuelled by Florence's décolletage, was amazingly true to life. The second letter Butler showed the perspiring Williams was the overseer's own complaint against the unfair cut in wages. Fortunately for Uncle Habakuk, Butler was not a close observer of handwriting, so to him the two letters seemed to have come from the same hand. The poor overseer was entirely ignorant of Uncle Habakuk's literacy and his past career as a portraitist, so he couldn't come up with a satisfactory explanation. In any case Butler was so angry that nothing would have satisfied him. Butler shouted at him and then resorted to physical violence, since challenging his wife's seducer to a duel was out of the question; the overseer was too far beneath him socially. That same evening the disheartened Williams left Butler's plantation, never to return. The crafty Florence convinced her husband that the love letter had been written by a famous New Orleans painter of miniatures called Besançon, who had recently attempted (unsuccessfully) to seduce her and was now trying to get revenge. The painter's social position did permit a duel, in which Butler lost an ear and Besançon a brand-new jacket from Paris, which the enraged plantation-owner slashed to ribbons with his sword. As for Uncle Habakuk, he went back to fiddling at the Saturday-night dances. He reopened his insect catering business, which he brought with him to Mr. de Ribordeaux's, to whom Butler sold him to cover the debts incurred by Miz Florence's passion for betting at horse races. Then Uncle Habakuk moved to Texas with his new owner.

"Let me touch you," said Cyril, "to make sure I'm not dreaming."

"Not here where everybody can see us," said his girl. They heard a clatter of hoofs, and a little gig appeared with a snooty-looking black footman in livery sitting beside the driver. A pretty young lady with a blue parasol sat in the gig.

"Miz Scarlett," whispered Dinah.
"Who's that?"
"You know, the girl Massa Étienne's engaged to marry."
"He's engaged to her?"
"He probably never told your Lida about that," said Dinah, "but he is."

★

General Carlin stood staring through his field-glasses at the meadows be-yond the palisade. The two men in the blood-soaked shirts were discussing something nervously. Groans came from the woods behind them, and the stretcher-bearers ran over from the palisade. The man they were carrying on the stretcher was holding onto his abdomen with both hands. Blood and a phlegmy substance oozed between his fingers. The grey line had stopped. The Rebels had taken cover behind the conquered palisades and the rem-nants of the wall, and in the underbrush. General Bate was nowhere to be seen. Several batteries of Rebel artillery were moving north, and there was a racket from that direction that sounded like a load of rocks rolling down a steep paved street. Sparse smoke from small-arms fire rose from a low, wooded knoll.

"Morgan," Carlin said to his aide. "They got around him and he at-tacked their flank. Now they're concentrating on him."

"Are we going to counter-attack, sir?" the aide asked.

Carlin looked around. Exhausted soldiers were resting among the trees. Nearby lay a caisson, one wheel ripped off; two men were lifting it, a third was removing the spare wheel. Several others were reloading their rifles. Carlin looked back at the hillside that lay before their palisade.

"You'll ride to General Slocum for orders. Attacking now wouldn't make sense. We have to regroup." He looked across the field. "Hardee's doing the same thing. And he outnumbers us. We have to hold him at this line, no matter what."

The two blood-soaked men came up to him again. Carlin shook his head. "No. We need every man we can drum up. Unfortunately, the wounded will have to stay where they are."

He stopped to think, looked over at Lieutenant Bellman. "Lieutenant!"

Bellman snapped to attention.

"Pick five men. If the Rebs break through this line, those men will stay with the wounded and be taken prisoner along with them. I doubt the Rebs have any medics to spare."

He brought the field-glasses back to his eyes. Grapeshot was still raining down over the groves on the hills to the north, and he could hear the constant clatter of rocks rolling on paving-stones. The sound of the cannonade was becoming a deep bass growl.

"Good God!" said General Carlin. "I haven't seen this kind of concentrated fire since Gettysburg."

The lieutenant hurried over to the men who were left of his platoon.

★

General Meade dismounted and walked up the steps to the main platform, where the unkempt beard of the sergeant's general was reflected in the new president's top hat. Abe Lincoln had been buried for twelve days now, and this morning they'd taken down the black banners from the buildings and raised the Stars and Stripes to the top of the flagpoles. The sun shone on the flags flying in the hot late May wind, while a steel river of bayonets—Grant's army—flowed past the platform where the sergeant stood with Cyril and Shake, a new medal glinting on a new uniform. Meade's corps filed past in ranks of twelve, marching in regulation twelve-inch paces to the tune of "Yankee Doodle" coming from the polished horns of Meade's big battalion band. There were wild cheers, fluttering handkerchiefs, glistening top hats, the rustle of bright ladies' dresses under beige and pale blue hats, and suddenly the sergeant caught a glimpse of her. She had the countenance of a young, suffering Madonna, but what gazed out from under the shadow of her broad hat was hard defiance. In the brilliance of gay ribbons—white, blue, yellow, pink, and other festive colours—her white hat bore a ribbon of black, a ribbon of mourning. The defiance was hardened by humiliation, by repeated misfortune.

Such as when they'd been harvesting the corn. She was working in the field shoulder to shoulder with her father, her mother, Josef, and the two servants, Washington and Jefferson. Little Deborah was sitting on the edge of the field, throwing a stick for their dog, Spot. Lida was dressed in a coarse linen blouse and skirt, her hair stuck to her forehead. She was shiny with sweat, and she poked out her tongue to catch the salty drops of sweat running down her nose.

Whatever was going through her head?

She saw a gig moving lightly and noiselessly along the road, almost floating, as if made of nothing—shiny gloss on fine wood. It was driven by a black coachman who had a liveried black footman beside him with a supercilious manner, his arms folded and concealing his white-gloved hands. Unexpectedly, the gig stopped and the footman leapt down in his glittering uniform of red and gold, braid and buttons and buckles. He put a tiny stool on the ground, then reached out a strong gloved hand to help a young lady in a pale green dress with a pretty—no, a lovely—face, powdered in the noonday heat. Green eyes, green parasol. She stood at the edge of the road, surveying the cornfield, until her haughty gaze fell on Lida. Lida straightened up and brushed her hair out of her face. Their glances met. The green eyes looked Lida over thoroughly and mockingly, then looked at her father, who was already standing on the path asking, "Can I help you, ma'm?"

She examined him, her eyes contemptuous, even hostile, and she replied, "Perhaps."

Then she turned, placed a hand on the Negro's muscular arm, and gracefully got back into the delicate gig. Like a black and gold bird, the Negro flew back to his seat beside the coachman. The gig floated away with a clatter of hoofs.

Who was she?

Lida felt a suspicion, but the heat and the toil drove it out of her mind.

Cyril saw her too, that unfeeling, suffering face beneath the hat with the mourning ribbon. Whatever was going through her head anyway? Her husband, Baxter Warren II, wore the brand-new uniform of a colonel in the volunteers; his face was unclouded by any knowledge of complex realities, and radiant with the bliss of victory. He had passed through the war unscathed, just as he had passed through his entire life with only minor scratches, and now he had his lovely reward at his side. When he had cast a questioning glance at the black ribbon, she had replied coldly, "I know they took them all down today. But I'm not going to forget."

He squeezed her hand, and he felt ready to burst with joy. His wife was not only beautiful and exotic, she was also a real American, a patriot who, amidst the excitement and cheering, couldn't forget that tall, thin, homely man who had made this victory parade possible. Without Lincoln the Union would have split and the war would have been put off for twenty or thirty more years. But it would have happened in the end, because the country could not exist half slave and half free. And that war would have affected his sons, the sons his beautiful, exotic American wife would bear him.

★

"I hoped I could take care of it so you would never find out—"

"So my father had to tell me. Did you know your father invited him to talk about it?"

"No, I didn't." Étienne was surprised.

"You probably weren't home," she said scowling. "You were either in bed with the perfume factory or off somewhere with your fancy fiancée."

"No, Linda, I swear—"

"And do you know what he wanted?"

"My father's a fool."

"No, I'm the fool," said Lida. "The way she looked me over."

Little clouds drifted over Bentonville, white and sad. Lida's hands were clenched in her lap and Cyril, his left arm bandaged to the shoulder, puffed on a corncob pipe, letting the hatred inside him cool. All that was left was fear for his tea-rose.

Old Toupelik couldn't imagine why Mr. de Ribordeaux had summoned him, or why he had sent a carriage to pick him up—not the light gig, but a formal black box of a coach with a liveried coachman. Half an hour later, he was sitting in the big parlour again, with the naked woman rising from the seashell over the mantelpiece and the fleshy faces of people in lace collars peering down at them. This time they were not served by the yellow girl; Mr. de Ribordeaux himself poured him a cognac in a brandy snifter. Toupelik took a sip right away. Clearly this summons did not augur well, but it took him a while to realize that this had happened to him once before, in the old country, and then there had not been a child. And this was America.

"Oh no, Mr. Ribordeaux." He shook his leathery head—and what was going through it? "I can't tell Lida what to do. One time I—" He wanted to explain how he had once helped kill his daughter's fortune—or was it her misfortune? If it was, he hadn't been responsible. "And then I—she—" He wanted to say that he had bartered the bride and brought her all the way to Texas, not for the slaves Mr. de Ribordeaux was offering him now, because farmer Mika had had none, but for the fare to America and Cyril's freedom. In short, it had been a good deal. What was going through his head? It had been good for him, good for his family, and he thought it had also been good for Lida, for there was a procession of suitors, not just from Cat Spring but all the way from Dubina, Hostyn, and the nearby German villages. To these men the illegitimate child didn't matter. They were in America now. But she had turned them all down, and now, over a glass of cognac, he finally knew why. History was repeating itself. "Oh no, Mr. Ribordeaux! And you let them be too!"

"Étienne," said Mr. de Ribordeaux from under the canopy of smoke rising from the big cigar, "is engaged to be married. Scarlett is the daughter of my good friend Delatour. They've known each other since they were children. They grew up"—Mr. de Ribordeaux hesitated—"if not together, then at least both on plantations."

History was repeating itself. With one difference that old Toupelik was not aware of. "Well," he said, "until the priest has bound them together, such engagements can always be—"

De Ribordeaux rose, thought for a moment, and refilled the other man's glass to the brim. He took a fresh cigar out of the humidor, sliced off the tip, and lit it with the waxed end of a wood splinter that he ignited from the candle.

"Think about it," he said. "There's a war on. The Confederacy needs soldiers."

So history was indeed repeating itself. In the old country he had been prepared to use subterfuge, connections, bribes. Here he found these measures repugnant. "You mean Cyril?" And he also felt fear for his son. "He's a young man, not twenty-six yet," he said. "We came here to the American republic, not the Confederacy." His defiance was rising like bread dough. "We have no slaves—just the two Mr. Carson lent us."

"The South acted on its constitutional right to secede," declared old de Ribordeaux. "You are now citizens of the Confederacy. As for slaves"—he corrected himself—"I mean servants, most citizens of the Confederacy don't own any. They just know that this conflict is about our inalienable rights. The right to own servants is simply one of those many rights. If that were the only thing we were after—"

Toupelik knew he was lying. What else could they be after? Was anything else being taken away from them? He too stood up. "Leave them alone. If they love each other—" He looked up to see a distinct sneer on de Ribordeaux's face. He suddenly understood more than he wanted to. He understood that his daughter, being who she was, could hardly be in love. He looked around the parlour. It reeked of gold and the smoke of fine cigars. And they were in America now. "—then leave them alone!"

"If they love each other," said de Ribordeaux sarcastically, as if to confirm Toupelik's realization. "Are you so sure that both of them—that they truly love each other?"

Defiance crumpled his brain like a ball of paper.

"Leave them alone, Mr. Ribordeaux!" he shouted. "I—" He looked around at the dull lustre of the walls of the parlour impregnated with the smell of money, at the unattractive faces in the pretty lace collars, and his eyes came to rest on the shameless girl on the seashell. "I have nothing to talk about with you."

He ran out of the parlour, out of the hall, out of the big house. He waved off the Negro in livery and walked, almost ran, towards the north-west, where his still poor but now beautiful farm was located.

As he went, de Ribordeaux's words kept running through his head: "The Confederacy needs soldiers."

★

"When I think back on it, I finally understand. It was awful! Awful! Awful!"
Only afterwards did she see herself as she thought Scarlett in the shiny gig would
have seen her, a drudge in a coarse skirt and a sweat-stained blouse, obviously
stinking of labour and probably—or so the young lady whose own odours were
masked by perfume would have thought—of other, worse things. "Awful!" she
yelled. "How could you do this to me?"

"I intended to tell you about it after I'd taken care of everything, Linda
darling—"

"Awful!" She was weeping convulsively. He had never seen her this way be-
fore. He thought he knew why she was weeping, but he didn't.

The previous evening, she had walked into the sitting room at home and
found her father at the table over a glass of last year's home-made slivovitz. "Sit
down," he said.

"What is it?" Her spine was tingling.

"Sit down." Then he told her everything. He saw her turn pale. "Have a
drink," he said.

She hadn't expected this. That bastard Étienne. She had known it wouldn't be
smooth sailing, but she hadn't counted on this. But she would settle it right away.
And she'd settle Dinah right away, too. Cyril would find his happiness, or what-
ever. And so will I. That is, I'll get what's coming to me. He'll crawl like a worm.
Like a worm.

Suddenly, like a red-hot dagger in her heart, came the memory of the sweaty
afternoon on the field, and the gig—

Étienne. The bastard.

She was being perfectly honest. There was nothing to pretend any
more—not now that Vitek was dead. Nothing at all. So Cyril knew everything. He sat resting his wounded arm in its white bandage, and sad little
clouds drifted over Bentonville.

She took a drink and poured herself another. Her father didn't stop her.

"Do you really love him?" he asked.

Whatever was going through her head?

"He loves me," she said.

"Then why didn't he tell you about the other one?"

She laughed. He had, in fact, told her about the other one. It was the third
one he hadn't told her about, the third person in their tangled pentangle.

"He was probably too afraid to," she giggled.

Her father hesitated. Then he took a sip.

"And do you think—"

"What?"

"That he won't jilt you?"

"Him?" She laughed again. "Don't worry, Father. I've got him tied to my apron-strings!"

She was an American now.

Cyril didn't know that for a time she thought he had lost his fragrant beauty. That night they were awakened by horses' hoofs, then a banging on the door, then the shouting of wild interlopers.

Father burst into the room. "Cyril!"

Cyril sat up in bed.

"It's the Rangers!" Father exclaimed hoarsely. "Out the window, quick! Head for the woods! I'll bring you some clothes tomorrow."

By then Cyril was halfway out the window, in his drawers and undershirt. The door was broken open and their mother started screaming.

★

The girl was reading faster than before. She was getting interested in the story now. The author had shifted from describing tactics—which he had studied after the war as a colonel—to an account of the battle he had witnessed first-hand, as a lieutenant. She was no longer stumbling over words, and the pleasant cadence of her voice spoke to the sergeant of his old comrades.

"The carnage that erupted in Hardee's rear lines forced him temporarily to set aside the order to storm Carlin's division. Morgan's units, which had circled around Hardee's corps, now attacked him from the flank. The battle-scarred Rebel veterans fought hand to hand and forced us back to our hastily constructed defences. We advanced again, and the enemy, gaining his second wind, once again quelled our attack. General Hardee, intent on improving the even odds, ordered cannon moved from the forward line, whereupon the men, fighting for their lives, experienced a hail of shrapnel, which mowed them down and ripped the needles off the evergreens like a merciless tempest. During a lull in the fighting brought on by the exhaustion of the men on both sides, our company could look up and see nothing but bare pine trees, trunks and branches stripped even of their bark. During that lull, I looked out at the field of battle, covered with dead and wounded, rifles dropped by men as they fell, knapsacks and caps riddled with bullet-holes, but also many other less predictable objects. For example, I spied a leather-bound book, although I am not certain it was a Bible. Nearby I saw a jar of preserves undisturbed by the rain of shrapnel and shining in the sunbeams like a warning light; a wooden flute; a pipe with smoke still rising from it; a lady's pink garter. . . ."

The girl stopped reading. "Garter?" She turned her eyes, a forget-me-not blue, to the sergeant.

"Mmm, that," said the sergeant, quickly trying to think of a way to explain such a human object in such inhuman surroundings, "that must be a mistake of Colonel Bellman's."

"It's not a mistake," said the girl. "It says right here: 'a lady's pink garter'."

"No, it must be a mistake," said the sergeant. "In a battle like that, you can think you see things you don't," he said. "A battle is like a bad dream, and memory mixes things up too. After years go by, you don't know what really happened to you and what you just imagined. Soldiers have bad dreams too, you know, Terezka? Once I dreamed—" he said, and he became so caught up in the memory that he almost forgot he wasn't telling stories to a bunch of his buddies around a campfire but to a child, though she was a farm child and accustomed to seeing a hog killed with a blow to its head or her mother slitting the throat of a terrified chicken, and one morning she had even seen their tomcat crawling home from the woods on its two front legs, having lost its hind legs in some nocturnal forest tragedy, and he had had to shoot the cat with his old army pistol and she had been inconsolable. "It was before Atlanta—I cut the heads off three Rebel officers with a single stroke of my sword, and during the entire assault those three heads rolled along behind me, yelling the Rebel yell and snapping at my heels." The girl was staring at him, horrified, and he realized that he shouldn't be telling her a story like this, even if it was God's truth. "You see, Terezka, it was just something I imagined. It was a bad dream. And yet now, years later, I sometimes get the feeling that it actually happened. Sometimes, before I fall asleep, I even believe it."

"But what if it really did happen, Daddy?" asked the girl, fearfully.

He smiled. "It didn't," he said.

"How do you know, if you're not sure yourself?"

"Because I was only a sergeant in the war, child," he said. "I didn't carry a sword. Only in my dreams."

The little girl looked up at him doubtfully.

"Don't worry, Terezka," he said. "Your daddy never cut anybody's head off. I just shot a rifle, and the last time I did that was at Collierville in '62. After that, I was with General Sherman's staff, and from then on I never fired a shot."

Reassured, the child turned back to the book, but she didn't resume reading right away. She looked at her father, obviously thinking things over.

"Well, but that's different," she said, "bad dreams. But why has—" But thinking and expressing complex ideas in Czech was too hard, so she switched to English. "Why did Colonel Bellman dream about a lady's garter?"

"It—" he began in Czech, but, unable to come up with something sensible to tell the child, he finally said, "I really don't know. Stop asking questions and keep on reading!"

"Well," she said, "what if all the rest of it was just a dream too?"

"Just read, please!"

"All right," said the child compliantly, and she began reading military jargon and style in a halting voice. "At four-thirty in the afternoon, General Braxton Bragg's battalion joined the fray on the battlefield and the battle resumed with renewed fury."

But the sergeant wasn't listening any more. The memories drifting through his mind were of things and events he could never tell his daughter about. Memories of the books in Corporal Gambetta's private lending library, with pictures handled so often that the ladies on them were actually clothed again, in grubby fingerprints. And reminders of women, both remote and agonizing. His mind wandered all the way to the little house on Gottestischlein—and he felt a wave of shame. He felt even guiltier than Zinkule had when the sergeant once caught him staring at a piece of lace torn from a petticoat. Zinkule had blushed and stuck the lace in his pocket. "Okay, Franta, just wait, you'll get your chance," he had said.

He didn't know if Zinkule had finally got his chance, or what it would have been if he had.

★

"Father did bring me clothes," said Cyril. "But he had to bring them to the Fayetteville jail. They caught me right after I jumped out the window. It was all Ribordeaux's doing, of course. He and Colonel Fenton were hand in glove, and Fenton was commander of the band of Rangers in charge of conscripting soldiers around Austin. Father tried arguing with them—said we were aliens in Texas and didn't intend to settle there, so that, according to the law on transient aliens, the most I had to do was serve in the state militia, not the regular army. They just laughed at him. 'So why did you buy a farm here, and twenty acres of woods this year, so that you have a hundred acres all told?' He told them he was going to sell it all after the war and move to Iowa. He shouldn't have said that. The Ranger lieutenant jumped right on it. 'Oh, to the Yankees, is that it? You, sir, are not a transient alien; you, sir, are a hostile alien!' Father saw he'd made a mistake, so he quickly invented a brother in Iowa and, to make things more convincing, a sweetheart for me. Naturally it was no use. They took my shirt and trousers from him and booted him out. Literally. And they left me sitting there for three weeks with nothing but bread and water while they were out trolling for others.

When they had collected enough of us, they escorted us to the Galveston training camp. I finally gave them the slip and travelled by night north to Austin. It took me two weeks to get there, almost two months after they picked me up."

It had been a foolish plan, though he'd almost pulled it off. It was autumn, and the Germans in the counties around Austin were on the verge of revolt. Central Texas was full of German villages, and because they were interspersed with Czech villages the revolt spilled over to the Czechs, although they were inclined neither to rebellion nor to war. Pro-Union petitions were circulated, some brave souls convened public meetings, and at one meeting in Austin there was talk of organizing armed units, even a cavalry, to stand up to the conscription units. A.J. Bell, commander of the crimps, had already asked General Magruder for reinforcements, and rumour had it that a regiment of the regular Army of the Confederacy was on its way to Austin, Lafayette, Washington, and Lavaca counties. Getting through hornets' nests like those with a light brown girl in tow was a fantasy he could support only by day, in brief, wild, runaway dreams when he lay sleeping in the forest undergrowth, waking up every few minutes. By night, moving northward, he thought it might be nothing but a pipe-dream. All the same, he kept going. Perhaps he just wanted to see his tea-rose. He kept on moving.

There was no light in the little house on Baywater Street. He knocked, but no one answered. He walked round to the back, broke a thin pane of glass, and climbed inside. The house had only one room. He opened the shutters and the darkness gave way to moonlight and he could see that the room was empty. A bare mattress on the bed. Nothing in the chest in the corner, not a trace of any of the clothes that belonged to the girl who had lived there two months before.

It was almost morning. He lay down on the bed and, in brief snatches of sleep, he went on in his fancy to the de Ribordeaux plantation. Daylight dawned, and he knew it was only a pipe-dream. But when darkness fell again, instead of heading north to the Oklahoma Territory and on to Kansas and the Union Army, he set out for the de Ribordeaux place.

He strode carefully through streets lit only by the lights from house windows, and when he got to the Davidson Hotel he saw, in a circle of brighter light, the familiar black carriage—a cage on wheels. A Negro in livery was dozing in the driver's seat.

He looked around, walked across the street, and gave the Negro's foot a pull. The coachman opened his eyes and stared at Cyril as though he'd never seen him before. Of course, in the two weeks on the road from Galveston his beard had grown, and in wrinkled trousers and a dirty shirt he must have looked like a beggar.

"It's Cyril," he whispered. "Towpelick."

"Oh, Massa Cyril!" the Negro said out loud. "I couldn't hardly recog—"

"Shhh! Where's Dinah? What happened to her?"

"Dinah got sold, massa," he whispered.

"Sold? Who bought her?"

"Nobody knows. They said she gone all the way to Columbia."

The fantasy collapsed, and hope along with it. It wasn't strong enough to support a journey to Columbia. And the coachman was still whispering. "Massa Étienne gone too."

"Where? Why?"

The Negro told him. Quarrelsome voices came from inside the hotel, above the sound of clinking glasses.

So he set off northward and, as the miles passed, his sorrow, deep as a well, filled with growing hatred.

In the spring of '63, he arrived.

★

When the gunfire from Morgan's division reached another fortissimo, Carlin decided to counter-attack. The whistle of bullets filled the air around them like a swarm of wasps. The first line fell like dominoes, and Lieutenant Bellman was relieved when he heard the signal to retreat. They leapt back over the palisades and lay down behind them. Before the counter-attack, they had sent Bellman's squad farther north, to a hilltop position that overlooked a group of hills in the distance, where Morgan's defence was. It was five in the afternoon. Metal flowers kept blossoming over the hilltops, and scattering fragments into the woods.

"Hardee's got reinforcements from Bragg or Taliaferro, so he didn't have to weaken the line against us," said one of the staff officers.

General Davis nodded.

"How long can their ammunition last?" the general asked. "They're firing those cannonades as if the war were just beginning, and not—"

"They're on their last legs," ventured one staff captain.

"Who knows?" Davis and Carlin again turned their field-glasses to the hills, where the metal flowers were blooming and fading in the growing dusk. Under the gathering clouds, Morgan's savage shooting machine rattled away.

General Davis listened to the noise of the machine. "They have two firing lines," he said. Four years of war had taught him to see with his ears. "If Morgan can hold out, all will be well." The machine was going at full blast. "If not, they're whipped. We have no reserves to send in, not so much as a single regiment. They'll have to help themselves."

The machine ground on and on.

"Who knows how long Morgan's ammunition will hold out."

★

"—your father!"

Whatever had been going through her head? A Negro regiment marched by in perfect ranks of twelve, with white officers on horseback, and the joyful breeze of victory blew the black mourning ribbon into her face. She pushed it back.

He tried to kneel before her, but his wooden leg made it awkward. So he reached out to take her hand, but instead she took his hand in both of hers, and squeezed it so hard he grimaced in pain. "And your father sent Rangers after my brother Cyril and now he's locked in Fayetteville jail!"

"I'll get him out, Linda!"

"Don't you be a fool too," she said. Cyril's tea-rose, her benign rival. But Dinah belonged to Cyril. Pegleg's traditional Southern sexual morality was an affront to both her and her brother. And now Cyril was doomed. They'd kill him in the war, and if not, if he came home—because some of them would come home—Pegleg's Southern mores were an affront. Then she thought of a solution.

"Linda! Darling!"

"Cyril is gone," she said. "You have other things to worry about, don't you?" She squeezed his hand again, then let go. He caught her hand and began kissing it.

"What are you going to do?" she asked frostily.

He glanced into her eyes, then looked away. He mumbled something.

"Say it out loud."

"I'll give her back the ring."

She took his hands again. There was nothing on his right hand, and only the large, angular signet ring he used to seal his correspondence was on his left.

She dropped his hands. He reached guiltily into his pocket and took out a gold band set with an impressive diamond.

She grinned to herself. She had never thought people like Étienne and Scarlett exchanged engagement rings. It was beyond her world, beyond her experience. It suddenly made her angry. "You're a coward, Étienne!"

"Forgive me, Linda! Darling! I swear to you, first thing tomorrow—"

"Today," she said. "Not tomorrow. It's not late yet. Only seven. You eat dinner at nine, no?"

His fear was obvious. He was foolish, spineless, crippled. But he would be her husband.

"And by the way—" she said.

★

The girl read on, but the sergeant wasn't listening—he was seeing. The Thirteenth Ohio was indeed firing in two ranks. Sergeant McAdams, whose reminiscences Colonel Bellman had translated into his officer's diction, was kneeling in the front rank. He kept shooting till the magazine of his repeater was empty, then passed it back behind him without looking, felt Mike Huddleston take it and place a loaded one in his open hand. It was still hot. He started firing again. The ragged line of Bragg's veterans advanced towards them, running across the meadow at a slow trot, past the shadows of shorn pine trees that formed dark stripes on the sunny grass. As they ran forward the shooting machine mowed them down, but more kept advancing. The sun was dropping low in the west. The big standard-bearer coming towards McAdams flew into the air, a tangle of intestines unravelling from a gaping wound in his belly. Before the banner hit the ground it was caught by another ragtag soldier, who had a bandage around his forehead displaying a darkened badge of honour. Sergeant McAdams passed the empty rifle behind him, someone grabbed it, his hand closed again on the butt of a loaded one. Mike's hot breath in his ear said, "For God's sake, Mac, the rifles are too hot!"

"So spit on your hands," hollered McAdams, and shot down the new standard-bearer.

In the end, the Rebels withdrew. Piles of corpses lay not twenty yards from the palisades, among them painfully wounded men writhing and thrashing or lying still and moaning.

They were ordered to collect ammunition from the casualties. Sergeant McAdams went from corpse to corpse, rolling some of them over to get the bullets out of their cartridge boxes and stuffing them inside the knapsack he had brought along, or, when it was full, into his pockets. A wounded man tried to sit up, but fell back into the blood-soaked grass. He was screaming, "Oh, my God, won't anybody help a poor widow's son? God! God!" Sergeant McAdams crawled over to him. The man opened his eyes wide and stared at him. "No help, God?" he whispered. "For the son of a poor widow!" McAdams saw that the man's side was torn open and blood was streaming from a wound in his abdomen. "None," he said to the wounded man. "And even if there was, I'd have no time." The wounded man's eyes stared at him in horror, but if they saw anything it was more likely some merciless, unchristian God. "You aren't going to need your bullets any more, friend. So let's have them!" said McAdams, reaching for the Rebel's cartridge box and stuffing the bullets into his pockets. Then he noticed that the wounded man had a knapsack on his back. Dozens of dead men and a vast supply of ammunition lay all around, but McAdams's pockets were full already. "You aren't going to need that knapsack either." He tried to roll the wounded man over onto his belly and pull it off his shoulders. The man screamed in pain, until his words were literally drowned by the blood spurting from his mouth.

The cannon in the groves and behind the stone walls down in the valley opened fire, and the Rebel yell echoed against the hillsides. The ranks rose again.

Sergeant McAdams jumped up and, bending low, dashed towards the barricade. Metal insects whirred past him. One bit him in the leg and he keeled over. Mike Huddleston dragged him to safety over the palisade.

"I don't want to read any more," said the girl. "It's too scary!"

The sergeant returned to the present. The clock was striking nine. I'm an old fool, he told himself. I have no business asking her to read that. He had thought that, like most such books of memoirs, this one too would resemble the coloured prints he had framed and hung on the walls of the room.

"Couldn't he have helped him?" asked the child. "What would happen to his poor widowed mother? She was left alone with the farm."

"Well, maybe they didn't have a farm," said the sergeant. "And it wasn't always possible to help, child. Back then there wasn't anything they could do for that kind of wound. And it was in the middle of a battle—"

"Then why didn't he at least give him a drink of water?" asked the girl indignantly. "That's what you do for wounded soldiers, you give them water."

The picture on the wall over the little girl's head depicted a soldier in a colourful, clean zouave uniform offering a drink from a canteen to a prone Confederate soldier wearing an equally clean uniform. Neither man bore a badge of honour or courage on his forehead. In the air above them, right next to the sun, a canister was picturesquely displayed in mid-explosion.

★

"—you'll sell that black concubine of yours!"

He blushed like a little boy.

"Southern ladies can maybe accept such customs," she said, "but I am not a Southern lady."

But I will be someday.

He began assuring her that he'd sell Dinah to a slave-dealer the very next day,

*just as he'd said he would when he'd lied about it, but this time he would really
do it, and he wouldn't even know where she ended up.*

Lida interrupted him. "You won't sell her to a dealer!"

He was taken aback. "Why not? It would—"

"Because I say!"

*"Well then," he said uncertainly, and then he remembered. "But before, you
said you had a buyer."*

"Now I have no buyer. You must find one."

"That won't be hard."

*"But don't sell her to some young rooster," Lida said with sudden intensity.
"Or to an old one either. Sell her to a widow who will be kind to her. And who
has enough money so she won't hire her out to some rooster."*

"And did you believe her?" asked the sergeant. Kakuska dropped a cog-
wheel and it fell with a tinkle on the pile of other clock parts on the floor.

"No," said Cyril. "But what if she was telling the truth?" He was babbling already. The gift of whisky was keeping its promise. "What if my tea-
rose"—his eyes filled with tears—"what if she—" There was yearning in the
groggy voice, or was it anger? Probably a little of both. Cyril fell asleep. The
sergeant glanced out the window. A fire was blazing somewhere off in the
distance, and the Negro voices were singing:

*Oh Freedom, oh freedom, oh freedom over me,
And before I'd be a slave—*

Columbia, thought the sergeant. So far away.

Pegleg's face was still red.

*"I have a spinster aunt. But she has more than enough servants. I don't know
if she'll want to buy her."*

"Then give her away as a Christmas gift."

*The aunt's address was simple—the de Ribordeaux residence on Main Av-
enue—that was how she memorized it. But Cyril didn't believe her. Not till
Columbia—and then he never set eyes on his sister again until near Bentonville.*

*A few days afterwards, Dinah set out on the long journey to the home of
wealthy old Mademoiselle de Ribordeaux, who lived on the backside of hell.*

★

Beyond the peaks and the rolling hills that stretched like a stage set all the
way to Bentonville, two kinds of smoke drifted skywards: the thinner smoke
from rifle-fire, its constant clatter drowned out by the thunder of the can-

non, and clouds of darker smoke rising from artillery batteries. The two kinds of smoke met and mingled above a forest that was still beyond the range of vision. But because all of them were old hands at war, they didn't need sight to see. When the courier had galloped up to the Twenty-sixth Wisconsin with Slocum's order to drop what they were doing and march to the aid of the beleaguered division, anxiety had spread through the ranks, because every soldier had secretly hoped to spend what was left of the war in the rear, where, at worst, they might work themselves to death laying new corduroy roads. Because they were old hands at war, the dance of smoke over the distant hilltops and the din of battle, which hadn't been that loud for a long time, spoke to them with perfect clarity. Shake put into words what nobody needed to explain: "Davis is in a fix."

A problem arose. When they had formed roughly into ranks, the naked Zinkule jumped off the ambulance cart with a rifle in hand and insisted on going with them.

"Are you crazy, Franta?" Shake held his nose. "A forced march? In your condition?"

"I'm not wounded," insisted Zinkule mulishly, trying to hide his genitals with his musket.

"In a certain sense you are," said Shake.

"It's just that I smell bad, that's all."

"But you make it harder for others to fight," said Shake. "It's as if you had your leg shot off and we had to carry you."

"I don't have anything shot off!"

"But you're buff-naked, Franta," said Houska.

Zinkule's clothes had been burned in the campfire, and everyone else was in rags. Sherman's great army had run out of uniforms. The new ones weren't due to arrive until General Schofield brought them to Goldsboro.

"It wasn't that long ago we were all fighting buff-naked," said Zinkule, and he was right. They had been bathing in a creek when they were attacked by Wheeler's cavalry. There was barely time to grab their rifles and shoot back. The skirmish lasted about a minute. The cavalry rode past, shooting as they rode, hitting nothing at all, and then galloping away out of range.

"We were all naked, though," said Stejskal. "Now you'd stand out like a sore thumb with all of us dressed. Everybody would be aiming at you."

A group of officers walked over and stopped while a black-bearded colonel glanced at the platoon with the naked man in its midst and snapped, "What's this?"

Then a breeze carried the smell to the officers. The colonel swallowed whatever it was he wanted to say, waved his hand dismissively, and spurred his horse. The rest of the staff followed him. They saw a long-haired captain pull out a handkerchief and press it to his nose.

When the sound of hoof-beats faded, Stejskal said, "No, it won't work. You know why, Franta? Everybody will think we all shit our pants in advance."

"On the other hand, we could blame it on Franta," said Shake.

"Blame what?" asked Houska.

The Third Company marched up behind them and its captain was annoyed at them for just standing around and getting in the way. Then he got a whiff of the breeze himself and yelled a hasty order, and they set out. Zinkule tried to line up behind the last trio, but the captain of the Third Company yelled at him so loudly that he crept back into the ambulance cart. The card-players pulled up their handkerchief masks again and went on playing.

★

"Is it a big city?" asked Lida.

"It's a port city. Very impressive. The house is on Bay Street."

"Does it belong to you?"

"Yes. Uncle Jean-Paul left it to me." He paused. "But Linda—"

"Is it ready to move into?"

"The caretaker used to be overseer in our plantation in Louisiana. He and his wife are living there, in retirement."

"Fine," she said.

He looked unhappy. "Linda, darling, I'm really not certain—"

"You want to or not?" she interrupted him pointedly. He had returned the ring to his fiancée. The lady and her father had left the very next morning. The arrogant footman had ridden in front, looking offended.

"I want to," he said. "My mother's jewels are yours."

She had seen them gleaming in their cases—necklaces, a diamond tiara, jewellery carried across the Atlantic many years earlier from a land that did not tolerate the faith of the women, now long dead, who had owned it. Rings, bracelets, some of them purchased later in the jewellery stores of New Orleans, a few of them for the more recent owner, now also deceased. "For your bride," said Lida.

"Linda—"

She broke in: "How much are they worth?"

"I don't know. A lot."

"Good," she said. "We won't sell them. Pawn money will support us until your papa changes his mind."

She was gambling everything on that. Despite the distance across the At-

*lantic, she saw that it was the same the world over. If the old veteran Vitek's fa-
ther had hired hadn't come hobbling up when he did, she might not even have
had to go to America. Vitek was Mika's only son. There were no other heirs.*

*Pegleg's sister, Hortense, was married and apparently expecting already. But
Pegleg too was an only son. The old world and the new, as Papa de Ribordeaux
had proved when he summoned her father and gave him his ultimatum, were
the same, though separated by oceans and continents. She was going for broke because she had nothing to lose.*

Nothing to lose and everything to gain.

Fortune favours the fearless, as the Czech saying goes.

*She had been Mrs. de Ribordeaux for several months, bound in wedlock in a Sa-
vannah church—although in her mind only one thing in the world had bound
her inseparably, and she had already been separated from that—when the letter
arrived. She grinned; Papa must be changing his mind. But it was still too soon.
The letter was just a first step towards getting back his inheritance.*

"Hortense," her husband sobbed, "Hortense is dead."

"How did it happen?" She could hardly conceal her pleasure.

"In childbirth," said Étienne. "The baby died too."

*Perhaps there is a God after all, thought Lida. The lovesick Father Bunata's
good and kind Lord God.*

*Étienne was no longer just the only son. He was now the only living heir.
Now it was a matter of time.*

Then the Lord God played another cruel trick on her.

★

It was twilight. The eastern sky was turning dark and the stars were coming
out. The smoke dissipated as night fell, but there were still flashes coming
out of the woods and from positions near the ground. They were close to
the battle now. Whenever there was a lull in the noise they could hear a tired
echo of the Rebel yell, but it was soon drowned out again by the crack of
muskets and the thunder of cannon. On they marched, at a half-trot, while
Shake cursed. He was cursing because K Company of the Twenty-sixth
Wisconsin had slogged through North Carolina like a pack of mules, and
now they had to step in and bail out a fop like General Carlin, doing the
dirty work for his men so they'd be fresh and rested for the march into
Washington and would look the way the ladies of Washington imagined
Sherman's great army to be. "And not like the pack of exhausted mules they
actually are," Shake complained.

"Calm down," said Stejskal. "We're worn down and worn out, but we'll still look better in Washington than Carlin and his dandies."

"If we look like anything at all," stated Fisher.

For a while no one said anything, and they could only hear the occasional clink of a rifle against a canteen, and the breathing of men who were exhausted but sustained by a second wind.

The order to halt came down and the lieutenant trotted off to the head of the column. By now they were very close. They could hear officers' voices nearby; units were beginning to spread out in the dusk, the first of them already disappearing among the trees. A shrapnel shell exploded, but it was still pretty far away.

"Neighbours, I got a premonition," Houska ventured.

"You know where you can stick it," growled Paidr.

Shake sniffed the air loudly. "We should have brought Zinkule along. We could have undressed some poor corpse along the road and made him decent. He'd come in handy now."

"Is it a punch in the face you want?" said Houska angrily. "If anybody's scared shitless here, it's you!"

"Figuratively, you're right," replied Shake. "Neighbours, I often thought about it whenever I saw the rockets' red glare and bombs bursting in the air. If I'd a brave bone in my body, I'd have deserted long ago."

Somewhere in the distance, not far away, several projectiles exploded one after another like flashes of lightning in the sky, and a weak Rebel yell sounded. The lieutenant came running back and commanded, "Follow me!"

They plunged into the forest but they were moving more slowly now. It was hard to see the ground. Then a few kerosene lanterns appeared up ahead. They soon reached an area cut out of the darkness by a yellow glow. Several men—in shirts so bloody they looked as if someone had poured a bucket of gore over them—were working in such a frenzy that they seemed like madmen. Saws rasped on bone. Without a word they advanced more quickly, because some of the light from this place of weeping and gnashing of teeth illuminated the ground between the moss-covered trees. As the flashes of light came closer, they could see a palisade occupied by a handful of ragged soldiers.

"We're relieving the unit in this area," said the lieutenant.

They flopped down on their stomachs.

"High time!" snarled a bearded soldier wearing an illegible insignia, as he walked quickly away from the palisade.

They peered over the rough, ill-trimmed log fortifications. Half a mile or so ahead of them they could see the flickering lights of battle. Small black figures were running across a meadow to the woods on the hill. The Rebel yell now sounded like the plaintive cries of dying men.

Shake leaned against the palisade beside Houska and philosophized, "No offence, Vojta. Let's not leave this world in a state of disagreement. What do you say?"

"Who's arguing?" asked Houska.

"Me," said Shake. "The difference is that I'm shit-scared and pretty soon I'm going to need Zinkule here to cover up for me!"

"Just wait till after the battle," Houska snapped at him, "I'll bust your mouth like I've been promising since Savannah!"

"Tell the truth, Vojta," said Shake. The shooting machine on the hill across the meadow rattled into action again. "You said you had a premonition."

"That's right." Houska placed the musket on the palisade in front of him, pulled out a handkerchief, and blew his nose. "It's a strong one, Amos. I think Ruzena is going to leave him."

Shake was taken aback. "Leave who?"

"That Ferda fellow, the one she married," said Houska, putting his handkerchief away. "When I get home from the war, I'll be a hero. And what will he be? Nothing but a plain ordinary yellow-bellied war-dodger."

★

"But what does it mean?" Lida wanted to know.

"Lincoln's getting cold feet," said Captain Culloch. The empty sleeve of his threadbare uniform was tucked behind his faded gold belt, and he twirled a glass of bourbon on the smooth tabletop with his left hand, which had the three middle fingers missing.

They were sitting in the Grenier Hotel and Lida was frowning.

"It's supposed to win him the full support of the abolitionists," said the captain, "because discontent is spreading through his Yankee empire. Have you heard of the Copperheads?"

Lida shook her head.

"They're openly opposed to the Emancipation Proclamation," said Captain Culloch. "They say the question of the peculiar institution is up to the individual states, not the federal government. So Lincoln has no choice, that's why he's betting on the abolitionists. We, Madame de Ribordeaux, can only watch with pleasure. When our enemies fight among themselves, we—"

She had stopped listening. In her mind she could hear filly-face, the woman

Cyril had jilted for his yellow rose, saying, "Daddy says the South can't win. We live in an age of machines, and the North has machines and keeps inventing new ones. Have you heard about the one Mr. Gatling invented?" She had shaken her head. "It's a rifle with ten barrels," said filly-face. "It shoots more than two hundred rounds a minute, my daddy says—"

The Emancipation Proclamation did not bring Papa de Ribordeaux to his senses. They pawned the tiara. Months flew by. They argued more and more. Pegleg started drinking heavily. They stopped talking except to argue.

Finally, the letter came.

★

The clock struck again, eleven. The sergeant rose, walked over to the chest, took a bottle out from under the folded shirts and underwear, and poured himself a generous drink. The glass depicted President Lincoln collapsing to the ground, his white vest displaying a red badge of courage. Glass in hand, the sergeant gazed at another Lincoln. This one was leaning out of a tiny window on the clock face, waving the Stars and Stripes in time to the music as brightly painted hand-carved figurines in the uniform of the Twenty-sixth Wisconsin band played "The Stars and Stripes Forever". One little figure was pushing and pulling the slide on a wooden trombone, and beside him two other red-cheeked musicians were puffing away at a trumpet and a tuba. On the right, a figure with a fat wooden belly was pounding on a big drum. The bells of the trombone, the tuba, and the trumpet were turned so they pointed backwards, because the woodcarver had remembered marching behind bands like that on his way to battle. Now, on a farm a few miles from Manitowoc, Vojta Houska spent long winter evenings carving these cheerful clocks, which he sent as Christmas presents to his old buddies from the Twenty-sixth. "I got the idea from old Kakuska, may he rest in peace," Houska would say. "Remember how he made spurs out of clock gears in Savannah?"

The sergeant recalled the memorable day after Appomattox, when the band marched back and forth across the camp with a sauced-up General Mower leading them himself, a big drum on his belly. He remembered Cyril, who was God knew where on the other side of the world, and Dinah, who was simply God knew where, and how Cyril had told the story of showing her a classified ad in a section called Escaped Slaves that said "Gabriel escaped with a very good bassoon." He had laughed, and Dinah had retorted, "What are you laughing for, white boy? He wants to get to Canada, where they say our kind get to play in army bands!"

"On the bassoon? Hardly. In a castle orchestra, maybe."

"*Have they got castles in Canada?*"

"*I don't know. Maybe. They have a queen.*"

"*So Gabriel's going to play in the queen's band in Canada.*"

The little carved band finished playing, and Lincoln withdrew behind a shutter that had a picture of the American eagle on it. The sergeant settled back in his armchair, picked the book off the chair where the child had sat earlier, took a drink, and started reading:

"Dusk had fallen when the Rebel troops circled around our positions and unexpectedly struck from behind. All we did, however, was to jump over the palisades and fight from the other side. At that point, General Hardee committed an incomprehensible error. If he had divided his forces and used only half of the men under his command to hit us from behind, we could hardly have successfully defended ourselves, having to fight on-slaughts from both directions. As it was, however, standing and kneeling once again in a double rank, we laboured like the ideal diligent soldier boys, so that after the victorious battle, our commander Colonel McClurg was absolutely truthful when he declared, 'I have rarely been witness to gunfire so incessant, so merciless. It seemed to me beyond human endurance. The soldiers under my command, veterans of dozens and dozens of terrible battles, had never before experienced anything resembling the carnage at Bentonville.' It was only when night fell and Hardee learned that fresh units had arrived as reinforcements to Carlin's divisions that he ordered his troops to withdraw to their original positions. Hence Colonel O'Carleen of the Confederate Army was also correct when he wrote in his memoirs, 'We came, we attacked, we fought, we accomplished nothing.'"

"*Daddy!*"

His daughter stood in the doorway in her nightgown. He tried to hide his glass under his chair, and spilled whisky on the floor.

"*What's happening, Terezka?*"

"*I can't sleep,*" *announced the child.* "*Something keeps bothering me.*"

He was worried that his story about the three disembodied heads might have given the child nightmares, but she said, "*Is it true that you never fired a shot in the war?*"

★

The white bride rode off in the cabriolet, the radiantly innocent Baxter Warren II by her side, towards the bristled array of bayonets floating forward through the morning fog as Logan's division of Sherman's great army marched on.

"*I once knew a girl who lived on Goat Street—*" *Shake said.*

And Stejskal interrupted him: "It really is nice, though, a Moravian girl finding happiness in Savannah, Georgia!"

But Cyril knew there had only been one happiness, and she had been robbed of that. Whatever had become of Vitek? She had no idea, there in Savannah, and if she couldn't have Vitek then at least she would have a substitute happiness, the kind that would enable little Deborah to find a happiness of her own. And no Mika, no de Ribordeaux, could—

The letter had arrived too late.

"Go alone," she said. "I would be in the way."

"But he wants to reconcile with you."

"It's you he wants to reconcile with," she said. "You are his heir." Then she added, "If there's anything left to inherit."

That startled him. "You don't believe the war is—"

"Of course not," she stopped him. "Go and come back. . . . If you want to."

It was the worst time in her life. Except of course for that day in Amberice. Once again she was gambling everything. True, Papa de Ribordeaux had come to his senses, but Pegleg arrived at the plantation just in time to close his father's eyes. Cirrhosis of the liver caused by excesses of cognac, a heart steeped in the smoke of thousands of cigars, the spectre of emancipation, the death of Hortense and her baby, though it was just a girl. His world and all his erudite theories had collapsed, a world of murders and bloodhounds and people like wily old Uncle Habakuk, and underneath all the learned knowledge had been the awareness that it had to end, but if only the end could have come later. Later. Pegleg, evidently by the miracle of passion or love, managed to return to Savannah. The inheritance was worthless. Sherman fought for Kennesaw Mountain and Lida knew she was gambling on the wrong card.

But fortune favours the fearless.

Sherman's great army marched up to Savannah and in fifteen minutes took Fort McAllister by storm. By the grace of Tecumseh Sherman, General Hardee led most of his troops across a bridge that had been built by slaves. The next day, the same men who had built it were singing,

Massa Sherman come to Savannah
And he set us free. . . .

Étienne, steeped in bourbon, was babbling and stammering about evenings made hellish by quarrels, about Linda, who was cruelly withdrawing from him, about having lost everything in the world. Cyril kept topping up his glass, horrified, hardly recognizing him. What had become of Dinah? But the cripple was beyond reach. Cyril put off asking him any further questions till morning, and left the drunken wretch on the chaise-longue in the parlour of his mansion (all that was left of the inheritance), and went to drink himself into oblivion in the little house where Kakuska was manufacturing spurs out of clock gears for the battle of Columbia, for the final battle at Bentonville.

Captain Baxter Warren II was in command of one of the companies that stormed Fort McAllister, the last obstacle that stood between Sherman's great army and the saloons and whorehouses of Savannah. On the way to Madam Russell's Bakery, where he had every intention of losing his virginity, his eyes fell on Linda Toupelik, and he changed course. Instead, he lost his virginity in the Grenier Hotel.

She hadn't even had to concoct a story, as Shake assumed she had. Baxter was an innocent, a true son of the land where he was born. "Your mother couldn't read?" Lida was astounded.

"No, she was from Ireland and she never went to school," he said. "I taught her to read myself." He swallowed. "I wrote to her about you."

"Nice things, I hope," she said, "or else!"

"I told her they married you off against your will. That happened to her too. Ma was fifteen when it happened."

"But you were—"

"Her first husband died on the boat. She married my pa in America and went with him to California. Pa's a Forty-niner."

"You mean there was a rebellion here then too?" she asked.

"No. What was here was gold," said Baxter Warren II.

So she didn't have to concoct a story, she just mixed some realities and some silences about her life into a cocktail for innocents. Later, she realized she needn't have bothered. Even had she told him the pure, unvarnished, European truth— about Vitek, old man Mika, the veteran, and Deborah the illegitimate, instead of Deborah with Huguenot blood coursing through her veins (she explained it to him just as Pegleg had explained it to her), which appealed to him, for all he knew of history was the Pilgrim Fathers, and in his veins there was an American aversion to oppression—even had she told him the naked truth, she wouldn't have offended against any taboo. For despite his name, which to Lida's Central European ears sounded so aristocratic, Baxter Warren II was a young man at the very beginning of his line, in a land at the very beginning of its history. A robber baron, he respected only money, which he possessed, and had opinions only about freedom. Freedom was the Union, that was what he had gone to war for. But Lida's cocktail was better, after all, than the bare truth about her big brother and his Uncle Tom's Cabin *love story, better than silence around Vitek, Mika, and the causal chain of hatred that had led her to gamble on the wrong card. Instead of the truth and nothing but the truth, she offered a slight fabrication—an overbearing farmer father, a rich Southern bridegroom, a daughter Deborah with Huguenot blood, and a hatred of the peculiar institution that had frustrated her unfortunate brother's love, a hatred that focused on her unloved, imposed, wealthy (she failed to add that he was wealthy no longer) husband.*

"You'll get a divorce," said Baxter Warren II.

But fortune favours the fearless.

The maid banged on the white door of the white house. There was no response—nothing but silence.

"He's probably asleep," she said. "But it's after ten."

Across the street, Madam Russell's Bakery was just waking up. A sleepy houseboy was sweeping the sidewalk. A woman with a large bosom appeared in an open second-storey window.

"He's probably stinking drunk," said the soldier with the terrible accent. "If it was me, I'd be drunk. She's a real looker, too! What else can he do but get drunk?" He pushed the maid aside and pounded on the door with his fist. Nothing. "Wait here," he said to the girl, and stepped over the low white fence protecting a flowerbed that ran around the house.

"Captain!" squealed the whore in the second-storey window. "One of your soldiers is trying to break into Mr. de Ribordeaux's house!"

A fellow in shirt-sleeves appeared in the window. All he could see was the maid, who was sitting on the doorstep. The soldier had vanished around the corner of the house.

Two large shuttered windows faced out onto the garden. The soldier looked around. There was a love-seat in a bougainvillea-covered pavilion. He carried it to one of the windows, climbed up, opened the shutters, and peered in. It took a while for his eyes to adjust to the gloom. Something was lying on the carpet in front of the dining table. It looked like a club of some sort, but he soon realized what it was, for a year earlier he had spent a month in hospital with an infected thigh wound. Then he looked up at the ceiling. He jumped off the bench, ran around the front of the house, yelled at the maid to get out of the way, then threw himself against the front door.

The half-dressed captain in the second-storey window across the street yelled, "Private! What's the meaning of this?"

The soldier looked around and saluted, more in mockery than in respect. The officer wasn't in uniform, but it could only have been an officer; the civilians of Savannah hardly had time for tarts.

"He could still be alive!" he yelled back with his heavy accent. The soldier,

whose name was Frank Vorastek, was a solid blacksmith's apprentice from Man-itowoc, Wisconsin. With good food and plentiful exercise during the march through Georgia, he had regained the strength he had lost in hospital. The door gave and he stumbled inside.

On the floor lay a wooden leg and overhead, suspended by a rope like a strange butterfly's cocoon, hung a man with one leg, his swollen purple tongue protruding from his mouth. Two days before, he had learned of the existence of Captain Baxter Warren II, having observed him and Lida, as the sergeant had, through a window of the Grenier Hotel. He had confronted her, she had denied nothing, a final quarrel had erupted, and he had attached himself to her like a Pinkerton agent; then Cyril had intervened on the main street of Savannah and saved her future husband's life. Later, up to his gills in bourbon, the cripple had wept on Cyril's shoulder, babbling about the hellion named Linda and how he had lost everything he loved in the world. Cyril kept topping up his glass, horrified, hardly recognizing the man. He left the poor drunken wretch on the chaise-longue in the parlour of the big house—where next morning Lida would send Private Vorastek and the maid from the Grenier Hotel to get her things—and went to drink himself into oblivion as well, in the little house where Kakuska was making spurs out of clock gears.

And so there was no need for a divorce. And because it was wartime and Baxter Warren knew no taboos, the wedding could be held immediately. He was a Yankee, sober but in love. The war was still creating casualties, and if he left a widow and perhaps an unborn child, he didn't want them to bear the name of a Rebel slave-holder. She had at last found good fortune—a substitute for the real thing, but still real in its way. Deborah was re-adopted by Baxter Warren II, who was either the prospective head of the Warren Bank in San Francisco, or a dead hero with widow and child. And she was his wife—Linda, formerly de Ribordeaux, née Towpelick, formerly Toupelik, from Lhota, Moravia, Austria, Europe.

"And you believe she wanted to rescue Dinah for you?" the sergeant said, shaking his head.

"Yes," said Cyril. "I used to think she was bad. But she's not. It's just that life taught her—"

The fires in the turpentine forests were burning out. Storm clouds over North Carolina were bursting at the seams. Spring was coming. The final battle at Bentonville was approaching.

★

He could see disappointment in the child's sleepy face. She hadn't learned hypocrisy yet, and he was glad. The sergeant had never regressed to the point where he became an ordinary farmer with manure on his boots and hay on his clothes. He was a veteran warrior. A Springfield rifle hung on the wall over the wooden armchair. It was the same rifle he had cleaned every morning long ago in the Thirteenth Regiment of the regular army of the United States, polishing it until he could see his face mirrored in the metalwork. And every time, he recalled the one and only time his general, still a colonel in a tattered hat, had run a white-gloved index finger over the metal trim on that very same rifle and had seen his own creased face scowling back, slightly more wrinkled than usual since the metal trim had been struck by a minnie that had knocked the rifle out of Kapsa's hand at Vicksburg, making a dent in the metal he never could even out. Yes, he was an old veteran. He had never missed a regimental reunion, and at the last one he had seen his general, who otherwise appeared to him only as a wild, spectral image in the metal trim of his old rifle. He was delighted with the disappointment of his daughter, who apparently thought her daddy was a shirker who had survived the war in a safe staff position.

"But I fired many shots, Terezka. At Vicksburg, at Collierville—I did enough shooting there to last me a lifetime. We attacked to the sound of music."

"Music?" asked the girl, wide-eyed.

"That's right. And General Sherman—"

They mounted their horses. It was already dawn. As the daylight grew brighter they rode hard to the north-east, past the apricot orchards, along the road they had travelled the day before to Howard's headquarters. Sherman rode far ahead, and his staff followed behind on sweating horses, spurring them on to keep up. The sergeant rode with them. The general's red hair—his hat had flown off when they rode into the first sunlight—shone the whole morning like flame. After noon, they reached Slocum's post in the pine woods. To the east they could hear cannon and rifle fire and from time to time a Rebel yell.

The sergeant rested against the trunk of a pine tree and watched the general listening to Slocum's report with one ear, and to the echo of the fighting with the other. It was ebbing and increasing, waning and waxing, like the irregular throbbing of a huge, sick heart. They all stood in a cluster around the general—Davis, Carlin, Morgan, Williams, Geary, Ward, Kilpatrick, and also Hazen from Howard's corps, who had just arrived with his Second Division. Carlin had found time to change into a clean uniform that symbolically confirmed Slocum's words.

"I think the day has been saved," Slocum was saying. "Morgan held on, and his officers and men deserve the highest praise. The battle rested with them. If they hadn't fought as they did, Johnston might have destroyed both divisions, Carlin's and Morgan's." Slocum nodded appreciatively at Morgan.

Morgan, embarrassed, looked down at his feet. His left sleeve was torn off. He ran his fingers through his beard and a light dusting of ashes fell onto his coat; part of his beard had caught fire in the battle.

"Our position has been consolidated," said Slocum. "After noon yesterday Baird's division moved to the front line, and last evening and overnight all three divisions of the Twentieth Corps moved up too. Before midnight Hazen arrived, and we're expecting more units of Howard's army in the course of the afternoon. By morning we'll have the advantage on them and we can attack."

The pulse of the distant battle throbbed again.

"Will you have advantage enough?" asked Sherman. "Johnston knows he's lost the benefit of surprise." He stopped to listen to the distant cannonade. "I don't understand why he's still fighting—" He looked around. "Where's Mower?"

"He ought to be here any minute," said Slocum. "He's on the far right wing." He listened again to the thunder of the distant fighting.

Sherman began pacing silently around the clearing. That was unusual. As a rule, he would talk while others were silent. Then he stopped and pulled a notebook out of his pocket.

"Kilpatrick," he addressed the horseman, who had removed his hat and was running a comb through his thinning hair. The comb was set with mother-of-pearl and did not appear to be government issue. "Can you name the units you identified from the prisoners you took?"

"Lee," said Kil, raising a finger.

"Four thousand," said Sherman, writing the number down.

"Cheatham."

"Another four."

"More like five," said Kil. "Maybe even more."

"Say five."

"Hoke, a good eight."

Sherman nodded, writing.

"Hardee—"

"Ten," said Sherman.

"If not more," declared Kil. "All the other units together, say another ten. Add Hampton's, Wheeler's, and Butler's cavalries—"

"Nearly forty thousand," said Sherman, and turned to Davis. "I made one blunder in this battle. I don't intend to make another one." He smiled at Davis.

General Davis laughed. "Right, Billy. After we almost got buried, I couldn't help remembering your words of wisdom: 'No infantry in our path, Jeff. Just a few squadrons of cavalry'!"

The general grinned. "It happens to the best of us, Jeff." He looked at the others. "Perhaps it was one of the occasional fits of madness the gentlemen of the press have enjoyed attributing to me."

They all laughed except Blair, who was just lighting a cigar.

"But I'm perfectly lucid for a change and I think we must avoid a general battle. Our numerical superiority isn't big enough, and I have no wish to emulate Pyrrhus."

"If you'll permit me, Billy," Carlin said.

The general looked approvingly at the neatly pressed figure, then glanced at his own muddy boots. "Now, there's a soldier!" he said. "Not like me!"

"It's my superstition," said Carlin stiffly. "We all have our superstitions."

"I wish I had yours," said Sherman.

Carlin didn't respond. Instead he said, "I think Johnston's numbers are considerably lower than we've estimated. I saw Hardee attack. His regiments seemed more like companies."

"Hmm," said Sherman. "And even so, he really gave you what for. I understand you scampered like rabbits."

Carlin's blush was visible. "They had the element of surprise."

"All day yesterday? Hardee at three o'clock, Bragg at five, and McLaws after dark? And artillery fire like at Gettysburg?"

No one said anything. Then Kilpatrick said tentatively, "Even if we subtract a third of them, it's still almost thirty thousand."

"Two to one," said Slocum. "We can take those odds into a general battle."

"Hmmm," said Sherman. He started pacing again, his hands folded behind his back. The heart of the battle on the other side of the forest pounded harder. Sherman halted, listened, then resumed pacing. A messenger galloped into the clearing and handed Slocum a dispatch. Slocum read it, then said, "Billy!"

"Hmm?"

"Hardee just sent his junior reserve into the first Division's sector. None of them is a day over eighteen. Their commander is a Major Clout. If he's seventeen, I'm a hundred. You know what that means?"

"I do, I do," said Sherman. He continued pacing in a circle, and when he got to Slocum he added, "They don't even spare their children!"

As he walked he pulled out a cigar, then noticed Blair and the smoke from his cigar curling up in the sunlight. He stepped over to him and gestured for a light. Blair passed him the burning cigar; the general lit his own from it and, without thinking, tossed Blair's cigar away. Blair stiffened indignantly and looked around at the others. Slocum and Hazen were trying hard not to laugh. Kilpatrick was grinning. So Blair smiled too, bent down, picked up the cigar, and lit it. The general approached him again. Deep in thought, he had forgotten to keep puffing and his cigar had gone out. He nodded to Blair for another light, but this time Blair hung onto his cigar while the general puffed his own back to life.

The general went on pacing. The shooting in the distance died away. Williams pulled a handful of peanuts from his pocket and a few of them fell onto the pine needles that covered the ground. A squirrel scampered down a nearby pine, grabbed one of them, and ran back up the tree. A bumble-bee flew past the sergeant. The general stopped.

"I don't understand why Johnston hasn't withdrawn. He was trying to destroy your flank, that's clear, Henry," he said to Slocum, "and he almost succeeded. That suggests his numbers aren't as bad as all that. And that's the only explanation—as far as I can see—why he hasn't turned tail and run. But Johnston is no fool. He learned that we're too much for him, and he has only one line of retreat, that last bridge across Mill Creek. I'm willing to wager he'll wait until nightfall and withdraw to Smithfield under cover of darkness. You see, Henry, I'd still rather avoid a general battle. Of course"— he looked around at the others—"if Johnston leaves us no choice, we won't deny him the experience."

"Real music?" the little girl persisted.

"Yes, real music," said the sergeant. "And on my orders."

What happened at Collierville was a minor skirmish, not a battle. A mere twelve dead and twenty-four wounded. The general had been moving his army to Chattanooga, and the Thirteenth Battalion, functioning as a guard unit with the general's headquarters, had gone by train with him from Memphis to Corinth. When the train stopped at noon at a depot near the village of Collierville, a nervous colonel stood waiting beside the tracks. From his report they learned that they had ridden into a trap. There were several squads of Rebel cavalry in the woods to the north of the depot. The scouts estimated their strength as at least three thousand, with a battery of field artillery. The colonel commanded fewer than five hundred men of the Sixty-sixth Indiana, half of them volunteers. He had positioned them in rifle pits around a little stockade with woods to the west and south of it. One unit was inside the stockade.

No sooner had the colonel finished his report than a rider with a white flag emerged from the woods. Everything was suddenly clear. The Thirteenth Battalion had about two hundred and thirty men, so the entire Union contingent now numbered under seven hundred, including Sherman's staff officers and the group of wounded who had hitched a ride with them to Corinth. The Rebels outnumbered them four to one. Sherman sent the colonel to negotiate with the messenger, with instructions to delay matters but to refuse to surrender. The colonel ambled over to the messenger, who had reined in his mount in the middle of the meadow, while Sherman and his men got off the train.

Inside the depot, Sherman telegraphed General Corso, whose division was camped about ten miles from Collierville, with orders to relocate by forced march to the site of the impending battle. Then he and his staff took up positions in the woods south of the stronghold. Three platoons of the Thirteenth took shelter behind an earthwork in front of the stockade, five more were placed in the woods to the east and south of it. The sergeant and his platoon reinforced the unit inside it.

The little stockade was nothing more than a rough-hewn log shack, almost completely dark inside because the shutters were pulled to and the only light came through the loopholes. A bunch of musicians, the unit band, huddled on the floor, and what little daylight there was reflected off the bells of their instruments. It looked as though they were sitting among many glimmering lanterns.

A cannon went off outside; the negotiations were over. The trombone player lubricated his slide with tobacco juice, and slid it back and forth as if he were playing. The sergeant looked through a loophole and saw the first canisters exploding at a safe distance from the trench in front of the stockade. The trench was almost crowded. The sergeant imagined what would happen when the artillery found the proper range. He looked back inside the room. The man with the trombone was still working the slide in and out, for the same reason that General Burnside always tugged at his monumental side-whiskers in battle, or Captain Smith had kept twirling his amazing moustache around his moistened finger at Vicksburg. Watching the musician calm himself, the sergeant had an absurd idea. It slipped his mind right away, because Chalmers's cannoneers had found their range and the first cries of pain were coming from the crowd in the trench. Fragments of iron buried themselves in the walls and roof of the stockade, and through the crack the sergeant could see a jagged line of dismounted cavalrymen rounding up a handful of inexperienced scouts of the Sixty-sixth Indiana. The battle had begun.

For almost four hours the fighting shifted back and forth across the meadows around the depot and the little stronghold. Chalmers wasn't expecting a lot of re-sistance; he was aware of his numerical advantage, and though he knew his ex-perienced cavalry would have to deal with the green troops of the Sixty-sixth, he wasn't counting on facing the Thirteenth Regiment of the regular army, with Chickasaw Bayou, Arkansas Post, Deer Creek, and the bloody massacre at Vicksburg behind it. All those had been fought in full view of General Sherman, and here too the general watched from the woods south of the depot as assault upon assault on the green meadows failed, and the depot and the stockade re-mained in the hands of his guard unit.

Only one little square on the chessboard changed figures. The cannon found the range of the train, and when several wagons caught fire the Rebels attacked from two directions. Only a hastily armed group of wounded had remained in the train and they were unable to defend themselves for long. Through his field-glasses the general saw the Rebels herd them out of the wagons, line them up in a rough formation, and drive them, limping and stumbling, into the wood, where a new unit was just emerging.

From the stockade, the commander of the Thirteenth, Captain Smith, saw them too. The men in the rifle pits had just beaten back another assault, and the sergeant couldn't tear his gaze away from a cavalryman with a bloodied leg drag-ging himself back across the meadow towards the shelter of the woods like a half-crushed beetle. The ball had apparently struck an artery because a red fountain was spurting from the wound. The cavalryman didn't get far before he fell face down in the grass and lay still.

The sergeant heard Captain Smith's voice ordering Lieutenant Griffin to counter-attack. He turned from the loopholes and saw the band, their instruments glimmering in the dull light, and the trombone player trying to calm himself. The commander of the Thirteenth was nervously buttoning and unbuttoning his grimy uniform.

From a rise in the woods, the general trained his field-glasses on the log shack. The door opened and Lieutenant Griffin appeared, followed by a sergeant and then, one by one, the soldiers of the Thirteenth. They spread out and ran towards the train. Intermittent puffs of smoke poured from the stockade's loopholes as the troops inside covered Griffin's assault.

Suddenly the stockade became a music box.

The general turned to his aide. "Do you hear that?"

The aide nodded.

They both listened. The band was playing "Rally Round the Flag, Boys!" The general smiled.

"Now, that's what I call soldiers. The Thirteenth are bored in there—"

A stray shrapnel shell exploded above the treetops and both men ducked.

Then the general raised his field-glasses again and saw a private in A Company swing his rifle and slam it down on the head of a Rebel officer who was firing a pistol from the train steps. He saw the officer fall and watched the private step over him and push his way to the wagon—apparently, or so it seemed, to the rhythm of the music still emanating from the stockade.

"But Daddy, that wasn't heroism, was it?" asked the little girl uncertainly. "Ordering a band to play?"

"Probably not," admitted the sergeant. "But the general was amused. And it got me transferred to his staff."

"And you never smacked anyone in the head with a rifle butt like Mister Zinkule?"

"No," said the sergeant. "All I did was slap a man in the face."

"A Rebel officer?"

"No," said the sergeant. "His name was Vallandigham."

★

The stable was silent and smelly. Cyril leaned back against the wall, sniffing occasionally at a handful of hay he clutched in his right hand. Pain shot through his left arm, which was splintered and bandaged. He was poking his nose in the hay to mask the stench of rotting flesh given off by gangrene-infected amputees.

The military chaplain was mumbling over a doomed Rebel casualty in the corner—both his legs were gone and pus was soaking through his bandages. A wounded man on a filthy straw mat beside him was rubbing a clove of garlic between his fingers and raising them to his nose. The Irish priest had been summoned by an orderly on the request of the dying Rebel. Cyril knew the priest. One time, back in South Carolina, he had been passing by their campfire when Shake and Zinkule were arguing about the Immaculate Conception. Zinkule claimed it referred to the conception of Christ, and Shake said it was the Virgin Mary.

"Father! We need some theological guidance," Shake had called out to him, and the clergyman stopped, sat down with them at the campfire, listened to the dispute, and then said Shake was right.

"We often encounter that error among laymen," he said. "Are you a faithful Catholic?"

"I'm a Catholic, yes," Shake replied. "But I have a mortal sin on my conscience."

The priest dropped his voice. "Would you like to confess?"

"It's not something I can atone for by confessing," said Shake. "The only way would be to make restitution."

The priest frowned. "Don't you believe in the grace of God?"

"Ah, but I do," Shake said. "If I didn't, I'd have gone crazy long ago."

Cyril buried his nose in his handful of hay. He caught a whiff of potato leaves and his inner eye took him from the stinking stable to an autumn evening in the mountains, and little fires burning. But why? Suddenly the priest stood up and looked around, and the campfires went out. He came over to Cyril.

"Good evening, father," said Cyril.

"You're one of the Bohemian bunch, aren't you?" asked the chaplain. He looked at the dying amputee, then back to Cyril. "The fellow barely speaks English."

"Is he a goner?" asked Cyril.

"I'm afraid so," said the priest. "He's delirious. He's babbling, it could be something about Texas, it's hard to understand. But I'm sure he's Bohemian."

"OK," said Cyril, and he rose painfully and, holding his arm out at his side like a broken wing, walked over to the man. The Rebel's eyes were closed; his skin showed a deathly white through the stubble on his beard. Cyril felt as if he were hallucinating, perhaps from the stink of rotting limbs, the fragrance of the hay, the smell of burning leaves. He leaned close to the dying man's face. "Jesus!" he gasped in Czech. The dying man opened his eyes. "Mary, Mother of Jesus!"

He turned and hobbled quickly, almost running, to the farmhouse where they had put the wounded officers. In the kitchen, Captain Warren sat at the table with a bandage wrapped around his head. It wasn't a serious wound. During an assault by Hardee's cavalry a minnie had grazed his skull; he had lost consciousness and had come to just in time to hear the jaded doctor say, "It's nothing, just a concussion." Now he sat at the table with Lida and Lieutenant Ferguson, who had sprained his ankle at Bentonville. They were playing Marias, a card game from Austria that the captain's wife had introduced them to.

Regardless of what he thought of her, Cyril had to admire his sister. "I's with Massa Captain Warren now!" Sarah declared proudly. She was a black woman whose owner had fled with Hardee, and she patted Deborah's head. The little girl grasped her pudgy hand. "Now that Massa Fitzsimmons is gone, I's with Massa Captain Warren and Miz Fitzsimmons!"

"You are indeed," said the innocent.

"I'm with Captain Warren too," said Lida, pressing up against her husband. "And I won't let him go!"

At the time, neither Sarah nor Baxter Warren II knew that she meant it literally. But when Sherman's great army set out to the north-east, and Captain Baxter Warren II with it, the ambulance at the rear of the captain's company was empty except for Lida, wearing the grey dress of a nurse. The captain protested, but in fact he was glowing with pride. What other man in Sherman's army had a wife like her? The ambulance gradually filled with casualties, and his exotic wife bandaged bleeding bullet wounds and sword cuts as if she had been doing it all her life. They had left Deborah in safety under the protection of the captain's sister, Mrs. Fitzsimmons, whose foolish husband had joined the retreating Hardee. Both of them were under the protection of Sarah, who was now working for Captain Warren. Although she was free, she had decided to remain a nanny to children of the wealthy. She had never done anything else and didn't want to start now.

"Lida," whispered Cyril.

His little sister, playing-cards fanned out in her hand, turned her eyes to him. "Yes?" Then she noticed Cyril's face and added, "What's the matter, Cyril?"

"Come with me," he said softly.

She collapsed. The doomed Rebel had died without opening his eyes. The Irish priest made the sign of the cross over him, and Lida broke down and cried, in awful, racking sobs. Under the grey fabric of her nurse's uniform, the farm-girl's sturdy shoulders heaved with a bottomless, endless agony. Captain Warren stood helplessly over her. Cyril met his unknowing eyes.

"It's her older brother," said Cyril. "God only knows how he ended up here, of all places. My God!"

God only knew, not Cyril. But it was Vitek, inexplicably here in North Carolina, a few miles from Bentonville.

Cyril looked at his sister, and for a second he thought Linda's heart might break.

But her heart didn't break. She wouldn't give God that satisfaction. Her heart had already been broken, years ago, in the country she had had to leave alone, without the man who now lay dead at Bentonville. But like a broken bone her heart mended, and afterwards it grew stone-hard, as healed bones sometimes do.

★

Around midnight it started to rain. The battle had slowed down. Now and then, when the rain let up, the sergeant could hear the creaking of axles; vehicles at the rear of the Rebel line were on the move in the darkness. The general had been right. Johnston was taking advantage of the cover of night and retreating to the bridge across Mill Creek. That would mean the war was over.

Shake had fallen asleep on the palisade. He was having a beautiful dream. Suddenly he was what he had never become, and he was celebrating the May Mass in gold-embroidered vestments. He had just turned to the missal and started back to the Epistle side of the altar when a rose-bush popped out of the carpet on the steps, spread rapidly, and soon covered the Epistle side with scarlet blossoms that gave off a pungent fragrance. He turned and the same thing was happening on the Gospel side. He turned towards the worshippers but he couldn't see them, for the entire altar was surrounded by rose-bushes. They smelled so strong that he felt faint and began to panic. He turned quickly back to the altar, climbed the tabernacle, and scrambled up the gilded baroque façade, where statues of Saint Peter, Saint Paul, Saint Cyril, and Saint Methodius gazed out at him from their niches. Suddenly, like snakes, rose-covered boughs emerged above their heads and began twining down the altar. Startled, Shake fell to the altar, and the rose boughs attacked him from all directions, twining around his arms and legs like vines, and the odour became so strong that it was practically a stench— he woke up. Behind him on a tree stump sat a man dressed in tails. A Negro who looked familiar was sprinkling him with liquid from a tiny gilt flagon. Shake decided that he was still asleep and had just moved from one dream to another.

Then he heard Paidr say, "I'll be damned, Franta! You're all we needed here!"

"You bet you need me," said the fellow in the formal suit. "I'm not wounded, so my place is with my unit."

The Negro stopped sprinkling Zinkule and corked the bottle. The cruel smell of roses awakened everyone around them.

"Franta!" exclaimed Javorsky. "Is that you?"

"Who do you think it is?" the fellow in the tail-coat replied irritably.

"What's that you're wearing?" Houska chimed in.

"Tails," replied Zinkule tersely.

"You sure you've come to the right place? This isn't a fancy-dress ball," said Paidr.

"It's all Breta could find," said Zinkule.

"He's in the right place, all right," said Shake. "It looks like the devils will dance here tonight."

As if in response, the thunder of artillery-fire rolled in from the right, where Howard's wing had joined Slocum during the night.

★

Long after the war, the younger Toupelik son Josef told the story. That was after Cyril had gone back to the de Ribordeaux plantation. It was being managed, more or less, by the Negroes, since there was no one left of the family and no one knew who the new owners would be, or even who should be selling it to whom. Nobody knew anything: neither Beulah, nor the foul-mouthed Benjamin. Uncle Habakuk was dead, and Samuel, the footman, was now a groom in the stable, still wearing his faded livery, though there was no one left to be escorted any-where. Cyril had come because he hoped Dinah would do the same. She must know that if he survived he would try to find her. But where should he start?

And Josef said, "It was on my first trip to Matamoros. I got myself hired on with the ox teams, otherwise I'd have gotten drafted into the army too. That way I was exempted."

They had been transporting bales of King Cotton through the wastelands of South Texas to the Rio Grande, because all the Confederate ports were blocked by the Yankee flotilla, and unless the Rebels could export their cotton to Europe there would be no arms, nothing. The Southerners had hoped that old aristo-cratic Europe—England and France—would come to the aid of the new aristo-cratic Americans, but for Europe it was simply business. Perhaps Maximilian, the new Mexican emperor, who was also a Hapsburg, would be an ally. But that hope too proved illusory. "Well," said Josef, "he had barely ten thousand men, about one Confederate division. And a lot of them were like him—looking for a free ticket to America so they could go off on their own."

In Matamoros they unloaded the cotton, found a stable for the oxen, and went into town—that is, into the taverns. Josef and Matej Vosahlik picked a tavern on a square, ordered something they had never heard of called tequila, and were soon in seventh heaven. Then a soldier began to irritate them, a non-com with stripes on his sleeve and a silver bird on his cap.

"What does he keep gawking at me for?" Josef asked Vosahlik.

"Maybe he knows you from some place," said Matej.

"That's impossible," said Josef. "He's the first Mexican I've ever seen in my whole life."

"Except he's no Mexican," said Matej, who had been in Matamoros twice be-fore. "He's Austrian."

"*Balls!*" *Josef snapped.* "*What would an Austrian be doing here?*"

Matej, who was an old hand, explained to him that there was an Austrian expeditionary army in Mexico under the command of Count Thun-Hohenstein; it had come to help the archduke, now Emperor Maximilian, occupy a precarious throne. And Josef looked back and said, "*He keeps staring at me. Is he a nancy-boy?*"

The Austrian noncom rose—the two-headed bird on his cap glinted and flapped its wings, or so it seemed to them—and addressed them in Czech: "*Look here, I heard you. You talk our language.*" *Then he turned to Josef.* "*Aren't you one of the Toupelik boys?*"

★

"Everything gets perverted into its opposite," said Shake. "Courage turns into cowardice, cowardice turns into courage."

They were back around a campfire again, many days later. Three geese were roasting on a spit. Breta was catching the dripping fat in a ladle and basting the golden-brown birds with it.

"That's what Hegel says," added Shake.

"How about translating that into Czech for us?" said Javorsky.

They were all wearing the new uniforms that General Schofield had brought to Goldsboro. Even Zinkule, although he was still—through no choice of his own—sitting apart from them with a little bottle in his knapsack. Now and then he would take it out and sprinkle something onto a handkerchief and tuck the handkerchief inside his shirt.

"It doesn't need translating," said Shake. "It just needs interpreting. To make it simple, the skirmishers were shocked when the smell of roses hit their nostrils, and when the smell was followed by Zinkule jumping over the parapet in his tail-coat they were scared out of their wits. So the three of us, Breta, Vojtech, and me, took advantage of the element of surprise, and out of sheer courage—without being ordered to—jumped over the parapet and gave chase. But when we got to the edge of the woods, Rebel cavalry burst out of the trees and cut off our line of retreat. So we had to advance until we found a hiding-place in the rushes of a swamp. We caught our breath and then it started to pour, so we took advantage of that and set out for the woods to the south, towards our line, until we got within range and saw the Stars and Stripes flying over the palisade. We ran towards it but we were met by gunfire. Thank God their aim was rotten." Shake paused, reached out and poked the closest of the geese, then licked his finger and said, "A little while longer and we'll have a feast."

"You were so crazy scared," said Salek, "you couldn't tell the Stars and Stripes from the Confederate rag."

"Not so, friend," said Shake. "It was the Stars and Stripes all right, but the ones flying it couldn't tell us from the Rebels, and who could blame them? When they've got a fellow in tails and a nigger with a rifle coming at them—and remember, word had got out that Jeff Davis had finally ditched his theory and armed the slaves. And everybody knew the South had finally run out of uniforms. So in the end it was a Carolina skunk that prevented us from rejoining the Twenty-sixth Wisconsin. On the other hand, it got our names written into the annals of the most famous chapter of the Battle of Bentonville."

"Even if their aim was rotten," said Paidr. "But, as usual, you high-tailed it out of there."

"And so would you!" Houska said angrily. "We didn't know their aim was rotten. There were only the four of us, and any damn fool could have hit us in that downpour just by accident."

"That's God's truth," said Shake. "We were simply forced to retreat back towards the enemy again. But the rain made it so hard to see that we weren't sure which way we were going. Every so often, flustered riders would appear from behind the curtains of falling water and then disappear again, but they never seemed to be on our side, so all we could do was retreat one way, then the other, until we got our directions confused. We knew we were in North Carolina, but that was about all."

"Never seemed to be on our side?" Paidr repeated scornfully. "How could you tell, when it was pissing rain and you couldn't see your hand in front of your face? Do Southern fillies smell different from Northern ones?"

"They do!" Zinkule chimed in.

"Look at who's the expert!" said Paidr. "How could you smell anything besides yourself?"

"I couldn't," said Zinkule. "Southerners look different. When they charge, they hold the reins between their teeth and shoot with both hands. At least that's what they did at Bentonville. They think they're hot and they're barely out of kneepants."

"By then you must have been near Hardee's wing," said the sergeant. "So you'd have retreated some distance. Three miles, if not more."

"You lose track of time and distance when it's pouring like that," said Shake, taking another poke at the goose.

"When you've got a fire under your butt and you're shitting your pants," said Paidr, "you can work up to speeds that brave men can only dream of."

"Fire under our butts? In that rain?" Shake said incredulously.

"That's just a way of putting it," said Paidr. "Have you forgotten everything Czech?"

"What was driving us was the desire to get back to our side," said Shake. "But we'd lost our bearings and we were getting farther away instead. When it was obvious we weren't getting where we wanted to be, we decided to hide in the woods, wait till nightfall, and follow the stars west."

"And it was a cloudy night," said Paidr.

"Probably," conceded Shake. "But we found our troops at four in the afternoon—not our own unit, but General Mower's famous division."

"Pop," said Breta, "I'm ringing the dinner bell."

★

"Matej ran away that night," Josef continued, while Mother Toupelik piled food on their plates. Everyone was there but Lida. In a month she was expecting to give birth to Baxter Warren III in San Francisco (she gave birth instead to Linda Warren II, but two years later a third male Warren generation would finally see the light of day, followed by Maureen, named after her grandmother). "On those earlier trips Matej had heard there was a Yankee consulate in Matamoros, and if you signed up there they'd send you north by boat. If you enlisted in the army, that is. I knew Matej was going to run off. We were best friends and we'd planned to run off together, but when Vitek showed up out of nowhere—"

"But how did he get to Hardee? All the way from Texas, in the spring of '64?" Cyril asked. He was still astonished.

"I don't know that part of it," said Josef. "They took him on with the ox teams in place of Matej. He gave me money to get him some civvies in Matamoros, which I did. But as soon as we got to Galveston, the Rebs grabbed us for the army. By then they were taking anybody they could get. They put us in General Kirby Smith's army and sent us with General Taylor to Louisiana, where General Banks was on the offensive. I lost track of Vitek at Shreveport. What happened to him after that I don't know. He hardly knew any English at all. I got slightly wounded, and when I rejoined my company half of them were gone already. They'd sent them somewhere else, or they'd deserted—"

"Wait a minute," Cyril interrupted. He desperately hoped for a moment that, just as Vitek had been blown to Bentonville by the winds of a crazy war—though late, when it was practically a lost cause—perhaps his own Dinah might have been carried by the same madness of coincidence, or by the laws of love, or of the novels she so loved to read—

But his tea-rose was lost. She seemed to have vanished into the huge maw of the rebellion. Nothing of her remained, not a trace, not a thing.

"Wait a minute," he said. "Did you tell Vitek that Lida had escaped to Savannah?"

"I didn't know that then. Not even Father knew. She just left him a letter saying she was marrying de Ribordeaux and taking Deborah with her. She never said where she was going. Maybe she forgot in the rush."

Had Vitek found out somehow? During the march through Louisiana, Mississippi, Alabama, Georgia, all the way to Savannah? And why hadn't he stayed there? Had he deserted from Kirby's army as he had from Thun-Hohenstein's expeditionary force? Or had they driven him there in some ravaged outcast unit, and then across a hastily constructed bridge with Hardee's troops, through South Carolina and North Carolina, until his trek ended when he got his legs shot off during the last desperate charge at Bentonville?

Cyril never did find out. But that was how it came about that, during the Washington parade, Lida pinned a black mourning ribbon to her hat in memory of her dead "brother".

★

They ran through the downpour till they got to the woods. Steam rose from the moss, making it hard to see between the trees. The wind flung sheets of water through the waving crowns of the pine trees, and grey-black clouds flew by over their heads like an ocean turned upside-down. Gunfire crackled from every point of the compass, and cannon barked like hoarse St. Bernards. They advanced in single file—first Zinkule in his now torn and water-soaked suit, then Breta, barefoot and in shirt-sleeves, then Houska in a uniform that looked like a bundle of rags, and, bringing up the rear, the relatively neat-looking Shake. They had no idea where they were.

A row of bushes loomed ahead in the mist. They walked faster. Soon they were sitting on the ground surrounded by dense foliage, isolated from the battle by a sense of safety. Speaking softly, they agreed that it made no sense to leave their hiding-place with the rain pouring down and the overcast skies making it impossible to determine direction. They disagreed about how long they had been running around in the rain and fog, trying to evade the enemy and avoid being shot by their own men firing at shadows. To Shake it seemed like five or six hours. Houska kept tapping a looted pocket-watch he had wound that very morning; it had stopped on the Roman numeral II so this must be afternoon, but the question was, how late was it? There was nothing to do but wait till the rain stopped and the ragged clouds parted to let the sun or the stars through. So they stretched out on the ground under a shelter of dense brush, and neither the rain nor the rising and falling music of battle could keep them awake.

It was actually the silence that awakened Shake, between the occasional clanking of iron on tin, musket on canteen, revealing the nearness of a still invisible army. His eyes opened wide. The downpour was over but it was drizzling. He realized that he was staring into a pair of equally wide eyes in a black face. He sat up, and that awakened the others. On all fours they set out through the mist rising from soil and moss, towards the sounds of the marching army.

They crept to the edge of the bushes. Beyond them lay a broad ravine, rain-washed and green, and, winding through it, a forest path thick with pine needles.

Through the leaves they saw a reconnaissance unit striding quickly down the path, wearing Union caps. They were reluctant to reveal themselves, for they knew that scouts don't think until after they've pulled the trigger. A man in tails, a Negro, and a soldier who looked more like a scarecrow would hardly encourage a thoughtful response.

The forward ranks of the army emerged from the mist. Rifles at the ready, they strode with the rapid gait of Sherman's swift troops. At the very head of the army marched a black-bearded general on foot, between two men in captains' uniforms.

Farther down the path, around the bend where the scouts had disappeared, there was a sudden commotion of gunfire.

★

The proceeds from the ladies' dance party had vanished, possibly to Siberia, and the prospect of red trousers for the militia unit had shrunk to practically nothing, because John Hubatty's tailor shop had given them an estimate of three dollars and fifty cents per uniform. Many recruits couldn't afford that, so the business-minded Hubatty had come up with a less splendid but more practical uniform with ordinary grey-blue trousers for only two dollars and ninety cents, but the idea of going to war outfitted so drably put most of the recruits off. Of the original fifty-two volunteers, the unit's first drill on the green behind Slavik's Tavern was attended by only twelve men in civilian clothes and Captain Mihalotzy, who arrived in the uniform of Hungary's Honved Infantry. Another twenty potential defenders of the Union sat inside the tavern, squeezed around the tables by the window, waiting to see what would happen.

"They were soon sorry," Shake said. "Even though Lincoln's Slavonic Rifles

without red trousers weren't nearly as colourful doing their drill as the zouaves had been, the prettiest girls in all of Czech Chicago stood smiling at them from around the green, including many of the wives of the fellows watching from the tavern window. Schroeder, banned from taking part for reasons of Czech chauvinism, was scowling from the sidelines beside Molly Kakuska, who was wearing the folk costume she'd worn to the party. Though they didn't have red trousers, they did have the handsome Captain Geza Mihalotzy. The fellows in the tavern realized this when Geza bellowed out the first order: 'Marschieren, marsch!' *The squad stepped out smartly, if not entirely in step, and Vasek Lusk—though soldiering was in his blood—got his feet tangled up and fell on his face—"*

"Marschieren, marsch?" *Houska interrupted Shake.* "In a Slovak company?"

"Slavonic," *Shake corrected him.* "And how did you expect Mihalotzy to give his orders? In Hungarian? The only people who could understand that would be him and Tonda Kovacz."

"Why not in English, then?"

"All the English Geza knew back then was what he needed as a physician's valet: 'Come in, please,' and 'The doctor will see you now, madam.' The Czechs hadn't had an army of their own since the Battle of White Mountain, except Oxiensterna's in the Thirty Years War, and there the orders were given in Swedish. Nobody in Chicago knew how to give orders in Czech or in English, so Geza used German, like the Austrians did."

Language aside, Mihalotzy was such a virtuoso commander that the girls and ladies on the sidelines kept breaking into spontaneous applause, and would-be soldiers started drifting out of the tavern to join the men on the green. By the end of the exercise—which lasted three hours, thanks to the intense interest of the women and the resulting enthusiasm of the participants—a full forty warriors were marching up and down the green in tight ranks, and at the next training session, three days later, the company showed up in full strength.

Because Captain Mihalotzy—

When a delegation consisting of Slavik, Padecky, and Kafka arrived at the front door of the white house on Canal Street with its gold-lettered sign: "William Walenta M.D., 3 PM – 6 PM and by appointment" *(it was after office hours), they were startled to hear groans coming from behind the door.*

"He must be operating," *whispered Kafka.* "Let's wait, neighbours."

They waited. The groans sounded odd.

"And the door isn't quite shut," *said Kafka,* "He wouldn't be operating behind an open door." *His curiosity got the better of him and he poked the black mahogany door with his finger. It opened noiselessly. A massive fellow in a grey valet's tunic had a bald-headed man in a physician's smock in a vicious full nelson.*

The delegation stopped in the doorway and the bald man noticed them. The tips of his black patent-leather shoes were dangling several inches above the floor.

Padecky came to his senses and yelled, "Let him go!"

The bald man gave a bit of a moan and said, "Won't you come in, gentlemen. I help others, but I can't help myself. Damned lumbago! You can let me go now, Mister Mihalotzy."

That was how they first met their future commanding officer.

"It was all the same whether he was a Slovak or a Magyar," Shake explained over what was left of the campfire. Only he and the sergeant remained; the fire was down to smouldering coals, and the North Carolina horizon was dotted with dying fires in the turpentine forests. "When he used to indulge at Slavik's Tavern, he'd say, 'We all share a single nationality,' by which he meant Slavonic. When he got drunk, which wasn't that seldom"—Shake sighed—"he'd recite Hungarian poetry, which I would say was pretty fiery stuff, considering how excited he got. He was strange for a valet, and the fact is that he wasn't a valet at all. He was a soldier. Sometimes he claimed he was an officer, but he was very vague about it, so personally I think his first officer's rank was the one he got from us when we elected him Commander of Lincoln's Slavonic Rifles. He translated the rank of 'setnik' into English as 'captain', though I'd say he was a corporal in the Austrian army, a Feldwebel at best. But in the long run he was a better commander for the Twenty-fourth Illinois than many a Yankee career officer would have been. He was a Forty-eighter. He had a cause."

"What cause?" asked the sergeant.

"Freedom, of course," said Shake. "The rest of Lincoln's Slavonic Rifles were more interested in the red trousers." Shake laughed. Was it a bitter laugh? Perhaps. "To be fair, twelve of us saved the honour of the banner, and in fact one was a Jew, Eda Kafka, though he was also an anti-Semite, which made him a true Slav. They discharged him after Chattanooga, because he got yellow fever or something. After that he married Sara Ohrenzug, daughter of our honorary colonel, which goes to show that his sex drive helped him shuck his anti-Semitism. Except that he died soon afterwards. The first to drop out of the company was Joska Neuman, who lost a leg at Perryville. His dad was German but a Forty-eighter, and his mom was born Krepelickova and hadn't got a Teutonic hair on her head. In America Joska got Americanized, but obviously not entirely, since he joined up with the Slavonic Rifles. Josef Jurka—they amputated his foot at Murfreesboro, and I hear he's in a veterans' home somewhere. And Lojza Uher used to be a pastry chef before he joined up, but he was absolutely fearless and

dedicated to Lincoln. When the company was attached to Haecker's regiment, he made sergeant. Poor Franta Kouba they say died in a Southern jail." Shake took his pipe apart and put the sections in his knapsack. "Twelve. Two more than the Good Lord required in Sodom. But the rest?"

After that first successful drill, which ended up with forty men participating (there were a full fifty-two at the second one, and the women's circle also increased in size after Geza Mihalotzy showed up with a waxed mustache), the captain told them that, if their unit was to become part of the Union army, they had to send a formal petition to the Governor of Illinois asking him to grant them the status of a regular volunteer regiment, and to issue them with weapons. They called a meeting where Trevellyan (there with Schroeder, who was there because of Molly Kakuska, who was holding hands with Kouba) formulated an English letter according to Mihalotzy's instructions, whereupon they celebrated by getting drunk.

After recovering from their hangovers, most of the company met again next evening at Slavik's. Kabrna, a cigar-maker, was upset. "Nobody translated it into Czech for us! God knows what they sent the governor. What if that Hun sold us out? What if he's put us in some kind of danger? What if they send us west to fight the Indians? What then?"

"In short, some of them began to realize that red trousers carried a certain risk," said Shake, "and the result was a near mutiny. They were afraid of Indians and proceeded to fortify themselves with more drinking, and in the end not even the intrepid Barcal could disabuse them of the notion that Geza Mihalotzy had sold them down the river to the Indian wars, where their scalps were definitely at risk. They demanded that the petition be translated into Czech."

Mihalotzy himself wasn't up to the task, so he turned it over to Molly Kakuska, and at the next meeting she read it to them out loud:

"Resolved that we, American citizens of Slavonic and Hungarian language, in demonstration of our love for our new homeland, form a company of militia; that in so doing we gladly offer our services to the Government of the United States to defend the flag and Constitution if the need should arise; that our secretary forward a fair copy of this resolution to the Governor of the State of Illinois with a request that he call upon our services as soon as the need shall arise."

When she finished, they were silent. In the back of the room Schroeder was also silent. He didn't understand this version of the petition, but he listened attentively because he liked the sound of Molly's voice. The silence persisted until finally Kabrna, the cigar-maker, rose at a table in the rear.

"'If the need should arise', " he quoted ominously. "What is by anybody meant by that?"

"Say it in Czech," said Shake.

"*I just did. 'If the need should arise',*" *said the cigar-maker.* "*How else I should say it?*"

"*What it means is secession,*" *said Mihalotzy in Slovak.* "*It means if the South takes up arms to defend slavery against the Union—*"

"*But have got a family,*" *said the cigar-maker.*

"*There's not going to be a war,*" *declared Padecky.* "*They'll shit themselves before they let themselves get shot over a bunch of niggers.*"

"*It's not about niggers,*" *said Kafka.* "*It's about them having to slave away on the plantations for nothing.*"

"*It's about freedom,*" *said Mihalotzy.*

Once again the tavern was silent.

"*Yes,*" *said Talafous, the butcher,* "*but would you want to go after a pack of Indian cut-throats?*"

"*You might,*" *said Shake.* "*With that cue-ball head of yours, you're not risking a thing.*"

The butcher reached up involuntarily, ran his hand over his bald scalp, and said, "*Seriously, now. Would you go fight red cannibals?*"

There was silence for a while, then Salek-Cup said, "*If it's over freedom, I would.*"

"*That's because you've got a bad conscience from '48,*" *said the cigar-maker.* "*You told us yourself how you fired on the students.*"

"*I was young and stupid then,*" *said Salek-Cup,* "*and loyal to my emperor. Now I'm a grown man and an American!*"

In a voice like a bull-horn Mihalotzy began declaiming a poem. Unfortunately it was in Hungarian, so they could only guess what it was about from his emotional recitation. In any case it failed to dispel the butcher's fears of an armed encounter with Indian cut-throats.

Frowning, Talafous reread the translated petition, and Vasek Lusk said, "*I wouldn't mind having a go at the Indians. I'm ready for a fight. I'm tired of all this drilling.*"

"*You've already got it in your blood,*" *said Shake.* "*Some people still have to get it there.*" *He glanced meaningfully at the butcher and the cigar-maker.*

"*This is easy for you to talk,*" *said Kabrna.* "*You don't have wife and kids.*"

"*But it still shouldn't be in here,*" *the butcher interrupted, glowering at the translated document.* "*Now the governor can snap his fingers whenever it suits his fancy and we have to march to his tune.*"

"*Why did you sign up if you're scared already?*" *Padecky yelled.*

"*Don't insult me, neighbour!*" *the butcher retorted.* "*You can never be too careful.*"

"*This is terrible!*" *Shake rolled his eyes over the translated missive.*

"What now, dammit?" hollered Padecky.

"The phrase 'gladly offer our services to the Government of the United States'," said Shake with a horrified expression. "It should say exactly what kind of services it's talking about."

"What do you mean, what services?" bellowed Padecky. "We're a company of soldiers, aren't we? What are we supposed to do, go and shovel manure for the governor?"

"'If the need should arise'—" Shake shrugged.

"Soldiers!" thundered Mihalotzy, who could follow just enough of the Czech to know it was time to intervene. "The governor will use our company if war breaks out with the South."

"It's not going to," said Shake. "Not according to Padecky here."

"Exactly," said the butcher. "So what else can the governor ask us to do as soldiers? Fight the Indians. They're the only ones making war right now."

"The governor has his regular army for fighting Indians," said Mihalotzy. "We'll march against the South."

"Yes, but Kabrna has a family," said Shake.

Suddenly the door opened and Marticka Lusk sailed into the tavern, radiant with good news. Tailor Hubatty had told Mr. Ohrenzug about the stolen proceeds from the ladies' dance and that patriotic gentleman had first flown into a rage and then asked how much uniforms with red trousers would cost. Then he'd done some figuring on a piece of paper and worked out that for fifty-two volunteers the cost would be a total of one hundred and eighty-two dollars.

"And, neighbours, he's offered to pay for them out of his own pocket!" raved Marticka.

"The man is too generous," said the cigar-maker gloomily. "There got to be a catch."

"There's no catch," said Marticka, "but there is a condition. He's too old to go to war, but he wants you to name him honorary colonel."

"How old is he?" Padecky asked darkly.

"Just short of fifty," said Marticka.

They were silent. Padecky, who had turned fifty in September, flushed a little, but the thought of the red trousers silenced him. "He's not in very good shape for his age, and that's the truth," he grumbled.

"He has one other condition," said Marticka.

"What else? Being a colonel ought to be enough, for a miserable hundred and eighty-two bucks," snapped Kafka the anti-Semite.

"He wants you to hang an oil painting of him in the assembly room," said Marticka.

"Does that mean here?" asked Slavik, glancing at the front wall, where

two portraits were hanging already: Frantisek Palacky and George Washington.

Over Kafka's protests, it was agreed that Honorary Colonel Arpad Ohrenzug would hang to the left of George Washington. And so Lincoln's Slavonic Rifles were saved, at least for the time being.

★

Dawn brought the sounds of daytime and the sounds of war, which drowned out the noise of creaking axles and the occasional braying of a mule. Dawn also brought a rider from General Carlin, which was how Sherman found out that he had lost the wager from the previous day. Johnston's army was still in the field, with a single avenue of retreat, the bridge across Mill Creek. They had remained there, however, not because the experienced commander had suddenly decided to go for broke, but because the relentless battle with Carlin's and Morgan's divisions had overstretched the capacity of Johnston's field hospital, and tending to all the wounded was more than his medics could handle. The only bridge was in constant use by ambulances transporting their bloody cargo across the river to Smithfield. Johnston hadn't expected such high losses, and there was a shortage of vehicles as well. Once in the town, the casualties were placed in churches and schools, and the ambulances returned for new loads.

After reading Carlin's dispatch, Logan suggested launching a general battle. The sergeant knew what his general's response would be.

"No, John," Sherman said. "Have you seen this?" He indicated the preliminary report of the chief medical officer. "Our casualties are up to about a thousand already." He glanced out from under the lean-to set up among the pines to protect the staff and the less than useful maps from the rain. The sounds of war were muted by the drumming of raindrops on the slanted canvas fly. "Johnston's on his last legs. Even without a general battle."

"The war could be over in one fell swoop," argued Logan.

Sherman turned away from the view of the green meadows among the trees, veiled by the driving rain.

"How many more weeks or days do you think it could take, John?"

"Today could be the last day."

"For how many men?" asked Sherman.

He did not issue the order for a general battle.

But then another messenger came, with news of a sudden and unexpected battle on the far end of the right wing shortly after four in the afternoon.

"It must be Mower," the general said. "He's one of our best young commanders." The sergeant smiled to himself. Mower was only seven years younger than Sherman, but the general was "Uncle Billy", the elderly, congenial leader. "Did anyone give him the order to do this?"

No one had. They bent over the map and saw that Mower's flanking manoeuvre was an imaginative way of striking at the enemy's Achilles' heel. But they also saw it as a risky decision. Mower was a brawler who sometimes relied too heavily on the exceptional skills of his soldiers and on luck.

Until that afternoon, Mower's division of Blair's Seventeenth Corps had stood almost idle at the far right flank of Sherman's army. Then Mower discovered that the enemy ranks in that sector had thinned out considerably, since Johnston had moved his troops to reinforce the centre. Like everyone else, Mower knew that the bridge across Mill Creek was Johnston's only avenue of retreat, and he reasoned that he could close that retreat off by a swift offensive march; the only resistance would come from a few units, and they were likely to consist of reconnaissance rather than combat troops. So he set out at the head of his division along a forest path that curved north-east and then, after emerging from the forest, wound across meadows and skirted marshes until it reached the bridge a bare two miles away. By the time Mower's first courier arrived at Sherman's headquarters, the van of his division had already broken through the sparse line of defence—cavalrymen on foot, there to protect Johnston's left flank—and were approaching the bridge. The courier reported that hastily assembled reserve and cavalry units were trying to slow them down. The bridge, however, was already in full sight.

They all looked to the general. He scratched his dishevelled hair and pulled on his cigar.

"We must skirmish along the entire front," he said, "otherwise Johnston will move all his reserves and all of Hampton's and Wheeler's cavalry units against Mower. And if that's not enough, he'll even yield his position against Slocum to keep Mower from getting to the bridge. We have to keep them busy, or he'll do to Mower's division what he failed to do to Morgan's."

He looked around at his staff. No one said a word.

"He has the very best reasons to defend that bridge. He's moving his wounded out. When that's done—well, I won't make any bets like yesterday's, but I'd say that he'll take what's left and withdraw to Smithfield tonight."

"All the more reason for us to initiate a general battle," insisted Logan.

The general shook his head. "Skirmishing along the whole front line is enough. Johnston won't be able to leave his defences, and Mower will manage against the reserves."

But would Mower close off the avenue of retreat, the sergeant wondered. If he did, Sherman couldn't avoid a general battle even if he wanted to.

The general walked out from under the lean-to and looked out over the verdant, rain-soaked North Carolina landscape rolling away before him. Flashes of faraway gunfire poked through the grey curtain of rain. He could feel spring in the air. A gust of wind brought a whiff of gunpowder from the battlefront.

★

Thanks to the generosity of Colonel Arpad Ohrenzug, participation in training exercises was now one hundred per cent. The circle of ladies and girls from the Czech community had widened again, especially when Captain Mihalotzy started drilling the soldiers in the art of man-to-man combat with fixed bayonets. True, they were using broom handles instead of rifles and bayonets (the brooms came from Salek-Cup's warehouse), but the glint of steel and stench of hot blood were provided by the imaginations of the blood-thirsty female patriots and the battling defenders of the Union, who in turn were inspired by visions of red trousers, the fabric for which was already being cut in Hubatty's workshop. Alone in a corner of the meadow, the outcast Schroeder stood balefully observing the mock battle.

One time there was almost a mutiny. The postman had brought Mihalotzy a letter at Slavik's Tavern. It was a letter he had written to Lincoln, and Lincoln had sent it back from Washington with a signed comment in his own hand appended to it. That evening, Molly Kakuska read it aloud at a meeting.

"Dear Sir," Mihalotzy had written in English (transcribed from the draft by Trevellyan), "We have organized a company of Militia in the city, composed of men of Hungarian, Bohemian & Slavonic origin. Being the first company formed in the United States of said nationalities we respectfully ask leave of your Excellency to entitle ourselves 'Lincoln Riflemen' of Slavonic Origin. If you will kindly sanction our use of your name, we will endeavour to do honour to it, whenever we may be called to perform active service. Respectfully on behalf of the Company, Geza Mihalotzy, Capt."

Under it stood, in Lincoln's hand, "I cheerfully grant the request above. A. Lincoln."

The phrase "whenever we may be called to perform active service" once more evoked fears of combat with the Indians. Honorary Colonel Ohrenzug, sitting beneath his own portrait at Slavik's Tavern that night, was aghast. "Men," he said, "when you join the army, you expect to fight. If I were younger, I'd lead you to the battlefront myself."

"But not against Indians," insisted the stubborn butcher.

"Why not?" Vasek Lusk chimed in. "If Bondy and Weiner could join John Brown fighting slave-drivers, why couldn't Colonel Ohrenzug—"

"But not against Indians!" exclaimed the cigar-maker, obviously obsessed with the fear of losing his scalp. Unlike the butcher, he still had a thick head of hair, which he had recently—perhaps preventively—trimmed short.

Colonel Ohrenzug was furious and threatened to cancel the order for the red trousers. If he weren't such an old man, he said, he would even go and fight the Eskimos, if need be.

"They're no danger," retorted the cigar-maker. "And besides, Hubatty already has cut the fabric for the trousers."

"Who cares?" said Colonel Ohrenzug. "So I sell them, maybe at a profit, to the Swedish zouaves. I hear they've organized a company too, in Decorah, Iowa."

"You can't do that," objected Padecky. "Zouaves wear Turkish trousers."

"They can be altered," retorted Colonel Ohrenzug.

"Then we'd take your picture down!" Kafka said with malice in his voice.

"Go right ahead," said the colonel. "Do I want my picture to hang over a bunch of cowards? I'd rather buy the synagogue a new Torah and get my picture hung there."

"Pictures aren't allowed in the synagogue!" said Kafka triumphantly.

The cigar-maker broke in: "I won't be insulted. I'm no coward!" He got up to leave.

"It's just that you've got a family," said Shake.

"So have I!" the butcher chimed in. "And I won't be insulted either!" He too got up, but not before quickly finishing his beer.

In the end, they managed to calm the two men down and Colonel Ohrenzug retracted his threat. They resolved that an addendum to the petition be sent to the governor, explicitly stating that the company must not be sent to fight Indians, and setting limits to the types of active service that the company could be called upon to perform. On the urging of the faction eager to do battle, led by Lusk and Salek, the more circumspect elements finally agreed to add that Lincoln's Slavonic Rifles would be willing to fight if the Southern slave-holders attacked Chicago, after Padecky reassured them once more that there wasn't going to be a war. They composed the addendum on the spot, and Shake offered to deliver it personally to the governor.

Later that night, he put a match to it.

★

The dismounted general barked an order, and the column spread out along the hills on both sides of the road. A scout appeared around a bend in the road and dashed to the head of the column to deliver his news to the staff. Several soldiers approached the wall of bushes on the edge of the woods, where Shake and Houska were lying observing the unfamiliar unit.

"Hey," Shake heard Houska whisper beside him, "isn't that Pepik Balda?"

The soldier nearest the bushes had a snub nose not unlike Houska's, and on his feet were boots of a decorative quilted leather that were obviously not government issue.

"Yes, it's him!" Houska said. "So this must be the Twenty-fifth Wisconsin!"

"Mower's division," said Shake. "So we made it through, then. We're on the extreme right wing."

"At least there won't be a lot happening here. Pepik!" Houska yelled, and crawled out of the bushes.

The soldier in the quilted boots first greeted Houska by aiming his musket at him, but then he recognized the tattered Union cap, and finally the moon-face of his countryman from Manitowoc.

Officers and sergeants fanned out from the general and ran to their units bellowing orders. In a few minutes, Shake, Houska, Zinkule in his tails, and Breta, along with the rest of the Twenty-fifth Wisconsin, were attacking the wretched grey line of defence at the bend in the road. Their company led the attack and lost only seven men. The soldier with the non-regulation boots was among the casualties.

★

They continued to drill while Hubatty sewed the trousers. Then a message came from the governor instructing the company to pick up their weapons, and the following day bayonets flashed on the meadow behind Slavik's Tavern as four-man ranks of Lincoln's Slavonic Rifles strutted before the women more smartly than ever before. Following Captain Mihalotzy's orders, they carried out complex manoeuvres in perfect unison, as if they were a group of Prussian professionals training for an imperial review, not an amateur volunteer militia.

In the first rank, the cigar-maker Kabrna had a determined look on his face, and his legs swung back and forth in the one pair of red trousers Hubatty had brought as a sample. He glowed like a cherry in the presence of the largest gathering of applauding women to date, one that included his own seven-member family. The men were still drilling tirelessly at sundown, when the metallic glint of bayonets looked particularly menacing and the red trousers glowed brightly in the dusk. During the post-drill drinking party, another twenty-seven men joined the ranks of Lincoln's Slavonic Rifles. Even before they could be properly registered and the gratified Colonel Ohrenzug could order more trousers, something happened that would alter the face and the fate of the Slavonic company.

The governor had provided two cartridges with each of the old Mexican muzzle-loaders, so at the next training session Captain Mihalotzy demonstrated the proper way to load a musket. After a break, they were to try some target practice with a life-size figure. The captain drew the outline of a man in chalk on the back of an old sign donated by Salek-Cup, nailed a brace on the back, and stood it up in the corner of the exercise grounds in front of Slavik's wooden storage shed. Mihalotzy had drawn a pair of trousers and a jacket with two rows of buttons on the figure, and he had added a heart on the left side of its chest. When he called a break, some of the men hurried to the tavern, and the rest went to talk to the women. The only exception was Vasek Lusk, who went over to the figure and began going at it with his bayonet. From the dreamy expression on his face, it was easy to tell that in his imagination he was far from the meadow behind Slavik's Tavern, on a battlefield in the middle of some bloody hand-to-hand encounter. It was almost dark, which helped to reinforce his fantasy.

Captain Mihalotzy was chatting with the ladies, twirling his waxed moustache around his finger as if he were in the lounge bar at the opera in Pest. Something had to happen because, on battlefields, shots are fired.

"Did Lusk fire a shot?" asked Houska.

"What else?" said Shake. "Not only that, his aim was excellent, though as a matter of fact he didn't take aim. He hit the figure not in the heart but in the right knee, and when he did there was a shriek of pain."

"The shot ricocheted?" said Stejskal.

"No, it went through the sign. The trouble was, Padecky had gone behind it to take a leak, because there was a lineup for the toilet."

"Did you wear the red trousers at the funeral?" Fisher asked.

"Padecky wasn't killed," said Shake. "But he was still out of commission when we were unexpectedly called up not long afterwards. The ball had hit his left knee and it was still in plaster. Fortunately they didn't have to amputate, but even when he got better his leg was as stiff as a stump and he limped. And Vasek Lusk didn't go to war with us either, for all he had soldiering in his blood."

"Why not?" asked Stejskal. "That sort of thing can happen to anybody. I had a rifle go off in my hand three times, and once I shot Captain Lidwell's cigar to bits as he was about to stick it in his mouth, and his beard caught fire from the burning tobacco."

"What did he give you?" asked Houska, intrigued.

"I had to walk around the camp for three days with a sign that said, I ALMOST SHOT CAPTAIN LIDWELL. The sign was in two sections, like a sandwich board, but some wag got hold of it at night and added, TOO BAD YOUR AIM AIN'T BETTER! to the back half and I never noticed, not even when so many of my buddies started ribbing me. Usually it's just a few jackasses who laugh. Finally Colonel Brummel stopped me and he wouldn't believe I didn't know about it, so he stuck me in a disciplinary squad for a week and I had to work on the palisades with three deserters who'd been condemned to death and then pardoned by Lincoln."

"What happened to Lusk?" asked Zinkule.

"Nothing. He ran away and disappeared," said Shake. "He probably withered away from shame."

★

The bridge was already in full sight, and the rain had started to come down harder again. For two hours now they had been marching double-time and running, and they'd been through several skirmishes. They kept encountering groups of armed men trying to link up with larger units to create a continuous line of defence. One wandering squadron of Wheeler's cavalry managed to slow them down, but they wiped it out of the way. General Mower was still marching in the ranks of the company heading his division. They forded a marsh, crossed a rise, and there was the bridge. Ambulances were slowly trundling across it, and sparsely placed riflemen lay in hurriedly dug pits along the banks of the creek, defending the gateway to safety. As soon as the first blue line appeared over the rise, they opened fire.

The order came to retreat. Behind a cluster of rocks, Shake said to Houska, "Is this enough for you? Or, as a man who wants to return home a hero, do you have higher standards?"

"Always the joker. Just wait, some day you'll be laughing on the other side of your face," said Houska, rolling over on his back. "Something's going on in the rear," he said.

Shake turned to see an officer gallop across the meadows among the soldiers, and stop in front of Mower's staff. Shake glanced at the sky. The clouds were breaking up. He saw Mower making authoritative gestures, then saw orderlies scatter in all directions. The lieutenant commanding the company they had joined hollered, "Fall back!"

"What for?" snapped Houska.

"A soldier doesn't question, a soldier obeys!" said Shake, rising.

They soon found out why. Strong squads of Rebel cavalry had attacked the division's left flank from the front and Mower was concentrating all his forces against them.

They were running towards a few isolated trees where they were to take up defensive positions when they caught sight of the Rebel cavalry, a cluster of wild riders galloping up to the trees, their reins in their teeth, beards flying in the wind. Each rider had a heavy navy pistol in each hand and was blazing away. The squad scattered. Shake ducked to the right of the lead rider, and as he did so he glimpsed Houska diving into the grass, Zinkule's tails fluttering, and Breta on one knee, firing at the second wave of riders. One of them veered to the left and cut off Shake's retreat to the hedge the rattle of gunfire was coming from. Shake hesitated; the rider swung his horse around and started towards him. Shake, his rifle slung over his back, sprinted towards a grove of pine trees and clambered up one of them. The rider didn't waste a shot on him, but just rode around the grove to join the next wave of attack. From his perch in the pine tree, Shake saw Hardee's wild warriors gathering for a fresh assault. He heard gunfire and the boom of cannon around him, all the way to the north. Suddenly the clouds parted, the sun came out, and a rainbow formed over the heads of the wild riders. Shake looked around. He could see several dead men on the grass between the grove and the hedge, and a horse lying on its side. The rider placed a navy pistol to the horse's head and fired; the horse jerked and went limp and the rider dropped behind it for shelter.

In an irregular line of running soldiers, Houska and Breta arrived at the hedge just ahead of Zinkule. Shake remembered his rifle and took it off his shoulder. The cavalryman behind the horse had his back to him, a good target. Shake took aim and pulled the trigger. The recoil knocked him out of the tree.

The man behind the dead horse jerked and went stiff. Hardee's riders were just launching a new attack through the grove, and Shake fell right on top of them.

★

"The catastrophe came the day after Vasek Lusk put Padecky out of action. In the morning Hubatty delivered fifty-one pairs of red trousers, but there was no drill

that afternoon. The tavern was packed but the trousers lay neatly folded in a pile in the corner and everyone ignored them. Why? Because Padecky wasn't there to reassure us that the situation wouldn't lead to war."

"You mean it was after the South fired on Fort Sumter?" asked Paidr.

Shake nodded. "Three days later, on April 15, Lincoln issued an appeal for seventy-five thousand three-month volunteers, and the day after, April 16, Lincoln's Slavonic Rifles were issued ammunition, twenty-eight cartridges in all, and we marched off to the field of honour and glory."

"Twenty-eight cartridges for the whole company?" Stejskal asked. "The army wasn't that short of ammunition back then. That's less than one cartridge per man."

"Not for Lincoln's Slavonic Rifles it wasn't," said Shake. "Only fourteen of us marched onto the field of honour, and two were Hungarian, one was a Czechified German, and one a Jew. All the rest decided to forgo the glory. They had families, livelihoods, rheumatism, or the red trousers were either too loose or too tight. Geza Mihalotzy almost became the first casualty of the war, because when only twelve of us, plus Tonda Kovacz, showed up at the tavern on the thirteenth he practically had a fit. It was Schroeder who finally saved him, except—"

The absent soldiers sent their daughters and wives to the tavern, some with verbal messages, some with written resignations. Mihalotzy was outraged and later he personally made the rounds of the Czech community till long after midnight. In some places they came to the door when he knocked, in others the men were terribly ill and in bed. Some gave an excuse that was so lame that he said later he'd "punched them in the mouth". Next morning, Schroeder found him at Dr. Walenta's, covered with blood (not his own) and sodden with booze. "The excuse," said Shake, "was so feeble that only the Czechs could have come up with it. No other nationality I know of has that kind of logic."

The suckling pig broke the spit it was on. They jumped up and rescued the meat from the fire with sticks, and forgot to ask about the excuse that could only have occurred to a Czech. Years later, Kapsa would find out anyway, but not from the lips of Jan Amos Shake, who by then had vanished into the Czech anthill of the Windy City, not to be seen by the sergeant until a quarter of a century later, in Milwaukee. No, the sergeant heard about it from the lovely wife of the Austrian consul in Chicago, a woman he had once known and had long presumed dead.

"Schroeder had a newspaper with Lincoln's appeal in it," said Shake, as pieces of the suckling pig, lightly powdered with ash, rapidly vanished into the ironclad stomachs of the Twenty-sixth Wisconsin. "He waved it in Mihalotzy's face and exclaimed joyfully, in German, of course, 'Don't worry about it, cap-

tain, sir'—he was a soldier in spirit already—'if you don't insist on having Czechs—and you can't any more because where will you find Czechs to replace the deserters?—I'll fill your ranks quicker than you can wink!' And so," Shake said sadly, "before long a full company of Lincoln's Slavonic Rifles was marching off to war, but they weren't Slavonic any more, just Lincoln's. The Slavs were in the minority. There were only twelve of us, and sixty-eight Germans."

"At least you had the red trousers," said Paidr.

"Unfortunately, we didn't," said Shake. "The Germans wouldn't wear them. Schroeder arranged for the issue of brand-new blue field uniforms, so we marched into combat wearing what any ordinary Union Army infantry regiment would wear."

"What didn't the Germans like about the red trousers?" growled Houska.

"They were all seasoned veterans. They said they weren't going to risk their necks just to be dressed up fancy."

"At least you had your armour," said Paidr.

"At least I had my armour," Shake conceded. "Colonel Ohrenzug palmed off the red trousers on a company of Italian volunteers. Most of them lost a leg, or both legs. The trousers turned out to be a perfect target."

★

The sergeant arrived in Milwaukee by the noon train, and was annoyed that Terezka wasn't at the station to meet him. But her husband, Premysl, was there, and in the carriage on the way to the Schroeders' residence he apologized for the inconsiderateness of the sergeant's beloved daughter, who had never disappointed her father like that before. When the carriage drew up in front of the big house with the carved balustrade over the entrance he still felt peeved, but his irritation vanished in the foyer when Terezka welcomed him with the usual embrace and kiss and he saw his granddaughter, Heidemarie, standing on a stool in front of a mirror while Identity, the black maid, tied red bows embroidered with doves into her blonde braids. The child wore a folk costume and, although the sergeant didn't know much about folklore, he thought it might be the kind he'd seen his mother wear to church in Eastern Bohemia, except for the green dirndl with the beautiful alpine chamois embroidered on the back.

"Oh, Daddy!" sighed his daughter in a mixture of American Czech and English, "I'm a nervous wreck! Will Heidi look pretty on the stage, do you think?"

The little girl's grey eyes gazed at her grandfather. The eyes, the dirndl, and the blonde hair evoked in him a vivid memory of a long-forgotten alpine valley, with brief, beautiful sunsets among tall, snow-covered peaks.

"*She will indeed,*" *he said quickly.* "*But what she'll look like in this get-up is another question.*"

The child was wearing riding boots, the kind Kilpatrick had worn many long years before—a little smaller, but also with spurs.

From his daughter's somewhat confused and nervous chatter, the sergeant gathered that a group of Czech itinerant players were in Milwaukee for a Sunday matinée. They were going to put on the hit play of the Prague season, Our Braggarts, and they had recruited a group of local Czech kids to appear in the tavern brawl scene as the progeny of a dishonest tailor.

"*Aren't they supposed to be poor children?*" the sergeant asked his daughter.

"*Oh, I know that,*" said Terezka, "*but Daddy, surely you don't want Heidemarie to be on stage looking like some beggar's brat!*"

Heidemarie looked like the brat of a rich farmer. That didn't trouble the sergeant, but the dirndl did. It seemed too far removed from how people dressed in a Czech village.

"*Well,*" said Terezka, "*I wasn't sure about the dirndl either, but it was a birthday present embroidered by her great-aunt in the Tyrol, and Grandpa Schroeder won't hear of her going on stage without it.*"

The man she spoke of strode into the room. He was no longer the slim surveyor who had walked into the Kakuska cabin with bad news all those years ago, and no longer the vigorous corporal who not long afterwards had fought mit Haecker, and then mit Sigel, and finally mit Grant. Now he was partner in a brewery and a prime consumer of his own brand of beer, called Milwaukee Bock. Milwaukee Bock was very nutritious.

He gave his granddaughter an admiring look and asked Kapsa in German, "Nu, how does she look?"

"*She looks—interesting,*" said the sergeant. The little boots didn't fit the Czech costume. But somehow he didn't mind. He looked at the girl, and suddenly he didn't mind the dirndl either. When all was said and done, the child was one-quarter German and—

The stout grandfather lifted the cherubic little girl with his meaty hands, rested her on his forearm, and gazed at her fondly. "Du mein Roeslein," he said, "My little rosebud," "du siehst wie eine kleine Prinzessin aus"—"you look like a little princess."

"*Grandpa,*" squealed Heidemarie in English, "*you stink like a beer barrel!*"

"*What!*" chuckled the old man.

"*That's what Mom says. Like a beer barrel!*"

The sergeant sighed, but then he smiled. When all was said and done, the child was an American.

·   ·   ·

The old German, who was also a veteran of the rebellion of forty-eight, had loved his wife, Molly, née Kakuska, and when she died before she turned thirty-five it seemed for a while that he would soon follow her. But it's hard to drink yourself to death with beer, and Schroeder only managed to get immensely fat. Time, the great physician, finally healed his wound, and he transferred his devotion to his son, Premysl, who, despite his legendary Czech name, was going to be German if his dad had anything to say about it. He succeeded only in part. When Molly died, her son spoke broken German, fairly good Czech, and excellent English. Having inherited a penchant for Czech girls from his father, he courted the sergeant's daughter in American Czech and eventually married her. The mulish grandfather did succeed in getting them to christen their first-born daughter Heidemarie, to compensate for her father's Czech name. But while the little girl knew fragments of her mother's native tongue, the only German she picked up was a few expressions that her grandpa strictly forbade her to use.

★

According to the script of the play, poor tailor Fiala had seven children. But because the Czechs of Milwaukee were breeding profusely and the proprietor of the itinerant theatre company didn't dare alienate his potential audience, Fiala brought eighteen youngsters onstage in the first act. And while the play called for the tailor's progeny to appear only in Act One, the mothers and fathers didn't feel that was enough, so the director included the children in the tavern scene in Act Two, although only seventeen appeared; one little fellow had been so nervous before the second act that he'd wet his pants. None of this mattered; the play's realism had already been sabotaged when the children described in the script as "hungry babes of the poor tradesman" had appeared looking more like pages and little ladies-in-waiting at the coronation of the Queen of England. One lad was even dressed in a faithful replica of the Union Army uniform that Kapsa had worn years earlier.

To prevent the children from getting in the way during the dramatic tavern scene—which took place in what looked like a Wild West saloon—the director seated them along the bar, and the actor playing Ehrmann, the Jewish tavernkeeper, kept pouring them ginger beer. Thanks to the anti-Semitic imagination of the play's author, Ehrmann wore a red wig and a nose enlarged with some kind of putty, and this caricature was enhanced by the requisite gestures and posture: the wringing of hands, the ingratiating stoop, the slavering mouth. The actor playing him did it all with bravura artlessness. But the sergeant noticed that he was pouring—or rather sprinkling—something from a pocket flask into the children's glasses of ginger beer, something too golden to be lemonade. When he set it on the bar, the sergeant saw that the label on the flask read "Black Crow Whiskey".

At that moment, behind the exaggerated gestures, the false nose, and the red wig, the sergeant recognized an old friend.

"Me? No! What woman would want me, when I don't want a woman?" said his old friend Shake, minus the false nose and with a head as bald as if he'd used Fircut's potion on it. The Black Crow sat on the bench between them and they could smell in the air the pleasant aroma of the final decade of the century: coal smoke from the Milwaukee railroad station. "Married? No," said Shake, "I'm a classic example of a man with a broken heart and a guilty conscience."

"Whose heart did you break and why did you jilt her?" asked Kapsa. "You never admitted to anything like that during the war."

"During the war I was young and taciturn," said the veteran. "Now I'm a garrulous old man. I feel the pangs of guilt not because I deflowered a virgin— although Rebecca was a virgin to end all virgins—but because her biblical beauty made me renounce my biblical calling."

"So they were right? All those rumours about you being a defrocked priest?"

"Rumours? I don't know about rumours. Paidr spread the word among the Czechs, and not only in the Twenty-sixth Wisconsin. He also wrote to Bublina, the bugler with the Sixteenth, and Bublina blew my history all over the place, until even K Company of the Twenty-second Iowa heard about it, and they were all Czechs, right down to the fourteen-year-old drummer boy, Honzik Sala. Wait a minute. . . ." Shake rubbed his high forehead. "He was actually with D Company, and he couldn't have spread the word there because he was the only Czech in the company. But after demobilization the others saw to it, unless of course they'd laid down their lives for the liberation of the slaves. So I was the most infamous ex-theology student in the whole Middle West of Bohemia. As a result, I got invited to Sunday dinner by every free-thinker with a marriageable daughter. Former seminarians have a reputation of being good and mainly hard-working husbands. The trouble was, the only girls who appealed to me were from Catholic families. Maybe they really were prettier, or maybe it was my bad conscience at work. Those were the houses I never got invited to."

Shake sighed, and it seemed to the sergeant that his old friend was being serious for the first time since they had met,

"You know, sarge," said Shake after a while, "I ran away from the only profession I would have been good at—if it hadn't been for Rebecca. I would have been ideal. I was by far the best preacher in the seminary. Monsignor Kotrly, who taught us rhetoric, used to say that I was going to be a second Savonarola—and *when he'd had a few too many, a second Master Jan Hus, and he only hoped I wouldn't let the Church down like that damned heretic did, gifted by God though he was. And I did, neighbour. On account of a girl—what's worse, one from the nation that has the Lord Jesus on its conscience. And I let down Monsignor Kotrly. He was such a good preacher that when he was preaching on a Sunday afternoon in the Church of the Templars, the nearby theatre was empty. He used to take the afternoon sermon deliberately, because he was a sworn enemy of the lascivious Muses. When he served Holy Communion, more wafers were consumed than during anyone else's service."*

Shake fell silent while the trains, puffing smoke, came and went.

The sergeant said, "He must have been a good teacher, too."

"The best. Still, I was weighed and found wanting. But with Rebecca—it was all so biblical. Even though, according to the Bible—"

★

Dusk was falling. The seminarian in the black robe—slender, good-looking, androgynous—strode the cobblestones of the town square, formulating an exemplum about Rebecca, the obedient one, Isaac's happy wife, when suddenly she appeared to him. At first he felt that he was being blessed with a holy vision, that he had been chosen—the square with a stone fountain in the middle of it, a damsel with a pitcher on her shoulder, walking towards the fountain, and she was indeed very fair to look upon, a virgin, neither had any man known her, and she went down to the well, and filled her pitcher and came up.

The seminarian, however, was unlike Isaac's servant. According to the Scriptures the servant was moved by the girl's beauty but, true to his master and his mission, only ran to meet her. The seminarian, on the other hand, was not simply moved by her beauty, he was infatuated with it, with the inexplicable osmosis of feeling touched off by Cupid's arrow. In his black robes he ran to meet her and he said, "Let me, I pray thee, drink a little water from thy pitcher."

The girl stopped, thought a moment, and then said in German, "You can speak German if it comes easier to you."

And the holy vision suddenly became a sturdy Jewish girl. The seminarian looked her over hungrily and the words that came to his mind—though unsuitable for a seminarian—were equally biblical: how fair and how pleasant art thou.

"Why German?" he asked, stunned.

"Because your Czech is so odd."

"I beg your pardon." He swallowed. "Allow me to introduce myself: Jan Amos Schweik." Cupid's arrow had dried his throat and he sounded hoarse.

"Would you like a drink of water, Father? Here!" And she handed him her pitcher.

Embarrassed, he tipped it up and drank, spilling water over his robe.

"God bless you," he said.

"I'm glad to be of help," said the girl.

They were facing each other, both ill at ease—the seminarian in black, the girl in a grey skirt and a grey blouse of rough linen. Under it, like two young roes that are twins—

"I'm not ordained yet," he said. "I'm only in my third year."

She looked puzzled.

"That means I'm not a priest yet."

"Oh, you'll get there," she said, and just then he had a different vision. He tried to drive it away but he couldn't.

"I—" the girl said reluctantly, "I'm Rebecca Goldstein. My father is the cantor at the Old-New Synagogue."

"May I—walk with you?" Then, firmly, "Here, I'll help you with your pitcher."

"I can't," she said.

"Why not?"

"People will see us," she whispered.

He looked around, glanced down at his robe. She was right. "So come to the park around the corner," he said softly. "There are benches there in the bushes, so you can't be seen in the dark."

"That's not possible."

"It is," he said. "No one will see us."

"You're a priest."

"No, I'm not."

"Well, almost."

At that moment he understood the story of Faust, which he had always found hard to believe. Faust had traded eternity for wisdom. He would have traded it too, though not just for wisdom.

He cleared his throat. "Please don't think ill of me, Miss Rebecca. I only—" He realized how awkward it sounded, but he couldn't think of anything more intelligent. "I just wanted to talk to you."

"I can't." She looked around nervously. "I don't know." Then she said, "If you were a rabbi—"

"Come!"

"I have to go home." She picked up the pitcher and put it on her shoulder, turned, and set out resolutely towards the lights of the houses down the street that looked like Mephisto winking at him.

"Come! I'll wait for you there!" he called to her softly.

It was the time of May masses and he could get out in the evening. He skipped mass, but she didn't show up.

A few days later, though, when he managed to slip away from the seminary again, there she was, drawing water at the well.

"Come with me!"

"I don't know."

"What if I were a rabbi?"

She didn't answer. For quite a while. Then she said, "I won't meet you there because people can see. I went to look. People can see from both sides."

He became Faust; the agreement was signed and sealed. He went to see an old schoolmate, a prosperous farmer's son who owned a bachelor's apartment on the Lesser Town Square.

"I need to borrow—" He hesitated.

"Well, well!" smiled his schoolmate. "They even gamble in the seminary, do they? Of course, Reverend Father, for you I'll do anything. How much do you need? A hundred? Two hundred? Any more than that will be a problem. Lady Luck hasn't been very good to me either these days."

"No. I need to borrow your apartment. Just for an hour or two—"

His buddy gave a whistle. "Well, what do you know!" But he gave him the key. "I'm going away tomorrow for a week. The place is yours. It's right around the corner from the Church of St. Kliment. Confession there, as I recall, is from five to seven."

Rebecca also sold her soul. And they were one.

He left the seminary. Monsignor Kotrly wept. "Oh, lad, you've disappointed me! Really disappointed me."

"But Reverend Father, it's just that I—I—"

"I know, I know." The monsignor wiped away a tear with a fleshy thumb. "You're not the first, and you won't be the last. But you've still disappointed me. Well, what's to be done? Go with God. But remember, even as a layman you're still a Catholic, and that binds you."

He kissed the old priest's hand. "I swear to you, by the Mother of God—"

"Better not swear. Pray. Like every seminarian, you've surely read Saint Paul. As long as you don't end up burning in hell, Amos, my lad!"

He didn't burn in hell, but he didn't follow Saint Paul's advice to marry either—nor could he have, because in the end Rebecca did what her biblical namesake did.

Cantor Goldstein was a stone wall. It wasn't because the former seminarian was now working as a clerk in a textile warehouse, and a Jewish-owned one at that—a job his classmate the rich farmer's son had obtained for him through friends. Even the fact that he had quit the seminary might not have mattered if—but Papa Goldstein was a stone wall. Rebecca was an only child. There was no one else. And like the vision in the first Book of Moses, she was an obedient daughter. Sinful, but obedient. The loss of her virginity was a secret she carried with her into her marriage with Isaac Karpeles, a shy, decent, and equally obedient young partner in the ironmongers' firm of Abraham Karpeles und Sohn in Olomouc. The secret remained a secret.

"You're not of our faith, young man."

"I could—" Schweik, the Gentile, tried to say, but he turned red when he looked into the deep-set eyes of the righteous old man. He couldn't even say the words to the old man's face. So the pact with Mephisto was never ratified. And that was that. He left for America.

"Oh yes, Rebecca has children. Six of them," said Shake, "each one prettier than the last. They all have her eyes."

"How do you know?" asked the sergeant.

"Well, I was there, you know. After the war."

It wasn't difficult to find Karpeles's shop in Olomouc. Besides, Rebecca had just leaned out of a third-storey window. Either she hadn't changed, or he was being revisited by the vision from the stone fountain on the square.

She opened the door and saw a man whipped by the wild winds of war who removed his foreign-looking hat and said, "It's me, Rebi. Remember?"

She was still sturdy but she almost fainted.

She too was a sinner—not in deeds any more, only in words—for she introduced Shake to Isaac Karpeles as the cousin of the husband of her distant cousin Rachel, the one whose marriage had caused such a stir. Isaac couldn't recall any stir or any distant cousin, but even at forty he was a gullible nebbish. He invited Shake to stay for supper.

There he saw Rebecca's four sons and twin black-eyed daughters. When Isaac said the prayers, Shake almost forgot himself and made the sign of the cross; then he folded his hands on the table in front of him.

Isaac even suggested he stay the night. The house was roomy, with a small guest chamber upstairs, but that was impossible. The pact might not have been ratified but he still felt desire for her. The vision remained. It was there at the table with the flickering candles, with the children smacking their lips over the gefilte fish. A vision come to life. He suddenly wished for it to remain with him, just as it was, for ever. He thanked them for the offer, told them he was staying with friends in Olomouc, then returned to the inn and carried the vision back to America.

Just the vision. Not so much as a photograph of her and her six children.

"Is that why you never married?" asked the sergeant. "After all, it's water under the bridge."

"Old love never fades," said Shake. "Besides, I still have a bad conscience. On account of the Holy Church, but mainly because of Monsignor Kotrly, may he rest in peace."

"You never took your vows. And anyway, why didn't you study for the priesthood in America? A confession would have put things right."

"It was too late. I should have gone back to the seminary in Prague when the thing with Rebecca was over. It would have delivered me from temptation."

"Hardly," said the sergeant. "You aren't the deliverable kind."

"I don't mean Rebecca, or women in general. I mean the American war."

"How was the war a temptation?"

"It shook my faith," said Shake. "After I was discharged, I could never have become a priest any more."

Train whistles hooted. A young Negro couple walked by arm in arm. By their fruits ye shall know them, the sergeant thought to himself. He said, "You may still change your mind. I agree with Monsignor Kotrly, you'd be good in the pulpit. Sure, your beliefs were shaken by what you saw, but you could still bring others to the faith."

A week later, in Iowa City, Shake was run over by a train.

★

"No," said the general. "My order is: withdraw to your initial positions. And that is an order, captain; that applies to General Mower as well."

The sun filled the glade with yellow-green light, and shone through the smoke of the battlefield till it seemed to be pouring molten gold on it. Rain was still falling in some places and a rainbow arched across the countryside.

"Yes sir!" said the captain. "Of course, the bridge has really been—"

"I said that's an order!" the general interrupted. "Now, ride!"

"Yes, sir!" The captain strode over to the horse on the edge of the clearing, jumped into the saddle, and disappeared in the woods.

The general turned to Captain Foster. "And Howard will stop Blair's corps. Mower will withdraw to his initial positions. He won't need help from Blair's two remaining divisions to do that."

The second courier rode off among the trees.

The general pulled a cigar out of his pocket and looked around. Logan stepped over to his commander and held what was left of his burning cigar butt to the general's. "All right, Billy," he said. "You're commander-in-chief. But why did you do it?"

The general raised his creased, weather-beaten face to the sky and the sun. "Hardee attacked from the flank and thrust at Mower's rear. If he'd managed to cut the division off, he might have destroyed it, the way Johnston tried to destroy Morgan."

"Yes, but Hardee could only have succeeded if Mower didn't retreat and didn't get reinforcements." Logan looked towards the sun too. It was going behind a cloud. "I don't understand you, Billy," he went on. "Let's say Hardee did have a chance to destroy Mower's division. But you had a chance to destroy Johnston's whole army. You know that. That single bridge was the only way out of a trap and Mower was just about to take it."

The general said nothing. He just stood there, his head enveloped in a dense cloud of cigar smoke.

"You could have won a great battle, Billy. You never won one like that before, and now you probably never will. This was your last chance."

"Precisely," said the general. "The thing is this, Johnny: we don't need to win battles any more. We're winning the war."

The sun emerged, molten gold, from behind the cloud and illuminated the puff of tobacco smoke, so it looked as if the general were standing with his head in a bluish lantern.

★

Looking over the hedge, Houska saw Shake jump from the crown of the pine tree, grab the Rebel rider around the neck, and pull him off his horse. After that, Houska had to turn his attention to the cavalry bearing down on Mower's line of riflemen, and it was only the concentrated fire, with Houska's generous contribution, that forced the riders to turn and, in a broad arc, disappear into the other side of the forest. A dead horse lay on the meadow in front of Houska, surrounded by fallen soldiers. Then he saw Shake again, running towards the hedge, stooped under the weight of a rider he was carrying on his back. He pushed through the hedge and Houska rose and went over to his buddy.

"Amos," he said to Shake, "you've got guts. Jumping on him out of the tree like that!"

"What?" said Shake. He was breathless. The wounded rider was not a small man.

"Jumping on him from up in that pine tree and pulling him off his horse!"

"Oh, that," said Shake.

The captain stepped over to them. "A prisoner?"

Shake dumped the wounded man onto the ground. The cavalryman swore fiercely. He turned out to be a major.

"Captain," said Houska, "Private Shake jump out of tree and pull him off horse to ground!" His moon-face radiated admiration, even if his English left something to be desired.

"What?" asked the captain.

Houska pointed to Shake. "He shoot. From top of tree. Then jump. Pull major off horse. Take prisoner."

The captain turned to Shake. "Is that true, private?"

"Well—" Shake cleared his throat. "Yes," he said, and then he added, "more or less."

A new assault by Hardee's cavalry interrupted them, and after that no one pursued the details of Shake's actions.

Each of them got a goose leg; the rest they cut up and shared, stuffing themselves to bursting. Now they were passing around a gallon of confiscated bourbon.

"If Shake were telling it," said Paidr, "I'd know it was a tall tale. But you, Vojta, you tell things straight, don't you?"

"Is that your way of saying I'm lying through my teeth?" snarled Houska. "I saw it with my own two eyes."

"You're going to have to get a pair of spectacles when you go home, my friend," said Paidr. "From what I saw"—he glanced at Shake—"the branch busted under you, right? And the major more or less broke your fall."

"I swear that you are more or less mistaken," said Shake, and took a swig of bourbon.

"Swearing falsely is a sin," said Paidr. "A fellow who goes to war in armour, and wears it backwards so he can urge the rest on with his back to the enemy, can't possibly be much of a hero."

"Well," said Shake, taking his meerschaum out of his knapsack and screwing it together, "as far as heroism goes, it's like Hegel says: everything turns into its opposite."

"Hegel who?" asked Stejskal.

"He's a—a wise man," said Shake, holding up his meerschaum for Paidr to light. "He saw God as something like a government official, and imagined heaven as a Prussian barracks."

"Look!" called Zinkule, who was still forced to keep his distance. He was pointing to the path below the hillside.

General Alfred Terry's Second Division was approaching. Unlike the Twenty-sixth Wisconsin, the soldiers had freshly issued blue uniforms. And they were black.

The sergeant and his buddies stared at them in silence. The vigorous young men marched as if on parade, their faces solemn. They looked nothing like the enlisted men sipping bourbon around the flickering campfire, nothing like Sherman's great army. Nor did they resemble the Negroes that the sergeant and his men had seen on the long march across America that was now coming to an end.

They stared without a word. When the last foursome had passed, the sergeant pulled a new bottle out of his knapsack and passed it around.

The war was over.

*The
Writer's
Fourth
Intermezzo*

MY FLAGGING SELF-CONFIDENCE was revived when I realized that the therapeutic power of my little novels had helped Maggie overcome the worst. I wondered initially if she had somehow discovered that Laura A. Lee was in fact her old friend Lorraine from Liberty, and if this—rather than anything inherently good in my writings—was why she devoured them. But Maggie assured me she had had no idea about my sinful intellectual life; it was the Roman bust in my parlour that made her put two and two together, though the bust had received only a passing mention in the novel *Heart of Marble*, when the poor but clever young Barbara received it as a gift from James Connington III, the handsome antique collector. Maggie always was good at noticing details.

Humphrey didn't think my literary efforts amounted to much, intellectually. Of course, he had nothing against my contributing to the family finances (in fact I made more than he did), but he would still make fun of my novels and declare he could write nonsense like that himself. Sometimes he would grow solemn and deliver a half-sermon, half-lecture on the noble role of literature, which was only worthy of the name, he would say, when it either held a mirror up to life and the world—and as he spoke he would pull volumes of Thackeray and Hawthorne out of his shelves and hold them up in both hands, like a Catholic priest raising the host—or responded to serious questions about the meaning of life and the world—at which point he would hold up Emerson and *Faust* by Johann Wolfgang von Goethe, which I had never finished (and thus didn't know whether Faust succeeded in duping the Devil or not), for I didn't care much for Faust or his sweetheart. The third category of acceptable literature Humphrey referred to in a condescending tone: "If women must write," he said, "then"—and he picked up *Uncle Tom's Cabin*—"for the less intellectually mature reader, they must enlighten him on matters worthy of his attention."

For a while I tolerated his pleasure in being didactic, but it annoyed me. Eventually I took him at his word and made him sit down and write a novel himself. The result was *Dawn on the Prairie*, a romance about a trapper's daughter and a professor of entomology. He wrote it under the pen-name of Lorraine Everett, and it was so awful that I had to threaten to take Laura Lee to another publisher before Mr. Little finally agreed to publish it, and then he was so upset he had to spend two weeks recuperating on Cape Cod, drinking heavily. Humphrey meanwhile strutted around like a peacock, and when he had finished the proofreading I visited Boston again and the publisher—who by now had returned from Cape Cod, unrefreshed and still upset—told me, with some reluctance, "Mrs. Tracy, your friend Miss Everett has dealt with the proofs of her book the way Balzac is said to have done. When we finally finished with the galleys and page proofs, we had been through what amounted to three different books. Could you please explain to your lady friend that changes this extensive are far too costly and that I will have to deduct at least fifty per cent of her advance to cover the corrections?"

"You can pay her the full amount," I declared, sounding like a literary prima donna, "and send the bill for the corrections to me."

"But that's something neither I nor Miss Everett can—"

"If it weren't for me," I interrupted him, "she never would have taken up the pen. She wrote it out of jealousy."

"All the more—"

I interrupted him again. "And you see, Mr. Little, I love her, do you understand?"

Mr. Little gave me a strange look and I hastened to add, "She's my maiden aunt. The book's appearance will be a gift for her sixty-fifth birthday."

"For heaven's sake," my publisher said, "why didn't you tell me straight out that this—this"—he faltered, trying to find a word to describe Humphrey's horror—"thing was the work of your aunt?"

"I didn't want you to see it as nepotism."

Mr. Little grew thoughtful. "That explains a lot, of course," he said. I preferred not to ask him what he meant.

Dawn on the Prairie was Little and Brown's greatest flop; they gave away more copies for review than they sold. Mr. Little asked me what magazine my aunt read and I told him it was Horton's *Girls' and Ladies' Weekly Visitor*, an obscure publication from Chicago. He knew what the critics' response to Lorraine Everett would be, and to make sure I'd stay with his firm he bought a superlative review in that journal. How he did it, I don't know. It was shortly after a series of scandals around paid book reviews, and editors were reluctant to print unalloyed praise even when it was sincere, for fear of being accused of taking bribes. Money can buy anything, though, if there is enough of it, and I think the review cost Mr. Little as much as Humphrey's proofs had. I also think he charged me for at least part of it, concealed in the amount that went for "corrections". What he didn't know was that the bribed editor would want to protect himself. The next issue of Horton's *Girls' and Ladies' Weekly Visitor* carried another review of *Dawn on the Prairie*, this time what is called a "devastating critique", which tore to shreds not only Mr. Little's paid advertisement, but also the novel itself.

Humphrey was shattered by the response. He was particularly upset by the unanimity of the reviewers, who concluded, with only varying degrees of contempt, that Lorraine Everett didn't know the difference between a novel and natural lyricism, and between lyricism and watered-down transcendentalism. One of them even came up with some statistics: a full six hundred and eighteen pages of the book's six hundred and seventy-eight pages consisted of descriptions of forests at various seasons of the year, and on four hundred and ninety-two of those six hundred and eighteen pages the lyrical evocations of nature were merely springboards for philosophizing on the principles of the universe. The story itself, according to the statistician, comprised a mere sixty pages, which was about right for the literary form the Germans call *die Novelle*, but certainly not what is implied in America by the term "novel".

But even this novella—Humphrey's clumsy attempt to tell a story of true love overcoming amusing obstacles—dealt with a serious question: the trapper's daughter and the professor of entomology, captured by Indians, discover that the noble savages (one of them makes a speech in which he sounds like Rousseau) are hiding an escaped slave. The Indians have taken the lovers captive solely to prevent them from revealing their black friend's where-abouts to the bounty-hunters. The professor allays their fears with a speech summarizing the main ideas in *Uncle Tom's Cabin.*

After that catastrophe, Humphrey stopped criticizing my lucrative liter-ary activity and I in turn kept silent about *Dawn on the Prairie,* since I truly loved my philosopher husband. To make up to Mr. Little for his mental an-guish and financial losses, I quickly wrote a novel called *The Pious Prevarica-tion of Liza Thompson.* It broke all my previous sales records and financed the building of Mr. Little's Provincetown mansion. Meanwhile, all memory of *Dawn on the Prairie* passed into merciful oblivion.

And yet how full of surprises life can be. If poor Humphrey had lived to my age, he might have started lecturing me about literature again. Today Laura A. Lee is forgotten, and not even professors of American literature know who she was. The last book she published was a quarter of a century ago, and that was an abbreviated edition of her first novel, reissued only be-cause Mr. Griffith had turned it into a successful motion picture in which, of course, the story was shrunk to a ten-minute farce and the text reduced to a single heavily edited title. And as for Humphrey—

The other day I had a visit from my great-granddaughter—or was it my great-great-granddaughter?—who brought me a brand-new edition of *Dawn on the Prairie,* which is now required reading in a seminar on nine-teenth-century American literature at her college. I could hardly believe my eyes. They had added seventy-five pages of notes and a thirty-seven-page in-troduction by a Harvard professor, which said, in essence, that if we set aside the predictable melodramatic plot and the cumbersome didactic passages the novel was an exceptionally fresh evocation of the virgin American wilderness, unlike anything left to us by any other American writer of the last century with the possible exception of James Fenimore Cooper, whose influence on the book was in any case obvious. I don't know if Humphrey was ever in the wilderness, but I doubt it. He was born in a brownstone house in Stuyvesant Park, New York, and spent his entire life, as unfortu-nately brief as it was, surrounded by books, even at our summer home in the Catskills. His "fresh evocation" was the result of a literary process similar to the one that produced my standard plots, those trips to the altar while over-coming amusing obstacles. My stories weren't grounded in reality either but, rather than imitating another writer, I drew them out of thin air. The difference is evidently an essential one, which may be why my grandchil-dren are now reading—or perhaps merely studying—Humphrey's sole ex-cursion into literary prose. There is no cause for dismay, however. Fashions change, and perhaps some day someone will notice that all my heroines are "smart" while all my heroes are merely "handsome", and will publish an annotated edition of *The Pious Prevarication of Liza Thompson* with an introduction showing that, like the unhappy Margaret Fuller, I too was an early proponent of women's rights.

I hope he will not conclude that this tame dichotomy is all I had left of Margaret's fighting spirit. But that will hardly happen. Literary criticism is, I sometimes feel, the art of seeing ghosts.

"I promise you the next novel I write will be true to life," I told Maggie. I was thinking of the story of Jasmine and her distant love, Hasdrubal. We said goodbye on the front porch. The sky over Cincinnati looked like a coloured Christmas illustration.

"Don't try it," said Maggie. "You said yourself that you're no Thackeray."

"I know that, but I'd like to be better than I am."

"You'll only manage to be worse." She tapped the pink spine of the book she held in her hand, my first author's copy of *Who Got the Best of Whom?*, containing a long and impassioned dedication I had penned into it for her. "Stick to what you do best."

"A person should aspire to higher goals," I said.

Maggie smiled wryly. "Perhaps. But in the final analysis it's not what you want in life that counts, it's what you accomplish."

She kissed me and climbed into the cab I had ordered. The driver snapped the reins, the horses started off, and I never saw her again. In Liberty they told me she had come back for her mother's funeral in the last year of the civil war, when she was a nurse in the field hospital with Meade's corps of Grant's army. After the war, they said, she moved to the South, but no one I knew had heard from her after that, so what she did with the rest of her life remains a mystery. But then, what she wanted in life remained a mystery too. Except for Ambrose. But that was just a wild, youthful infatuation—the kind that lasts a lifetime only in novels like Laura A. Lee's.

2

Because Ambrose was loyal but insensitive to the personal motivations that often lay behind deeds that appeared to be for the common good, he was frequently clumsy in his handling of politics.

His final fall—which was actually fortunate, for it was what made him leave Chicago politics, which he had never understood, for the battlefields of Corinth and Knoxville—apparently began with the Carrington affair. He had hesitantly asked me about Carrington at the outset of his stay in

Cincinnati, when he almost let slip what Halleck, Lincoln's commander-in-chief at the time, thought of that thoroughly bureaucratic general.

He didn't tell me what Halleck thought then, and I didn't find out until long after the war, in a dissertation written by my grandson Brendan. Brendan was possessed by an inexplicable interest in the Civil War in general, and in dear Ambrose in particular, although I had never told my own children, let alone my grandchildren, about that painful week in Liberty so long ago.

Halleck's assessment of Carrington was a good one: he thought Carrington was only playing soldier, and that might be why he could hear grass grow a bit more than it actually did. But heaven knows—it isn't clear from Brendan's dissertation, or from my memories. "The extent and plans of treasonable societies are not realized," Carrington wrote Ambrose. "Even men dare not speak loyalty for fear of fire and murder in some counties." The correspondence lacked details about specific instances of arson and murder so motivated, and Ambrose was at a loss about what to do—whereupon Halleck wrote to him to express misgivings about Carrington's judgement, and his conclusion was more than clear to the hesitant Ambrose. "General Carrington has never been tried in the field," Halleck wrote. "Perhaps he may do better there." Ambrose may not have even read the letter through to the end—if he didn't, it was unfortunate—but he went straight to work. He removed Carrington as commander of the District of Indiana and replaced him with Milo Hascall. Although it soon became apparent that Halleck's reservations about Carrington's abilities applied equally to his replacement, in one respect Hascall differed profoundly from his predecessor: he virtually stank of gunpowder. He was a veteran of Shiloh and Stony River, where he had commanded an army corps. What Halleck had only feared that Carrington would do, Hascall made a reality. He didn't worry about the probability of complicated conspiracies, but took preventive steps against them. Soon Halleck had occasion to resume his correspondence with Ambrose.

Unfortunately, the next letter was not as specific as the previous one. Halleck simply reflected on "the difficulty of finding district commanders with enough common sense to avoid conflicts with civilian authorities." Hascall's name was never mentioned in the letter. His actions can hardly have seemed those of a man lacking common sense, from Ambrose's point of view, given his antipathy to anything remotely treasonous.

I said it was unfortunate if Ambrose didn't read the first letter through to the end. The statement that General Carrington had never undergone trial by fire was followed by a subtle insinuation: "He owes his promotion entirely to political influence."

Of course, he must have read the letter to the end, and he must have known that in this context "political influence" meant Governor Ollie Morton. Before Carrington's appointment as district commander, he had been the governor's choice to advise him on matters of sedition in Indiana. But Morton had once made a hat for Ambrose with his own two hands, whereas Carrington was a mere adviser. Ambrose's call for resolute action against the Copperheads was in keeping with Morton's opinions, of course, and so Ambrose knew that, Carrington notwithstanding, he was acting in the spirit of Morton's intentions when he issued General Order Number thirty-eight, putting Vallandigham out of action.

Hascall also acted in the spirit of those intentions, but by then, unfortunately, Morton's intentions had begun to change. Ollie Morton was a politician, and he weighed matters on the basis of how the voter would respond, not on consistency of principles. And his fingers were long enough to reach Washington.

He might have overlooked the fact that Ambrose hadn't consulted him before removing Carrington, his protégé, but he soon discovered that Hascall was creating bedlam in his election district by infuriating not only the Peace Democrats—Ollie couldn't have cared less for them—but also those committed to the war. As a result, Ollie's radical opinions quickly began to flag and he demanded that his main connection in Washington, Secretary of War Stanton, order Ambrose to replace Hascall. Stanton seemed in no hurry to comply.

Then, on May 28, Hascall arrested and detained the influential Senator Douglas. Ollie appealed again to Stanton, and sent a personal courier to Ambrose with a dispatch whose contents can only be deduced from the telegram Ambrose sent to Lincoln immediately afterwards, which Brendan quotes in full in his dissertation. It implies that, although several days earlier Lincoln had approved Ambrose's actions, including General Order Number Thirty-eight, Ambrose had just learned from Ollie that not a single member of the president's cabinet had agreed with Lincoln on that point. From Morton's dispatch, Ambrose deduced that his action must have been an embarrassment to the president, and he reacted in his own way: "My views as to the proper policy to be pursued in this department are only changed," he wired Lincoln, "in the belief that the present policy should be increased in rigor. You know my views upon the subject of command and you must not allow me to stand in the way of the carrying out of any general policy which you may choose to adopt. . . ." And then he offered his resignation.

That was no help to Lincoln in his dilemma. At a time of military defeats, gathering political storms, and the approaching presidential elections, he was besieged by worries from all sides. Besides, he was fond of Ambrose. What man who didn't hold unyielding grudges wouldn't have been fond of him? So Lincoln's Pythian response to Ambrose's telegram read, "When I shall wish to supersede you, I will let you know." Lincoln went on to say that the entire cabinet regretted the necessity for Vallandigham's arrest but that, now that the affair was ended, "all are for seeing you through with it."

Could Ambrose have interpreted these words as anything but approval of his actions? And Ollie's dispatch? Unyielding himself, Ambrose interpreted it in his own way. After all, Ollie was a friend from Liberty. It may never have occurred to Ambrose that political life had taught his old friend flexibility.

Life had indeed taught the governor flexibility. Ollie wrote to Lincoln again—because the situation in Chicago was intensifying—questioning the wisdom of General Order Number Thirty-eight, which he had earlier agreed to. His view now was that it increased Democratic opposition to the war. Expressing his sudden disaffection with General Hascall's radicalism, Ollie said that military commanders were in fact unnecessary in the Department of the Ohio. Given Washington's support, the governors themselves could find ways to solve the problems that Hascall was dealing with so ham-handedly.

Lincoln met with Stanton to discuss Morton's letter, then instructed Stanton to explain to Ambrose that, with his lack of diplomatic tact, Hascall was upsetting public opinion, which was upset enough already. Ambrose was to avoid anything that might jeopardize the position of officials loyal to Washington, like Governor Morton. Lincoln's message ended with another oblique bit of counsel: the president did not expect General Burnside "to be able, under any circumstances, to satisfy everyone". The most he expected was that unnecessary irritation be avoided.

Stanton passed these instructions to Ambrose on June 1, not by telegram but by letter. Meanwhile Ambrose, still believing that Lincoln expected him to continue as before, issued General Order Number Eighty-four, and closed down the Chicago *Times* for running a disparaging article about the president.

3

Unlike Ambrose, I am inclined to expect the worst rather than the best from people, and to suspect their motives. I had to ask myself, therefore, why a politician as experienced as Stanton would send instructions to Ambrose by letter rather than by telegraph, when everyone in Washington was enamoured of that new and useful toy.

If Stanton had put his advice into Morse code, the *Times* wouldn't have been banned, and many people—including Lincoln, but mainly Ambrose—would have been spared considerable humiliation. Could Stanton have made such an incredible gaffe because he didn't know what to do himself, thus leaving the decision, as it were, to technological Providence?

The fact that a few days later Stanton did send a telegram gives credence to my assessment.

So does the fact that he sent it to the wrong address.

4

As soon as the cab bearing Maggie vanished around the corner, I sat down with the manuscript of *Carolina Bride* and examined my conscience. I kept the manuscript in the left-hand drawer of my writing-desk, while in the right was the manuscript of a little novel-in-progress with the working title *Prudence and Premonition*; it was pure Laura Lee, complete with the half-borrowed title. I had written about twenty pages of *Carolina Bride*, and at least ten times more of *Prudence and Premonition*. As usual, inventing things came easily to me.

Well, inventing things. . . . I read the pages of *Bride* and found that there were only eighteen; then I delved into *Prudence*, and on page forty I felt a wave of heat flood over me. The story's hero, a handsome farmer called Frederick, is flirting with the clever Maureen, daughter of a small dry-goods merchant who drinks whisky to excess. In the course of Frederick's stealing a kiss, his shotgun goes off (he's on his way home from a hunting expedition), and though Maureen is unharmed, her new dress is irreparably scorched. It's impossible for a girl wearing a badly burned dress to walk home through the village unnoticed, so Fred takes a dress belonging to his sister Kate from the clothesline in the garden and his sweetheart goes upstairs to change in his parents' bedroom, where she is observed through the open window by the village gossip, Miss Peters. This basic situation would lead to the usual trip to the altar in the face of amusing obstacles.

But had I really invented this story? Feverishly I went back to the eighteen pages of *Carolina Bride* and read them again. There could be no doubt. I hadn't invented the Labiche-like farce with the coquette and the hunter; I had taken it lock, stock, and barrel, so to speak, from *Carolina Bride*, where it was based on fact. I had merely adapted it slightly to make it fit.

But was it really based on fact? The fact was that Gospel, the cook, had lost her leg. As a seventeen-year-old chambermaid she had been polishing silver while, beside her, the devout slave Henry was no doubt pondering more spiritual matters as he cleaned Massa Sinclair's shotgun. He had forgotten to check if it was loaded.

I felt another flush of heat. My serious intentions had converted a real story into the drama I had set in motion in the first chapter of *Carolina Bride*. In fact I had written two variations. The first, rejected and blue-pencilled, turned the pious Henry into Gospel's beau and his fateful absence of mind into the flirtation of young lovers. The shotgun goes off as it did and hits Gospel. Justifiably frightened of the wrath of Massa Sinclair, whom I transformed from a good-natured idler into a slave-driver, Henry attempts to escape to the North but is caught and sent down the river. I abandoned this variation because Henry's motivation to escape struck me as unconvincing, and because I didn't know how to handle a crippled girl in a novel, even a serious one. But the main reason was my fear that the drastic impact of selling Henry down the river would be hard to surpass in the novel's climax, which I hadn't come up with yet. I had learned my poetics from Poe and so, without a qualm, I deleted the passage. The flirtation became an attempted rape— not by Henry, of course, but by the plantation-owner's son John, who was carrying a loaded shotgun on his back. The shot did not hit Gospel, but shattered a valuable Meissen porcelain vase, and John pinned the blame on Henry. That relatively non-dramatic incident set Henry's calvary in motion and it was to culminate, exactly according to the lessons I had learned from my mentor, Poe, in his sale down the river at the end of the novel.

I compared the three stories. All they had in common was a simple shotgun blast. The fact that it really happened was irrelevant.

How in God's name was literature supposed to mirror life?

5

Ambrose issued the order to halt publication of the *Times* on June 1, and immediately left for Hickman's Bridge, Kentucky, to prepare for the campaign against Braxton Bragg.

Storey and his editors ignored the order, which was delivered to the *Times* on the morning of June 2. Storey quickly obtained a restraining order from Judge Thomas Drummond and attempted to serve Drummond's edict on the officer overseeing the implementation of Ambrose's order in the *Times*'s editorial offices. The officer refused to take it and returned to Camp

Davis, apparently for reinforcements. Storey sent spies on horseback to follow him, and a rumour went round the city that the army was preparing to march on Chicago.

The morning of June 3, just as the paper was being typeset, a fellow rode up to the *Times* building and reported that General John Ammen's units were marching towards the city. The rumour turned out to be true; the units arrived at half past two. When Storey refused to admit them, the soldiers broke down the door, rushed into the print-shop, stopped the rotary press, carried the bundles of finished newspapers out into the street, and ripped them to shreds with their bayonets.

They missed the smaller job-printing press in the neighbouring workshop, however, and handbills were rolling off it at full steam. "All good and loyal citizens of Chicago who favour Free Speech and Freedom of the Press," they said, "are invited to assemble in mass meeting in front of *The Chicago Times* on Wednesday evening, June 2, at 8 o'clock. . . ."

That was the beginning of the drama, or the farce, that raised a philosophical question we Americans will probably be grappling with for as long as America exists.

Soon crowds of people started to stream towards the *Times* building, and about the same time word got out that armed units of Copperheads would be attacking the Republican *Tribune* building, which was loyal to Lincoln. The *Tribune* staff barricaded themselves in the building and declared that they would defend the paper even if they were outnumbered by the Copperheads. The Republicans had no intention, however, of leaving the fate of their newspaper in the hands of pressmen and typesetters, and so eight hundred men of Colonel Hauck's Home Guard took up combat positions around the *Tribune*, each man with thirty rounds of live ammunition. My old friend Colonel Jennison appeared as well, with his John Brown beard flying. He marched up and down the ranks of guardsmen, proclaiming in a clear and audible voice that if the traitors dared to attack, the street would be "carpeted with Copperhead corpses."

To make a long story short, by twilight of that day nebulous terms like "disloyalty" and "weakening the combat morale of the army" had the makings of a very tangible threat.

At half past seven that evening, the street in front of the *Times* building was so jammed with peace supporters that an appeal was made to them from the windows of the editorial offices to move to a bigger square two blocks away. As the milling crowd walked over to the square, there was a lot of confusion, pushing and shoving, and the occasional fist-fight, while over it all hung a thunderous roar. Humphrey said that from his vantage-point in a colleague's window he could smell the stink of rot-gut whisky rising from twenty thousand throats, and the slogans they chanted were certainly not flattering to Lincoln and his generals. Now and then the very chantable name of Vallandigham rang out, but mostly the demonstrators were calling on Storey to speak.

Storey was no orator, though, and he knew better than to mount the podium. So the crowd—including some three thousand Copperheads sporting their buttons—had to make do with unremarkable substitute speakers, and then a resolution was adopted which included the statement that they would sacrifice life and fortune "and all but liberty to preserve the Union" but that "they would not sacrifice their liberties, though life and fortune go together." Clashes with the police increased but the constabulary maintained control, so that nothing happened to give General Ammen a reason to declare martial law. One tipsy fellow in a linen coat sporting a big copperhead in its buttonhole put his hat on a walking-stick and waved it over the heads of the crowd, shouting that he could "rally enough Copperheads to squelch the *Tribune*", then set out unsteadily towards the offices of that newspaper, where a frowning Colonel Jennison was eagerly observing his progress. But the police picked him up before he could get into trouble.

Next day, the Republicans held a rally. Colonel Jennison publicly reiterated the suggestion he had made privately at our house—that his people would be glad to hang the Illinois traitors if the namby-pambies from Chicago were too soft for the job, because there was nobody left to hang back in Kansas. Even so, the Republicans' meeting was far more peaceful than the stormy demonstration of the Peace Democrats. Just before the speeches started, they learned that Lincoln had ordered General Burnside to rescind the order to suppress the *Times*, and that Burnside had done so.

6

What had happened? Telegrams had flown back and forth across the country. The first was sent from Chicago to Washington right after lunch on June 3 by a group of businessmen and politicians, all in positions more or less dependent on public opinion and alarmed at the approaching cries of an incensed mob. It asked the president to revoke Burnside's edict. Two of the telegram's authors were professional politicians, Lyman Trumbull and Isaac Arnold, who appended an urgent postscript asking the president to give the resolution his "serious and prompt consideration".

As the president was reading the wire from the Chicago businessmen, Ambrose was reading another telegram in Kentucky, this one from Halleck: instead of marching against Bragg in Tennessee, he was to organize reinforcements for General Grant and send them to Vicksburg in all haste. No sooner had he started working on that problem than yet another telegram arrived, this one from Secretary of War Stanton asking him to rescind the order suppressing the *Times*, on the president's orders.

With no way of knowing what was going on behind the scenes, how could Ambrose, in Kentucky, have grasped it all? He apparently cursed but immediately wired the requisite instructions to General Ammen in Chicago. Then he turned his attention back to Vicksburg.

Later, it turned out that the president, assailed by requests, resolutions, reports, calls for help, and appeals, finally made his decision after reading the urgent addendum from the old congressional professionals, Arnold and Trumbull. He conferred with Stanton and thought he had settled the dilemma. But not even half an hour after Stanton's dispatch to Burnside, the telegraph in the Office of the President was tapping out a new message from Congressman Arnold in Chicago, stating that his postscript to the earlier telegram did not imply any opinion in the matter of rescinding the order to stop publication of the *Times*. The president, accustomed to finding his own way through allegories and chaos, was far better than Ambrose at reading between the lines, and so at six o'clock that evening one more telegram flew across the wires from Stanton to Burnside in Kentucky with a message that was clear despite the tangled syntax: "The President directs me to say that if you have not acted upon the telegram, you need not do so but may let the matter stand as it is until you receive a letter by mail forwarded yesterday."

7

All of this reinforces my contention that Stanton left the solution of the dilemma to the technical possibilities of communication. It is hard to believe, for example, that he didn't know about the telegram Halleck had sent to Ambrose in Kentucky the previous day, ordering him to stand down from an offensive against Bragg and organize reinforcements for Grant at Vicksburg. He was, after all, Secretary of War. And yet his own wire vaguely but unquestionably revoking the previous order to rescind the suppression of the *Times* was sent not to Kentucky but to Cincinnati, where Ambrose most certainly was not, and had not been for quite some time. Had the telegram been sent to the proper address, it would have reached Ambrose before half past six on the evening of June 4, when Ambrose wired General Ammen that the *Times* could proceed to publish as usual. In Cincinnati, the captain on duty who received Stanton's dispatch took a while to realize that it had been sent to the wrong address and to redirect it to Ambrose at Hickman's Bridge.

The normally prompt Ambrose didn't send his reply to this last (or so he thought) unclear order until seven hours after he received it. It may have been that his hands were full with the difficult transfer of troops to Vicksburg. Or perhaps he finally lost his temper. When he sat down at the telegraph at two o'clock in the morning, he dictated a message to Stanton that was not entirely coherent. "Your dispatch revoked the order of the President in reference to the Chicago Times came too late. I had already sent telegraphic orders revoking my order. I am very much embarrassed and beg to ask for specific instructions in such cases."

Despite stylistic or perhaps grammatical ambiguities, Lincoln and Stanton must have understood the wire. Of course, what they read was the brief, amended version. Ambrose had written a longer, more coherent message, but deleted his conclusion. My grandson found it among his papers and included it in his dissertation. Originally, Ambrose had written: "I am very much embarrassed and beg to ask for specific instructions in such cases or be allowed to resign my commission. The latter will be most agreeable to me if it is for the interest of the public service, and I really believe that it is. I cannot change my views as to the policy that should be pursued in this department, and I am sorry they do not coincide with those of the government. I respectfully ask to be allowed to resign."

Lincoln did not accept his resignation and Ambrose continued to serve, with his usual verve and devotion. They say that no Union general stood on so many battlefields as my friend.

8

The letter which, according to Stanton's June 4 telegram, had been mailed June 1, did not reach Ambrose in Kentucky until June 12. In addition to various suggestions concerning Hascall, Morton, and general circumspection, Stanton added, a little late, a postscript that must have seemed at the very least ironic to Ambrose by then: "Since writing the above letter the President has been informed that you have suppressed the publication or circulation of the Chicago Times in your department. He directs me to say that in his judgment it would be better for you to take an early occasion to revoke that order.

The irritation produced by such acts is in his opinion likely to do more harm than the publication would do. The Government approves of your motives and desires to give you cordial and efficient support. But while military movements are left to your judgment, upon administrative questions such as the arrest of civilians and the suppression of newspapers not requiring immediate action the President desires to be previously consulted."

Ambrose did not respond to this, he merely confirmed receipt of the letter by telegram on June 12, noting that it had "only come to hand today".

The entire difficult, precedent-setting comedy of errors was hardly Ambrose's fault. And yet, because of it, General Burnside will apparently be remembered as an accomplice in the suppression of freedom of expression. The incident has a postscript of its own, to be found in a letter Lincoln sent May 17, 1864 to Congressman Arnold, the author of that guardedly neutral second wire which caused the president to attempt to rescind the rescindment. Lincoln wrote: "I am far from certain today that the revocation was not right."

A Pythian, grammatically contorted sentence. It hardly indicates, however, that the president was convinced he had made the right decision.

9

When the war was over, Jasmine left Cincinnati and vanished without a trace. We didn't get a single letter from her. Shortly afterwards we moved to Chicago, where Humphrey had been given a professorship at the university. A letter I sent her from there care of Mr. Carmichael's plantation was returned as undeliverable several months later.

Weeks and months passed, and then years. The newspapers carried strange and unpleasant news from the South. Hordes of freed slaves poured into Chicago, and they soon created a ring of poverty around the noisy and dynamic city centre. There were also spectacular, if not entirely respectable, tales of success. Humphrey tried to see things in philosophical terms; the first step is freedom, he would say, then comes knowledge, then better living standards, and finally full equality of rights and prosperity. He spoke beautifully about it, and everything seemed simple and only a matter of time. I must say that he didn't stop at philosophy. He became the heart and soul of all kinds of committees founded by the abolitionists while liberated slaves still interested them. He opened schools for Negro children and set up night courses for their parents. Then, unexpectedly, he died.

I was barely forty. I was still writing novels—not as many as before, because I didn't need to. I had money enough. The children were growing and I had already put more in their bank accounts than they deserved—but no, they were good children. Loretta was a pretty and surprisingly feminine young lady. Jimmy was a diligent student and a star pupil at the Latin school in Chicago. And I went on writing. Why? Because I enjoyed it. Because my female readership was growing. And because, in between assembling the stories my readers were waiting for—stories that resembled reality as they wished it to be—I was working on *Carolina Bride.*

I never stopped thinking of Jasmine. It occasionally struck me as odd that I should think of her so much; I felt almost guilty about it, because I thought far less about my own former tomboy, even after she got engaged to a young New York attorney who had entered politics and was starting to get rich, quickly, steadily, and considerably. I preferred not to ask how; it was during General Grant's infamous second term as president.

Once, a few years before Humphrey died, after I had spent a week wrestling with my serious novel without managing to get a single line on paper, I was overcome by an unbearable longing to see that lovely girl who used to pour Ambrose's cognac in silence and then stare out the window at the stars over Cincinnati—who had once asked me anxiously, "Miz Tracy, do you think that—they'll make peace?" My longing was so great that I dropped everything and set out by train to Mr. Carmichael's plantation in Carolina.

I had never been there, and the ruins that remained of the plantation could only hint at its former beauty. The big house had been hit by cannon-fire and only a few scorched timbers remained, along with four Doric pillars that had nothing left to support. Even the Negro cabins looked run down. A few goats grazed behind them and an old man in tattered clothes sat in front of one of them, watching me with bloodshot eyes as I stumbled amid the wreckage of faded glory. I spoke to him and he mumbled something in reply.

"I'm looking for a young coloured woman called Jasmine," I said.

The old man just shook his head.

"Or a cook that everyone here knew. She had only one leg. Her name was Gospel."

Nothing.

"Wasn't this Mr. Carmichael's plantation?"

"Can't say," said the old man. "I ain't from here."

This poor unfortunate had joined the northward exodus, but when he couldn't go any farther he'd been left to die at the Methodist manse in the village. The minister's wife had fed him chicken soup and put him back on his unsteady feet, and now he was tending the minister's goats out here and gazing longingly to the North, where he no longer had the strength to go.

I returned to my hired carriage and drove into the village, with the image of the lovely girl and her no-account Hasdrubal before my eyes.

The minister didn't know them either. He had come to the village during the last year of the war, and had only witnessed the general exodus of Negroes from the plantation. The owner had died earlier, during a bombardment by General Sherman's wild cannoneers. I went home to Chicago.

I reluctantly returned to *Carolina Bride* and, with much editing, the kind my editor would have sought in vain in my other manuscripts, I tried to put into words reality as I remembered it, not as I wished it could have been. I reread what Poe had to say about consistency of tone, about how close poetry is to music. I even made a fair copy of excerpts from Jasmine's story for Humphrey to read, something I had never done before. Humphrey used to tease me about my novels, and after his own literary fiasco I was reluctant to hurt his pride. But by then he had gotten over it, and besides, Jasmine's story was no trip to the altar. It was serious; it mirrored real life—not mine, of course, but the life of my lovely girl and her race. Like so many professors, Humphrey understood literature better than I did; he just didn't know how to write it.

Humphrey endorsed my theory about consistency of tone, although he did remark that Poe was thinking of forms smaller than a novel. And in Dickens, he reflected, one could hardly speak of consistency of tone, but there was no denying that Dickens mirrored life. "It's odd. If there is anything at all to your—mm—artifacts, Lorraine, then it is consistency of tone. They are essentially farces in which nothing serious happens and nothing serious is said."

This got me thinking. That couldn't have been what Poe meant by consistency of tone. Or was it? He said, *"In the whole composition there should be no word written of which the tendency, direct or indirect, is not to the pre-established design."* If my trips to the altar had any compositional quality at all, it was in the way the tones harmonized with each other. There were no dissonant modulations to disturb their simple melodies. And hadn't Poe also written that *"He who pleases is of more importance to his fellow men than he who instructs"*? Yes, perhaps—but I recalled Humphrey lifting a volume of Thackeray as if it were the host, and I thought of Gospel and her spell-casting son, of the gastronomical passion of the plantation-owner killed by Sherman's artillery, of the philosophical debate between the benign slave-owner and the abolitionist manufacturer from the North as Jasmine had described it to me. And I struggled with my *Carolina Bride*.

Then Humphrey died, and in my grief, which lasted many long months, the work started to go amazingly well.

Everything in the manuscript was based on fact; unlike my stories of nuptial fun and games, *Carolina Bride* was written with exhaustive preparation. Everything I wrote was based on first-hand testimony and evidence I found in abolitionist newspapers, in Harriet Beecher Stowe, in Frederick Douglass, in Dickens's *American Notes,* or in what Jasmine herself had told me or what I had observed myself during our occasional trips to the South.

And the plot unfolded. Jasmine and Hasdrubal attempted to travel north with the Underground Railroad, but only Jasmine made it. Bounty-hunters caught Hasdrubal and after many dramatic vicissitudes (all taken from life) the former domestic slave and the object of so much feminine attention found himself on a rice plantation in the deep South. Old Gospel, now an invalid living on the charity of the inheritor of the plantation, hanged herself soon after they sold her son Hasdrubal down the river. The novel was already five hundred pages long, and everything in it had actually happened. I had merely gathered all these authentic tales into a single story. But because I had managed to maintain a consistency of tone, the effect was not that of an unrealistic compilation, but rather that of a mournful epic critique of the times, and of one part of our beloved and afflicted Union.

The bass line—no, the ubiquitous lovely soprano—of the story was Jasmine, that sad caramel damsel, and her fear when she drummed up the courage to ask Ambrose about the war—because my assurances were not enough for her, since I was not a soldier—and the general, upset by his difficulties with Vallandigham, looked out at her from behind his chestnut side-whiskers and moustache and said, "When we defeat them, child! Not sooner!" Jasmine stepping off the train, going all the way to the Carmichael plantation on foot but finding it in ruins. The ancient Negro couple who had stayed there, eking a living out of what they could harvest from a wretched little field, telling her how Hasdrubal had been sold on the eve of good old Massa Lincum's great war, and Jasmine travelling south, asking around, trying to get close to her sweetheart through the chaos that was Dixie.

The ugliest of the strange new events that the papers had started writing about was the appearance of a hitherto unknown organization of white Southerners. Jasmine finally meets Hasdrubal, but their bliss is only a few days old when the organization strikes. Hasdrubal winds up hanging from a tree, a burning cross behind him.

Jasmine stands above the morass of failed escapes, all of it painted in the sombre colours of mourning, the sombre consistency of tone, all of it the awful truth. As I dipped my pen to finish writing that song—and I'm not ashamed to admit I had tears in my eyes—the postman arrived with a large coloured envelope bearing the letterhead of a Chicago restaurant.

10

The disgrace—and if it was a disgrace, then whose was it?—in Chicago was not Ambrose's final calamity. "*The evil that men do lives after them, the good is oft interred with their bones,*" wrote Shakespeare, and this applies exactly to Ambrose, if we replace the word *evil* with *calamity* or *muddle* or the greyer word *set-back*. Fredericksburg, Chicago, the bungled opportunity at Petersburg that entered the history of the war as "The Crater". I heard about what preceded the latter long after the war, from the lips of first Lieutenant Duty, in a Chicago restaurant called The Witches' Kitchen.

Ambrose's only successes were in trivial matters. They were not the stuff of ballads. Two months after the embarrassment in Chicago, after he had managed the exemplary transfer of troops to reinforce Grant at Vicksburg, while he was pondering the operation against Braxton Bragg across the Cumberland Hills to Knoxville in eastern Tennessee, he came up with an idea that might have inspired military bards to poetry, had it not originated with Burnside the bungler. He even carried his idea out, but—how else?—in a manner far less spectacular than Sherman would do it later, in Georgia.

He simply abandoned the clumsy wagons, which were the standard means of transporting supplies but a terrible hindrance on the steep hills, and ordered his soldiers to live on what they could pillage during their march across the picturesque mountain ranges. As a result, the advance of the Twenty-third Corps was so rapid that it took Rebel General Buckner completely by surprise in Knoxville. Two and a half thousand bewildered prisoners fell into Ambrose's hands, along with eleven field-guns. Before leaving Knoxville, he developed a strategic plan for a march from eastern Tennessee across Georgia to the sea and wrote to Halleck, "It is proposed to take no trains but to live upon the country and the supplies at the enemy's depots, destroying such as we do not use. . . . from the celerity of our movement and the destruction of bridges, etc. in our rear, the chances of escaping material injury from pursuit are in our favour. Our chief loss would probably be from stragglers."

Halleck's reply back then was terse and negative: "Distant expeditions into Georgia are not now contemplated." The letter travelled the labyrinths of Washington corridors and eventually came into Sherman's hands, and exactly a year later it was he who marched his great army swiftly across Georgia to Savannah and the sea. Later on, he was heard to say that he had had Ambrose's plan "in his mind's eye".

It's just as Maggie said: it's not what a person wants in life, it's what he accomplishes.

Ambrose wanted a lot—above all, to help the Union win the war. But what he accomplished were trivial things, or rather, the kind of things they don't write ballads about: the orderly retreat at Bull Run, the first, though minor, Union army victory at Roanoke Island, the picturesque if undramatic march across the Cumberland Hills, and the defence of Knoxville, organizing all sorts of troop transfers, often in large numbers, which were always successfully (that is to say, professionally) executed. There was nothing in them to inspire the bards.

And then he caught Vallandigham.

II

Whenever I think of that man, I see in my mind a stretcher and on it a dying old man being carried to the gallows. The final court case of Vallandigham's life also took place in the shadow of that inhuman apparatus. By then, in 1871, Vallandigham's political career was only a memory. He'd finally realized that he was washed up and had returned to his law practice, which he conducted on the same principle as he had politics: nothing mattered but winning. He saw the presumption of innocence not as a challenge to the court to prove guilt, but as a challenge to himself to prove his skill as a lawyer. So he sent a dying old man to Golgotha on a stretcher.

Thomas McGehan was not a dying old man. The face in the drawing that stared out at me from the *Dayton Evening Herald* was that of a brute from a dark back alley, who hires out his fists for dirty work and who therefore has friends among politicians. Those friends asked Vallandigham to defend him, and Vallandigham accepted.

When Vallandigham was escorted to General Rosecrans's headquarters to be shipped across the lines to the Rebels the following day, they say that Rosecrans, who saw the Copperhead hero as a traitor, said his farewell to him over a dinner that lasted until well past midnight, like a maudlin Pilate with freshly washed hands. I believe it, because in the courtroom in Warren District, when Vallandigham described the fist-fight between two scoundrels that put an end to the earthly sojourn of a blackguard named Tom Myers, he brought tears to the eyes of eight of the twelve jurors. That was why, at three in the afternoon, the judge adjourned the court until the following morning.

It was a sunny afternoon, and Vallandigham and the young lawyer Snopes went for a stroll in the woods. There, in the green shade of the elm trees, Vallandigham told Snopes his hypothesis about the encounter between McGehan and Myers.

The two men had got into a fight—all the witnesses agreed on that—and McGehan had knocked Myers to his knees. The furious Myers had reached into his breast pocket for a pistol and, as he tried to get up and pull out the gun at the same time, the trigger had caught on the edge of the pocket, the pistol had gone off, and the bullet had penetrated the left ventricle of Myers's heart, with fatal results.

"And do you believe that's what happened, sir?" asked young Snopes.

"I think it could have."

"It sounds improbable," said Snopes.

"It must be presented to the jury so as to sound probable."

"But do you really think that's what happened? After all, McGehan fired a shot too—"

"I think it could have happened. That's why it's my duty as attorney for the defence to convince the jury that it did."

The young lawyer looked at the sun-drenched landscape, the butterflies, the beauties of life. "What if the prosecution brings in evidence that it wasn't like that at all?"

Vallandigham smiled at the innocent youth. "There is very little evidence a good lawyer can't discredit."

"Even if he believes it's true?"

"All the more reason to discredit it. He could be wrong in that belief, and defending a client is a matter of professional honour."

After that, Snopes said nothing. When the trial was over he wrote an article about it, which was in fact Vallandigham's obituary. During their stroll in the woods, Vallandigham had fired several shots at a piece of tweed fabric that he had Snopes hold at various distances from the gun barrel, to find out how close the fabric had to be to show powder burns. Then they returned to the hotel, where Vallandigham invited Snopes up to his room for a drink of whisky. He placed the pistol on the mantelpiece and poured Snopes a drink from a bottle that stood beside it.

Snopes noticed another gun on the mantel, identical to the one Vallandigham had been experimenting with. He didn't mention it, though.

The next day the courtroom was crowded. Some of those present had faces like McGehan, others like Myers, and their rumpled clothes indicated that they had had to fight their way into the courtroom. Vallandigham entered, and the jury—or most of the jury—softened even before Comely Clem could open his mouth and start to demonstrate his hypothesis about the unfortunate accident. He stood with his feet apart, pulled a pistol out of his pocket, cocked it, and addressed the jury: "This is about how Myers was holding his weapon. Of course, he wasn't standing, he was rising from his knees." As a mouse's eyes follow a snake, the jury watched the barrel of Vallandigham's pistol as he turned it towards his chest.

"Something like this," said Comely Clem.

12

Witnesses differ on what exactly Vallandigham said when the bullet entered his chest from the loaded pistol, the one that had lain on the mantel beside the whisky bottle. According to some he said, "God, I've shot myself!" According to the *Dayton Journal* he cried out, "Oh, murder! Oh, what a blunder!"

I think the latter version fits him better.

He fought for his life until the morning of the second day. He fought hard, the way people fight for their lives when they are convinced there's nothing beyond this life. They even brought McGehan to see him, and McGehan shed tears as well—probably genuine tears, since his chance to escape the gallows lay on that hotel-room bed.

In the end, though, McGehan did escape the gallows. Vallandigham's death affected the jury like a final unspoken oration for the defence, and not even the insipid performance of his successor, young Snopes, was of any help to the prosecutor. McGehan, who would not have needed a stretcher, eluded the gallows. Several years later, he died by another man's bullet, and that event did not end with a hanging either, because the gun had clearly been fired in self-defence.

Such was the end of Vallandigham. He defended freedom beautifully, but what was he really after? He wasted his extraordinary ability playing gallows games.

Perhaps I have not been unfair to him.

13

I never saw my dear friend Ambrose again after the war. He too went into politics. For a while he was Governor of Rhode Island, the state where he had once tried to become a manufacturer. Then he represented Rhode Island in the Senate, and then, unexpectedly, he lost his wife, Mary. I never did meet her. She was young, just forty-nine years old, and Ambrose survived her by only five years.

It was said, as it often is, that his wife's premature death killed him. I believe that. Ambrose had never lived primarily for himself.

The last time I saw him was in Chicago in the spring of 1864, when the war was still dragging on. Ambrose was preparing the campaigns that would lead him through the nightmare of the battles of The Wilderness to the disastrous Crater at Petersburg and his discharge from the army. He had come to Chicago from Virginia, where he was reassembling his old Ninth Corps, which would soon join the Army of the Potomac to plunge into The Wilderness. On March 20, the Chicago Republicans held a banquet. Ambrose had been invited to make the formal speech. I went with Humphrey, who had so neglected his professorial duties during the recent election campaign that I began to fear that he would soon have to bid adieu to the academic life I found so comfortable, since it demanded so much less of a wife than the life of a political candidate. All the same, I found time during the campaign to write a novel about clever Maud and her skilful manoeuvring to bring the handsome Jonathan—who had fallen victim to the recurrent madness of politics—to his senses and, eventually, to the altar.

Many Republicans in Chicago had not forgotten the unpleasant situation Lincoln had inflicted on them by rescinding Ambrose's order to suppress the *Times*. Storey took malicious advantage of that, too, though only briefly; Gettysburg and Vicksburg and the overall reversal of the fortunes of war had taken the wind out of the sails of those who, like the publisher of the *Times,* were wrapping themselves in the Constitution. The Chicago Republicans read this shift in fortune in part as evidence that Ambrose had been right about the *Times*, and even contended that his vigorous action against Vallandigham, and the slap in the face he had given Storey, had broken the Copperhead conspiracy almost as effectively as Grant and Meade had defeated the Rebel forces on the battlefield. The hope was that, now that the president was riding on a wave of battlefield victories and criticism could no longer do him any damage, Ambrose would remind him that, less than a year ago, in Chicago, he had miscalculated.

Ambrose disappointed them. "I entirely acquiesce in all the president has done," he declared in his powerful yet quiet voice, standing tall behind the lectern draped in a colourful Union flag, "and I feel now, tonight, just as I felt the moment I issued that order that was later rescinded." In his beautiful blue uniform, his ruddy face framed by his incredible chestnut whiskers, he stood there and said, "I am as much an advocate for the liberty of speech and of the press as any man on the face of the globe can be, but when I am sent into a department to command soldiers who are to be strengthened in all possible ways by giving them encouragement, and by giving them clothes to wear and food to eat, and recruits to fill up their ranks; when I find men in the department opposing all these means of strengthening the soldiers in the Army, I will strike these men in precisely the same way that I would strike an enemy in arms against them." Ambrose's eyes gleamed in the light of the chandeliers, the gold tassel on his sword glimmered against the fine fabric of his trousers, the kind that Jasmine had once spilled cognac on and that soldiers deserve because they so often die. I had tears in my eyes, I who was perfectly capable of evoking them in my gentle readers but rarely shed them myself, and at that moment, at that pretentious banquet in the Republican Club of Chicago, surrounded by gentlemen in tails and ladies in elegant gowns from Worth's, I loved that grand, childlike man. Tomorrow he would gallop off along muddy roads towards a winter of savage combat in order that those here might live as they did, but also in order that Jasmine and her shiftless Hasdrubal might live at all. "I would fail in my duty if I did not risk all I have in the world in the way of reputation or position, or even of life itself, to defend and strengthen those poor soldiers who are in the field risking their lives in defence of their country. That is all I have to say with reference to this order which I issued and which was rescinded."

Applause, ovations, the dear, masculine, somewhat comical countenance—its whiskers already a synonym for dandyism. I never saw him again in my life. It is with this demeanour and with those words that he has remained alive in my mind.

Chicago

THE LANTERNS rattled like little tin drums in the rain. They were brass, polished and new, and they bordered the entranceway. Raindrops glinted coldly in the light of the lamps. A beige carriage drove up; a Negro pulled down the step and raised a large beige umbrella. The rain poured down. A lady's foot in a patent-leather laced shoe emerged from the darkness inside the carriage into the golden light and placed itself on the step. The Negro footman took the lady delicately by the elbow and helped her down. She lifted her pretty face to look at the sign illumined by the glow of lamplight. In gold and red letters on a black background it read THE WITCHES' KITCHEN, and beneath it, on a banner hanging down like a flag, were the words GALA OPENING. The lady walked under the umbrella to the door, and her red locks swung above the iridescent taffeta that covered her shoulders. The rain drummed down.

Houska gave a low whistle.

"Houska, shush!" said his pretty wife, Ruzena.

"Don't be vulgar!" said Salek. "You're not in North Carolina any more."

"It's my asthma," said Houska, and they all turned to watch the lady walk through the frosted-glass doors, past the Negro doorman, who bowed to her, and past the restaurant owner, who attempted a similar bow but couldn't quite do it because of the rheumatism in his back. The lady entered the restaurant, the music, and the dense cigar smoke.

Shake approached the owner and handed him a book.

"For your newly arrived nephew," he said.

Puzzled, the restaurant owner looked down at the book, and then he remembered. "Oh, yes, yes. Much obliged to you. What do I owe you?"

"That's all right, I'll take it out in drinks," said Shake. "And in food."

He kept watching the red-haired lady. She gave off a coppery glow as she made her way among the tables.

"Who is she, colonel?" Bozenka Kapsa asked Mr. Ohrenzug.

"Some woman author," replied the restaurateur. "They say she's famous."

They stared at the lady, who shone like a candle. At a booth at the head of the dining room, beneath portraits of Lincoln and Grant, a youngish high-yellow woman also dressed in iridescent taffeta got up and ran over to the author. The lady opened her arms and they floated towards each other like two glittering birds, down the aisle between the richly laid tables under the red, white, and blue streamers. They met in the middle of the dining room and fell into each other's arms.

"And who's the other one?" asked Bozenka.

The sergeant felt a spasm, as though he'd been struck by a minnie. He had never seen Cyril's yellow tea-rose; he had only an imaginary picture of her in his mind, drawn from Cyril's sorrow and from people they saw in deserted plantation houses. This was what she would have looked like, though she would have been younger back then.

"Her?" he heard Mr. Ohrenzug say. "She runs a sort of—well, it's a restaurant too, on South Street. She's the one who told me that this author woman is so famous."

A new guest walked through the door, and the doorman bowed to the sound of the little tin drums.

Burning snow was falling on the Congaree River.

"She died?" Cyril's voice cracked. The sergeant saw the old Negro woman nod. He looked around. A drummer boy was marching down Carolina Avenue; his drum—riddled with bullet-holes—sounded hoarse, almost malevolent. He looked about twelve years old. A general's field-glasses stuck out of his back pocket and a smoking cigar protruded from his boyish lips. Behind him, under a ragged banner, marched a platoon of bearded men carrying a long pole on top of which was a dummy made of cotton-filled burlap sacks topped with a painted tin pirate's head. They had cut the effigy down somewhere in a looted tavern and hung a sign around its neck that read JEFF DAVIS. A red-bearded soldier in the first

rank, right behind the drum, tossed an empty bottle at the window of an ornate building across the street, but he missed and the bottle shattered against the wall. A young Negro in a lace shirt that was too small for him jumped out of a group of dancing blacks on the sidewalk and placed a fresh bottle in the bearded soldier's hand. The damaged drum sounded as though it were drumming a man to the gallows. The sergeant had witnessed a number of executions, and they were always worse than any death in war.

"From the de Ribordeaux plantation in Texas? No. Weren't nobody. And Missy Ribordeaux, she died. Who? Some old white lady? Sorry, massa," said the Negro woman, "my memory is full of holes."

A pipe joined the drum. Cyril took off his cap and wiped his forehead. "It would have been an older white woman," he said. "Not old. Just older than her. And she wouldn't have been a lady, more like white trash. She was supposed to bring her here, to Miss de Ribordeaux."

The Negro woman thought hard, the drum pounded, the pipe trilled. "About three years ago, you say?"

"It would have been in the summer of '61," said Cyril, "at the very start of the war. And she wasn't a lady. Her husband was a blacksmith in Austin."

"The last company Missy Ribordeaux have was almost a year ago, and she wasn't no white trash, it was Miss Sullivan from the Glenwood plantation."

"No, that's not it. This would have been right at the beginning of the war. And she wouldn't have been a lady."

The old woman closed her dim eyes. "Sorry, massa, my old head. Beginning of the war, you say—like before Massa Lincum—?" She opened her eyes. "Long about then Missy stopped walking. She'd just sit here in the armchair, never move," and she pointed behind her at the big room full of furniture. By the leaded glass window stood a velvet armchair with a lace antimacassar on the back. Burning snow was falling outside the window, and the drum was pounding.

"A white lady," repeated the old Negro woman pensively.

"She wasn't a lady," Cyril insisted.

"Once, towards fall, Missy de Ribordeaux had a visit from the widow of Mr. Lemaître—used to be overseer at her cousin M. de Ribordeaux's plantation. But"—she paused, the drum sounded—"she wasn't no white trash. I don't know, massa," she said anxiously. "I'm awful sorry I can't help Massa Lincum's soldiers. It's just this old head of mine. . . ."

★

"I swear to you, big brother, I swear to you," Lida said miserably, clutching a basin with some solution in it while a wounded man behind her moaned, "by everything that's holy—"

"What's holy to you?" he interrupted her, but his voice was as full of misery as hers. A strange light flashed in his sister's eyes.

"I swear by his memory," she said softly, almost in a whisper.

★

They paced in the smoke and noise of the house where the sergeant's general had set up his quarters.

"Why?" said Cyril. "She must have made it up. Otherwise I'd have killed her."

"Her story's too complicated to make up," said the sergeant.

"Protect Dinah?" said Cyril bitterly. "She should have left her in Austin, in that little house. In the end, she badgered Étienne all the way to Savannah. And when he got there she badgered him to death."

"That was before she knew the old man was going to disinherit him," said the sergeant. "She didn't want Dinah anywhere near Étienne. You know what she's like—"

"To Columbia!" Cyril struck himself in the forehead. "That's more than a thousand miles! Did she expect me to believe that?"

"In the summer of '61 it wouldn't have been so hard. By train from Vicksburg. . . ."

They walked around the demolished building, which had taken a direct hit by Captain DeGress. An old Negro man was gathering bricks from the ruins and piling them on a cart.

"Maybe Dinah ran away from the blacksmith's wife on the trip," said the sergeant.

"Then she'd have been waiting for me in Austin."

"She didn't make it. Something—" He stopped short.

"They caught her," said Cyril bitterly. "Without papers!" He looked around at the burning cotton floating down over the scorched roofs. "Where could she be?" he wailed.

"It's still harder to believe that Lida lied," the sergeant said softly. Although, he thought, a thousand miles is a long way. But at the beginning of the war, a blacksmith's wife and a black slave girl travelling together? Still, the men of the South are gallant. And she had sworn to Cyril, on the memory of—

Cyril sat down on a pile of bricks and put his head in his hands.

"Cyril, my friend," said the sergeant, *"maybe she found a place to hide and she's waiting till the war is over. It's almost over now."*

Burning snow, on the Congaree River.

The sergeant stepped over to the window, leaned his forehead against the cool glass pane with the raindrops running down it. The rain tapped on the brass lamps. The band was playing and couples in evening dress were swirling around the dance floor. The famous lady author was dancing with an officer, and his own Bozenka was dancing with Houska. Padecky was clutching a beer stein, his stiff leg stretched out in the aisle between the tables, a hazard to guests on their way to the dance floor. Scowling, Padecky watched Molly Kakuska on the arm of Schroeder in his colonel's uniform. She looked offended but she carried herself like the great lady she was quickly becoming back home in Milwaukee. She disappeared from Padecky's sight on the crowded dance floor, and he glowered around the room as though looking for someone.

"If they so much as stick their noses in here," he raged, "I'll tear them off and feed them to the dogs! This is an American party, and subjects of the emperor are not welcome!"

"They had wives, children, and businesses," said Shake.

"And their pants were full of shit," declared Salek.

★

"Ja, das war wirklich unerwartet und—unangenehm," said Ursula.

"Sorry," said the sergeant in English. *"I forgot my German over all those years."*

"Unexpected, and unpleasant," said Ursula, placing a finger on the back of his hand. She wore a beautifully engraved wedding band on her third finger, and on her middle finger was a huge stone that looked like a glass egg. One from the nest that Fircut—

"Mein lieber Mann," she said. *"You still understand that much,* nicht wahr?" He turned his hand over and tried to clasp her fingers, but Ursula pulled her hand away, laughed, and continued in English. *"My husband didn't understand it right away. He knew them both. One of a consul's duties is to keep an eye on people like that. Our agents often filed reports on them. They never missed a gathering."*

★

"It's easy to beat your gums so patriots will buy more of your sausages, right?" hollered Padecky in Slavik's Tavern. *"But when the going gets tough—"*

"It's easy for you to talk, neighbour," said Talafous the butcher. "Now, with your leg, you don't have to go to war—"

"What do you mean, don't have to? Can't, Ferda! I can't! That's a Jesus big difference! If I could"—Padecky slapped his plaster-encased knee and howled with pain—"I would, wife or no wife, kids or no kids—"

★

"I rather enjoyed reading the reports," said Ursula, smiling. "I'm not exactly an admirer of the house of Hapsburg, even though I married a member of the imperial diplomatic corps. But I didn't marry again because I was forced to, as I was when I was sixteen—"

★

"It's not just the cowardice!" Padecky yelled, his eye lighting on Molly, who was all dressed up and looking lovely on the arm of the portly officer. She had noticed Kapsa, Bozenka, and Shake, and was pulling Schroeder over to their table. But Padecky snapped at her as she went by, "Not here, you don't!"

Molly was startled. "Why not?"

"You know perfectly well why not!" Padecky exclaimed. "Your husband is barely cold in his grave—"

"I got the letter. General Schofield signed it himself." Molly blushed. "Franta died in September of '64."

"Died!" hollered Padecky. "They tortured him to death at Andersonville! Franta's a martyr! And you're a martyr's widow. The cannon-fire barely dies down and you—"

"Was sagt er?" Schroeder couldn't understand this tirade in Czech.

"And a bloody German at that!" Padecky ranted on. "One bloody German torments her husband to death at Andersonville and she can't wait to marry another one!"

"He was Swiss," Molly objected. "And Fritz here fought the whole war on our side. With Haecker. And that Wirz fellow got hanged after the war!"

The colonel understood only that they were talking about him. He smiled. *"Jawohl,"* he nodded, *"mit Haecker."* He started counting on his fingers, comfortably mixing his mother tongue with English. "And *mit Siegel und* in the end *mit General Burnside* at The Crater, where *mein Glueck* left me and I got *eine kugel in den Arm."*

Schroeder's bullet in the arm shut Padecky up for a minute. He stared at the German with the expression of someone proved wrong, then growled at

him in Czech, "You could at least learn to talk right, instead of your gob-
bledygook. After all, you've got yourself a Czech girl!"

Shake asked, "What do you speak at home, Molly?"

She blushed. "Well, German," she admitted. "Fritz isn't good with
languages."

"*Jawohl,*" nodded the colonel complacently.

"*So my husband told them he didn't understand them, and he quoted something to the butcher from his informant's report,*" Ursula said, *raising her coffee
cup. The glass egg on her finger glittered and Ursula noticed the sergeant's glance.*
"*You see,*" *she smiled,* "*my jewels brought you luck. Of course,* mein lieber
Mann, *I don't know if it still is luck—?*" *The sergeant turned red and Ursula
quickly touched his sleeve with her bejewelled hand.* "*Aren't you sweet?* Wie
damals, *like back then . . . but that's so long ago. Today it is just* eine Legende,
a—legend?"

"*I—*" *The sergeant's voice cracked.* "*I'm married now. And I love her. Very
much!*" *He felt like a wretched sinner, but he had had to come here.*

And Ursula said, "*I also married again, for love. That doesn't—or should we
forget about it all?*"

"*No,*" *he said quickly.* "*Forgetting would be impossible.*"

"*Na,* siehst du, *you see?*" *she said.* "*Let us remember, and be glad of our good
fortune. You survived the war, I survived—*" *She stopped and looked at him.* "*It
was by a hair, though, you know?*"

He knew. The old nightmares flashed through his mind.

"*But back to my husband. In his official capacity, I mean,*" *said Ursula.* "*He
quoted what the butcher had said publicly about the emperor on June 6 of '63,
the day you celebrate your heretic, John Huss. And then he said to the butcher
and the cigar-maker, 'And now, gentlemen'—pretending not to understand—
'you presume to restore your allegiance to the Hapsburg line?' The two of them
looked at each other and the one who makes cigars, I forget his name, said, 'If it's
about that speech he made, your honour, Mr. Talafous just said that to help out
his business.'*"

"*Did they actually intend to go back to Austria?*" asked the sergeant,
amazed.

Ursula laughed.

"*Of course not. They just wanted to become subjects of our most merciful
Emperor and King Franz Josef here in America. Then they could claim the status
of naturalized aliens, and President Lincoln's conscription order wouldn't apply
to them. They came to this country for economic reasons, and as economic émigrés, the cigar-maker said, they had no involvement in American internal political disputes.*"

The sergeant didn't say anything. Images of war flashed through his head. His fellow soldiers, Houska, Kakuska, Paidr. . . . Then he closed his eyes, opened them again, and asked:

"Did your husband restore their status as subjects?"

"He sent their request to Vienna," said Ursula. "There was no precedent. Vienna didn't know what to do with it, and in the meantime another thirty or more of your countrymen applied for the same thing, some of them from as far away as Minneapolis."

"So they got conscripted?"

"Vienna finally decided that if the applicants paid a stamp tax proportionate to their income, from five to fifty gulden, they'd be restored as imperial subjects. So the two of them bought the stamps—each of them paid the fifty gulden, I think, and most of the others did too. Business was brisk at the consulate." Ursula laughed. "But the Chicago sheriff got wind of it, and all the newly restored imperial subjects were notified that if they were citizens of the United States before their status as imperial subjects was restored, military service was compulsory for them both in Austria and in America. There was a huge outcry, and you can imagine the crowd that rushed the consulate."

Now the sergeant laughed. "Who was Austria at war with?"

"Denmark," said Ursula. "It was a brief war, so there was no danger there. But in Chicago the pot was boiling. The Copperheads were revolting and the Union suffered a big defeat at Chancellorsville. Lincoln needed soldiers."

"So they had to go after all!"

"Most of them paid for substitutes," said Ursula.

"At least they gave something for the Union cause," said the sergeant. "And the other fifty gulden for Austria, that must have stuck in their craw all right. After all, what worried them most was losing money. Their problem was more greed than fear."

"I don't think so, mein lieber Mann," said Ursula. "You know better than most that there was reason to fear."

The rain rattled down on the lanterns. The sergeant turned and sat back down at the table but he wasn't listening to the conversation. He was hearing Cyril, and where was he now?

She wasn't an old woman, forty perhaps, and rather pretty—a stout, tanned villager—but her eyes reminded Cyril of the Madwoman of Cachtice, who killed young women and bathed in their blood. Behind her, her new husband was pounding something flat on his anvil, and the woman stood leaning on a pitchfork.

"If you believe some Negro witch more than you do a white woman," she said to Cyril, "then—" He looked into those eyes, and he had to look away.

"She didn't say you never brought her there, she just said she couldn't remember. She said she's getting forgetful."

"She certainly is. Head like a sieve," said the woman. He didn't believe her. Eyes like that were not to be believed. "Young Ribordeaux paid me and he paid me well. I'm not in the habit of taking money and not delivering."

Cyril realized she was laughing at him. What did she care about his tea-rose? About whether she arrived or got lost along the way? If the girl ran away, how could anyone fault a blacksmith's wife? If she sold her—everything could be fixed to hide the truth. And who could prove anything against her today? Her eyes showed—what? That she was capable of anything. The anvil rang like a bell in the courtyard. Was it sounding an alarm?

"Mrs. Smith," he said. "Look here, if she ran away from you along the way—"

Rain drummed down on the lantern lids.

"No," said Josef. "Miss Rosemary didn't go back to England with Mr. Carson. She got married."

"Married," Cyril repeated absently. He suddenly felt a longing to see the girl with the face of a pretty pony, her red dress like a red butterfly. Another world. "She and her husband—are they still running the Carson plantation?"

"Oh, no," said Josef. "She married some Yankee captain. I heard they have a business in Indiana. But she came to ask after you before she left, to find out if you came home safe from the war."

"She did?" whispered Cyril.

"Yes. And she sends you her regards."

Little tin drums. Burning snow.

"She ran away from you, more likely," the woman said maliciously. "You're telling me some brother of hers in Chicago wants to find her?"

"That's right!" Cyril replied, irritated. The woman's nasty eyes stared right through him. "And even if it weren't, it's none of your business."

"Well, if you say so," she said scornfully. "All right, then. Tell her brother that Columbia was full of good-looking house-nigger boys. Pretty as pictures. And you know what they say," she said mockingly. "Birds of a feather. . . ."

Cyril felt weak. It isn't possible, is it, that such mean eyes could—

"Of course," said the blacksmith's wife, "I'm just guessing what probably happened."

The big Negro opened the frosted-glass door wide. The rain was still coming down and the lamps clattered like little tin drums. He shut the door again and looked around the restaurant. Mr. Ohrenzug joined the table. He was wearing a formal set of tails with the Slavonic linden cockade sewn beneath his heart like a medal, and he put Shake's book down on the table in front of him. The famous lady author caught their attention again. She walked past their table with the pretty Negro girl, and they had their arms around each other's waists.

"I read one of her novels. It was called *She Played It Safe*," said Bozenka, quoting the title in English. The sergeant thought his wife pronounced it as if she'd been born in America. He felt proud, and then a memory flashed through his mind: a sad, tragic memory, but funny all the same. He remembered Shake asking, "Who speaks English best, the doctor, your old lady, or you?" and poor Kakuska. . . . Apparently the doctor's English had been at fault, or else Bozenka had made immense progress when they opened the English school in Manitowoc and she got a wonderful teacher, Miss Woodford, who spoke no Czech but lent her books, turning her into an ardent wintertime reader, since in spring, summer, and fall she was too busy on the farm.

"Some sort of foolishness," said Padecky.

"I'll have you know it's not," objected Bozenka. "Read it, Mr. Padecky, I'll lend it to you."

"Not interested," snapped Padecky.

Molly Schroeder retorted pointedly, "You would be if you knew how to read."

Padecky's temper rose. "What do you mean, Molly? You trying to say I don't know English? My English is plenty good enough for that kind of nonsense."

"That's not what I said," replied Molly sweetly. "But you still can't read anything but Gothic script."

Padecky grabbed the book from the table in front of Mr. Ohrenzug, opened it, put his finger on the first line on the page, and opened his mouth. Then he gradually turned purple; he snapped the book shut and shoved it across the table, where it came to rest against the beer stein in front of the sergeant. Kapsa picked it up.

"Damn foolishness," Padecky growled, but then he added softly and uncertainly, "I left my spectacles at home."

The sergeant brought the book up to his eyes. The Negro opened the door for someone to the sound of little tin drums.

At first the sergeant failed to notice the glitter at the young woman's throat. His attention was on the warmth coming from the cardboard box in his pocket containing the forget-me-not earrings he had come to Chicago to buy. They were genuine, imported from Bohemia, and he had paid all of two dollars for them in Mr. Pancner's shop on Dearborn. So he didn't really register the beautiful gleam at the young woman's throat as he hurried along Lake Street towards the train station, eager to see the forget-me-nots in the tiny ears of his newborn daughter, Terezka. But in the light pouring out of the restaurant window a splendid stone glittered at the stranger's throat—

He spun around. The girl in the fancy cloak and her companion in the derby hat were just turning to enter the restaurant.

He hesitated, and looked down. His shoes were still shiny from the honest efforts of a shoeshine boy at the train station when he had arrived. He was wearing his Sunday suit and, though his hat wasn't new, it was still quite dapper. He took a deep breath and followed them through the revolving door into the restaurant. He watched the waiter help the girl off with her cloak and take her companion's derby. They sat down at a table, the gold light from the long bar shining on them from the left. He walked over to the bar, sat on a bar stool, and glanced at himself in the bar mirror that doubled the size of the already spacious restaurant. He was presentable. He even had a tie tack in his cravat that Vojta Houska had made from a Rebel belt buckle back in the hospital where they'd been treated for the Kansas quickstep. She was wearing a dress that revealed a lovely alabaster throat, but he could see only the gold chain. He glanced at her companion and was so startled that he didn't hear the bartender saying, "What'll it be, sir?"

Seated opposite the girl was Hauptmann von Hanzlitschek.

"What'll it be, sir?

"Pardon?"

"What will you have?"

"Oh," he said. "Bourbon. With ice."

He stared at von Hanzlitschek until his heart slowed down again. It couldn't possibly be the Hauptmann, even if he'd risen from the dead. Today he would be in his fifties, perhaps even his sixties. He had been fifteen years older than Ursula. Then he remembered a park, a tiny girl, a pug dog, a lace bonnet, then a slap and a howling miniature of the Hauptmann. The young woman's companion could only be that miniature, now grown up. Even the moustache was smaller, more American, and he wasn't wearing a monocle. But he sat straight as a candle, as if he had a corset on, and he was smoking a slim cigar. Ursula's son.

He turned to the bartender.

The bartender shrugged his shoulders. "But his lady friend is Miss Faber," he said. "Eberhart Faber, don't you know?"

"Faber?" he repeated absently.

"Pencils." The bartender's eyes fell on his tie tack. "You a veteran?"

The sergeant nodded.

"Twenty-first Michigan," said the bartender, offering his hand over the bar.

"Thirteenth United States."

"I see," said the barman. The sergeant shook the proffered hand.

"You said Miss Faber?"

"Her uncle has a pencil factory in New York. Her father heads the branch here in Chicago."

The girl rose, turned. A flash like a canister exploding.

"Did you stay in the army?" asked the barman.

The sergeant didn't reply. The bartender followed his stare. He said, "Nice, isn't she?"

But the sergeant wasn't staring at the girl. He was staring at what she had around her neck.

Diamonds, like a nest of crystal eggs.

The bartender kept trying to engage him in conversation, but the sergeant sat there like a pillar of salt. The bartender gave up and poured him another drink. "This one's on the house, buddy," he said. "Because we won."

A whirlwind was howling inside the sergeant's head. Madam Sosniowski hadn't known for sure. And diplomats get transferred. Ursula's necklace, stolen by Fircut—now on the neck of the niece of a pencil magnate. . . . The sergeant's head was spinning.

The next bourbon was no longer on the house. Nor was the one after that. He was drinking for courage. When von Hanzlitschek rose and the waiter placed the fancy cloak around Miss Faber's lovely neck, the sergeant slipped down from the barstool, waved the couple through the revolving door ahead of him, and then pretended to look surprised. "Excuse me, aren't you Mr. von Hanzlitschek?"

Von Hanzlitschek looked at the sergeant suspiciously, not recognizing him. How could he? He had been a tearful ball of rage in a sailor suit at the time—

"Yes?" von Hanzlitschek replied tentatively.

"You're the living image," said the sergeant, "of your father. I served under"—von Hanzlitschek was now staring at him intently—"served with your father many years ago, in Austria."

"Ah," said von Hanzlitschek, "In Helldorf? Or in Viertal?"

"In Viertal," said the sergeant quickly. "I was—a sergeant back then," he said, wondering how much von Hanzlitschek knew about his father's demise. But the young man smiled, his hard Austrian eyes softening, and he shook the sergeant's hand.

"Sergeant—" Kapsa started to introduce himself, and stopped. Then he translated his name into German. "— Tasche."

"Tasche?"

"That's right," said Sergeant Kapsa. "What are you doing in Chicago?"

He gave his head another shake. He was back in The Witches' Kitchen.

Meanwhile, the famous lady author and her companion had made their way over to the doorman and the companion was introducing him to the author. The sergeant opened Mr. Ohrenzug's book. On the title page, in an alphabet the sergeant couldn't read, in a language he didn't know, it said, *The English Language for Émigrés from Russia*. He looked at Padecky, smiled to himself, then he shut the book and put it back down in front of Mr. Ohrenzug.

"Who's that fellow, Mr. Ohrenzug?" asked Molly.

"You mean the nigger?" asked Mr. Ohrenzug.

Padecky said, "Nigger, German, Babylonian, as long as he's wearing trousers." Molly decided to ignore him.

"That's Jasmine's hubby," said Mr. Ohrenzug. "I hired him as a waiter back in the old place on Dearborn, but he had two left hands so I put him to washing dishes. That was even worse. Fortunately that woman of his—" Mr. Ohrenzug hesitated and looked around at the ladies present. "Are any of you from Chicago?"

The three women exchanged glances. "No," Ruzena Houska said, and shook her head. "We're the closest and we have a farm south of Manitowoc."

"What was fortunate about his woman?" asked Molly Schroeder eagerly.

"Well," said Mr. Ohrenzug, "she opened a—place of her own. So she hired him. I just kept his mother on. He offered to help out today because of the gala opening, so I put him at the door with orders only to bow. He knows how to bow. That's what he does at his wife's place, at her—restaurant. Even so, he slipped once already and broke the glass in the door. It'll cost me at least twenty bucks to fix. It's special glass."

The famous author was laughing heartily at something the doorman had said, her red locks swinging over her iridescent shoulders. "He's a talker," said Mr. Ohrenzug, "but that's all he's good at. The truth is that before Jasmine gave him a job in her place, he was what you might call my silent partner."

"Why silent?" asked Molly.

"Mrs. Schroeder!" Mr. Ohrenzug sounded surprised to have to explain. "In Chicago it's bad enough being a Jew. If a Jew is known to be in business with a nigger—"

"Where did he get the capital, Mr. Ohrenzug?" asked Shake. "Compensation, so to speak, for years of slavery somewhere in the South?"

"Just let me finish," said Mr. Ohrenzug. "He invested, so to speak, his mother into the business." And he proceeded to tell how he'd wanted to get rid of him, after the débâcle at the door and the damaged dishes, but it turned out that he wasn't totally useless, though the one skill he had was useless in the restaurant business. Mr. Ohrenzug had actually hired him as a tagalong with his mother. She'd moved from the South to Chicago with him after the war and soon became famous as a cook, but when Mr. Ohrenzug fired her son she started scorching the sauces. She said that her son knew black magic and that he'd put a spell on her as revenge for getting fired. There was nothing left for Mr. Ohrenzug to do but take him on as a silent partner. And then the spell-caster's wife had opened her own establishment.

"How did she get to be friends with Mrs. Lee?" asked Bozenka. The sergeant glanced at his wife.

She had been so exhausted then, after two years of bad harvests. And it had rained all summer, and then the hailstorms had come, and then a tornado had collapsed the barn, and little Cyril needed a doctor, and she was worried to death that the farm her late husband, Kakuska, had built up was going to go under now that she was in charge.

He had decided to go and talk to Cup, and so he took the train to Chicago. The grocery store, Cup & Co., had survived the war under the management of an honest man from Nebraska too near-sighted for the army, and then the business had expanded, growing from one store into five.

At one of the stops, a fellow in a ten-gallon hat and a chequered suit got on the train and sat down opposite him. It was hot. The man took off his big hat and—

"Fircut," said the sergeant. The man blinked and then cringed, as though expecting a slap in the face.

"Kapsa!" he exclaimed. "Man, you don't know how hard I looked for you!"

"Me too," said the sergeant. "And I never could find you either." He examined Fircut's face. It had grown jowly, but the eyes were still shifty. "Till now," said the sergeant. "That's what I call a coincidence." He raised his hand and pulled up his sleeve a bit. The war had marked the sergeant, but differently from Fircut. The scoundrel had grown a belly and was soft and flabby. He looked scared. He's afraid I'll hit him, thought the sergeant.

"I owe you, Kapsa," said Fircut, his double chin trembling.

"Really?" said the sergeant, irony in his voice.

"With interest, I figure it'll be seven, eight hundred"—he assessed the look in the sergeant's eye—"say a thousand—"

"It'll be more than that," said the sergeant, "even without interest." He gave his sleeve another tug. Fircut stared at him with his puffy eyes. He's certainly afraid I might hit him, the sergeant thought. But he soon discovered that that wasn't what Fircut feared most. "Fifteen hundred," he said.

Later the two of them sat in a saloon at Clinton and Monroe and ordered drinks while "The Battle Hymn of the Republic" jangled loudly on a player piano.

Fircut pulled out a thick wad of bills held together with a gold money clip. "Here, take two."

The sergeant looked at him in amazement. The puffy eyes were swimming. Should I have asked for more, he wondered. Fircut in tears? And the money— well, it was heaven-sent, he thought to himself. From Ursula. It solved the problem of the farm he had inherited, along with the farmer's wife, from poor Kakuska, and there would be enough left over for a new reaper.

"It's three times what I got for them," Fircut was saying. "You can imagine, I had to go to the Jew with them, I didn't know my way around yet. But they brought me luck back then, Kapsa, and I—"

★

"So they brought you luck," said Ursula.

"In the long run they did."

"Exactly what do you mean, in the long run?" Ursula pouted, but she didn't sound particularly serious. By then it was just—a legend.

"They brought everyone luck," he said, and started enumerating. "Your boy Georg was lucky that you saw them on Hannelore; that was lucky for Hannelore, too—"

"That is, if Georg is good luck for her," she said. "There are days when he's far too much like the Hauptmann, and not just in the way he wears his moustache. But for you they did bring luck."

"Didn't they for you?" he asked boldly, and immediately felt like a wretched sinner, but still he reached over to cover her hand sporting the single glittering diamond. Gulls stared down at them from the sky as they sat on the bench by the edge of Lake Michigan, surrounded by hedges.

She pulled her hand away and said, "In the long run they did. I was afraid for you. Afraid they'd catch you, you know? But it turned out all right. And they brought you luck. Of course, he cheated you."

"I could get back at him. It's just that—" He stopped. He didn't have to finish his sentence.

Ursula spoke quickly. "No! Don't tempt your luck. They say luck is fickle."

It certainly is, he thought. Ursula said, "When I saw them on Hannelore, my heart stopped. I knew then that you'd made it to America."

"Why didn't you answer my letters, Ursula?"

"I never got any letters," she said.

Didn't you, thought Kapsa.

"Her uncle, the pencil magnate, bought them for Hannelore," said Ursula. "He has three sons but he always wanted a daughter. I've never met him, to ask him where he got them."

"That doesn't matter," said Sergeant Kapsa. "The main thing is, they brought us luck."

★

"— I've got cancer, Kapsa," said Fircut. "It's no use."

In the saloon, a player piano played "The Battle Hymn of the Republic".

★

"His woman was a servant of hers in Cincinnati," said Mr. Ohrenzug.

"What's it about, Bozenka?" said Padecky, changing the subject glumly. He had been silent for quite a while, mulling over the book he couldn't read because of his ignorance of the Latin alphabet, an ignorance reconfirmed over *The English Language for Émigrés from Russia*.

"It's hard to explain," the sergeant's wife replied. "Lots of things happen in it. You'd have to read it for yourself."

"I don't have my spectacles, dammit!" swore Padecky. "Anyway, don't bother your little head. It must be full of straw if you can't even tell a fellow what a stupid book's all about!"

"Why are you interested, if it's stupid?" asked Molly Schroeder, but again Padecky ignored the merry ex-widow.

"It's about a girl named Geraldine," said Bozenka. "At the beginning she gets engaged to someone called Patrick who's a doctor. In the end they get married, but in between it keeps going back and forth between looking like the wedding is never going to come off and looking like it is. Mainly because, if you ask me, he's a dimwit."

"See? Stupid," said Padecky. "I didn't even have to read it to know that."

"It's a very nice book," Bozenka protested. "And a big one. I just wonder, if the fellow is such a dimwit compared to Geraldine—"

"So?" Padecky looked out on the dance floor in annoyance. "Look at him!" he said, pointing to Houska's face moving in and out of the cigar smoke like a sweaty moon as he spun around with his pretty wife. "He too got himself married! He even broke up her first marriage, although it's true it was a bad one!"

"But he came back from the war a hero," said Shake.

"And didn't you?" yelled Padecky. "With a medal and all! But you're still batching it!"

"I have my reasons," said Shake.

"What reasons, I ask you? Is it that you're—" Padecky stopped short. "Well, you know what I mean. There's ladies present."

"You mean us?" Molly Schroeder asked impudently, but Padecky continued to ignore her.

"Yes, I know what you mean," said Shake. "No, that isn't why. Actually, I think Miss Laura Lee would understand," he said, with a wistful glance towards the famous author standing with the doorman, who was still bending her ear. "God knows," he said, with feeling. "Maybe I should tell her my story. She might turn it into a beautiful novel." He paused. "It could be called *Between the Devil and the Deep Blue Sea*. And, my dear lady"—he turned to Bozenka—"it would contain a similar problem: how someone so pretty and apparently so smart could fall in love, even though just briefly, with, as you put it, such a dimwit."

"You're a jester, Mr. Schweik," said Bozenka. "But that wasn't the strange thing about the book. Sure, a girl who's pretty and smart can marry a—" She hesitated and glanced at the sergeant, who just made a face. "Although it doesn't often happen."

"Hardly ever," Shake interjected sadly.

"What I wondered," she went on, "was how such a fool as this Patrick fellow ever got to be a doctor. I wouldn't let him write me a prescription for Hoffman tonic."

"Well, doctors like that do turn up now and then," said Shake. "I knew one, a German called Schlaflieber, and he was a past master at messing up prescriptions."

Bozenka blushed beet-red. But that had been long ago, and time was a better healer than Schlaflieber, M.D., or the fictional dimwit Patrick. The sergeant smiled at his wife and she flushed an even deeper red, although that was impossible. He felt a pang of conscience, but that had been more than long ago—it was deep in the abyss of time. And more recently—

When he returned from Chicago to the farm and got into bed beside his wife, deep in the well-deserved sleep of a young farmer's wife, he stared at the summer stars and meditated on the many mysteries of love that his wife read about in her novels. He looked at her face and love poured over him like honey. He recalled the summer sky long ago in a distant land, in a mysterious cottage on a hill, on God's own little table, in a beautiful time now deep in an abyss that the war had covered over, the same war that had buried Kakuska.

Six months later he had to go to Chicago again, and in a fancy lawyer's ma-

hogany-panelled office he received a cheque for a staggering five thousand dollars willed to him in a moment of deathbed guilt by Fircut, who—as he admitted in a hastily penned note attached to the cheque—had not sold the nest of crystal eggs to a Jew, but had discovered a more lucrative market, which in turn had moved the goods by some uncanny route to the lovely throat of the pencil magnate's young niece. An hour later the sergeant found himself standing in front of a mansion by the lake, with a heraldic eagle scowling down at him from over the door—an eagle different from the bald one that had witnessed his entry into a new and better, though cruel and dangerous, chapter of his life—and moving to a side entrance, pulling the bell rope, and saying in English to the chambermaid who answered the door, "Tell Madam Consul that someone would like to speak with her, a sergeant—" He hesitated. "Sergeant Tasche," he said.

He gave his head a shake. The doorman had opened the door for someone else, and the drumming of the rain interrupted his thoughts and brought him back.

"I mean, she was her servant," said Mr. Ohrenzug. "Only until she made it in—in the restaurant business. You know, neighbours, it's like something Mrs. Laura Lee might have thought up."

The doorman was standing alone again. The sergeant looked around and saw the author and the young woman sitting in a booth, the author's mouth open as if in astonishment at what her companion was telling her. She took a handkerchief from her décolletage, patted her pale forehead—was it that hot in here, wondered the sergeant. Mr. Ohrenzug was telling the others how the abolitionist Mrs. Morris had asked her father for the girl as a birthday present and then drowned in the lake, and how the girl had got a job with the famous woman author, whose real name was not in fact Laura Lee.

"Anyway, Mrs. Lee hired her as a chambermaid," continued Mr. Ohrenzug, "and the girl was going to save her wages to buy her husband's freedom. That shouldn't have been a problem—how much could they want for someone as lazy and useless as Hasdrubal? His mother"—Ohrenzug grew thoughtful—"now, that was another matter." But even that they had figured out. The liberated loafer would put a spell on her and her price would drop to zero, especially since she was short a leg. "But man proposes and God disposes," said Mr. Ohrenzug. "Before they could do anything, the South seceded, the chambermaid was stuck in Cincinnati, and Hasdrubal was still on a plantation. Luscious as she was, the girl was so gone on the loafer that she only cheated on him once, and that was with a general who was here in Illinois arresting journalists."

"Burnside?" asked Shake, amazed.

"You leave him out of this!" Padecky cried. "He's the one who nabbed that bastard Vallandigham!" A memory burst in the sergeant's mind like a shooting star. "And he should have given him the noose, too!" Padecky went on. "Big mistake, not stringing him up!"

"You mean the one with the *peyzes*?" asked Mr. Ohrenzug. "No, it wasn't him, he was a decent fellow. This one's name was Rascall, and that's exactly what he was. Not because he locked up reporters—I approved of that. But he was a libertine. She only did it as a way of thanking him for fighting to free her race. He was sneaky, that rascal. He thought nothing of taking advantage of nobler emotions." Mr. Ohrenzug was gradually getting as angry as Padecky, but he forced himself to calm down and went on to tell about how, as soon as the war was over, the Negro girl packed a suitcase and got on a train to South Carolina. In the suitcase she was carrying her wedding dress.

"I'll bet that's who the Carolina Bride is going to be!" exclaimed Bozenka.

"What bride, damn it?" growled Padecky.

"In the book I read, *She Played It Safe*," explained Bozenka, "it said at the end that Mrs. Lee was working on another story, 'a tragic romance of the War of Secession'. It said the new book would be called *Carolina Bride* and would be a big surprise for all her readers, because there'll be entirely new tones in the story, never used before by Mrs. Laura Lee." She glanced over at the booth, and so did the sergeant. The famous writer was just setting down a liqueur glass. The pretty Negro woman was gesticulating earnestly, the way people do when they are eager to be understood.

"Tones? What tones?" Padecky asked.

"What?" Bozenka responded absently.

"I said what tones? Is it about bagpipes or what?"

"Mrs. Kapsa was speaking figuratively," said Shake. "The new novel will contain new stories, told in ways the author hasn't used before."

"I don't know about that," said Padecky. "A girl packs a wedding dress in her valise—what kind of new stories or tones or what? Just maybe she was too sure of herself, since she'd cheated on him, only once, true, but still. Dumb biddy. If it was me—" Padecky fell silent, because two waiters stepped up to the table with trays laden with steaming food, and he was overcome by the long-forgotten fragrance.

— and the sergeant, a sparkler exploding in his mind's eye, saw the training camp in Washington where he had tormented volunteer recruits by drumming Austrian-style drill into them, but all for a good cause, for the kind of freedom he

had found in this country, even in the army, and the kind that was missing in Cyril's story.

One day a politician came to the camp. He was elegant and he made eloquent speeches, and the recruits—defiant and reluctant to obey orders shouted at them by some kid from the village back home just because he happened to have stripes on his sleeve—stood around a hastily constructed platform, their faces growing darker as the congressman from Washington pontificated against the war. They never let him finish. They lifted him bodily down from the platform and sat him on a rail. Four men went for a barrel of tar and two more came running up from the mess hall with five freshly slaughtered chickens, plucking them as they ran, but then Colonel Farrar blocked their way and rescued the speaker. But before the handsome politician climbed off the rail and was escorted out of camp on the colonel's orders, the sergeant approached him and—

★

"You slapped his face?" the little girl asked, astonished. "What did he do to you?"

"Nothing personal, Terezka," said the sergeant. "But—" He had just received a letter. Paidr had died in the veterans' home in Racine. Two sentences, that was all. The sergeant glanced at Houska's clock, the wooden band started playing, Lincoln leaned out of the window like a cuckoo and waved the starry flag nine times. The sergeant recalled his old buddy Paidr, one name in a wreath of names that included Gettysburg, the Army of the Cumberland, Chattanooga, Wauhatchie, Lookout Mountain. The clock played other names in his head too. Kabinus—had he ever gone back after the war to the girl whose age the chaplain listed in the marriage certificate as sixty? He had lost a hand at Resaca. He was a man of few words, a friend. Kennesaw Mountain, Vojta Houska, Yazoo River, Stejskal, the Twentieth Corps of the Army of the Cumberland, the Twenty-sixth Wisconsin, Svejkar, Zinkule, Fisher, Javorsky, Kakuska—

"No, he did nothing to me personally, Terezka. Now read some more to me. You read so nicely."

"Oh, sure I do," said the little girl, and she picked up the book and, in a mechanical voice, started reading where she had left off.

"And General Sherman, having averted a general battle, waited at Bentonville until Schofield's boats delivered the accoutrements so desperately needed after the long march through the Carolinas, the frequent and brutal skirmishes and ultimately the final intensive encounter at Bentonville having demanded their own, and Sherman's army, albeit victorious, resembling for the most part a pack of scarecrows in ragged dress, bare-chested and in many cases barefoot (though with weapons spotless), arrived at the Neuse River, where, only a month later—when on April 18th General Johnston finally laid down his arms—the war finally ended in glory for General Sherman's brave troops."

★

"Hadn't he waited for her?" Bozenka asked, disappointed, glancing over at the handsome doorman. Two silhouettes appeared behind the frosted glass, and the Negro opened the door. It was raining. A man with a rough, weather-beaten face walked in, slipped the cape off his shoulders, and handed it to the doorman. He was followed by a second man, shorter, with hunched shoulders and a large nose. The rain continued falling. The brass lantern roofs clattered like little tin drums.

"You're on the right track," said Mr. Ohrenzug. "She was too trusting. It was a long way to go—all the way to South Carolina by train, right after the war—and when she finally got there, her fellow was long gone. A week earlier, on the next plantation, the owner's daughter had turned up with her own chambermaid. She'd married an ink manufacturer who later became a general in our Union army, and the chambermaid, whose name was Bee, was a wedding gift, but in Chicago her slave status hadn't lasted; either she was given her freedom, or else everyone just ignored her lack of it. When the war broke out the ink manufacturer became a colonel, and after the battle on Little Round Top, where he lost an eye but kept on fighting, he was promoted to general. In the meantime Bee had become her former owner's confidante and best friend. In fact, they had always been close, since they'd grown up together. So the two of them arrived at the Cooper's Ferry plantation, which was half demolished and deserted, for the funeral of the lady's widowed father. They came without the general, who had gone back to manufacturing ink and loved to brag about his glass eye in cities both north and south. They stayed at the plantation only a week, but that was enough. The general's wife returned to Chicago with her chambermaid, a new footman, and a new cook. The following day the bride from Cincinnati arrived at the plantation next door, and never even unpacked her wedding dress. She caught the next train back."

"But there was a happy ending," Bozenka reassured herself, glancing at the famous author. The Negro woman in the iridescent silk was still talking and gesticulating eagerly.

Mr. Ohrenzug hesitated. "It's all in how you take it. She had the footman's mother on her side, the one who's responsible for the dishes making your mouths water," he said, looking around the table.

Shake declared, "The lady's cooking is beyond reproach. What I don't understand, though—"

"She gets it straight from God," Colonel Ohrenzug interjected hastily. "You don't need schooling for that. In fact, you can't learn to cook like this in any school."

Shake looked him firmly and silently in the eye. In a nervous tone, the colonel asked, "Would you like some more?"

"Did I hear you say this Jasmine opened a restaurant?" asked Shake.

"So to speak."

"And you also said the footman's mother is on her side?"

"I did," admitted Mr. Ohrenzug, and stopped short.

"What I don't understand, then," said Shake, without taking his eyes off the colonel, who lowered his gaze, "is why the mother stayed with you when her daughter-in-law opened a restaurant and her son waits on tables there."

"He's really a bouncer," Mr. Ohrenzug explained. "What I mean to say is, it's not all that fancy a restaurant."

"Are you saying that your cook refused to work in a low-class place?"

"That's what I'm saying. She resents it that Jasmine is—" He halted.

Shake was still looking into his eyes. He asked, "Where is this place?"

"I'm not exactly sure. Some place between Dearborn and Clark."

Houska, who was busy cleaning his plate, looked up as though he wanted to say something. But Mr. Ohrenzug, with considerable effort and forced levity, quickly changed the subject: "Things looked pretty dim for the girl," he said, nodding towards the booth where the famous author was shaking hands with the man with the weather-beaten face. The Negro woman had stopped gesturing and was gazing at the man as though he were the president. "To that fool over there"—the colonel nodded towards the handsome doorman—"the Chicago chambermaid seemed like a better match. Both girls were good-looking, both were pale yellow, and both were chambermaids. Bee was employed by a general's wife. The two girls got into a fight over him, and Bee whipped Jasmine. Trounced her! Almost tore one of her ears off. She'd have lost it for sure if Dr. Walenta hadn't sewn it back on. Meanwhile, the general's wife started planning a wedding."

The sergeant noticed Bozenka frowning at Ohrenzug. "For Bee and Hasdrubal?" she asked.

"Yes. For Bee and Hasdrubal."

"So Jasmine can't be the Carolina Bride," Bozenka remarked sadly.

"She was some Bee!" chuckled the colonel. "She should have been called

Hornet! The big fight happened the night before the wedding. The general was off on one of his frequent business trips, bragging about his glass eye somewhere in Albany, and the wedding dress was laid out on the double bed he shared with his wife. Jasmine's dress couldn't compare. The general's wife and Bee were as close as sisters. And what do you think happened?"

In a shed in the courtyard where Gospel had put her, Jasmine was thinking of poison and considering suicide, but a sudden outburst in the general's home made her prick up her good ear. It was female voices screaming in the master bedroom—the general's wife and Bee. "Pandemonium broke loose," continued Mr. Ohrenzug. "Twice a male voice grumbled something amid the female screams, but each time Jasmine could hear a resounding slap. Bee has a nasty temper."

"So what was wrong?" asked Vojta Houska. All three women looked at him as if they couldn't believe their ears. Padecky tried to comment but couldn't; his mouth was full of sauerkraut.

"It's obvious," said Shake.

With a painful gulp Padecky swallowed the sauerkraut and went into a rage.

"As close as sisters? She was an officer's slut!" he yelled. "But what can a fellow expect from women? Vipers is what they are, each one as bad as the next!" He seemed to be responding to some profound experience, rather than sounding off for the sheer pleasure of it as he normally did.

"Calm down, Padecky!" Ruzena scolded him.

"Why should I calm down?"

"Not every woman is a bitch," said Molly.

"That, from you, who—"

"She doesn't mean herself," Bozenka tried to help out. "I mean to say—"

"— a merry widow?!" Padecky roared.

"*Was sagt er?*" Schroeder asked.

"Who was she?" asked Shake.

Padecky looked startled. "Who was who?"

"The one," said Shake, "who makes you damn the whole female race."

Padecky stiffened. "You knew her?"

"No, I didn't," said Shake. "I haven't the faintest idea who she is."

"So why are you asking? And why don't you mind your own business, dammit? And why am I getting so excited if you don't know what you're talking about!"

"You're shouting," said Shake. "It's upsetting the customers."

"What customers?" Padecky looked around. The people looking at them seemed more interested than upset.

"So will I ever find out what the fight was about?" asked Houska.

Almost softly, Padecky said, "You? Probably not."

The door opened to the drumbeat of rain. The sergeant turned and saw a tall, straight figure with a gigantic general's moustache, but it was just Stejskal, who had made sergeant too by the war's end and had become one of General Williams's bodyguards. Beside him was a tiny, wiry fellow who also wore an immense moustache. They approached the table and joined them.

"But there was a happy ending, wasn't there?" insisted Bozenka.

In the booth, Jasmine was pouring a drink for the man with the weather-beaten face, from a carafe of lovely liquid that gleamed in the candlelight.

"It depends on how you take it," said Mr. Ohrenzug. "Bee packed up that very night and left by carriage. A week later she came back for her wedding dress. Now she's married to some consul in the Republic of Haiti, they say. Dr. Walenta fixed up the general's wife—he was already experienced in that kind of thing—and Hasdrubal got off unscathed. When he saw that things were getting serious, he didn't hang about for a third slap in the face."

For a while no one spoke. Then Houska said, "Aha!"

They all turned to look at him, but Houska didn't notice. He said, "But it's odd she married him, if he cheated on her like that."

"Don't you know women, stupid?" exclaimed Padecky.

"I don't," said Houska. "That's why I'm asking."

"Maybe she's the Carolina Bride after all, then," said Bozenka. "They don't say love can move mountains for nothing."

The sergeant took a swig of his beer. He had secretly poured a shot into it from the little bottle he'd refilled at the bar earlier, and now he allowed his thoughts to flow back and forth through time. Ursula, Josef, burning turpentine forests, Vitek.

It was Martin Touska who spread the news back in Lhota. Vitek's neighbour Vantouch brought it back from town, where he'd gone to the mill. Touska sat in the driver's seat of the buggy, his empty right sleeve pinned up, but it didn't matter. Lida had long since been "out of sight", but the rest of the proverb didn't apply to Vitek. He had almost made up his mind, but his father wasn't letting him have any money. The fellow with one arm was like a sign: an idea, a possibility, opened up. Vitek ran away. The crimps were in the district capital. A month later Vitek was in the Tyrol, in two he was on a ship, in half a year he was undergoing trial by fire in Matamoros, in the hot and humid summer of a far-away land, but near the place where she had disappeared from sight, so love does move mountains. Then he met Josef in Matamoros, and Josef told Cyril, and Cyril told the sergeant. By then Mother Toupelik had died. The turpentine forests were burning. After that, Cyril too vanished in the tropical shade of war—Jamaica, Trinidad, Barbados.

He heard Stejskal's voice making introductions: "Jake Duty. The one who laid the mine at Petersburg. They made him a first lieutenant for that." The whisky rose to the sergeant's head.

"I looked it over through a crack in the palisade," said the diminutive man with the big moustache, "and I said to myself, if we tunnel under the parapet and pack a big enough charge inside, we can blow up the whole damned fortress, leave a big hole like pulling a giant's tooth." He sniggered. "We were going to do something like that, only smaller, at Vicksburg, but the Rebs got the same idea. There we were, digging a shaft; I stopped for a nap and what did I hear—a shovel scraping. I look around, all our crew are taking a snooze—" The little guy tipped up his beer stein, took a huge swallow, and began to choke.

Ruzena pounded his back with her fist, but Stejskal shook his head. "It's no use, his lungs are full of dust from working in the mines." The little fellow was desperately gasping for breath. "Come on, Jake," said Stejskal, helping him to his feet. They all watched as Stejskal took his friend towards the room marked "Gentlemen".

"All the same, colonel," Shake piped up, "if the cook and her son were so close—"

"They had a disagreement," Mr. Ohrenzug interrupted, his face reddening.

"What about?"

"She—" Mr. Ohrenzug turned a shade darker. "She wanted him to marry Bee. He could be living in a consulate in Haiti today, if—"

"I thought you said she favoured Jasmine," Bozenka said.

"Did I say that? I must have been mis—"

"And if Hasdrubal had married Bee, how could she have been a consul's wife in Haiti?" asked the sergeant's wife.

Mr. Ohrenzug said feebly, "I suppose I. . . ."

"Mr. Ohrenzug, you're lying through your teeth!" Molly Schroeder said sternly. The sergeant furtively poured another shot into his beer while his wife scowled at the colonel. He took a swig and the voices faded.

When Lida (or Linda) went home to her mother's funeral, she was pregnant again, this time with Baxter Warren III, a son and heir. Once again she gave Cyril her word of honour. He didn't believe her, but she said, "Why would I lie to you, Cyril, tell me that? She was really gone. In Savannah I could easily have said I had troubles enough of my own. But I didn't, I really tried to keep an eye on her for you."

"But why, Lida? Why?"

"Well," said his sister, fashionably dressed now, rich—that time in Washington she had also had a mourning ribbon on her hat—"partly on account of you. That tea-rose of yours, heaven knows what kind of abracadabra—" She looked across the fields towards the de Ribordeaux plantation in the distance, past the graveyard where a fresh mound of soil lay on the family grave where they had laid their mother to rest beside their father. "I could have made him sell her south, you know. But I went through all that rigmarole with the blacksmith's wife—"

"Crash!" he heard Jake Duty exclaim. Kapsa hadn't noticed him return to their table. "Crash!" Jake repeated. "The head of the tunnel started shifting and in the light of my lantern I saw a fellow in butternut with a spade. Like I said, they'd had the same idea and we were tunnelling under the parapet from opposite sides. So I swung at him with my pickaxe, he swung back with his spade—and boys, we fought the Rebs underground, hand to hand."

"Did you take any prisoners?"

"We fought off their attack, but we had to retreat. Our plan was blown and any more digging was out of the question. But at Petersburg I saw the chance right off, as soon as I took a look through the crack in the palisade. Somebody behind me says, 'Think we could do it?' I turn around and there's Lieutenant-Colonel Henry Pleasants. All of us in the Forty-eighth Pennsylvania were black-coal miners from the Schuylkill. 'You bet, colonel!' I say. 'What about ventilation?' he asks. 'You'd have to dig almost two hundred yards.'"

Cyril never told Lida about the bug the blacksmith's wife had planted in his ear. He went back to Chicago, where he was a partner in a machinists' firm, but the idea was firmly planted. They say love moves mountains. "God knows," he admitted to Kapsa, "maybe she just gave up. Besides," he said sadly, "I'm not of the same blood she is."

"As if that mattered!" the sergeant said.

"God knows," said Cyril, and left.

The sergeant got up and walked towards the gentlemen's room, stopping at the bar on his way.

When she saw him, Ursula exclaimed, "Ach, Tasche! Kapsa! Mein lieber Mann!" and she took him by the hands. "All that is not true," she said.

"It's not," he replied. "But I never even thanked you, Madam—"

"Ursula."

"Ursula."

"And what about me? Who should I have thanked?" She smiled, and that

*was that. Something rose up in him, a strong sensation, gratitude, but that was
that.*

*Then he said, "This cheque really belongs to you. I couldn't even manage to
hang onto your precious gift."*

"But the jewels brought you luck."

"That they did," he said.

"I gave them to you. And now they're actually back in the family."

"But this cheque—"

*She interrupted him: "You said you have a daughter?" So the nest of crystal
eggs would buy a dowry for Terezka. He looked into her eyes. Gottestischlein. She
stepped closer to him, then they embraced, and as they were kissing, his mind
turned into a kaleidoscope—the soothing sweet water, the miracle, and how she
said in her sweet German, so unlike that of Hauptmann von Hanzlitschek,
"Oh, you dear man! You're even making progress with the German language!"
Then the bloody welt on Ursula's back where the bullwhip struck . . . he felt the
happiness that could not have been real rising in him, centering on his under-
belly—and she extricated herself from his embrace, and whispered passionately,
gently, joyfully, "Danke, thank you, mein lieber Mann, thank you, thank you,
thank you!"*

*He came to his senses, felt ashamed, then grateful, then joyful. He walked out
of the house, glanced back at the two-headed eagle, and never saw her again. It
was with the last, whispered, gentle, passionate words that she had remained
alive in his mind.*

He came out of the gentlemen's room and saw his general, hesitated, and
returned to his table.

"A thunderclap!" Jake Duty was saying. "An explosion like the world
never saw before or since. A huge mass of earth, dirt, palisades, cannon, and
Rebels flew straight up in the air, with a column of fire and a head of smoke
like a great mushroom. Then it all fell back down again, men—whole ones
and parts—a caisson wheel, a horse's quarters with a leg attached—"
*Cornflower-blue serpent's eyes. How was it Bozenka put it? Some proverbs prove
true, some don't.* "The plan," he heard Jake Duty go on, "was to launch an attack through that gaping hole. And it should have worked, they could have
been in Petersburg in an hour, but the blast was so awful that everyone was
scared. To top it off, our artillery cut loose and made a racket like the world
had never heard. Ledlie's division was supposed to lead the assault but they
stood there with their mouths hanging open, and when they finally got
moving, instead of securing the gap, they jumped into the crater and started
helping the wounded and buried Rebels. It wasn't until two more divisions

joined them that the shooting started in The Crater, and soon it was such a mess that nobody knew who anyone was. To top it off, General Ledlie stayed out of it, probably because he'd been drinking under the palisade, shitting bricks. Small wonder. Then a well-drilled nigger division came marching into all that madness as if they were on the parade ground and, on top of everything, they were singing! Of course, their commander turned them loose into that madhouse by themselves, while he stayed under cover, boozing with Ledlie. Some commanders we had! Burnside wanted to send the niggers in first, partly to prove to the doubting Thomases that they were as good as anyone else, and in fact he'd drilled them to do this for two weeks before. But then Burnside thought it over and instead he sent the white divisions, who hadn't trained for it. He bungled it the way he did at Fredericksburg."

"*Remember? Remember, buddy? Perryville. And us among all those awful bubbles!*" *It was a happy Salek-Cup. How things changed. Somebody called it the alchemy of time. The sergeant took a drink of his fortified beer. That was alchemy too. They had fought at Perryville with their tongues hanging out. All that was left of it were the tales of Jan Amos Shake. Cup, first widowed, then divorced, now happy again—*

"An apartment house?" asked the sergeant.

"He has two of them, in Prague. One in Zizkov district, one in the Lesser Town," said Cup. "And a fruit and vegetable store on the Small Square. My father-in-law and I, we're colleagues," he declared happily. "Both of us were patriots, we belong to the Sokols. Me in Chicago, him in Prague. The first time I saw Jirinka, my second wife, was with the Sokols—"

"And how come you weren't afraid to go home for the Sokol Assembly?" the sergeant interrupted him. "After all, they're such patriots and you're a deserter. You bombarded the Lesser Town."

"I'm Andy Cup now," said Salek, "and I have the papers to prove it. American papers. So I was in the artillery—I was young and foolish. Besides, that was a long time ago."

They were sitting in Slavik's Tavern, and they were older now, the farmer and the wholesaler.

"Aren't you too old for Jirinka?"

"I'm an American," Cup said proudly. "I served honourably in the great war for liberty!"

The sergeant looked around. "Not that her restaurant is such a bad place," said Mr. Ohrenzug, getting himself in deeper and deeper. "It's just in a bad neighbourhood."

"Funny I don't know it," said Shake. "I associate exclusively with poor people."

"Where did you say it was?" asked Houska.

"Somewhere between Dearborn and Clark," said Mr. Ohrenzug.

"Isn't that Little Cheyenne?" said Houska, then stopped.

Ruzena asked, "What's Little Cheyenne, Houska?"

"But that was before we got married," said Houska.

"Ah," said Shake.

"You know that part of town, Mr. Shake?" asked Ruzena.

"That was before you two got married," said Shake.

"Married or not," Houska's wife retorted, "we were engaged, Vojtech and me, during the war."

"But then you married Freddy!" Houska protested.

"But I divorced him because of you!" snapped the angry Mrs. Houska. "And now he's a candidate for the Sixth District in Berwyn!"

Bozenka, who had been listening closely, said, "Well, I don't think she's going to be the Carolina Bride after all. This doesn't sound like the kind of story Mrs. Lee writes."

The famous author sat at the head table in the dining room with her head in her hands. But then she stood up and tossed her head abruptly, setting the red curls in motion. The man with the weather-beaten face rose as well, and bowed. The author took his arm and they walked onto the dance floor and began dancing a jig to the music of Mates's band.

Those strange paths across the mountains.

"There was that one letter," said Lida. "Somebody was supposed to have seen her in Jamaica."

"So the blacksmith's wife—"

"I don't know," said Lida. "A drowning man will grasp at straws."

Some proverbs prove true, some don't.

The sergeant rose.

"And then nothing? No news from Jamaica?"

"Nothing," said Lida. "It's been three years now. Poor Cyril. Strange stars we had in our sky, didn't we, sergeant?" She stood there in her green hat on the corner of Randolph and Green, Cup's brightly coloured oranges like burning torches behind her, the cornflower eyes from that distant land, the turpentine forests, here now for ever.

"Not necessarily," Mr. Ohrenzug consoled the sergeant's wife. "It's a fine place, otherwise. They have a salon band from New Orleans. Imported—"

"Have you been there, Mr. Ohrenzug?" Bozenka asked him.

"Strictly out of professional curiosity," said Mr. Ohrenzug. "You can go there just for a drink. A glass of wine, I mean. Some of the ladies even speak French. It's just that patois of theirs, but still—"

"There's one thing I still don't understand," Shake said. "Where did she get the money?"

Mr. Ohrenzug flinched. "The capital came from Dr. Walenta," he replied hastily. "I suppose he got the idea when he was stitching up her ear."

"So she certainly isn't the Carolina Bride," said Bozenka flatly.

The sergeant began walking over to the VIP table, then hesitated. The famous author was returning from the dance floor and he heard her tell the man with the weather-beaten face, "I don't know if I'll ever write anything again, general. I had apparently written everything I knew how to write. Then I tried something . . . I tried hard. But what I wanted doesn't count. What counts is what I accomplished."

The farmhouse door was opened by the rosy-cheeked woman in the picture, the one with the miniature portrait of her husband in the background, painted by the jack-of-all-trades from Wilber. He knew then that his footsteps hadn't been guided here merely by the people who gave him directions at forks in the road. She wept wretchedly, inconsolably. Finally, however, she allowed herself to be consoled.

His wife.

"No, general," the famous author was saying. "Burnside should not have let them draw lots. He should have picked the most experienced commander for the attack, and Ledlie was certainly not the right one. He just drew the short straw. But why did he fail so miserably?"

"Why indeed?" said the man with the weather-beaten face. "Burnside was a capital fellow. But he bit off more than he could chew."

"I don't know about that," said the famous author. "I only know how important it was to him that this battle create not only a breakthrough in the Rebel line at Petersburg, but also a breakthrough in the technology of warfare—" *He saw him on his huge horse, Sam, his staff closing the gap and falling behind like a pendulum in the burning snow.* "And that the battle at The Crater be associated for ever with his Negro division. He was genuinely proud of them. He respected them. It's a story that goes way back, back to the Mexican War, even further, in fact. And you gentlemen did not permit it."

The sergeant plucked up his courage.

"That was why there was the foolishness of drawing lots," said the famous author.

"Meade was afraid," said his general. "If there had been a massacre, the reporters would have accused Grant of sending the coloureds to certain death to spare the whites."

"So at the last minute you changed Burnside's orders, and now the reporters are accusing you of regarding the coloured soldiers as trash," said the author. "You were afraid to trust them with an untried task."

"You can't win," said the general, scowling. *To General Logan he had said, "We don't need to win battles any more." Then Terry's Negro Second Division had been marching past in their new blue uniforms and Lida had said, "What can you know, Cyril?"* What could he know? The sergeant stepped over to the booth, and out of the corner of his eye he noticed the rapid approach of Mr. Ohrenzug, who had put on his spectacles and had finally noticed the presence of the man with the weather-beaten face. The sergeant snapped to attention. "General, sir!" he said hoarsely. The weather-beaten face turned to him and he knew the general was searching his memory. Lida in her hat with the black mourning band and, marching past the reviewing stand, Sherman's army. The general looked into his eyes.

"Wait—it's Kapsa, right?"

"Yes, general, sir!" replied the sergeant.

Toronto, 1984–1991
DEO GRATIAS

Postscript

In the Czech archives of the University of Chicago, while doing research for my novel *Dvorak in Love*, I came across 19th century issues of the Czech-American farmers' almanach *Amerikán*. In them I found stories about the Czech soldiers of the Civil War, and also brief memoirs written by the veterans. Searching on, I discovered other sources: *Josef Cermak's* invaluable *History of the Civil War with Experiences of Czech Soldiers Attached* (1889) which gives the names of Czech participants in most major battles of the conflict; Rudolf Bubenicek's *History of the Czechs in Chicago* (1939); Thomas Capek's *The Czechs (Bohemians) in America* (1920), and other books and articles.

My interest was aroused and I decided that, after I finish my Dvorak book, I'll try my hand at a novel about the war from an angle which, to my knowledge, had never been attempted. My intentions were patriotic in the old-fashioned sense: I would do my best to create a sort of memorial of the men who, far from their native land then under Austrian despotism, fought for the country which, unlike Europe, promised hope for a life worth living.

With the exception of Jan Amos Shake, all other Czech soldiers are real. They fought in various units of the Union Army, some in 26 Wisconsin. For the purpose of my novel I put them all there.

Trying to compute their numbers I failed, as others before me. I went through the card catalogue in the U.S. Army Military History Institute in Carlisle Barracks, PA, but after examining several hundred cards, I gave up. The trouble was that far too many Czechs have German names, and since army registers almost never gave the ethnicity of the common soldiers it is impossible to decide whether a Konig, a Miller or a Frohlich was Czech, German, Austrian or Jewish. Besides, Czechs in America also anglicized their unpronounceable names, or Army clerks distorted them, so that a Skrzkrk became a Skirk, a Frkac turned into a Fircut, and a Machane, due to Yankee pronunciation, metamorphosed into a Scot, MacHane.

For these reasons it is hardly possible to determine exact numbers. Thomas Capek quips that "the Czechs provided the United States Army with more musicians than generals," but, except for adding that the number of Czech generals was zero, he does not give any data either for the musicians, or for the common soldiers. He mentions four officers, of whom I found only two listed in the *Official Army Register.*

My own, admittedly unreliable, estimate is about 300 combatants. The U.S. Department of Commerce *A Century of Population Growth* (1909) lists 26,061 immigrants from the Austrian countries recorded by the census of 1860, on the eve of the war. Josef Chada in *The Czechs in the United States* (1981) opines that the "largest fraction" of these Austrian immigrants were Czechs but he, too, fails to provide numbers: the census did not take notice of ethnic origins. If I, rather arbitrarily, take 20,000 for the basis of my computation, assuming that more than half of these were women, children and old or infirm men, the percentage of able-bodied men who joined the army would be about 3 per cent.

However, those who saw service, judging by their brief memoirs and by the few honorable mentions in unit histories I have read (e.g. Zinkule acknowledged in Captain U.G. Alexander's *History of the Thirteenth Regiment United States Infantry,* 1905) acquitted themselves well on the battlefield. Perhaps, even in a huge army, it is quality rather than quantity which counts.

Having lived over one-half of my life in a Communist country, I became allergic to Marxist interpretations of the Civil War. They tended—and for all I know, may still tend—to dismiss or, at best, grossly underestimate concepts that see the conflict also—if not mainly—in terms of the liberation of the slaves. The communist historians I read described the war exclusively as a clash between the interests of northern capitalists and southern plantation owners for which, in the North, emancipation only provided a smokescreen and, in the South, the issue of states' rights served a similar purpose. This seemed to me like spitting on the graves of the soldiers—an emotional reaction, to be sure. But there is also a rational argument: "Although there were serious differences between the [South and the North], all of them except slavery could have been settled through the democratic process . . . [Slavery] was not the only cause of the Civil War, but it was unquestionably the one cause without which the war would not have taken place." (Bruce Catton, *Short History of the Civil War,* 1960).

I resented another popular recent opinion which sees in Sherman the originator of total war. As a youngster, I encountered this killer-warlord image of the general in the Nazi weekly *Signal*. There Sherman's military strategy was used to mock allied criticism of Goebbels' notorious *Totalkrieg* speech, and to defend the *Propagandaminister* against allegations of being the one who instigated universal butchery.

I see Sherman differently.

It has never been clear to me how historians can blame Sherman for this kind of warfare. All one needs to know in order to refute the dubious credit is to read the Old Testament, or be aware of the 15th-century Hussite warriors' battle song "Hit hard, kill, don't spare anyone", or remember the war practices of the *condottieri* in Italy, etc. Compared to them, Sherman is a true American innocent who scorched enemy land to shorten the war but never killed civilians on purpose.

The revisionist criticism of the general brought to my mind Graham Greene's recommendation that writers should focus on characters ripe for universal condemnation rather than on heroes whom everybody likes. I felt I found such a character in the much maligned and ridiculed General Ambrose Burnside, and tried to treat him in the light of my late friend's and patron's advice. For this I found support in Craig Davidson Tenney's dissertation on Burnside.

J.S.

Main American Book Sources

Angle, P.M. *Created Equal? The Complete Lincoln Douglas Debates of 1858.* The University of Chicago Press, 1958.

Argument of Hon. Aaron F. Perry, Vallandigham Habeas Corpus. U.S. District Court, 1864?

Barnard, G.N. *Photographic views of Sherman's Campaign.* Dover, 1977.

Battle of Bentonville, The. Bentonville.

Bierce, Ambrose. *Bits of Autobiography.* Gordian Press, 1966.

Botkin, B.A. *A Civil War Treasury of Tales, Legends and Folklore.* Random House, 1960.

Bowman, S.M., Col. and Irvin, R.B., Lt. Col. *Sherman and His Campaigns: A Military Biography.* New York: Charles B. Richardson, 1865.

Burton, W.L. *Melting Pot Soldiers: The Union's Ethnic Regiments.* Iowa State University Press, 1988.

Catton, Bruce. *Reflections on the Civil War.* Berkeley Books, 1984.

Catton, Bruce. *Short History of the Civil War.* Laurel, 1984.

Commager, H.S., ed. *The Blue and the Gray: The Story of the Civil War as Told by the Participants.* 2 vols. New American Library, 1973.

Crawford, R., ed. *The Civil War Songbook.* Dover, 1977.

David, Donald. *Lincoln Reconsidered.* Vintage, 1961.

Davis, Burke. *The Civil War: Strange and Fascinating Facts.* The Fairfax Press, 1982.

Davis, Burke. *Sherman's March.* Random House, 1980.

Dyer, F.H. *A Compendium of the War of the Rebellion.* The Press of Morningside Bookshop, 1978.

Faust, D.G., ed. *The Ideology of Slavery: Proslavery Thought in Antebellum South 1830-1860.* Louisiana State University Press, 1981.

Foote, Shelby. *The Civil War: A Narrative.* 3 vols. Random House, 1958-1974.

Gardner, Alexander. *Photographic Sketch Book of the Civil War.* Dover, 1959.

Genovese, E.G. *The World the Slaveholders Made.* Vintage, 1971.

Hagerman, Edward. *The American Civil War and the Origins of Modern Warfare.* Indiana University Press, 1988.

Haythornthwaite, Phillip. *Uniforms of the American Civil War.* Blanford Press, 1986.

Hitchcock, Henry. *Marching With Sherman.* Yale University Press, 1927.

Klement, Frank L. *The Copperheads in the Middle West.* University of Chicago Press, 1960.

Klement, Frank L. *The Limits of Dissent.* University of Kentucky Press, 1970.

Korn, B.W. *American Jewry and the Civil War.* Jewish Publication Society of America, 1951.

Lewis, Lloyd. *Sherman, Fighting Prophet.* Harcourt, Brace, 1932.

Liddell-Hart, B.H. *Sherman: Soldier, Realist, American.* Dodd, Mead, 1929.

Lonn, Ella. *Foreigners in the Union Army and Navy.* Louisiana State University Press, 1951.

Lossing, B.J. *Mathew Brady's Illustrated History of the Civil War.* The Fairfax Press.

Marszalek, John F. *Sherman's Other War: The General and the Civil War Press.* Memphis State University Press, 1981.

McAlexander, U.G. *History of the Thirteenth Regiment United States Infantry.* Regimental Press, Thirteenth Infantry, Frank D. Gunn, 1905.

McPherson, James M. *Battle Cry of Freeedom: The Civil War Era.* Oxford University Press, 1988.

Menendez, A.J. *Civil War Novels.* Garland, 1986.

Merrill, James M. *William Tecumseh Sherman.* Rand McNally, 1971.

Official Army Register of the Volunteer Force of the United States 1861-1865, 9 vols. Ron R. Van Sickle Military Books, 1987.

Olson, Kenneth. *Music and Musket: Bands and Bandsmen of the Civil War.* Westport: Greenwood, 1981.

Russell, A.J. *Civil War Photographs.* Dover, 1982.

Schuyler, Hartley and Graham. *Illustrated Catalog of Civil War Military Goods.* Dover, 1985.

Sherman, William Tecumseh. *Memoirs.* Da Capo Press, 1984.

Simonhoff, Harry. *Jewish Participants in the Civil War.* Arco Publishing Company, 1963.

Slotkin, Richard. *The Crater.* Atheneum, 1981.

Stampp, Kenneth M. *The Peculiar Institution: Slavery in the Ante-Bellum South.* Vintage, 1956.

Symonds, Craig L. *A Battlefield Atlas of the Civil War.* The Nautical and Aviation Publishing Company of America, 1983.

Tenney, Craig Davidson. *Major General A.E. Burnside and the First Amendment: A Case Study of Civil War Freedom of Expression.* Indiana University, 1977. University Microfilms International, 1987.

The Civil War, 27 vols. Time-Life Inc., 1987.

Todd, F.P. *American Military Equipage.* Charles Scribner's Sons, 1980.

Vasvary, Edmund. *Lincoln's Hungarian Heroes: The Participation of Hungarians in the Civil War.* The Hungarian Reformed Federation of America, 1939.

Walters, John B. *Merchant of Terror: General Sherman and Total War.* Bobbs-Merrill, 1973.

Wheeler, Richard. *We Knew William Tecumseh Sherman.* Thomas Crowell, 1977.

Wheeler, Richard. *Sherman's March.* Thomas Crowell, 1978.

Wiley, B.I. *The Life of Billy Yank: The Common Soldier of the Union.* Louisiana State University Press, 1978.

Wiley, B.I. *The Life of Johnny Reb. The Common Soldier of the Confederacy.* Louisiana State University Press, 1978.

Williams, T.H. *Lincoln and His Generals.* Vintage, 1952.

Woodbury, Augustus. *Ambrose Everett Burnside.* Providence: N. Bangs Williams and Company, 1882.

Wyatt-Brown, Bertram. *Yankee Saints and Southern Sinners.* Louisiana State University Press, 1985.

Czech sources are listed in the Czech edition of the novel which, as *Nevesta z Texasu*, was published by Sixty-Eight Publishers, Corp., Toronto in 1992.

Illustration Credits

p. x. Ward, Geoffrey C., et al. *The Civil War: An Illustrated History* (New York: Knopf, 1990), 320. Courtesy of the National Archives.

p. 3. Goolrich, William K. *The Civil War, "Rebels Resurgent: Fredericksburg to Chancellorsville"* (Alexandria: Time-Life Inc., 1985), 151. Courtesy of the Rochester Museum and Science Center.

p. 30. Nevin, David. *The Civil War, "Sherman's March: Atlanta to the Sea"* (Alexandria: Time-Life Inc., 1986), 105. Courtesy of Ronn Palm.

p. 133. Wiley, Bell Irvin. *The Life of Billy Yank: the Common Soldier of the Union* (Baton Rouge: Louisiana State Univ., 1952), 320. Courtesy of the National Archives.

p. 158. Bailey, Ronald H. *The Civil War, "Forward to Richmond: McClellan's Peninsular Campaign"* (Alexandria: Time-Life Inc., 1983), 28. Courtesy of the Library of Congress.

p. 233. Murphy, Richard W. *The Civil War, "The Nation Reunited: War's Aftermath"* (Alexandria: Time-Life Inc., 1987), 43. Courtesy of the Lightfoot Collection.

p. 376. Korn, Jerry. *The Civil War, "Pursuit to Appomattox: the Last Battles"* (Alexandria: Time-Life Inc., 1987), 54. Courtesy of the National Archives.

p. 400. Cermak, Josef. *History of the Civil War* (Chicago: August Geringer, 1889). Courtesy of the Library of Congress.

A Note About the Author

JOSEF SKVORECKY was born in Bohemia and emigrated to Canada in 1968. He and his wife, the novelist Zdena Salivarova, run a Czech-language publishing house, Sixty-Eight Publishers, in Toronto. Skvorecky's novels include *The Cowards, Miss Silver's Past, The Bass Saxophone, The Engineer of Human Souls, Dvorak in Love, The Miracle Game,* and *The Republic of Whores.* He has also written many short stories and filmscripts, and was the winner of the 1980 Neustadt International Prize for Literature and the 1984 Governor General's Award in Canada.

A Note on the Type

This book was set in Adobe Garamond. Designed for the Adobe Corporation by Robert Slimbach, the fonts are based on types first cut by Claude Garamond (c. 1480–1561). Garamond was a pupil of Geoffroy Tory and is believed to have followed the Venetian models, although he introduced a number of important differences, and it is to him that we owe the letter we now know as "old style." He gave to his letters a certain elegance and feeling of movement that won their creator an immediate reputation and the patronage of Francis I of France.

Printed and bound by Quebecor Printing Martinsburg, Martinsburg, Pennsylvania